MORE THAN A THREAT SERIES

COMPLETE BOXSET

KENNEDY L. MITCHELL

Copyright © 2021 by Kennedy L. Mitchell

This is a work of fiction. Names, characters, businesses, places, events, locales, and incidents are either the products of the author's imagination or used in a fictitious manner. Any resemblance to actual persons, living or dead, or actual events is purely coincidental.

All rights reserved. No part of this publication may be reproduced, distributed, or transmitted in any form or by any means, including photocopying, recording, or other electronic or mechanical methods, without the prior written permission of the publisher, except in the case of brief quotations embodied in critical reviews and certain other noncommercial uses permitted by copyright law.

Cover by Bookin it Designs

Edited by Hot Tree Editing

Proofread by Sisters Get Lit.erary

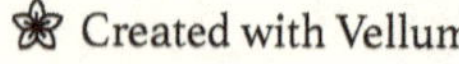 Created with Vellum

MORE THAN A THREAT

MORE THAN A THREAT BOOK 1

1

———

I hated mornings.

Truly loathed them.

To me, mornings were evil, and morning *shifts* were the sole work of the devil himself. And if having to get ready for work before the sun was even up wasn't cruel enough, I was awoken by some country artist singing about his stupid truck. Country music and morning shifts, both sent to this Earth to torture me, I just knew it. I rose up just high enough to smack the snooze button and rolled back over to gain eight additional glorious minutes of sleep. The pillow and plush feather-down duvet were so cozy, I never wanted to leave. But before I could fully nod off again, the question of how that song got on that playlist to begin with swirled in my mind.

Ah. Mark. My lovely ex-boyfriend Mark.

Mark had loved country music with a passion and made me listen to it constantly during the year we were together. He thought it would change my mind regarding the sorry excuse for music. But in the end, the only thing it changed my mind about was *him*. There was no way I could be compatible with someone who listened to that crap. It could have been worse, I guess; he could have liked Justin Beiber and forced me to listen to that instead.

The song going off for the second time signaled it was *really* time to get up. Those extra eight minutes of being snug in my soft bed would now make me rush, but it was worth it. I groaned, turning off the alarm, and blindly felt around in the dark along the bedside table, searching for my phone. The screen lit up the dark room, momentarily blinding me. Surprisingly there were several missed texts. I knew this early, there were only two people the texts would be from: Eric or Meagan. They were the only two people who had messed-up work schedules like me, and really the only two friends I had. Well, the only two people who I had allowed close enough to be considered friends.

> Eric: You better be awake.

> Eric: Are you awake?

> Eric: You're my relief today. Get your tiny ass up.

> Eric: If you're late and make me stay one minute longer than I have to, I get the right to punch you in the boob.

> Eric: That's if I can find them…

My brows furrowed at the phone. Boob punching was a tad dramatic for the possibility of being late.

> Me: You're an asshole.

> Eric: Knew that would perk you up. Now GET UP.

> Me: You suck as a BFF.

> Eric: Whatever, you love me.

> Eric: Don't be late.

He did actually have a point; if I didn't hurry, I *would* be late. Tossing the covers off, I lay in my king-size bed, letting the cool air snap my body awake before rolling out and practically crawling to the shower.

After a glorious shower that I enjoyed ten minutes too long, I was definitely running late. *Good thing it wasn't a hair wash day or I'd be even later.* At least choosing clothes for work was simple. Every day, every shift was a simple choice between blue or green scrubs. It was nice not having to put thought into matching clothes, pairing everything with jewelry and cramming my feet into high heels on a daily basis. Don't get me wrong, I loved getting dressed up, but scrubs made rushed days like this one easy—well, easier.

I raced down the stairs toward the kitchen, brushing out my long dark hair with one hand as I attempted to brush my teeth with the other—neither attempt very successful. But first coffee. And lots of it before comprehending English was even a thought. Coffee had always been a necessity, but after the long and late hours during med school and residency, it was now my lifeblood. There was no functioning Kate without it.

Setting both brushes down on the kitchen counter, I quickly poured water and coffee grounds into the pot and bounded back up the stairs to finish getting ready for work.

Not bad. Borderline impressive, really. Thirty minutes after waking up, I was dressed and ready to walk out the door without a minute to spare. At this rate, I would be on time, which would make Eric happy. My two-bedroom townhouse was close to downtown Dallas, conveniently located just a few blocks from the hospital I worked in. Which meant walking to work was the norm, leaving my Ninja motorcycle unused most days.

Travel mug filled to the brim clutched in one hand, I headed out the door, grabbing a Luna bar and my backpack along the way—and stopped. A bouquet of flowers—well, maybe two days ago they would have been called flowers, but now they were just sad versions of their former beauty—was sitting on the welcome mat.

"What the hell?" I whispered.

No idea who these could be from. My father wouldn't buy wilted, bargain bin flowers. Plus he would just bring them to work, not leave them on the doorstep in the middle of the night, and there was no boyfriend in the picture. Even Mark wasn't a possibility considering he was *still* angry at how I had walked away from a yearlong relationship without even a tear or glance back. If it were a dead cat or armadillo, then yeah, Mark could be a possibility. But flowers? Nope.

Setting my mug and backpack down on the entry table behind me, I grabbed the flowers, closed the door with my foot, and brought them into the kitchen for closer inspection.

Now that they were up close, I could see a note tucked into the green tissue paper the flowers were wrapped in. Well, no need to wonder; at least whoever it was had the decency of letting me know who sent them instead of making me wonder all day. That would be torture.

Mornings. Country music. Leaving my curiosity to run rampant. The list of things that tortured me was growing by the minute. Maybe that said something. Maybe everything annoyed me. Eh, that was too deep a thought this early in the morning.

Pulling the card from its resting place, I opened it so I could know who sent the awful flowers and then sprint to work.

My stomach flipped as I read the message.

TELL YOUR FATHER TO DROP THE SALAZAR CASE OR ELSE

"SHIT." I wrapped my trembling hand around my neck and then slid it to my chest, where my heart was on the verge of thumping out. I attempted to take a deep steady breath in and out, trying to calm the strike of panic and fear that had just raced through my entire body. The note trembled in my hand until I set it down on the counter. I needed to figure out my next move. Obviously, there was no way I would actually tell my father that he needed to drop his current case. It was a big deal. He'd mentioned a few times in the past couple months that the case he was working on was bad, but he didn't go into too many details. Being the district attorney for the city of Dallas put him first in line for the major cases. This was just one of the many that were on his plate.

Closing my eyes to help trigger memories, I tried to remember some of our conversations. He'd mentioned the case involved one of the notoriously vicious gangs. A lead member was arrested for murdering a family of five in their south Dallas home when they wouldn't hand over the drugs they'd muled over from Mexico. The case wasn't that far along either; jury selections were just starting.

Picking at my lip—an awful nervous habit—I stared at the counter, thinking about my options. If I told my dad about the threat, he would insist on twenty-four-seven protection or worse. It had been a fight in the past when he had high-profile cases; anything gang related always put him on edge. But with those previous cases, I'd been able to talk him off the ledge since there was no direct threat. But now? These flowers. The note. It not only said "I know where you live," but it also sent a more direct threat. It said "I know how to cut you to the core," considering I was the only family my father had left after my mother passed away a couple years ago in a car accident. Whoever gave me these flowers and threat knew exactly what they were doing and knew it had the potential to send my father into a downward spiral.

Once my vision refocused, pulling me back to reality, I glanced up at the clock and swore. No matter how fast I walked, I was going to be late to work, and Eric was going to be pissy.

"Glad to see you could make it to work today," Eric snipped when I rushed out of the locker room toward the computer where he was waiting for me.

"Sorry, really crappy morning. I'll tell you about it later. Let's go over the patients from last night. I know you're ready to get out of here." With a deep sigh, trying to calm my still frayed nerves, I clipped my badge onto my scrubs and attempted to log into the computer. My hands were shaking so badly I was having a hard time typing in my password to clock in for my shift.

"Hey, you okay?" he asked, staring at my trembling hands. "You seem a little more on edge than normal. Maybe you should lay off the coffee. You know, detox or something." While Eric was talking, he handed me a stack of charts for the patients he was trying to wrap up from the night shift.

Thankfully, it had been a slow night in the emergency room, so there weren't too many patients for us to discuss. Most had been assessed, treated, and released. Only a handful were left, either waiting to see someone or waiting on test results.

After the rundown and a quick hug and kiss—no boob punching, thank goodness—Eric clocked out and headed toward the locker room to change before heading home.

My mood slipped yet another rung when I found my coffee mug nearly empty. Draining the last of it, I grabbed the charts and headed to the first patient.

The day-to-day life of an emergency medicine doctor was all I'd hoped it would be. The fast-paced, always-changing environment was exactly what I needed considering I got bored quickly. Thinking on my feet, dancing on the line between being crazy and brilliant was exhilarating. From patient to patient, seeing anything from the flu to gunshot wounds was what kept me coming back. A regular doctor's office setting, seeing the same thing day in and day out, would cause me to gnaw off my arm from boredom.

My father was supportive now, but initially not so much. He'd wanted me to follow in his, and my mother's, footsteps and go to law school. My mother, on the other hand, hadn't cared which major I chose as long as I sought to be more than anyone expected me to be. The best version of myself. Career focus was my dad; life focus and making a difference was my mom.

Undergrad, medical school, and emergency medicine residency all brought me to where I was today—an emergency medicine doctor at one of the largest hospitals in downtown Dallas. It was all worth it. Well, most days. The long hours of studying, getting paid less than a dollar an hour during residency, all the hard work I had put in had been worth it. Every shift, I made a direct impact on someone's life. But sometimes I found myself wondering what was next. I'd worked so hard to get where I was, pushing everything else aside—relationships the most affected by that determined focus—and now that I was here with everything I could possibly want... I wanted more. But I had no idea what that "more" even was. Right then it was just a feeling, a feeling that this wasn't it for me.

A nurse who looked about eighty from the too-tan leathery skin that pulled at her cheekbones stopped in front of me. "Kate, there's a boy in area one waiting to see someone. Looks like the flu. Might want to wear a mask," she said before depositing another chart on the stack already in my hands.

I couldn't help my deep sigh, this time to set my feet and mind in motion. Grabbing a disposable mask, I headed in the direction of area one.

WHAT SEEMED like forty-eight hours later, though only ten hours in reality, my shift was finally done. Now it was time to start my actual day.

With morning shifts, I tried to fit in the gym right after. If I didn't force myself, then I would simply go home and lie on the couch all afternoon until it was time to change locations, then zombie-walk up to bed and just to do it all over again the next day.

After changing and cleaning up in the locker room at the hospital, I headed in the direction of my gym. It was a long enough walk that I had plenty of time to call my dad and get the whole death threat discussion started on some level.

He picked up on the second ring. Of course he did; I was his life. He always made time for me no matter what was going on at work. That thought put a smile on my face, which quickly faded when I remembered what was going on and the reason for the call.

"Hey there, pumpkin," he greeted.

My eyes rolled at the term of endearment, but I felt my lips twitch upward, trying to smile.

"Hey, Dad, I was wondering if you were free to stop by tonight on your way home from the office. There's some stuff I wanted to talk to you about."

"Of course, sweetie. Do I need to come over now? Everything okay?" His voice shifted from cheerful to sounding full of worry.

"No. Everything's fine, just come over when you're done. I'm headed to the gym now, so I won't even be home for a while."

His disappointed sigh echoed down the line, making me roll my eyes once more. "I really wish you would pick up something less aggressive for your workouts. What about Pilates or yoga? I just don't understand why you have to get punched around to feel like you've gotten a workout in."

Here we go again. He wouldn't let it drop.

"Don't start with all that, Dad. I'll see you tonight. Love you." Pulling the phone from my ear, I shoved it into my bag and picked up the pace to jog the rest of the way to gym. Even though it was over one hundred degrees outside, I figured I could use the warm-up.

THE GYM WAS A PRIVATELY OWNED KICKBOXING club, and I loved every inch of it. There was a large section in the back with dozens of mats spread out for sparring and private lessons, and toward the front was the cardio equipment and free weights. Everything I needed for a full-body workout was here, including several punching bags in the back-right corner, where I loved to work off stress from the job.

As soon as I entered the gym, I hit the mat, foregoing my normal routine of cardio and weights. It was exactly where I wanted to be. Kickboxing was the best workout and stress reliever I'd found, and the self-defense piece was a bonus. I never had to actually use it on anyone outside the gym, but knowing the moves and ways to defend myself was huge considering I fell into the petite side of the petite category.

"Kate, you're up," the instructor called from across the mat. He was attractive in a big guy way. His chest and arms were huge, but his legs were so thin it made me wonder if a leg day ever crossed his mind. "You're up against Jessica today. You two are equally trained, so this should be interesting." He waved a hand between me and the other woman and gave a soft chuckle as he stepped off the mat.

Glaring at the instructor, I gave him my best cocky smirk. The long-legged blonde who I was to spar with was significantly bigger than me in every sense—height, weight, boobs—but I knew I could take her. One of the benefits of my bite-size frame was that I was unsuspecting in my attack and ability. People had no idea how far my competitive spirit could drive me. Just like the blonde now standing in front of me.

The girl got a few good punches and kicks in, much to my surprise. One of her kicks was a direct hit to my ribs, knocking all the air out of my lungs from the force. Trying to recover, I stumbled back and took a second to regain my composure. In the end, I took her out with a quick sweep to the ankles, knocking those long lean legs right out from under her. The sound of her back slamming against the mat brought a smile to my face.

I really, really liked winning.

Even after the challenging sparring session, I still had some pent-up energy to burn, so instead of heading home, I walked toward the area with the punching bags to work on my technique. I needed to work off some anxiety before the conversation with my dad. It would be challenging, and I needed to ensure I had a level head.

It was well past eight when I finally walked into the house, dripping sweat from the workout I'd just put in. As I set down the gym bag and toed off my tennis shoes, pain rippled up my right side. Apparently that kick from earlier was worse than I initially thought. Each step up the stairs toward my room caused pain to reverberate from my side all the way down to my toes.

Once I disrobed and climbed into the shower, I attempted to prod around the area while I cleaned up for the visit with my father, trying to see if a rib was cracked or just badly bruised. But every time my fingers skirted around my lower right ribs, my body involuntarily jerked away. Somehow my body knew the pressure would cause blinding pain. Someone else would have to look this over. *Good thing all my friends are doctors.* And even though I had the day off tomorrow, I could still pop in to the hospital and see if someone would give my side a once-over.

Groaning into the hot stream from the shower head, I tried to let the water wash away the remaining stress from the day, plus my now building annoyance toward that Jessica woman, plus the anxiety that was creeping up with each minute that passed, thus bringing me closer to the conversation I was dreading.

I had just slipped into a pair of black cotton sleep shorts and a tank top when I heard a knock at the front door. Without looking to see who it was, I opened the door and smiled, knowing it would be my father on the other side.

When my eyes connected with his, I wondered if I should have been more cautious, maybe looking through the peephole to make sure it wasn't someone coming to follow up on the death threat. But the thought pushed through my mind as quickly as it had come when I saw my father coming in for a warm embrace. Considering the pressure of my tank against my bruised side was almost enough to put me in the fetal position, I had to dodge his attempt at a hug. I opened the door as wide as I could, gesturing for him to come in. Thankfully he didn't question the hug dodging; the last thing I needed was for him to add *another* concern to our soon-to-be intense conversation.

He walked toward the flowers that had caught his attention. Still dressed in his workday suit, he shrugged off his gray pinstriped jacket and laid it carefully across one of the stools scooted under the kitchen island. "Who are these dreadful flowers from?" he asked, his brows knitted together. "Are you dating someone new? You haven't mentioned anyone recently." He paused when his eyes landed on the card.

I wanted to kick myself for not putting that damn note away before he got here. Panic set in from not having a plan and not knowing how he was going to react. My hands were stretched out in front of me, palms out, hoping it would calm him down. "Dad, just let me explain before you—"

Too late. His eyes widened and his face flushed with anger as he read the card over and over. His face began turning a deep shade of red bordering on purple, causing my panic to turn into fear. Not fear from what he would do to me but more from the type of security suggestions for my safety that were about to flow from his mouth.

"When?" he demanded. His tone made it very clear it was not a rhetorical question.

"This morning. The flowers were on my doorstep when I opened the door to leave for work."

"These flowers were on your doorstep." His eerie stillness and intensity were intimidating and growing. It was the calm, calculating badass attorney standing in my kitchen now, not the loving, soft dad he became when he was around me. "Did you *read* the card before you left for work?" His focus turned from the card to me, glaring.

"Yes, I read the note." I glared back at him. There was no way I could back down now. If I gave him an inch, he would run with it and have me locked away in some remote compound before I had a chance to object.

"Let me get this straight. An educated, smart woman has flowers with a *death threat* left on her doorstep, and she shrugs it off and walks to work? What the hell, Kate? Do you know how much danger you're in? They know who you are, they know where you live, these people know—" As he spoke, his face visibly paled to a clammy white before my eyes. As if he was replaying all the gruesome crime scenes he'd seen over and over in his mind. He knew what could be done.

"I'm sorry. I know it wasn't the smartest thing to do, but I didn't know how to handle the situation. This is my first death threat, after all. I wasn't sure on the fucking protocol."

He shot me an incredulous look from across the kitchen. With the note in hand, he had begun pacing around the whole first level of my townhouse. It wasn't that big, but with how fast he was walking, he was getting quite a workout in.

"You're not staying here tonight. Pack a bag. You're coming to stay with me until we can figure this out. I'll make some calls. Maybe we can get you into some kind of safe house for the next few months. Until the trial is over. It should only take four to six more months." The way he wouldn't meet my stare, one I knew he could feel, told me he knew what he was suggesting was over the top. And nothing I would ever consider.

"Dad, you have to be kidding me. I'm not going to put my life on hold. That isn't even an option, so don't mention it like it might be. You know I would never say yes to something like that. I have a job. I have friends. I have a life."

The job part was true, and I did have two friends. But the life part, well... that was debatable. Depended on who you asked.

"I don't know how else to keep you safe, Kate. These people, they're vicious, extremely dangerous. If I thought I could protect you, I would, but I can't. You can't even protect yourself against them. Your kickboxing moves won't do anything against a bullet." He took a deep breath in and let it out slowly. Without breaking eye contact, he walked toward me and placed his hands on my shoulders. Face-to-face, toe to toe, I could see the swirling fear and pain behind his eyes. It cracked my resolve to stand up against him. If even the thought of me being in danger did this to him, what would he do if something actually happened?

"I get it, Dad, I do. You want me safe, but there has to be something less drastic. Can we figure it out where we meet in the middle on the security piece? Please."

Dropping his arms with an exaggerated sigh, he furrowed his forehead in such a dramatic fashion that his hairline almost met his eyebrows. At least with all the pacing the blood had come back to his face and he was back to his slightly tan, peachy self. "Let me make some calls. Maybe we could get twenty-four-hour security detail or something along those lines for you. I'm not sure what they offer to the family members of the DA office. But even if I have to pay it myself, we'll figure it out."

Crossing my arms over my chest, I gave him the same incredulous look he gave me earlier.

"I don't want a group of guys following me around all day and night. Maybe just some unmarked car outside the house to watch me get to and from work safely... something like that would work. The hospital would be a safe place, so I definitely don't need someone with me there."

"We'll do whatever it takes to keep you safe. Now, go upstairs and pack an overnight bag. We're leaving here in twenty minutes, even if I have to drag you out kicking and screaming." He held my gaze for several seconds, conveying his resolve on the matter, before pulling out his phone and turning toward the living room.

Even though it was childish, I stuck my tongue out at his back as I sulked toward the stairs to do as he asked. There went my big plans of sleeping in and lying on the couch all day tomorrow. Just the thought made me roll my eyes at the controlling storm of a man downstairs.

2

———————

The gentle but loud purr of someone vacuuming directly outside my bedroom door pulled me from a restless sleep around eight the next morning. Rubbing the sleep from my eyes with my thumbs, I tried to calm the uneasiness that started to set in the pit of my stomach. Ever since my mother died, it had been hard staying the night in this house. Waking up in my old room with all the familiar smells and sounds had my grief starting to bubble up again, slowly taking over my mind and body. Rapid breaths and clammy palms were all too familiar from the cruel drop of hope in the back of my mind that tried to fool me, telling me it was all a dream. That my mother wasn't gone from my life but would walk through my bedroom door any minute now, talking up a storm and forcing me to go downstairs to eat a healthy breakfast.

It sounded crazy. I knew it did. But this house was our family home, and now it was just a reminder that my mother's joy no longer filled every inch. The house seemed empty now, and if I wasn't careful, if I let myself lie there much longer, dwelling on the absence of her, it would swallow me whole.

I scooted my body up the bed and winced from the pain shooting from my ribs. Resting my back against the tufted upholstered headboard, I glanced around my childhood room, attempting to get my mind off my mother. Nothing had changed. Every award, poster—yep, Gavin Rossdale's beautiful face still graced the ceiling right above my bed—even the stockpile of Beanie Babies were still in the corner.

As I focused on the trophies on the shelf, thoughts of how much life had changed since those accomplishments began running through my mind.

Going from the all-girl college prep school to the enormous campus of the University of Texas was a huge culture shock. The first year was incredibly hard, not academically but socially. It was hard having to start all over with new friends, trying to learn to trust and let people in—which had never been a strong suit of mine, though I had no idea why. If you believed my father, he would say I was cursed with indifference and had been since I was young. It made keeping relationships with men almost impossible, but it did make the cattiness and brutal years of middle school and high school easy—*easier*.

After graduating with a 4.0 in undergrad and breezing through the MCAT, I had several options for medical school. In the end, I came back home to Dallas. Medical school, then rolled right into emergency medicine residency, which was difficult. But at least at that point I'd met Eric and Meagan. We supported each other every step of the way after meeting during orientation that first day at UT Southwestern. They'd been my two best friends ever since.

Twisting my body to find my phone, I choked on a breath. If I ever saw that Jessica girl again, she'd better hope there were too many witnesses around for me to consider following through on the evil thoughts that were running through my mind.

I lifted my ratty University of Texas T-shirt, my eyes widening as I took in the black/blue bruise running down my right side. It was roughly the size of a large man's hand. Dropping my shirt, I checked my phone and found I had just missed two texts from Meagan.

Meagan: I need help.

Meagan: You awake?

What in the world had she gotten herself into now?

Me: What's up, buttercup?

Meagan: This guy last night, so fun….

Me: And?

Meagan: And now I have to figure out how to sneak out of his place without waking him.

Me: You have to be kidding me, Meagan.

Meagan: What? It was fun. No strings attached.

Meagan: Should be right up your alley.

Me: Ouch.

Meagan: I'm just saying, have fun. It doesn't have to be serious to get laid.

Meagan: Gotta go. Have to figure out a way to sneak out… and on my OWN since you have no brilliant ideas.

I groaned, pushing my phone aside when it buzzed again with an incoming message.

Meagan: Shit, he has a dog.

Laughing at my phone, I peeled myself out of bed to shower and change. Hopefully someone at the hospital would be open to giving me a quick assessment.

THE CHARGE NURSE wasn't scared to let me see she was more than slightly annoyed at my asking for help. Finally, I wore her down with my begging, and she sent me in the direction of the cafeteria to find Eric, who was on break during a midmorning lull of patients.

"Hey, bestie." I smirked as I sat down in the chair across from him. Without having to look down, I knew what was going to be on his plate. One of Eric's endearing quirks was going in phases of certain foods. He would eat the same thing for every meal until he got tired of it and moved on to the next choice. During residency, he went four months eating Chick-Fil-A for every meal, and on Sundays, when they were closed, he wouldn't eat anything, claiming he was fasting.

"Hey," he said, surprise written on his soft features. He was pretty for a guy, nothing rugged about him. His perfectly cropped blond hair accentuated his green eyes and round cheeks. Maybe that was why I'd allowed myself to get so close to him; I knew I wasn't his type and he definitely wasn't mine. Even the first time I met him, the only thing I was attracted to was his humor and uncanny ability to read people. "What are you doing here? I thought you were off today."

"It *is* my day off. I just really wanted to see you, so I thought I would surprise you." I popped a fry in my mouth and reached for another as he scowled at me.

"Stop eating my fries. Those are the best part. And whatever, stop lying to me. Why are you here?"

Sighing, I snuck another fry. "I need a favor."

"Oh, and what's that?"

"At the gym yesterday, I... ugh, this is kind of embarrassing. I took a bad hit in the side. Can you check it out and make sure nothing is cracked or broken? I can't check it myself. I can barely touch it."

Eric leaned back in his chair, balancing on the two back legs, and gave me a cocky smile. "Gotcha. We should probably give you a full-body exam too while I'm at it. Any other areas bothering you, like maybe your tits? I should probably take a look at those too. You know, just in case."

He batted away the stolen fry I threw at his face with ease.

"You are such a boy," I said, smirking back at him.

"I'm taking that as a compliment."

Once he was finished eating, Eric pushed back his chair, grabbed his tray, and headed toward a trash can. Glancing back at me, he inclined his head toward the exit, "Come on, let's get this peep show started."

"Do you want some music?" Eric chuckled. The pull of the metal curtain rings against the metal rod above made me grimace as he slid the curtain closed in one of the exam areas. That sound haunted my dreams since I heard it about a billion times a shift. When he turned around, his smile grew wider when he took in the look of utter annoyance written on my face.

Rolling my eyes, I began lifting my shirt for him to start.

"Wait, do it nice and slow...." Eric waggled his eyebrows up and down.

I'm glad someone finds my pain funny.

"Stop dicking around."

"Fine," he said with a dramatic sigh.

Pulling my shirt up enough for him to see the full bruise, I leaned to the left to expand my ribs. The move alone had me biting my lip to hold back a whimper.

"Damn." He gently prodded around my ribs, pushing harder in certain areas. "This is from one kick?"

Concentrating hard on keeping my breathing steady, I could only nod in reply.

"You're always telling me and Meagan how amazing you are and a total badass at this gym of yours. How did you let *this* happen?" He grazed his fingers along my ribs one last time, then pulled my shirt back in place and stood staring, waiting for my response.

"I was distracted. I had a really bad morning yesterday, remember?"

"So what happened yesterday to distract the amazing Kate Wheeler?"

"I... ugh—"

"Oh, I forgot to tell you. Meagan is off tonight too, so she and I are going to dinner. You want to come with?"

"Sure, I'll tell you about everything then. I know you need to get back to work. Thanks for looking me over. What's your professional opinion, Doc?"

"Not broken or cracked. If anything, just a bone bruise, but I'm not sure it even goes that deep. It's just in a really bad spot. We can get X-rays done if you want to be sure."

"Nah," I said over my shoulder, walking toward the curtain. After yanking it open, I turned to give him a quick hug. "Thanks again. Text me when you know the details about tonight. See you then."

I passed through the hallways in a daze on my way toward the parking garage. Death threat, staying with my dad, bruised ribs—the past twenty-four hours had not been good to me.

Just when I was thinking it couldn't get any worse, I rounded a corner and some idiot ran directly into me, their hand connecting with my bruised side.

Stars appeared in my vision as I doubled over from the impact. I began taking in little gulps of air, trying to shorten the expansion of my ribs. Still doubled over, I felt two large hands grip my shoulders and try to raise me upright. I could barely make out that he was mumbling; all I could focus on was getting my breathing under control.

Several seconds passed before my vision cleared and the roaring in my ears dulled enough that I could make out the male voice above me.

"I'm so sorry. I didn't see you... sorry. Are you hurt?"

The man was mumbling and still had his hands on my shoulders. Now my shallow breathing was from him touching me; the thought of ripping his arm out of its socket or biting his hand off ran through my mind. Instead of resorting to violence, however, I took as deep a breath in as I dared and slowly stood up, gathering all the foul words I was going to yell at this stupid, inconsiderate, waste of—

As I stood, my eyes scrolled up his body. The man was fit. His trim waist, broad chest and wide shoulders were accentuated by a white button-down shirt that clung to all the right areas. And then I saw his face. It was perfection. All the profanities I had prepared slipped from my mind. *Everything* slipped from my mind, actually, and by the smirk on the man's face, which made his blue eyes twinkle somehow, he knew I was just stunned into silence.

He had to be one of the most beautiful men I had ever seen in person. This guy could be the son of Brad Pitt and Chris Hemsworth if that was physically or even genetically possible. His heart-shaped face, delectably plump lips, and broad nose were accentuated by his smooth golden skin. Even his dirty-blond hair pulled back in a tight man bun was damn sexy, making me wish I could run my fingers through it, disheveling its perfect placement.

Still smirking down at me, he retracted his hands from my shoulders—which I immediately missed.

"Are you all right? We didn't bump that hard."

For the life of me, I tried to regain some composure. I really did, but seriously, how in the hell was anyone supposed to form sentences from words with a man looking like him standing in front of them? So close that I wouldn't have to reach far to touch him, to run my fingers down—

Wait, did he ask a question?

"Yes. Fine. I'm bueno."

Damn it.

That *just came out of my mouth. And when did I start speaking Spanish?*

Way to use your million-dollar education, Kate.

His smile grew at my response. His turquoise blue eyes had a hold on me and were keeping me in some kind of erotic thought laced trance.

"You know, you should get that checked out," he said, pointing toward my right side. I was lightly holding it, trying to protect myself from other dangers. "You might have a cracked rib or something if you're in that much pain."

Again. No words. Not only that, but I couldn't even smile back at him. I blamed it on some rare disease, that I swore I read about somewhere, that caused temporary paralysis of the face. And vocal cords. And rational decision-making ability. Surely that was what was happening to me at that moment. There was no way I, Kate fucking Wheeler, was put in a partial coma-like state by some guy.

"Listen, I have to get going. Again, I'm sorry for running into you." He brushed past, careful of my right side, and continued on his way down the hall I had just come from.

Once he was several feet away, I could breathe easily again. Think again. That was the first time ever in my adult life that had happened. I had never been *that* girl who lost it around attractive or powerful men. I was stronger than that. I was better than that. Except when beautiful blue-eyed men who made you think of all the naughty things you wanted to do to them ran into me in the hallway. Apparently.

Shaking the whole encounter off, I headed toward the Audi that would be parked out front waiting for me, something my father demanded until we had the security situation figured out. With a glance back down the hall, I was glad for the chance run-in, because for those thirty seconds, I'd forgotten about my shitstorm of a life.

THE THREE OF us being off at the same time was a rare occurrence, which was probably why Eric still showed up for dinner even though he was clearly falling asleep in the chair beside me. They had decided on an authentic brick oven pizza restaurant in an area of downtown known as Deep Ellum. The food was amazing, and they had Huge Ass Fans—seriously, that was the name of the brand—and misters out on the patio so it could still be functional in the Texas heat. Even late-summer nights were hot with the day's heat still beating down from above plus seeping up from the concrete below, smothering you in a heat sandwich from the intensity. But here, with the fans and misters, it was decent enough that we chose to sit outside.

Glancing over, I eyed a sleeping Eric. His head rested in his hands, elbows propped up on our table.

"Wakey, wakey, sleepyhead." I smacked one of his elbows, causing his arm to wobble and drop his head. "We haven't even gotten our food yet."

Leaning back in his chair, he closed his eyes again. "Sorry, stupid busy day. Keep talking, I'm listening."

Right. I snorted, knowing he was doing no such thing.

Not that Meagan even noticed. She was too busy flirting with the young server assigned to our table. That was Meagan for you, an insatiable flirt. She had no type when it came to hitting on men; she just wanted some kind of attention, good or bad. Sometimes it bothered me, I realized, as I took a sip of water and watched her from across the table. I didn't understand her need for that kind of attention. Why couldn't she have an ounce of self-respect?

But who was I to judge? My love life was nowhere near perfect. Actually, it was nonexistent. To have a love life, you would actually have to get close to someone to love them, and well, that always seemed to be the catch with me. To love someone, you gave up some level of control and a little of yourself. I'd never been good at that. In fact, Eric had been the only male to truly know me and me know him. Ever.

The warm metal of the chair pressed against my back through my light tank top as I leaned back in my chair and wondered if maybe I was jealous of Meagan. She loved easily and rebounded just as smoothly. Maybe I was jealous, since that ability was something I wasn't gifted with.

Plus Meagan had the advantage of being noticed wherever she went. She was tall, with long legs and fiery red hair, and every head turned when she walked in. Her huge boobs helped too. Very different from me. I was so short I had to wear heels just for people to see me. But what I lacked in height, I made up for with thick dark brown hair that most women paid a fortune to have. And my almond-shaped hazel eyes gave me a slightly exotic look. Some of my features were striking, others not, which was fine by me. What I really wanted men to be attracted to were my wit, charismatic personality, smarts. Meagan didn't care what they were attracted to, just that they were.

A loud laugh pulled me back to the present, and jolted Eric awake. I rolled my eyes and watched Meagan graze her fingers up and down the server's arm, whispering something into his ear.

"Hey, you never told me your horrible morning story from yesterday. What happened?" Eric mumbled, trying hard to keep his eyes open but losing the battle.

"Oh, nothing big. I found a death threat waiting for me on my doormat on my way to work, courtesy of one of the gangs my dad is about to put on trial." Yes, it was blunt, but how else was I to gauge if they were both truly listening?

They were.

Meagan's green eyes snapped to me, and she shooed the disappointed server away in a dismissive wave. Eric leaned forward, his eyes popped open, now fully awake and engaged, as soon as he heard the words "death threat."

"What did you just say?" Meagan asked, her eyes so wide it was almost cartoonish.

My hair stuck to the back of my neck, and it was driving me insane. While pulling it up in a makeshift bun, I dove into the story. "My dad has a big case in front of him right now. It's still in jury selection, but apparently the gang the accused is associated with isn't all that happy that my father has the case. So, they left a note on my doorstep yesterday morning saying he needed to drop the case or else."

The sounds of the crowd around us amplified the silence from the other side of the table. Both of my friends stared at me. Neither moved.

"What are you going to do?" Eric asked after several tense moments.

Sighing, I sat back in the chair and folded my arms across my chest. "My dad made me stay with him last night, and I'll continue to until we get something figured out. He wants me in a safe house for a few months, but I don't want anything at all, so we're in the process of finding a happy medium. You know him. Everything is a battle."

Meagan was still gaping at me when she finally said something.

"You need some kind of protection, Kate. I know you put up this whole tough girl act, but these people, it's not a joke. You need to take this threat and take *them* very seriously."

"It's not an act," I snapped. "I can handle myself."

"Meagan's right, you need some kind of protection. Even if it's simply someone watching your back or keeping an eye out while you sleep," Eric said, which didn't sit well. Even though we all met at the same time, I always felt closer to Eric, and his support of Meagan's comment kind of stung.

"Listen, I agree I do need some kind of help. But anything full time would be a ridiculous waste of money. Can you imagine someone being with me twenty-four-seven? That poor person wouldn't last a week." Even with everything going on, the thought made me smirk.

"If it's a guy, yes. You do tend to have trouble keeping them around," Eric joked, clearly trying to lighten the mood when the server reappeared with our food.

As we ate and talked, our conversation drifted to work drama, but I could tell from their body language that they were nervous for me. Several times, I caught Eric's eyes darting around the restaurant looking for any signs of a threat. Not sure what he would do if he actually spotted one, but it made me happy that he was doing what he could to watch out for me.

When the waiter brought our check, Meagan smiled up at him and wasn't bashful about watching him walk away.

"Dang, he is cute. Look at that perky ass," she crooned, biting her lower lip.

I shook my head and smiled at her. "He's also young, my friend. Are you sure he's even legal?"

"Very funny. He isn't that young. Besides, while we were in school all those years, studying and going through residency, all the hot guys our age got saggy and started growing beer guts. All I want is to live out my twenties in my thirties. Is that so bad? We spent so much time trying to get to where we are now. I say live it up." She crossed her arms and gave me her best pouty lip while trying to hold back a playful smile.

"Do whatever you want, just use protection. The older guys might be getting less attractive, but with what all we've seen come through the ER, the younger ones are more contaminated."

3

─────────

I covered my wide, open-mouth yawn behind the disposable coffee mug in my left hand the following morning. The *one* good thing about another overnight stay with my father was he made a quick pit stop by Starbucks for me before driving me to work. The venti coffee made up for the nonstop talking he did on the drive in. He'd gone over *every single detail* of the various security firms he had lined up to interview later that morning. I stopped paying attention halfway to work, zoning him out completely to the point that when we arrived, it took me a few seconds to gather my internal thoughts and step out onto the sidewalk. The passenger window rolled down, and he called out behind me, saying he would have everything figured out by the end of the day.

Taking a sip of coffee, I wondered where someone would even start to look for a bodyguard. Surely Craigslist would be a bad place to start, or maybe—

My thoughts were cut off by the smacking sound of charts being plopped on the desk in front of me by the doctor rotating off the night shift.

"Everyone else has been cleared. Just patients in area one, three, and four for you to check on." He covered his mouth with the inside of his elbow as he yawned. "Oh, and by the way, we have a new trauma surgeon starting today. I hear he's an ass, so watch out."

Great, just one more thing I needed this week. Another know-it-all jackass surgeon. "Thanks for the heads-up, Christian. I got this, go home. You look like the walking dead." I patted him on the shoulder and headed deeper into the emergency department to see the first patient of my morning shift.

The smell of alcohol, tobacco, and urine engulfed me as soon as I pushed the curtain back, causing me to hold back a gag and begin breathing through my mouth. Without looking up from his chart, I introduced myself and started right into the reason for the emergency visit. My goal was to make this as quick as possible so the urine smell wouldn't seep into my scrubs and make me stink all day.

"Mr. Street, I'm Dr. Kate Wheeler, and I'll be assisting you today. Can you tell me what brought you to the emergency room?" When I didn't get a response, I glanced up from the chart and found him passed out on top of the gurney.

"Mr. Street?" I said a little louder, hoping it would wake him.

It didn't.

The smell grew stronger with each step I took closer to him. Grabbing his shoulder, I shook him gently, trying to get him to wake up. I said his name again. And again. Still no response. His chest was heaving up and down, visually proving to me he was alive but, unfortunately for me, unconscious.

I had my hand around his wrist, my attention on my watch while checking his pulse, when I felt him start to stir awake. He was startled as he came to, glancing around, obviously not knowing where he was. When he looked down and found my hand on his wrist, he began yelling. Loudly.

His words were too slurred, I had no idea what he was trying to communicate to me. There were definitely some profanities and a few unique ways for me to screw off mixed in. Clearly he did not approve of me touching him or ignoring his requests. Done with talking, he grabbed my wrist with his other hand, pulled my grip from him, and shoved me backward.

Stumbling back against the wall, I tried to stay on my feet. The patient took the open opportunity and began swinging his legs over the gurney and pushing himself off in an attempt to leave. Without thinking, I launched myself in his direction, grabbing him by the shoulders and pushing him back down with all my weight.

"I need some help in here!" I yelled, trying to draw attention to my desperate need for assistance.

Not enjoying being restrained, he continued yelling and now added in, much to my dismay, flailing around. His wrist struck me on my right side, directly on my still tender bruise. The pain that shot through me morphed my concern and care for the patient into something angrier.

Enough of him hurting me and possibly himself.

One hundred pounds. That was about how much I would wager he outweighed me by. But he was drunk and sloppy, and I was pissed, making me stronger than my one-hundred-pound frame made me look. Bracing my hands on his forearms to keep him from hitting me again, I hopped on top of the gurney, straddling him as I slammed my size five feet around his shins to keep him from kicking me or attempting to swing them back off.

Still wiggling, trying to break free, the look on his face was one of pure shock. Even in his drunken state, he knew this was not protocol. I was about to yell something completely inappropriate for a work setting when I heard the curtain behind me rip back. Several sets of feet entered. And stopped. It must have been a sight to see, me on top of a yelling, urine-soaked patient still thrashing beneath me, because no one moved.

Glancing over my shoulder, I barked, "A little help here, please. I can't fucking hold him down all day."

Feet and bodies rushed into motion. Just as my arms started to tremble from exhaustion, someone appeared beside me and administered what I assumed was a sedative into his IV. Within thirty seconds, the man stopped trying to buck me off and relaxed beneath me.

My hands hurt when I released them from the death grip I had on his arms. Crawling off the gurney, I scowled at my wet scrubs. Wet from the urine that had seeped from his pants into mine.

Disgusting.

Just as I turned from the patient to head to the locker room to change, a man in a white doctor coat stopped me. I glanced up at the person blocking my path and found beautiful turquoise eyes staring back at me.

My eyes widened in shock when I found the man from yesterday's hallway incident smiling down at me, clearly amused. When my brain cleared from the fog his intoxicating cologne had over me, I narrowed my brows at him, completely confused as to why he was here. In my hospital. Wearing scrubs. And looking damn good in them. In his blue scrubs and a white doctor coat, tall and gorgeous, he was a walking fantasy come true—the rich, handsome, marriage-material doctor.

"Dr. Austin Lockwood," he stated, shoving his hands into the pockets of his scrubs. "I'm the new trauma surgeon." Still smiling, showing off his straight white teeth, he glanced to the patient now snoring behind me and then back again. "That was quite impressive, I must say. He outweighs you by fifty pounds, at least."

"I was going with one hundred. Dr. Kate Wheeler. Nice to meet you." I made to move past him but turned too quickly. Pain radiated down my right side, making me wince.

He studied me, his eyebrows furrowing together. "Are you still in that much pain? Let me take a look," he said, starting to reach for the hem of my scrub top.

I smacked his hand away. "It's just a bad bruise."

"It's okay, Kate. I *am* a doctor and have seen ribs before. Don't be shy." He chuckled, once again reaching for the hem of my shirt, this time getting close enough that his fingers grazed the bare skin underneath as he started to lift my top.

Swatting his hand away more forcefully a second time, I took a step back out of his reach. "Well, you haven't seen mine, and we're going to keep it that way. It's just a bad bruise. I already had someone look at it. That's why I was here yesterday when you ran into me."

I needed a shower; the wet scrubs clinging to me had started to make my stomach turn with each movement. Pushing past Austin, I started toward the locker room. But before I could get away, he grabbed my wrist, stopping me in my tracks.

"Suit yourself. I would have been gentle, Kate. I always am," he whispered into my ear before releasing my wrist. With a flash of a sensually laced smirk, he was gone.

CONSIDERING the first part of the shift was filled with drama, the remainder seemed... quiet, boring even. The hospital was bursting at the seams with patients, but no interesting cases came in, and to top it off, Austin had made it a point to keep his distance since the earlier encounter. Maybe I'd scared him off. But it seemed that every time I stole a glance in his direction—while he roamed around the emergency room familiarizing himself with the surroundings and introducing himself to other doctors—he was already looking at me. The first couple times, I shook it off as pure coincidence, but the third, fourth, fifth, and now sixth time, it made me wonder. What if he was walking around pretending to take in his surroundings while using this time to monitor, maybe even study me?

The unsettling thought of him sizing me up made my stomach clench in a way that hadn't happened in a long while. Just thinking about it made me glance around once more. This time when our eyes connected across the emergency room floor, he smiled. Clearly he was enjoying the little cat-and-mouse game we were playing.

I tucked my head behind the chart in my hand to hide the smile I couldn't suppress. There was no reason to feel happy about a perfectly gorgeous man staring at me. Instead I should have felt offended or called human resources about sexual harassment. But the thing was, I kind of liked it, knowing he could be just the fun distraction I needed right now from my mess of a life.

Before I knew it, thanks to the eye-flirting with Austin, the remainder of the shift flew by and I was clocking out and cleaning up in the locker room. The locker door slammed closed with a push of my shoulder after I pulled my backpack out. I blindly rummaged through it, searching for my phone. Plopping down on the bench between the lockers, I finally located and pulled the phone out of my bag.

Dad: Worked it out, screened a few candidates today. Someone will be at your house tonight when you get home from work.

Dad: Do not put up a fight. This is going to happen.

Dad: Just got the confirmation. His name is Casey Weston. Ask him to identify himself before you let him in.

Dad: There will be a car waiting out front after your shift. Do not walk home alone.

Eric: Juicy gossip spreads fast. I hear the new surgeon is gorgeous and has his eyes set on you.

Eric: Good luck not getting knocked off tonight. If you need anything, just let me know. I'll call 911 for you.

Meagan: This isn't fair. The hot new surgeon apparently has a thing for tiny brunettes. You are so lucky. Once you scare him off, I call dibs.

Wow. News traveled fast in the hospital. But how did it go from me and him catching each other's glances to getting texts about it? Whatever, I now had bigger things to worry about. Like dealing with this Casey guy, whom I assumed would be a total meathead, sexist prick. Someone who wanted me to be the scared Disney princess so he could be my knight in shining armor.

A mischievous and calculating grin spread across my lips as I slipped out the back door, avoiding the awaiting car to walk home alone. I was going to enjoy proving his dumbass assumptions wrong.

A drop of rain slid down my arm, causing me to glance toward the sky. Dark ominous clouds loomed overhead; the green color of the sky had me saying a quick prayer that it wasn't going to be a long night with tornado warnings. It looked like it was about to pour any second. More and more cold drops hit me and the pavement below me, pushing me into a slow jog, hoping I could make it home before the floodgates opened.

THROUGH THE DOWNPOUR, I could barely make out the silhouette of someone standing on my limestone-framed front stoop. Whoever it was, they were standing close to the front door, attempting to keep themselves somewhat protected from the rain. My breaths were ragged from my quick-paced jog as I leaped up the stairs to my landing and fumbled around in my soaked backpack for keys.

"Casey?" I shouted over the rain and loud crack of thunder rumbling through the sky. Locating my keys, I pushed the door opened and lunged in, thankful for the reprieve from the cold rain. Assuming the man would follow me in, I continued walking toward the kitchen, leaving the door open. But he didn't. Halfway to the kitchen, I turned and frowned at him still standing at the threshold. Door still open, allowing rain to blow in on the sporadic gusts of wind.

"What are you doing? Are you coming in or what?" I demanded, placing my hands on my hips. I was in no mood to deal with formalities.

Finally he spoke, his frustration *very* clear in his tone and annoyed expression. "You were *told* to ask me to identify myself. Not give some random person the name of the man you're expecting," he said. He took a step into the entryway, just far enough for the door to close behind him, then retreated a step to lean his back against the door.

"You can't be serious."

The man said nothing, only cocked one eyebrow at me. Waiting.

I rolled my eyes in the most dramatic fashion I could muster. Crossing my arms too, I decided I could wait in silence just as long as he could. Cold, soaked, and with time to kill, I took a few moments of our stubborn standoff to assess the man in my home.

He wasn't Austin hot—though really, who could be?—but he wasn't unattractive. The first thing I cataloged was how massive he was, almost the size of my front door. He had medium-length wavy dark hair, a straight nose, a strong jaw, and a dark shaggy beard that was nasty. There was something unnerving about how still he was as he leaned against the door, like a predator waiting to strike. It was a stillness that came from someone already knowing they would win if a fight were to break out, aware of the killing blow required. The way his black T-shirt clung to his broad shoulders and trim waist indicated he was fit. And his arms... well, his arms looked hard enough to break a knuckle or two if I chose to hit him there.

My casual perusal stopped when our eyes connected. The coldness in his dark brown orbs sent a shiver down my spine. So emotionless; no joy or warmth seemed to lurk behind them.

Enough. I tossed my hands up in the air and sighed loud enough for him to hear every ounce of my exasperation. "Fine. Please identify yourself."

"That's better. Casey Weston. I'd say it's a pleasure to meet you, but based off the past two minutes, I'm pretty sure neither of us sees this as a pleasure."

What an ass. I gaped at him as he walked past me toward the kitchen, an army green duffel bag in hand.

"Listen, Casey—"

"I go by Weston, actually."

"Fine. *Weston*, I need to get out of these wet clothes and take a hot shower. It's been a long day. We can have our lovely discussion after." Without waiting for a reply or dismissal, I headed toward the stairs, leaving Weston in the kitchen to fend for himself.

· · ·

IN A MUCH BETTER MOOD AFTER getting clean and dry, I made my way back downstairs to face him. One glance at Weston leaning against the kitchen island had me rolling my eyes and heading toward the coffeepot. In the few minutes I'd been around him, I'd already learned enough about him to know we would not be getting along. This conversation about security and what I needed was probably going to be a long one—coffee was the first order of action.

Pressing the brew button, I turned to face the quiet menace and found him staring at me, arms crossed and his stance wide. Prepared for a fight, it seemed. I made my way to his side of the island and plopped down on one of the leather-covered barstools.

"Listen, Weston, I'm not sure what you were told about this situation, but I can guarantee I don't need someone shadowing me all day every day. I'm thinking some kind of unmarked car out front so you can monitor the house while I'm at work. That way I know it's secure when I come home. I can take care of myself."

Weston laughed. Scoffed was more like it.

"Sure you can, Miss Wheeler," he said so condescendingly it set my blood boiling. "I have a couple rules we need to cover before I unpack my stuff—"

"What stuff? You don't need to unpack anything. You're not staying here. That's absurd," I snapped with a quick glance around the room, wondering where his duffel bag from earlier disappeared to.

"Absurd or not, I am in fact staying here until I'm told otherwise."

"Who approved all this? I sure as hell know I didn't. I am not okay with a strange man living in my house for the next several months."

"Your father hired the security firm I work for, he interviewed me today, I got the job, and now I'm here. I'm absolutely staying here with you to keep you safe at all times, like I was hired to do. And quite frankly, I don't *care* if you like it or not. I have a job to do, and I will do it," he said, glaring down at me. Each word he spoke seemed to make ice frost over his features. I'd never met anyone so... intense.

"I have no idea what you have against me, considering we've spoken all of fifty words to each other, but you can lay off with the attitude and intensity. I'm sorry you were pulled from some super-cool hipster convention and now you're all bent out of shape, but don't take it out on me."

That eerie stillness leaked back into him, making me casually slide farther back on the stool, putting more distance between us.

"Hipster convention?"

"Your beard, tight T-shirt. I figured your duffel bag was filled with skinny jeans and ironic T-shirts as well. Maybe a fedora or two." I smirked up at him, knowing I was getting under his skin. He didn't look like a hipster at all. In fact, he looked like the type of guy who would have no idea what I was even talking about. My favorite wall to put up was built with sarcasm, somewhat truthful jabs, and anything I could use to annoy the person encroaching on my space. And it seemed to be working with this jackass. Maybe he wasn't as smart as he looked.

"I landed two days ago from a six-month assignment in Afghanistan. The beard was to fit in and not draw attention to myself."

Oops.

"I would suggest you shave it off. It does the opposite and makes you stand out here." I slipped off the barstool and stood in front of the coffeemaker, pouring myself a steaming cup of liquid love. Stealing a scalding sip, I turned back around to face him. "I'm not trying to be rude, I just don't think all of this is needed. This isn't something I need or want. Can't we compromise?"

"No compromises. I read your file on what's going on, who's threatening you. You absolutely need protection. The people who sent you that threat will make an attempt on your life if your father doesn't back down and drop the case. I'm not sure what game they're playing by placing a death threat in flowers. Maybe they just wanted to terrorize you before they moved forward with their actual plan of kidnapping you and using you as leverage against your father. Either way, they will follow up on their threat. It's only a matter of when and where. When they do follow through, I'll be here." He sighed, resting his muscular forearms against the edge of the granite countertop. "I understand you don't want someone following you around all day, living in your home, but know that this is just a job for me. It's all strictly business, so you can go about your life as normal but with minor adjustments. That leads me to the few rules I have for all this to work out—"

"For what to *work out*?" I asked from behind the coffee cup at my lips. This conversation was already draining.

"So you don't end up decapitated in some part of Mexico, leaving your father devastated and unable to recover from the loss," he said flatly, not blinking.

A pulse of fear ran through me at the thought. I hadn't considered what could actually happen if they did get their hands on me. "Don't sugarcoat it on my behalf."

"The rules. Please focus. First, you're not to go anywhere alone at any time. I don't care if it's the middle of the night—if you need to leave, I'm going with you. Second, no standing out on the patio or in front of the doors or windows for long periods of time. Too much exposure. Third rule, I will not sleep with or fall in love with you."

I laughed, hard. So hard I had to set my coffee mug down on the counter to keep the scalding liquid from sloshing out on my hand. A snort might have even escaped.

What in the hell? Why would he even think that would be a possibility?

"What makes you think *I* would want to sleep with *you*? That's very arrogant, don't you think?"

When he ran a hand through his hair in obvious exasperation, it drew my attention. Now that it was dry, I could tell it was healthy and shiny for a guy. I wondered if maybe his longer hair was also from his long overseas stay or if maybe he always kept it that floppy.

"It just happens," he said, pulling me out of the internal hair debate I had going on. "Women love to fall for the guy who's the hero. The person protecting them, keeping them safe. I'm just telling you this now so there's no confusion in the future."

I chuckled again, picking up my mug and taking a long sip. "Believe me, if you think I'm going to swoon over you because I see you as the hero in this whole story, you can think again. I don't need a hero."

A brief nod was the only acknowledgment I got in return.

"Final rule, no random men over to the house. If you want to invite someone over outside of your current circle of friends, I need a twenty-four-hour notice. That way I can have time to run a background check. Once they're cleared, you'll be good."

"Me. Having random men over." I laughed as I poured myself a second cup of coffee. *Maybe I should offer him some... nah.* "I can guarantee you *that* won't happen."

There was long enough silence from his end that I looked up, only to find his face flushed—almost blushing. "Apologies. No random women in and out of the house—"

"I'm not a lesbian, you idiot," I snapped, moving so quickly that hot coffee sloshed on my hand, but it didn't fully register considering our current topic. "I'm saying me having random men in and out of my house is comical. I don't hook up with random guys. I don't even date."

His flush from embarrassment rose first up his neck and then crept across his face. As quickly as it appeared, it disappeared, his body absorbing any wayward sign of emotion.

Four rules. The only one that really bothered me was the one about not going out alone, and there were ways around that. Having someone monitoring my moves the next several months, not having a say in my own life, my actions, was hard to swallow. But what was the alternative? I knew balking against this guy would only result in another overbearing man appearing on my doorstep as his replacement.

After analyzing the hell out of my crappy situation, I set my coffee mug down and crossed my arms over my chest. "I agree to your terms, but I have some rules of my own."

Weston nodded, keeping his eyes trained on me.

He really needed to learn to use words.

"Rule one, don't bring up my eating habits. It's none of your business. Rule two, I don't clean, so deal with it and pick up after yourself.

Rule three, I don't cook. If you get hungry, figure something out on your own."

Uncomfortable silence filled the kitchen.

"I already put my bag in the downstairs bedroom," Weston said eventually, not acknowledging my rules.

I rolled my neck back and forth, trying to stretch out the tension building in my neck and shoulders. "This is so... unnecessary. Don't take this the wrong way, but I really don't want you here."

"Don't take this the wrong way, but I would rather be back protecting someone more important than some rich Dallas brat," said Weston. He started toward the guest bedroom, now his room for the next few months.

"Excuse me?" I pushed myself away from the counter and strode across the kitchen to catch up with him. He could take me out in one move, but there was no way I could let that comment go without saying something.

"I read your file. I know who your family is." When he turned to me, his face finally showed some emotion. His eyebrows shot up in surprise at finding me now standing directly behind him.

"You know nothing about me. Do not even pretend to know who I am based off a report some assclown in the back of a dusty room put together from what he found on the internet. I am more than that. I am more than you will ever know. Stay out of my way. Don't interfere with my life. In fact, just be as fucking invisible as possible and we might not end up killing each other by the end." Breathing was difficult, as if I were actually drowning in the contempt that was filling my chest. I wanted to hit him. Wanted to hit anything.

Knowing it would be a fight I would lose, I held his now amused gaze for a beat before shoving past him and storming toward the stairs.

I couldn't calm down. His words, what he thought of me, the way he assumed he knew who I was were nothing new. But it still ripped me apart and poured salt in a wound that would never heal. My family's money caused everyone to toss me into the spoiled rich brat club, but it wasn't me. It had never been me. My house, career, friends were all because of the effort I put in, not bought from gliding through life gripping the coattails of my family name or fortune.

I hated him. Truly hated him. He had no idea who I was but couldn't stand me based off the false information he'd been given. From what he read, I bet he expected to be dragged to every charity event and high society gathering in Dallas. Instead of what it would actually be—ten to twelve hours, five days a week at the hospital, and the other hours of the day at the gym or trying to catch up on sleep.

If this was going to be pleasant for either of us—or at best not end in bloodshed—he needed to know I wasn't the Dallas version of a Kardashian.

Cupping my sweaty hands around my face, I started counting to ten, taking a breath with each count, hoping it would calm me down enough to get some sleep.

It didn't work. The only way I was going to calm down was to confront him.

Right now.

The bedroom door slammed against the wall as I shoved my way through it. Taking the stairs two by two, I raced down to clear up any misconceptions Weston had of me. His door shook from the pounding of my fist against it.

When the door finally opened and he was standing in front of me, I realized this was a bad idea.

A very bad idea.

Weston was shirtless with one hand braced on the open door as he stared down at me. His face was white, covered with shaving cream. Almost covering the annoyed expression on his face.

Almost.

Annoyed or not, I couldn't pull my eyes from his chest. It was covered in tattoos that flowed up his shoulders and down his arms, stopping at his elbows. I wondered if they went down his back too....

"What, Kate?"

I heard him say something, or ask something, but I couldn't stop staring. How could I not stare? He looked like the bad-boy version of an Abercrombie poster. It really caught me off guard; I didn't expect him to be so attractive when he was such an ass.

"I work the midday shift tomorrow, so I'll want to work out in the morning."

He nodded, took a step back, and closed the door in my face.

Okay, I didn't accomplish what I had originally come down for, but there would be plenty of other opportunities to correct his judgments of me.

I couldn't help the sly smirk that grew as I calmly climbed the stairs back up to my room.

4

———

Curious as to what Weston would look like after shaving off that nasty beard, I popped out of bed the following morning. Curiosity was another weak point of mine. Everyone knew it, and with Weston being so damn reserved, it sent my curiosity churning at a rapid pace. After last night, it was apparent that the next several months were going to suck, but maybe the puzzle of piecing this Weston character together would keep me distracted enough that it wouldn't end up being too bad.

Halfway down the stairs, the smell of fresh brewed coffee tickled my senses. Huh, maybe having this guy hanging around wouldn't be too bad if it meant having coffee made for me each morning as part of the security package.

When my feet hit the final stair, I glanced around the lower level, searching for my new roommate. I found him sitting on *my* couch reading, cup of coffee in hand, looking way too comfortable. He didn't look up from his book as I made my way to the kitchen to pour myself a cup of coffee.

Lifting the carafe out of the coffeemaker, I found it empty. Not even half a cup of deliciousness left.

"Dick," I said loud enough for him to hear.

When I went to dump the used coffee grounds into the trash, I thought I caught an almost smile tugging at his lips. Apparently he found making my life hell amusing.

While making another *full* pot of coffee, I used the distraction to watch Weston out of my peripheral. He did in fact shave the night before, and it was a *much* better look on him. It made him look about ten years younger. His skin was a golden tan and looked baby soft, but that was where using the word soft to describe any other part of his face and body stopped. His dark brown eyes never glanced up to notice my stare, totally unaware of my scrutiny.

Turning my attention back to the coffeepot in front of me, I cataloged all his features and came to the conclusion that if I did have a specific type, it would probably be someone like him. Well, he would be my type if he didn't see me as some rich brat, or even worse, someone who *needed* him around. As someone who couldn't protect themselves.

Unfortunately, my petite frame typically attracted the "protector" type guy. I'd always known my short stature put me at a disadvantage. Maybe that was why I started taking kickboxing. I wanted to know that if I needed to, I could get out of any situation. I wanted to take care of myself, not rely on someone else. Maybe that was also why my trust fund had sat untouched all these years. The need for me to make my own way was just short of obsessive.

With a mug full of fresh coffee, I walked to the living room and sat on the couch opposite Weston. Placing my cup on the coffee table in front of me, I pulled my long hair back in a messy bun, tucking it into itself to make it stay.

"What gym do you go to?" he asked without even looking up from his book.

Sitting back into the couch, I kept my eye on him to gauge his reaction. "It's a private gym a few blocks away."

"Of course it is." He scoffed under this breath.

"Do you have a problem with me?" I asked, focusing on not throwing my coffee in his face.

He looked up from his book, finally, and answered with a quick "No."

"You just seem to, so I wanted to make sure. If this is going to be pleasant for either of us, we should probably set aside our assumptions and figure out who the other person really is."

He held my gaze for a few seconds before nodding and turning his attention back to his book.

Laying my head against the back of the couch, I closed my eyes and began to dread the next few months of my life.

The sound of the doorbell a few minutes later startled me, mostly from Weston's overreaction. He was on his feet before the first bell had finished sounding.

Staring the door down like it was about to attack us, he asked, "Are you expecting anyone?"

Hmm. Was I expecting someone? No. But *something*, yep, I was sure I was. I was always expecting something; my online shopping had grown into an unhealthy obsession the past few years. So much so that the UPS and Fedex guys on my route knew me by name, and the UPS guy went as far as harmlessly flirting with me when I was home to receive the packages in person.

Before I could respond to his question, he was halfway across the house, stalking toward the door. Gun by his side.

Where the hell did that come from?

"Stay in the living room," he barked over his shoulder, clearly having zero concerns about how he spoke to his employer. Well, kind-of employer.

The pure command and annoyance in his voice pissed me off. So, instead of doing as he demanded, I followed him to the front door, not wanting him to think he could boss me around like that.

Keeping the gun hidden behind his back, Weston opened the door so slowly I thought I would combust.

"Can I help you?" Weston demanded to the person on the other side of the door, whom I still couldn't see.

"Where's Kate?"

"Give me the package and I'll give it to her."

"Um, who are you? I can't just give her stuff to anyone. I have a job to do, man."

I watched Weston stand with his hand out, holding the door open with his foot—since the other hand was still holding the gun—saying nothing, just waiting.

This was insane. From the voice, I knew exactly who was on the other side of that door, and he was no threat. Having had enough, I pushed past Weston, who glared down at me as I opened the door wider and reached for the package Darrell had in his hands. "Stop being a dick, Weston. It's just the shoes I ordered last week, or the dress, or maybe the cute leopard print belt. Whatever it is, it's mine, and Darrell is just delivering it to *me*."

Darrell looked back and forth between Weston and me, assessing the new male addition to my household. I inclined my head toward Weston and rolled my eyes.

"Good to see you, Kate," Darrell said as he smiled down at me. His smile always made me smile in return. It was so... honest. "Not sure how I feel about this new guy in your life. What about me? What about us?" he joked.

"Don't worry, Darrell, he'll be gone soon enough. Our little meetings will continue long after he's gone." I gave him a wink and backed away to close the door.

Standing in the entryway, package in hand, I rolled my eyes at Weston's furious glare. "It was just my UPS guy. Lighten up a bit. You're going to have an early heart attack stressing over every little thing like that."

He opened his mouth to say something but was cut off by the doorbell. Again.

Hmm, now who could that be? What day is it?

Not giving Weston the chance for another overbearing security guy scene, I grabbed the knob and pulled open the front door once more without looking to see who it was.

Sharon, my weekly housekeeper.

It must be Tuesday, then.

The heat from Weston's frustration burned into my back as I

opened the door wider for her to enter. She shrugged past me but was stopped by a scowling Weston.

This man was insufferable.

"Weston, meet Sharon. Sharon, meet Weston. Sharon is my housekeeper. She comes every Tuesday. Weston is my new roommate. He'll clean up after himself, so don't worry about too much extra work, Sharon."

She nodded and walked deeper into the house, glancing back a few times toward Weston's merciless glare that followed her in.

"I told you to stay in the living room," he growled. "Do you always have this kind of problem with direction?"

"That was not direction. That was a pure command, and I didn't like it. So next time, how about you try approaching your demands in a nicer tone? Maybe then I'll listen. *Maybe*."

I could have sworn I saw a hint of humor on his face as he kept his eyes on Sharon.

"Any other unexpected surprises?" he asked after a beat.

"That should be it for now. I'm only expecting a few more packages this week."

Grumbling something I couldn't quite make out, he turned and followed Sharon into the house.

"They should be fine with you being here, working out with me. I'll just explain the situation to the owner," I said, reaching up and pulling open the glass door of the club for us both to enter. While Weston scanned the facility, I watched him, wondering what he was thinking. Maybe I didn't want to know. I started to ask him what he thought of the place so far, if it met his security standards, but was cut off by one of my favorite trainers.

"Hey," Matt called out as he approached Weston and me, "I'm surprised to see you back so soon. I figured that sparring session the other day would have you down and out for a while. You took a few hits before you worked your tiny-body magic and got her down."

We continued walking into the gym until we met Matt, halfway between the reception desk and the front door. Weston's gaze and demeanor toward Matt as he spoke was so impassive and unimpressed that it came off rude.

"Good to see you again, Matt. Yeah, it took me a while to get her down, and one of her kicks really stung. Check out this nasty bruise." I raised the hem of my workout tank high enough for both men to see. It actually looked worse than it had a day ago, which was good. It meant it was healing, even if the yellow-green tint looked like I'd caught a case of gangrene.

"That is nasty," Weston exclaimed. "You need to focus on your defensive moves if you let that get by. No sparring for you until that thing heals."

Matt's attention shifted from my side to Weston, his eyes scrolling up and down the newcomer's body, sizing him up. I once thought Matt was a big guy, but standing next to Weston, he looked... well, average. Or maybe Matt just made Weston look that much bigger. Neither male moved or said anything, only stared. I had to do something to break the silent pissing contest going on in front of me.

"Fine, I'll just do some cardio or something today. Hey, can you grab Bobby for me? I have a question for him regarding this guy." I jabbed my thumb in Weston's direction. Not sure why, as there was no other guy standing around me for Matt to wonder who I was talking about.

He broke his stare from Weston and nodded, heading toward the office. He called over his shoulder as he strode off, "Sure. See ya next time, Kate."

While we waited for the owner, I leaned against the front desk and eyed Weston only to find him already staring down at me. He inclined his head toward the inside of the gym and raised his eyebrows, asking a silent question.

"It's a kickboxing gym, club, whatever you want to call it. It's a full workout gym, plus we have trainers to help with form and lead the sparring session. Since I'm healing from that dumb blonde's kick to the ribs a couple days ago, we can just hit the treadmills or something."

Glancing around the gym, he nodded. I assumed that meant he approved of the facility, but I wasn't quite sure. It was going to take a while to understand this silent man's body language. It really would make my life a lot easier if he would use actual words.

"You know, you really should start using your words more often —" I started to say but was cut off by Bobby, the owner, approaching us.

"Hey, Kate." He gave me a firm handshake and took a step back. "Did ya need somethin'?"

"Yeah, I have a question for you. This is my... friend, Weston, and he's going to be staying with me for a few months. I didn't know if we needed to sign him up for a membership, guest pass, or whatnot. So...."

Bobby turned his attention from me to Weston and did just as Matt had, looked him up and down, assessing. His eyes stopped on the large tattoo inked on Weston's left forearm.

"If you're talkin' about this guy beside ya, he's welcome anytime free of charge." Bobby extended his hand to Weston, who clasped it loudly, giving it a firm shake. "It's always a pleasure to meet one of the military's finest, and it would be an honor to have ya at my gym. Anything ya need, man, just let me know." He dropped Weston's hand and turned his attention back to me, this time a little amused, like he and Weston were in on some inside joke that I wasn't. "Maybe he could teach you a thing or two, Kate." He laughed under his breath and walked toward his private office.

Now it was me asking Weston a silent question. I furrowed my eyebrows together as I looked from his face to the tattoo on his forearm and back up again. The tattoo didn't mean anything to me, but it clearly triggered something with Bobby. I glanced down again, trying to get a better look at it; maybe if I could memorize it, I could research it tonight. Seeming to know about my potential research project, he tucked his forearm behind his back and gave me a knowing smirk.

This man truly is insufferable.

Shaking my head slowly, I extended my hands in front of me in surrender. "Okay, okay, I won't ask. Even though I'm more curious than ever. Let's go get started. I have to be at work later, and I want to run a few miles and get to the weights before we have to leave." Turning on my heels, I headed in the direction of the treadmills.

The cardio area of the gym was empty, as everyone else was on the other side sparring—where I wanted to be. I stepped onto a treadmill and grabbed my iPod and earbuds out of my bag before tossing the bag to the side. As I pressed the speed and incline arrows up to ease myself into a slow jog, I noticed Weston beside me doing the same thing, but with no headphones—no music at all.

How could anyone work out without music? Wasn't that some form of torture they used to break traitors?

Slapping the red Stop button in front of me, I grabbed my bag from the floor and fumbled around, looking for my spare iPod. I always kept a spare, just in case.

Once I found it, I reached over toward Weston and tapped him on the bicep to get his attention off the soundless twenty-four-hour news broadcast playing on the TV in front of us.

He glanced down and shook his head. "No, thanks," he said and pressed the button on his treadmill to increase his speed.

"Just use the damn thing and stop being so damn smug. I'm trying to be nice here. You should try it sometime." Frustrated as to why I even bothered, I tossed the iPod in his cup holder and turned my attention back to my own workout.

I was shocked when I heard him speak up.

"Pretty sure we don't listen to the same music, and there is no way in hell I'm going to listen to Justin Beiber or Meghan Trainor for the next hour."

Snorting at his complete inaccuracy regarding my music choices, I faced him once again. "Remember this morning when I said let's try to put all assumptions aside? How about we try that? I think you'll like that playlist. It's my favorite nineties mix," I said, pointing at the iPod. "Just try it, and if you hate it, then you get to remind me the rest of the day how I was wrong and you were right."

A hint of a smile tugged on his lips, making me feel as if I'd accomplished something unobtainable. I turned back toward my own machine and rapidly pushed a button to increase my speed, sending me into a slight jog for a brief warm-up. Out of the corner of my eye, I caught him reaching into the cup holder. I knew he would like the playlist; it was one I was about to listen to as well. Beastie Boys, Nine Inch Nails, Hole, Green Day, and Rage Against the Machine would accompany me on the six-mile run I was about to accomplish. Beastie Boys' "Body Movin'" poured through my ears just as I lengthened my stride and eased into a steady rhythm.

Six miles later, I was drenched in sweat and panting as Green Day closed out the cardio portion of my workout plan. Reaching for my towel, I found Weston still running, and I could have sworn his lips were moving, barely singing along to the music filling his ears.

A QUICK GLANCE over the schedule as I logged in let me know I would be sharing the shift with Eric and Christian. Briefly, I wondered if Austin would also be working—not that I cared... too much. Okay, yes, it was wrong to date someone at work, according to my personal ethical code, but it was nice to be pursued. Especially by someone as attractive as Austin was. If he really was interested in pursuing me, of course. I'd only heard secondhand that he was through the hospital gossip, so who knew?

I turned from the computer and stumbled back against the desk behind me, startled. A smiling Austin looked down at me.

"Geez." I gasped from the shock of someone being behind me and the pleasant surprise of it being Austin.

"I just finished with a patient and was heading up to the OR when I spotted you across the room. And I thought I would come over and say hi. So, hi." The sexy smirk on his face made my breathing falter slightly. He really was breathtaking. And that damn man bun pulled tightly back accentuating all his pretty features had some kind of bad-boy allure to it.

A bit frantic, my eyes darted around the busy ER, looking for a way out. I needed to get away from him. He was way too close and smelled so good that I was having to hold myself back from completely forgetting our surroundings and running my nose along his throat, up to his ear to inhale the scent deeper.

"Hi," I mumbled as I reached past him to grab the stack of charts needing my attention. Trying to do anything to give him the hint that he needed to keep moving.

"Kate, the man in area four has a large laceration down his arm. He needs stitches," a nurse shouted from the other side of the room, drawing both our heads toward her.

With a quick nod in the nurse's direction, I turned my attention back to Austin. "I have to go. Bye."

I made to step around him to head toward the man needing stitches, but Austin moved with me, blocking my path.

"Do you have a boyfriend?" he asked, that same damn flirty smirk plastered on his face.

"I'm not sure how that's any of your business. Now move. I need to start my shift." Glaring up at him, I moved to the left, trying once again to sidestep him.

He mirrored my movements, taking a smooth step to the right and blocking my path again.

Relentless.

"It's just that I've never had this kind of reaction from a woman before. So I just assumed you did have one. A boyfriend, that is. Because why else would you be avoiding me?"

Something between a laugh and a snort rushed through my chest and out my nose at his audacity. Who did this guy think he was, assuming every woman would fall susceptible to his good looks and charms without him having to put forth any effort? Locking eyes with him, all lust gone and only annoyance remaining, I started to make some smartass comment, but a warm hand grasped me on the shoulder, stopping me.

"Be careful with this one, Austin. She's meaner than she looks." Eric inclined his head toward me. "In fact, I'm shocked she hasn't punched you by now." Turning his eyes to me, he said, "I need you to go check out the guy in area four, please. I don't want to be forced to come up with some lie because you let that guy bleed out on our watch."

He grabbed my waist carefully, remembering my injury, and pulled me away from Austin. Once we were far enough away, I took a quick glance back and found Austin watching us walk away, his gaze a little lower than my waist.

"Thanks, friend, but I really didn't need you to rescue me."

"I know you didn't. Believe me, I would have loved to hear what you were about to say, but I wasn't kidding about the guy bleeding out. And I'm not doing your stitches just so you can flirt with the new hot-as-hell surgeon."

"Hmm, sounds like you're a little jealous. Do *you* have a crush on him?"

My backside stung from the quick smack Eric gave it to hurry me along to the waiting patient. "Who wouldn't? But from the sound of things, I don't think I'm his type."

HALFWAY THROUGH THE SHIFT, I was able to sneak away for somewhat of a lunch break, leaving Weston unaware in the emergency waiting room as I headed toward the cafeteria. Soggy fries and stale coffee were the best I could find with what was left over from the lunch rush. Grabbing a table in a back corner away from other hospital employees and the various families visiting with loved ones, I plopped down in the lone metal chair around the table, ready to savor the alone time.

I was staring into space, thinking of nothing—thinking of everything—and failed to hear Austin's approach until he pulled up a chair from a neighboring table and sat down across from me.

It was sweet at first, but now his presence was interrupting the small amount of peace and quiet I knew I would be allotted for the day.

"What do you want, Austin?"

"Tell me again why you're so offended by me that you won't even carry on a civilized conversation?" His turquoise eyes twinkled with amusement, as if he knew his words would annoy me and force me to talk to him.

I smirked and rolled my eyes as I leaned forward to grab my disposable coffee cup, not confirming or denying his claim.

"What do you have against me, Kate? I don't recall doing anything to offend you other than running into you by accident that first day."

What did I have against him? I was pushing him away because I thought I knew the type of guy he was. The type that always got his way because of his looks, typical jock ego.

Okay, if I was throwing him in that category, maybe I did hold that against him. If that was the case, I was just as bad as Weston in letting my assumptions dictate how I treated someone.

"I don't have anything against you. But why are you so desperate to get me to talk to you?" I smiled at him, trying to play nice as best I could. As soon as my eyes met his, a now too familiar haze settled over my brain. His eyes were the color of the Caribbean ocean, various blues and greens swirling together, unlike anything I had ever seen.

A cocky smirk played on his lips, like he knew he had me in his thrall. "Why do I need an angle when trying to get a beautiful woman to notice me, talk to me?"

My cheeks heated at his words and the way his eyes seemed to grow hungrier and hungrier for me the longer our gazes stayed locked together. It took every ounce of willpower I had to pull my eyes from his, focusing on the empty coffee cup in my hands instead. I cleared my throat as a verbal cue that the topic needed to be changed, and also hoping it would help clear my mind. "How do you like the hospital?" I asked, staring at the loud table of nurses behind him.

"I like it. It's not that different from the hospital I came from in San Antonio, but the city of Dallas is amazing. I needed different. Which is why I had to leave. I grew up there, went to school there. I guess I just needed a change of scenery and opportunity to taste new people."

"You mean taste new food."

When a few seconds passed and he didn't correct me or respond, I shifted my gaze to him—only to find him staring at my mouth.

Damn, and I thought I was blushing before. My face was now on fire, and my palms began to sweat.

"Why do you care if I have a boyfriend, Austin? And don't give me some bullshit story. I'll know."

He broke his hungry stare from my mouth and met my eyes as he sat forward in his chair, leaning against the ceramic table in between us. "I wanted to know, Kate, because I'm attracted to you and wanted to know if there were any... hurdles that might hinder me from pursuing you. Boyfriend or not, I still would have asked you out, but it's good to know if there is any competition lurking around."

"Interesting. Scared of a little competition, Austin?" I asked, raising an eyebrow at him.

A loud, sensual laugh came from him as he shook his head and looked down at the beeping pager hooked on his belt. "I've gotta go. Gunshot victim coming in." He stood gracefully and pushed his chair under the table. "This will be fun, promise," he said, turning and breaking into a jog toward the exit.

Well, that conversation was interesting. Diverting, even. A nice diversion from the shitstorm my life was currently in. It was a lot to process, and unfortunately I had to get back to work.

Filing the conversation away to dissect later, I grabbed my tray, dumped the leftover fries in the trash, and walked back to the emergency room.

I couldn't help the smile on my face the remainder of the shift. The more I thought about it, the more I liked the idea of Austin. He could be a good distraction over the next few months. And an easy one, since I was well aware what he wanted from me, and it wasn't anything serious.

While I finished writing up final notes in a patient chart, eager to end this shift and get home to a hot shower, a nurse walked by and plopped a new chart in my arms, mumbling something as she walked away. I gave an annoyed growl and picked up the chart, then headed to the indicated exam room to see my last patient of the night.

My hand paused on the cloth curtain separating me from the patient within while I quickly scanned over his chart. My heart sank at what I read. I knew exactly what I was about to see once I gathered up the courage to open the curtain. Fourteen-year-old male, multiple visits to the emergency room over the past year—too many—mostly broken bones, a few times with second degree burns on his body.

Taking a deep breath, I closed my eyes, trying to regulate my emotions, and stepped behind the curtain. It took every ounce of self-control to not gasp as I looked over the boy in front of me. There was no way he was fourteen. He looked about ten, twelve years old at the most. The clearly malnourished boy kept his eyes trained on the floor as I slowly approached, not wanting to startle him.

"Hello, Patrick. It's Patrick, right?"

Without looking up, he nodded.

Good. He was responding, even if he wouldn't look at me. I wanted to cry, scream, or hit something in disgust at what other humans could do to each other, and to a child at that.

Fighting against revealing emotion in my voice, I swallowed against the lump forming in my throat and said, "My name is Dr. Kate Wheeler. You can call me Kate, okay? Can I take a look at the arm you think is broken?"

Another nod from the boy as he slowly lifted his arm toward me, still keeping his eyes trained on the eighties-style linoleum beneath his feet.

As I gently grasped his arm, bending and prodding along the bones to see what exactly was broken and how badly, I couldn't hold myself back from asking questions. Wanting to know more, anything that could be beneficial to the report I would be creating and sending to Child Protective Services as soon as I was done with my evaluation. Someone had to help him, to stand up for his rights, because obviously the adult looking out for him wasn't.

"This is a nasty break, Patrick. How did it happen?"

"Practice," he said far too quickly for my liking, like it was rehearsed or the go-to excuse for all his broken bones.

Setting his arm back down on his too thin thigh, I kept at it. "Practice, huh? Must have hurt when it happened. What sport do you play?"

Something in my question had him looking up at me, surprise filling his gaze. Maybe he wasn't used to people digging further, caring enough to take the time. The desolation in his eyes, the lack of hope made me want to hug him until he couldn't breathe. Then he lowered his gaze back to his clasped hands.

"I noticed in your chart you've been to the ER a few times in the past year. Do you want to talk about it?"

Please say yes.

Please say yes.

Tell me anything.

Tell me everything.

Help me stop this.

"No," he whispered through a deep sigh.

My heart shattered. My hands were tied if he wouldn't tell me, if he didn't trust me enough to help him.

"We need to get some X-rays, but I can tell you now it's broken and will need a cast." I stepped to the side, stripped off my latex gloves, and tossed them in the trash can. "I really wish you would tell me what happened. I know that isn't a sports injury. It looks like your arm was gripped and twisted."

His only response to my accusation was to hang his head lower, slightly shaking it back and forth.

My minuscule amount of self-preservation wanted me to get the hell out of there. Pull me away from what was causing me so much heartache that I was finding it hard to breathe normally. But my anger, which I sided with most of the time, wanted me to do a little digging in his chart, find his home address, and take care of the situation myself. Especially now that I had my own personal brute by my side at all times.

Before walking out, I grabbed a piece of paper, scribbled my name and cell number down, and placed it beside him. "If you ever need anything, remember my name and ask for me. I want to help. I wish you would believe me."

As I turned to leave, I watched his hand slide down his leg, drop to the gurney, and crumple the piece of paper, squeezing it so tight his knuckles turned white. Knowing that he at least had some way to reach out, in case things got worse or if he ever changed his mind, was the only thing that stopped me from fully hating myself for leaving him in that room.

MULTIPLE PAPERCUTS and two hours later, I had completed all my patient files and the CPS report on Patrick. The report to CPS was what took me the longest; I wanted to make sure I documented every-thing clearly, detailed enough that hopefully someone would take some kind of action. Even though I knew no one would. The system was too broken. Too many kids slipped through the cracks, leaving them in awful living situations until they turned eighteen and could "adult" themselves.

It was a cool seventy-three degrees as Weston and I walked home in the dark, the streetlamps lighting our way. Thinking back to the hopeless look in Patrick's eyes had my hand at my mouth, picking at my lip nervously. Why he wouldn't tell me, why he didn't trust me enough. I wasn't really watching where we were going; I let my feet guide me home by memory alone.

"Did something happen at work tonight?" Weston asked, his deep voice cutting through the silence.

"Huh?" I dropped my hand from my lip. "Oh. No, I just.... Tonight there was this boy who I treated. It got to me, I guess."

Weston kept his eyes trained straight ahead for the most part, shifting across the street every now and then, assessing for any threats. He didn't ask for details—honestly, he didn't look like he even cared if I ever spoke again—but *I* needed to talk.

"This kid came in tonight. He had a broken arm. It was the kind of break that 99 percent of the time comes from child abuse. It's called a twist break. In his chart, I noticed he's been into our ER several times in the last year, so this isn't the first incident. I asked him to tell me what happened so I could tell someone, get him help, but he wouldn't. He didn't trust or believe in me enough to tell me the truth. Why wouldn't he just tell me? I can't do much if he won't talk. My hands are tied." I sighed and closed my eyes, saying a silent prayer for the tension to release from my gut and shoulders.

"Maybe he's only been hurt by adults his whole life and doesn't trust anyone because everything in life has been a lie," Weston responded. I whipped my head in his direction in astonishment. "You said you wanted to help him, but he's been told that by too many people who did nothing, maybe even making his situation worse. Don't take offense to him not trusting you. It has nothing to do with you. He's just.... His hope of things getting better is gone."

"I can't accept that. I could have done more. Maybe if I go back or call the caseworker directly...."

Weston slowed his pace and stopped completely to stare down at me, his expression unreadable. The glow from the streetlamp over-head made him look even more domineering, casting shadows on his face while illuminating his broad shoulders.

"Why do you care so much?" The words shouldn't have shocked me considering he thought I was just some spoiled brat, but they still did.

"Why do I care? He's a kid. But even if he was an adult, no one should treat another human being that way. We're not on this Earth to be someone else's punching bag."

He inclined his head, considering my words, probably deciding if I was even worthy of a response.

"You will never know how deep the distrust and anger in that kid goes, Kate. You will never understand why he won't accept help."

I snorted, widening my stance and preparing for a fight. "Are you saying you do?"

He hesitated and looked at the dark street behind me. "Yes."

For a split second, I thought I was looking back into Patrick's eyes.

The bleakness that flickered behind Weston's made me hate my laugh and words to him.

He recovered quickly, putting that emotionless mask back on, and began walking again.

As soon as we arrived home, Weston checked the windows and doors. When he found everything as secure as they were when we left, he mumbled a "Good night" and closed the door to his bedroom behind him.

I stood staring at his door for a few minutes, trying to piece it all together. How did he understand Patrick's point of view so clearly? What had he been through in his life that made him who he was now?

My curiosity started creating various versions of answers in my head, but in the back of my mind, I wondered if I really wanted to know the truth, or if the reality would be more than I could fully understand.

5

———————

I read the same line over and over again on a patient's chart, but after the fifth time, I still couldn't retain the information. Over a week had passed since the abused boy, Patrick, came through the emergency room and a sliver of Weston's past had slipped out. He never did elaborate, and, not wanting to die in my sleep, I didn't probe any further. Hopefully someone had taken the CPS report I sent out seriously and something had been done.

The sound of someone yelling my name pulled my attention from the chart in front of me. Scanning through the hordes of people in the ER, I located the source. Eric was on the other side of the emergency room floor with his hands on his hips, glaring at me.

"What?" I shouted back. *Why does he look so frustrated?*

"I've been trying to get your attention for the past five minutes. Finish up with that chart and get your ass to the next patient. We're swamped. I swear there are a billion people waiting to see one of us. It has to be a fu—freaking full moon or something."

"Seriously? A billion, Eric? It's 2:00 a.m. I highly doubt a billion people are out there—" I kept talking as I walked toward the waiting room but quickly stopped my commentary. The waiting room was packed. "Well, hell," I said to no one in particular. Grabbing a pair of latex gloves, I started toward the charge nurse to see who needed to be seen next.

FOUR HOURS LATER, I could barely tolerate pressure on the bottom of my feet. It really did seem like we'd seen a billion patients altogether. When we started comparing notes on the different types of illnesses/injuries we'd seen, we laughed at how it sounded like a Christmas carol:

Twelve false alarm heart attacks.

Eleven sick babies with panicked parents.

Ten broken bones.

Nine high fevers.

Eight mysterious abdominal pains.

Seven lacerations needing stitches.

Six sprained ankles.

Five cases of whooping cough.

Four addicts needing a fix.

Three drunk and disorderly.

Two gunshot victims.

And the best of the night...

One woman who was in labor and had no idea she was even pregnant.

It was a hell of a night shift, and now all I wanted to do was go home, soak in a scalding hot bath, and binge-watch something trashy on TV until I fell asleep.

Heading toward the locker room to get cleaned up, I found Austin leaning against the doorframe. He seemed to be waiting for someone, and by the half smile on his lips as our eyes met, I guessed me. He must have been scheduled for the day shift, since I hadn't seen him at all during the shift. In fact, this was the first time I'd even seen him since that day in the cafeteria.

Right now, however, was not a good time for this; I was too tired and in no mood for his games. Giving him my best attempt at a smile and a brief nod, I walked past him into the locker room.

He followed.

The locker room was empty except for the two of us. I lifted my backpack, though it felt like it held a hundred pounds of rocks in my weak arms. When I closed the locker door, Austin was casually leaning against the lockers, staring at me with the same cocky smirk he always wore.

"We haven't gotten a chance to talk much, have we?" he mused, daring a step closer to me.

"We've both been a little busy." My words were almost a whisper; I couldn't muster enough energy to speak any louder. Just breathing was draining my last few ounces of reserved energy. I had so little energy that I didn't fight it when Austin wrapped his arm around my waist, pressing his palm to my lower back and pushing me closer to him until our bodies connected.

And just like that, I no longer cared about my exhaustion or where we were. All thoughts swept away at the heat flowing through my body. It intensified when Austin twisted us so his warm body had my back pressed against the cool metal of the lockers. The thud of my backpack on the floor was the only sound except our mingled deep, shaky breaths.

Holy hell.

His lips brushed against the shell of my ear. I could almost feel his smile as he breathed, "Do you want to talk now?"

Absolutely not was what I wanted to say, but instead I focused all my energy on simply shaking my head back and forth.

"Good." His lips hovered dangerously close to mine.

Reflexively, my eyes closed at the promise of his lips connecting with mine. He was so damn good at the buildup, there was no doubt that when our lips connected, it would be phenomenal.

Austin gently swept his lips against mine, back and forth, teasing, before migrating down my jaw to the nape of my neck, where he continued brushing his lips against my skin, causing a shiver to crawl down my spine. His lips never fully connected with mine or my skin, only teasing, knowing full well what he was doing to me.

Just when I was ready to grab his face and force his lips against mine, he pulled away, making my eyes snap open. As I stood in utter disappointment and not understanding the reason for his withdrawal, the corners of my lips turned downward. Then, to my horror, I watched him pull farther away, even going so far as taking a step backward, leaving the front of my body hungry for more of his warmth.

That freaking cocky grin was back in full force. "See, I knew you were attracted to me too. I'm not sure why you're hell-bent on fighting it."

My mouth gaped open. "Is that what this was about? You wanted to know if I find you attractive? Fine, yes, I find you attractive. Who wouldn't?"

His grin turned into a full smile as he reached out once more, wrapping both hands around my thin waist and pulling me toward him. "Good point."

"Arrogant son of a bitch, aren't you?" Placing my palms on his chest, I pushed back, trying to prove to him—or myself, I didn't know which—that I wouldn't give in to his charms and games that easily.

His grip didn't falter; instead, he pulled me tighter against him, smiling down as he did.

"Now that we know we're both attracted to each other and know there is something between us, say yes to going on a date with me."

Something between a sigh and a laugh came out as I tried to come up with a way to explain my current situation. "An actual date might be difficult for the next couple months." I was still pushing against his chest, trying to put a little distance between us so I could think clearly. When we were this close, the fluttering in my belly made it hard to focus on anything other than the need for him.

His smile faltered and he released his grip on my waist. Since I was still pushing against him, my back slammed hard into the lockers behind me. "Oh? And why is that, Kate?"

"There's some stuff going on with a case my father is working." *Bastard.* I rubbed a spot on my lower back that ached from the impact. "Apparently some people want me dead or something, so I can't really go out to public places without protection. Plus, it would be awkward, the three of us going out together."

Austin took two more steps farther away, his mood shifting to something unreadable. "The three of us?"

"You, me, and Weston, my security detail."

"Are you being serious, or are you just trying to get out of going on a date with me?"

"Unfortunately I am being serious, so until the trial is over, no dates." Plus, I was still trying to figure out exactly how I felt about this whole scenario. Yes, of course I was attracted to him, but... dating.

"Fine, no dates. We can just keep it casual. There are plenty of supply closets we can investigate until then," he said with a wink. "I gotta go start my shift. Until next time, Kate," he whispered as he kissed my cheek.

As soon as he was out the door, my exhaustion came back in full force, making my knees buckle. Grabbing my bag from the floor, I slung it over my shoulder and made my way to the waiting room to meet Weston and finally head home.

I swayed on my feet for a moment when I rolled out of bed around noon. Four hours in my bed wasn't nearly enough, but another night shift was on the books for later, and I didn't want to sleep the day away. When I stumbled down the stairs, Weston was in the kitchen, standing in front of the coffeemaker and going through the motions of starting a fresh pot of coffee. He must have heard me stirring; he looked like he'd just rolled out of bed too in his wrinkled T-shirt and mesh shorts. His wavy dark hair was going in every direction, making him look young, less harsh. The cuteness of it made me smile.

Sliding onto the barstool, I quietly observed him. There was a brute force, chiseled, commanding attractiveness there. I found myself wishing I knew more about him, about his life and what all he'd seen and been through to be as hard as he was now. Maybe if I knew more about him, it would make the next few months easier. Up to this point, we'd simply stuck to head nods and, on occasion—way more than I would like to admit—vulgar hand gestures behind the other's back.

Weston hit Brew on the coffeemaker and turned to face me. He said nothing, only stared with his piercing brown eyes. The way he looked through me, read me when he held my gaze, was unnerving. He made me feel like all my thoughts and emotions were an open book for him.

I gave him the best smile I could muster after four hours of sleep and leaned into the countertop. "Good morning, sunshine."

From the snarl on his face, he didn't quite like my new term of endearment, which meant I was going to keep using it. Poking at him and finding new ways to annoy him had somehow become my new favorite hobby. Annoying him made me smile a bit and forget everything else that was going on. A bit of a reprieve from my life. A life that even before this whole "gang might kill me" crap felt empty, lost even.

For a while now, I'd been wondering what else was out there for me. Like I knew I was destined for more than this life, but I just hadn't found it yet.

"I'm going to take a shower."

Six words in a row. We were making progress.

Giving him my best sly grin, I said, "Okay, are you asking for permission, or is that an invitation?"

He narrowed his eyes before stalking off toward his room and partially closing the door behind him.

I knew better, but I couldn't help myself. Looking through his cracked door was an invasion of his privacy, but then again, he was the one who didn't close it all the way. It was like he wanted me to sneak a peek inside. The coffee wasn't fully done brewing, but I still poured myself a cup and walked to the couch in the living room where I could read... and have a better view into his room.

Of course, Weston was oblivious to my curiosity. I watched him go into the bathroom, heard the sound of the shower running just before he walked back into the bedroom. The coffee mug froze in front of my lips and my breathing turned shallow, not wanting to make a sound. Afraid it would distract him, or worse, make him stop undressing. He removed his T-shirt by grabbing the back and pulling it over his head. How in the hell did guys do that? It seemed so natural to them, yet I'd tried a million times and just got tangled up in my own shirt.

He turned to toss his dirty shirt in the laundry bin, putting his back in my direction. Even from several feet away, I could tell his back was solid muscle; it flexed and moved with every movement of his arms. Plus, every inch of skin was covered in ink from his shoulders down to the middle of his back. I was too far away to see exactly what it was, but I could make out that it was all done in black and shading, no color anywhere.

Closing my eyes and gripping my warm coffee mug between my hands, I leaned my head back against the couch, trying to stop myself from becoming a full-fledged voyeur.

Just when I thought one more look wouldn't hurt anyone, I felt something land on the crown of my head.

Deep breaths in and out, I told myself as I carefully reached up to explore the top of my head. Whatever it was, it was now crawling along my hair and tickling my scalp. "Please don't be a spider. Please don't be a spider" I whispered the mantra over and over again while my trembling fingers combed through my hair. Not many things grossed me out or scared me, but spiders, they were my kryptonite. When my fingers grazed a tiny creature but it scurried away, hiding itself in my wavy hair, I lost all control of my body.

Coffee sloshed on every piece of furniture from my mug being chucked across the room. Both hands were needed to get the arachnid out of my hair. Standing on the couch, I began screaming and flipped my hair over to start scrubbing my scalp.

"Get off me! Get off me, you nasty creature!" was all I could get out in between ragged breaths.

Within two seconds of my initial scream, Weston was out in the living room with only a towel wrapped around his muscled waist, gun in hand.

"Kate, what the hell is going on?" he yelled over my screaming.

"Get it off me! Please get it off me!" I screamed and whimpered in the same breath. My heart was racing, almost pounding out of my chest.

As I continued my spider dance on the couch, I heard laughing —*loud* laughing—coming from across the room. It was a harsh laugh, like it was something new or just remembered. I paused my head shaking long enough to look up and see Weston slumped over, hands on his knees laughing. Hard.

"This isn't funny," I hissed.

"Oh, but it is, Kate. You put up such a tough act, yet you're still such a girl, scared of a bug."

"It's not just a bug, you idiot, it's a spider. They are nasty, and it's probably laying eggs in my hair right now. Its babies are going to crawl into my ear at night and invade my brain. I'll end up on some medical mystery TV show on how a woman is now brain dead due to spider infestation."

Still chuckling, he shook his head and headed back in the direction of his room.

What the hell? The one time I actually needed him, and he simply walked away. *What a jackass.*

As I debated shaving off my hair to make sure the nasty creature was indeed gone, Weston reappeared. He'd ditched his towel for a pair of basketball shorts, but the upper part of him was still naked.

Sitting on the couch, he grabbed my hand and pulled me down beside him. My cheeks flushed as his agile fingers combed through my hair, inspecting each section for my eight-legged nemesis. He didn't say a word as he searched. Neither of us did.

Once he was done, he dropped his hands and scooted away so our thighs were no longer touching. Almost like he needed the distance, building up some invisible wall between us. "I don't see anything, Kate. I'm pretty sure your scream scared it off. If not that, then all the flailing around you did sent him flying."

Taking a deep breath in, I attempted to calm myself. After my fifth breath, I glanced up at him, wondering what he thought of this whole thing. Because if I was being honest, I felt exposed, vulnerable. Him seeing this side of me was not in the plan. But when you were living together, I guessed all the sides of someone came out eventually. Mine just happened to be a slight case of arachnophobia.

"Thank you for your help," I said sincerely. "I *hate* spiders."

"I can tell. Well, as long as I'm around, if you see one, just come get me and I'll take care of it. I would much prefer that than hearing your bloodcurdling scream, making me wonder if you're being gutted in the living room." Even though his words were reprimanding, the small smile on his face conveyed something very different. "*Now* I'm going to take a shower."

Ink and muscle flexed with each move he made toward his room, making it impossible not to stare and fantasize a little. He was spectacularly built from the size of his arms and the strength in his back. I was willing to bet he could toss my small frame around like a doll.

A small, unfamiliar part of me hoped I would find out one day. And soon.

6

It was a rare day off, and I was lounging on the couch in the living room attempting to read a book I'd been trying to get into for weeks. But my thoughts kept drifting. In the past month, nothing unusual or life-threatening had happened, leaving me to wonder if Weston's presence was necessary or if it was simply my father being overzealous about my safety. He seemed to think I was still in grave danger, and Weston... well, Weston took intense to a whole other level. It seemed every move and every thought was with my safety and protection in mind.

The tension between us slowly dissipated since my near-death experience with the spider, and much to my surprise, he'd started to grow on me. I even started *enjoying* having him around most of the time. He wasn't the dumb sexist brute I thought he was initially, and it seemed he was slowly coming around to the truth that I was... well, just Kate. Nothing extravagant or showy, just me.

Our time at home mostly consisted of him reading on the couch while I played on the iPad or watched TV. He wasn't much of a talker but happened to be a great listener. I found myself talking nonstop simply to avoid the silence that fell between us when I stopped initiating the conversations. We mostly talked about surface-level topics, but sometimes, when I was too tired from a long shift and my walls were down, I talked about my life, past, and what I dreamed of for a future. There had been a few times when something I said or did made him laugh, really laugh, and it made everything in the world right for those few moments.

Then there was Austin. I couldn't figure out what was going on with him. Gorgeous, flirty, and a little-too-handsy Austin. We flirted and snuck in short supply room make-out sessions every shift we overlapped, but that was it. No long talks on the couch or asking about the other's day. We'd even started to skip the basic pleasantries knowing our time alone was short. It had become a fun distraction from the hectic, demanding life in the emergency room, one I found myself looking forward to a little too much. And to top it all off, much to my chagrin, everyone at work had started teasing me if I was in a foul mood, blaming it on Austin if we weren't sharing the shift. Eric and Meagan were by far the worst. The bastards.

An incoming text pulled my attention from the book and my internal thoughts.

SHELLY: I know things are crazy for you right now, but can you come by today? I just found out we have several women and a few kids coming through.

GROANING AT THE TEXT, I tossed the phone on the couch and stared at the closed book in my hands. There were two options: tell Weston the truth, or simply sneak out now. Even though I knew he would catch me and murder me for attempting an escape before I could get one foot out the door.

Tossing the hardback book beside the phone, I pushed off the couch with a low groan and walked toward his room. The door was slightly open, my knock causing it to open wider, revealing him laid out on his bed. He had one arm tucked behind his head while the other held a nondescript hardback book. When I met his gaze, he looked surprised to see me standing in his doorway.

"Hey." No idea why it felt awkward to talk to him about this, to talk to him in his room—with him on his bed—but it did. My eyes shifted around the former guest room and noticed it had never been this clean before. The dresser was clear of all the random clutter I stored there, and the couch, which normally held anything I didn't want to deal with or something I needed to return, was clean except a couple of throw pillows that I had no idea even existed.

Sensing my apprehension, he set the book aside and sat up straighter on the bed. "What's going on? Is there something wrong?" he asked.

"No. Well, yes. Not really wrong, per se, but I do need to go out for a little bit. It's really complicated, so I was hoping you would let me go alone. I promise I won't be gone long and will go directly there and back. No pit stops." I leaned my hip and shoulder against the doorframe, hoping my acting casual about the request would put him at ease and help him say yes. This whole asking to go out was so degrading, like I was a teenager begging to stay out past my curfew.

"Sorry, Kate, but I can't let you go anywhere alone. I know it seems over the top considering it's been quiet the past month, but I can't risk something happening to you. Is there a reason you don't want me to come?"

"It's not that I don't want you to come with me. It's...." I sighed and closed my eyes, leaning my head against the doorframe while I tried to pull my thoughts together.

Why was this so hard? He would understand, of course. But what concerned me was it would give him a glimpse into me, of who I really was and what I truly cared about. What made me anxious was the pull going on inside my heart and mind. Half wanted him to see this side of me, but the other half wanted to keep it hidden so in case... well, in case... hell, I couldn't come up with a good excuse. Not anymore, and not with him.

"If this is about you wanting some alone time with that guy you've been seeing at the hospital"—he gave a half shrug, trying to act casual, but his words were clipped and his shoulders tense—"I don't care, Kate. You do whatever you want. I won't judge you, if that's what you're worried about."

Damn. I knew he was observant, but since he wasn't back in the emergency room with us every day, I kind of thought I'd been doing a good job of keeping the whole thing a secret. Now that I knew he knew, my cheeks burned and flushed pink with embarrassment.

His body tensed when I sat on the end of the bed. He pulled his legs back and swung them over the side of the bed, situating himself beside me.

"Why would you think it has anything to do with Austin?" I asked, turning to face him head-on. We were sitting so close, our thighs grazing one another. This was the closest we'd been to each other since he arrived that day in the rain. The urge to reach out and touch him in some way was almost overpowering. I tucked my hands under my thighs to help fight the urge.

He turned to face me to answer my question, but when our eyes locked, my stomach sank and flipped inside me. Yes, he was attractive, but this was the first time my body had reacted like this *for him*. And just when I thought I was the only one with overactive hormones reacting to our close proximity, I caught Weston's shallow breaths and him casually clenching and unclenching his fists.

"You two seem to have something going on at work, but you never see each other outside the hospital. I thought maybe you two were taking that next step or something. Am I wrong?"

"Well, yes and no. We do have fun at work, but that's about all it is at this point. He is gorgeous, yes, but it's just all surface with him. Flirting but nothing that... matters." I watched his brown eyes harden and his lips press into a thin line at the mention of Austin's looks. "But today has nothing to do with the hospital or Austin. It's something I do on the side. It's a volunteer thing at this nonprofit, but...." I sighed and plopped back on the soft feather-down duvet. "It's complicated if you go with me. If I tell this group I can come help today, you'll need to stay out of my way. I can't risk them because of your obsession with needing to be around me at all times. If you go, you'll have to promise to stay out of the way. That you'll stay where I tell you to. Do you think you can do that?"

"Did you just tell me to stay... like a dog?" He lay back on the bed beside me, head propped up on his elbow, his body twisted to face me. The corners of his mouth twitched up in an almost smile. That tiny smile. It slayed me every time I saw it. They were so few and far between, I began taking a lot of pride in knowing I was the reason that almost smile was on his face.

I kicked my foot out to the side, nailing his shin. "I didn't mean it in a derogatory way, you know that. I'm just saying you'll need to listen to me, for once, if you do come with me. The whole thing is complicated even without you tagging along."

He was giving a fake scowl at his shin, making me chuckle at how comfortable we were becoming with each other, when his eyes flickered to my mouth. He stilled and his fake scowl faded, his lips parting with a quick intake of breath. Before I could question what was going on in his mind, he was pushing himself off the bed.

He held out his hands in an offer to help me up. "As long as it's not putting you in danger, fine, I can give you marginal control for one afternoon. But don't get used to it. This is a once-in-a-lifetime offer, and I'm really not happy about it."

Once my feet hit the floor, he immediately dropped my hands, wiping his own down the front of his jeans.

"Um, hate to break it to you, but I'm always in control. I just let you think you are the majority of the time. We can take my bike, but since you don't know where we're going, I'll drive."

I bolted toward the entry table where I knew my keys were waiting, but out of nowhere, he reached around me and snagged them out of my hands.

That stealthy bastard.

"Absolutely not. You can direct me on where I need to go just fine. I know this city better than you, I'm sure," he said, already heading toward the door that led to the garage.

Grumbling a slew of nasty words, I grabbed the stocked medical bag I kept in the downstairs closet. After locking the back door and checking it twice, per his barked orders, I climbed on my bike behind Weston and began securing my helmet.

"So, Your Majesty, which way are we heading?" Weston asked, pulling on a spare helmet I bought hoping Eric would trust me enough for a ride or two. He hadn't yet.

"Your Majesty... I could get used to that. Head North on I-35."

I wrapped my arms around his waist as he started the bike, the loud rumble filling the small garage.

WE MADE great time from my perspective, and twenty minutes later, we were at the warehouse and I was dismounting the bike. I could feel the unease rolling off him as he surveyed our new surroundings. We were not in a great part of town. The area was known for drugs, prostitutes, and had about 90 percent of the city's strip clubs in a ten-mile radius from where we stood. There were still a few good companies in the area, but most had left back in the nineties, their abandoned buildings now used for squatters and areas where the local prostitutes could conduct their business. It was late morning, and on our drive in, we were approached by a lady suggesting her services when we stopped at a red light a couple blocks away. What I would have given to see Weston's face. It must have looked terrifying; she got half a sentence out before turning and bolting down the street away from us.

At least the weather was nice, the summer heat taking pity on us overbaked Texans and cooling down to a pleasant ninety-five degrees.

Gravel crunched beneath boots behind me, signaling Weston's approach. "Kate, what are we doing here?" he asked tensely as he tucked his helmet under one of his powerful arms.

I shook my head, not knowing what to say, and started toward what looked to everyone else like an abandoned building. But he needed to know, needed to understand. Taking a deep breath in, I turned and held up my hand, signaling for him to stop his approach.

"This is where you need to stay put. Please. Guard the door, walk around the outside of the building, juggle guns or knives to ward off bad guys, do whatever you need to do, but please do *not* come inside this building," I said, lifting my arm behind me and pointing toward the building I was about to walk into.

I couldn't read Weston's body language. That unnatural stillness had somehow leaked back into him, taking away the warmer Weston I'd started to call my friend.

"Kate, what the hell are you doing? What are we doing out here? Fuck, if you're doing something illegal, I have to report it. Don't put me in this situation. I—"

"Calm down, you idiot. You really think I would do something illegal? Something that would ruin everything I've worked for? We've been living together for over a month. Do you actually think I would do that to me, or you, or even my family?"

"No," he said hesitantly, "but look where we are. What are we doing here? You have to give me some kind of explanation, Kate."

I gave a sidelong glance back toward the building while I gathered my thoughts, then sighed and turned back to Weston. Maybe if he knew, maybe he would understand why it had to be this way.

"I volunteer at a nonprofit, and this, the building behind me, is their transition building."

"Okay, good start. Now what the hell is a transition building?"

"The nonprofit is called Second Chances. It focuses on helping women, men, and sometimes children transition out of prostitution. Or on occasion, they're asked to help women who are rescued from human trafficking situations." I took a step toward him, showing him the most open and honest face I could for him to realize how vulnerable the people in the building behind me were. "They do not trust men. They barely trust me. That's why I've asked you not to come inside. Why you *cannot* go inside. You, you will terrify them just by being a guy and being one who's so hulky."

The few seconds of silence that followed were surprisingly calm, as if he knew he would give in to my request and stay outside. But for those few lingering seconds, he seemed to be assessing me. As if this part of me was a surprise to him.

A warm breeze swept a few loose strands of hair into my face, but

I didn't dare move. Not while he was still forming new judgments, a new perception of me.

"I'll wait out here. If you need me or if you're in danger, or if you sense any kind of danger, just call out. How long do you think you'll be?" he asked, walking back to the bike and hooking his helmet on to the handlebars. A sharp glance back let me know he was waiting for a response.

I pushed those wayward strands of hair behind my ear, tucking them out of my face. "I don't... I don't know. The text said they had a few women and kids for me to look over. It's usually a few hours, just depends on how many, really. And when it's kids...."

"What do you do for them?"

"I give them basic exams. Most need heavy antibiotics, or if they're addicts, then I get them in touch with a rehab facility in the area we partner with." Nausea rose in my belly knowing what waited for me in that building. Most of the time, it was young to middle-aged women, but when kids were involved, it made everything much, much harder.

Taking a deep breath in, I turned and began walking toward the building.

His voice was deep and clear, cutting through the traffic noise coming from the busy interstate nearby. "I'll be here."

WHEN I STEPPED out into the sunlight six hours later and found Weston sitting on the concrete steps, I must have looked as exhausted as I felt. One look at my drained face and the distance in my eyes had him leaping from his perch and grabbing the black bag from my hands. I was too exhausted, emotionally and physically, to demand that I could carry it myself, that I didn't need his help.

We walked in silence to the bike. He handed me my helmet and proceeded to put his on. The day had grown hotter, and combined with the lingering heat in my body from the stuffy building behind me, my head began sweating before I secured the chin strap. Climbing onto the back of the bike first, I scooted as far back as possible, giving him ample room to swing his leg over. In a daze, I stayed scooted back until two solid hands gripped my thighs and pulled me in close, securing me to him. His hands left my thighs and grabbed my hands, wrapping my arms around his waist, and giving my hands a gentle squeeze before releasing them to grip the handlebars.

As we weaved in and out of traffic, the strong hold I had on my imagination slipped, allowing all the images of what those women's lives had been like, sold day after day to the scum of the Earth, to flash over and over in my mind. There was nothing I could do to take away the horrors that would most likely chase them until the end. Nor was I able to make it stop for all the thousands of other women and children out there who had hope and love ripped from them day after day. Choking on my own helplessness, I squeezed Weston as tightly as I could, causing my arms to tremble from the tension. I closed my eyes and rested my head against his strong back, giving up all control and letting him take me home.

My helmet was off and I'd started to hop off the bike before the engine was even off. Tossing the helmet on the bench in the garage, I headed straight into the house and up the stairs. I could hear loud grumblings from Weston. I couldn't quite make out what he was saying through the numbness in my mind, but I assumed it had something to do with me barging in the house before he could give the all clear. Not today; I was in no mood for that crap today. He could get over it or lecture me about it tomorrow, but now... now I just wanted to take a shower so hot it melted the images of the day from my memory. And hopefully cleansed me of the realization that the difference I was making at Second Chances was just a drop in the bucket compared to what all was truly going on in the world.

THE SMELL of brewing coffee lured me down the stairs into the kitchen. My feet came to a halt as I took in the scene before me; I knew complete disbelief was fixed on my face. Weston was standing over the stove cooking what looked to be dinner with a full pot of fresh coffee brewed on the counter beside him. The gesture of both, that kindness and awareness of my day, made my breath hitch. No one had ever....

Shaking my head, allowing the shock to move into a true smile, I made my way to the stool that had a steaming cup of coffee sitting in front of it on the counter.

With all his security training, I was sure he heard my approach, but he said nothing, only banged a spoon around in a few pots. A few minutes of comfortable silence passed before he verbally acknowledged my presence.

"I'm not that great of a cook. Don't get your hopes up. It's nothing fancy, just spaghetti," he said, not turning to face me as he spoke, still stirring what I now knew was pasta sauce.

Where the hell did he even find the supplies in this house to make all this?

I wrapped my hands around the warm mug as my smile grew. Just when I had seen all the indecency a human could offer another, here was Weston proving there was still some kindness in the world.

"Sounds great," I said before taking a sip of coffee. Of course, it was prepared the way I liked it. Weston apparently was more observant than I gave him credit for. It made me wonder what else he'd noticed about me. Maybe he'd already seen how broken I was in the love department, making him realize that, rules or no rules, I wasn't worth the effort he would have to put in. A small—but growing—part of me hoped he hadn't.

He finally turned to face me, I assumed once he realized I wasn't going to mock him for his show of kindness. He was wearing an old army T-shirt and a pair of mesh shorts, looking so comfortable and casual in my home, making my heart flutter again as I took in those tattoos peeking down his arms. His hair kept falling in his eyes, he really needed a haircut, but the longer hair didn't look bad on him. I suspected nothing really did. Not sure how I didn't notice it before, but he was handsome. His massive size, tattoos, and soul-reading brown eyes made him extremely alluring.

Needing to stop my gawking, I gave a pointed look to his T-shirt, then back up to him. "Army, huh?"

"Yep," he said back, not breaking my gaze.

Whether it was the heat from the stove warming up the house or the intenseness in his stare, I didn't know, but something caused my body temperature to start creeping up.

"Why army?"

"It was the closest recruiting office to where I lived at the time."

"Oh, interesting. Where did you live at the time?"

"Here, Dallas." He paused for a second, looking like he was contemplating telling me more. "I grew up in Dallas."

My eyebrows shot up in surprise. "Where in Dallas? You know I grew up here too, so maybe we ran into each other at some point or know some—"

"Nowhere you would know or ever go."

The ice that laced those words had me flashing back to that night in the emergency room. The night I called CPS and he'd seemed so empathetic to the young boy's home life. Damnit, my curiosity was swirling again. I was going to find out more about him, whether he wanted me to or not. So I continued with my questioning.

"Where did you go to school?

"A high school in Dallas. I didn't go to college."

"Did you join the army after high school, then?"

Silence.

Then more silence. It turned uncomfortable as he stared me down. I wanted to know what was running through his head so badly.

I set the cup down on the counter and raised my palms toward him. "Listen, you know everything there is to know about me from that dumbass report on my life and my insistent ramblings the past month. We're living together and will be for the next few months, so I think I deserve to know *some* things about my roomie."

His lips twitched at the corners. "First off, Kate, that file they gave me was nowhere close to being accurate. The facts might have been correct, but it did not prepare me for *who you are*." The sound of something bubbling turned his attention from me to the stove. His back was to me as he continued. "Second, I didn't join after high school. I worked for a construction company for a few years. Then 9/11 happened. I joined the day after."

"Wow, that is...." I didn't know how to respond. The fact that he'd opened up at all, plus his story, made my mind go blank.

He set down the spoon he was using to stir the cooking noodles and faced me once again. "Most people say it was a stupid emotional decision." He looked like he was trying to read me just as I was trying to read him.

"I was going to go with admirable, amazing, sacrificial. You did something I would never be brave enough to do. I was in undergrad when it happened, I wanted to go help so bad it hurt, but I didn't know how. I wasn't a doctor yet, so I knew if I went to New York, I would just be in the way. I felt so *useless*." Pride for his sacrifice and bravery simmered in a part of my heart that I didn't even know existed, making my eyes soften as I gazed back at him.

"I wouldn't go as far as admirable, but once I enlisted, I found a home. The military was exactly what I needed."

"What do you mean? What did you need?"

"A purpose, a mission, a family," he said quietly before turning back to the food cooking on the stove.

The smells wafting from the boiling pots made my stomach grumble. I wanted to keep him talking since he seemed to be in a good enough mood to deem me trustworthy. But when I opened my mouth to urge him on, he started switching the flames off and moving around the kitchen, grabbing a strainer, plates, and silverware.

Once everything was cooked and mixed, he prepared my plate and set it in front of me on the counter before turning back to the stove to make his own. I stared down at my plate; the massive amount of food that was on it was enough for four of me. Where did he expect all of it to go?

I stole a glance in his direction. I didn't want to hurt his feelings by not eating it all, but I didn't eat this much food in a whole day, and now he was expecting me to eat it all in one sitting.

I ate slowly, moving the noodles from one side of the plate to the other, hoping he didn't notice. It was delicious, but again, way too much food.

"Do you want to talk about today?" he asked between shoveled bites.

Sighing, I set my fork down, thankful for the reprieve of having to eat even if it meant talking about the day's events.

"There really isn't much to talk about. It's the same every time I go. I know what to expect, but each time, it takes me by surprise. Does that make sense?" I stared at my plate; it didn't even make sense to me.

"Yes, it makes sense to me. You can be prepared for anything or feel like you've seen everything, but every situation is different, and you're different with every new situation. You can't expect yourself to feel the same just because the job is the same each time."

"Wow. That's extremely insightful. Did you just come up with that on your own?" I started eating again, hoping the quick break had made some magical cavern appear in my stomach to shove the rest of the food into.

"I wish I could take credit for that, but someone once told me that when I was struggling with things I had seen, had done time and time again."

"Like therapy?"

He glared at me, obviously annoying by my persistent questions, but continued.

"Yes, we're offered help after we return from deployments. Some guys don't take advantage of it, but I did. I knew I had to. Between what I'd seen in the army and my childhood... I was pretty messed up for a while. The first time I went, I thought it was a bunch of shit, expecting me to open up about myself, but afterward I felt better. The lingering tension had eased enough that I could get a decent night's sleep. I kept going after that, especially after difficult assignments."

"Oh." I knew about therapy. Everyone tried to get me to go after my mother died, but I had refused. Hearing how much it helped him, maybe I was wrong in denying that help. "The other day at the gym... the owner saw your tattoo." I glanced down at the symbol on his forearm so he knew which of his tattoos I was referencing. "What does it mean or stand for?"

He rested his arm on the countertop and faced his forearm toward me so I could get a better look. "I got it when my service was up. I'm proud of the time I spent in the army, but the tattoo was stupid. It feels more like a brand now. Everyone knows who and what I am just in one glance. Like that guy at the gym."

"You didn't answer my question. What does it *mean*?"

"Special forces."

I blinked, the only reaction I would allow myself. I didn't want him to see the chill that ran down my spine at what he admitted. A highly trained killer living under my roof. The emotions running through me were contradicting—half terrified while the other half was extremely turned on by that power.

Weston began speaking again, pulling me away from dissecting my body's response.

"Why do you volunteer at that nonprofit if it makes you feel miserable every time you leave?" His plate was practically licked clean. I caught his quick look at the food sitting out on the counter, seeming to debate seconds before turning his dark eyes to mine.

I'd given up on eating—one more bite and I would vomit—but there was still so much more on my plate. His casual glance back to the stove had me pushing my half-full plate to him with a slight nod. Maybe it was the soldier in him or just being such a large guy needing additional food, but he didn't even flinch. Pushing his empty plate aside, he grabbed mine and began digging into my leftovers.

Folding my arms on the counter, I tried to answer his question even if I didn't fully understand why I did it either. "It makes me feel like I'm making a difference, however small. Most of the time at the hospital, I feel like people treat the emergency room as their regular doctor, or I'm treating the people who are too lazy to take good care of themselves, so they ended up having to come see me when it could have been prevented with regular care." Grabbing a hair tie out of my pocket, I began fumbling with my dark hair, attempting a bun. "When I volunteer, I'm making an impact on those lives, and they're so grateful. They don't take what I'm doing for granted. They've either been held captive in that industry by a pimp or someone else owning them or sold, never even having a choice of that life. Even if it's just a kind word or sitting holding their hand, they're grateful for that gesture. That someone remembers them and that their life matters to someone. I wish I could do more. I wish I could make a bigger impact, but I don't know how."

Wiping his mouth with a napkin, he tossed it onto the second empty plate in front of him. "That isn't what I expected you to say. Actually... I should have expected what you said since everything about you has been unexpected since the day I met you." His unyielding stare burned into me, sparking excitement that rushed through me in a wave of heat.

"Is that a compliment?" I quirked an eyebrow up at him, smirking.

"Absolutely."

We sat staring at each other, our faces a mirror image—half smirks, eyes wide with the thrill of the light flirting. Weston was the first to break the hot stare, turning to face his plate. I watched him briefly close his eyes as he took in deep breaths.

If his breathing was anything like mine—short and quick—maybe I should try that calming technique too.

HE COOKED AND I CLEANED, which was a small miracle in itself that I did it willingly without *too* much complaining. I shoved all the plates, pots, and glasses into the dishwasher before turning it on the heavy-duty cycle. For anything to survive in my house, it all had to be dish-washer safe; it was the only way anything ever got cleaned.

It was 9 p.m. by the time I finished up in the kitchen, and I was itching to get out of the house, to do something instead of lying around and thinking about the day. Weston seemed to be in a good mood, especially after getting food in him, and I wondered if he would be open to going out and having a little fun.

Walking to the living room to discuss the idea, I found him sitting on the couch reading—again. I plopped down next to him and leaned closer, trying to get a glimpse of what he was reading. Sensing my invasion of privacy, he closed the book and turned to face me.

"Can I help you with something?" he asked, sort of smirking. For anyone else, it would have been a grimace, but I had learned this look was his "I'm not annoyed, you're kind of funny in a funny way" smile.

"What are you reading?" I asked, peeking over his shoulder.

"Nothing." He pushed the book farther away from my curious eyes.

"Wait! Is the stoic Weston reading something naughty?" I exclaimed, leaning closer to him to get a better view of the title. "It's some romance novel, isn't it? Or are you reading about that fabulous Mr. Grey?"

I couldn't hold myself back any longer; I had to know why he was keeping this bit of knowledge from me. I shot a mischievous smile at him before launching across his body, reaching for the book. I thought I was being smooth as a ninja, but apparently not nearly quick enough. Weston's hands wrapped around my waist midair, turning me and pushing my back onto his thighs. Not willing to give up easily on anything, I stretched my arms overhead, smacking my hands around on the couch, trying to feel for the book.

His strong hands wrapped around my delicate wrists and held my arms above my head. Breathing became difficult when I met his intense stare. I couldn't tell if he was holding himself back from killing me or devouring me.

He closed his eyes and shook his head, releasing my wrists and running both his hands through his hair.

Somehow the moment had gone from fun to awkward in the matter of a millisecond. Pushing off the couch with my elbows, I moved to slide off him to hopefully get playful Weston back. It was hard and completely awkward trying to climb off him without touching him further. Sensing my dilemma, he grabbed me around the waist, picked me up, and sat me down beside him. Far enough away that not one inch of our bodies was touching, like he needed the distance.

That didn't sit well with me; it even had a hint of rejection, which pissed me off.

"I need to get out of here. I need to do something fun," I said, staring at the wall.

Cautiously, he replied, "What did you have in mind?" He kept his eyes trained ahead as well.

Turning to face him, gaining his full attention, I gave him a wicked grin. "Nope. I wouldn't want to ruin the surprise."

7

———

With every alley we walked past, his head swiveled, trying to assess as much as possible. He bitched about the dark, being too exposed, blah blah blah.

"Where are we going, Kate?" he asked, taking a moment from his surveying to peer down at me.

Ignoring the annoyance and stress in his voice, I gave him a casual shrug. "I come here when I'm stressed out, sad, angry, frustrated. So I guess I come here quite a bit." I smiled up at him. "No one knows about this, not even Eric, so *you* should feel special."

"I'll feel fucking special when I know where we're going and that it's safe," he growled.

I gave his shoulder a light pat, trying to comfort him and ease his tension. "We're here. Stop worrying." Turning right, we stopped in front of a red nondescript door directly under a blinking BAR sign. The older building was original, the brick façade slightly crumbling from the decades out in the elements. Before I could grasp the handle, Weston stepped around and opened it for me, gesturing with his free hand for me to enter first.

We made it two steps into the packed bar before I turned to face him to gauge his reaction.

"A karaoke bar." A mix of surprise, relief, and humor laced his words and forced a larger-than-normal smile to surface.

I smiled and continued walking in, trying to find a good table. Keeping a firm hand against my lower back, Weston stayed unnervingly close. Halfway in, I inclined my head toward a table near the front of the stage, and he followed my lead. Like a Texas gentleman, he pulled my chair out for me before dropping into his own. Even now that we were here and he could see there was no imminent danger, he still looked uncomfortable. His eyes darted around the bar, searching the patrons, as if there were assassins hidden in every shadow ready to pounce.

After only a few minutes of waiting, a waitress appeared, one who I'd had in the past but never got *this* kind of immediate attention from, and took our order before sashaying back to the bar with a glance back to see if Weston was watching. For some reason, I wanted to hiss at her.

"Seriously? You ordered not one but two shots of Goldschläger? Big plans of getting hammered tonight?" he joked as he played with a few cardboard coasters that were left on the table from the previous occupants.

"Yep. And now the fun really begins. I'm going to choose a song. Would you like me to pick a duet for the two of us?" I asked, jabbing my elbow into his side.

There was no need for words; his look back to me said it all. *Hell no.*

I gave him a dismissive shrug, walked up to the main stage, jotted down my favorite request, and made my way back to sit beside him. Evidently, me arriving with a handsome man made the service faster than usual; the two shots and beer I'd ordered were waiting for me on the table when I returned.

"Cheers." I lifted the tiny glass high in Weston's direction, knocked the bottom on the table, and then proceeded to dump the cinnamon liquor down my throat. The IPA waiting for me was exactly what I needed after the second shot. The coolness of the beer soothed my burning throat and warming stomach.

Needing to break the silence between us, I started to tell Weston the reason Goldschläger was my drink of choice.

"One night, when I was in Europe doing study abroad, I was hammered out of my mind at this tiny bar with several of my friends. It was my turn to buy rounds for everyone, so naturally I bought what I wanted to drink—Goldschläger. The bartender was pouring the shots in front of me and got distracted, spilling some on his fingers. I pushed myself up onto the bar, leaned over, and started sucking it off his fingers. He had no idea what to do with this tiny American woman sexually harassing him." Tears dripped down my face from laughing so hard at the memory. That trip and the people I'd gone with would be forever memories, ones I would never forget.

Weston's hair swooshed back and forth against his forehead as he shook his head and scrunched his nose. "That's disgusting. What if that guy never washed his hands?"

"I was way too drunk to even think about hygiene. Plus, any germs would have been killed by the amount of alcohol in my system."

"You were so drunk you licked some stranger's germ-infested fingers. Was that safe?"

"Yeah, I'm sure one of the guys we were with was holding back. Pretty positive. Maybe. Honestly, I can't remember, but we all made it back safe. No harm done. Well, except for the hotel room we left utterly destroyed. Three girls and one toilet to vomit in did not work out well. It looked like fucking rock stars stayed there instead of three college girls backpacking around Ireland."

"Doesn't sound very smart, or safe for that matter."

"Relax. You can't teleport back in time and protect me from myself or others. Just focus on the here and now. And look, we're perfectly safe, just like I said we would be."

The waitress reappeared to check on us, though more so to check on Weston and see if he wanted more boring water. Since she was already there and asking, I took the opportunity to order another shot and beer, considering all the glasses in front of me were now empty. *Just one more,* I told myself. That would be plenty to help me forget and get some decent sleep.

The MC called out my name, signaling it was my turn to embarrass myself in front of all these strangers and Weston. Narrowing his eyes, Weston glanced behind me toward the stage and grumbled something I couldn't quite make out over the noise in the crowded bar. Whatever it was, a lecture on proper security measures was surely coming my way tomorrow, but that didn't matter now. Now all that mattered was losing myself in the music. Becoming someone else for a few minutes, leaving behind my life and worries, and just allowing myself to be carefree for a little while.

The pulsing beat pushed away the remaining images of the day. When the words for my new self-proclaimed theme song—Elle King's "America's Sweetheart"—popped up, I began. My smile widened when I looked over at Weston and found him smiling back.

I knew I was a bad singer, but it'd never stopped me before, and watching him cringe at some of the high notes I clearly didn't hit made me smile more. Being good wasn't the point.

Through the dismal applause, I gave a dramatic bow that made the Earth shift on its axis slightly from the movement. Maybe I didn't need that third shot. My steps slowed and my smile faltered as I approached our table. Weston's attention was no longer directed toward me, making me immediately miss being his sole focus. Now his intense focus was on the beautiful—*if you like extensions and too much makeup*—waitress. I paused, watching their interaction from a distance. He was smiling up at her while she giggled at something he said, lightly touching his shoulder as she flipped her long blonde hair over hers. Anger and loneliness filled my every pore watching them talk, flirt. He was flirting, and not with me. No, I was just a *client*.

Tipsy Kate wanted that sly smile directed at her.

Tipsy Kate wanted him all to herself.

The liquor flowing through me spun my next actions before I could even contemplate the consequences.

Regaining some composure, I approached, forcing a pause in their conversation. When I was beside Weston, I slung my arm around his shoulder and collapsed in his lap, taking both him and the waitress by surprise.

"Did you like my singing?"

The shock on his face turned to utter confusion. The waitress was just as confused, looking back and forth between us, trying to assess our relationship and the fading potential of a partner for the night.

Adjusting myself, I snuggled in deeper against his chest and planted a soft kiss on the smooth skin beneath his ear.

"Thank you for bringing me my drink. I think that's all we need for now." I spoke to her but kept my eyes locked with Weston's seething gaze. His breathing was shallow and fast, his heart thumping against my shoulder in a rapid beat.

Taking the hint, the waitress sauntered back to the bar, mumbling something as she slipped into the crowd.

As soon as her long blonde hair was out of sight, I turned back to Weston, grinning at my victory. He didn't return the smile. Apparently my antics were more transparent than I realized. Lifting me from his lap, he set me down in my own chair and proceeded to scoot his farther away. He folded his arms across his chest as his whole demeanor shifted into something foreign, guarded.

"Come on. That was funny," I said, crossing my arms, putting up my own wall.

His eyes shifted anxiously around the room. "What was that, Kate?"

"It was a joke. You can't tell me you were actually enjoying the conversation with that girl. What were y'all talking about anyway?"

Weston ran his hands through his hair, clearly exasperated by me.

"We were just talking. She asked me if I was from around here. We talked a little about living in Dallas. She asked me if we... if you and me are together."

"And?"

"And what?"

"What did you tell her about us?"

"I told her no, we aren't together, that it wasn't like that."

"I'm sure she perked up at that," I snapped.

I downed the shot in front of me, allotting myself a few seconds to regroup. Trying to understand what was going on with all these feelings swirling around inside. It almost felt like jealousy.

"What did you want me to tell her?" he asked, balancing his chair on the back two legs, effectively putting even more distance between us.

My cheeks flushed pink. I didn't have an answer. I was wondering the same damn thing.

Weston leaned forward, setting the front two legs of the chair down once more, and rested his elbows on his knees, hanging his head. He stayed like that long enough that one singer had gone through his full song and a second person was being called up. When he finally looked up, his eyebrows were furrowed as he stared, considering me. Once, twice and then a third time, he opened his mouth, looked at me, but then would suddenly close it and look away.

This couldn't be good.

Finally, he found the words he was searching for and held my gaze as he spoke.

"Kate, listen. I know it's hard considering we're together all day every day, but you need to keep your distance from me. Don't go down that road of feeling anything for me. You know my rules. I won't allow myself to feel that way about you. I'm sorry if today... if tonight made you think I could offer something more. The last thing I want to do is lead you on."

Air.

I needed air.

The embarrassment from my drunk-ass actions and feelings made it hard for me to look him in the eye.

"It was a stupid joke. Stop being so damn serious," I snapped. "I'm going to the bathroom."

Without waiting for a dismissal or another word from him, I pushed my chair back, almost knocking it down with the force, and headed toward the back of the bar where the bathrooms were located. Standing in front of the black door that led to the ladies' restroom, I hesitated. Another door down the dark hall was calling to me. The bright red Exit sign seemed to beckon me toward the fresh air, away from the disapproving looks from *him*. I knew the dangers surrounding me, but the need to feel free—alone—just for a few moments had me pushing those concerns aside. I would only be a few minutes anyway; what he didn't know wouldn't hurt anything.

The faint cool evening breeze caressed my face through the open door, urging the first relaxed breath in weeks to escape. Letting the door close behind me, I leaned against the brick, still warm from the hot Texas day, and closed my eyes as I laid my head back. This was what I needed to clear the fuzziness from my mind.

I cannot believe I did that. What an idiot. Now he thinks.... What was I thinking? How will I ever be able to look him in the eyes again?

The back door swung open beside me with so much force it rattled against the brick before slamming shut. I didn't need to open my eyes; only one person in that bar was strong enough and pissed enough to almost rip the door off its hinges.

"What the *hell* do you think you're doing?" Weston shouted, his voice getting louder as he approached me.

Giving him a dismissive shrug that I knew would send him into a rage, I simply said, "I needed air, so I came out here for a minute. It's fine. See? I'm safe."

His yelling turned into something quiet and deadly. "You're an idiot for being out here alone, you do realize that, right? Or are you too self-absorbed to see that you're now putting yourself and me at risk by being out here? I have one job to do, Kate, and it's to keep you safe. Let's go. Now. We're done here."

Knowing I was on dangerous ground and really not caring, I slowly opened my eyes and tucked my hands into the back pockets of my jeans.

"First, don't yell at me, and second, no, we're not leaving. I'm not done."

"This is not open for negotiation."

"You work for *me*, remember? You have to do what I say, not the other way around, and I say we're not leaving yet." I knew that would get a response out of him. I was pushing his buttons on purpose, just itching for him to make the first move.

A mean smile spread across his face, making me wish I could take a step away from him, but with nowhere to escape to, I could only press my back flatter against the brick. He took another step closer, his face just a few inches from mine.

"I was wondering when you were going to show the true bitchy, self-centered Kate that I knew has been itching to come out. Is this who you normally are? 'The girl on a mission' mask has finally worn off. Or did your embarrassment pull it out of you?"

My eyes widened in shock at his cruel words. I wanted to rattle his cage a bit but hadn't expected *that* response. But the shock quickly morphed into something angrier and wild.

My hands stung from slamming them against his solid chest. "Screw you, you obnoxious bastard."

Weston had the audacity to laugh at my attempt to hurt him. He grabbed my wrists and held them tightly in his grasp, but what he didn't see was my left leg. When it connected with the back of his knee, he stumbled forward, giving me enough of a distraction to slam my right elbow directly into his rib cage. The look of surprise in his eyes quickly faded into fury as he regained his balance. Unable to stop him, he grabbed my arm and twisted me around, slamming my back against his chest and pinning my own arms against me.

I struggled to get out of his hold, but his grip wouldn't falter. The only other option I had was using my legs again. Drawing my knee up, I slammed my foot down hard on the top of his, causing a pained and annoyance-laced grunt to escape his lips.

"Damnit, Kate. Stop. Fighting. Me," he growled into my ear. Even though his voice was harsh and I knew he was boiling mad at me, the way his lips touched the shell of my ear as he spoke made my legs wobble slightly.

I pushed against his hold one more time, but he squeezed me tighter against him, forcing me to take shallow breaths to get any air in my lungs. He was so furious with me, I wondered if he was debating how much trouble he would be in if *he* killed me instead of the gang.

All the quick movements mixed with the alcohol still flowing through my system made the asphalt sway. Still pinned against him, I could feel every deep, rapid breath of his.

"Are you done with your little tantrum?" Weston whispered against my neck. His warm breath tickled my skin.

My voice caught in my throat, making it sound deep and breathy. "I'm done venting, yes." Which was the truth. The sharp edge of my temper was dulled.

When it became apparent I was done fighting and would listen to his orders, he slowly released me from his arms. Done with being out in the open, too exposed, Weston strode to the exit door and gestured for me to walk through first.

Tossing some cash on the table to cover the bill and tip, I grabbed my purse and walked out the front door, not caring if he followed. Even though I knew he was. He stayed two paces behind while we walked home surrounded by tension-filled silence.

I hated myself for making everything so uncomfortable, my damn temper getting the best of me once again. I picked at my lip as we walked, contemplating what I could say or ask to make things normal between us again. Thankfully Weston beat me to it.

"That song you sang at the bar, it reminded me of you."

Keeping my gaze straight ahead, I smirked. "I'm taking that as a compliment."

"You should."

When I gathered enough courage to look up at him, he was looking straight ahead, always on the watch for danger.

"I'm going to have a bruise tomorrow from your damn pointy elbow. You might be small, but you know how to hit using every ounce of the force you do have."

So many compliments. Maybe he was trying to make up for being an ass back there.

"Thanks," I mumbled, not really sure what to say back.

We walked in silence for another block, my townhouse finally in view down the street. As we got closer to the house, he started fidgeting, crossing his arms, putting his hands in his pockets, running them through his hair. I started to say something about it, since it was odd for him to be anxious, but he spoke up again.

"I didn't mean to call you out back there. It's normal for you to start to feel something toward me. I guess... I guess it took me by surprise. I wouldn't have thought it would happen to you. You seem to enjoy being on your own, being so independent. I prepared myself for you to never... well, honestly I prepared myself for you to never warm up to me. When you reacted like that to the waitress, I didn't know how that would affect me."

My feet stopped moving, frozen in place, which, of course, made Weston pause. It was too much trying to process everything he just said in those few sentences and walk at the same time. First he knew and appreciated my independence—score, Weston—yet then again, he saw me as cold and distant, which was not good. Second, what did he mean by "affect me"?

"It was nothing. Too many shots too fast. I just wanted to forget the day, that's all. Let's just say it was a stupid drunk thing and move on. Okay?"

Gripping my elbow, Weston gave me a forceful tug, urging me to keep walking. "We need to keep moving. I can't protect you well out here in the open."

Forcing my feet back into motion, I allowed him to pull me along the sidewalk toward home.

8

―――――

"Wʜat about tonight?" Austin asked, brushing his lips against mine in the back of the supply room closet. It wasn't the ideal place, cold and stuffed with medical supplies, but it would have to do for now. It had been a few weeks since that day in the locker room, but it seemed the universe was against us. Our schedules never aligned to make an actual date possible. However, we were both wrapping up a morning shift, meaning we would both be free this evening.

His lips connected with my tender skin at the base of my neck, his tongue flicking softly, eliciting a moan. His answering smile against my skin let me know he approved.

"So how about it, tonight? I can come over for dinner since you still have that *security* guy watching your every move."

When I didn't answer, too engrossed in the sensation of his teeth scraping the shell of my ear, he stopped and pulled back. Staring down at me, he raised his eyebrows, waiting for an answer.

"Yes, whatever you want." That must have been the right answer, because he gave me one of his dazzling flirty smiles and went back to the sensual torture on my neck and ear. "Oh wait." My eyes popped open when I remembered what day it was. Austin raised his gaze to mine. "I forgot what day it was. Meagan and Eric are coming over tonight to watch this new ER show on TV. We love to watch them together and make fun of how inaccurate and dramatized they are."

I leaned my head against the hard metal of the storage rack and held his gaze, giving him time to contemplate the change in plans.

"It's not ideal, but I'll take what I can get. I guess. What time."

I bit my lower lip, trying to stifle a stupid happy smile.

"Eight-ish would be good. Are you sure?"

A nod in return was all I saw before he pressed his lips against mine while he slid one hand around the back of my neck, into my hair, and the other pressed on the lower half of my back, urging our bodies closer together. There were still a few minutes left before anyone came looking for us, and it was apparent that Austin was ready to make full use of the remaining time we had together.

EVEN TREATING and almost getting thrown up on by a woman with a blood alcohol content five times the legal limit—without drinking, so she said—the goofy grin across my face wouldn't fade. Even on my walk home with Weston, I couldn't stop thinking about what the night might hold.

"Why in the hell are you so giddy? Didn't you just have a grueling day? The waiting room was packed."

I shook my head, making the tip of my ponytail whip against my face, attempting to shake the memory of Austin's hands and lips from earlier. "Yeah, it was brutal. I felt bad for leaving knowing it was probably going to get worse for the night shift team. But I don't know, I guess... I'm just excited. Eric and Meagan are coming over tonight. Oh, and Austin too."

"Excited that they're all coming over or just one person in particular?" Weston asked, keeping his gaze straight ahead. Somehow he seemed tenser now than when we first left work and started the walk home.

"One person in particular, I guess. Come on, even you have to admit he's gorgeous." I gave him a friendly shove with my shoulder.

"Hell no. I'm not going to say another guy is gorgeous, especially one with girl hair. That's just weird. Do you trust him enough to have him over?" Weston asked, giving me a friendly shove back. The force almost sent me flying to the other side of the sidewalk.

"I do. Plus, the hospital did a background check when he first started, so he's in no way gang related, if that's what you're asking. Anyway... what do you do all day in the waiting room? It has to get boring."

"I work the majority of the time, updating everyone on the previous day and setting up expectations for the next. I let everyone know your schedule, what I suspect you'll do before and after. It just helps keep you safe if more people are in the loop."

"Sounds boring."

He smiled. "I also read and get other personal stuff done."

"What other personal stuff?"

"Are you always this curious, or is it just me that brings it out in you?"

"A little of both. Now spill it."

Chuckling, he wrapped his arm around my shoulders, pulling me in close to him as we walked. "Nah, I think it's more fun making you wonder."

"So cruel," I grumbled, making no move to shrug out of his hold.

Eric was early, making me love him a bit more. I loved that he was so predictable. Eric eyed Weston suspiciously when he was the one to greet him at the door—a security measure Weston would not back down on—before walking into the kitchen and wrapping me in a warm hug.

"Hey there, gorgeous. Ready for a fun night of horribly inaccurate depictions of our daily life in the ER?"

"Always. Alcohol will help it not seem too bad. Beer is in the fridge."

"Oh, you know the way to my heart. Please tell me it's something local." He kissed my cheek with a quick release of my shoulders and made his way to the fridge. I followed him, sitting on the stool beside Weston, who was watching Eric search for his beverage.

With his head still inside the fridge, he called out to Weston, "So, man, how's it been living with Kate? I lost the bet a long time ago on how long you would last."

Weston looked over at me, bracing his forearms against the counter as he held my gaze. "It hasn't been that bad. She isn't as bad as she makes herself out to be."

I held his gaze in return, raising an eyebrow at him. "Whatever, I'm scary as shit. I've been going easy on you until you get settled in. You know, reining in my inner bitchiness so you don't hate your life every second of the day."

"Okay, tiny queen. You're a badass, and we're all scared of you. Is that what you want to hear?" He folded himself over in a mock bow.

Placing two fingers under his chin, I raised his gaze back up to mine. "I might be tiny, but remember... I have very sharp elbows and can take you down at any moment."

"Highly doubtful."

"Is that a challenge?"

Eric cleared his throat, reluctantly drawing our intense, humor-laced gazes from each other to him.

"Kate, as much as I would like to see you try and smack your highly trained, no-mercy bodyguard... there's someone at the door." Eric pointed the neck of his beer bottle toward the front door.

"Another time maybe," Weston said to me before walking toward the front door to see who was knocking.

My gaze followed him, eyes slightly lower than his waist, admiring the view.

"Seriously, Kate?"

Ashamed that I got caught, not that I was checking out Weston's ass, I smirked at Eric. "What?"

He shook his head, smiling down at me. "And you call men animals. You were just eye-fu—"

A familiar cheerful female voice called from the door cutting him off.

"Hello, Mr. Bodyguard," Meagan crooned. "Aren't you the hottest thing I've seen in days?"

"Meagan, stop. Leave him alone." I leaned as far back on the stool as feasibly possible before toppling over to watch their interaction.

Not paying my demands any attention, Meagan placed a slim, fair hand on Weston's chest and flipped her beautiful red hair over her shoulder. "He doesn't seem to mind, do you, handsome?" Giving his chest a soft pat, she walked toward me, mouthing, "OMG," as she did. "Kate, you didn't tell me the guy protecting you and living with you was the sexiest bodyguard on the planet. I mean, have you seen those arms? They are just begging to be nibbled on. Why haven't you been sharing?"

I couldn't hold back my snarl at her words as she rummaged through the fridge. Weston was making his way back to the kitchen, his head hung, staring at the floor as he ran a hand through his hair. My whole body tensed, wondering if he would fall for her antics. Every other male seemed to; not sure why I would think Weston would be any different.

Meagan popped the cap off her beer and came to stand beside me and Weston around the center island. Not letting up with the in-your-face flirting, she jutted out a hand to him. "I don't think we've been properly introduced. I'm Meagan, and I'm single."

"Seriously, Meagan!" Either Eric was as tired of her antics as I was or he saw the look of promised death on my face directed toward her.

The unsure look on Weston's face made me stifle a laugh. A hesitant Weston was a first. Looking back and forth between the three of us, he grasped Meagan's hand. "Casey Weston. Nice to meet you."

"He goes by Weston. Don't ask me. It's some military crap." I stole the beer from Meagan's hand and took a long drink.

"Military *crap*?" Angling his body toward me, he leaned his side against the counter and peered down at me.

"I assumed that's where you got the idea to go by your last name instead of your actual first name."

Meagan stepped between us, breaking our back-and-forth. "I like both."

A knock at the door had Weston taking a relieved step away from the two of us and heading to see who was there. Both Eric and Meagan shot over a questioning look, wondering who else was coming since I'd failed to tell them Austin would be joining us.

Not wanting to miss a single moment of Austin and Weston's meeting, I hopped off the stool and peeked around the corner. The front door was held open by Weston's firm grip along the edge, effectively blocking Austin's way inside. There was no telling what those two were saying to each other, and I knew it was best to keep their interactions as brief as possible. Not that Weston had ever said anything outright, but I got the feeling he wasn't a huge fan of Austin. Wasn't sure if it was just Austin being Austin that he didn't like or if it was the fact that he and I were... whatever we were.

"Come on in, Austin," I said from behind Weston's back. I watched his back muscles tense as he stepped aside, clearly frustrated at my intrusion.

Grabbing my waist, Austin pulled me against him and kissed me hard—laying claim. "You weren't kidding about the bodyguard shit, were you? For a second I thought he was going to pat me down."

Stealing a quick glance over Austin's shoulder toward Weston, I found his stare focused on Austin's hands around my waist. The look on his face made me hold a breath in, as it looked like the one I gave him and the waitress that night at the bar. Pure jealousy.

"Don't tempt him. He would probably enjoy it a little too much." I stood on my tiptoes and gave Austin a brief kiss before pulling one of his hands from my waist and dragging him into the kitchen where Eric and Meagan were waiting.

As the conversation between the group picked up and turned toward work and catching up on other things, I casually watched Weston head to his room, where he would hole up for the rest of the night until everyone left, not fully shutting the door behind him. I must have been focused on his actions longer than I realized, because Austin snapped his fingers in front of my face, trying to draw my attention back to him.

"Sorry, zoned out for a second. Y'all ready to watch *The Real life of the ER*? I can't wait to see how romanticized it is versus the real crap we see."

The look Austin shot me was dripping with jealousy, but I wasn't sure why. Maybe I was reading too much into it.

Grabbing his hand, I pulled him with me to the couch, Meagan and Eric following, and picked up the remote.

AFTER THE SHOW, Eric stood up while yawning, making to head home.

"That show was so awful. Do they actually think we get those kinds of fascinating cases every shift? What morons. I should write the writers. They need to make a real-life ER show. It could go something like 'Hi, Mr. Smith, I see you have gangrene in your foot because you chose not to take your diabetes medication which has been prescribed to you on multiple occasions. Oh, what's that? You didn't think they were that necessary? Well, hope you feel the same about your foot, because it's coming off.'" He threw his hands up in the air and walked toward the kitchen to toss out his empty beer bottle. Both he and Meagan only had a couple beers each; morning shifts always demanded a calm evening the night before.

Meagan stood up and stretched, making to follow Eric out. "I don't think anyone would watch that show. I know I wouldn't. No drama. Now, if it starred Austin, well, then maybe."

Austin smirked but didn't say a word or make any moves to leave; instead he pulled out his phone and began checking his email as I stood to say goodbyes.

Eric was waiting for me in the kitchen, staring at Austin with a look I couldn't read. Austin had been a little standoffish to him and Meagan all night. Maybe it had something to do with that. "Bye, love. See you soon," I said, giving him a bear hug and nuzzling my cheek against his chest.

Wrapping his arms around me, he squeezed me tight and released me, holding me at arm's length. "Hey, your birthday is coming up next month. If you want us all to be off on the same night, you need to let us know the plans now so we can request off. You know how quickly those requests come in."

"Yeah, yeah, I know. I've been thinking about it, and I think it would be fun if we all went dancing: you, me, Meagan, and some of the others from work. There's this new dance club downtown. We could get bottle service so we could have a reserved booth. What do you think? Are we too old for that?"

"Sounds fun to me." I jumped hearing Meagan's voice so close behind me. "You know I'll take any opportunity to get dressed up. Just let me know the date and I'll put my request in. I'm going to say bye to Weston before I head home." I turned to face her, but she was already walking toward Weston's room. Knocking slightly before pushing the door wider and entering, she shut the door with a quiet click behind her.

A warm breath tickled against my ear. "You might have an unexpected sleepover tonight. Tell me, how do you feel about that, Kate? Honestly." The elbow I sent into his ribs earned a barked laugh from him. "See ya, Kate. Thanks for tonight." Kissing my cheek, he turned, giving Austin a goodbye wave, and headed for the front door.

Curiosity got the best of me as I walked back to the couch where Austin was waiting. Opening Weston's door, I peeked my head in, taking a quick glance around. They were sitting side by side on the bed talking. My eyes stopped when they landed on her hand on his thigh. "Eric just left. Thought you would want to know. I locked up after him. No need to stop... doing whatever y'all are doing" Keeping my eyes on her hand, fingers stroking back and forth, I took a step back and closed the door.

What the hell?

I plopped down beside Austin and rolled my eyes. "What is with her? Why does she have zero restraint and do that with every guy she meets?"

Tucking his phone into his back pocket, Austin faced me. "You sound a little jealous."

"Of Meagan?" I snorted.

"Jealous that she's in that room with him instead of you."

Shit.

"Do you have a thing for him?" Austin asked as he stroked his fingers up and down my inner thigh.

"No. Why would you ask that? Not at all. No."

"Say it one more time and I just might believe you."

"It's complicated. We're just together a lot, that's all. It's nothing."

"Good." He pressed his lips against mine, stroking his tongue along my lower lip. "That would make all this harder."

Pulling my face back far enough to speak, I asked, "All *this*?"

His soft lips brushed down my jaw, sending a shiver down my spine. Each word of his reply was punctuated with a soft kiss down my neck. "You. Me. Us doing our thing."

Pulling his mouth back to mine, he used the tip of his tongue to part my lips, a gentle request. The hand in my hair pressed me closer to him, deepening our kiss. It was the kind of kiss that would normally make me forget where I was, but this time, it couldn't pull my thoughts from what was happening behind that damn closed door thirty feet away.

"I heard Eric talking about your birthday coming up. When is it" he asked, yanking the collar of my shirt down, giving him full access to nibble on my collarbone.

"Next month. November 30. This year it's the Wednesday after Thanksgiving. Do you want to go out with us?"

"Hmmm."

Well, that really wasn't a response, but he was kind of preoccupied. Grabbing my hips, he twisted me so I was on top of him, straddling him on the couch. His eyes were burning with lust and arousal, which he kept trained on me as he shifted his hips up so I could feel all of him through his jeans. The pressure of him against me at just the right spot forced an audible gasp. Grasping my cheeks with both his hands, he yanked my face an inch closer to his. "Are you thinking about *him* now?"

The possessiveness in his hold on my face and his question caught me by surprise. It made me feel small. It was something that I worked every day of my life to avoid.

"Bye, Kate," Meagan called out on her way toward the front door. "Bye, Austin. You two have a fun night. Don't do anything I wouldn't, which would be… never mind, you two have fun."

Pressing my hands against his shoulders, I pushed out of his grasp and slid onto the couch beside him. I could almost feel Weston's gaze burning into the back of my head as he followed her out.

"I think you should go too, Austin."

"Seriously?"

"Yes."

"Why?"

"I'm exhausted and—"

"And we've been waiting weeks to have some alone time together away from the hospital. I'm not leaving."

I heard Weston pause at the threshold of his room at those last words, but he continued inside, except this time he left the door wide open.

"And I'm just not ready for all this tonight," I said, pointing back and forth between us.

He sighed and leaned his head against the couch, utterly frustrated. "Are you always this uptight, or is it just me that brings it out in you? It's just sex. Don't overthink it."

Was I overthinking it?

I stood and walked to the kitchen to put distance between us. Grabbing a bottle of water out of the fridge, I leaned against the counter facing the living room, waiting for him to break the silence. Sixty long, silent, and tense seconds passed as I stared at him on the couch and he stared at the TV in front of him.

"Fine. Sorry if I'm being a little pushy," he said as he stood from the couch and began walking toward me. He wrapped his hands around my waist and pulled me close. "I just really want you, and we've been waiting for a while now. You felt how you affect me."

After a few seconds, he groaned in frustration at my lack of response.

"When I told people at work I wanted you, they laughed and told me I had my work cut out for me. But I had no idea it was going to be this difficult. Lucky for you I've always loved a challenge."

His words cut through me like a knife to the heart. I'd heard various versions of how challenging dating me could be from men since I started dating in high school. I wasn't trying to be difficult, it was just who I was. And from what I could tell, there was no reason outside my inability to give up control.

With a quick peck on the cheek, he started toward the door. "I'll concede tonight to a Kate win. You might have won this battle, but I *will* win the war. I always do."

Before Austin was fully though the door, Weston was walking toward him, preparing to lock up for the night now that everyone had left. If he heard the slight creak of the door opening, had he heard everything Austin said? My gut tightened at the thought.

Downing the bottle of water in my hand, I tossed it into the recycle bin and headed toward the stairs to get ready for bed. It was a little early for bed since I wasn't scheduled until midday the next day, but the conversation with Austin had left me exhausted and feeling retrospective.

"Why did you let him talk to you that way?" Weston asked from the bottom of the stairs.

I paused halfway up and turned to him. He was leaning against the doorframe to his room, his tattoos rippling as he crossed his strong arms over his broad chest.

Too tired to stay standing, I groaned and gently sat down on the stairs.

"You heard all that?"

"Yes. I almost came out there, but I know how you like to handle things on your own, so I stayed out of it."

"Thanks for not barging in. I had it under control." I closed my eyes and leaned my head back, hoping he would drop the subject and go back to his room. This really wasn't a conversation I wanted to have with him. I didn't want him to know how defective I was in the love department.

He didn't take the hint.

"It all seemed really disrespectful to me. No guy should keep pressuring after you've said stop. He was practically begging for it, the tool."

I smiled. Weston calling Austin a tool was kind of the highlight of my night.

"Also," he continued, "it shouldn't matter how long you two have been seeing each other or how long you make him wait. If you aren't ready, he needs to back the fuck off."

My eyes fluttered open at the sound of his voice close by. He'd moved from his doorway and was now sitting a couple stairs below mine with his back propped up against the wall. Turning my head to face him, I found him looking at me; the emotion pouring through his eyes was a mix of concern and annoyance. And for once I knew that annoyance wasn't because of me or my actions.

"It's complicated. *I'm* complicated," I said, trying to find the right words.

"I 100 percent agree that you're complicated, but why does that matter? He shouldn't talk to you like that or treat you like that."

I sighed and leaned back, propping myself up on the stair behind me by my elbows.

"I guess... I know guys have needs, and Austin is just wanting those needs met. Did you hear when he said, 'Everyone said I had my work cut out for me'?"

"Yes," he growled.

"Well, I've heard different versions of that my whole life. At least since I started dating. And if you're told something enough, you start to believe it. I don't try to be difficult, it just comes off that way, I guess. It takes a lot of work for someone to get to know me, or for me to trust someone enough to let them see the parts of me that mean the most. I'm not great at it. I haven't... I guess I don't let myself get close enough to someone to have a strong emotional connection. I don't get attached. I don't invest myself in someone so I don't have that pull or need for the physical side of a relationship. Some of it is that I don't like giving up control, and that's what being intimate is with someone, isn't it? Trusting the other person enough with your inner self, giving up a piece of you to them, hoping they don't shatter it. Once things get physical, it's more because I know it's what's expected, that it's fun, but really it's kind of meh. I could take it or leave it.

"So I guess that's what people mean when they say I'm difficult to be with, because I don't let them in. A relationship has never been something I couldn't walk away from, and that frustrates most men. They give so much of themselves to me and I can't, or won't, return it. And that leaves me where I am today. Single with only two friends, but even letting a friend in is hard for me."

Weston picked at the carpet runner that ran up the stairs, focused —thinking. When he looked up at me, he had a devious smirk on his lips.

"Okay, but did I hear you right? Did you say sex is meh?"

"Yeah, I guess I did. From my experience, it's never been something that I couldn't live without."

His smirk grew. "Then the guys you've been with haven't been doing it right. Sex is fucking amazing." His eyes were shining with memories, stories that would prove my theory on sex wrong.

"Pretty sure the problem is with me. I don't let myself get emotionally invested enough to enjoy it."

He looked down at the hole in the carpet he was making. "There isn't anything wrong with you, Kate. Don't let anyone ever say that about you, and don't you ever think it about yourself. You just haven't met the person who makes you *want* to let go, or maybe no one has ever built up enough trust with you so you can let yourself open up." Looking up, his eyes locked with mine. "You deserve to be with someone who respects you, someone who's willing to wait for you to be ready. Not that asshole Austin. Was he even the slightest bit concerned as to *why* you have to have twenty-four-seven security?"

Come to think of it, he wasn't. I frowned at the thought. Austin was more frustrated by the inconvenience of Weston than worried about my safety.

"But he's so pretty." I pouted at Weston, knowing it would get under his skin.

"Why doesn't he get a damn haircut?" he grumbled.

I reached up and pushed his dark wavy hair out of his eyes. "You're one to talk. Your hair is getting frizzier and frizzier every day."

He stilled as my fingers played in his hair. His eyes shuttered when I lightly scraped my nails along his scalp.

"I haven't had a chance, you know," he practically purred, eyes still closed. "I've been busy keeping your ass safe."

"It is a good ass, if I do say so myself. And I'm quite glad you're the one keeping it safe."

He glared at me as I laughed and dropped my hand from his hair.

There was still so much I wanted to know about him. Picking at my lip, I debated asking personal questions, but then again, I didn't want him to think I was getting too attached like he assumed that night at the karaoke bar.

"What?" he asked.

"What?" I said back, totally confused.

"You're anxious about something. You only do that"—he pointed to the hand at my lip—"when you're anxious or nervous. So, what are you thinking?"

I immediately dropped my hand. It was frustrating that he could read me so easily when I had such a hard time reading him. "Can I ask you a personal question?"

"Sure. Depends on the question if I'll answer though." He sat up straighter, preparing for the worst.

My hand tried to go back up to my lip, but I sat on it to keep it still. "Are you dating anyone?"

He eyed me for a moment before responding. "No. Why?"

Nodding, I didn't say anything.

"Why do you ask, Kate?"

Lying back on the stair again, I smiled up at the ceiling. "Couple reasons. I haven't noticed you on the phone or texting with anyone, so I assumed you didn't have one. But tonight when Meagan was hitting on you, you didn't give her much back. In fact, I think her leaving tonight was a huge blow to her ego. Meagan gets who she wants when she wants. You must have asked her to leave, because she would have never left of her own free will, at least not until she was done with you."

"Well, it wasn't hard turning her down. Meagan really isn't my type."

I sat up quickly, wanting to know more about his "type," and leaned forward, placing my elbows on my knees.

"I figured any woman who was ready and willing to have sex with you was any guy's type. Am I wrong?"

"Maybe shit-for-brains Austin, but not me."

I snorted, the sound causing the corners of his lips to twitch. "Do tell, then. Who or what is your type?"

"I guess I wouldn't say have a physical type. I definitely have a type when it comes to personality. All the women I've dated in the past have had one thing in common."

He paused. The bastard paused, knowing it would drive me crazy. Punching his shoulder, hurting my hand more than him, I gestured for him to continue.

He grinned, loving the fact that he was torturing me. "They were themselves, comfortable in their own skin. I date women who accept their flaws, accept who they are and love themselves for it. They don't need me to reinforce who they are; they already know who they are. I guess I fall for a woman who's so secure in herself that she doesn't need me, she simply wants me. Wants us."

"Interesting. That's not what I would have guessed. At all. With the type of gig you're in, I figured you would be the type of guy who would want to be needed, playing up the 'protector against all the evils in the world' role."

"A man's natural instinct is to protect, and the army has helped me hone that skill, so I may feel it a little more intensely than others, but that's not what I'm talking about. I'm talking about being so secure in themselves that they enjoy life, they see the good in any situation, and they think for themselves."

Drumming my fingers against my shins, I mumbled, "They sound like someone I would be friends with."

A few seconds of silence fell between us as I gathered the courage to ask my next question. I wasn't sure if I wanted to know the answer, but I was kind of hoping he was as messed-up in the relationship department as I was. "So, have you ever been so completely wrapped up in someone that you wanted to give everything to them? You know, ever truly loved someone?"

His broad shoulders lifted in a shrug, his eyes skirting around the room, avoiding me. "I thought I was once, but looking back, I don't think I actually was. I still had some distance between us, like I knew it wasn't right for the long term. I was still in the army, and I think I just wanted someone who was waiting for me back home, you know, someone who missed me. That's the completely wrong reason to be with someone, but they were in the military too, so I think we both felt the same way. Plus I was really fucked-up for a while even after I got out. That's when it ended." He turned back to me. "So, what about you? Have you ever, or just always kept that distance?"

"There was this one guy...."

"What happened?"

"He kicked me in the shin on the playground for jumping ahead of him in the twirly slide line. Apparently our relationship hadn't reached that level yet. I've been my fucked-up self ever since."

His loud rumbling laugh that bellowed through the stairwell made my heart smile. Making him laugh, catching him off guard, making him happy really was the best.

I covered my mouth as I yawned and glanced down at my watch. It was close to midnight.

"You're tired. It's been a long day. You should go to bed," Weston said, pushing himself off the stairs and standing over me.

"Yeah." I yawned again. "Good night, Weston."

He pulled me off the stairs, and his hand stayed wrapped around mine a little longer than necessary. Halfway up the stairs, I heard him say a quiet "Good night" as he watched me until I was at the top of the landing.

Unsure of what was going on between us, I gave him a small wave and ducked into my room.

· · ·

AFTER WASHING MY FACE, then pulling on a pair of sleep shorts and a tank top, I crawled into my big bed and almost cried in relief as I snuggled in. I turned the bedside lamp off and grabbed my phone.

Fourteen missed texts.

What the hell?

Sliding the screen open, I started reading through the group text Meagan and Eric had started just a few minutes prior.

Meagan: Damn, he is scrumptious. You really need to learn how to share, Kate.

Eric: He's not a cookie, Meagan.

Eric: But if Kate does decide to share, I want a bite too.

Meagan: I don't think you're his type.

Eric: Oh and you are? You don't seem to be warming his bed.

Meagan: I wasn't in the mood.

Eric: Right…

Eric: I think he has his eyes set on our tiny friend.

Meagan: Him too?!? Damn it, Kate, leave some of the hotties for us.

Meagan: She doesn't get Austin AND Weston. That's not fair.

Eric: Who do you think she would toss?

Meagan: Ohh, this is fun, ummmm….

Eric: I'm going with Austin. She's always had a thing for tattoos.

> Meagan: See, I'm going with Weston. Austin is educated and has these bedroom eyes that are just begging to be staring at you from between your legs.

THEY CAN'T BE SERIOUS.

> Me: Y'all can't be serious. Don't you have better things to do, like sleep?

> Meagan: Come on, this is fun. Tell us, who is right? Eric or me?

> Me: I couldn't toss Weston out.

> Eric: I knew it! I win.

> Me: Because he's not mine to toss. Eric, why do you think he is?

Silence. Nothing from either of them.

> Me: Answer me.

> Eric: Shhh... I'm asleep.

> Me: I'm going to kick your ass the next time I see you.

> Eric: Could you have Weston do it for you? I would enjoy it so much more.

> Meagan: Oh me too! Me too! We all need spankings.

> Meagan: To clarify, I want my spankings from Weston.

> Eric: Have you asked him to frisk you yet?

> Me: No

> Meagan: Yes.

> Me: What, Meagan?

Meagan: What?

Meagan: You aren't taking advantage of that smoking hot deadly weapon in your home, so I thought I should.

Meagan: Or are you saying I shouldn't because…

Eric: Oh oh, I know the answer to this one.

Me: Both of you STOP IT.

Eric: Weston and Kate, sitting in a tree…

Me: I hate you both.

Tucking the phone under my pillow, I couldn't drop my grin as I closed my eyes and quickly fell asleep.

9

———————

I sat up straight in bed and glanced at the clock.

One in the morning. I had only been asleep for an hour, but something had startled me awake. A feeling of dread washed over me as I sat in the dark listening for any sound or movement that could be the reason behind the sleep interruption. The silence that filled the room was deafening. My eyes were wide open searching the dark, allowing them time to adjust. It wasn't a loud sound, a simple creak of the floor downstairs, but I heard it and instantly knew something was wrong. That sound was out of place at this time of night.

I swung my legs out of bed and reached for the side table. Quietly pulling the drawer open, I took out the nine-millimeter I'd given myself as a birthday gift last year. Snapping the clip in place, I checked the safety and tiptoed toward my door, determined to investigate.

All the lights were off, but my eyes had already adjusted to the darkness, allowing me to make out enough to not tumble down the stairs. Each step was slow and calculated, trying not to make any sound just in case the worst-case scenario was waiting for me.

When I reached the last step, terrified panic set in, sending my heart racing a million beats per second as tiny beads of sweat began rolling down my back. With my back flat against the wall, I held the gun close to my chest and strained, trying to hear, but I couldn't hear a damn thing because of my own damn body. My breaths were too loud, my heart beating too fast. I needed to calm myself down to hear, to be prepared to act, to form some kind of plan. If I had a plan, then everything would be fine. Ideally.

Then I heard it. The noise was much louder this time now that I was so close. And what I heard next sent another spike of fear throttling through me, making my hands shake. It was the faint sound of the back door scraping against the hardwood floors as it was opened.

Shit.

The sweat beading up on my palms forced me to take a moment and wipe each hand down the tank I wore to maintain a decent grip on the gun.

I stopped breathing completely when the door closed, followed by the sound of near silent footsteps growing louder as the person now in my home came closer and closer to the stairwell where I was partially hidden. Trapped. I was trapped. No way to escape out the front door or get up the stairs fast enough for them not to see me. In that moment, I knew what I had to do.

Listening to each step grow closer, I waited. I had to wait for the unknown person to round the corner to face me. If I attacked at that precise moment, I would have the element of surprise on my side.

Straining to hear each tiny movement, I held my breath.

Five more steps.

Four more steps.

Three more steps.

I let out a quiet breath to calm my shaking legs and hands, tucking the gun in the back of my shorts so both hands would be free.

Two steps.

One step.

Gathering all the courage I could—and a slight amount of stupidity—I swung my right fist around the corner, aiming high to connect with the person's face. My knuckles split as I made contact, and a cracking sensation reverberated from my fist to my shoulder.

Moving forward with the second part of my genius plan while the person was still in shock, I stepped around the wall, placing myself directly in front of intruder. Wrapping my hands wrapped around the person's shoulders—*large, broad... male*—I positioned myself and rammed my knee into his groin.

"Fuck."

I stilled. I knew that voice.

"Weston?" I exhaled in surprise and frustration. Why in the hell was he creeping around the house at night? In the dark?

He didn't respond, but even in the dark, I could tell he was crouched down close to the floor, hands gripping his hurt male parts. I did feel bad about that.

"What the hell are you doing sneaking around the house at night?" he yelled in between breaths, still crouching.

"Me? What are *you* doing creeping around in the dark? What if I shot you?" I pulled the gun from the back of my pants and held it by my side.

His head shot up, eyes landing on the gun in my hand.

"Please tell me that thing isn't loaded."

I held the gun in front of me, examining it as I spoke. "I always keep one loaded by my bed and one in the junk drawer in the kitchen. You know, just in case."

He grunted as he stood from the floor. "I heard a sound." A loud thump filled the air as he fell against the wall for support.

Who knew I had such crippling power in my knees? Good to know for future altercations.

"Huh?" Maybe the lack of oxygen was getting to his brain.

"You asked me why I was walking around down here in the dark. I heard a sound. It sounded like someone running around outside the door, so I went to check it out."

I put my hands on my hips and asked, "Did you see anything?"

"No. I was about to check the front door, but I was surprised and taken down by the tiniest tough-as-shit woman I've ever known."

The darkness was perfect for hiding the flush and smile that rose to my face at his compliment.

Fully recovered, he pushed off the wall and stalked toward me. Yanking the gun out of my hand, he mumbled, "Give me the damn gun before you shoot us both." He placed it on the kitchen island and released the clip. "Do you even know how to use this thing?"

Giving him my best cocky smile, I said, "Of course I do. I've seen it done thousands of times on TV. I'm a quick study."

I had to stifle my laugh as his mouth popped open in utter disbelief.

"You have to be joking, Kate. You can't…. It doesn't work that way. And you have *multiple* loaded guns in this house!" The gun scraped along the counter as he pushed it farther away from me. "You are an idiot. These things are dangerous if you don't know how to use them. And you leave them loaded. We're lucky you haven't killed us both being so reckless."

My shoulders shook from my silent laugh. Oh, he was getting so riled up about this, and it was hilarious.

"Weston, I'm kidding. I've taken classes on gun safety and go to the range often. Calm down. It was a joke."

After a minute, his glare morphed into a smirk that mirrored mine. We stood staring at each other in the shifting moonlight from the windows that illuminated the kitchen. My stomach tightened and tingled with the anticipation of what could happen here in the early morning moonlight between the two of us.

The sound of glass shattering coming from the back door broke the spell of the moment.

Both our stares were trained on the back door, waiting to see what would happen next. My eyes widened when a hand came through the shattered pane, feeling around for the deadbolt.

The sound of the deadbolt unlocking was still in my ears when Weston shoved me behind him, shielding me from the person now turning the doorknob to enter my home. Grabbing the gun, he clicked the clip in place and leaned toward me, keeping his eyes fixed on the door.

"Stay here. Hide behind the island. Stay out of sight no matter what happens," he whispered into my hair.

The ability to speak escaped me, so I nodded while keeping my eyes on the back door that was now quietly opening.

"I need you to say yes, Kate. Stay out of this."

"Yes," I squeaked and dropped to the floor. Crawling on my hands and knees, I moved to the other side of the island as he directed. As degrading as it felt, I knew it was the smartest thing to do, to let him handle it. Half of me wanted to go help him while the other half—the wiser, smarter side of me—wanted me to crawl into one of the cabinets to get even farther from danger.

My ears pounded with the beat of my heart, making hearing anything difficult. A distraction, that was what I needed while I sat on the cold tile waiting. I began counting the passing seconds in my head.

One Mississippi.

Two Mississippi.

Three Mississippi.

Four Mississippi.

A thud of a body slamming against the wall, pictures rattling against it, sounded through the downstairs.

Five Mississippi.

Someone yelling—not Weston.

Six Mississippi.

Things crashing and breaking in the living room.

Seven Mississippi.

The door banging open and someone running, then a second set of feet following.

I let out a relaxed breath. Whoever was attempting to break in and do who knew what was now on the run with Weston hot on their heels. Even though I hadn't seen him in action, I was 100 percent sure the person who was being chased would live to regret the moment he tried to break into this house.

Uncurling from my spot on the floor, my legs tingled from the tension in my entire body. The sound of cracking wood coming from the front door stilled me immediately. *Maybe it was my overactive imagination?* The cracking sound came again, louder this time.

Crouching down on the floor, I moved so I could have a good view of the front door while still being semi-protected by the island.

It was hard to see in the dark, but the sound of wood cracking and breaking sounded through the whole house as the front door broke open and two large men slipped inside. The two crept farther into the house, one pointing toward the stairs, saying something in Spanish to the other.

Dragging myself back against the cabinets, I used the shadows as cover, angling myself so I was tucked into a dark corner. It was only a matter of time before they found me. My whole body started shaking as I realized how bad this situation was.

Think, Kate. Think. Make a plan.

The second man stomped down the stairs, saying something to the other. Silence engulfed the townhouse. Both now knew I wasn't upstairs, meaning I had to be hiding somewhere downstairs. At first only my legs were trembling, then my heart, arms, and now my teeth. Adrenaline was not my friend at that moment.

Maybe this was their plan the whole time, to distract him, get him out of the house away from me. Then the real plan to attack me went into action.

Clamping a sweaty palm across my mouth, I tried to silence my chattering teeth. I hoped it wasn't as loud to the men in my house as it was to me.

"Hola, señorita," said a deep male voice in the dark.

Shit. Shit. Shit.

Sliding my back up the cabinet, I stood, keeping my back in the corner. I knew I had a better chance of defending myself that way.

You can do this. You can do it on your own.

Taking a deep, shaky breath, I forced my breathing and panic to calm just like I trained myself that first year of residency.

My other gun was tucked away six drawers down; there was no way I could get to it before both men were on me. Feeling around the counter behind me, I blindly searched for anything I could use to defend myself.

I'm going to kill Weston for running off with my gun.

A whimper of relief almost escaped me when my fingers felt the smooth wood of the knife block. Gliding my fingers up, I grabbed the first handle I could grip and pulled out a large carving knife. The men would have to get closer for me to use it on them, but at least it was some way to defend myself when they did attack.

I tried to make a move toward the front door, but the larger of the two men cut off my path, smiling down at me with a devilish grin.

Turning, I found the other man blocking my escape from the other direction.

I was trapped. Trapped in my own home. My legs were useless rubber things hanging from my hips, I couldn't move at that point, could barely even breathe. My fight-or-flight instinct set in, and it was telling me to get the hell out of here, but there was nowhere to go.

"I wouldn't do that if I were you," said a voice from the living room.

Weston. My knees wobbled with relief when I saw him inching toward us with my gun trained on the male closest to him.

"Kate, watch your six." His voice was calm and steady.

Distracted by the sight of him, I'd failed to notice the larger man creeping closer and closer. Taking the opening, the second man lunged toward me, arms stretched out. The bang of the gun being fired rattled my eardrums as I watched the man fall in midair, landing at my feet.

The second man, seeing Weston wasn't bluffing with the gun, turned and ran out the front door.

Wounded but not dead, the man on the ground reached out and grabbed my bare ankle, pulling me toward him and causing me to lose my balance. Before my backside had a chance to hit the ground, Weston was there beside me, pulling my ankle from his grasp. He jammed his knee into the wounded man's spine as he jerked his hands behind his back, wrapping both in a tight grip.

Pulling my leg farther away, I gripped my thigh in pain. Blood was beginning to seep through my shorts. Glancing down at the knife lying beside me, there was a streak of blood down the razor-sharp edge. Blood seemed to be everywhere in the kitchen. My attention shifted to the man slowly bleeding out, his dark blood already pooling on the tile, making little rivers through the grout lines.

"Kate," Weston said gently.

Even with all my training, with everything I'd seen, the sight of the wounded man on *my* kitchen floor was unnerving. So much blood.

"Kate, look at me," he demanded.

My eyes were transfixed on the blood. I couldn't pull my eyes away.

"Kate!" he yelled.

His voice and tone snapped me out of whatever daze I was in, pulling my attention from the floor to him.

"I need you to grab my phone. It's beside my bed. Call the police."

When I didn't move, he smacked my foot with a bloody hand. "Damn it, Kate, go get my fucking phone."

"Don't yell at me," I snapped and pushed myself off the floor, gripping my sliced thigh. "This is a first for me, remember?"

I grabbed his phone off his nightstand and limped back to the kitchen. His face hardened when he noticed the blood dripping down my leg.

The way his face contorted in anger had me pausing several feet away from him. Even from where I stood, I could see his grip on the man's wrists tighten and his knuckles go white, a scream of pain bursting from the man beneath him. "Did they do that?" he asked with lethal calm.

"No."

Damnit, I didn't want to admit that I did it to myself accidentally, but if I didn't, then Weston might finish the guy off right there on the kitchen floor.

Walking closer to hand him the phone, I explained, "I must have cut myself when I fell backward."

He snatched the phone from my hand and began dialing. I cocked my head to the side as he punched in way more numbers than needed to dial 911. Before hitting Call, he glanced up at me. "Go upstairs and clean up your leg, then pack a bag. We can't stay here tonight." That was the end of the discussion, apparently. He pressed the green button and placed the phone between his ear and shoulder.

"No, you might need—"

"For one fucking second of your life, just do what you're told." His nostrils flared as he narrowed his eyes at me.

Ready to prove a point, I stayed, listening to his conversation.

"The police and ambulance are on their way." He placed the phone on the counter and turned his focus back to the man beneath him.

"If you ever speak to me that way again, Weston, I swear on my mother's grave I will take your balls off." I didn't wait to see his reaction before heading toward the stairs and up to my room. By the time I closed the bedroom door behind me, the glare of flashing lights was pulsating through the windows.

10

The wound on my leg was deep enough that I had to rummage through the cabinet to find gauze and something to wrap it with. I needed to remind Weston that injuring myself while trying to protect myself needed to be our little secret. If Eric found out.... I rolled my eyes at the thought.

I packed an overnight bag and gingerly sat on the bed. Just a few hours ago, all my friends had been here, having a great time, and now I had two busted doors and a crime scene in the kitchen. Plopping my back on the bed, I rubbed my temples with my thumbs, trying to keep the approaching headache at bay.

What I wouldn't give for a good cup of coffee right now.

"Kate," Weston whispered and shook my shoulders. "Kate, we need to go."

I swatted his hand away. "Go away."

In my daze, I heard him huff a laugh.

"We have to go. You can sleep in the car." He grabbed my hands and gently pulled me off the bed.

Practically sleepwalking, I followed him down the stairs and out to the sidewalk in front of the townhouse.

"Wait, my bag." I turned to go back inside, but he grabbed my wrist, keeping me close to him.

"I grabbed it."

"Where are we going?" I yawned.

"My company arranged for a hotel room for the night, right down the street."

My head snapped up. There were *no* good hotels around me. "Um, no."

"Excuse me?"

"I'm not staying somewhere that also rents by the hour. I'll get us a room." I pulled out my phone and began scrolling through the contact list.

"Get one room. After tonight, I'm not going to let you out of my sight. Where are we going?"

I smiled at him, which was amazing considering the night we'd had. "Somewhere with a big bed and good breakfast." I found the contact I was looking for and called the reception desk to book our room.

Sliding my phone into the pocket of my sweatpants, I looked up at him. "We're all set. Are we taking the bike or waiting for a car?"

"Waiting for a car. I need to make a few calls on our way."

"Oh? What kind of calls at three in the morning?"

He sighed. "Your father, for one. He needs to know what happened tonight. And second, to my company to debrief."

"So official."

Wrapping my arms around myself to keep the early morning chill from sinking in, I looked up and down the street, wondering if we were targets standing on the sidewalk with only the streetlight protecting us. Looking back at Weston, my eyes landed on the gun tucked into the back of his pants. Just the sight of it made me relax.

A dark SUV approached. Weston stepped beside me, wrapping a hand around my elbow and holding me close.

"I want my gun back."

"You can have it back once the police release it."

Weston opened the car door and helped me in, then tossed our bags into the back and climbed into the front passenger seat.

He turned to face me. "Where are we going, Kate?"

"The Ritz." My eyes shuttered closed just thinking about the big comfortable bed that was waiting for me.

I was fuming as we entered our hotel room. He knew I could hear his conversations with my dad and his boss from the back seat. His retelling made it sound like I was trying to take on the two men who had me cornered, not just preparing to defend myself while he was off somewhere chasing the other guy. Okay, yes, I could have called out to him, done something to let him know I was in danger inside the house instead of grabbing a knife and preparing to go down swinging. But I had it under control. I wasn't stupid enough to engage them like he was making it seem.

Tossing my bag on the bed, I stormed to the bathroom and slammed the door shut just to have it open again. Gripping the top of the doorframe, he angled his body into the bathroom.

"Why are you pissed now?"

"You know why."

"Oh really? Were you or were you not standing in the middle of your kitchen with a knife in your hand ready to attack the two men tonight?"

"It wasn't like that and you know it. I had to do something while I waited for you."

"You didn't even try to call out to me. You thought you could handle it on your own, didn't you?"

"Why would I call out to you? I knew I could hold them off until you came back."

He scoffed. "Do you even hear yourself? There were two of them, Kate. They had you trapped in your own kitchen. Wake the fuck up. This is way more than you can handle on your own. Let me help. Let me do my job. Let me protect you."

Lunging for him, I pushed him away and slammed the door in his face.

The almost scalding hot shower did nothing for the tension building in my whole body. After wrapping my leg in a fresh bandage, I stood in front of the steamed mirror towel-drying my hair, wondering if maybe he had a point. Maybe this was bigger than me. Maybe I did need help.

It wasn't that I always avoided help—hell, in the ER, I needed help all the time and it never bothered me to ask—so why did Weston helping to protect my *life* get under my skin so bad? Even I didn't have an answer.

"Damnit," I muttered as I realized my bag was in the other room. Wrapping the plush towel tightly around me, I opened the door and tried to walk as evenly as I could, not wanting to draw attention to my leg again, to my bag. Weston was in the process of making a little pallet on the floor. He stood up at the sound of the door, looking like he was about to say something, but as soon as he saw me partially naked, his mouth closed and his eyes widened a fraction.

Bending over to search through my bags, I snuck a peek behind me and found Weston blatantly looking me over. "Like what you see?" I joked, pulling my sleep shorts and tank from my bag.

He grumbled something before grabbing his own bag and heading into the bathroom.

My tossing and turning had nothing to do with the comfort level of the bed I sank into minutes after Weston entered the bathroom. The different versions of how the night could have ended up kept sleep from me. My leg throbbed under my weight, causing me to roll over on my back and stare at the ceiling. Maybe I was an idiot for what I tried to do tonight, for even thinking me being able to do it all on my own was an option.

If I was being honest with myself, it was just second nature. I'd been pushing people away for so long that I didn't know how not to. With Weston, he was encroaching on dangerous territory, and my first reaction was to do anything to get him to back away from the wall he was starting to tear down with each day that passed. He was the one I needed to watch out for, not Austin. No, Austin was a distraction, something easy that would pass the time. But Weston, he was more, and I had no idea what to do with more besides keep pushing until he stopped coming back.

It would make him leaving easier if I did. That was what all this came down to anyway—our time together had an expiration date, and we both were just trying to make our way through these next few months so that when the time came, we could emerge still whole, no emotional scars left from the other.

So I had my answer to the question I hadn't even realized I was asking. Keep pushing him away, protect myself, because if I didn't, he might be the one who left me unable to trust ever again.

The sound of him slipping into his makeshift bed on the floor had me rolling over to face his direction.

"Good night, Weston," I whispered as I gazed down at him in the dark.

"Good night, Kate."

I could tell his eyes were open, sleep evading him too.

"What happened with the guy you chased?"

Through the dark, I saw him angle his face toward me.

"I chased him a few blocks, had him down on the ground, but then I realized it was too easy. He'd let himself get caught. It only took me a few seconds to piece it all together and realize he was the distraction and the real danger was in that house with you."

"Yeah, and you had my gun. I'm still a little pissed about that one."

"So your next best option was to grab a knife?"

"I had to figure out something. I thought it was pretty resourceful, honestly."

He snorted. "Right, the knife which you used to stab yourself in the leg."

I gripped the unused pillow beside me and flung it down at his face. A yelp of surprise echoed through the room as it connected with my target.

"We are not talking about that ever. Do you hear me?"

He chuckled and tucked the pillow under his neck. "Yes, Your Majesty."

Tracing the folds of the sheets, I asked him something that I would never have been brave enough to ask in the light. "I did okay though, right? I'm still alive, so that says something, doesn't it?"

Weston sat up and turned to me. "I want to beat your ass for not calling out to me. If I'd been just a few seconds later, they would have...." His head drooped and I heard him sigh. "But yes, Kate, you did great. How you could hold your own in that kind of situation is beyond me. Most men would have pissed their pants."

The shock of the whole evening wearing off had to be the reason tears slid down my cheek. "Good." I turned and placed my back to him. "Good night, Weston."

"Kate." The way his voice projected, I could tell he was still sitting up facing me.

I tried to keep my sniffle quiet, but I knew he heard it.

"Kate."

"What, Weston? I'm trying to sleep. Now go to bed," I snapped, using the sheets to wipe my face, then nose.

I heard his sheets rustling, and I knew what was coming. The bed dipped against his weight as he sat beside me.

"You're not sleeping, you're crying. Talk to me."

A sob shook through my body; I clamped my hands over my mouth, trying to stifle the sound. His hand wrapped around my shoulder, trying to angle me toward him, but I yanked it out of his grasp and pulled the covers over my head.

There was no way I was going to let him see me like this.

"Stop being so damn stubborn and talk to me," he growled as he jerked my duvet wall away from my face. "It's just the shock wearing off. It happens to everyone."

I wiped my nose with the back of my hand, my voice full of unshed tears as I said, "You don't seem to be affected by it."

The weight of his body lifted from the bed for a moment, then was back again. He had a box of tissues in his hand. "I am affected by it. Tonight was tough for both of us. I'm still reeling, which is why I can't go to sleep even though it's five in the morning and I've had an hour of sleep."

Weston admitting his vulnerability while he was witnessing mine had me reaching across the comforter and grabbing his hand. The physical connection helped enough that when my eyes closed, I was able to drift off into a peaceful sleep.

THE SOUND of an unfamiliar phone ringing urged me awake. It was loud and obnoxious this early in the morning. Without opening my eyes, I attempted to crawl across the bed, but my hand landed on bare skin instead of soft sheets. Opening one eye and then the other, I looked at what my hand was pushing on.

Weston's bare chest.

Pulling back an inch, I tried not to panic. He was clothed from the waist down. Good. That was when I realized my other hand was restricted, held tight. Looking down, I found our hands still connected, just as they were earlier that morning before I drifted to sleep.

Groaning, I climbed over him toward the phone and lifted it from the receiver. The perky voice on the other end notified me it was noon, and this was a courtesy call to let me know we needed to be out within the hour or they would charge us another night. I grumbled a thanks to the woman and slammed the phone back into the receiver, fumbling around a few times to hang it up properly.

Lying back on the bed, I turned on my side to face Weston.

"Who was that?" he asked, eyes still closed like he was attempting to fall back asleep. He wasn't embarrassed or concerned that he'd fallen asleep in the bed with me and somehow held on to my hand all night.

Stretching my arms over my head, I arched my back and lengthened my body as I yawned. "Front desk. We have an hour to get out of here."

Reaching back over, I grabbed the phone and dialed room service to order breakfast and several carafes of coffee.

When I rolled back over, Weston had fallen asleep once more. He looked so peaceful that I snuggled back into the covers and watched him. His hand was lying on top of the covers, fingers out like it was waiting for mine. Running my fingers along the duvet, I paused right before our hands would connect and looked at him. The softness in his face had turned to concern as his brows furrowed in his sleep. I slipped my fingers into his, our palms connecting, and in that instant, I felt... more. I wondered if he felt the same thing.

This time when I looked up to his face, I found the worry and concern replaced by a sweet side smile that looked remotely of contentment.

Me: So last night was interesting. Two guys broke in. Weston saved the day. Stayed at the Ritz.

Eric: WHAT! Are you okay?

Me: Yes I'm fine. Besides the huge gash down my leg. I got stabbed.

Meagan: Is Weston okay?

Eric: One of the guys stabbed you?

Me: Um, not so much one of them...

Eric: Weston stabbed you?! I'll kill him. Well I'll hire someone to kill him. Pretty sure he would kick my ass.

Meagan: Um, are you going to answer me? Is Captain Too Hot okay?

Me: I might have grabbed a knife to protect myself, then fell on said knife.

Eric: Somehow you just made my day by telling me you stabbed yourself with your own knife.

Me: Yes, Meagan, he is fine. If you think he's
hot normally, you should see him with a gun.

Meagan: I think I would combust.

Eric: Me too. Did you take pictures?

Me: No… do you want me to ask him to
reenact it so I can?

Meagan: Yes.

Eric: Please.

Me: You two are pathetic. I will add that he
did it all with his shirt off, so it was kind of
amazing.

Eric: Tease.

Meagan: Bitch.

TUCKING my phone into my scrubs, I headed toward the charge nurse to see who was up next. Even with the absolutely shitty night, a smile tugged on my lips every time I thought of Weston's hand engulfing mine all night, never letting go.

I hadn't been at work very long when an arm wrapped around my waist while I was making notes in a patient chart at the nurses' station. My stomach dropped knowing it was more than likely Austin, not Weston, who had his arms wrapped around me, pulling me close.

"Hey, beautiful. Let's step away for a few minutes. I need to talk to you. In private," he whispered into my ear.

Shrugging a shoulder to brush his lingering breath off my skin, I mumbled, "I just got here. I can't take a break yet."

"I'll cover for you. Go with Austin," Meagan chimed in with a little smirk after overhearing my protests.

Not wasting a second, Austin gripped my hand in his and dragged me in the direction of the locker room. Closing the door behind us, he scouted the empty room, making sure we were alone and had privacy for whatever conversation he wanted to have.

He perched on the edge of the long metal bench situated between the rows of lockers, leaning forward and pressing his forearms against his thighs. "Listen, I know I was out of line last night. And I'm sorry. Really I am. I was being a complete dick and wasn't listening to what you were asking, what you needed. If you need more time, I can give you time. Just don't cut me out. Not yet."

I sat straddling the narrow bench and scooted closer to him. "Yes, you were being a dick, but I do appreciate you admitting it and for trying to understand me needing some time."

"Just so we're both clear on expectations, how slow are we talking?" He raised an arched eyebrow in questioning, but his eyes sparkled with amusement.

Without answering the question, I cupped his face, pulling him in close and pressing our lips together. His answering groan rumbled across my lips as he slid his hands up my arms, over my shoulders, only stopping once they were snagged in my hair, pushing our lips tighter together.

I must have let out a soft moan of my own. He pulled away slightly, peering down with a cocky male grin. "See what you missed out on last night?"

When his lips grazed down the nape of my neck, I couldn't help my own cocky grin. He alternated between kissing, sucking, and gliding the tip of his tongue along my collarbone. With every touch of his lips against my skin, goose bumps rose in their wake, sending shivers of warmth down my spine.

Easy. No complications. That's what I need.

And for half a second, I believed it, that this was all I needed. But then the image of a brown-eyed boy flickered in my mind, and I found myself wondering. Wondering if I would have the same reaction for Weston if his lips were on my lips and skin. If he, instead of Austin, were pulling me closer and closer just to have my body pressed together a fraction more.

Releasing my hair from his grasp, Austin leaned his forehead against mine, dragging in deep ragged breaths.

"Please don't push me away next time. We could be so great

together. I promise. Just give me a chance to show you. You don't have to be anxious with me."

I smirked up at him, finding it hilarious that he thought I was anxious about being with him. "Maybe I'm protecting you, Austin. You don't know anything about me. I could be into some crazy stuff. Speaking of which, do you have a safe word?"

"For you, I wouldn't need one. I will do whatever you ask me to do." He attempted to stand up but abruptly sat back down again, swearing as he did.

"What?" I asked, giving him an innocent look but knowing full well why he couldn't stand. Scrubs didn't cover things well on aroused men.

"Look at me, Kate." He ran both of his hands through his long blond hair. "Look at what you do to me. This is why it was so hard for me to leave last night. It's why I pressed so hard. I need you. Bad."

Pushing off the bench, I stood and started toward the door. "Be glad you didn't stay or you would have found yourself in a war zone."

"Huh?"

"Last night, my house was broken into. Everything turned out fine in the end. Weston shot the guy—"

"He did what?" he shouted as he bolted to his feet.

"Someone broke in, the guy had me cornered in the kitchen, he made a move toward me, so Weston shot him. He called the police, and then we went and stayed the night at a hotel since both my doors were damaged."

He shrugged, dismissing the awe in my voice as I retold the story. "I'm sure anyone could have done all that if they had a gun. Not that impressive if you ask me." Austin reached around, placing his hand on the door, holding it closed no matter how hard I pulled on the handle. "You said *we* stayed at a hotel. Did he have his own room?"

I snorted. There was no way in hell I was going to let him make me feel bad about the sleeping arrangements. After all, we were simply make-out buddies at this point, nothing more.

"No," I said, giving the door one more strong pull.

"So he slept in your room. Let me guess, for protection." He laughed under his breath. "How noble of him. Did he sleep with you?"

Hell no.

"Listen, you asshat. He's just doing his job. Stop making this out to be more than what it is. He's protecting me. Obviously I need it. Oh, and by the way, you forgot to say, 'I'm so glad you're safe. How are you feeling?' Now get out of my way before my knee makes sure you never have an embarrassing man situation in your scrubs again." My glare conveyed my level of annoyance and resolve to uphold the threat.

He slowly pulled his hand from the door, allowing it to open just wide enough for me to duck under his arm and slip through it.

"Kate, wait."

I didn't turn around. I was at my limit with him. Plus, I'd been off the floor long enough; Meagan's generosity would only last so long.

He gripped my forearm, forcing me to stop and hear him out.

"You're right, I'm sorry. I'm glad you're safe. It's just... I think he has a thing for you, and knowing you two are together all the time makes me, I don't know...." He ran his free hand through his hair as he struggled with the word. "Jealous, I guess."

"Let go of my arm. Now. I need to get back to work."

"Just say you forgive me."

As hard as I yanked, I couldn't get my arm free from his grip. With how hard he was holding on, I knew bruises would appear by tomorrow. "It's fine, Austin. I get it, but you have to cool it with the jealousy crap. I'm not the type of girl who likes the type of guy who smothers."

A familiar musky scent wrapped around me, making me feel at ease and alive all at once.

"Everything okay over here, Kate?" Weston asked in an icy tone. I was relieved that his annoyance and anger weren't directed toward me or because of me, for once. His intense focus was on the white-knuckled grip Austin had around my arm.

Austin might have been attractive, but damn he was dumb when it came to knowing his match. Squaring his shoulders to Weston, he gave him a dismissive smirk, not dropping my arm out of sheer defiance. "She's fine. We're just having a conversation. You can go now."

Reluctantly dragging his focus from my arm to meet my wide-eyed stare, Weston asked, "You good, Kate?"

These men. And they thought *I* was exasperating.

"I'm fine, Weston. Austin, let go of my arm. Now," I snapped, giving my arm one more strong pull just as he released it. The two stared each other down in some male dominance bullshit. "If you two want to have a pissing contest, do it somewhere else. I need to get back to work."

Pushing past Weston, I headed toward the nurses' station.

Five hours later, we had a slight lull in patients, allowing me the opportunity to step away for a rushed dinner. My shoulders slumped with exhaustion and relief when I found Eric sitting alone in the cafeteria. Setting my own food down beside him, I plopped down and laid my head on his shoulder.

"You okay?" He wrapped his arm around my shoulders, holding me close.

"I don't know. To be honest, it was all too much: the guys breaking in, Weston shooting him, my home being a crime scene.... I can't believe it actually happened. Is this really happening? Is this my life now? It makes me sick thinking about what *could* have happened if he wouldn't have been there." I stared at the tray in front of me. Rehashing the memories again made my stomach churn and the food look undesirable.

Eric pulled his arm from my shoulders, which I immediately missed, and began eating, knowing we wouldn't have long on this break. It was a luxury that we had this time now.

"Can I ask you something?" He wiped his mouth with a paper napkin.

"Of course."

"What's *really* going on between you and Weston?"

My back straightened at the question. "Nothing, why?"

He laughed under his breath and took a sip of coffee. "Why are you denying it? He's a great guy."

"What am I denying?" I couldn't look at him. I knew exactly what I was denying. I knew it the second I woke up that morning with my hand still wrapped in his. And liking it.

"Last night, Kate, you were happy. With all the shit going on around you, you were so happy just sitting in that kitchen going back and forth with him. I don't know if I've seen you that relaxed with a guy before. And Weston, damn that man, he gives you your shit right back, and it's amazing. He's challenging you, pushing back on your bullshit. I think you've met your match in him, Kate Wheeler." I pulled my hand from my lip to grab the disposable coffee cup filled to the brim with burned coffee. "And don't worry. It's not just you. He feels the same way. The way I see it, I think he's simply happy to be in the same room with you."

"I don't know about all that. He likes being in the same room with me because he can see me, protect me better, that's all. That's what you're seeing from him. He's made it very clear that something between us would never be an option," I said skeptically.

This doesn't change anything. Weston is off-limits. He's still leaving.

"Believe what you want, Kate, but what I saw was you happy with a guy who was just as happy with you. What you do now is up to you. He has a job to do, so he won't be the one to make the first move. Honestly, he's so focused on your safety, I don't know if he'll ever relax enough to let himself act. You two might have to vacay to some remote island, far away from all this crap, to get laid."

I snorted and shook my head.

"You saw me with Austin. What did you see when you saw us together, oh wise one?"

He shot me an incredulous look and went back to eating his food.

I shoved his shoulder hard. "Remind me again, what makes you the subject matter expert on all this?"

"Well, I know guys, and I know that look, and believe me, he has that look when he looks at you. And I know you. We've been friends long enough that I've seen you with other guys, and he's different,

Kate." His chair scraped against the floor as he pushed back from the table and picked up his tray full of trash. He paused, tray in hand, glancing nervously around the room. "Have you told Weston what tomorrow is?"

My stomach dropped. *Tomorrow.* "No, I haven't heard from my dad yet on the plans. I was going to wait until I heard from him," I said quietly, my gaze unfocused on the wall behind him.

"I know it's a hard day. If you need me, I'm here for you. I know you like to go out alone with your dad, but if all this that's going on is too much with tomorrow...."

Closing the distance between us, I reached across the table and grabbed his hand, giving it a strong squeeze.

"You offering means so much. Thank you. I don't deserve you as a friend, you know that?"

"I know," Eric said with a cocky smile. "Call me if you need me."

Focusing on my tray of soggy cold food, I gave him a slight nod.

"And, Kate?" Eric's voice brought my attention back up to him. "Don't waste this time you have with him. He's worth the risk."

As I watched him walk away, I wondered if he was right.

PLOPPING down on the couch beside Weston, I propped my feet up on the coffee table and set my plate on top of my outstretched legs. It felt amazing to elevate my feet; the past twenty-four hours had been brutal. When we got home just an hour or so ago, the doors had been fixed and were now installed with Shawshank-level deadbolts.

The sound of his book closing drew my attention. He glanced down at my plate and pressed his lips tightly together, clearly unhappy about whatever he saw.

"Do you ever eat anything other than cereal or peanut butter sandwiches?"

I cocked an eyebrow at him as I took a bite of the sandwich he was judging. "You do realize you just broke one of my rules, right?"

"Yes, but it's just a question."

"Hmm. If you get to break one of *my* rules without any repercussions, does that mean I get to break one of *yours*?"

His smirk turned into something mischievous. "I think you've broken enough of mine already that I get this one free."

"Fine," I grumbled. "Oh, and I need to talk to you about something."

He turned, giving me his full attention.

"Tomorrow is...." My eyes skirted around the room as I tried to find the right words to explain. "Tomorrow is the anniversary of my mom's accident. My dad and I go out to the cemetery together to... oh, I don't know, pay our respects, check in with her, say hi... whatever. But my dad called earlier while I was at work and wants us to still go tomorrow even with everything that's going on. I know it's important to him. It helps him get through the day, gives him a bit of distraction. It's a nice distraction for both of us, really. That way we aren't watching the clock count down to the hour and minute our hearts shattered into a thousand pieces."

When I finally gained enough courage to look in his direction, I couldn't read the look on his face. Concern was there, yes, but there was something else mixed in with it. For once, after talking about my mother's death, there seemed to be understanding instead of pity mixed in, which was a relief.

"I understand you wanting to still go tomorrow, but I'm not okay with you being out there alone, unprotected. Anything could happen."

"I know. I already talked it over with my dad. His security detail will be with him, and you'll be with me. But I do need you to keep some distance while we're there so we can have some sense of privacy. I haven't been out there in a while, so I have a lot to catch her up on." Giving him a half smile, I shrugged and went back to eating.

"Whatever you need. I'm here for you."

Even as the thought of what tomorrow would bring made exhaustion seep in faster, causing my eyelids to get heavier with each passing second, the thought of him being with me, by my side, stilled my nerves. With him, I knew the day wouldn't be as lonely as it had been in the past.

11

Zipping up the black three-quarter-length sweater dress, I stared, unseeing, at myself in the full-length mirror. Today, everything would be a struggle. It seemed as if this date held some kind of magical property that would transport me back to *that* day. That day when my mom came bounding in, sharing an endless stream of ideas for Thanksgiving before giving me a hug to head to Second Chances, where she volunteered helping with grants and other legal situations.

My eyes shifted from the mirror to the door. I would give up everything I owned, everything I'd worked so hard for just to get one more minute with her. With the friend who was taken too soon, taken before I was ready, taken just when I needed her most.

A ghost of a smile crept up my face wondering what she would think about Weston. What she would think about the whole situation, really. More than likely she would have told me to stop holding myself back. To enjoy life but to stay true to myself. That was one of her mottos that she latched onto at the end of every piece of advice she dished out. In the past couple years, I'd begun to wonder what she even meant by it. At the time, I thought I knew, but now it wasn't as clear.

Shaking my head, I grabbed a set of headphones and iPod off the dresser. Dwelling on that day wasn't healthy, but sometimes being alone with my thoughts helped me work through things better than anything else. Setting Disturbed's "The Sound of Silence" on repeat, I lay down on the bed and let myself slip into happy memories.

A familiar scent wrapped around me, letting me know he was in my room, and from how strong the scent was, he was close. Opening my eyes, I found him standing beside the bed, eyes narrowed as he stared down at me, looking completely conflicted. Maybe Eric was right. Maybe I needed to be the one to make the first move.

A few soft pats on the comforter was all it took. Without hesitation, he lay down beside me, tucking an arm under my shoulder and folding me into him. I wrapped my free arm around his waist, and something happened that I didn't think was possible on a day like this.

I smiled.

It was beginning to spit rain from the cold front pushing through when our car pulled up behind my father's black SUV at the cemetery. I took a deep breath in and held it as I swung open the car door and released a black umbrella to protect me from the cold rain. It was finally starting to feel like fall after so many days of unseasonably warm weather. Thankfully I'd thought ahead and brought a jacket and wore my Hunter boots just in case.

It was only fitting that it was cold and rainy today. Exact same conditions that had a major part in my mother's accident. The weather gods seemed to have a sick sense of humor, it seemed.

Turning toward my father's Escalade, I found him waiting under his own umbrella. A look of soul-crushing agony covered his face, almost bringing me to my knees. It was hard for me to be here, but for him, it was just a reminder that he lost the love of his life, that his best friend was never coming back. It had taken him months to pull from the hollow shell of a person he'd become after the accident.

Hopefully today, amid everything else going on, wouldn't send him spiraling back into that darkness.

A strong, warm hand pressed against my lower back as I started toward him, giving me the strength and support to continue walking. Large streams of water began pouring over and down the umbrella in my hand as the rain picked up.

"Ready?" my father asked so low I could barely hear him through the drumming of the rain.

His hand was ice cold when I grabbed it and nodded. Taking two steps toward the gravesite, away from Weston and the other security detail, I immediately missed the hand warming my back. My tear-rimmed eyes connected with his in a stolen glance back in his direction.

A sad, pained half smile played on his lips. "I'm not going anywhere."

I mouthed, "Thank you," before turning and following my father down the rows of headstones.

MY FATHER LEFT me alone at the headstone an hour or so ago after giving me a bone-crushing hug. But I couldn't leave. Not yet. There was still so much I needed to tell her, to ask her. Without a doubt, Weston was having a panic attack back by the car from me being out here alone and exposed for so long, but he would just have to get over it.

With my hand on her gravestone, I kept going with my one-sided conversation.

"Shelly from Second Chances says hi and that she misses you. She says she misses your friendship every day and wishes you could see the women we're helping there now. I've been volunteering more and more. It's becoming the thing I look forward to and dread the most out of my week. I just wish... I don't know... I wish I could do more, but I don't know how. If you could just give me some kind of sign of what I should do, that would be great. Not sure if it works that way up there or not, but hey, it's worth a shot. What else?" I drummed my fingers along the cold wet stone. "Oh, I met this doctor at work, Austin. He's gorgeous, Mom, and his hair is to die for. He's kind of an ass though. Then there's this other guy, Casey. Well, he goes by his last name, Weston, don't ask me why. He's the one protecting me during all this crap going on with Dad's big case, so he's around all the time, and he hasn't run off yet. I know part of it is his job, but a part of me wonders if he's sticking around for more than that."

The sound of approaching footsteps stopped my rambling.

Weston.

"Do you need something?"

"I just came to see if you were ready. We need to go."

My contemplative gaze floated back to the headstone. "Okay, I'm almost done. But can you give me one more minute?"

"Of course." He turned to head back toward the idling SUV.

"Wait." I placed my free hand on my hip. "Do you want to meet my mom?"

A genuine smile crept up his face as he said, "Of course."

My smile mirrored his. "Weston, meet my mom, Rachael. Mom, this is Casey Weston."

Weston shifted on his feet, not knowing what to do next. It was a little crazy asking him to meet my dead mother.

"I know it's weird. Just humor me, okay?" I shrugged and angled my head toward the gravestone.

"Hi. Nice to meet you...?"

I chuckled at the effort. It was sweet. "Okay, your time is up, Weston. I'll meet you back at the car in a few minutes."

He nodded and started to walk off, then stopped abruptly and turned. Reaching past me, he patted the headstone. "Bye. It was nice to meet you."

Once he was far enough away to not hear my words, I said, "He's kind of adorable, right, Mom?"

WESTON WAS STANDING NEXT to the passenger door, waiting. The look of frustration on his face caught me off guard.

"Sorry to keep you waiting, but you don't have to look so pissed." Stopping in front of him, I gave him my best scowl.

He pursed his lips in a thin line. "I'm not pissed. Get in the car."

A quick step back had me just outside his reach. "Um, no. What's your problem?"

"Kate, just get in the damn car. Right now. This isn't a game." With each word, his voice rose.

"No. Not until you tell me what the hell—"

Before I could finish the sentence, he tossed me over his shoulder, holding on to me with one hand while the other opened the passenger door.

"What the hell, Weston? Put me down right now!" I beat against his back with my fists.

Without flinching from my hitting or anger, he flung me into the car, pushing me across the seat so he could slide in behind me.

The car door slammed behind him as he yelled, "Go, go," to the driver, Carl.

It was a command he'd obviously been prepared for. Carl pressed on the gas, my back slamming against the seat from the force.

What the hell was going on.

Situating myself and fastening my seat belt, I asked him just that.

"I'm sorry I had to manhandle you," he grumbled, keeping his eyes trained on the back window. "Carl and I noticed the same blue Toyota drive by four times in the past twenty minutes. I'm not taking any chances, no matter how pissed you are at me."

That was a pretty good excuse. And who was I kidding? I kind of liked him manhandling me. Crossing my arms over my chest to emphasize that I was indeed still mad, I huffed, "Are we safe now?"

Weston grabbed his gun from its holster and held it against his leg, finger poised over the trigger. My mouth went dry at the sight. The whole situation was a little terrifying, but my body was reacting to him holding that gun. It was dangerously attractive.

Realizing he hadn't responded to my question, I turned my head and stared out the back window, mimicking him. Fear pooled in my gut when I saw a late-model blue Toyota following close, only one car separating us from them.

His eyes were fixed on the car as he called out to Carl to run the next red light, wanting to see if they followed. But it hadn't been forty-eight hours since their last attempt at me, so why would they try again so soon when all our guards were up?

Carl yelled at us to hold on as he gunned it through a red light. Tires screeched, and our car swerved back and forth, dodging the cars that had already ventured out into the intersection. When we made it through, thankfully unharmed, I snapped my focus to the back window once more only to see the blue Toyota still on our tail.

Weston swore, then shot me a nervous glance before looking back out the window.

Keeping his full focus on the car weaving between lanes to catch back up to us, Weston said, "Carl, get on the interstate when you can. We'll have to lose them that way. There's no way that piece-of-shit car will be able to keep up."

My back slammed against the leather seat once more as Carl sped through traffic, searching for an onramp. Heart fluttering from the anticipation and the unknown, I closed my eyes, trying to calm down.

That was when I felt it. It wasn't much, but for a few seconds Carl lost control of the SUV at our high speed on the slick road. Weston cursed at Carl. Carl yelled at Weston. But I didn't hear what they were saying. That slight hydroplane aligned my scattered subconscious thoughts.

Interstate.

Today.

My mother.

Rain.

Wreck.

Images from the wreck, of her Lexus flattened and pinned between two other cars, flipped through my mind like a silent film.

All the blood drained from my face.

This can't be happening. This can't be happening.

Wild panic crept up from my stomach to my throat, shrinking my airways, making it difficult to breathe. Hyperventilating. I was hyperventilating, and I couldn't do anything to stop it.

"Kate, I need you to pull it together." His voice was muffled through the roar pulsing through my ears.

Air. I needed air. But none could squeeze through the strangled passageways. Desperate to breathe, even just half a breath, I began clawing at my neck, trying to do anything to open my airways. Darkness pooled in the corners of my vision, spreading quickly with the lack of oxygen.

Everything went dark and quiet, my body shutting down. But just before I gave in to the deep sleep that beckoned, I felt sweaty palms grip my face, shaking me.

It felt like someone took a sledgehammer to my head. The throbbing was so intense that even opening my eyes was a struggle from the intense pain it caused.

Once the room came into focus, I relaxed, recognizing my surroundings. Home. And sitting across from me on the other couch in the living room was Weston. He was still in his slacks and jacket from earlier, staring at the wall, worry etched in the wrinkles from his furrowed brow. His knee bobbed up and down as he bounced his leg in an anxious habit I hadn't seen before.

The pounding worsened when I attempted to sit up, forcing a pain-laced groan to escape. It was too much. Giving up, I lay back down, and the pressure lessened immediately. At the sound of movement, his head whipped to me, his throat bobbing slightly in relief at seeing me awake.

"What happened? Did I pass out?" My throat felt like I'd swallowed gravel. Every word burned.

Standing from his place on the couch, Weston walked out of the room, immediately returning with a bottle of water and what looked like headache medicine. He placed the tiny white capsules in my palm and set the water within reach on the floor below me.

"Yes, and it scared the shit out of me. One second you were fine, the next you were pale and attempting to scratch all the skin off your neck."

The water felt amazing, soothing my throat as I washed down the medicine he'd given me. "I remember that part, but what happened after that? How long have I been out?"

"We lost the other car on the interstate, though it took longer than expected. We finally ditched them and came back here. You still weren't awake when I carried you into the house, so I called Eric. He left about thirty minutes ago after giving you the all clear."

Draining the last of the water, I set the empty bottle on the floor and closed my eyes. Damn, I was exhausted. "You didn't answer my second question. How long have I been out?"

"A little over two hours."

Two hours?

"That's a long time for a panic attack, right? What did Eric have to say about it?"

Weston ran a hand through his dark hair. Bending forward on the couch, he rested his forearms on his thighs, one barely bouncing as the leg beneath tapped up and down. "He said the same thing, but when I told him what was going on when you passed out, he seemed to think it was okay. He said something about your body shutting down, being overwhelmed with emotional triggers, or something along those lines. It was like your body was hitting a reset button when you couldn't process everything going on around you anymore."

His knees cracked as he crouched in front of me, putting our eyes at the same level. "I was worried about you. I didn't know what to do," he said, his voice hoarse with emotion.

My eyelids drooped with the heavy weight of exhaustion. "Can I just go back to sleep? You know, get this shitty day over with?"

"Do whatever you need to do, but after this afternoon, I would prefer it if you stayed down here and slept on the couch so I can watch after you. Seeing you... unresponsive... it messed with my mind. I just... I need to make sure you're okay."

Eyes closed, I smiled. I wondered if his past clients had gotten this kind of detailed attention or if it was just me. A small—but growing by the minute—part of me hoped it was just me. "Who knew you were such a softy, Weston? Fine. I'll sleep down here so you can watch me sleep."

"You're making it sound creepy."

"It is a little, isn't it?"

"I'm only trying to take care of you, so no, it's not creepy."

"Whatever, you just want to stare at me without me knowing." I opened my eyes and found him still crouching, smirking.

"So conceited, thinking that's how I want to spend my time. It's only four in the afternoon. I do have other things I could be doing."

I smirked back, the movement worth the pain. "No you don't. The only thing you need to be doing is me."

What I thought was pain before was minimal compared to the ice pick that went through my brain as I sat straight up, horrified at my words and how they could be interpreted by him. And judging by the expression on Weston's face, he was reveling in my embarrassment.

"I swear I didn't mean for it to come out that way." The pounding against my skull was so forceful, I wondered if my brain would turn to mush if I stayed sitting up much longer. "I just meant I'm all you need to be doing because you can't leave, since you're here to protect—"

He cut me off, laughing under his breath at my backtracking. "I know what you meant. Lie down and go back to sleep. I'll get you up in a couple hours for dinner. You haven't eaten all day."

The couch shifted as Weston sat down and settled in. He patted his thigh, motioning for me to lay my head on his broad lap.

I wanted to balk, but I found myself asking why. This gesture, he wasn't trying to be anything other than kind. Once I was settled in, he tossed a blanket over me and reached across to the coffee table, picking up his book. In one hand he held his book while the other unconsciously raked fingers through my long dark hair, easing me into a deep, peaceful sleep.

. . .

Night had fallen when I woke for the second time; the clock was too far away for me to read it to see what time it actually was. The pounding in my head had subsided enough that it was only a mere annoyance in the back of my skull. I stretched my short body along the couch, arching my back and hitting Weston in the arms and chest with my arms as I lengthened them over my head. Rolling onto my back, I adjusted my head so I could look up at him. His eyes were glued to his book, but I could tell he wasn't reading.

Without looking away from the book, he smirked. "Hey, you, feel any better?"

Half my face was tucked against his muscled abdomen, making the vibrations of his words when he spoke tickle my cheek. "Yeah, a little. My head doesn't feel like someone took a sledgehammer to it anymore, so that's improvement. What time is it?"

"Seven. I was going to finish this chapter, then wake you up to figure out dinner."

"What are you reading this time? Anything good?"

Blatantly ignoring my question, he pressed his lips together, suppressing a smile.

"You're insufferable, you know that? I don't care what you're reading, even if it *is* naughty. I'm just curious."

Closing the book, he looked down at me with humor in his eyes. "You are the most curious woman I have ever met. Keeping something this small from you is kind of fun. Not knowing is driving you insane. Consider it payback for all the hell you give me on a daily basis."

"Whatever. I'm a perfect client," I said, giving him an innocent smile and batting my eyelashes.

My cheeks flushed when the deep rumble of his laugh vibrated against me. Being this close was making my body react; heat filled my core and twisted, making my stomach tingle with hope of our bodies getting closer. His musky scent filled my senses as I took a deep breath in, trying to commit it to memory for those months ahead when he would be gone, having moved on to his next client.

A loud echoing growl erupted from my stomach, making us both peer down at my belly in amusement.

"Let's go to this brick oven pizza place a few blocks from here," I said. "The food is amazing."

Pushing a lock of hair from my forehead, he narrowed his eyes at me. "Are you sure you want to go out? Are you up to that?"

Reluctantly pulling my head from his lap, I pushed myself to a sitting position. "Give me twenty minutes and I'll be ready to go." I swayed as I stood, light-headed from lying down for so long and having nothing in my belly.

Weston grabbed my waist with both hands, his thumbs sketching small circles beneath my ribs as he held me steady.

My breathing faltered slightly and my heart raced at the feel of his hands on me in such a sensitive area. Pulling my focus from his touch up to his beautiful face, I rested my hands on his shoulders, steadying myself as my vision refocused. The moment our eyes met, the movement in his thumbs stopped, his grip tightening slightly as he took in a deep breath.

His voice was deep and husky, with need, want, restraint—I couldn't tell—when he finally spoke, breaking the tension between us. "Put on something warm. It's gotten a lot colder out."

He was insufferable.

Patting his shoulders ever so slightly, I pulled out of his grasp and headed to change for dinner.

As I put on a pair of dark-wash jeans, a cream sweater, and over-the-knee flat brown boots, I wondered what was going on between the two of us. If I did make the first move, would he want me to? Maybe Eric's evaluation of us was all wrong and Weston only saw this as a job. I would die from embarrassment if I opened up to him and he pushed me away, not wanting me like that. But then there was the look in his eyes just now when his hands were around my waist. I could have sworn I saw… more.

Somehow he'd been tearing down the walls I'd so carefully constructed the past few years. And the sneaky bastard had done it a little at a time so now, today, when I looked at him, I felt like he could see me. It was slightly terrifying, but at the same time, it was exhilarating, something new. He was the first one to ever get this far past my defenses. Maybe it was due to anything intimate being off the table, so our only option was getting to know each other, for him to understand who I was with each day we spent together.

What annoyed me was he still knew way more about me than I knew about him.

As I situated my gray floppy hat, I grinned at my reflection.

Tonight, that was going to change.

12

My phone vibrated just as we sat down at our table.

Eric: How are you feeling?

Me: Better. Thanks for coming over and checking on me.

Eric: Of course. Glad you're alive.

Me: Me too. Dying would have sucked.

Eric: How's Weston?

Me: He's fine.

Me: Why are you asking about him?

Eric: I almost had to treat him too.

Eric: I thought he was going to die from worrying about you. Or punch a wall. He's very hard to read.

Eric: But I can tell you, the look on his face while you were passed out on that couch. It broke my heart.

Me: He just didn't want to get blamed for me dying on his watch.

Eric: It's more than that and you know it.

Me: We just sat down to dinner. I'll call you tomorrow.

Me: Thank you again. You're the best.

Eric: I know. You're welcome.

"Who's that?" Weston asked from across the booth as he looked over the menu. If I was hungry, he must have been famished.

"Eric. He was checking in on me." I omitted the part where he described Weston's worry. "Thank you for today, by the way. I know it was a weird day all around, especially when I asked you to meet my mom."

The waiter approached our table to take drink orders, which put a pause on our conversation. Weston ordered water—shocker—and I ordered a glass of red wine. Alcohol the night before a morning shift wasn't my norm, but with the completely shitty day I had, I figured the rules could be bent this one time.

Weston's eyes darted around the restaurant, always looking, always assessing. When we arrived, he asked—demanded—a booth near an exit door, and when we got to our table, he forced me to switch sides so his back could be toward the wall, facing all points of entry.

"Do you miss her?" he asked after the waiter had set off to put in our order.

I started twirling the roll of silverware on the table in front of me while I pieced together my thoughts. "Sometimes I miss her so much I can't breathe. Then other times I find myself not even thinking about her." I smiled and looked up at him. "She's the one you can blame for my fierce independence. She taught me to be the best version of myself, challenged me to not settle for anything. She loved seeing me live my own life, apart from our family's name, no stereotypes or restrictions. All the money my family has is from my dad's side, old oil money, and she was never the kind of wife or mother to spoil me or herself since she grew up with nothing."

His gaze landed on me. "She sounds like you, or you sound like her, however you say it. Remind me next time we go out there to thank her for that independent spirit that made my first month with you an absolute living hell."

"Whatever. You loved the challenge." I threw my napkin at him.

He chuckled as he snatched the napkin from the air, inches from his face.

The question about my mom had memories popping up everywhere in my mind. "You know what I miss the most?"

He leaned forward, placing his crossed arms on the table. "What?"

"The way she and my dad made each other so happy. I loved watching them interact. They loved each other and truly liked being around each other. My dad was everything to my mom and vice versa. Maybe that's why I'm so screwed up in the relationship department. They set the standards too high."

His gaze lowered, landing on the table between us. "I would think having high standards for relationships, for love, would be better than having none like your friend Meagan."

I snorted. He had a point.

Taking the opening, I turned the question he asked back on him. "What were your parents like?"

His warm smile disappeared. An icy calm washed over his face, and I could have sworn his eyes glazed over, as if he was sorting through thousands of memories. "Let's go back to talking about you and your family. I want to hear more about you."

My nostrils flared in annoyance. "No, we're talking about you for once, damnit. You know so much about me. You've seen me at my most vulnerable moments. Now you will tell me something personal about yourself, Casey whatever your middle name is Weston. Even if I have to... well, I don't know how to torture you because I don't know anything about you," I shouted.

"I think one of my weaknesses is pretty clear at this point."

I angled my head, not understanding what he was referencing.

He chewed on the inside of his cheek, another nervous habit that presented itself today. "What if you don't like what you hear?"

I rolled my eyes. "It won't change my opinion of you. Promise," I said as I held my right hand over my heart.

"Don't make promises you can't keep."

Folding my arms across my chest, I gave him the best annoyed look I could muster.

"Fine," he said, placing his palms flat on the table. "You're relentless, you know."

He huffed a laugh at the cocky grin on my face, very satisfied that I was getting what I wanted.

"I grew up in Dallas. East Dallas, to be exact. I never knew my dad, but my mother... when she was sober or too broke to buy more drugs, she was a great mom. But those moments were few and far between. We lived with whichever boyfriend she was living off at the time. In between, we would stay with my grandmother in her tiny trailer. My mom tried to protect us from as much as she could, but ultimately she was a mess and really shouldn't have had kids—"

Wine sloshed on my jeans at the abrupt movement of sitting up straight and leaning forward, totally caught off guard. "Kidssss? As in multiple? As in, you have siblings?"

"I have a younger brother, three years younger. He was a shithead then and still is. So, anyway, it went on like that for years. House after house, new boyfriend after another until...." He shifted in his seat, keeping his focus on the straw wrapper he was tying into knots.

"Until what, Weston?"

"Until she was gone."

"She abandoned you and your brother?"

"Not exactly."

"Then what? You have to give me more than that."

The frustrated, annoyed sigh that pushed from his chest was loud enough that most of Dallas could hear it. "She was killed. Murdered, if you want to get technical about it."

"I am so sorry, Weston. I had no idea or I wouldn't have pressed you so hard. Did they ever find the person that did it?"

"Yes. I was there when it happened."

No words. I couldn't find the words to let him know how deeply his story affected me. But for the first time without my prompting, he opened up, telling me what I wanted to know.

"We were staying in yet another boyfriend's mobile home, and I had woken up from the sounds of my mother and her boyfriend arguing. I didn't see it happen, but I heard the first gunshot, then the other. I was terrified that whoever was in the living room was going to come after me and Ryan, so I crept back to where he was sleeping and stayed there, wide awake, watching and waiting. Eventually the cops busted down the door. Someone had called the gunshot in. The police labeled it as a murder-suicide. After that, we were taken to my grandmother's."

He cleared his throat and took a sip of water before continuing. "Where my mother got her kindness, I'll never know, because my grandmother might have been sober, but she was mean. She only saw us as a burden and made sure we knew it. Of course, my brother didn't help anything. He always seemed to push her buttons, causing her to fly off the handle and lash out at him." His fist clenched around the nearly disintegrated wrapper. "I tried to step in so many times that she started locking me up before she 'disciplined' him.

"It got so bad that CPS, once again, got involved and pulled us out. I don't even know what happened to her after that day. I do remember Ryan giving her the bird as we walked toward the police cars while he held his other arm, which was in a cast, against his chest. After that it was the foster home life for us. We got to stay together, Ryan and me, until I aged out of the system."

The grip I had on the booth seat beneath me was all I could do to stop me from reaching across the table and wrapping him in a fierce hug. Tears formed in my eyes as I tried to find the words. He'd lived a completely different life than me; I had nothing to relate it to.

"Casey...." I couldn't hold back a second longer. My hand flew across the table for his, but before I could grab it, he yanked his away, tucking it under the table.

"I told you it wasn't a pretty story. Don't feel sorry for me, Kate. I turned out fine. I don't need or want your pity."

The hardness in his eyes made me instantly miss the Weston who was playing with my hair on the couch just an hour ago. The two were the same person, but recalling those childhood memories seemed to put him on edge. Like a rage he kept buried down deep most of the time was now simmering right at the surface, begging for anything to set him off.

"What do you expect after that? For me to sit here and smile while you tell me about a childhood that couldn't be more opposite than my own? You're an idiot if you think that."

His fists clenched and released as he attempted to calm himself down. "You wanted to know. Now you do. Happy?"

"You have no idea how glad I am that you opened up and told me something about yourself. Good or bad, Weston, I want to know more about you. My heart is breaking for you, not for you as you are now but the kid version of you. You never got to have a childhood, to feel so loved and secure that you could be free. That's what I'm sad about. You're still 'badass' Weston in my eyes, but adolescent Casey... I want to hug him so tightly he can hardly breathe in an attempt to take away some of his pain."

"Those years with my grandmother and in the system molded me to who I am today. I'm stronger because of it. Stronger physically and mentally. Being able to shut everything out, to hide in a dark room in my mind was a priceless talent that aided me during special ops training."

I nodded like I understood, but I didn't. Wanting to do something to pull him back to me, to bring back the warmth in his eyes, made me ask my next question.

"I assume she was pretty," I mused.

He cocked his head to the side. "Huh?"

Smiling behind my wineglass, I said louder, "Your mom. I assume she was pretty since you're pretty."

The change in subjects had him relaxing and the distance fading in his eyes as relief washed over him.

"I think I would rather be called ruggedly handsome. Sounds manlier." My sigh of relief was obviously loud enough for him to hear, as I saw the corners of his mouth twitch in a faint smile. "But yes, she was very pretty."

"Tell me about this brother of yours. Is he pretty too?" I asked, giving him a mischievous smile and waggling my eyebrows.

"Stop that. You'll never meet him. He looks more like his dad. We don't look anything alike really."

"Does he still live in Dallas?"

"Yes and no. He roams. He gets into more trouble than anyone I know. I've tried everything to help him, but he just has this anger inside him that I don't know how to calm. I don't think even he knows how to manage it."

"So Ryan is your...."

"Technically half brother, but after going through our shitty childhood together, he's my brother."

Nodding, I smiled at the approaching waiter bringing our large half veggie, half meat lovers pizza.

"WHAT'S up with you and food anyway? If you don't mind me asking," Weston said between bites.

Putting my hand over my mouth so I could respond while chewing, I said, "I eat small meals, I guess. I hate cooking. More like I don't know how to cook, really. Sandwiches and cereal got me through undergrad and med school, so I just never went back to normal food or normal eating patterns. Does it bother you that much?"

"I wouldn't say it *bothers* me, but it does make me worry about you. With as little as you eat and pouring gallons of coffee into your body, I'm surprised today was the first time you've passed out around me. You never slow down. You're either at the hospital, volunteering, or working out. You don't stop unless you're asleep."

Shaking my head, I smiled at him. He was trying to protect me from myself, and I found it adorable.

Wiping my lips with a napkin, I set it aside and leaned against the edge of the table. "You're in the perfect job for you."

"What does that mean?"

"You're OCD on protection, having control over everything in your life and the lives of the people around you."

He thought about it for a minute and nodded while taking another bite of his pizza.

"Once the trial is over, what do you think you'll do next?" It was a question I'd wanted to ask now that the answer had the potential to affect me so deeply.

Leaning back in the booth, he dusted off his hands with his napkin and took a long drink of water. "I don't know where I'll go next. That's the fun part of the job. Once an assignment is done, I get shipped off to the next, never knowing where I might end up. I wouldn't mind going back to the Middle East, taking the more dangerous jobs so the guys with families back home don't have to."

"Do you think there would ever be a chance to stay local?" I asked, my stomach in knots.

The look he gave me was full of understanding as to why I was asking these questions. I hated that he could read between the lines so well.

"Doubtful. Your case was rare. It caught my eye because of how dangerous it could potentially be—and after the past couple of days, I was correct in my assessment. I enjoy the action, the challenge of thinking on my feet. No day is the same, which I like."

I tried taking a sip of wine but found the glass empty. "Would you ever want to do anything else?"

"I don't think I would ever be happy doing something that wasn't challenging, something that wasn't pushing me to the edge of my capabilities." He chuckled. "Saying it out loud makes me sound like I'm trying to challenge death, but I'm not, I don't think."

The reasons for him loving his job sounded a lot like mine. I wondered if he felt like he could do more with his life too.

. . .

Yawning, I marched through the morning shift; even the five cups of coffee did nothing to alleviate my exhaustion. The past several nights of little to no sleep were finally catching up to me. As I wrote in the previous patient's chart, I thought about everything Weston had shared the night before. The brother thing threw me for a loop, that was for sure. He was never on the phone or had anyone stop by to visit, so I'd just assumed he didn't have any family or that they lived far away.

Austin was also working the morning shift and had already come by twice to see if I had fifteen minutes to spare. That man was sexy as hell but a horny pest the majority of the time. What Austin and Weston wanted and could offer couldn't be more opposite. Austin wanted my body, and that was it. I knew once he got what he wanted, he would move on to his next challenge. And Weston... well, I really didn't know what he wanted from me at this point besides keeping me safe.

As I walked toward the next patient, chart in hand, a hand gripped my shoulder, stopping me in the middle of the emergency room floor.

"Kate, I need to talk to you. It's urgent," Weston said quietly from behind me.

Whirling around, I found a worried look on his face, sending me into panic mode. Something was wrong. "What's going on? Is it my dad?" The way he was keeping me at arm's length while still gripping my shoulder felt like he was bracing me for bad news.

"It's not your dad. It technically has nothing to do with you. It's my brother. Something has come up, and I need to take a few days off to go handle a situation in South Texas. I already called my employer, and they're sending someone to fill in for me until I get back. I need to be gone by the time your shift is up."

"Is everything okay? Anything I can do?" I asked, wanting to do anything to ease his worry and concern.

"No. Thank you, but no. I'm sure it's just another 'misunderstanding' that my brother has gotten himself into. I should be back in a few days. I wanted to tell you before…. I didn't want you to think I just left. I'll be back as soon as I take care of all the shit he's gotten himself in to."

"Yeah, yeah, I get it. Be safe. I'll see you when you get back. If you need anything, call me or text me." Not knowing what to do with all the mixed emotions running through me, I wrapped my arms around his neck, pulling him against me in a tight hug. When his arms wrapped around me, I held him tighter.

"I'll be back by your birthday, promise," he whispered into my ear before slowly releasing me. "Stay safe, and please be nicer to my replacement than you were to me. Not even my enemies deserve to be on your bad side."

The sound of someone calling my name had me glancing away from him. When I looked back, he'd already turned and started walking away.

13

Me: You have to be kidding me. Weston, this
guy is a joke.

Me: I AM being nice, but this guy... I'm
scared for my own safety, so you know it's
bad! What will this guy do if someone tries to
come after me? Sit on them?

Weston: Hmmmm, that doesn't sound very
nice.

Me: I didn't say it to his face. He did seem
very disappointed in the lack of food in my
pantry. I told him he could run to the store, I
would just wait here.

Weston: Please tell me he didn't leave you
alone.

Me: It's fine really, I have my gun from the
kitchen out and a knife just in case. I've seen
all the Die Hards. I know what to do if
someone tries to break in.

Weston: I'm calling him to get his ass back over there NOW.

Weston: Don't move.

Weston: Actually, take the gun and go lock yourself in the bathroom. Leave the knife. We both know you'll just end up stabbing yourself again.

Me: Asshole. I'm kidding. He's in the chair beside me, snoring.

Me: Haha?

Weston: Not funny. I don't want to come back to you dead.

Me: Yeah, that would suck for both of us.

Weston: You are so strange.

Weston: Looks like I'll be here for a few days. My dumbass brother somehow got himself mixed up with a group, and now the DEA has him in interrogation.

Me: I'll be glad to have you back. I might not sleep until you do. There is no way this guy could hear anyone breaking in over his snoring. I might just go sleep at my dad's.

Weston: You'll be fine. Just do what he says and don't give him any lip about it.

Me: You like my lip, don't deny it.

Weston: You have no idea.

Weston: Gotta go. Stay safe, and please eat something more than cereal today. I don't want the call that you passed out again.

Weston: Anything exciting happen at work today?

Me: Yeah, some meth head tried to bite my arm off.

Weston: Austin working today?

Me: Yes.

Weston: How is the tool?

Me: Okay I guess. We don't really talk a lot.

Weston: I don't need to know details.

Weston: What do you see in that guy anyway?

Me: Nothing really, it's just a fun distraction. My life is kind of a mess right now, if you haven't noticed.

Me: Well, besides my hunky bodyguard.

Weston: Glad to know I've moved from pretty to hunky.

Me: I was talking about Joe. He's starting to grow on me.

Weston: Stop.

Me: Oh yeah, he's so sexy when he snores and drool dribbles down his chin.

Weston: I hate you.

Me: No you don't, you find me oddly entertaining.

Weston: Yes, Your Majesty.

Me: I hate men.

Weston: What did we do to offend you this time?

Me: I just got back from volunteering.

Weston: Oh, then yeah, men suck. You okay?

Me: Not really.

Weston: Want to talk about it?

Me: Not really.

Weston: So the point of you texting me was just to throw around your sexist prejudice?

Me: Yep. Cool?

Weston: Yep.

———

Weston: My brother is an idiot.

Me: At least he's a hot idiot.

Weston: Don't start with that shit. He really doesn't think past the next five minutes when making his decision.

Weston: Drives me insane.

Me: Well, we all can't be perfect like you.

Weston: So time away has given you insight to how amazing I am? Good to know.

Me: I just rolled my eyes at the phone, thought you should know.

> Weston: Nice, I've been missing those lately.
> Good to know you're keeping them in shape
> until I get back.

Me: Which will be...?

> Weston: Not sure, he's in it pretty deep here.
> Do you miss me?

Me: I miss feeling safe and getting a good
night's sleep.

Me: Hello... you there?

Me: Weston...

Me: Fine, I somewhat miss you.

> Weston: Good, because I somewhat miss
> you too, but on a larger scale.

Me: Huh?

> Weston: Gotta go, bye.

D ay four of Weston being gone and I was starting to have withdrawal symptoms. The days revolved around wondering if he was okay, where he was, and what he was doing. At night I couldn't sleep; I would lie there staring at the ceiling, thinking about the past few months and the memories we'd already made together. It all came down to the fact that I missed him. A lot. More than I had anyone before.

It didn't help that I was a little scared for my own safety with Joe being my first line of defense. He was nice, yes, but he wasn't nearly as dedicated to my safety as Weston had been. Which meant I needed to step up and be prepared for anything. What I really needed was a quick trip to the gym, get some practice in just in case.

Joe was sound asleep in the buddy chair in the living room. I rolled my eyes, knowing there was no way he would want to go. He looked too comfortable to be disturbed—at least that was what I told myself to help justify sneaking out. At least I left a note on the counter telling him where I was headed, in the rare chance he woke up before I was back.

The whole walk to the gym, I smiled at my perfectly innocent plan.

Besides, where would be the fun in not giving the new guy a challenge?

Two hours later, sweat dripped down my temples and my hands were numb from pounding the bag in front of me. My coming here had been to release all the pent-up worry and anticipation that had built up in my gut, keeping it in knots. But it hadn't. It was all still there, and I still missed Weston.

After pulling the wrappings from my hands, I reached into my gym bag in search of my phone.

When the screen came to life, there were several missed texts and calls.

This couldn't be good.

> Weston: You have to be fucking kidding me, Kate.

> Weston: You think leaving a fucking note is okay? Damn it, Kate, you told me you wouldn't pull this shit while I was gone.

> Weston: Joe is on his way to the gym now. DO NOT LEAVE without him.

> Weston: I am so pissed at you. Be glad I'm not there.

> Weston: Do you even know what I go through when you pull crap like this? AND I'm fucking hundreds of miles away.

Weston: Text me. Let me know you're okay
so I can start planning how I'm going to
kill you.

Whoops. Who would have thought he would overreact like that?

Checking the front door of the gym, I found Joe leaning against the wall, still slightly panting from rushing over. His dress shirt was soaked in sweat even though it was cool outside.

Me: I needed to work out.

Me: What do you go through?

The phone bobbed in my hand as I waited for a response to appear, or even that little thought bubble indicating the other person was typing, but nothing came. Damn it, I felt really bad for making Weston worry. And for almost causing Joe to die of cardiac arrest from his brisk walk to find me.

Meeting him at the front doors, I apologized profusely and promised to make it up to him by ordering something delicious for dinner. He was clearly still pissed off, but the offer of food smoothed away some of the anger lines on his face. With my hand on his back, we headed home.

NIGHT SHIFTS WERE my favorite for a lot of reasons. It was the craziest, most hectic shift to be on, but for someone like me, it was the good kind of crazy, and I thrived in the chaos. The threat of being overwhelmed by the sheer number of people waiting to see a doctor was exhilarating, and so far, this shift was no exception. Four hours in, I'd already seen as many patients as I'd seen in my full ten-hour morning shift yesterday. The most interesting case being a patient who flatlined and went into full cardiac arrest *while* I was examining him for chest pains. Thank goodness I'd read up on the training for the new top-of-the-line defibrillator the hospital installed two weeks ago.

Chaos was fun, for a while, but I was no Energizer bunny. After six hours on my feet with no breaks or lulls in patients, I was worn out and needed five minutes alone to regroup. My hand was poised over the Staff Only door handle to grab a cup of coffee when I heard someone call out my name.

With a loud annoyed whimper, I stopped and turned toward the nurse walking my direction. She was just as tired as me at that point, so I tried to reel in my annoyance at the delay to the break I desperately needed.

"Dr. Wheeler, some kid is here and is asking for you by name. I tried to tell him other doctors could help him and the girl he has with him, but he said he would wait for you. Only you." The young nurse pointed to the exam room at the very end of the hall.

My stomach lurched, causing bile to rise in my throat. Thank goodness it was empty or dinner would have been on the verge of making a reappearance. I knew who was waiting for me behind that curtain, and if he had someone else with him....

Swallowing down the panic that was making it hard to think straight, I headed in the direction of the exam room, dreading to open the curtain.

Inhaling a shaky breath in an attempt to settle my nerves—which didn't work—I gripped the cloth curtain and pulled it aside, the scraping sound of metal on metal annoying my already frayed nerves. The boy was just as I remembered him. Patrick was the first to turn and face me, and as he did, a too thin arm tucked a tiny body behind his back in the only protective move he could make. The panic brewing up in me flipped to rage as I took in the condition of the boy in front of me. His eye was swollen shut and his lip was split, along with other cuts and bruises trailing down his arms and hands. And that was just what I could see.

As I took a step back toward the curtain to go call the police, national guard, anyone who could help these two, the small frame tucked behind Patrick stepped around and locked eyes with mine, freezing me in place.

Her tiny, delicate face had streaks down her cheeks where tears had streamed through the dirt and dried blood. So much dried blood that I couldn't quite tell where it all had come from.

Sinking to my knees to put myself at their eye level, hoping that small act would help them know I was here for them, I was on their side, I asked, "Patrick, right? What's going on, and who is this with you?"

His lip trembled. When he attempted to bite it to keep it steady, he winced as his teeth sank into the bleeding cut. "It's... she's... she's my sister. I didn't know where else to go. I tried to protect her, but...."

The next thing I knew, his frail body flew against me so hard I had to catch myself with an outstretched hand so I wouldn't fall backward from the force. His arms wrapped around my neck as he sobbed into my hair.

Images of Weston as a child going through the same thing, having the same cuts and bruises with no one to trust, had me wrapping my arms around him and holding him so tightly he almost couldn't breathe.

Pulling back from our embrace, I held him at arm's length to look him over again. "Let's get you two cleaned up." I paused as my voice cracked. "Then we can figure out where to go from there, okay?" I said as I brushed away his tears with my thumbs.

Sobering a fraction, he stepped out of my arms and nodded toward his sister. "Her first."

That sweet, strong spirit reminded me so much of the man I was longing to see.

After cleaning Patrick and his sister enough to see where their actual injuries were, I moved on to patching up their lacerations and checking them over for any other trauma. I was wrapping the last bandage around Patrick's hand when I asked a passing nurse to call the police. Every inch of me wanted Weston there. He would know what to do. He could and would stop this from happening again. Somehow.

At the mention of the police, Patrick's frail and beaten body began trembling in fear. "No, don't, please. He won't allow it. No one can help us."

Fury like I'd never known welled up inside me at his words, kindling the natural instinct to protect these kids at all cost.

"He won't know until it's all over with. You'll be safe with the police by the time he even—"

Patrick's eyes darted in the direction of the waiting room.

Realization sank in as he held his worried gaze out the curtain.

"Is he here? The man who did this to you and your sister is here?" I grasped his shoulders, demanding an answer from him before years of reason kicked in.

"Yes, but—" he whispered.

Before he could finish, I was halfway to the curtain to find the lousy excuse for a human. Hand on the cloth, I turned back to the two kids who were staring wide-eyed, wondering what I was about to do. "Stay here. Do not leave unless it's with a nurse or a police officer," I hissed.

Ripping the curtain aside, I grabbed their charts and stormed toward the waiting room.

Gripping the wall, I took a deep breath in before stepping out into the waiting room. I had no idea what I was going to say to this guy or what I *could* do in this setting, but none of that mattered. Right then, all I knew was I had to find out who this piece of shit was.

With a plastered-on fake smile, I stepped around the corner into the waiting room.

"Father of patient Patrick Gardner," I called out into the sea of waiting patients and family members.

Scanning the room for any movement or glances toward me, I found nothing.

I called out the name again. Louder.

Nothing.

On a whim, I decided to look one more place before giving up on my mission. The cool air was refreshing as I walked out of the emergency room doors toward the designated smoking area, where I found one man sitting on a bench, smoking and playing on his phone.

"I'm sorry to interrupt, but I'm looking for the father of Patrick Gardner," I said to the man as I approached.

"Good luck ev'r findin' that li'l shit's dad. Who knows where he gone? Ditched 'em when he could. Patrick is a kid staying in our house. You know, one them government kids. Did you see his sister too? I can't remember her name."

Everything in my vision went red. All reason, education, and sense of self-preservation flew from my mind.

"Her name is Betty, you dumb fuckstick."

The man's deep-set black eyes shot up as he sneered. showing his yellowed and brown teeth. "Ya can't say that, stupid bitch."

"The hell I can," I shouted down at him. "Those kids are beat to shit, and I know you did it."

The man stood in slow motion, just like in the movies, making me take a step back. It was a very, very poor decision coming out here alone. He was huge. And from what I saw from the beating Patrick and his sister had taken, he was also violent.

You can do this.

"Really?" His sneer turned into an evil smile. "Do ya have proof that I'm the one that did it to those kids? 'Cause I can promise ya neither told ya that. I've made sure of that the past year."

All breath was knocked from me as if he'd hit me in the stomach.

A year. A year in that house.

A shiver went down my spine.

"It doesn't matter. I've already called the police, and I will do everything in my power to make sure you can't lay a hand on them or any other kid again."

He took a large step toward me, forcing me to retreat two, my back nearly against the brick building. Taking a quick look toward the emergency room doors, I wished for Weston to magically appear just like he had that night in the townhouse.

That second of distraction was all the man in front of me needed.

Lunging toward me, he wrapped a large, thick hand around my throat and clamped down, raising me so high the tips of my tennis shoes frantically scraped the cement trying to gain traction. He slammed my back against the brick to hold me in place. Coming close enough that I could smell the stale cigarettes and alcohol on his breath, he leaned down to whisper in my ear.

"Ya will do nothin', or I will find ya and make ya wish ya were never born. Stupid stupid bitch, did ya actually think somethin' would be done?"

My nails left marks, and blood caked under them as I scratched at his hand. Only sporadic spurts of air were passing through, barely enough to keep me conscious.

The sound of running feet and shouting voices had the man's grip loosening, then freeing completely as a group of men pulled him off me. Sinking down to the cold concrete, I kept my back against the brick, taking in deep gulps of air.

IN JOE'S DEFENSE, he'd just run to the restroom when I stormed out in my stupid yet gallant display of protection—at least that was what my father deemed it. He was pissed. Joe felt awful, apologizing over and over again, but I kept trying to explain to him it was my damn fault for going out there anyway. He felt bad that it happened on his watch, and I think he was a little terrified of what Weston was going to do once he found out. So, to relieve *both* of our fears, we made a pact that neither of us would tell him anything until his return. Besides, he would be back soon enough, and there was no hiding the five long bruises wrapping my neck.

That next day, as I lay on the couch, staring blankly at the ceiling analyzing the previous night's incident, a knock sounded at the front door. Frowning in the direction of Joe's room, I wondered if he planned to open it for security reasons like Weston always did. But Joe's door didn't budge as the knocking became louder and more insistent.

With a loud exhausted groan, I rolled off the couch and headed toward the door, not bothering with a knife or gun. If they were knocking, I figured they were most likely friend, not foe.

"Coming," I shouted at the continued knocking. Looking through the privacy hole, a mixture of excitement and disappointment shot through me.

See, I'm learning. I used the peephole for the first time in... probably ever.

"Hey, Austin," I said as I opened the door. "What are you doing here?"

He shoved his hands into the front pockets of his light-wash jeans and gave a half smile, so different than the cocky one he normally wore. Pushing the door open wider, he stepped around and didn't stop until he reached the kitchen. "I heard about yesterday. It's the talk of the hospital. I wanted... I needed to make sure you're okay. You know... to check on you." He perched himself on one of the barstools. "Why didn't you call me after it happened? I had to find out during my morning shift from one of the nurses instead of you. I've been worried since and haven't been able to get away until now."

Okay, that was sweet. It would be nice to have someone to talk to, to distract from all the what-ifs running through my overactive imagination. I pushed off the fridge where I had been leaning and came to stand between his legs.

"I don't know. You know me. I think I can handle it on my own, I guess."

He skimmed a knuckle down my neck where four of the bruises were. "You don't have to get through this on your own. I'm here now."

My lids fluttered closed at his touch, not wanting him to see what my eyes would surely give away. What I didn't want to admit to even myself was how much I needed and wanted another person's touch after everything. But what I didn't want him to see was the hint of disappointment that it was his hands around my waist instead of Weston's.

"I'm fine," I whispered, eyes still closed. "Meagan looked me over after it happened and it's just bruised, along with my ego. I can't believe I was that stupid going out there alone. Plus, I don't know which was worse, the fact that he had the opportunity to pin me against the wall or that I couldn't do anything to defend myself."

The feel of his soft lips brushing promised kisses along each purple mark had my stomach fluttering. "Yes," he murmured, his warm breath causing goose bumps down my neck and arms. "You're an idiot for going out there on your own, for even thinking that kind of behavior is okay for a doctor. Maybe we should find some way to punish you for such erratic behavior. To teach you to *think* before you act next time." His teeth nipped my earlobe. "What do you suggest we do to get this lesson of personal safety through your head? Hmmm? I've had all day to think about what I would like to do to you, but I'm always open for suggestions."

Not able to hold himself back any longer, he pressed his lips hard against mine as he yanked me closer, holding our bodies tightly against each other with a firm hand on my lower back.

The distraction did sound appealing, even if it wasn't with the one I truly wanted to be comforted by.

He released my waist and grabbed my hand. With each step up the stairs, my anticipation built, so when we reached my room and he pushed me down on the bed, I was ready for almost anything. Kneeling on the floor in front of where I sat on the bed, he slipped off one shoe, then the other, massaging each foot as he slid off my socks.

The rolling pressure of his dexterous fingers on my feet nearly had me moaning. It felt amazing. Lying back on the bed, I groaned when he pushed against a particularly sore spot.

A sensual chuckle coming from the floor had me propping up on my elbows and peering down. His turquoise eyes sparkled with promised pleasure as he kissed across my stomach, keeping his eyes locked with mine.

"You'll be begging me in no time, Kate. And when you do, I will remind you that your irresponsible actions affect us all. When you admit that, when you concede to never being that idiotic again, well, then we can have the real fun."

I collapsed against the bed at his words. Closing my eyes, pushing everything else out, trying to forget that this was not what I wanted, but it just might be what I needed.

14

Thanksgiving had come with the typical stuffy, formal dinner with all the extended family at my grandfather's estate and gone with still no Weston. I began to wonder if he would uphold his promise and be back for my birthday, which was in just a few days. The bruises from that night at the hospital were still very visible, but luckily it was cold enough that turtlenecks or scarves kept it covered and the curious stares at bay.

The "comforting" Austin provided had helped me move past the incident and relax. Now when my eyes closed, I pictured Austin's peering up from between my legs, smiling, instead of that man's black eyes bearing into me inches from my face. It was a small miracle Austin had understood I wasn't ready for sex. He didn't press the issue, and when we were done, he held me, exhausted from his talented fingers and tongue, until I fell asleep. He was gone by the time I woke hours later.

Cleaning up in the locker room after a long morning shift, I grabbed my bag from the locker and headed toward the waiting room to walk home with Joe. He'd started to grow on me, even if I still preferred Weston. For many reasons beyond the fact that Joe was lacking in the eye candy department.

As soon as Joe and I walked through the front door, a familiar scent wrapped around me, making my stomach flip in anticipation. My eyes didn't need to see who it was; the rest of my body was reacting in such a way that I knew instantly. Weston was finally back and waiting somewhere in the house.

Joe had no idea anything was different, pushing past me as I paused at the threshold. Taking a shaky breath in, I walked deeper into the townhouse, peeking around each corner, wondering where I would find him. Relief washed over me and my heart rate picked up when I spotted him on the couch, book in hand, glaring at me.

It was a bit awkward since we hadn't talked since his angry texts several days ago. Complete radio silence from his end, and I wasn't about to be the one to break it. If he wanted to talk, he would have reached out.

"Hey," I said as casually as I could even though my voice was a little too high-pitched to be normal. "Welcome back. I was beginning to wonder if you actually would."

His intense gaze drifted from me to Joe. "I've got things covered here, Joe. You're good to go. Call Seth on your way out. He needed to talk to you." Bringing his focus back to me, his eyes then dropped down to his book, dismissing me.

Oh hell no. Is he seriously still pissed?

I rolled my eyes. "I'm going to take a shower. Let's catch up after." There was no mistaking the bite of annoyance in my voice. If he was still pissed, then so was I.

His narrowed eyes met mine once again. "Can't wait."

Without thinking about anything other than my annoyance, I held his gaze before turning and flipping him off behind my back as I ascended the stairs to get cleaned up.

THE SHOWER MIGHT HAVE BEEN a bit longer than necessary, since I was dreading the conversation with him. I slipped into sweatpants and an oversized hooded sweatshirt before heading down to face him. The sweatshirt was strategic; the way the hood gathered around my neck helped conceal the lingering bruises. With him already being angry, I didn't need to add another reason for him to be even more pissed.

Looking in the guest bedroom, I found no signs of Joe. Weston was still sitting in the same spot on the couch. Now, however, instead of reading, he was looking straight ahead, burning a hole into the wall with his stare.

"Do you want to do this now, or can it wait until after we eat?" I asked, still standing, keeping my distance. With that livid look, I was a little nervous of what he might say, that it might be something he couldn't take back.

"No, I don't want to fucking eat. I can't... I can't think past what you pulled while I was gone. That you didn't give a shit about what your actions would.... I'm so angry at you, Kate. Do you even know...?" He hung his head and stared at the floor.

Daring a single step closer, I asked, "Do I even know what, Weston?" My heart was on the verge of pounding out of my chest.

Still staring at the floor, his response was so weak I had to step even closer to hear what was being said. "Do you even know what kind of danger you're in? Do you think this is some kind of game? At any moment you could be killed, or worse, taken, leaving me and your father agonizing about what was being done to you while we searched. How can you be so fucking selfish to not even consider the people who love you when you pull shit like this?"

My breathing stopped.

Taking a step back and stumbling against the couch, I caught myself on the armrest and took another step away from him. "What did you just say?"

"Yes, people who love you. Your father, Eric, Meagan, and I would say Austin, but let's be honest, we both know he doesn't love you. He just wants to fuck you."

I blanched.

The all too familiar wall I used as a defense, the one he'd torn down, started to rebuild. I had no control over what happened next.

"At least he's acting on what he wants."

Weston's head snapped up, his icy focus fully on me. "What is that supposed to mean?"

"It means," I spat, "at least Austin has the balls to go after what he wants instead of sitting on the damn sidelines waiting."

He prowled toward me. With each step he took forward, I took one backward until my back was against the wall and he was standing an inch from me. I could feel his body heat radiating off him; it leached through the soft cotton of my sweatpants, making my whole body pulse with longing to be pressed against him.

"I am not sitting on the fucking sidelines, if that's what you're referring to. What do you want me to do, Kate, give in to every—"

He stopped mid-sentence, his breathing growing rapid and erratic. That intense focus was trained on my neck, and I knew by his reaction what he saw.

Keeping his eyes on the bruises, he spoke in an eerily calm voice that sent chills down my spine. "Austin?" he asked, or demanded. I couldn't tell which.

"No," I whispered, all strength and anger gone from my voice.

"Who?"

"It's not import—"

The wall beside my head vibrated as his hand slammed against it, inches from my head. I knew he wouldn't hurt me, though the fact that he let his anger slip that much surprised me, but I wasn't scared. Not of him. Never of him.

With an agonized look, he turned, but I gripped his hand in mine to keep him from walking away.

"He came back," I said.

"Who came back?"

Even though the knuckles on his other hand were white from his tight fist, the one I held was gentle. His thumb brushed against my palm softly, urging me to continue.

"Patrick, that boy I called CPS about a while back. He came back to the ER, and this time with... with his younger sister. They were really banged up. I treated them both and then went to call the police. I couldn't just send them back to that house knowing what was going on, not when... not when his story hit so close to home," I whispered. Everyone had heard about the incident secondhand, but this was the first time I was actually having to tell it, besides the statement I gave to the police. "When I mentioned the police, he freaked out, and I knew the guy who did that to him and his sister was somewhere in the hospital, so I went to find him."

"Shit."

"Yeah, tell me about it. Anyway, I found him outside, and... well, I won't go into all the details, but it ended up with his hand wrapped around my neck and me pinned against a brick wall until some guys pulled him off."

With a gentle squeeze, he dropped my hand and walked away, sending my heart plummeting into my stomach. He bent over the kitchen island, shaking his head back and forth. I didn't move from the wall. I couldn't.

A few seconds passed before he pushed himself off the counter and strode back to where I was standing. Waiting. His strong hands wrapped around my waist, pulling me close. His body shook against me as he held me firmly. The feel of his arms around me, of him being so close, had me reaching up and gripping the back of his shirt and pulling him tighter to me.

"I'm going to find him, and I'm going to kill him."

I believed him.

"I missed you," I whispered into his chest, not sure if he could hear me.

His grip on me tightened.

"Weston." I pulled back far enough to see his face. Tears rimmed my eyes as I tried to find the words to tell him how I felt, or what I was starting to feel, starting to know. "Weston, I mean I really missed you. I missed you being here with me, I missed our random conversations, watching you read on the couch. I want—"

Hands that were capable of such violence, that had been trained to kill at an expert level, were gentle as he cupped my face. "I know, Kate." He pressed his forehead against mine.

We waited in silence with our eyes locked, holding each other close. Both of us knowing what we wanted—desperately, it seemed. But I wasn't ready to act on my feelings just yet, and he... well, it seemed that with my safety still in jeopardy, it would take an act of God for Weston to act on what he wanted.

"So now I have two things to be pissed at you about," he said, smirking down at me. All the pent-up anger had faded, as if all he needed was our physical connection to lower his tension.

"You know what I'm pissed about?"

"What?" he asked, pulling his forehead back a fraction yet still cupping my face in his hands.

What surprised me about his hands on my face was that I liked it. A lot. The way he held it was different than the way Austin had that night. Weston was holding it as if he needed to keep his hands on me to keep me from disappearing. It was gentle, calming, not possessive.

"That I didn't defend myself. He had me, and I couldn't do a thing about it."

His eyes darkened again at the mention of the incident. Dropping his hands, he walked to the kitchen and opened the fridge.

"You just need to learn some key moves. You can defend yourself against anyone. You have enough force in that tiny body, believe me. You just need some coaching."

Pushing off the wall, I followed him into the kitchen. "Is that an offer?"

The water bottle he pulled from the fridge paused an inch from his mouth as he debated. "Yeah. You already know a lot, but I can walk you through a few moves the next time we're at the gym."

The way his lips wrapped around the bottle made me wonder what they would feel like against my lips, against my skin.

Catching my assessing stare, he arched an eyebrow.

Snatching the water bottle from his hand, I took a swig and handed it back. "Then let's go. I need to work out anyway. We can eat after."

His eyes darted to the clock. "It's almost eight. Won't they be closed?"

Halfway to the stairs, I said, "They gave me a key a long time ago because of my crazy hours. I'll be ready in ten."

WHEN WE ARRIVED, only a few of the members and coaches were still milling about. Most were wrapping up their workouts or had already packed up their bags to head out since the gym was closing soon. By the time we were on the mat and ready to square off, everyone had gone home except the owner, who was busy in his office.

Rolling my neck, I attempted to ease the tension that was building. It wasn't a bad or stress-related tension. Somehow, since the last time I'd seen Weston, the sexual tension between us had increased. The air between us was now strung tight, and neither of us seemed ready or willing to relieve it.

Yet.

With a smirk, I decided to take it up a notch.

"Damn, it's hot in here, don't you think?" I pulled my black workout top over my head, leaving me standing in a pair of leggings and a sports bra.

His gaze fell to my bare stomach, his dark eyes turning darker with hunger for me. Even from across the mat, I could see his nostrils flare before turning as he ran his hands through his hair. When he turned back to face me, all of that emotion was wiped from his face.

Fine.

"Okay, let's get started. Let's go with you trying to attack me first. Try to hit me," he said.

Even I knew I didn't stand a chance. I was stubborn, not a fool.

After an hour of me trying to attack him and failing horribly, Weston shifted into coaching mode. Which wasn't such a bad thing since that meant he had to correct my stance—a lot.

"No, you can't lean back like that. If you do that, then someone can knock you off balance, and if you're on the ground, you're vulnerable. Keep your feet planted, don't dance so much. Here...." For the third time in just a few short minutes, Weston dropped his sparring pads and grabbed my waist, correcting my stance. If I didn't know any better, I'd say he was looking for any tiny thing wrong as an excuse to touch me. Also, if I didn't know any better, I'd think *I* might have been standing wrong on purpose just so he could correct me.

"Now, if someone comes at you like this—" He lunged toward me, making to punch my side. "—you grab their arm and pull them down at an angle and take them off their feet, then ram your knee into their ribs or head."

Beads of sweat slid down my stomach and back. He was *very* serious about this. When I turned to face Weston after wiping off my face and grabbing a quick drink, he was wiping his own face. But not with a spare towel like me. No, he was using his shirt. It was in his hands, meaning it was no longer on his back.

Damn.

I'd seen him without a shirt before, but now that my mind and body had shifted to the idea of more, he looked different. Sexier. Stronger.

And those fucking tattoos.

Hot. Damn.

My fingertips itched with want. I wanted to touch him, anywhere and everywhere all at once.

He was the picture-perfect bad boy with his tattooed chest and arms. And his abs... oh, his washboard abs. The kind of man who every woman and some men fantasized about. It didn't help that underneath that hard exterior, I knew he was a good guy. That made him even sexier.

"Now," he commanded, tossing his shirt aside and striding toward me, "let's practice if someone grabs you from behind."

Yes, please.

It's just Weston. Protective. Over the top. Sexy as hell. Kind. Caring. Tattoos that I want to bite every inch of.

Shit. I'm in deep shit.

I couldn't help it when my breathing hitched as he wrapped one arm around my waist, holding my back tightly against his stomach and chest. The other wrapped around my shoulders, and he placed his hand against my mouth.

"Now try to get out of my hold. Shove me off you."

Can I say, "No, thank you"?

A distraction, that was what I needed. It was the only way I would ever be able to accomplish what he was asking. I bit the palm covering my mouth not so gently and held on, running my tongue against the small bit of flesh between my teeth.

His grip around me tightened. "Kate," he said, his voice raspy.

Damnit, I loved his arms around me. Skin to skin was overwhelming.

Reaching one hand up, I dragged my fingernails along his forearm and up to his bicep. With each inch I moved, his fingers dug deeper into my hip and his breaths became more frequent.

Just where I wanted him.

Gripping his shoulder with one hand and his wrist with the other, I pushed my hips back, knocking him off balance, and shoved all my strength into his right side, flinging him to the floor.

The sound of his bare back smacking the mat sounded through the empty gym. Wide-eyed, he stared at me in utter disbelief. Tossing my arms up in the air, I began circling, dancing around, savoring the victory.

"You fight dirty. I like it."

Putting a pause to my celebration, I smirked down at him. "Maybe, but I'll do whatever it takes to get you on your back."

A mischievous smile spread across his face, making him look like a hot-as-hell deviant. "Isn't that the guy's line?"

Snorting a laugh, I offered my hand to help him up. "Enough of the coaching. Let's go back to sparring for a bit."

"Okay, but now that you've won one round, I'm going to kick it up a notch. If I get too rough, you'll have to let me know. I don't want to hurt you."

"It's fine. I like it rough anyway."

"Kate." His response was tight, clipped.

I was toeing the line and loving every moment of it.

Faking innocence, I shot him my best doe-eyed look, knowing he would see right through it.

. . .

AND I THOUGHT I was sweating before. Thirty more minutes of sparring and I was exhausted, hot and hungry. On the verge of turning hangry.

"One more round, and then let's go get something to eat. I'm starving."

He nodded as he downed the last of his water.

Fists up, we danced around the mat, dodging kicks and punches just like we had been the past half hour. In between one of his attacks, I saw an open shot for his ribs. Taking the chance, I didn't realize it was a trap until it was too late. Before my foot could connect with his side, Weston's hands were wrapped around my leg, twisting and sending me face-first into the floor. All the air in my lungs came out with a loud whoosh.

Flipping over, I lay on the mat trying to catch my breath and figure out how in the hell he'd pulled that off.

"If an opening looks easy in a fight, there's typically a reason why," he panted as he bent over me, hands on his knees.

Now I was the one with the opening.

"Sure." I smiled and flung my legs behind his knees, sending him tumbling down on top of me. The look of pure shock on his face as he fell was all I'd hoped for and more. He lay on top of me, our bare stomachs connected, sending tingling sensations spreading through my whole body before settling between my legs.

"Cheap shot again. Is cheating the only way you can win against me?"

He didn't move.

I didn't move.

Staring at the overhead lights, I remembered something he'd said earlier, the same thing he'd texted while he was out.

"Kate."

He still wasn't moving, and I still wasn't making him.

"Kate."

I had to know what he meant. Maybe if I knew, it would calm this wanting that was now surging every time I looked at him.

Pushing himself off, he lay beside me, head propped up by his elbow on the mat.

I had to ask.

"What do you go through?"

He furrowed his brow, obviously not understanding what I was asking.

"Your text while you were gone and earlier tonight. You said, 'Do you even know what I go through when you pull that crap?' You didn't respond to my text, so tell me now, while it's just us. What do you go through?"

His eyes shuttered at my request, and I wondered if he would answer.

"I've been through a lot in my life, from my childhood to my time in the army. I've known true fear—crippling, lose-all-the-breath-in-your-lungs fear. That's what I felt when you were gone during that hour. Anytime you disappear or I lose sight of you, that fear eats at me each second until I see you again. Have you not noticed that each time you're unaccounted for, any long periods of time apart, I have to physically touch you even if it's just for a moment?"

I shook my head. I really hadn't noticed before, but now looking back....

"I have to have that connection to know you're okay. Once I do, the fear dissipates. But if that fear was because of your selfish, idiotic antics, then it morphs into anger. Anger because I can't control you, and if you only knew why it affects me this way... more than anyone else. But you don't know. You can't know."

A single tear slid down my cheek.

"I get so angry that I want to shake you, yell at you, kiss you... there are a lot of things I've thought about actually."

I stopped breathing. "When you're angry at me, you want to kiss me?"

He nodded slowly. "In relief for knowing you're okay, that you're not hurt, that you would still be here *for* me to kiss."

My throat began swelling closed, or at least that was what it felt like.

"What about now? Do you still want to kiss me even though you're not angry with me?"

"Yes." His voice cracked, giving away the deep emotions he felt for me running through his body.

In a deliberate move, I ran my tongue along my lower lip. His gaze turned hungry as his eyes followed the movement. "Then what are you waiting for?" I asked.

An audible groan escaped his mouth, confirming the tether he had on his restraint was on the verge of snapping.

Enough.

Enough of waiting.

Enough of not going all in.

Enough of being afraid.

Grabbing his free hand with mine, I skimmed it across my waist and wrapped his fingers around my side. "What. Are. You. Waiting. For?"

His eyes shifted from mine to my lips, to my chest, and then my waist, his gaze growing darker with each inch. Releasing my waist, his fingers skimmed along the curve of my body until he was cupping my jaw. Reflexively, my eyes closed as he brushed his thumb against my lower lip.

Everything inside me was on fire, throbbing with each rapid beat of my heart.

"Kate." My name sounded reverent on his lips.

His lips hovered above mine, allowing us to share tight breaths as our bodies thrummed against the other's. When they finally pressed against my own, a shock ran from my head to toes and back up again. *More, lots more.* I tugged his dark wavy hair, pulling him tighter against me.

An answering growl rattled through me, making me pull harder.

Angling his mouth over mine, he brushed his tongue against my lips in a gentle request. The moment I opened for him, he took control, total possession with his talented tongue massaging my own, coaxing various sounds from me that I hadn't ever made or heard before.

There had been boyfriends in the past, but this... intensity between us in this moment was new. No one had ever made the whole world fade away like this. If he could do that with a single kiss, I wondered if the whole universe would shatter once I had all of him. Just the thought had me writhing beneath him.

When the warmth of his lips left mine, a soft whimper slipped out. Opening my eyes, I found him gazing down at me, his face unreadable.

"Why are you stopping?" We couldn't stop *now*.

He pulled his face farther back, putting more distance between our lips, as if he was trying to figure out the same damn thing.

"You know why, Kate. But one day... one day when all this is done and you're safe and I don't have to be on guard, I won't hold back. I won't stop. I'll take you at any time, against any surface." Bending back over, he kissed me lightly and pulled back again. "Until then, I have to make myself stop *now*."

Pouting was a new low, but he was worth it. My lower lip stuck out, eyes pleading up at him.

His nostrils flared in frustration. "Don't do that," he growled.

A smile crept up my lips. Having this kind of effect on him was empowering in a way. Plus, I was very glad it wasn't just me.

"Fine." I pushed up on my elbows as Weston stood and adjusted himself. The deep ache crept back through my body when I saw just how *much* he needed to adjust in his shorts. Still staring at his crotch, I asked, "How much longer until the trial is over?"

With a laugh laced with the same need that pulsed through my body, he said, "Not soon enough." Helping me up, he wrapped his arms around me, groaning as our bodies connected once again. "Forget the gang. *I* might ask your dad to drop the case."

With my cheek pressed against his bare chest, I listened to his steady heartbeat and smiled knowing there was nowhere else I would rather be and no one else I would rather be with.

And he felt the same way.

15

———

The actual day of my birthday wasn't very exciting from my perspective. Volunteering in the morning, then a ten-hour shift made the day seem like it would never end. By the time my mid-shift was finished, all I wanted to do was take a long hot shower and snuggle in bed for some much-needed sleep.

All hopes of a decent bedtime were dashed when we were greeted by one of my father's security detail on the front stoop of my townhouse. Tossing my bag and coat into the corner of the entryway, I searched until finding my dad and the rest of his team waiting in the kitchen. As disappointed as I was that my long shower and sleep were delayed, I was excited to see him, and at least he had a fresh pot of coffee going. That, of course, was my first course of action.

"Hey, pumpkin. Happy birthday. I wanted to stop by and wish you happy birthday in person, but maybe that wasn't such a good idea. You look exhausted."

The warm mug in my hands brought some renewed strength. "I *am* exhausted but still very glad you stopped by. It is my birthday, after all."

"Here." He jutted a perfectly wrapped gift onto the counter. "Happy birthday, Kate."

Setting the mug down, I began unwrapping the small square package. With a flip of the lid, I found a beautiful David Yurman bracelet resting in the black velvet inside.

"It's beautiful," I said, slipping it on my wrist. "You really shouldn't have though."

"It's your birthday! Of course I should have. Plus, I hate that your life has been turned upside down because of me and my work."

"If this is how you pay your penance for feeling guilty, I'm totally open to that. You could get me the matching ring and earrings if you feel *really* bad."

He looked down at the floor and sighed. Apparently he didn't find the death threat or my life being in danger a laughable matter yet.

With a stretching reach across the island, I grabbed his hand and gave it a strong squeeze, making him look up at me. "Dad, it's a great present for my birthday. You shouldn't feel guilty about anything. We'll get through this. It'll all be over soon."

The sound of someone clearing their throat from the living room drew our attention. "When are you expecting the trial to be over?" Weston asked.

There was no hope in trying to hide my amusement at the question. I knew exactly why he'd asked and was pretty sure my father would not be happy at all if he knew Weston's motives.

"Probably another few weeks. Maybe sometime after the first of the year depending if the judge breaks for the holidays. Speaking of which, Kate." He turned his attention back to me, taking my other hand in his. "I want to get out of Dallas for the Christmas holiday. Let's go up to the house in Vail, spend a couple days there. It'll be good for both of us to get out of town, get away from this mess."

At the mention of the trip, Weston and the other security team members' heads snapped in our direction, listening to every word.

The head of the small security force surrounding my father spoke up first. "Sir... Mr. Wheeler, I wouldn't feel comfortable with you two going alone, even if it is far away from the threat here in Dallas."

Nodding, Dad smiled at the man. "I've already thought of that. That's why I've decided to charter a private plane so we can all go together. Kate, you can even invite that guy you've been seeing from the hospital if you want to."

My back went ramrod straight at the mention of Austin. I still hadn't told Weston about Austin's "comforting" that night while he was away. "I'll think about inviting Austin, but I would want Weston to come too. Not that I don't trust your team, it's just...." I didn't know how to finish the sentence. Silence hung in the air until Weston finished the thought for me.

"We know each other's routines, Mr. Wheeler, so it would a good idea if I were there, solely focused on Kate. That way your team can focus on you."

I wondered if he meant to say solely focused on my safety instead of just solely focused on me. The latter sounded much more enticing.

Dropping my hands, Dad tucked his into the pockets of his slacks. "It's settled, then. We'll plan on leaving the day before Christmas Eve. I'll start making the necessary arrangements. Kate, don't forget to ask off work."

He wrapped his lean arms around my shoulders, pulling me in close for a warm hug. After a kiss and whispered "Happy birthday" into my hair, he and his security team headed out, closing the door behind them.

FRESHLY SHOWERED, I was sitting on a barstool at the kitchen island, eating a bowl of cereal and playing Clash of Clans on my phone, when Weston sat down and slid a poorly wrapped box toward me.

"Happy birthday," he said, running a hand through his dark hair. He never did get it cut, but I wasn't complaining. The longer hair looked good on him, making him look younger by softening his features.

Biting my lower lip to hold back a grin, I slid the bowl aside and began ripping the wrapping paper away from the box, excited to see what it was. Lifting the lid and peering inside, I couldn't hide my confused expression. "A cookbook?" I questioned as I removed the enormous white book from the box, turning it over in my hands and trying to understand the gift. He knew I couldn't cook.

Sliding to the edge of the stool, he gestured to the book, "There's more, open it."

Opening the heavy book, I wondered why the word joy was anywhere in a cookbook title. There was absolutely no joy in cooking. As I flipped through the pages, an envelope fluttered out and landed on my lap. With an amused look, I tore open the envelope and read what was tucked inside. "Cooking classes." *Oh, he's good.* "Your obsession with my eating habits knows no bounds. You're relentless."

"You mentioned that you didn't enjoy cooking because you didn't know how to, so I thought...." He sounded hesitant, like he was wondering if I would be upset.

"It's perfect," I said, easing his fears. His shoulders relaxed at my admission. "I love it. Thank you."

Shrugging a shoulder, he stared at his hands on top of the island. Nothing had happened physically between us since that night in the gym. He'd once again morphed into the all-business "protection at all costs" guy he was before. Yes, he was right in not wanting to let his guard down since it would put us both at risk, but now I knew what his lips felt like linked to mine and trailing down my skin. I found myself thinking about that more often than not throughout my days now.

I wanted it again. The trip to Vail couldn't come soon enough. I just hoped he would lower his guard enough to have a little fun.

I guess the same could be said for me. Maybe Weston would be the one I could give up all control for and let myself enjoy the moment, enjoy him.

Glancing up, Weston opened his mouth to say something but was cut off by a knock at the door. He lifted his eyebrows, asking a silent question, I shrugged in return; I wasn't expecting anyone.

Pushing off the counter, Weston strode to the door. I heard a grumble, then the sound of the lock clicking and the door opening.

"Oh good, you're back." The voice echoed through the townhouse.

Austin.

Well, hell.

My palms started to sweat from anxiety. *Why is he here? What if he brings up our time together?*

The sound of their footsteps grew louder as they rounded the corner.

"Hey, beautiful," Austin crooned as he wrapped his arms around my waist, pulling me tight against him. "Happy birthday."

Releasing me, Austin glanced down at the discarded wrapping and box still out on the counter and frowned. "Looks like I'm late to the party. Sorry, I would have been here sooner but one of my patients had some complications."

Weston choked on a laugh.

Shooting him a glare, knowing the last thing I needed was for him to provoke Austin, I said, "You're fine. Thanks for stopping by."

He reached up, gently tucking a damp piece of hair behind my ear. His touch was no longer electrifying as it once was. "I didn't come empty-handed though. You're going to love it."

"Oh, I love gifts," I said, trying to convey excitement I didn't feel.

My stomach was in knots with both of them in the same room. That kiss with Weston had changed our whole dynamic. The tension radiating off both men was palpable. I wiped my sweaty palms on my shorts when I noticed Austin reaching for my hand.

He guided us away from Weston's stare, and we walked hand in hand to the living room. Settling onto the couch, he wrapped one arm around my shoulders while the other pulled something from his back pocket. That damn cocky smirk made a reappearance as he placed a nondescript envelope on my knee and began drifting two fingertips up and down my bare thigh.

No, no, no. This couldn't happen, not with Weston here. Not before I had a chance to tell him, to explain what happened and how things were different now. My breathing grew rapid from the increasing levels of anxiety with each stroke of Austin's fingers on my skin. I needed to get him out of here and fast. If Weston found out about that night with Austin... I wasn't sure how he would react. Not that he could be mad since we weren't anything then... not that we were anything now. But now we had the promise of more, and Austin wasn't a part of the equation.

Impatient for me to discover what was tucked inside, Austin reached across and pulled out two pieces of paper. The excitement radiating off him was contagious, and I started to get excited too. He held the tickets close to my face so I could read the tiny print.

Concert tickets. To Justin Beiber.

All my excitement rushed out and was replaced by pure disappointment. There was no way to hide the fall in my expression.

What the hell?

Is he serious?

This had to be a joke. He had to know I would rather play with spiders than go to a Beiber concert.

Letting out a confused laugh, I said, "Thanks, Austin. But Justin Beiber?"

He beamed at what he thought was a generous gift. "Yeah, he's awesome. I've been wanting to see him live for a while now, and now I get the chance. His music is amazing, so talented."

"So these tickets, this concert... is more for you?"

"Well, I figured it would be a fun night and you could come with me."

Unable to take one more pass of his fingers on my leg or his arm around my shoulders, I straightened off the couch, letting his arm fall behind me. "Let me get this straight. You gave *me* concert tickets, *for my birthday*, to a performer who *you* like, not me, then say *I* would be coming with *you*, not *you* coming with *me*?"

Weston was right. Austin was a fucking tool.

And I was the idiot who couldn't see past the damn man bun and beautiful eyes.

Weston must have heard the tension building in my voice, knowing a fight was about to ensue. Out of the corner of my eye, I saw him not so casually walk into the living room and sit on the couch opposite us.

"You sound pissed," Austin stated. The cocky smirk was gone, replaced by a slight downturn of his lips, the tension in his voice mimicking my own. "I thought it would be fun."

Afraid for his safety—from Weston or me, I wasn't sure—I scooted down the couch, just out of reach of his long fingers.

He glared at the gap between us, eyes widening and his face flushing. "So what, now that he's back, I'm not allowed to touch you?"

All focus went from reining in my annoyance at the tickets to his words. "Austin, stop talking now. In fact, I think you should go."

Instead of listening, he stayed seated, turning from me to face Weston.

Shit. Shit. Shit.

"She wasn't this hesitant the other night," he gloated.

Damnit.

Weston's brows furrowed, clearly not understanding what Austin was referencing. Austin grinned, obviously loving that he'd blind-sided him. Reaching across the couch, Austin wrapped his hand around my upper thigh, clamping down in a possessive hold that made my jaw drop. "Oh, she forgot to tell you? After her incident at the hospital, she needed some *comforting*, and I was more than willing to help. Where were you again?" He gave Weston a perfect cocky smile. "You should hear the sounds she makes—"

My brain started functioning again, making me realize I needed to cut him off, to stop this conversation. Now.

I lunged off the couch, slamming my shins into the coffee table, but the pain didn't register.

"Austin," I yelled. "Out. Now."

To get where he was in his career, he had to be smart, but what he did next was the stupidest thing he could have done in that moment. One second I was standing, pointing toward the door as I seethed that this asshole was still there. The next, Austin gripped my hand and yanked me back down beside him, the whole time keeping his sneering gaze locked on Weston, who slid to the edge of the couch, preparing to take him out.

"Austin, let her go. Go home. This isn't a fight you'll win." With his voice calm but direct, there was no question Weston would follow through with his indirect threat.

Fuck. Fuck. Fuck.

There were at least three moves I could think of in that moment to take Austin down, but the look in Weston's eyes, that aggression rolling off him, I knew if anyone was going to take Austin out, it needed to be him.

His hand pulled from mine as he stood and squared off with Weston. "Fuck you," he shouted, jabbing a finger at the larger man. "Stop it with this whole hero shit. I can see right through it. You want to fuck her just like me, so stop playing the damn chivalry card."

I stared gaping at Austin. *How could I have ever been attracted to this asshat?*

Both of Weston's hands balled into tight white-knuckled fists, and his muscles twitched. I could tell he was aching to close the distance between them.

"Go home now, Austin, before I make you."

"Fine." He snatched up the tickets that had fallen to the floor in all the commotion. His shoulders rose and fell in an exaggerated shrug as he stood. With a dismissive once-over glance, he said, "You're not worth the trouble anyway."

Before my brain could process his words Austin was flying backward over the couch, Weston's fist frozen in the air.

He prowled around the couch, clearly hoping for more of a fight than a single punch. Weston stood over Austin, but Austin didn't stand up and start swinging back. He didn't even sit up and start mouthing off again. No, Austin didn't do anything, because he was out cold. Or dead.

My knees popped as I crouched down beside him, pressing my fingers against his neck, checking for a pulse. In the back of my mind, I began thinking through all the places that would sell a shovel and bag of lye at this time of night—you know, just in case.

A relieved sigh pushed from my lungs when I found a pulse. "He's not dead, so there's something positive."

Even with my gaze glued to Austin, not wanting to face Weston just yet, I could feel his glare burning a hole into the back of my head. He was pissed. And rightly so, I mused. He hated being caught off guard, hated that Austin had the upper hand for that moment, knowing something he didn't.

"Tell me you didn't sleep with that tool," he growled.

Like a coward, I kept my eyes trained on the unconscious Austin. My nervous hands twisted and fumbled in my lap. "No, I didn't sleep with him. I'm sorry I didn't tell you. It was while... we just—"

"Stop," he shouted, forcing my eyes to look up and lock with his. There was no mistaking how angry he was with his scowling, flushed face. "I better not be around when he comes to. I'll be in my room."

Everything in me wanted to reach out, pull him to a stop so we could talk about it instead of leaving it like this. A few minutes just to explain what happened that night and how none of it mattered now, to tell him Austin didn't matter. Not now. Not with the hope of him.

But I didn't. Like the coward I was when it came to relationships, I let him walk away.

The bedroom door slammed behind him, rattling the pictures along the wall, effectively shutting me out.

16

———————

A quick glance at the clock showed it was noon. The sunlight pouring through the windows forced my eyes shut. Turning away from the light, I stared at the wall, not ready to face reality just yet.

Last night was a mess in so many ways. Once Austin came to, he was furious at Weston, at me, at the world. The punch was deserved, but he didn't see it that way. Once he was able to stand without needing assistance, he stormed out, spewing profanities as he slammed the door. With a morsel of hope, I waited downstairs for over an hour after Austin left, hoping Weston would come out of his room so we could talk. But he never came out, not even to check and secure the locks. Which was very unlike him, leaving me unsettled, tossing and turning all night.

The late nights with Weston, kidnap attempts, work, plus the volunteering were exhausting. Just thinking about it all forced a yawn. Pulling the blankets over my head, I snuggled in and immediately fell back asleep.

.   .   .

NOT BOTHERING with a bra or even giving myself a once-over in the mirror, I stumbled down the stairs around three, finally feeling somewhat rested. Weston's amused gaze followed me from the stairs to the kitchen. Maybe I looked worse than I realized. Perhaps I should have taken a second to at least brush my hair.

"Good morning, or should I say afternoon," he teased from his seat on the couch.

"No talk. Coffee. I need coffee," I grumbled back.

My brain was foggy. Rested, but foggy. Maybe sleeping in this late was a bad idea.

After filling my mug to the brim, I came and sat beside him on the couch. With a touch of bravery, hoping the lingering frustration from the previous night was gone, I leaned against him as I flipped on the TV.

Halfway through the coffee, my head began to clear. Unable to keep my curiosity at bay, I had to know if he was still mad. At least he hadn't pushed me off him yet, though he hadn't even muttered a word since I sat beside him. With the coffee mug at my lips, I peered up at him, finding his attention on the book in his hand. Of course he was reading.

"Sooo, Weston. Are we good? You know, after last night?"

The shoulder resting against his chest rose and fell with his exaggerated breath. "I wish you would have told me. You know, prepared me for what that fucker would try to throw at me. But yeah, Kate. You and me, we're good."

Turning back toward the TV, I smiled behind my mug. With that out of the way, now all I had to focus on was the fun night ahead.

SHOWERED and hair wrapped in a towel, I stared down at the three outfit options I had laid out. All three were rompers but varied in style. The first option was short with long flowy sleeves and a deep neckline, the second was short, black, and strapless, and the third was bright blue with a floral design, the more modest of the choices. Holding each up, I looked in the mirror and wondered which would get the biggest rise from Weston. My eyes skirted across the options before eventually landing on the strapless romper.

"Yep," I said out loud, confirming my brilliant yet devious plan to push Weston into action.

The plan was for Meagan and Eric to meet us for dinner before heading to the dance club to meet the rest of the group. As I applied eyeliner, my mind wandered to Weston. I wondered what he would do all night. Would he sit in the private booth with his eyes trained on me or follow me around, never leaving my side even out on the dance floor? Both were acceptable options, but the latter would definitely be more entertaining.

As I zipped up the black romper, I had to suck in to get it all the way up. It was *significantly* more revealing than it had appeared online. Even with my petite frame, the shorts barely covered my ass, and the strapless top was so snug, it pushed my small chest up, making my breasts look larger than they actually were. If this outfit didn't provoke Weston, then the goal of anything further happening between us before the trial was over would definitely be left unaccomplished.

I slipped on a pair of nude five-inch heels and practiced walking around the room to remind myself how to move in anything other than my daily tennis shoes. Hand on the doorknob, I paused in a last-minute attempt to steady my anxious nerves, taking a deep breath in and out. Ready as I would ever be, I opened the door and started down the stairs.

When the kitchen came into view, I halted. Weston was standing, back to me, in front of the island, typing on a laptop. Unaware of my presence, it gave me a moment to savor the sight of him. He was wearing dark-wash jeans that accentuated his trim waist, thick thighs, and firm backside. His boots looked newly polished, which made me smile, but as my eyes trailed up, I was confused by the plain white T-shirt. Even though I didn't fully understand his casual ensemble, he looked damn good. The shirt was snug around his muscular arms and stretched across his broad shoulders. There was something sexy about the way his tattoos ran down his arms; the black and shading were eye-catching against his olive skin. Continuing my walk down the stairs, I considered that maybe I would be the one who couldn't keep their hands off the other.

The clicking of my heels against the hardwood floor had Weston shutting his laptop and turning to face me. His smile faded, replaced by a blank, stunned expression. Ever so slowly, his eyes trailed down my body, cataloging each exposed inch, then back up again, pausing at my heaving chest. Lips pursed in visible restraint, he willed his gaze up until our eyes locked.

"Is that what you're wearing tonight?" he finally asked, breaking the electric silence, but not his hungry stare.

I couldn't help the mischievous smile that spread across my face. Having a man like Weston breaking every law of physics to keep himself from attacking me right here in my kitchen was beyond anything I had ever felt.

"You approve?" Turning slowly, I let him get a good view of my backside.

A deep growl made me turn back to him. The way he was gripping the granite countertop, I wondered if it would crack under the pressure.

"No, I don't approve. Isn't there more to that?" He waved his hand up and down my tiny outfit. "I think I'm more scared for your safety tonight than ever. You know every guy will want to put their hands on you if you wear that."

Feigning pissed, I crossed my arms. "You don't like it."

The movement of my bright red lips seemed to have him in a lust-filled trance. After a few seconds, he shook his head and started toward his room. "It's fine. We need to head out. Our car and backup are here." When he emerged from his room, he was shrugging on a long-sleeve white collared shirt.

"Backup?" I asked, now in my own trance watching his fingers work their way down the buttons of his shirt.

"Yes. Too many people tonight, too many ways for all this to go wrong. I'll need help watching the crowd."

"Fine," I said, shrugging, though it was a little disappointing hearing we wouldn't be going alone.

Before opening the door, he gave me another once-over. This time his look was more assessing than devouring. His brow furrowed at the goose bumps that had already appeared on my arms. "Do you have a jacket or something. A parka maybe?"

With a huffed laugh, I patted his chest. "Don't worry, *Dad*, I have a coat." Grabbing my long black wool coat from the hall closet, I shrugged it on.

As he locked up, I heard him grumble, "Can you leave it on all night?"

SWEAT TRICKLED down my forehead and neck as I swayed with the music. The hair I had taken an hour drying to form the perfect waves was now in a high ponytail that I hoped would keep me from succumbing to heat exhaustion while we danced. The club was packed, and the beat of the music thudded against my chest. The dinner before was amazing, and now dancing with my friends was perfection. Exactly the way I wanted to celebrate.

Eric reached across our group, pulling me close. Not understanding, I followed his nod across the dance floor and found some random guy blatantly staring at my ass.

"He was headed this way," Eric yelled into my ear.

"Thanks!" I shouted to him over the music.

"No problem. I didn't want Weston to kick that guy's ass just because he couldn't keep his hands off your hot ass."

"Yeah, he has a hawk eye on me tonight. Wish that stare was because he found me desirable instead of vulnerable."

"Anything since that kiss at the gym?"

"No. I have high hopes for Colorado though." My throat hurt from screaming at each other to be heard over the music.

"Right." Eric laughed, then grabbed my hand and started toward our private booth. "I need a drink."

It seemed everyone in our group had the same idea; the booth was full, and Eric took the last available seat.

I smacked him on the shoulder. "Hey, it's my birthday, and my feet are killing me. Scoot over!"

He squinted at me.

"What?"

He nodded in Weston's direction. Weston was sitting on the opposite side of the table, looking uncomfortable as everyone talked around him.

"Huh?" I was so confused.

With a groan loud enough for us all to hear even over the music, Eric stood, gripped my hips, backed me up to where Weston was sitting, and shoved me down into his lap. "There, now you have a seat." He smirked.

Thankfully Weston's reflexes were way faster than mine, and he caught me before I tumbled back into Meagan.

"Sorry," I mumbled as I tried to stand, then paused at the feel of his hand on my bare thigh.

"It's okay. At least this way I can relax a bit knowing you're safe. I am not a fan of you being out there alone."

I turned to face him. Damn, he looked good. He wasn't even sweating. Maybe the army had taught him how to control everything even down to his sweat glands. "That's your own damn fault. I asked you several times if you wanted to dance, and you said no, so don't make it sound like me being out there alone was my idea."

Our faces were only a few inches apart, making me wish we were here alone. The intense look he had made me think he was wishing the same thing. My skin burned and tingled at each place where our bodies were connected.

The sound of my name being called from across our private table had me pivoting in his lap, positioning my backside flush against him as I leaned forward to hear what my friend was saying. At the feel of him shifting his hips beneath me, I no longer heard my friend's story. When he moved again, I couldn't tell if he was trying to torture me or if he was trying his best to keep me from noticing the growing tension in his jeans. When he pressed his hips up as he held mine firmly against him, I had my answer. But he wasn't the only one who could tease in this position. Leaning farther forward, I pressed back against him, widening my legs by a fraction as I did. The sound of his answering growl was like tossing gasoline on an already blazing fire.

The new Pitbull song blared from the DJ booth, making the whole party jump from their seats in excitement and head to the dance floor. Everyone except me and him. Neither of us moved. Eric paused and turned back to us halfway to the dance floor. With a quick smile and wink at Weston's hands at my hips, he turned to join the rest of the group.

What a sly bastard. He knew exactly what he was doing.

I love him.

Two rough hands slid down my bare thighs, making my eyes involuntarily close.

He shifted behind me again, this time adjusting so he could lean forward and whisper into my ear. "Do you want to dance with your friends?"

His warm breath against my skin had me hanging my head back against his shoulder, aching for more. "Not right now. My feet hurt."

Truth and a lie.

When he leaned against the upholstered back of the booth, I followed, keeping my back pressed against his chest. At this angle, we were hidden from the dance floor by the shadows, making the tension between us climb higher.

"Kate," he said hoarsely. His fingers began brushing up and down my inner thighs.

Arching my back, I pressed myself harder into him, spreading my legs wider, wanting more. He answered. Long firm strokes of his fingers grazed up and down the sensitive skin of my inner thighs, each one higher than the last.

I couldn't suppress the moan that came out as his fingers inched closer and closer to where I wanted them. Where I desperately needed them. Chills raked down my neck when his lips grazed the shell of my ear. His breathing was as ragged as my own, but I could tell he was holding back.

"Kate, we need to stop. I need you to get up" was what he said, but his fingers were telling a very different story. Maybe he was looking for permission, a sign from me that this was okay. Taking that chance, I opened my legs wider. His roaming stopped and his hands clamped down on my knees. "I need your help, Kate," he choked out. "I can't stop on my own."

"No."

"Kate, get up now before I can't stop myself from ripping your fucking clothes off."

It was the hardest thing I had ever done, but I pushed off his lap and sat in the empty seat beside him. Neither of us could look at the other; we both stared straight ahead. His head was in his hands, and my hands were tucked under my thighs to stop from reaching out and touching him. This was torture. Both of us knew what the other wanted, but we still couldn't do a damn thing. Not until I was "safe" in his eyes. Yes, the initial threat was the reason he was brought into my life, but that same threat was the one that was keeping him from giving me more.

Frustrated, pissed, and way too turned on to be sitting next to the man I wanted to touch me but wouldn't, I stood up and stalked toward the dance floor to find the rest of the party. Before I could locate Eric and Meagan in the mass of people grinding against each other, I was grabbed by the waist and pulled against a smiling, attractive man. He seemed more than happy to give me whatever my body wanted. Knowing Weston was watching from some vantage point, I rotated, putting my back against the stranger's chest, grabbed his hands that had migrated from my waist to hips, and started dancing.

"Don't Let Me Down" blared from the DJ booth, making me forget everything that was going on between me and Weston, with my life. Shutting my eyes, I let the beat dictate the swaying of my hips back and forth. Losing myself in the music, I lifted my arms and wrapped them around my dance partner's neck. The feel of his fingers brushing along the inside of my elbow caught me by surprise. He trailed gentle strokes down my arms to my waist, then back up again. It felt good, but nothing like how it felt to have Weston's hands gripping my thighs.

When the DJ moved on to the next song, the spell I was under broke, making me realize I needed to stop this guy before Weston did. Opening my eyes to get my bearings, I couldn't believe what I saw.

Meagan was in front of me dancing provocatively, in a way that led one direction—being taken home and fucked senseless. And her dance partner was Weston. *My* Weston.

The music stopped playing, but the touch of the guy's hands at my waist failed to register as I tried to process what I was seeing. Her backside slid up and down Weston's strong body, and when I saw his hands gripped around her waist, I couldn't take it. Ripping my dance partner's hands from my own waist, I started my retreat into the sea of people without ever looking up at Weston.

A strong hand grabbed my shoulder, stopping me from moving farther away. No matter how hard I shook my shoulder, the grip didn't falter; in fact, it tightened. I didn't want to see his face, didn't want to hear his explanation as to why he would dance with *her* but not me.

"Kate, don't be pissed. Do not run," he shouted in my ear as he pulled me toward him. "That guy had his hands all over you. I needed to be close in case you needed me, and I couldn't very well stand in the middle of the dance floor staring. Meagan offered—"

His head snapped away from me. Scanning the room, his gaze darkened. "We need to get out of here." He grabbed my elbow so hard it almost hurt, making me worry about what he'd just heard.

We weaved in and out of the crowd of people, his hand still gripping my elbow as he talked to our backup through a headset. The back of the club was getting closer and closer, but from what I could see, there were no visible exits. It made me wonder if he'd scouted the club earlier and knew about some obscure exits and escape routes.

Once the crowd thinned enough, he pulled me in front of him, pushing toward a side hallway. In the hall, slightly protected from the blaring music, I heard him yelling instructions to the team about our escape and what he needed from them.

17

The black door he pushed us through didn't have an Exit sign above it. It was at the end of the dark hallway we'd passed through, and I prepared myself for the door to be locked and us to be trapped. But it opened, bitter winter cold and wind biting into my exposed skin as we stepped out into what looked like the club's back alley. Pressing me forward, Weston shut the door behind us and glanced in each direction.

"This way," he said, pointing toward the back of the alley.

Cold and too scared to put up a fight, I complied, walking as quickly as I could in five-inch heels. But the ground was uneven, making me go slower than Weston's liking.

"Come on, Kate. We need to get hidden in case they saw which way we went and follow us out here."

"I can't, you asshat." *Yep, still a little pissed about him dancing with Meagan.* "Do you see the shoes I'm wearing? And my toes are already numb."

He frowned down at my shoes. A quick apology and I was over his shoulder, staring down at his ass. To keep steady, I braced my hands against his lower back as he jogged down the alley, looking for a place to hide.

My feet wobbled when they touched the pavement, but his hands stayed on my waist until I was steady. It wasn't much, but Weston approved of the small area that looked like another company's back stoop. The spot wasn't very deep, barely enough space for us both to hide, but the shadows would help conceal us.

"Put your back against the door," he commanded, reaching down and pulling up his pant leg while digging into the side of his boot. The metal of a small handgun shimmered off what little light from the streetlamps reached this far down the alley.

Such a Boy Scout, always prepared.

Too scared and cold to talk, we stood in silence. Weston stood peering around the corner toward the door, pressing his earpiece and listening for any information from the others who were still inside.

"Shit." He slammed his back against my chest, pushing me harder against the cold metal door just before the sound of another metal door slamming shut echoed down the alley. In a near silent whisper, he notified the others that the two men were now outside and they needed to get their asses out here. Now.

The air was cold. The wind was cold. And the coldest of them all was the damn door my bare back was pressed against. It only took a few moments before my teeth started chattering. Maybe it was from the cold, or maybe fear, but either way, once they started, I couldn't stop. Before I knew it, my whole body was shaking so hard against the door that it began to rattle against the hinges. Staying hidden and keeping quiet were our best option for survival, I knew that, but I couldn't stop my body. And that was exactly what my look conveyed to Weston when he turned around, glaring at me for the racket.

Without making a sound, he pulled me in front of him, placing his back against the cold door and mine against him. Weston's arms wrapped around my chest, holding me tighter against him and allowing me to steal some of his body heat while we waited.

The sound of bottles being kicked and the crunching of pavement under shoes told us they were headed in our direction. I had no idea what he had planned, but being trapped in this tiny little area was *not* my idea of a brilliant plan.

It was strange feeling Weston's rapid breaths from our hurried escape slow to a steady rhythm as he willed his body to calm, preparing for a fight. His grip on me tightened as the two sets of footsteps grew louder. Metal banging against metal sounded down the alley as the two men searched every possible hiding spot. By the sound of it, they would indeed find us within the next thirty seconds.

Where the hell is our backup?

Silence filled the alley, and I knew they were done searching. Two men stepped into our view at the same time, one pointing a gun directly at me. Weston's arm tightened around my shoulders in a failed attempt to reassure me everything was okay.

"Let us have her and no one gets hurt," one man said. When he stepped out of the shadows, I immediately recognized him. He was the one who got away when he and his partner broke into my home.

Weston didn't respond. A warm hand wrapped around my shoulder, pulling me back and attempting to tuck me behind him, to get me away from the gun pointed at my chest. But I didn't budge. This wasn't just his fight. These men, this man, broke into my home. They'd made my life a living hell the past few months, and I wanted payback. Weston's protective instincts would just have to sit on the sidelines for one night.

Before, when those men broke in, I was scared. But now, I was pissed, and with the training Weston had been driving into me, I was pissed and prepared.

The cold air felt like ice in my lungs as I took a deep breath in and started out of his grasp. My head snapped back, nailing Weston's chest. His grip tightened around my waist, knowing what I was about to do.

"No" was all he said, his eyes still focused on the gun pointing directly at me.

Sweet, sweet Weston. I had to hand it to him for believing he could stop me.

The look I shot him was nothing short of pure condescension. It let him know this was going to happen with or without his consent.

Gripping his hand in my own, I pulled at his arm and again stepped toward our attackers.

What Weston did next made me want to kiss him and thank him for understanding.

He let me go.

Three short steps put me staring down the barrel of a gun. My panic started to rise. Maybe this plan wouldn't work and I had just made a very stupid mistake.

Too late now.

The man lowered the gun to his side and grinned at me. "Wise choice."

I forced a grin back.

"Yeah, well, I wouldn't want you to go back empty-handed *again*. What would the other guys say if you failed once again to kidnap a tiny female?" His vile smile faded into a sneer. "I mean, look at me. Here I am standing in front of you, and yet you still haven't grabbed me. Are you scared? That would be embarrassing, wouldn't it? Being scared of someone like me." His fist clenched, and I knew he was one more comment away from taking a swing. "Is that why they didn't send you alone? They knew you couldn't hack it by yourself, so they sent a fucking chaperone."

Yep. That did it.

Even in the semi-dark, I could see his fist coming toward my face. All the moves and training Weston had drilled into me snapped into place, giving me something to fall back on instead of spiraling into the panic that was desperately trying to seize my body.

A quick duck and his fist missed its mark. Before he could swing again, I grabbed his shoulders and kicked as hard as I could into his groin. The poor bastard let out a garbled yell and fell to his knees. Right where I wanted him. Gripping his head with both hands, I slammed my knee into his nose. An MD wasn't needed to know I'd shattered his nose and possibly his cheekbones as a cracking sound filled my ears.

The sound of yelling and something being shoved against a metal dumpster echoed as I retrieved the man's gun from the pavement.

The look of pure satisfaction smeared across my face when I pointed his own gun at his chest.

Moments later, several sets of feet charged down the alley.

Only once Joe had the man secure did I dare turn to see what had happened with Weston and the other guy. My whole being relaxed when I spotted him a little way down the alley with the man pinned against the brick wall. Another one of the security detail was heading in his direction, a pair of cuffs dangling from his hand.

"Remind me to never piss you off," Joe grunted as he hauled off the guy I'd just mangled.

Once everyone was out of sight and silence filled the area once more, I turned, finding Weston staring at me from several feet away. His shirt was red in various areas from the fight, but he didn't show any signs he was hurt or that any of the blood was his own.

"You're a piece of work," he said, shoving his hands into his pockets.

I couldn't help the smile that crept up my face as I looked at him.

"Thanks?" I said, daring a step toward him. "I was shocked you let me go so easily."

His dark hair shifted back and forth as he shook his head "I knew you could handle the situation. Plus, I had a plan B in case yours went sideways. They didn't know about the gun tucked in my back pocket. I'm just glad you're okay. If anything would have happened to you...."

"We make a pretty great team, you and I. We could do this for a living maybe, going around and beating up all the bad guys in the world. Although, we would have to come up with a catchy slogan—"

"It just about killed me, but what you did to that guy, how you taunted him to position himself right where you wanted him... it was brilliant, and so fucking sexy."

Him being proud of me, believing in me, *and* it being a turn-on. I lost it.

Walking toward him as quickly as I could in my heels, I slung my arms around his neck and pulled his lips down to meet mine. Not holding anything back, I jumped and wrapped my legs around his waist.

His eyes widened with surprise. With one hand, he gripped my backside to hold me while the other pushed against the brick wall behind him to keep us from falling backward. Without breaking the kiss, in one quick move he turned so my back pushed against the cold brick, his body hard against my own.

His whole weight was pressed against me, and it was the most beautiful torture. I wanted all our clothes gone, to vanish into thin air so nothing would be between us. My head thudded against the wall as he trailed kisses down my neck to collarbone and back up again. His fingers dug into my backside and thighs, urging for more. Arching my back, I tried to get the pressure of him to connect between my thighs where I needed it, to offer some relief. As if my movements were a question, Weston answered, thrusting against me and causing a few profanities to slip—from both of us.

Everywhere he touched and kissed made me want more. Even with the freezing temperatures outside and my nearly nonexistent outfit, beads of sweat were starting to form across my forehead and temples.

Pulling my lips from his, I started kissing and nibbling down his neck. His answering growl and thrust against me had me pulling back and meeting his fiery gaze.

All of this was unlike me, this insatiable hunger that wanted more and more.

Holding his gaze, I trailed my hands down his chest and abs, stopping at the top of his belt. One tug and the leather came free, my cold fingers fumbling with the clasp before finally undoing it. The sight of his dangling belt had me licking my lips, anxious for what I would find. I reached to pop the top button of his jeans. When he shifted, giving me room to work, the dim glow of the streetlights illuminated his chest, bringing my attention to his shirt. The right side was glistening with blood, and it seemed to be soaking, spreading.

Everything I wanted to happen between us left my mind. My only focus was finding out exactly how hurt he was.

His hands tightened under my backside as I leaned back to carefully lift his shirt, then his undershirt. There was too much blood to see the full damage, but what was visible was a ten-inch gash angling from the middle of his ribs toward his navel. I slid out of his grip to get a better look.

"We need to get you home," I said nervously, glancing up at him and then back to his wound, trying to see more, but it was too damn dark.

Warm fingers slid under my chin, angling my focus back to his face. I couldn't tell what he was trying to convey in the gentle kiss he pressed against my lips, but when he pulled away, he smiled and said, "Let's get your stuff."

"THIS MIGHT HURT." Wincing when causing someone pain for the greater good had been forced out of me early on in residency. But when I poured and wiped disinfectant over Weston's gash, I flinched, knowing how much it hurt. If I didn't do this, then it would get infected and hurt worse, but it didn't help the small bit of remorse in me for causing him pain. "It doesn't look deep enough to need stitches, but it's still bleeding. We'll need to wrap it in gauze tonight and clean it again in the morning."

His eyes stayed on me as I worked, applying gauze and securing it against his olive skin with tape.

"What happened, anyway?" I asked, putting my supplies back into the black medical bag.

He shrugged. "I guess when he slammed me against the dumpster."

"How did you let him slam you against the dumpster? You were twice his size."

"I was distracted."

With a very unladylike plop, I sat beside him on the bed, tucking one foot under me, and turned to face him. "I don't understand."

Sighing, he lay back on the bed and tucked one hand behind his head. "Distracted by you and making sure you were okay. He used that distraction to his advantage, I guess."

Careful of his wound, I wrapped my arm around his waist and lay beside him. "I kicked his sorry ass."

A near purr rumbled through my chest when I felt a slight tug against my hair as his fingers trailed through it. "Yes, you did, and in ridiculous shoes at that."

Propping myself up on my elbow, I frowned down at him. "They were not ridiculous, they were fabulous, and you loved my legs in them. Don't even try to deny it."

The beat of my pulse quickened as I watched him drag his tongue across his lower lip. His hand dropped from my hair to my lower back with just enough pressure to hold my body against his. "I can't deny it, but, Kate, I... we still.... What happened out in the alley can't happen again. I'm not going to risk you."

I smirked down at him, knowing what I was about to tell him would turn the tables. "Well, then it's a good thing I asked Joe to hang around for a while just in case I had to give you pain meds." His eyes shot to the closed bedroom door, then back to me. Before he could come up with an excuse, I slid one leg over him and sat up, straddling him. "We don't have long."

One second I was on top of him; the next the room was twisting in my vision as he flipped us over, pinning me underneath him. We picked up right where we left off in the alley. He was ravenously kissing down my neck, scraping his teeth against my already sensitive skin, down to the tops of my breasts. The heat from his breath seeped through my clothes as he caressed his lips over my stomach down to the apex of my thighs. His teeth nibbled between my legs. Even through my clothes, it was enough euphoria to force me to bite down on my forearm to keep from moaning too loud.

Without warning, he stopped his tormenting and started trailing kisses back up my body, nipping at each breast before connecting his lips with mine in a passionate kiss. It felt right, everything about this moment together, and I didn't want it to end. He pressed and nipped at my lips, already knowing what I liked, making me want more of his lips, and not just on my own but everywhere at once.

To my surprise, he reluctantly pulled away. Not ready for it all to end, I threaded my fingers through his hair in an attempt to pull him back to me. But he wouldn't budge.

"Kate."

Shifting my hands from his hair, I held his face, caressing his lips with my thumbs.

"Why are you stopping?" I panted.

I wanted more. Lots more.

"We don't have enough time for—"

Frustrated beyond belief, I gripped his shoulders and tried to shake him, shake the resolve out of him. "Damnit, yes we do," I begged. "Please, Casey, I'm lying here practically naked under you. Please."

His gaze softened at my begging, and a shy smile crept up his face. "We don't have enough time for me to do all the things I've been planning for you." Kissing the tender skin of my neck, he continued, "You told me once that you struggle with letting go, and I don't want it to be that way with me. When we do this, when I'm finally able to have you in every way, I want you right there with me. I want you to feel comfortable, safe enough to let me take control."

"Yes, fine. I feel that way now. Just take your damn pants off."

His laugh against my neck tickled and sent chills down my arms and legs.

Smoothing the hair from my face, he kissed each temple. "Soon. I promise, baby. Soon."

I hated terms of endearment, especially when men called their significant others something that equated to a tiny human. But when he said it, the softness and wanting that laced his voice made me want him to use that and only that ever again.

Realizing there would be no changing his resolve, I let my arms fall down to the bed with a muffled plop. "Then when, damnit?" I whimpered.

The begging was a new low. So was the whimpering. But this

man, what he could do to my body was new and amazing. Weston was turning me and my life upside down, for the better it seemed.

The bed shifted as he sat down beside me, lying on his back and staring at the ceiling, trying to calm his ragged breaths. He grabbed my hand, interlacing his fingers with mine, and turned to look at me. Locks of dark hair fell across his face. Without thinking, I used my free hand to move it back so I could see those chocolate brown eyes staring back at me.

"Soon, baby."

"Promise?"

"Yes, I promise, and nothing will keep me from making good on that promise, Kate." Keeping his eyes locked with mine, he gently pressed his lips against mine and murmured, "Nothing."

18

It had been a while since I'd been here in the winter. I had forgotten how cold Colorado was at that time. My gloved hands were shoved down into the pockets of my North Face jacket to protect them from the below-freezing temperatures. It was late morning and spitting snow as the seven of us walked from the plane to the waiting Tahoes. My hair whipped across my face from the cold wind as I turned around, searching for Weston. He was a few paces behind me, assessing the surroundings, eyes darting from one area to the next looking for dangers.

My father and his security team climbed into one of the black SUVs while Weston and I took the other. *Still unsure why he needs four guys to protect him when I only have one... though maybe his four only equal one Weston.* Once all the luggage was loaded and we were buckled in, the hired driver set off toward our destination—my family's cabin.

Now, I say cabin, but it was slightly more than that. It started out as a small A-frame log cabin, but as the demand for and price of oil grew year after year, so did the size of the cabin. Now it slept ten to twelve adults comfortably and was outfitted with all the necessary toys for each season.

The snow fluttered past the window, growing thicker with each mile we drove. Thank goodness the driveway was heated or we wouldn't make it all the way up. Weston was looking out the window, same as me, but he'd been quiet the whole flight except when he talked to my father's head of security halfway through. They'd discussed the ins and outs of the high-end security system that had just been installed. Between the cold shoulder on the flight and now him acting distant, I had no idea what was running through his head. The silence between us was uncomfortable.

"Hey," I said, punching his shoulder. "What's with you?"

His breath fogged the window he wouldn't turn from. "Nothing, just looking."

I knew that was a half-truth.

"Come on, out with it."

Sighing, he turned in his seat and leaned back against the head-rest. "Cut me some slack. This is a lot to take in. Private planes, houses in Vail…. You know my story, my life. This, you and your family, it's a lot to take in."

Reaching over, I grabbed his hand. "I get that, but you have to remember this isn't me. You know the life I live. Besides the online shopping addiction, I'm pretty normal." He snorted, making me scowl at him. "Don't go getting all pissy pants because my family has money. I can't help it. Plus, does it really matter? Just enjoy the trip. I'm not going to let you waste my two consecutive days off work because my grandfather knew where to drill for oil."

He huffed a laugh and turned back toward the window, never letting go of my hand. "Pissy pants?"

"Yup, so snap out of it and enjoy the trip. Stop overthinking it and try to relax."

"Relax, huh?" he asked, turning back to me. His gaze had gone from distant to ravenous.

Smiling, I pivoted back to the window. "I'm sure we can figure *something* out," I whispered just loud enough for him to hear.

. . .

As soon as I stepped over the threshold, it felt like Christmas. The smell of the fire burning in the great room and the pine scent that filled the air from the ten-foot pine tree made me smile. Of course my father had someone come in and decorate the place from top to bottom for Christmas. The ornaments on the tree reflected the twinkling lights, making the whole room seem to shimmer like it was anticipating our arrival.

Unwrapping my scarf, I tossed it on the long dining room table as I made my way to Weston. He was standing in front of one of the back floor-to-ceiling windows, staring at the snow falling onto the deck. The deck was another great addition to the cabin. One area was covered with comfortable seating around a fireplace while the other section was left to the elements. The entire deck, along with all the exposed furniture, was blanketed in several inches of snow. Even the hot tub cover.

His gaze fall on the hot tub and he arched an eyebrow, asking a silent question.

"I hope you brought your suit."

"Seriously? Why would I pack a bathing suit? It's the middle of winter."

"Right, sorry," I said, shrugging and taking a step back. "Don't worry, we have extras. Come on, I'll show you where the rooms are. If you hurry, you'll get dibs on one with a single bed so you don't have to bunk with someone."

The smile on his face was menacing, mischievous. "I thought I was sharing with you."

"I... um...." I was lost for words. *Is he serious?*

He prowled toward me, glancing around before pulling me to him. "It's a joke, Kate. Calm down. But I am open to taking your suggestion from earlier."

Suggestion? I pressed my hand against his solid chest, pushing back so I could peer up at him. Eyebrows furrowed, I shook my head, letting him know I wasn't catching on.

"To relax. I figured with the four other security guys being here, plus your father, I might be able to loosen my focus a little."

My mouth gaped open.

Please be serious and not playing some messed-up mind game.

Grabbing my hand, he pulled me toward the staircase leading to the second level. "Come on, show me which room has a single bed. I really don't want someone monitoring when I come and go... or if I even stay in there at all."

The lump in my throat made it hard to swallow my growing anticipation. The fluttering in my stomach grew worse with each step we took up the stairs.

AFTER DINNER, I wandered out to the deck with a cup of steaming coffee in my hand, decked out in thick leggings, a warm oversized sweater, and a beanie to keep me warm. Even though the house was used all year round, coming here in the winter had always been my favorite. It was so peaceful sitting by the fire and watching the snow fall all around you.

Sitting down on the couch beside the fire, I winced at the soreness in my thighs that had already started to sink in from our short cross country skiing outing earlier that day. Leaning closer toward the fire's warmth, I wrapped both hands around my mug and breathed in the fresh coffee aroma, thinking back on how great the day had been. Weston and my dad had gotten along fairly well, which helped put aside some fears of what my father would say when—if—he found out about Weston and me.

"There you are," Weston said as he closed the back door behind him. He sat in the chair opposite me and leaned forward, placing his forearms on his thighs. "You disappeared after dinner."

"Just enjoying my favorite part of the house." That and I couldn't be around my father any longer. I loved him, but sometimes he was relentless on trying to get people to agree with his views.

"You seemed frustrated with your dad during dinner. What pissed you off?"

I rolled my eyes. He was too perceptive for his own damn good. "His views on the punishment of the women instead of the bastards who are paying to use their bodies for sex is disgusting. We're prose-cuting the victims, and he doesn't see it that way. He hasn't seen what I've seen or really understand why my mom got involved with Second Chances to begin with." Taking a sip of my coffee, I looked out at the snow. "If men weren't willing to pay for it, then there would be no sex industry. We need to change the laws, focus on bringing them and sex traffickers to justice, not the women."

Weston nodded and stared into the dancing flames of the fire. "Sounds like you're regretting your decision to be a doctor instead of an attorney."

The way the light from the fire flickered in his eyes held me in a trance as I thought about what he said. "No, not necessarily. There are plenty of other people out there with the same passion as me about this who can change the laws. It just needs awareness. But I do feel like there is more for me out there. I'm just not sure what at this point."

"Whatever you do, I know you'll be this unsuspecting menace to anyone who stands in your way."

Smirking behind my cup, I shook my head.

"What do you want to do?" he asked.

"That's the thing. I don't know. I've thought about Doctors Without Borders, so that's an option, but it still doesn't feel right. I want to believe that when I find my overall purpose in life, it'll feel like a puzzle piece snapping into place. But maybe that's just me living in an unrealistic world."

He clasped his hands behind his head and leaned back against the chair. "Not necessarily. I knew when I found the army it was what I was called to do, then again when I focused on special forces. But I get what you're saying. Sometimes I start to feel that way about this job. I miss the action of the army, but more than anything, I miss the feeling of making a difference."

Tucking my knees into my sweater, I started to say something, but the back door clicked open and my father stepped out onto the deck. Leaning down to hug me from behind, he whispered, "Good night," before standing straight and heading back inside. Not even a "Good night" or nod in Weston's direction.

The lights in the house began turning off behind us, letting the darkness encroach farther across the deck and making the falling snow glitter against the slivers of light coming from the kitchen windows.

With my father asleep....

I dared a glance toward Weston. There was one thing on my mind, and I was pretty positive it was the same thing on his, based off his hungry gaze.

"Come sit with me." A mix of demand and hope filled his tone.

More than happy to.

It was a single-person chair, so the only option I had was to sit in his lap. Neither of us minded. He was a heater, my back warming against his chest the moment I leaned against him. With him heating me from beneath and the fire at my front, my eyes grew heavy with sleep. I felt safe in his arms, knowing nothing could hurt me. He wrapped his strong arms around my waist, holding me tight. The warmth, feeling of security, and the crackling of the fire had me drifting off to a peaceful sleep within minutes.

THE FEELING of being weightless was strange; I didn't quite understand what was happening as I rose to consciousness. Strong arms were carrying me, and from the way my body was moving, I could tell we were going up stairs. Willing my body to react to my command, I wrapped my arms around Weston's neck and laid my head against his chest as he carried me down the long hallway to my bedroom.

The sheets were freezing when he tucked me in, pulling the quilt and comforter over me to stay warm through the night. The feel of his warm lips against mine woke every inch of my body. When I finally opened my eyes, he was halfway to the door, sneaking out to not wake me.

Somehow I found the courage and words to beg him to stop. "Stay with me."

He turned and faced me but stayed in the same spot, not making a move toward the bed.

"I somewhat promise to keep my hands to myself," I murmured and rolled over, placing my back to him.

Footsteps approaching the bedside behind me and the sound of various things being set on the nightstand had me rolling over to find out what all he kept in those pockets. He'd started unbuttoning the top of his jeans just as I rolled over, and he paused at my movement. All reservations aside, I sat up and took over the task, undoing each button slowly as I looked up at him through my lashes.

When I reached the final button, I ran a finger along the waistband, tracing back and forth until I was rewarded with a deep growl. I hooked my fingers in the belt loops and pulled down until he was standing in only his boxers. Making sure he was watching, I licked my lips and began kissing along the waistband of his boxers, inching them lower and lower with each pass.

"Enough," he panted, sliding his hands under my arms and lifting me so he could climb in beside me. Lying on his side, he tucked an arm under his head. The sound of our deep breaths stood out against the quiet of the house. A finger tenderly traced my jaw and then lips as he gazed down at me. "What are you doing to me?"

Enjoyment raced through me at the fact that he was as affected by me as I was him.

"I could ask you the same thing," I said, opening my eyes.

Even in the dark, I could read his face. And what I found took me by surprise. I expected desire or lust, but his masculine face had astonishment, confusion, and longing written all over it. Which was good, since I was conveying the exact same look back to him.

The feel of his fingers in my hair massaging my scalp made me moan and press my head harder against him, begging for more. His deft fingers continued weaving through my hair as he pressed his lips against the sensitive skin of my neck, moving up to my ear. A not-so-quiet whimper escaped when his teeth lightly clamped on my earlobe at the same time he wrapped his lips around it, giving it a gentle tug.

"Enough, Casey."

His smile against my cheek made me want to smack him, kiss him, beg again, or all the above. When his lips finally pressed against mine, I opened freely to him, allowing him and his expert tongue to explore my mouth. His kiss was possessive, making me his and him mine. The feel of his hands skimming down my waist and thigh had my back arching, trying to get his fingers right where I wanted them.

A low chuckle rumbled through the room; the bastard knew he was teasing me and was fucking enjoying it. His rough hand moved from my thighs to pressing against my lower back, putting me flush against him. A gasp escaped when I felt all of him pressing against me through the leggings. Desperate to get our connection closer, I wedged my leg between his thighs, needing some kind of relief from the pulsing at my core. Knowing exactly what I was searching for, he rolled on his back, pulling me on top of him. Straddling him, I sank deeper against him, finding a small bit of relief that instantly turned into needing more. My head dropped forward as I savored the relief from the pressure from him and the friction of our clothes as I rocked back and forth.

Our bodies shifted as he scooted up, placing his back against the headboard and positioning us nose to nose. A single tug on the hem of my sweater was all the request I needed. My arms shot in the air, making it easy for him to pull it over my head. He released a frustrated growl when my sweater came free and he found yet another layer that needed to be removed.

With a husky laugh, I lifted the final layer over my head and tossed it onto the growing pile of clothes beside the bed. Weston wasted no time nibbling on my collarbone, making his way down to my chest as I tipped my head back, enjoying every place his lips touched. With a flick of his fingers, my bra clasp fell open, allowing him to hook his fingers through the straps and gently pull them off my shoulders before tossing the bra on the floor.

My lower back arched from the pressure of his hand pushing my chest closer to his lips. Stars floated in my vision when his lips connected with the tip of my breast as he gently rolled the nipple of the other between his fingers. I ran my fingers through his hair, pressing his mouth harder against me, wanting more of his tongue and teeth.

Without warning, he gripped my hips, flipping us. Tossing back the covers, he settled between my legs and began tracing the leggings' inseam up and down my inner thighs.

"Kate, I need you to look at me," he murmured. His fingers paused until my eyes met his. "I need to know you're in this with me. If you start to slip, if you start to feel yourself overthinking and not feeling us, I need you to tell me. I want you with me every step. This isn't just for me, it's for us." Wrapping his hands around my waist, he began inching my leggings down. "Do you understand what I'm asking you? I want you to relax, lose control. With me. Let me do that. Let me take care of you. Don't think about anything other than me and this moment. Can you get out of your head long enough to do that?"

What I wanted to tell him was in this moment, there wasn't any control left to hold on to.

It only took half a second after the pulling against my leggings paused to realize he was waiting for a response. "Nothing matters except me and you. I have *never* wanted something more than this. Take me. Take all of me," I whispered keeping my eyes locked with his throughout my confession.

The force of my leggings being yanked off had my hips arching and then flopping against the bed. Blazing-hot hands gripped behind my knees, pushing my legs wider and giving him a full view. Before, being exposed like this, allowing someone to stare at my naked body, made me feel like nothing more than an object, but the way Weston was drinking in every inch made me feel special, cherished. Like I was the only thing in the world that mattered to him, and not just for this moment but for a lifetime.

Running a hand up my stomach and down the curve of my waist, he kissed every inch of my inner thighs, making me moan various versions of his name. When he gently clamped down on the sensitive part of my inner thigh as he pressed his palm against my most sensitive spot, circling as he did, I screamed against my palm, trying to muffle the sound.

"Fuck, Kate, you're too much. I can't wait." He left me wanting on the bed to dig through his wallet on the bedside table. Before hopping back on the bed, he dropped his boxers, giving me the first view of all of him. My eyes widened; there was no way I couldn't stare.

"Enjoying the view?" he mumbled against the condom wrapper as he ripped it open between his teeth. My brain went into overdrive watching him roll it on, but the world stilled when he hovered over me, pressing his lips to mine.

"Are you with me, Kate?"

Unable to speak, all focus on the glorious feeling of his naked body pressing down on me, I could only give him a nod. At this point that was enough for him. He didn't ask for a verbal answer before grabbing both of my hands in his, stretching me under him as he rocked his hips, slowly gliding into me deeply. The connection was more than I could have imagined; the pressure of his body, his lips against mine with him inside me was exquisite torture. I felt myself on the verge of shattering beneath him, and he hadn't even started moving yet. It was the most fantastic, overwhelming sensation my body had ever experienced. *Ever.*

The roll of his hips had me biting his lower lip, trying to hold back a moan that would wake everyone in the house from the glorious sensations he was sending through my body. With each move of his hips, my body came closer and closer to tipping over the edge. I wiggled my hands free from his grip to grab the strong backside I'd been staring at for months, pulling him deeper just as he bit down on my lower lip.

Arching my hips against him as the world tilted on its axis, I yelled his name and thanked all the various gods I could think of. The feeling of free-falling made my entire body tremble.

After a few moments of catching my breath and scattered mind, I opened my eyes to find him smiling down at me.

"Again," he purred.

Yes. Hell fucking yes.

Flipping me so my stomach was against the sheets, he inched my hips up to meet his. I knew what was coming, and the anticipation made my whole body ready for him again.

"Oh fuck," he groaned as he began thrusting into me from behind.

I used the pillow as a silencer, burying my face in it to try and stifle the sounds of my profanities. My body was already deliciously sore, making this position a perfect mix of pleasure and pain.

His hand slipped from my hip, reaching around and settling just above where our bodies were connected. A flick of his fingers had me pushing against him, demanding more. With an answering growl, he pumped faster as his fingers moved back and forth.

When my body started quivering for the second time, the hand that was wrapped around my hip pulled away but quickly reconnected with a not-so-gentle slap on my ass, sending me over the edge once more. He drove deeper, cursing my name as he shuddered, finding his release.

The weight of his sweaty body pressed against my back made me smile, relishing in the feel of him. It only lasted a few seconds before he recovered and rolled off the bed to make his way to the private bath.

Turning on my side, I watched him walk away, appreciating the view of his muscular, nude backside.

A welcome burst of cold air wafted under the covers as he settled beside me, wrapping an arm around my chest and tucking my back firmly against him. He nuzzled his nose against my hair. "Now that I know what you feel like—what we feel like together—how will I ever be able to focus around you again?"

I rolled over to face him. "My thoughts exactly. Now that I know what you can do in bed, we might never leave. Screw skiing tomorrow. Let's just lie around and do *that* all day. That's my vote."

"Whatever you want, baby."

My cheeks flushed hearing the term of endearment I now truly loved and wished would pass his lips every time he spoke. "Is there anything you can't do well?"

"Resist you, apparently."

"You've done a damn good job these past few months. Well, until tonight, that is. Speaking of that.... Spanking? Really?"

"Don't you think you deserve it based off your actions the past few months?"

"So you've been wanting to spank me since...."

"Since that first day you disregarded orders, and every day since. Did you like it?"

"Surprisingly yes. Never been spanked before. Maybe I should do more naughty things to deserve it again."

With a push of the shoulder, he rolled me over, kissing my neck, then collarbone before making his way to my already sensitive breasts. The feel of his breath against me as he flicked my nipple with his tongue reverberated through me. "If you do anything else, spanking will be the least of your worries."

A fresh vein of excitement coursed through me when he moved to my other breast. He wasn't done tonight apparently. Leaning my head back, I let him once again take control of my body, and possibly heart and soul.

19

———————

The early morning light poured in from the floor-to-ceiling windows when the sound of the alarm going off pulled me from a deep sleep. Weston was making no attempt to silence it even though it was on his side. Crawling over his bare chest, I hit Snooze.

Two hands wrapped around my waist, holding me atop him. Lying prone against him, I rested my head on his chest, listening to the peaceful rhythm of his heartbeat.

"Good morning," he said in a husky voice as he skimmed his fingers down my spine. "Why do you have a shirt on?" His hand brushed over my covered backside. "And underwear?"

Resting my chin on his chest, I smiled up at him. "I hate sleeping naked, so I dug around in the dark after you fell asleep. Everything might be on backward. Why is the alarm set so early? We don't need to be ready for another two hours."

Giving me his adorable sly smile, he said, "We'll have to work on that. I wanted to wake up to you naked beside me."

"Maybe I like the idea of you undressing me."

"Now *that* I'm okay with."

"Now answer my question. Alarm, why is it set so early?"

"I figured your dad wouldn't enjoy seeing me leaving your room wearing the same clothes as yesterday, and...." He paused, biting his lower lip to stop his growing smile.

"And you were hoping to sneak in a quickie too."

Oh hell, could he get any cuter? His crazy morning hair only added to his boyish charm. Even though I hated mornings, his reasons for setting the alarm were warranted.

"That might have been a part of my plan, yes."

Faking a scowl, I said, "Cocky son of a bitch, aren't you, thinking I would be willing to give up sleep for you."

Rolling his body, he pinned me under him. I loved it. I wanted to be beneath him for the rest of the trip and beyond.

"Is that a no, baby, or just a maybe and you need some convincing?" he purred against my neck as he kissed down to my breasts.

My back arched off the bed when his lips wrapped around me, sending shots of adrenaline racing through me. Running my hands through his long hair, I held his head against me as he moved to the other side. "Convincing. Convincing for sure," I breathed.

He smiled up at me before biting at my nipple, causing me to yelp in pain and surprise. "Hmm, what can I do to convince you?"

"You're doing a damn good job right now," I said with my eyes closed, taking in every beautiful sensation.

"I think I can do better," he murmured, trailing brief kisses down my belly. Tossing the covers off the bed, leaving me fully exposed in the bright morning light, he raked his eyes up and down me, taking in every inch. "From the moment I met you, I've wanted... I've dreamed of you like this, naked under me, and...." His voice was guttural as he spoke. When his eyes finally met mine, he continued, "You are more beautiful than I ever allowed myself to imagine."

I raked my eyes up and down him just as he had, pausing between his legs, admiring all of him. Keeping my gaze on him, watching him twitch under my stare, I growled, "Enough convincing. Come here."

Reaching up, I grabbed his shoulders and pulled a compliant Weston down on top of me.

. . .

WESTON SAT to my right and my father directly across the table from us. After a full day of skiing—or for Weston, attempting to ski—Weston, my dad, his security team, a few local friends, and I were out for Christmas Eve dinner. Flame was packed, but with a couple words from my father, we were immediately seated beside a row of floor-to-ceiling windows so we could watch the falling snow.

Since it was Christmas Eve, I decided to dress up for the occasion, wearing black leather leggings and a long cream V-neck sweater, topped with my family heirloom fur vest and a long gold chain Kendra Scott knot necklace. The over-the-knee black wedge boots pulled the whole outfit together, even though Weston had voiced some concerns about their safety on the slick icy sidewalks.

Shaking my head at the memory, I leaned closer to him to engage in the conversation he was having with our Colorado neighbor.

After the first round of wine was ordered, my father's focus zeroed in on us, leaning against the table as he looked back and forth between Weston and me. I knew he could sense the shift in me. Not sure how, but from the evil eye he was giving Weston, I knew he knew.

"So, Weston, how did you like the slopes today?"

"They were great. It was my first time skiing, so the beginning of the day was tough, but I figured it out," he responded, taking a quick sip of his water.

"Did you figure it out on your own?"

"Sort of. Kate helped me some—in between making fun of me, that is."

I smirked, sipping my wine. "You deserved it. You're great at everything you do. I had to gloat about this one teeny tiny little thing that I'm better at than you."

"What is she referring to, Weston? What else do you do great?"

I choked on my wine. Weston's hand dipped under the table, gripping my inner thigh in an attempt to calm me.

"I guess she's referring to my army career. I was a part of a special forces unit. She seems to make a bigger deal out of it than it actually is." As he spoke, his fingers traced tiny circles along my inner thigh, driving me insane.

"Is that how you got into the security business?"

"Yes, sir."

"Do you like it?"

"I love it."

"Once the trial is over, where will you go next?"

Weston's fingers paused and I stopped breathing. That question—the deadline, really—was something he and I were doing a good job of avoiding.

"Dad, stop firing questions at him. He's not on the witness stand."

"It's fine," Weston said to me before turning his attention back across the table. "I'm not sure. It all depends on where I'm asked to go. I usually enjoy the overseas assignments, because I get to see so much."

"Sounds dangerous."

"Not as dangerous as you would think. The worst beating I've taken on the job recently was actually by your daughter. Did she tell you how she took me down one night?"

The wineglass at my lips hid my smile as he recounted the details of that night.

THE EMPTY DINNER plates were cleared, and everyone groaned about how full they were, yet almost every person at the table ordered more wine plus dessert. We weren't going anywhere anytime soon, much to my disappointment. All I could think about was getting back to the house and having Weston all to myself again.

Taking a subtle glance across the table, I adjusted in my seat, grabbing my wine with my left hand and casually draping my right on his upper thigh.

To his credit, Weston didn't skip a beat in his conversation with the person to his right. Sipping my wine, I began tracing the inseam of his jeans with my nails. With each pass, I pressed harder and rose higher, but he continued his conversation, ignoring me and my hand.

Not enjoying being ignored, I cupped my hand around him, stroking up and down. After a minute, he pushed away from the table, my hand falling through the air as he excused himself and headed toward the back of the restaurant where the restrooms were located.

The wine burned down my throat as I finished it in one large gulp. Maybe I had taken it a bit too far, but I needed to touch him. The night was dragging on and on; I was past the point of being able to hold myself back.

I need to apologize.

Excusing myself from the table, I walked in the direction Weston had headed a few moments prior. I waited outside the bathrooms, but when he didn't emerge, I started down the long hall leading deeper into the restaurant where the private party rooms were located. Each one was packed with families celebrating the holidays. My stomach sank with each step of my search.

When I reached the very end, I turned, disappointed that I'd missed him and wouldn't be able to apologize until we were alone later that evening. Just as I passed the only room that wasn't occupied, a strong hand wrapped around my wrist, yanking me into the dark. The door closed, and he pressed my back against it.

"What the hell do you think you're doing, Kate?" He sounded pissed, but his passionate, desperate kiss told a different story.

Each place he touched with his lips and hands sent shots of fire through my body, making me uncomfortably hot. "I know, I know. I'm sorry. I just needed my hands on you. I feel like we're wasting time being here. We don't have much time together before we head back to Dallas. I want you. Now."

"I feel the same way, baby, believe me," he said breathlessly as he nibbled on my earlobe. "But I don't want to start something here we can't finish here. If there weren't so many people around, and if I didn't think your father was half a second away from coming to look for us, I would fuck you right here against the wall like I want."

His words formed an image in my mind that made my entire body convulse. At that point, I didn't care if anyone did walk in and find us.

Squeezing my hands between us, I started to unbutton his pants, my anxious fingers fumbling. Two buttons left, he wrapped his hands around mine, pulling them away.

"I don't have any willpower left to stop you again, and fucking you here isn't what I had planned for tonight."

"What *did* you have in mind for tonight?"

The way he licked his lower lip had the back of my head tapping against the wall, trying to restrain myself.

"I wanted you to undress in front of me, slowly peeling off each piece of clothing, unwrapping yourself like the perfect Christmas gift you are. Then I want to kiss every inch of your body, stopping here" —he pressed his palm hard against the apex of my thighs as he ran his middle finger up and down the inseam—"where I want to lick you until you're screaming my name."

"Damnit, Weston," I groaned, banging my head so hard against the wall I just knew a dent would be left behind in the drywall.

"Oh, baby, I'm not done. After that, I want to fuck you until neither of us has enough energy left to breathe."

I couldn't speak. My throat was dry from the ragged breaths I was trying to drag in. The feel of his stare had my eyes opening to meet his.

"What about me, Kate? Did you have plans for me?"

Enough talking.

Pressing against him, I flipped us around so his back was now pressed against the wall. Not dropping his gaze, my fingers found his jeans once more, finishing the unbuttoning I had started earlier before I kneeled on the hardwood floor. "I'm not waiting until later. I don't care who walks in."

With a quick pull, his pants pooled around his ankles. I heard him groan when I wrapped my hand around him, gliding up and down. With the intensity of being in a public place, knowing we didn't have much time, Weston finished quickly as I moved my mouth up and down, taking in every inch of him.

When his shaking body stilled, I looked up from the floor. His eyes were wide with delighted surprise. "What the hell? That was amazing."

"Come on, people are going to be looking for us," I said, standing and reaching for the door. But Weston pulled me back, kissing me hard as he ran his fingers through my hair.

"Round one goes to you, baby. I look forward to round two back at the house," he said, situating himself in his jeans.

"Sounds good to me."

20

The near scalding water of the hot tub made me wince when I submerged into the water. Setting my glass of wine along the rim, I sank deeper into the hot water, letting it lap over my shoulders, easing the soreness there. It was serene, sitting here hot from the bubbling water, gazing into the snow-covered trees. I rested my arms along the edge and looked out into the darkness.

The sound of the back door opening and closing sent a pulse of excitement through me.

Water lapped around me, rising slightly as Weston climbed in and settled beside me.

"What are you thinking about?" he asked, spreading his arms out across the rim, mimicking me, and staring out into the forest that surrounded our cabin.

"You," I whispered.

"Me? Why are you thinking about me?"

"Our time in Dallas, last night, today…. All this, how I feel, it's… foreign to me, and it's all happening fast. In the past, I've been able to walk away from someone without a second thought, but now, with you… the thought of you leaving once the trial is over makes me nauseous."

"I know, I feel the same way, but I'm trying not to let it take away from what we have right now, this freedom from our normal life. Let's just take it one day at a time."

"But what happens after the trial? Where will you go? You know where I'll be, so where does that leave us?"

Moving off the edge of the hot tub, he positioned himself behind me and wrapped his arms around my waist, resting his chin on my shoulder. "I don't know, Kate. That's the most honest answer I can give you. Do you regret last night because we don't have an answer?"

"No."

"Then let's just leave it at that for now, because right now... I'm looking forward to round two."

My toes curled in the water as he pulled me against him, his lips connecting with the base of my neck. He had a point. Tonight was our last night together; tomorrow, Christmas Day, we would be heading back, and who knew what would happen then. Wasting this night debating the what-ifs was not how I wanted to spend our precious time.

I turned to face him and wrapped my legs and arms around him. "Round two?"

Leaning forward, he nipped at my lower lip, sending so much heat flowing through me that I started to sweat. "Ready?" he asked, pulling me flush against him, letting me feel *he* was definitely ready.

As our lips connected, Weston moved so he was sitting along the bench deep in the water, pulling me with him. As I flexed my hips against him, he reached up and grabbed my head, pushing me harder against his lips. I had no idea I would love being possessed and controlled by someone so much. It was amazing giving up the control for once.

Just as I started moving against him, ready to get round two started in the hot tub, Weston pulled back, breaking our connection.

He was breathless when he said, "We need to get upstairs now, baby. I don't have a condom down here, and if we don't stop now, I won't be able to at all."

Slightly annoyed, I groaned and peeled myself off him. "Why

didn't you bring one down? You're usually such a Boy Scout, always prepared."

That adorable sly smile made a reappearance. "I guess I was too distracted by the thought of you being mostly naked in a hot tub and me getting to be the one with you in it."

The cold air felt amazing on my too hot skin as I stepped out to grab a towel. "Well, if that's not the sweetest excuse ever, I don't know what is."

Padding toward the door, I was propelled forward when Weston smacked my ass, growling at me to pick up the pace. Once inside, he struggled between setting the alarm and following close behind me up the stairs. Thankfully Carl was still up watching TV, eyeing us suspiciously, and told Weston not to bother, that he would lock up for the night after his last cigarette before bed. I could see the wheels turning in Weston's mind, an internal battle of waiting to secure the house or following me. With a little sensual sway to my hips, he gave in and followed me up the stairs.

Before the door to my room was fully closed, I began untying my bikini top, eager to get it off.

"Stop," he commanded as he prowled toward me. "I changed my mind. I want to do it."

My stomach dropped at the feel of his hands pulling on the top and bottom string, allowing it to fall to the floor, exposing me to him. Dropping to his knees, he kissed along the top of my bathing suit bottoms, inching them down with each pass and making me moan with want for him to go faster. The bottoms met the same fate as the top, tossed aside and immediately forgotten. He gripped my hips tightly, pulling me harder against his mouth as he bit down on the soft skin surrounding my navel.

Dropping the borrowed swim trunks, he stood before me fully naked. While I was still admiring the view, he grabbed my hand and guided me toward the bed, sitting me down at the edge and pressing me back until I was lying down. I couldn't watch when he lowered his mouth to my already peaked nipple and began sucking and flicking his tongue against me. Grabbing his hair, I held him tight against me, enjoying every sensation that was making me start to sweat from anticipation.

Skimming his hand down my stomach, he moved to the other breast and pressed his palm hard against the apex of my thighs. I groaned his name along with a slew of profanities. He smirked, holding my gaze as he bit down gently on my nipple at the same moment he slid a single finger into me.

I was going to combust, truly burst into flames if he kept that up.

Kneeling by the bed without withdrawing his hand from me, he hooked one of my legs over his shoulder, opening me to him. Gliding another finger in, he pumped in and out as he kissed up my thigh, moving closer and closer to his ultimate destination.

When his lips finally connected with me, I grabbed a pillow and held it over my face to muffle my moans. He applied the same detailed attention between my legs as he did to my breasts, sucking and flicking his tongue back and forth. I pressed my back against the bed to lift my hips, trying to get more of him.

Puffs of warm air caressed my skin from his sensual laugh against me. With his free hand, he pushed my hips back against the bed, holding me firm despite my wiggling.

I flexed the leg over his shoulder, holding him against me just as he bit down and sucked, making me scream into the pillow as I came hard.

Yep, never giving this up.

Kissing down my leg, he pulled it from his shoulder and moved to lie beside me. Cool air brushed my cheeks, and the feel of him burying his face in my hair had me opening my eyes and gazing at the ceiling.

"I love the sounds you make. I can't tell which is hotter, your sounds or how good you taste."

"You win round two," I panted, still reeling, trying to figure out if I was dreaming or if this was my new reality.

Unexpectedly, he pushed off the bed and strode for the door, picking up a discarded towel along his way.

"Where are you going?" I questioned, sitting up and frowning at him.

He wrapped the towel around his waist and went through the door without looking back or answering my question. Ten seconds later, he returned with a hand tucked behind his back as he clicked the door closed.

Losing the towel, he sat on the bed and set a small square white box between us. "It's finally midnight. Merry Christmas."

To combat my exposure and the chill in the air, I tucked a blanket around my legs, even though he didn't seem to mind sitting around naked. Which was typical for a guy, I supposed, especially one who had a stunning body like Weston did. I tugged on the disheveled red ribbon holding the box closed. Lifting the lid, I looked at the strange object tucked into the white tissue paper.

"Read them." He picked up the long steel chain from the box and set the dog tags in my hand.

"You're giving me your dog tags?"

"Just read them, will you?"

Holding one between my fingers, I raised it closer to my face so I could see what was embossed on the steel. My smile grew as I read.

IF FOUND RETURN TO
CASEY WESTON

His cell number was listed at the bottom, making my smile widen until my cheeks hurt.

"I love it."

"It's for when you run off again. This way people know where you belong."

"Are you saying I belong with you?"

"Are you denying it?"

"Now, no. But we both know that won't always be the case."

"Even if I'm halfway across the country or the world, I know I will always be there for you, Kate. Assignment or no, if you need me, I'll be there."

The metal was cold against my skin as I put the dog tags around my neck and let them hang between my breasts. My bare backside stuck out of the covers, and I was rewarded with a smack against one cheek as I reached across the bed into the nightstand to pull out his perfectly wrapped gift. Setting it on the bed in front of him, I sat cross-legged and motioned for him to open it.

The ribbon and paper were ripped off in one pull. He tossed the trash aside and flipped the plain white box over in his hands, glancing up at me with a curious look. I held my breath as he tossed the lid aside.

The look on his face was everything I'd hoped for and more when he pulled the new Kindle Paperwhite from the red and green tissue paper.

"Are you serious?"

I grabbed it out of his hands and swiped the screen alive. "It's the newest version. I figured with as much as you read, this would be easier than carrying around all those hardbacks. And since you wouldn't tell me what you like to read, I had to guess. I downloaded several books from each genre. I did my favorite books last, so they're the first ones listed here," I said, pointing to the screen as I handed it back to him to play with.

The look of pure joy on his face made me want him again. Giving gifts had always been fun, but giving him this, seeing his reaction, made me teary with happiness.

He swiped through the pages and pages of books. "It's perfect."

Lying back against the bed, I fiddled with the dog tags. "Are you going to play with it all night, or me?" I asked, arching an eyebrow at him.

There was zero hesitation at my question. Tossing the Kindle aside like it was nothing, he lunged for me, grabbing and rolling so I was sitting astride him. He cupped both breasts, kneading them and rolling my peaked nipples between his thumb and finger. "You. Every damn day. Every fucking second. You."

It hit me as he said those words that there was no coming back from this. For either of us.

21

———

Something cold pressed against my forehead. I swatted the air, trying to figure out what was pulling me from my deep sleep; the numerous varied rounds of play had left us both exhausted. When my hand connected with skin, my eyes popped open, immediately alert. It was pitch-black in the room, so I felt down the arm I'd made contact with.

My breathing stopped and my heart raced at the feel of cold steel gripped by an unknown hand. A gun was pressed against my forehead. The trembling that raked through me from fear was enough to shake the entire bed. So much so that Weston began stirring beside me.

"Get up," the male voice whispered, then yanked my arm with his free hand, making me tumble off the side from the force.

"Baby, what are you doing?" Weston grumbled from the bed above me. I heard the sheets and quilt shift against each other as he felt around the bed searching for me. "Kate?"

The unknown man yanked against my arm again, pulling me across the carpet away from the bed, away from Weston. I tried to think straight, form some kind of plan that could get me, Weston, and everyone else in the house out of this alive.

The bedside lamp flipped on, and the pressure from the gun barrel shifted from my forehead to the back of my skull, holding me in place.

The air went tight as light flooded the room and Weston saw me on my knees with a gun pressed to the back of my head. Tears streamed down my face at his look. Anger, anguish, fury, desperation—it all swirled on the face that just hours before I'd held between my hands as I kissed him with a passion I'd never known existed until him.

The intruder pulled me up, and gripped my bicep, holding me in front of him, creating wall between him and Weston.

"Not so tough now, are you, bitch?" the man whispered in my ear, making me cringe and gag at the smell of his foul breath and body odor. He smelled horrible, like he hadn't bathed in days, maybe even weeks.

"Let her go," Weston said calmly, even though I knew he was anything but. His years of training were snapping into place.

I could sense the man's sneer as he hissed a breath, running the gun down my cheek. "I don't think so. This bitch is the reason my brother, my only family left, was killed. She humiliated him."

My knees buckled when the back of his hand connected with my face. I'd been hit before at the gym, but they always had pads. This feeling was so intense I wondered if I would black out from the pain, but I knew passing out would be the worst thing I could do. At least awake I could put up a fight, even if it meant feeling every second of the pain.

My hair tore from my scalp as he pulled my head back, exposing my throat. Blood filled my mouth as I tried to swallow at the odd angle. At least this time I was prepared when his fist slammed down against the side of my face. I screamed from the pain and tried to fall to my knees, but his grip on my hair tightened, holding me firm.

I couldn't look at Weston; I knew no matter what happened, I would never be able to unsee the look on his face as he had to stand there and watch me get beat to shit.

"Come on, bitch. There are some people who want to meet you," the man said, pressing the gun back against my temple as he started backing us toward the door.

I dared a look at Weston. He was standing, naked, glaring at the man behind me.

I couldn't stifle my sob as I gripped the base of my hair, trying to keep the intruder from pulling it all out as he dragged me toward the bedroom door.

"Don't follow or we'll make her death slower than planned."

The sweet relief from my hair being released so he could open the door was brief, but even without him holding on to me, with the gun still pressed against the back of my head, there was nothing I could do to escape. Nothing Weston could do. We all knew it.

"Not a sound or I shoot him," he whispered, pointing the gun at Weston's bare chest.

My heart cracked. One of us wasn't coming out of this alive, and I would rather that person be me.

I nodded, complying with each step we walked down the dark hall, our breathing the only sound. At the landing, I gripped the wood railing, not trusting my wobbling legs to get me down on their own. My moment of concentration allowed my captor a brief second to look behind him, making sure Weston was indeed not following. The huff of his satisfied laugh made me want to vomit.

He turned back to me, saying, "Not so tough now, is—"

It all happened so fast. One second his gun was at my ribs, and the next, three bodies were tumbling down the stairs. The back of my head smacked against the wall and stairs as we tumbled, causing my vision to tunnel. When I stopped moving, landing at the bottom, the sound of multiple voices faded out completely.

Something cold pressed against my face.

Not again.

In full panic mode, I began punching the air around me, trying to get free from my captor.

"Kate, you're safe. It's me. It's Dad."

My shoulders shook on the sob that broke from the throbbing pain in my face and relief. If my dad was there comforting me, I was safe.

Pushing up, I felt worn leather under my hands, letting me know I wasn't in my bed but possibly downstairs on the leather couches in the living room. I had to go by feel since I still hadn't braved opening my eyes, too terrified of what I would learn. What if Weston...? My body began shaking, hoping my new greatest fear hadn't come true.

"Where's that damn ambulance?" my father shouted so loud it felt like his lips were pressed right against my ear.

"On its way, along with the police."

I knew that voice.

I might love the person who owned that voice.

He was standing behind the couch, looking down at me when I finally opened my eye. One eye was swollen shut, and the other wasn't much better. The repulsion on his face made me wish I hadn't looked. What hurt even more was he held my gaze for half a second, then turned and walked out of the room.

I heard another man shrieking and sounds of heavy things being tossed around in the other room, making my good eye widen as I looked to my father for answers.

"The police will be here soon. He's just trying to get some information out of him."

Another scream for help from the neighboring room had me sitting up faster than I should have.

"What are they doing to him?" I asked, my voice shaking with panic.

"They?" The way my father laughed made it sound as if my question was a joke.

"Yes, they."

"It's not a they, honey. It's a him."

Weston.

As if simply thinking his name was a summons, he came stalking from the other room and headed toward the kitchen, eyeing me as he strode across the cabin.

My voice was weak and I hated it, but I wanted him, not my father, by my side. "Weston, come sit with me."

He heard me, I was sure of that, but he didn't turn from the sink.

"Weston, please."

Water dripped from the faucet as he turned to me, patting his hands dry on a kitchen towel.

"Please," I begged.

My father stood, leaving my side, when Weston finally gave in and started toward me. He squatted in front of me, looking up with a blank expression on his face that I hadn't seen in months. I hated it. I hated that look. I hated the man who took all the looks Weston had given me this weekend away and replaced them with this dull, distant one. If Weston hadn't beaten him to a pulp, then I wanted a turn.

I swallowed against the lump forming in my throat. "Say something. Talk to me."

His eyes focused on my face, making his expression harden further. The leather of the couch groaned under his grip; I looked down only to find his knuckles a bloody mess. Grabbing one, I began giving it a once-over, making sure no bones were broken.

"Are you okay?"

The hand I was holding jerked from my grip. "Seriously? Kate, your face is beat to hell, and you're concerned about my hands."

He stood and walked across the room, not once looking back.

THE EMT LOOKED ME OVER, confirming what I had already guessed: no broken bones, but a lot of swelling, and my face would be gorgeously bruised for a week or so. Watching the final police car head down the driveway with my would-be captor inside, I turned and joined the men in the living room. Even though they were mid-conversation, I knew what was being discussed.

"You cannot be serious." My father's face was a unique shade of purple.

"If the code isn't punched in and the system armed, then yes, nothing works," the head of security said to my father, glancing at me and wincing as I approached.

"Kate, go upstairs and lie down." The outright command in my father's voice had me widening my stance and crossing my arms over my chest. I caught an eye roll from Weston out of the corner of my good eye. "Kate, I'm not going to ask you again."

"Then don't. So what happened?" I asked, scanning the crowd with the same authority as my father.

Everyone stood silent, staring at the ground, the wall, ceiling, anywhere but at me, not wanting to see my face, the reminder they'd failed in keeping me safe.

Weston was the one who finally spoke up. "The alarm wasn't set. He walked right in through the back door. He's been watching us for the past two days, waiting for the right moment."

A shiver went down my spine.

"He was waiting for one of you to slip up, and you did. Now I want to know whose fault it was that the alarm wasn't set," my father shouted, forgetting about his command for me to go upstairs and now focusing on finding the weak link in our group.

"It was me." Weston stepped in the middle of the group. "I was the last one outside and didn't set the alarm behind me."

Thankfully, Carl stepped up beside Weston. "No, it was me. You asked me to set the alarm since I was still up and would be going back out to smoke at some point. I take all the blame." His grief-filled gaze shifted to me. "I'm sorry."

"You're both to blame. Look at her. Look at her face! Do you see what can happen when you're distracted, when your focus isn't on her safety?" My father yelled that last bit while glaring at Weston.

"Dad, I—"

"I don't want to hear it from you right now, Kate. Go upstairs. Now." I didn't move, partly from astonishment that he was speaking to me that way. "You're both fired. Go pack your stuff."

"No." It came out of my mouth before I even realized what I was saying.

"Yes, Kate."

"It wasn't Weston's fault. He didn't do anything wrong."

"He was distracted. Do we all need to talk about why? He's fired. He's no longer focused solely on your safety."

"No. He's *my* security, and I'm saying he's not fired."

"I'm paying his salary right now, and I'm saying he is."

"Fine, then I'll hire him."

We were only a few feet from each other at this point, growing closer and closer as we bantered. A mean smile crept up his face, making me cringe. "Interesting. I thought you were against people paying for sex."

For the first time in my life, I hated my father. Balling my hands into fists, I lunged at him, ready to make his face look as bad as mine, but a strong arm wrapped around my waist, holding me back. I pulled against it, stretching my arms out long, trying to get to my father, but Weston's arm held firm.

Not knowing what to do, my dad's security team formed a wall between us as I lunged again, trying to get at him.

I heard him say behind the human wall, "She won't hurt me."

Not backing down, I lunged once more. This time when Weston pulled me back, he tossed me over his shoulder and headed toward the stairs. "I wouldn't bet on it," he called behind him.

The bed in his room creaked against my weight when he set me down so gently it pissed me off, like he was scared I would break.

"This has to be the worst Christmas ever," I murmured, needing to break the tense silence filling the room.

He didn't respond; in fact, he didn't even look in my direction or acknowledge that I'd spoken at all.

Panic had my heart pounding and my breathing growing rapid with each intake. How could things have gone so wrong? Just a few hours ago, Weston had me wrapped up in his arms, whispering about never wanting to let me go, but now when I did catch a sidelong glance, he looked repulsed by the sight of me.

"It wasn't your fault."

"I didn't follow up. It was just as much my fault as Carl's."

"He's the one who didn't do what he said he would do. He's the one who forgot!" I shouted, pointing toward the door.

"I knew this would happen. It's why I have my rules. No exceptions." The sound of drawers opening and closing sounded behind me.

"Screw your rules. You did nothing wrong, Casey. *Nothing.*"

"I was distracted by you, by us. Which led to that piece of shit getting into the house." I watched him flex his hands open and closed, making the cuts along his knuckles shimmer with the fresh blood seeping out. "I am so angry at myself. I know better than to get involved with a client."

"A client. So now I'm just a client?"

"You've always been my client."

"Am I just a client now?"

"No, and that's why I need to go. I can't do this at the level you need anymore."

"It wasn't—"

"Look at your face!" he yelled, dropping the bag he was packing. "Do you not remember the last couple of hours, because I sure as hell do. Fuck! Every time I blink, I see that gun at your head, you crying and pleading with every look, begging me to make it stop. What if Paul hadn't heard your scream and been waiting in the hall?" He sat on the opposite side of the bed, keeping his back to me. "I failed you tonight. The second I gave in to the thought of us, I put you at risk. You might not see it as my fault, but I always will."

Tears streamed down my cheeks, my voice trembling as I said, "You're not leaving. I'm not letting you give up."

"It's not up to you anymore, Kate."

I stifled a sob, holding my hands over my face. My name. We were back to him using my name, making me ache to hear him call me "baby" one more time.

"Like hell it is," I said between sniffles. "I don't want you to go. Please don't go. If you leave, I don't... I don't want to go back to being me before you."

The sound of the zipper on his duffel bag made me cringe. Hands wrapped around mine, pulling them from my face. "You were perfect before I came along, and you'll be fine when I'm gone. I can't stay, Kate, knowing I'm putting you at risk if I do. I want you to know...." His eyes slid to my swollen eye down to my split lip. I watched him swallow the words he was about to say. "You'll be safer this way."

"Fuck you, Weston," I said, pushing him off me and making him tumble into the wall behind him. "You're running away."

"I'm not running," he growled as he stood. "I'm doing this for you."

I shoved him out of my way and strode to the door. "Is that what you're telling yourself, that you're doing it for me, instead of the real reason? That you got to fuck me and now you're done, nothing left to stick around for. Is this what you do with all your female *clients*? Make them fall for you, then make up an excuse to leave?"

The door slammed closed from the force of his hand. I pulled against the knob, hoping I could overpower him and get the door open enough for me to slip out. I needed out of this room. I needed away from him. Just a few minutes of silence to process everything, to work out a plan to make him to stay.

"I've never let myself get this close to a client. You're.... That's not what's happening here, Kate, and you know it. Stop making me the bad guy in this."

My shoulder rose and fell in an exaggerated shrug. "From my point of view, you are. You're the one leaving."

"Pretty sure the fucker who broke into this house and beat you to shit and the rest of his pathetic friends back in Dallas are the bad ones. Not me."

I looked him in the eyes so he could feel the anger and devastation when I said, "They're the threat, Weston. You're the asshole who's leaving on his own when I'm begging you to stay."

His voice broke as he whispered my name.

Enough.

I yanked on the door and ran down the hallway to my room. Peaceful silence engulfed me as soon as the door shut behind me. My back slid down the door until my backside connected with the carpet.

Tucking my knees against my chest, I wrapped my arms around my shins and buried my face in my thighs just as the flood of tears I could no longer hold back began to flow.

When my tears had stopped and I could think clearer, I pushed off the floor and headed to the bathroom, hoping a shower would help me piece a plan together to convince him to stay. Not wanting to see how bad I looked, I turned on the shower, stripped off my T-shirt and the sweatpants I'd slipped on before the police arrived, and stepped right into the cold water. The shock to my body was exactly what I needed.

First, I needed to apologize for saying those things to him. Maybe if I did and if we talked calmly—possibly with a brown bag on my head so he wouldn't be reminded of my beat-up face—he would stay. I knew in my heart he didn't want to leave, not really. It was just his twisted overprotective nature that was telling him all this was his fault. Which was insane; even distracted, he was ten times better at his job than any of the other guys downstairs.

Talk. That was what we needed to do. We could figure it out.

Tossing on a sports bra, a long sleeve T-shirt, and boyfriend jeans, I whipped my hair into a messy bun as I descended the stairs, ready to test out my convincing skills.

The look on everyone's face had me halting on the final stair.

Pity. The look of pity was written on all their faces. Everyone's except my father's. He looked sad, staring into the highball glass filled with some kind of dark liquor in his hand.

"Where is he?" I demanded, coming to stand beside him in the kitchen.

The ice clinked against the glass as he took a sip. "He's gone."

"I told you not to fire him. You have no right to do that without talking to me first."

He took another sip.

"Where is he, Dad?"

"He quit."

"What?" I deadpanned.

No, no, no, we have to talk.

"He asked me to book him on a commercial flight back to Dallas later today. He and Carl left in a taxi about five minutes ago."

My mind swirled. I began scrambling for the phone in my back pocket, hoping I could catch him in time, to let him know I didn't mean what I said.

I pressed the Home button, and one missed text lit up.

> Weston: You are and will always be my only exception. I'm sorry.

Angry at him, at the world, at the damn case that brought us together in the first place, I flung my phone across the kitchen and right into the damn door the bastard who'd ruined my hope of more snuck in through, officially ruining my life.

The glass pane shattered, sending shards raining down onto the deck and tile.

But I didn't care. I didn't care about anything anymore. He was gone, and the good part of me that he helped me discover left with him.

22

———————

The flight home was painful, and not only from the throbbing in my face. Everyone avoided me, even my father by having side conversations about what would happen when we landed, who would be taking over my full-time security. All conversations about me that they wouldn't include me in. From my father's perspective, I wasn't in the right state of mind to make those kinds of choices. Between his comment earlier and now treating me like a wounded teenager who couldn't make informed decisions, I was furious at him. So when we landed and he had the audacity to tell me I wasn't going to work, that I would be calling in and letting them know I was "sick," I laughed in his face and headed toward the waiting SUV, flipping him off behind my back.

Now I stood with Eric, recounting the story and begging for the charge nurse to let me work my scheduled shift. The bruises would make people question my choices, which would then make them question any diagnosis I gave them. That was her argument.

Unfortunately, she won.

When the charge nurse dealt out the sentence of not being able to return until my face was healed, Eric grabbed my hand and hauled me out of the ER before I could do or say something stupid.

The mobile coffee cart line moved at a snail's pace, giving us a few minutes to talk before I headed home and Eric went back to work. He turned to me, his forehead wrinkled with concern. "I tried to text and call you. What the hell happened?"

"Oh yeah, I need a new phone. I kind of shattered mine when I threw it against a glass door."

"Kate, what is with you? I've never seen you this hateful before. I'm actually a little scared of you right now."

"Well, let's see here. I had an amazing weekend with Weston until that bastard broke into our cabin, beat me to shit, and made me think he was going to torture me slowly before killing me. Then, to make everything worse, he left."

"You mean the police came and got him."

"I mean Weston. He left. He quit. He left me."

He wrapped his arms around my shoulders, pulling me in close before the last words were out. It felt amazing to be held after the past twelve hours.

The barista's cheerful voice asking what we wanted had me wiping my eyes and turning to her. "I'll be fine," I murmured, then ordered my coffee.

"I'm sorry, Kate. Have you tried calling him?" Eric asked as we were handed our beverages.

The coffee cup was deliciously hot in my hands, bringing some life back to my body. Hopefully the contents would too.

"No phone, remember?"

"Right. Well, I need to get back to work since we are down one tonight." He jabbed my bicep with his elbow as we walked back toward the emergency room. "I'll stop by and check on you after my shift. Love you. Oh, and Merry Christmas."

Rubber squeaked against clean linoleum floors as he walked toward the emergency room. It really did suck that I couldn't work, leaving them one person short. With all that was going on, knowing my friend would have to carry my weight at work because of the case made me even angrier. What I needed to do was go to the gym and hit something, or maybe hit someone. Anything to get this anger out of my body before I exploded, hurting myself or someone else unintentionally.

I made it two steps toward the locker rooms to change back into my leggings and sweater to head home when a delicate hand wrapped around my wrist.

"Excuse me, do you work here?"

No, lady, I just like to walk around a random hospital in scrubs. Idiot.

She was beautiful. Striking was more accurate, with her long blonde hair and piercing blue eyes. The grip she had on my wrist dropped when I turned to face her.

Shit, forgot about that.

"I'm sorry. I, um, thought you were a doctor," she stammered, taking a step back.

Inwardly I cringed. Everyone was reacting that way when they saw my face. From my perspective, it wasn't *that* bad.

"I do work here, just about to head home. They won't let me work like this." I gestured to my face. "They say it'll scare off patients. Is there something I can help you with?"

Her blue eyes were still pinned to my nearly swollen shut one. "I'm looking for my fiancé. He works here. He's a doctor. This is my first time to this hospital, so I'm a little unsure where to find him."

An unsettling feeling filled my stomach. Somehow I knew who her fiancé was without having to ask. Only one other person we worked with was as perfect as she was.

"What area of the hospital does your fiancé work in, and I'll point you in the right direction."

Please don't say trauma. Let me be wrong. Please don't say trauma.

"Oh, wonderful. He's a trauma surgeon."

This day really, really needs to end.

A small forced smile played on my lips as I tried to hide the boiling wrath that was building in me.

"I work in the ER, so maybe I know him. What's his name?"

"What a coincidence that I stopped you. I'm sure you know him. He is kind of hard to miss." She smiled. "His name is Austin."

"Of *course* he's your fiancé." It came out more hateful than I wanted, but when your whole body was full of hate and anger and more hate, that was what happened.

"Excuse me?" she said, taking a step back and shooting a suspicious look in my direction.

"You're both striking, that's all I meant," I grumbled. It wasn't her fault that her fiancé was a cheating, lying, cocky son of a bitch. "What's your name? I'll go find him and let him know you're here to see him."

"Brittany Jones. Can I go with you? I kind of wanted it to be a surprise."

Oh it will be when it's me telling him that his fiancé is here to see him.

"I don't think that would be smart, just in case he's in surgery or something. I'll walk you to the waiting room, and you can wait for him there. How's that?"

"Okay, if you think that would be best."

"How long have you two been engaged?" I asked as we walked toward the waiting room.

"Ten months, and we still don't have a date. When Austin got the job here in Dallas, he tasked me on setting the wedding plans aside and getting everything taken care of in San Antonio for the move."

I didn't know what to say. So instead of saying the wrong thing, we walked in silence the rest of the way. When we reached the waiting room, my stomach sank knowing Weston wouldn't be there waiting for me. Not today, not tomorrow. Never again.

Motioning for her to wait in one of the quieter areas, I stormed through the emergency room, nearly knocking Eric off his feet.

"What the hell, Kate?" he yelled from behind me, but I didn't stop. The doors to the surgery rooms swung open, banging against the walls from the force. The roaring in my ears kept me going, pushing the sound of Eric calling out to me to the background.

Each hall I walked down was empty, making me even angrier that I wasn't able to confront him. Wasn't able to see the look of fear on his face when I told him who I'd met and was currently waiting for him downstairs.

The sound of someone, two people maybe, talking around the

corner had me taking a right. Evil happiness filled my heart when I found Austin leaning against a wall with some nurse I didn't recognize beneath him.

She was giggling at something he said while he played with her ponytail, whispering in her ear. Eric yelling my name from down the hall had them both looking in my direction.

That damn cocky grin didn't fade as he took in the condition of my face, unlike the nurse beneath him, who ducked under his arm and took off in the opposite direction. She was smart; she knew the look of a scorned woman and got the hell away.

Austin glanced in the direction the nurse went. "Seriously, Kate? I had to find someone who was more willing."

That was it. It was all too much for even me to handle. Unfortunately for Austin, he was the final straw for the day.

Eric's voice grew closer, and I knew he would stop me, so I needed to act fast.

That cocky smirk still didn't fade, and what came out of his mouth as his gaze raked over my beaten face fueled my already burning anger. "I told you he wasn't a hero," he said when I was finally standing in front of him.

The first place I aimed was his nose. I knew how much he loved his perfect nose, and I wanted to break it. Not just break it, I wanted to shatter it like my life had just been shattered in the past twelve hours.

He screamed and grabbed his face, blood already starting to pour from his nose. The feel of my skin connecting with his made me feel slightly better, so why not do it again?

Pulling my fist back, I aimed for his cheekbone and was rewarded with a cracking sound from my knuckles as they connected with my target. Yelling for help, he fell to his knees.

An evil grin made the split in my lip pull farther apart as I watched him writhe on the floor beneath me.

One more hit. That'll make me feel a lot better. But with him on the floor, maybe a kick to the ribs would be best.

Before my foot could glide through the air, I was shoved from behind, sending me sailing over Austin and skidding across the floor.

"What the hell, Kate? What the fuck are you doing?" Eric was bending over Austin, trying to pry his hands from his face to assess the damage.

My palms stung from skidding across the floor. I pushed up and stood facing the two men on the floor, more people gathering in the hallway from the commotion. Both shrank back when they found me standing beside them.

"I met your fiancée downstairs. She came to surprise you," I spat at Austin. His eyes widened with realization. "You lying prick. She came to surprise you on Christmas. You made me—" My nails nearly punctured my skin, my hands were clenched so tight. I didn't want to think what kissing Austin, being with Austin, wanting Austin made me in this whole scenario with his fiancée. "I hope I broke your damn nose, you lying piece of trash."

Even though I knew I would get in major trouble for what I'd just done, maybe even fired—very likely, actually—I felt better. Much better. The only thing that could make me feel even better was a drink.

Good thing my fridge was already stocked.

A COUPLE HOURS or so after the incident, and five beers in, my iPad started dinging with iMessage after iMessage.

> Meagan: You're nuts, you know that right? What if they fire you?

> Meagan: Do you think Austin will file charges?

> Eric: You broke his nose. You're so fucked.

> Meagan: HOW COULD YOU BREAK THAT PERFECT NOSE

> Eric: He's engaged, Meagan.

Meagan: Oh.

Meagan: I haven't heard that part of the
story yet.

Meagan: Think I could take her?

Meagan: The fiancée, that is, not Kate. After
tonight I know I wouldn't win.

Eric: Yeah, she was a little scary tonight. Did
she tell you what happened in Vail?

Meagan: No. Tell me.

Eric: Call me.

Oh hell, they were having side conversations. This wouldn't turn out good for me.

Instead of responding, I decided another beer was in order considering the first five made me feel so good. Well, good was an exaggeration; numb might have been a better word for how it made me feel, which was a hell of a lot better than hateful and angry.

Meagan: Kate. I don't know what to say.

Yep, she and Eric talked. Hopefully he told her to cool it on all the Weston comments for a while or she might end up like Austin, or worse.

Meagan: I'll come over with ice cream, wine,
and a bunch of girly movies.

Me: Huh? What does that have to do with
anything?

Meagan: OMG you haven't been through this
before, have you? It's what happens when
you break up with someone and you actually
miss them or want them back. It's a form of
comforting. It's a girl thing.

Eric: I want in.

Meagan: Okay, a girl and Eric thing.

Me I really just want to be alone.

Meagan: That's the worst thing possible for a heartbreak. It'll fester and you'll end up drunk-dialing him one night begging him to come back, that you didn't mean to cheat on them or act crazy.

Me: Sounds like you know this from experience.

Eric: She's right, Kate. You need to be comforted.

Me: I am. His name is Bud.

Meagan: WHAT!

Eric: WHAT.

Me: First name Bud. Last name Light. He is of the Busch family.

Meagan: Oh great, you're drinking. Eric, she's drinking.

Eric: This is worse than we thought.

Me: Um, guys, I am on this group text. I can hear you.

Eric: Did you know, Meagan?

Meagan: Yeah, kind of. Did you know?

Eric: I caught on way before they even did.

Me: What are y'all talking about?

Eric: That you fell for Weston, and for the first time in your life, you wouldn't be able to walk away. This is what heartbreak feels like, Kate. It sucks. Sorry that you have to know how the rest of the world feels when someone leaves.

Me: Oh.

Eric: I'm sorry.

Meagan: Me too. Chocolate chip or plain chocolate?

23

Sometime during my four-week suspension, as I fell deeper into seclusion and despair, the stupid country songs I used to make fun of started making sense. Thankfully it was just a suspension—that was what the administrator said, anyway—instead of being terminated for workplace violence. The administrator was a nasty, sweaty man who reveled in the power he had over my fate, which, before my life going to absolute shit, would have made me fight back, but now I no longer had that kind of energy or passion in me. The sneer that was plastered on his face throughout the whole conversation made it apparent that he was not happy with the fact that Austin had not only chosen to decline pressing charges but was now saying he slipped—multiple times—on the wet floor, which caused his broken nose. It was satisfying hearing the administrator's discontent at the situation and that I would still have a job after the "explosive display of violence."

Since that day, almost three weeks ago now, all I'd had the energy to do was volunteer, shop online, and drink wine while watching trashy TV. It didn't help that I couldn't sleep at night; every night I would wake in a cold sweat, panting and trembling in fear from the reoccurring nightmares. It made me feel weak that I couldn't make them stop, so I chose not to tell anyone about them. When people stopped by to check on me, their voices just faded to the background. They all said the same thing: "You need to snap out of it, move on." Even Joe, sweet Joe, often tried to cheer me up. He happened to be the only person who could bring me out of my despondent state for those brief moments of time.

What everyone didn't know was that during those months that Weston and I were together, before we were *together*, I fell in love with him. He was—*and still is*—the only person I wanted to see when I woke up, the only person I wanted to argue with, banter with, spar with... and who I wanted playing with my hair as I fell asleep in his arms each night. More than anything, I ached for the friend I'd made.

But he left me without even a phone call. Just one single text that I still couldn't force myself to delete, that some nights I fell asleep reading while cuddled up in one of his soft army shirts I stole months ago.

My norm was now being drunk, slothful, and sad.

And I. Didn't. Care.

THE BLINDS on my bedroom window clattered open, causing brightness to burn through my closed eyelids. Without opening them, I tossed a blanket over my head and rolled over.

"You have four days to get your shit together, Kate," Eric said, pulling the blanket to the end of the bed.

"Get out," I moaned, yanking a spare pillow over my face and holding it tight just to also have it ripped from my hands.

"No, this is getting bad. You have to go back to work in four days, and you need to get your shit together."

"I'll be fine. Just let me sleep a little longer."

The bed shifted under his weight when he sat beside me, a warm hand interlacing with mine. "Joe said you haven't been downstairs since yesterday morning."

"So?"

"It's almost three in the afternoon. Are you even eating?"

"Yes, lots of fruit."

He rolled his eyes. "Wine isn't fruit."

"It's a form of fruit, just fermented."

If you asked me what I would have expected Eric to do next to snap me out of my sinking depression, I would have said something like "Take me to brunch," "Make me talk it out on long walks along White Rock Lake," or even "Go shopping," but what he actually did shocked me.

He yanked his hand from mine only to wrap both of his around my ankles. Before I could open my eyes, he jerked me out of bed, sending me crashing to the floor.

"What the—"

He didn't let me finish. Dragging me by the ankles, he pulled me into the bathroom and turned on the shower. My eyes widened when I realized what he was planning. Kicking my feet, I started screaming for Joe, but with all the exerted energy and very little to eat except delicious fermented fruit the past few days, I couldn't fight back when Eric pulled me in his arms and walked us into the freezing cold water.

I thrashed against Eric's vice grip across my arms and chest, trying to get away as the cold water soaked me, beginning to snap pieces of the old me back into place. Pieces that were left disjointed after Weston. The water poured over and around me, helping me remember that feisty, smart, tiny warrior who was still inside me, aching to resurface.

Giving in, I slumped against his chest, gathered up his soaked T-shirt in my fists, and let all the sorrow and pain pour out of me with each bone-rattling sob.

Tomorrow. Tomorrow was my first day back since "the incident," and I was nervous, really nervous about how everyone would act around me. All I wanted was normalcy; go back to work, gym, volunteer, and repeat—that was the pattern I needed to get back into to keep me from dwelling on *him*. It was hard not to think about him with Joe still lingering around, the trial thankfully almost over.

Closing statements from each side were coming up in the next few days.

Since that day in the shower with Eric, my mind was clearer, focused on moving forward with my life even if there was a hollow ache in my heart that hadn't been there before. I could live with that ache. I *had* to live with it and move on.

Getting back to the gym was the first thing I did, and it felt amazing to be exhausted from being active again. It made me want more and more. For the past couple days, the majority of my afternoons were spent running or smacking the bag around.

Except today. Tapping my tennis shoe on the tile floor, I glared at Joe asleep on the couch. I told him I needed to go to the gym as soon as we got home from Second Chances twenty minutes ago, but clearly he was too exhausted from our previous outing. Not wanting to wait for him to be ready, I quietly grabbed my gym bag and tiptoed to the front door. Easing it open, I made to slip out but tripped over several boxes piled right outside.

I slid the Zappos and Nordstrom boxes inside the house before I locked up, the January air biting at my face as soon as I turned to walk the few blocks to the gym. As I jogged, the wind swirled around, prompting me to zip up my jacket and pull the hood on, leaving Joe unaware inside and no note as to where I could be found.

Cold air tore at my lungs, easing me into a brisk walk to save my energy for the sparring ring, and a feeling of unease settled into the pit of my stomach. Glancing around, I didn't notice anything suspicious, but I picked up my pace once more just to calm my nerves. But it didn't work; it only made me more paranoid, the feeling of dread washing over me, turning my fast jog into a sprint toward the gym doors that were now in sight.

Just get to the doors. You'll be safe there. Get to the gym.

My heart pounded, urging me faster. Sweat dripped down my temples and the back of my neck, forcing a shiver as it made its way down my spine.

Twenty more yards.

The cold air felt like broken glass in my lungs as I took in deep breaths to keep myself moving forward, faster and faster.

Ten more yards.

I was so focused on those doors, on the false sense of security they offered, that I didn't glance to my right. If I had, I would have seen a late-model blue Toyota creep up next to me, window down. And maybe I would have dived to the ground as the person inside held a gun out the window, pointing it directly at me.

But I didn't.

All I was focused on were those damn doors.

MORE THAN A RISK

MORE THAN A THREAT BOOK 2

KATE

In the movies you watch, there are people shot multiple times crawling across the floor toward safety or standing up, fighting their way out of the danger. Maybe they're stronger than me or have more will to live. Because all I can do is lie here, on the freezing sidewalk, doing everything I can to stay fucking conscious while I bleed out from the multiple gunshot wounds I just sustained. Hell, I can't tell how many I have at this point. All I know is it fucking hurts worse than anything I have ever experienced.

So now I wait. Wait to either die of blood loss, which I know is quickly approaching, or for whoever shot me to come back and finish the job. I don't know which would be worse, because the pain is unbearable, but the thought of having to watch someone point a gun at my head, for that to be the last thing I will ever see, is terrifying.

The feel of the pavement vibrating beneath me and the sound of pounding feet approaching makes me realize my fate will probably be the latter. But much to my surprise, the person doesn't stop and hold a gun to my head or gloat at what he's done. No, instead this man drops to his knees beside me, places his hands over my abdomen, and begins to shout to someone I can't see. I wonder if I'm going to make it to the hospital in time. I wonder if I even care.

I want to live, I do. I want to see if he'll come back.

See if he'll come back for me.

The man bending over me starts talking, trying to keep me conscious. Asking who he needs to call. Telling me to keep my eyes open. Telling me help is on the way.

But I don't want to keep my eyes open. I don't want to see what's happening.

As the stranger's voice fades and I sink deeper into the darkness closing in, I'm scared to let go. The need for him here, to hold my hand, to keep me from slipping away is overwhelming. But he isn't. I'm here alone, wishing I wasn't.

1

My muscles and skin tingled, every nerve ending flashing like each square inch had fallen asleep and was slowly waking up.

Damn that insistent alarm for ruining this unusual dream.

I should wake up, but staying in bed and getting more sleep sounded way better. Even my eyes were too tired to cooperate.

Wait.

Something's not....

I *never* set the alarm for anything other than music. What was that rhythmic beeping in the distance? What the hell was going on? The unending darkness behind my closed lids was disorienting, plus not a single body part would respond to my commands to move.

Okay, the last thing I remember is... shit, what's the last thing I remember?

What the hell happened to me?

Getting my eyes to open was crucial. I begged them, pleading internally, but my eyes wouldn't cooperate. Nothing would. Everything felt too heavy, and, damnit, ache had started to replace the numbness.

Even breathing fucking burned.

My heart ratcheted against my chest, panic slowly taking over, the beeping mirroring the quickened beat.

What if I'm trapped like this forever? No way to communicate. No end to the throbbing pain consuming half my body.

What if—

Familiar, distorted voices pierced through my chaotic thoughts and the beeping in my ear. With one voice, my heart ached and came alive in the same beat, while the other wrapped around my soul like a soft, warm security blanket.

Before I could piece together who owned the two voices, oblivion swept in and pulled me back into the depths of darkness.

TEARS welled in the corners of my eyes as I blinked once. Twice. Finally, *finally* my body was responding.

With a quick prayer of gratitude, I focused on my unfamiliar surroundings. It was dark, wherever I was, but to the left, a sliver of light from a large window offered some visibility.

Where the hell am I?

My eyes grew heavy again, desperately wanting to close. I raised my brows, forcing my eyes to stay open, in order to learn everything I could, to make sure I was somewhere safe. The room wasn't much, tiny and square with monitors to my right which were familiar, and so was the uncomfortable, adjustable bed I was lying on. All that answered the most important question: I *was* safe. But why was I *in* a hospital bed instead of *attending to* someone who was?

A faint memory fluttered, teasing me to remember, but the answer was stashed too far in the back of my mind to make any sense of it.

His masculine, musky scent warned me he was in the room before I could find him in the darkness. That familiar aroma pulled my heart in opposite directions. One half boiled, wanting to scream for him leaving me like he did and for thinking he was welcome back, while the other half was already crying in relief because he was back—he came back for me.

"Kate?" Weston said, his deep voice cracking from the far corner of the room. Even though haziness still clouded my brain, the exhaustion in his voice was clear.

What the hell is he doing here?

Wait, where is here again?

As if he heard my internal question, he started to answer.

"You're in the hospital. Your hospital."

Finally adjusting to the lack of light, my gaze landed on where he sat, leaning forward, forearms pressed against his strong thighs. The same muscular thighs only a month ago held me close as he claimed me over and over again at my family's cabin in Colorado. Before the unthinkable happened—getting the shit beaten out of me while he was forced to watch, then dragged out by my hair until another bodyguard was able to make it all stop.

I pushed away the memory. *Focus, Kate.* So many questions, but I couldn't ask him, or wouldn't ask. No way I would give him the satisfaction of needing him again. Anyone but him.

On his own, he started giving the answers I needed.

"You were walking to the gym, unprotected because you left Joe at home. You snuck out, again." His tone was harsh, giving away anger and frustration.

My attention shifted to his hands, and I watched his fists clench and flex as he tried to rein in that temper of his. While living together last fall, we had learned so much about one another. He couldn't hide anything from me. Not anymore.

"Someone in the gym heard the gunshots and came to help before those bastards could come back and finish the job. They... he called 911, and the ambulance brought you here."

All the important questions answered, except one. *Why in the hell is he here?*

Pulling my reluctant gaze up to meet his, I poured every ounce of discomfort, pain, and disdain for him I could into it. He flinched. The Special Forces badass *flinched*.

Good.

"Get out." My burning eyes stayed locked with his.

"Kate—" he started, but his voice broke. The stronghold he normally had on his emotions cracked at the resentment in my voice and behind my eyes.

I wanted to scream, but the deep breaths needed would be too painful. "Get the hell out. Now."

He rose from his chair and paced around the room. "They shot you. Those bastards shot you in the street. If they hadn't found the dog tags I gave you...."

It was all too much, what he was saying and trying to explain. I needed sleep, my mind and body growing heavier each second I stayed awake. Plus, he wasn't listening—I wanted him gone, out of this room and out of my life.

I hated him.

I hoped he regretted leaving.

I wanted to rip his heart out like he did mine.

If he wasn't going to leave on his own, then I needed to find someone to *make* him leave. My joints and muscles trembled with each movement as I patted around the bed, attempting to locate the call button. Those dark brown eyes met mine once again, but this time I dismissed his concerned look and turned away.

He was at my bedside the next instant, wrapping his large hands around one of mine. When I turned to face him, ready to scream for him to leave me alone, all my hateful anger faded with one look. Those soulful brown eyes bored into mine, begging to let him explain, to give him another chance.

Wide-eyed, brows furrowed, his face was marred with anguish. "Please, Kate, let me explain. I—"

The door opening cut him off, bright light from the hallway shining in, momentarily blinding us both. A nurse entered and began going about her assigned duties: checking the levels of my saline bag, various monitors, and morphine drip before focusing her attention on me.

She leaned against my bedrail and peered down with a calming smile. "Dr. Wheeler, good to see you're awake. I'll let your doctor know. Do you know where you are?"

I nodded.

"Do you need anything?"

Again, my head moved up and down, gaining her full attention.

"Get him out of my room," I croaked. I needed water, my throat like sandpaper, but getting him out of sight was priority number one. Maybe then I could decipher if my pain was from being shot or from my shattered heart being too close to the one who caused the detrimental damage in the first place.

His grip on my hand weakened and slipped down my fingers as the nurse tugged on his other arm, urging him out the door, but he turned back one last time. My spiteful, hateful side wanted to revel in the heartache behind his dark eyes. It had to be a mirror image of the look I gave *him* this past Christmas before he left. Left when I needed him most, when I pleaded for him to stay. But I couldn't revel in that hurt. No, his devastated face ripped what was left of my heart and soul to shreds.

Plus, the moment he walked out the door, my stomach dropped and my heart raced from some new deep-rooted worry.

All together it made me wonder what the hell I really wanted.

Bickering male voices woke me, but I kept my eyes closed, hoping to learn more without the conversation being censored.

"Get the hell out of here." *Okay, that's Weston. What was he doing here again?*

"He's her surgeon, the one who saved her *life*, remember? He has every right to be in here. What I'm wondering is why in the hell *you're* here." *Oh, Dad sounds pissed.*

"Yeah, Weston, why are you here? Didn't you up and quit after fu—" *Damn that Austin.*

A loud noise erupted, like something hard was slammed against the wall.

"Damnit, Weston, don't kill the guy who saved her." *Ah, Eric. Hi, Eric.* "Mr. Wheeler, there is a lot of history you don't even want to know between these two and Kate. Weston is just trying to—"

Sweet Eric trying to get everyone to play nice in the sandbox.

Enough listening.

"Weston's trying to kick his lying ass, Dad," I said, my voice shakier than normal. Not knowing how long I'd been asleep this time, my eyes drifted to the window. The sun shone brightly through; must have been midday or later.

Eight wide eyes shot to me.

Tired of lying down, I pushed against the bed to sit up. I whimpered as stabbing pain throbbed in my side and shoulder.

The four men hurried to my bedside.

"Kate," Austin said as he helped me to lie back down. "You can't bend like that. Your incisions and wounds are still too fresh. I wouldn't want you to rip any of those meticulous stitches I sewed while saving your life."

I groaned, not from pain but his arrogant ass. "So what, that's all I'm going to hear from now on? How you saved my life?"

He winked and started to raise my gown. "It's a great story with an unearthly handsome surgeon as the hero."

I glared at Austin and gripped my gown to keep myself covered. "Are you serious? Do you have to do this right now, with everyone in here?" Dying on the sidewalk seemed like a missed opportunity at this point; now I had to deal with these men fussing over me.

With a cocky smirk, Austin stared Weston down as he spoke to the group. "Everyone out. You heard her."

Dad bent down to kiss my cheek and whisper how relieved he was I was okay and that he would be waiting out in the hall. He also mentioned we had a lot to discuss once Austin was done with his exam.

Not a word from Weston; he didn't even glance back as he stalked out of the room. *No, no, no, where is he going?* I hated him, but his nearness made me feel safe. I needed him to protect me. What if they came back?

Something heavy, like a chair or table being flung down the hall, rattled loudly. But it was Eric's hand gripping mine which paused those panicked thoughts.

He stood to my left, refusing to leave.

"I'm a doctor too, Kate. Plus, you've changed in front of me enough times that nothing under that gown will be a surprise."

"Fine," I grumbled, staring up at the ceiling. *This could not be more humiliating.*

As Austin inspected the wounds, he chatted about my injuries in a slight attempt to distract me. The gesture, from him, was surprising.

"You took one shot to the right shoulder, which was a through-and-through. Easy to patch up. What gave me the most trouble was this one here." His fingertips grazed across my upper abdomen. "It wasn't as clean. The bullet fragmented, shredding your spleen and nicking your stomach. You lost a lot of blood on the sidewalk while you waited for an ambulance, then more during the transport here. We've given you several transfusions since you were admitted forty-eight hours ago."

Austin laid the gown down and covered me with a blanket, tucking it gently around me.

When I finally gathered up enough courage to look at him, his eyes were on my chart. "I debated, you know, if I should pass you off to another surgeon since our last encounter was so… hostile. But I'm glad I didn't. There isn't another surgeon here who could have patched you up as fabulously as I did. I'm still pissed about that shot to the nose, even if I deserved it, but I'm not going to let you die over it."

He cleared his throat, his blue eyes meeting mine. "Plus, I didn't want to hear Eric bitch all day every day if I let you die. He really is relentless. Or have to watch my back wondering when your boy Weston would show up for payback. Now, everything looks good. If you want to sit up, have someone help you. You should be out of here in a few days." With a quick wave of my chart, he was gone, leaving Eric and me alone.

Hands on his hips, Eric stood staring out the windows. He had on hospital-issued scrubs, as if he were visiting on a quick break or stopping by before a shift. Sensing an observing gaze, he turned with a smile that didn't reach his bright green eyes.

I cocked my head to the side with furrowed brows. If I didn't know any better, I would think he just gave me his pissed smile.

Wait, that was *his pissed smile.*

"I'm so angry at you," he said as he turned back to face the windows.

My mouth gaped at his furious tone. "Excuse me? What did you just say to the woman lying in a hospital bed with two gunshot wounds?"

He turned to face me straight on and leaned his back against the window to keep his distance. "I said I'm so angry with you. You are one of the most selfish, stubborn women I've ever met. Your little antics almost got you killed."

"My antics." My lowered voice was a clear warning my patience was wearing thin.

"Yes, your antics. You left without protection. If someone were with you, they would have seen that damn car. They could have protected you. But no, Kate fucking Wheeler can't be bothered with following rules that are set up to keep her safe. You would rather disobey, get shot, and leave me broken with the fear of a future without you in it. So yes, Kate, I am beyond furious at you right now."

He stomped out the door before I could fire off a comeback.

The faster I breathed, the sharper the pain surged. I closed my eyes, started counting to ten, and focused on slowing my quick breaths. Somewhat calmer, I opened my eyes to my dad glaring.

"I'm with Eric. I can't even talk to you right now. What you did was... idiotic. Do you know what we've been through these past couple days? What your childish actions put us through? I was terrified. We all were. But now that I know you're okay, I'm pissed. At you."

"Dad—"

"You're my life, don't you realize that? You almost left me with nothing. Your actions, your stupidity, almost left me with nothing left to live for. Do you know how many people care about you and want you here with us? How could you be that selfish, Kate, to think only of yourself and your own damn independence?"

Dang, everyone was really pissed.

Weston strolled into the room, cutting Dad off before he could continue with his rant. He gripped Dad's slumped shoulder and tugged him toward the door. Dad easily complied and walked out, shaking his lowered head without another word spoken.

A few minutes later, the door clicked closed as Weston leaned against it.

The quivering in my stomach, which started and worsened those minutes I was alone, eased the moment he walked over the threshold. But I didn't want *him* to know that—hell, I didn't even want to admit it to myself.

"What do you want?" I growled as I stretched for my cup of water, just out of my limited reach.

Silently he pressed the toe of his boot against the table, sending it rolling to me, and stepped back to lean against the arm of an older green couch tucked in the corner of the room.

The water was divine, instantly soothing my rough, dry throat. Looking anywhere other than at him, my attention landed on an empty juice cup on my tray. "Who drank my apple juice?" My tone was more pouting toddler than adult woman, but the juice cup was the best part of being in the hospital. Even with the men in my life being pissed, and almost unbearable pain, that empty juice cup officially became the worst part of my recent consciousness.

"Eric."

"Of course he did."

"I think he knew how much it would piss you off and drank it out of spite. He might be the angriest of us all."

My annoyance shifted from the empty cup to him. "'Us all.' So you're mad at me too."

"I am beyond angry, Kate."

"Well, then that makes two of us," I hissed back.

His eyes narrowed, zeroing in on me. "What in the hell do you have to be mad about? You're the one who gave those bastards the opportunity they'd been waiting for."

There was no way he was that obtuse. "*Seriously*, you have to ask? Men... you're so ignorant sometimes."

He glared and started to say something back, but I'd had enough of these pissy-ass men for one afternoon. "You can leave now," I muttered and lay back on the flat pillow, closing my tired eyes.

The couch groaned and boot heels thudded back and forth against the floor. "We aren't finished here. We need to talk."

"No! I'm done talking to you, to my dad, to Eric—hell, anyone else who's pissed at me right now. I'm done. I'm especially done talking to you. You who just left. You left with nothing but that damn text. Well, guess what? I'm sorry too. I'm sorry our lives ever had to cross, I'm sorry I pushed you to break your stupid rules, and I'm especially sorry you weren't man enough to face me when you decided what was best for me. You. Just. Left."

Either from pain or the crack in my heart expanding, tears pooled behind my shut lids, trying to break free. "You don't get to tell me how mad you are, Weston. Honestly, I have no idea why you're even here. You quit, remember? You should go, and not only out of this room, but out of this hospital and out of my fucking life."

I wanted him to go, but then again, I didn't want him to leave.

His hoarse voice hinted at conflicting emotions he was trying to keep hidden. "I'm sorry, Kate. You've no idea how sorry I am. What I did... I did it thinking it was best for you. That you were better off without me."

I jumped when large hands—hands that wanted to protect and love, not control or minimize—wrapped against my cheeks. Warmth from his palms seeped into my cheeks, the smell of him so close, warming my chilled blood, spreading heat from head to toe before settling low in my stomach.

Letting out a low growl, frustrated for not having enough strength to smack his hands away on my own, I said through gritted teeth, "Get your hands off me."

His grasp faltered slightly.

Opening my eyes, I stared back at him. This close, there was no overlooking how disheveled his appearance was, which was not the norm for this clean-cut ex-military man. His hair was dirty and a mess, eyes bloodshot, and judging from the scruff along his jaw, he hadn't bothered to shave in days.

The exhausted strain in his voice matched his appearance. "I get you're pissed at me, I do, but I'm not leaving. Say what you want. Hell, you can scream at me all day every day if that makes you feel better, but I'm not going to let this happen again. Until the trial is over and the bastards who shot you are caught, I'll be here. By your side every second of every day."

A light rap on the door paused the conversation. The nurse entered but slowly backed out; murmuring quiet apologies; who knew what he thought seeing us like this.

Without shifting his attention from me, Weston instructed the nurse to come in. As the nurse scurried around the room, checking various machines and refilling my water, Weston's gaze held my own, conveying pure determination. After a minute, the nurse asked for some room, for Weston to release me so he could dispense my pain medication.

Weston brushed his soft lips against my forehead, and as he pulled away, he whispered, "Never again."

2

———————

Something was wrong.

I tried to open my eyes, but they wouldn't respond, the pain medication had taken me too far under. The sounds around me were just as they were before—the heart rate monitor, people milling about in the hall—and a new sound, that of rubber-soled shoes quietly squeaking against linoleum. With each squeak, the owner of those shoes grew closer and closer to my bedside. When the unfamiliar scent of cigarettes and body odor hit me, my pulse increased.

Something was definitely wrong. Very wrong.

Begging my body to respond, to do anything to get myself away from danger, tears began sliding out of my shut eyes. They rolled down my cheeks only to be wiped away by rough male hands.

Those hands briefly lingered before sliding away from my face and wrapping around my neck.

I'm going to die.

He's going to kill me.

Cold sweat drenched my clothes, and my body began to tremble all over. In my mind, I began screaming for help as the hand tightened around my throat, cutting off my air supply. I choked for air but it came freely, even with the hand around my neck squeezing the life from me.

The sound of someone roaring my name from somewhere in the room made the grip around my throat release by a fraction. When I heard it again, the anger and fear in the voice yelling my name so close made the hands vanish completely, and the seal on my eyes disappeared.

With a deep gasp, I flung my eyes open, finding it as dark in my room as it was locked in my mind. The weight had also been lifted from my arms, allowing me to push against my attacker as he shook my shoulders.

"Baby, it's me. I'm here. Only me. Baby, wake up. Please wake up," Weston pleaded.

Weston?

Wait, if he's here, then I must be safe. He wouldn't stand by calmly and allow someone to hurt me. I'm safe if he's here. I'm okay.

His firm but gentle grasp on my upper arms steadied me enough to take in a deep breath, giving me time to reorient with reality.

"You had a dream or something," he rasped. "You were screaming. I thought.... You're safe. I'm here. No one else, only me."

"Weston." His frantic eyes searched mine. "Not a dream, no.... Someone was in my room. They...." I pushed to sit up, to search the room, to find the person who had hurt me and make sure they weren't lingering—waiting to attack Weston, then me—but his firm grip kept me pinned to the bed.

"I've been outside this room since you kicked me out. No one has been in here except the nurses. You're safe."

Absolute trust—that was what I had with him. He wouldn't lie when it came to my safety. The anger and hurt from how things ended between us were one thing, but I still trusted him, more than anyone actually.

I shook out of his grasp with uncontrollable sobs escaping and pulled my hands to my face, only to have strong, gentle hands grasp them and guide them down to my sides.

"Kate, talk to me. What's going on?"

"I don't know. The dream, or whatever it was, was so real. I don't know if I was asleep or if I...." It was too real. I felt the man's hands, smelled his odor. It was like.... *Fucking dumbass Austin.* "Weston, grab my chart. Tell me what pain med they switched me to after the morphine drip."

A confused Weston obeyed with a press of the call button. When the nurse came by, I demanded to know what pain medication I was prescribed. She glanced at the chart and rattled off a few different types they had tried to help manage my pain.

My face heated. "I want off all pain meds. Nothing except 800mg ibuprofen."

Appalled, the nurse pushed back, telling me I had no right to discontinue, or prescribe, my own medications.

Weston chuckled at my dramatic eye roll.

"If you need Austin's approval"—her gaze shot up in surprise at the casualness of using his first name—"then call him, text him. If you won't, I will. But I'm done with pain meds. They're causing me to hallucinate that people are trying to kill me."

The nurse turned, mumbling something of discontent as she left, leaving Weston and me alone in the room once again.

"Even injured you're bossy." It was a sweet but failed attempt to break the tension in the room even as he held on to it, worse than me. His shoulders were tight, back ramrod straight, and with the deep creases in his furrowed face resembling pain more than fear, he might have been the one who needed the pain medication.

What if it wasn't the medication? What if the nightmares that started after Vail were only getting worse, to the point where I now couldn't differentiate between a dream and reality?

"I don't want to close my eyes," I admitted. He pulled my fingers from my lip, interlaced our hands, and tucked them beside me. "What if...? I can't go through that again." Recalling the sensation of those cold hands around my neck sent the pulse monitor racing.

"Stop. Stop thinking about it. I'm here. No one is going to get into this room without going through me first." He grazed the backs of his knuckles down my cheek. "What made it stop before? What brought you out of it?"

"You. I heard you, and I knew...."

"Good. Close your eyes. You have to sleep. I won't leave."

"You did before."

"Fuck, Kate. Are we really going to do this now? If you need to get it out, we can, but it's three in the fucking morning. Just close your damn eyes and go to sleep. I'll be here. I told you before, I'm not leaving again."

"Fine," I grumbled. But I believed him. When I closed my eyes, I would be safe. He wouldn't leave. Maybe, hopefully, his presence alone would be enough for me to dream of something other than the terrible night in Vail, the too-familiar nightmare of the gun pressed to my head, my hair being yanked out by the root, Weston's look—the soul-crushing look he gave me when he couldn't do anything to stop it.

He glared down at my still-open eyes, which made me narrow mine in return annoyance. "There's no way I can sleep now. Let's watch TV or something, okay?"

Long gentle strokes of his fingers brushed up and down my arm as his other hand continued to grip my own. "You know, the first time I met you, that day in the rain, I knew you were trouble."

With a covert peek, I watched him staring at nothing, looking toward—maybe through—the early morning darkness. Those featherlight fingertips relaxed me deeper and deeper with each stroke.

"I was so closed off from being on a long overseas assignment. Since before that, if I'm being honest. I didn't have any hope of.... I resented you because of what I read in the damn file. Who your family is, the perfect life you were born into, everything in your life had been easy, and I knew—without a doubt—you took all of it for granted. Then you stalked toward me in the rain, unfazed, unim-pressed by me. You gave half a glance before opening the door, completely against what you were told to do, and I knew. I knew in that moment you were going to be the one to challenge me. What I didn't know then was how much I needed it and how much I would love..."

My heavy eyes drooped and closed. I wanted to hear the story, our story, but sleep dragged me down deep, drowning out what I desperately needed to know.

AFTER TWO DAYS of being consistently awake and aware, I was ready to leave—*very* ready to leave—and the staff felt the same. The nurses were tired of my bossy ass; at least that was what they said every time they came in. It was brutal lying in bed all day when I was used to being active. Physical therapy was the only time I was allowed up, which, even though it was only a lap down the hall and back, was exhausting.

Being this weak was beyond frustrating.

Everyone visited as much as they could. Eric and my dad were done with the angry phase and now switched to doting, making me feel weaker and smaller than I already did; it made me pray for the angry phase to resurface.

Yesterday, while I was acting asleep after being *told* to take a nap, I overheard Weston and Dad discussing the terms of reinstating Weston to my full-time security detail. Weston guaranteed he would not make the same mistake again, that his full focus would be on my recovery and safety. It must have been enough to satisfy my father, as a loud clap from the two men shaking hands, settling their differences and moving forward, sounded soon after.

It was frustrating that Weston—or anyone—was still needed at this point. The day of my shooting, the trial that started this whole circus was paused. Within hours of my drive-by attack, the defendant was shanked in the neck while in his holding cell prior to closing arguments. Now there was an investigation into what happened to him, along with my shooting, and how they were connected.

When Dad updated me on the progress, he was clearly frustrated, and furious, at the delay. He'd paced around the room as he spouted off different theories for why all this had happened now. The most likely one was the leaders of the gang knew Dad would get a guilty verdict, making the defendant a liability, and with time to kill sitting in jail, it might have led to him cutting a deal and trying for a lesser sentence. So the gang sent someone in to take care of the issue. And it almost worked, except a bailiff found the poor bastard lying in the holding cell and got him help before he bled out completely. If the gang only wanted him silenced, they got what they wished for, considering he was in a coma at the county hospital from massive blood loss.

No one knew when the trial would resume, but with the assault in Vail and the one here, everyone—except me, of course—agreed continued protection was needed.

"You should get released in a few more days," Austin said as he looked over my chart. "Any more hallucinations?"

I hissed from the worn green couch where I was allowed to sit for an hour or so at a time to help keep fluid from settling in my lungs. "No, you prick."

Thankfully they'd let me put on real clothes, my sweatpants and T-shirt a much better option than the revealing gown I'd been forced to wear the first few days. Every time I'd gotten up to pee, I needed to cover my bare ass from Weston, who had stayed true to his word and hadn't left my room. His staying made it awkward as the days passed when there was nothing but silence between us, but the worst part was him showering in my en-suite bathroom. Even though he never paraded around naked or even in a towel, the image of him being completely naked, so close with only a thin door separating us, made my stomach flutter and warm each time.

My lovely shower scene daydream was interrupted by Austin's continued rambling. "Were they at least good hallucinations, like ones of me and you? Oh wait, that would be a memory, not a hallu-cination."

Weston walked into the room with two steaming cups of coffee in his hands, cutting Austin's sensual laugh short. A goodbye wave with my chart and Austin was gone.

I paused the wringing of my hands to accept the cup from Weston's outstretched hand.

"Ah, exactly what I needed. Thank you," I murmured into the disposable cup, blowing to cool the steaming dark goodness.

The clearing of someone's throat pulled my attention from the coffee I was ready to devour.

Shelly, Director of Second Chances, stood in the middle of the doorway, flowers in one hand and Starbucks in the other. "I'm sorry to interrupt, I just wanted to stop by to check up on you." She stared, not making a move into the room. Shelly was probably unsure of what to make of Weston and me in the same room without him ripped to shreds. She and Eric were who I vented to the most those weeks after Weston left; we sat in her office for hours trying to make sense of my rolling emotions.

Weston pushed from the couch and motioned for Shelly to come in and take his spot beside me. "I'll be right outside," he whispered as he grabbed the cup of coffee he'd just brought from my hand. With a polite nod to Shelly, he slipped out of the room, closing the door with a gentle click behind him.

She placed the gerber daisies—my favorite—in my lap and the venti Starbucks in my hand before she settled beside me.

"Thank you for the flowers and coffee. You really didn't have to do that. It's good to see you. I've missed you. How are things going?"

She shifted side to side, trying to get comfortable on the most uncomfortable couch ever made. "We miss you, of course, but things are okay. I wish I could say they're slowing down, but they aren't. It seems things are getting worse rather than better." Her head dipped, shoulders rounding inward. What the nonprofit accomplished on a daily basis was only a drop in the bucket as the sex industry and human trafficking became readily available and more profitable.

Seeing her look lost and defeated had me grabbing her hand and giving it a squeeze to draw her eyes back up to mine. "You're making a difference one life at a time, and that's all you can hope for. There are hundreds of women out there who have a better life because of you and what you do every day. Don't diminish that because you wish you could do more. We'll find a way to help more, to be more, but until then, you're doing all you can."

Her troubled gaze shifted from mine to the door and then back again as she opened her mouth once, twice, debating saying something but holding back each time.

"What is it?" She was nervous about something, which made me nervous. We'd always been open with each other; if she was holding something back, it had to be bad.

Shifting on the couch, she angled her knees to face me, cleared her throat, and kept her eyes on the closed door. "Yesterday, one of the girls we helped last year came back."

The blood drained from my face. *Where is she going with this?*

My anguish must have shown, because she clarified quickly. "She's doing great, has a good job and an apartment and has really... well, she's doing amazing, but that's not why she stopped by. She was watching the news one night last week and heard a voice from an interview that she recognized. Recognized from when she was *brought* here."

Thousands of women were brought over the border against their will to be sold for forced labor or worse. It had become more profitable than drugs. Unfortunately, we were seeing it more and more at Second Chances, women who were sold and forced into prostitution from human trafficking, forced to meet daily quotas, never paid, and drugged out of their minds most of the time.

"How was she able to recognize the voice? Aren't they normally drugged?"

"I asked her that too." Shelly sighed. "But she said it was something unique about his voice that jogged her memory. As soon as she heard it, her body began panicking, confirming her fears. This woman was terrified to come tell me, knowing they would hunt her down if they knew she could identify him like that."

My heart dropped into my stomach. Here I was, confined to a damn hospital bed, unable to do anything about the situation. "Are you getting her out of Dallas?"

"Yes, I reached out to a sister nonprofit in Atlanta. She left this morning."

My fingers pulled on my lip. Why was Shelly telling me all this when there was nothing I could do, no way for me to help? Unless she needed money, which I would freely give if asked.

"I hate dumping all this on you while you're in the hospital and recovering, but I was hoping... I'm telling you all this thinking maybe your father could help. Maybe prosecute him or something, or even have someone look into his business and background to see if it's true. I want you to talk to him, get his thoughts on it all and find out if it's even worth pursuing."

Right.

Without asking, I knew what his response would be: "No evidence, no way." Plus, Dad wasn't as empathetic to the growing issue as I was. No, if anyone was going to do something about it, it would have to be me. It wasn't like there was anything to lose at this point.

There was no way Shelly would give me the man's information if she knew I would take matters into my own hands. A part of me did question lying to her, but it was for the greater good, which was the new mantra on repeat in my mind as I leaned back against the couch, grabbed her hand once again, and lied to her sweet face.

By the time Shelly left, I was past exhausted. The conversation and sitting upright the entire time took more energy than I expected. Each step toward the bed was heavier and shakier than the previous one.

A deep relieved sigh passed my lips as I scooted onto the bed and lay back against the pillows. Eyes closed, I savored the wonderful feeling.

"I should have made her leave thirty minutes ago."

One eye peeked open. "She was fine. We had a lot to catch up on. Stop being such a worrywart."

The blanket at my feet lifted and stretched over me, and I couldn't help but smile. I still hated him for leaving me brokenhearted, but it was also nice having him back for the thoughtful things he did, like this one.

"You need to sleep."

"Okay, bossy pants, I'll let you win this one. Only because I happen to be tired at the moment and was already planning on taking a nap." I couldn't stop my smirk.

When he stepped away from the bed, my eyes shot open. Was he leaving me alone in this room? I needed him here for sleep to be a possibility.

My eyes frantically flitted around the room, but he wasn't at the door. Instead, he was now settled on the couch with the Kindle I gave him for Christmas in his hand.

Perfect.

The name Shelly gave me resounded over and over again as my breathing evened, deepening with each exhale.

Chase Smitson. Chase Smitson. Chase Smitson. Chase Smitson.

So, now I had the name, but what in the hell was I going to do with it?

3

————

"I'm calling your father."

Oh, he was furious. They both were. And for the first time ever, the two of them were agreeing on something.

"Kate, don't be a dumbass. You're not ready to go home." Austin leaned against the doorframe, glaring as he spoke.

With a dramatic shrug, I continued filling out the Against Medical Advice forms I requested from the nurse earlier this morning. *She* didn't seem to have a problem with me leaving. In fact, faint cheers sounded down the hall after the nurse dropped off the forms in my room.

The cheers were a bit dramatic. I wasn't that bad; I had tried to be on my best behavior—most of the time.

Weston yanked the forms off my lap and stomped across the room to stand by Austin. "Stop being so damn stubborn. You know this is a terrible idea. Why are you pushing yourself before you're ready?"

This was exactly why I was ready to go home. Being babied and worried about every fucking second was exasperating. Okay, yes, I still hurt, and yes, walking more than a few steps at a time without becoming winded and drained was challenging, but no way in hell would I tell them. Home was where I needed to be, away from everyone watching me, before all their hovering suffocated me.

Not to mention Weston had turned into a mother hen, not letting me out of his sight. He even went as far as keeping post outside the bathroom while I showered or used the restroom. It was brutal.

A few minutes alone to sort this mess out was all I needed. Basically, one minute I was recovering from a shattered heart, about to return to work after my four-week suspension for breaking Austin's nose, and the next I was here in *my* hospital recovering from gunshot wounds. And, to top it all off, the man I loved and hated in the same breath was the one who wouldn't give me space to think.

Once I was home, it could all be sorted out, I could make some sense of these roller-coaster emotions. If there was a plan, maybe this helplessness and sense of dread would fade. Plus, I needed time alone to research Chase Smitson.

All of it combined proved that even if leaving early from the hospital was against my better judgment, medically speaking, I needed to leave for my own sanity.

"Listen," I voiced as I stood but didn't move; there was no way I could make it across the room to them without assistance. "This is happening. You can call my dad, you can rip up those papers I've just spent half an hour filling out, you can call the damn Surgeon General for all I care. I. Am. Leaving."

Austin flung his hands in the air before interlacing them behind his head in complete exasperation. Damn. He was a complete jackass, but that man bun.... "I can't stop her, and neither can you." He pointed at Weston. "I'll get her meds sorted out for her release." He faced me again, shaking his head with a pointed look to my healing abdomen. "If you rip any of your stitches, don't come crying to me. I'm done saving your life. Once was enough." At the door, he glanced back to Weston. "Good luck, man."

The couch groaned beneath me as I held out a hand, giving a beckoning gesture with my fingers. "Papers. Now."

"You're insufferable." The papers smacked against my palm.

"Why are you doing this? I know you're smart enough to realize this is a bad idea," he said, shaking his head.

"I don't expect you to understand, and yes, if it were anyone else, I would tell them they were an idiot and needed to be in the hospital for a few more days. Hell, I can't even walk to the bathroom on my own without needing a break—"

"You're *not* making me feel better about this," he groaned as he sat beside me.

"So much has happened, can't you see that? I need... I need to be home. I'm comfortable at home. And I need somewhere to process all this." I gestured between us. "I can't do it with nurses, monitors, you, Eric, Dad all watching my every move, afraid I might break. I'm going to do this with or without your permission, so you better get on board quick."

He leaned forward, placing his forearms on his bouncing thighs and dropping his head as he ran his hands through his hair, which was shorter now. Almost shaved on the sides with the top longer but trimmed in a trendy style that made him look sexier somehow. Which reminded me of the almost five-week gap when we were apart. Where had he gone, stayed, and what else might have changed with him during that time? What if his feelings for me had changed, or maybe he'd moved on to someone new?

A breath caught in my now-dry throat.

"What do you need to process with me?" he asked, eyes still trained on the floor.

Reaching for the pen on the side table, I started completing the remaining pages of the AMA form.

"Well, one second you were with me, and everything was amazing. The next you were gone. I don't... I don't want to talk about it now." I handed him the stack of papers as I stood and shuffled toward the en-suite bathroom. "Now, I'm going to take a shower. Please take those to the charge nurse and have Austin sign. And when I'm done getting ready, I'm leaving."

A warm hand wrapped around my upper arm, making me pause.

"Um, Kate, there is one more thing. Your dad... you getting shot really messed with his head, so he...." Weston's eyes flicked to the ceiling, his face reddening. "He bought you a car. It will guarantee nothing will happen to you while you're in it."

"Okay, why are you acting so weird about it?"

"Because I know how you're going to feel about it."

"Now I'm nervous. What kind of car did he buy for me, Weston?"

Nothing.

"Weston, come on. I won't overreact. Promise."

"A Mercedes G550. Armored."

"A G-Wagon."

"Yes."

"What the hell? Of course he couldn't buy something less opulent. Did he say why he felt the need to drop over a *million dollars* on a damn car for me?"

"The safety part. Plus, I got the impression he never loved the idea of your Ninja."

"Oh I knew he hated it. He's always wanted me to be more... feminine. The Ninja plus the kickboxing was too much for him. Freaking Dad."

"I expected the typical Kate fireworks. You know, broken noses, knee to the crotch... the usual."

He was right. My temper normally dictated my overreaction, but right now, even though I was pissed, I didn't feel annoyance rolling beneath my skin.

"Maybe I've grown up a little in the past month. Not like you would know."

His hand slid down my arm, reluctantly pulling away. With a nod, he turned on his heel and went out the door, forms in hand.

WE HAD it out in the car. Dad and me. The SUV was ridiculous, but it was amazing inside—providing the luxury he knew I would appreciate. I was still frustrated at his overbearing intrusion when we arrived home.

Supported by Dad's arm, we followed Weston through the front door into the townhouse. Which seemed... different. When we rounded the corner to the kitchen, I cringed. Joe stood in the living room shooting me a look filled with utter disdain. But who could blame him? I *did* sneak out while he took a catnap, and I got shot in the process.

With wide, sincere eyes, I mouthed, "I'm sorry," hoping that would be enough for now. He deserved more, but it was all I could offer at the moment since getting to a barstool in the kitchen without passing out had recently climbed to the top of my priority list. But it wasn't enough. Without another glance, he walked past us to the front door.

Okay, add Joe to the pissed-at-Kate list.

I collapsed onto the stool, entirely spent from the short walk and car ride. Maybe leaving the hospital early *was* a bad idea.

Feet stomping up the stairs drew my attention to Weston, who was going up, my hospital bags in tow.

"New rules," Dad said from the opposite side of the kitchen island, drawing my gaze to him. "Let him do his job. Don't be a distraction."

"And how might I go about being a distraction, Father?"

"You know what I mean. Just keep your distance until the trial is over. He needs to focus on your safety and that's it. We can discuss what's next once all this is done."

My gaze fell to my lap. "Don't worry, Dad. He broke what we had when he left," I murmured and glanced up the stairs. My heart turned to lead, dropping to my stomach. Weston had paused on the final step, watching me with heartache burning behind his eyes.

Good. I was glad he heard me. He needed to know he might have broken me for good—he broke us, that was for sure. There was no way I would risk my heart again after... everything. My safety, yes. But nothing more.

"And, Kate, I don't want another word about the Mercedes. I bought it for you. It'll keep you safe, and that's what matters. I don't care how 'pompous' you feel in it. Now, all your meds are on the counter. Weston," my dad called, "make sure she takes them, all of them, as prescribed, and if she gives you any hell, call me."

His brief kiss grazed my cheek as he whispered, "Good night," and he turned to leave but paused. With a glance back to Weston, who was standing in the living room now, giving us space, he asked, "By the way, Weston, do you know anything about the bastard who assaulted Kate outside the hospital being found beaten within an inch of his life?"

My attention whipped to Weston, who stood shaking his head, all emotion lacking from his tense face.

"That's what I thought. Whoever it was, I would like to thank them for doing something I couldn't."

After a goodbye wave, Dad was out the door. The click of the front door sent Weston into action. He walked to the long hallway and started pressing several buttons on some new panel that had been installed.

I tilted my head at the new addition. "What's that?"

"An alarm system. They installed it while you were in the hospital." Beeping sounded through the house, signaling it was armed. "I was shocked they didn't install one after... anyway, you have one now, plus someone stationed outside the house while we're here. When we're out, Joe will wait in the house, making sure it's secure for when we return."

"Isn't that what the damn alarm is for?" I snapped.

"We aren't taking any chances."

"What's the code in case I need it?"

He turned, placing his back to me, an obvious attempt to avoid my question and demanding glare.

"What's the code, Weston?"

No answer.

"Damnit," I screamed. "Tell me the fucking code." Out of nowhere, warm tears trickled down my cheeks. When did I become so damn emotional? Throbbing in my abdomen and shoulder spiked and spread with my too-rapid breaths. Gripping the counter, I counted my breaths, focusing on making each one deeper than the last. The pain might ease a fraction if I could rein in my temper.

"I can't give you that code. It's for your own good. This way I'll know if you—"

"So I'm locked in my own home. Trapped. Just like I was in the hospital." A core-shaking sob broke free, forcing a whimper from the intense pain it raked in its path.

Strong arms tucked under my legs and shoulders and held me against his warm chest. Determined willpower kept me from giving in to the contact, from wrapping my arms around his neck and burying my face in his hard chest. With absolute gentleness, I was laid onto the long living room couch.

"This way I'll know if you try to sneak out again," he whispered by my ear. "If you promise—really promise me—you won't run, I'll give you the code. But you have to swear to me, Kate. I can't take you getting hurt again."

"Where the hell would I go, Weston?" I sniffled, opening my hazel eyes to meet the deep brown of his. He had crouched beside the couch where I lay. "Look at me. I can't even walk from the car to the kitchen without almost passing out, much less devise some grand scheme to make a run for it. Again."

A smile tugged at the corners of his lips. I had missed that almost-smile—so, so much.

"Your birthday, the date then month."

The frantic tears dried as relief flowed through me, calming my worries.

His fingers caressed the dark, thick strands of my hair. It was pure bliss. My lids grew heavy, and the idea of sleep sounded better and better. And since I was already slipping into sleep, I wasn't entirely sure if what he said next was real or a dream.

"I didn't mean to break us. I'll fix it somehow. I have to."

4

Every which way I moved, something ached, making getting comfortable nearly impossible. And to make it worse, each time I shifted to get situated, Weston was on alert, popping to the edge of the couch, ready and willing to help if I asked—which, of course, I never did.

Two weeks since the hospital and things were still uncomfortable between us. Every day, I missed those months we had pre-Vail. Before Colorado, things were simple; yes, we'd been at each other's throats most of the time, but at least then there wasn't this haunting topic of what happened in Vail—*everything* that happened. It sucked the simplicity out of our days. Now, every breath, every caught glance or long pause left us tense and uncomfortable.

The only positive from our aversion to discussing the past was the quiet time it allowed to research my new side project on Chase Smitson—Project SAND, aka Project Shitty-Ass Narcissist Dickhead. I thought, for a hot second, about looping Weston in on this endeavor but quickly concluded there was *no way in hell* he would allow me to participate while injured. So it meant I was going at this alone.

Which was fine. It would be fine.

Surely it would be fine.

As I started the research, I quickly found, unfortunately, his public relations firm had done one hell of a job. All the information about him online was what he *wanted* everyone to see. He was, without a doubt, Dallas's most eligible bachelor, which one local paper recently crowned him. He had started his own export business distributing authentic Mexican tortillas just outside San Diego in his early twenties. Since then the business had grown to offer chips, salsa, rice, and beans, and they were adding more each year.

This past year, however, marked a trademark year for the brand in launching his own tequila. So far the reviews on the tequila were not positive; most people were comparing it to other high-end tequilas, and his didn't meet the mark. Yet the revenue it brought in grew dramatically each month.

Based off Google images, he was in his early forties with golden skin, which accentuated his salt-and-pepper hair. Thin lips and a straight nose were overshadowed by almond-shaped, honey-colored eyes. He was very good-looking. Most women fell at his feet, I was sure.

As I scrolled through his online profile, one thing kept catching my eye. In each picture, he wore an impassive mask; not a single one showed him smiling. One after another, photos of him gazing at the camera, not mad or upset, simply... expressionless.

And he didn't appear to have a steady girlfriend. In each photo of him with a date, a different tall, long-legged, busty woman was on his arm, gazing at him adoringly. Meagan seemed to be more his type than me.

Then the beginnings of a plan started to form. It would be easy enough considering I'd never been able to hold back my smart mouth.

So there I had it, a vague plan, but how would I get in front of him to execute said plan? There was no listing of upcoming appearances, but many of his pictures were taken at charity and fundraising events around the city.

Maybe....

"Ugh," I groaned at the thought of what my next move was.

Weston sat up from lying on the couch, setting his Kindle aside. "What's wrong? Are you in pain? What do you need? Damnit, I told you, you should have taken those pain meds. You got off them too early."

I was still hurt by his past actions, but I still had to smile at his concerned response.

"I'm fine, thanks, nursemaid. I just... *ugh*... realized I need to reach out to an old friend. She's probably worried about me after all this."

Lie. Total lie. I hadn't talked to Courtney since high school, since I got the hell out of that batshit-crazy school and ran all the way to Austin. Courtney was the only person I knew who kept up with the Dallas charity scene; at least that was what I deciphered from her Facebook pictures.

"You need to eat. I can make us something or order in. Your call."

I scowled across the room at his hovering, which was on the verge of suffocating me. Previously a mention of my eating habits would have broken one of my preset rules. I brought it up the first day back from the hospital when he tried making me eat everything in my pantry for "healing energy." He laughed and stated since *I* chose to escape and get shot, my rules were null as part of my punishment.

"Fine. I just want cereal."

He returned my frustrated scowl. "You need to eat more than that. Now what do you want me to order?"

"I want cereal."

"No."

"Yes."

"No."

"Hate to burst your bossy bubble here, Weston, but you can't force me to eat. You've already won a battle with those awful protein shakes, so I get this one. I'll eat a respectable breakfast tomorrow, how about that?"

His eyes narrowed and his lips pursed together in a thin line, not saying a word.

With a loud groan, mostly for dramatics, I stood from the couch and shuffled to the kitchen, perching myself on one of the stools as he pulled out a bowl for me and a plate for himself.

"What are you going to eat?"

"I don't know. We have shit here. I'll tell one of the guys to run by the grocery store tomorrow. I might order a pizza or something," he grumbled into the fridge.

"Careful, it would be a shame if you lost those perfect washboard abs of yours."

Well, shit, that slipped. My face flushed warm.

A feline grin spread across his face as he turned. "*Perfect* abs, huh?"

"I'm trying to be a friend here. They really are your best feature since your personality is completely awful." My attempt to play it off was a complete disaster.

"Thanks for the warning. I'll watch my calories until we can get back to the gym." His smile lingered as he turned to the pantry.

"I want to go tomorrow."

"I don't—"

"But maybe we should find a different one, you know. Since I can't spar for a while, we could go somewhere else for a few months." I really hoped he couldn't read between the lines, but by the knowing look he was shooting me, he did. Merely the idea of being close to where the shooting had happened made panic rush over me like a wave of heat, causing my body to sweat and heart to tremble.

As I ate the cereal and he ordered a pizza, I savored the casualness of our conversation. I smiled around the spoon in my mouth. It was nice not bickering or being told what to do. I missed the comfortable us, missed being able to laugh with him and tell him anything and everything on my mind.

I nibbled on my lower lip and stared into my bowl.

But he left me and still hadn't explained. And now my side project.... Like a lead weight, my heart fell. I needed to keep my distance from him, like I promised my father, and not just for my sake but for Weston's too. If he found out what I was planning with the information Shelly gave me on Chase Smitson, he would get himself killed trying to stop me.

Yes, keeping Weston at arm's length was a good thing.

For everyone.

EACH NIGHT since waking up in that hospital room—since Christmas, really—was the same. Sometime in the night, I would be yanked awake in a terrified panic, drenched in cold sweat. I never knew if it was from pain, being alone, or whether a nightmare triggered me, but tonight seemed no different. Shutting my eyes, I took one deep breath in, one deep breath out—and repeat.

It was only a dream. I'm not on that sidewalk running for my life. No, I'm in bed. Safe.

Something moved in the corner of the room.

I froze. I couldn't think; the deep-rooted fear had me paralyzed in my bed. Over the thudding of my heart against my chest, sounds of deep breathing and light snoring carried through the darkness from the small sitting area near the window to the right of my bed. I squinted, eyes still fuzzy with sleep, at the oversized cream-colored wingback chair.

The pounding of my heart instantly ceased, and every lingering drop of fear vanished.

Weston.

He was asleep in the chair, facing me like he'd accidentally dozed off while watching over me as I slept. His chest rose and fell with each deep breath. As I watched, my breaths started to mimic his, calming me further.

He looked peaceful as he slept, arms relaxed, mouth slightly open. In the dark of the room, I wondered whether he came up to protect me or perhaps *he* needed the nearness to know I was safe for *his sake*. Either way, he was here, in my room.

I snuggled down into the pillow, turning on my side to continue watching him. Soon all the vivid memories of attacks, shootings, and hospitals drifted away, and all that remained was the image of him snoring in my bedroom chair, protecting me.

As I drifted to sleep—a peaceful sleep for once—I prayed my presence eased his fears enough that he too could sleep soundly through the night.

THE EARLY MORNING sun poured through the window, waking me earlier than I wanted, but for the first time in weeks, I wasn't exhausted. This morning my mind and body felt rested, and I couldn't help but wonder if it had everything to do with Weston's presence in my room all night.

I glanced to the chair. It was empty. The cashmere throw he'd used was folded and slung over the back, leaving no trace of his late-night intrusion.

I stretched my good arm over my head and smiled at the ceiling. At some point in the early morning hours, he'd woken, folded the blanket, and snuck downstairs to his room, believing I was none the wiser. *This* I wouldn't tease him about, not when I knew there might be another night in the near future when I would want his presence back in my room to chase away the monsters who pursued me in my dreams.

Stairs.

They were my new kryptonite. Okay, spiders were still up there on the list, but stairs were nearly as awful.

It took me five minutes to get down and would take at least ten minutes to go back up. Typically by then I was dripping with sweat, breathing hard, forcing Weston to follow me up in case I passed out. At least it was getting easier. Everything was becoming easier. With each day I was slowly healing, getting stronger.

I sat on the final step, not able to go any farther until my legs stopped trembling.

How was I ever going to get back to the old me?

"It'll take a while, but you'll be back to normal soon," Weston said from where he stared on the couch, Kindle in one hand and a cup of coffee in the other.

"How did you know—"

He gave a pointed look to the hand at my lip, which I immediately stashed under my thigh, hating that he knew my tell, and went back to reading. I frowned at his hand. The coffee looked delicious. It smelled like heaven too, but there was no way I could get to the kitchen and then to the living room without needing help.

"I'll make you some coffee. Just come sit on the couch and stop making that sad someone-stole-your-puppy look."

Pushing off the steps, I swayed, then steadied myself with a quick hand against the wall. I walked to the couch, pulling my phone from the pocket of my dark gray sweatpants.

With a swipe of my thumb, I scrolled through the missed texts from last night and this morning.

Eric: How are you feeling? I'm going to stop by sometime tomorrow and bring you food.

Eric: Is it awkward with Weston there? Every time you see him, do you want to do him?

Eric: If you do, I can relate.

Eric: I think he's gotten even hotter. How is that even possible? And that new haircut...

Eric: Helloooo... where are you, Kate?

Courtney: OMG KATEEEEEEEEEE. So glad you reached out on FB. Let's brunch soon and catch up. Want to get together in the next day or so? I'll check my calendar, but I think I'm free.

Courtney: Okay, I checked and I'm free on Sunday for brunch. Nick & Sam's, 10:00. So excited to see you and catch up on the past... 15 years.

> Eric: I didn't hear back from you. I'm worried. Coming over now.

I JOLTED on the couch when a loud knock on the front door echoed through the townhouse.

"That will be Eric," I sighed to Weston as I settled back against the couch. The full mug of delicious coffee he'd brought was on the side table within my reach.

A curt nod and he strode to the door. *All business this morning.* I laughed to myself. The alarm beeped as it deactivated, and the front door opened, then nothing. I strained to hear what was keeping the two men.

When Eric and Weston rounded the corner, I didn't know what to make of it. They were talking—really talking, like two friends catching up on old times and smiling. *Wait, Weston's smiling?* I thought only I could make that happen, but apparently Eric could too now.

I didn't understand. When had they become friends?

Eric kissed my cheek before plopping on the couch beside me. "Hey, beautiful. You look better."

"Thanks. I don't feel like I can sleep for eternity, so that's a positive sign. Plus, Weston and I have plans to work out today. That's something to look forward to."

Pivoting on the couch, Eric faced Weston. "Hey, man, do you mind giving us a minute alone?"

I snorted in amusement. There was no way in—

"Sure, just let me know when you're heading out so I can lock up after you."

My mouth gaped open. What the hell?

"Will do, W," Eric said to Weston but smiled to me.

W? When did they move to the nickname level of friendship?

Once the door to Weston's bedroom clicked closed behind him, I shot Eric a scowl, demanding answers. Fast.

"He never left your side while you were in the hospital, Kate. I had to drag him away those first couple days to get him to shower and eat. We got to know each other and... damn, he's pretty amazing, Kate."

"Don't you think I know that? I've seen him naked!" I hissed back.

"Is this awkward? You two being back together, stuck under the same roof, alone. Are any of the old feelings starting to come back?"

After a long sip of coffee, Eric grabbed my mug, took a sip of his own, and handed it back. "Yes, it's weird," I admitted. "Not sure what he makes of it all. I'm sure he approaches it as business as usual, and I'm back to only being a client."

"So you two haven't talked about what happened this past Christmas?"

"No. I'm not ready."

"Why not?"

"I don't know how I feel about it all, and"—*I'm about to do something so stupid you'd both rip me to shreds if you knew, so I'm keeping him at arm's length*—"I'm waiting until I know what I want from it all."

Eric stared through me for a few seconds before responding. "How can you not know? Yes, he broke your heart, but he's the only guy who has gotten to you like that. That means something and you know it. You two were in a shitty situation, and what happened over Christmas was awful. He didn't know how to handle it, and neither did you."

"It sounds like y'all have talked a lot about it."

He glanced away, stood from the couch, and made his way into the kitchen. While he poured his own cup of coffee, he didn't say a word. Silence lingered even after he returned.

To break the silence and set the stage for Project SAND, I said, "I think... I think I need to see who else is out there. Now I know that part of me isn't broken, maybe I should see if there's someone else out there who could be a better fit."

"You're saying date, with two gunshot wounds and a bodyguard by your side at all times. A bodyguard who...." He shook his head in what looked to be disappointment. "Not sure how many guys will look past that, Kate."

I set my mug down on the coffee table and pivoted to lie down, resting my head in his lap.

"I know, but we both know Weston will end up leaving eventually anyway. I'd be a fool to set myself up for another heartbreak by him. Let's stop talking about me. What about you? Anything new?"

His answering smile didn't reach his eyes. "Nothing new. My best friend was gunned down in the street, and it's all I can seem to focus on."

"Come on, there has to be something." In a not-so-subtle hint, I grabbed his free hand and raked his limp fingers through my hair.

"Let's see here. Meagan is Meagan. By the way, she said she would stop by soon. She's been all wrapped up in this one guy, who she won't tell me anything about. Oh, I did hear through the gossip channels at work that Austin and his fiancée split up. He had to explain how he got the broken nose, and, well...."

"Good. She deserved better than him. Glad she found out now before they were married. A broken engagement is easier than divorce."

Minutes passed. I rested and he sipped his coffee as we sat in comfortable silence, simply enjoying being with each other.

"Hey, I need to run," he whispered. "Want to do brunch or something this weekend? Maybe Weston will let you out of the house for a few hours." As he spoke, he raised my head from his lap, scooted down the couch, and tucked a pillow under my head where his lap had been.

Brunch with Eric *would* be more fun than going with Courtney, but I had to stick to the plan. No matter what.

"I wish I could, but I'm actually meeting up with a friend from high school on Sunday."

He paused halfway between the living room and kitchen and turned, his lip curled to the side with mock disgust. "I thought you hated all those girls you went to high school with. Who is this hussy you're choosing to brunch with over me?"

I smirked at the jealous tone of his voice. He was precious and my favorite person in the world. "I hated most of them, yes. Girls that age really do suck at life. But Courtney was the least sucky. I'm hoping she can introduce me to some of the eligible men around town. You know, see what else is out there, like I was saying earlier."

He pursed his lips together so hard they turned white. He wanted to say something about me dating, but instead he turned away. "I'm heading out, Weston," he shouted. "Bye, Kate. Be careful, and don't overdo it at the gym. It'll push back your recovery if you do."

"I love you." I blew a kiss from the couch as Weston reappeared.

Their whispering as they walked made me curious as to what was being discussed. It kind of irked me that they were friends, like I was being ganged up on.

When Weston returned, his expression was hard, unreadable, ratcheting up my curiosity to unhealthy levels.

"You need to eat real food, like you promised. Then we can go check out gyms." He stood over me, hands on his hips, indicating he meant business.

"Fine. I want scrambled eggs, toast, and orange juice. Oh, and will you get me more coffee while you're at it?" I raised my mug as far as I could muster with my injured shoulder and gave him a sweet, innocent smile.

"Yes, Your Majesty."

My eyes followed him into the kitchen. Keeping him at arm's length didn't mean I couldn't admire from afar, which was good since my gaze always seemed to dip to his backside, or the way his shirts stretched across his broad chest and back, or his cut, muscular arms with those teasing tattoos. What made it worse was I remembered what the man's body could do to me—what we could do to each other.

Damnit, Kate. Stop it. You have work to do.

Arm's length.

Arm's length.

Arm's length.

Arms.

Muscles.

Tattoos.

Shit. Arm's length might not be far enough.

5

———————

Snow in late February was odd, considering yesterday was a pleasant fifty degrees, but Mother Nature didn't run by our calendar. The wintry mix landed and immediately melted against the windshield of my black Mercedes as the driver weaved through the streets of uptown to meet Courtney for brunch. My outfit options were limited, considering leggings were the only pants that fit comfortably—okay, fit at all; I blamed it on swelling—and the top needed a high neckline to keep the bullet wound hidden. The snow made it easy to justify the practical black Hunter boots, making Weston happy.

The restaurant was a few miles away when I gathered up the courage to turn and say to Weston, "Today, please give Courtney and me some space while we're in there. *Please.*"

His observant gaze shifted from the street with a faint shake of his head. "Sorry, Kate. Before, it would have been debatable whether you could defend yourself until I got there. But now you're hurt and can't react as fast."

Whew. As much as I didn't want him around, I needed him close. This insistent need for his protection needed to subside and soon.

"Fine," I said, faking annoyance. "But no talking from you. Got it?"

A curt nod was all he gave before turning back to watch out the window. Which, of course, really did annoy me, so in return I gave a dramatic eye roll to his back and flipped him the bird.

His deep voice, which sounded faintly amused, rumbled against the window. "I saw that."

Damn.

Another eye roll, but this time I scrunched my face and stuck out my tongue.

"And that too."

Insufferable.

Good thing the place we were headed had booze. I needed a drink, or two. Stat.

THE RESTAURANT WAS CROWDED—THEY were known for having one of the best brunches in town—but even through the crowd I spotted Courtney quickly. She hadn't changed a bit, which said a lot in the plastic-surgery-addicted culture of Dallas. She was beautiful in her own way. Not striking like Meagan with her stunning red hair and flirty personality, no, Courtney was girl-next-door attractive with her long, straight brown hair and dark eyes. But her best feature, what made every man's head turn, was her smile. Somehow even the smallest upward curve of her lips had yours doing the same. It was a genuine smile, and as soon as I saw it, I was thankful it hadn't changed.

"Kate!" Courtney rushed to where we stood at the door, her over-the-knee wedge boots clicking loudly against the tile floor, and flung her arms around my neck. I stumbled backward from the force and would have fallen on my ass if it weren't for Weston's strong hand stabilizing me against my lower back. "I cannot believe we're doing this. It's been way too long, you know? You didn't even make it to the reunion. We all missed you—"

"Hey, Courtney," I said, cutting her off. "It's good to see you too. You look amazing, as always." Forming words into sentences was a struggle as I breathed to work through the pain caused by the impact of her hug. The edges of my vision were still dark as I said, "This is Weston, a friend from college who's in town. I hope you don't mind I brought him along."

Her brown eyes swept up and down his massive frame, devouring every edible inch. I liked Courtney, but the look she just gave him... I kind of wanted to punch her in the throat. "Oh, it's fine. Hi, Weston, I'm Courtney Reynolds." She held out a delicate hand and yelped a little when he clasped it hard with a curt but polite "Hello."

We waited a few minutes before we were led to a booth in the back by a very young, bouncy hostess who couldn't keep her eyes off Weston. Shimmying down the dark leather, I scooted in to give Weston room beside me. When the waiter arrived, Courtney ordered three mimosas, not even bothering to ask if we wanted one. This was brunch in Dallas, after all; there was a high possibility of being verbally accosted if you didn't drink on Sunday Funday.

"So, Kate, tell me everything that's been going on with you. Where are you now? I think someone at the reunion mentioned you're a doctor?"

Weston's sharp, narrow-eyed glare had me shifting uncomfortably in the booth. Earlier in the week, I made it sound as if Courtney and I had remained close, but clearly from her question, we hadn't talked in years.

"Yeah, after high school, I went to Austin for undergrad, then UT Southwestern for medical school. Now I'm here in Dallas, working at Baylor in their emergency room as one of their full-time doctors. It's been fun. Exhausting but fun. What about you? What did you end up doing after graduation?"

The conversation paused when the server appeared with the mimosas, ready to take our food orders. I caught a look of warning from Weston at the champagne flute in my hand.

One glass wouldn't hurt anything. Plus, it tasted delicious, so he could be irritated somewhere else if he was going to put a damper on my fun.

"Oh, I hung around here. I was accepted to the dance program at SMU and finished up there. Now I own a little studio in Snider Plaza, where I teach scheduled dance classes and private lessons. It's what I always wanted."

The words were right, but her tone made me think otherwise. And now, when I really looked at her, she didn't seem happy at all. Unsettledness seeped out of her. I wondered if she saw the same in me.

We talked for over two hours, catching up on the past fifteen years while Weston kept his comments to a minimum, only speaking when Courtney asked him a direct question. With all the catching up, I ran out of time to ask nonchalantly about Chase; plus, Weston was listening to every word. It was time to adjust and move forward with plan B.

"So, I was... do you maybe want to hang out one night? I noticed you still attend all those charity events, and I was hoping I could tag along to one." I kept my head down as I spoke, calculating the tip and signing the bill.

"Yes! Yes, please! They are so fun. I think I'm signed up for one next Wednesday night. I forget who it's benefiting, but anyone who is anyone will be there." She leaned forward, arching one brow high. "I have to admit it's weird, you reaching out to me randomly and now wanting to attend an event with me. What the heck are you up to, Kate Wheeler?"

Well shit.

"I... uh...." Maybe if I gave up a half-truth. "I need to meet new people, find someone to help me get over this guy I dated last year. You know, move on."

Courtney bit her quivering lip in an attempt to keep it hidden; apparently, my confession hit a familiar chord. "I get it. You have no idea how much I get it, Kate. Yes, come with me next Wednesday. With us together"—she gave an exaggerated wink with a mischievous grin—"the men won't know what hit them."

I scooted out of the booth toward Weston's outstretched hand, which I didn't take. "Thanks, sounds perfect. Text me the details."

When we reached the rotating door, she started through but I called out, making her pause. "I really am looking forward to it, Courtney."

The happy, carefree smile I remembered from high school shone back as she waggled her fingers in a goodbye wave and pushed through the doors into the wintry mix.

My smile faded as she rounded the corner out of sight. Now I had to deal with Weston, to play off what all he heard. Me calling him my friend from college, being in contact with Courtney recently—the list of lies I needed to keep up with had doubled the past few hours.

When I glanced up through my dark lashes, Weston was staring out the window, face void of emotion, watching. But a quick look down at his wide stance and tightly fisted hands showed the anger he was trying to hold at bay.

"The car will be here in five," he said, not looking down.

Fine, so no talking about it here.

I rolled my eyes and crossed my arms over my chest the best I could, staring out the door while we waited in tense silence.

Not a word was spoken the entire ride home. He had to be fuming and questioning my motives for lying to him about Courtney and lying to Courtney about who he was.

The moment Joe was out the door and the alarm was set, Weston turned, and I knew the questioning and fighting was about to start. But it didn't. No, something worse happened, worse than him yelling, questioning, or even giving the silent treatment. His eyes locked with mine, grief pouring through, before he turned to his room. His bedroom door quietly clicked closed behind him, officially shutting me out.

Fine. This was best anyway. I could deal with hurting him for now, even if my heart was in my stomach and every shred of my soul wanted to run through his door and tell him I didn't mean anything I'd said.

Yes, I would deal with his hurt and my own. I had to.

Heavy fog prevented me from seeing too far ahead, but I continued down the street toward the gym. An eerie chill enveloped me, making me aware of my doomed fate, but there was nothing I could do to stop the inevitable.

I was going to die.

Running away from the danger was the best chance of survival, but as the thought entered, my feet sank deep into the concrete, as if the solid surface had turned into quicksand, preventing me from going anywhere. I clawed at my legs, trying anything to get them free while I waited for the person slowly approaching from the adjacent alley. Each heavy step of my attacker thrummed in my skull like the tolls of a church bell. I couldn't look; I didn't want to see who would be holding the gun against my head. My head bowed, a pair of men's tennis shoes came into my line of sight, and I knew what he would say next.

Every night. Every single damn night it was the same. I knew what to expect, yet...

The cold metal of the gun pressed against my temple.

"You brought this on yourself."

No!

I bolted up in my sweat-drenched bed, my breathing short and sharp, heart trembling. The nightmare was back, haunting my dreams, but this time I wasn't comforted by Weston's presence in the bedroom chair.

Everything ached, from my pounding head down to my toes. All I wanted was sleep, but as soon as my eyes shut, I would be right back on that damn sidewalk. Dying.

Groaning, I crawled out of bed, changed into fresh clothes, and tiptoed to the stairs. Each step was difficult, forcing me to support most of my weight along the wall using my good arm as I crept down. This was a bad idea, but I was too exhausted to talk myself out of it. The only other option was taking the prescribed sleep medication, but I hadn't taken any yet—why start now?

The door to his room opened noiselessly as I pushed it wide enough to slip through before closing it behind me. I knew the layout of the room well enough that no light was needed as I carefully, quietly stepped through the dark toward the tufted love seat along the wall opposite the door. Not surprising but still frustrating, the fear and anxiety that had built since I woke alone dissipated completely when the form of his massive body, hidden under the quilt, shifted restlessly.

Stubborn, volatile, bossy, fantastic—those were words that could be used to describe me, but foolish wasn't one of them. I knew he was awake, probably from the moment I opened my door to creep down the stairs. Not even a ninja could get past him when he was on alert, but he didn't acknowledge my presence, and his breathing stayed deep and even, faking sleep—same as I had all those nights. In the soft queen-sized bed beside him was where I wanted to be, but there was still too much anger and hurt from his actions over Christmas to give in to that urge. The love seat would have to suffice for a bed, if only for a few hours. A couple hours of decent sleep were all I needed; then I could sneak back up to my own room just like he had many nights before.

The instant my head hit the decorative satin pillow, I nodded off into peaceful sleep.

His skin was as soft as I remembered, the black lines of his tattoos rough against my fingertips as I raked them up and down his arms and bare chest. This was exactly where I wanted to be; I loved being in his strong, protecting arms, breathing him in, savoring every inch where our bodies were connected. Lifting my head, I looked into his deep brown eyes, trying to piece together how we got here, but at the same time I didn't want to know how it happened, only that it had. His calloused hand wrapped around my cheek and stroked a thumb along my full lips, sending sensual chills down my spine. His touch drove me wild, making me want and need more. He pressed his lips to mine, and it was like my life was complete. Anything could happen in that moment and nothing would matter except us. Together, he and I, like it was meant to be now and forever.

"I love you, baby," he whispered, gliding his teeth along the outer rim of my ear. His lips connected with my neck, trailing soft kisses down past my

collarbone. He paused, lifting his head to look at me, and asked, "Do you love me?"

"Yes, I love you, Casey. I've never stopped loving you."

His full, genuine smile made my heart burst with joy. My love for him, that reassurance meaning so much to him.

My smile faded when his lips began grazing down my bare chest to my stomach and below.

This, this was what I missed. Being in his arms, cherished, devoured.

The aroma of coffee wafting into my room, begging me to come out and savor the deliciousness, woke me from the perfect, slightly erotic dream. But something wasn't right. This wasn't my pillow or my down comforter. Eyes closed, I moved a hand around the soft sheets and the light quilt lying over me. I opened one eye to confirm what I already knew. Yep, I was in his bed, tucked in tight. I squeezed my eyes shut again. The wonderful dream was probably due to us being so close, sleeping side by side all night.

I would never hear the end of this. The only thing I could pray for at this point was him having the decency to not bring it up like I hadn't in the past. Maybe he wouldn't—hopefully he wouldn't. I might die of embarrassment if he did, or lash out with words I didn't mean, the latter seeming most likely.

When I finally peeked out of the room, he was standing over the stove. Eggs cooking mingled with other delicious scents, making my stomach growl.

"Good morning," he said, not turning.

Maybe he was as embarrassed as I was.

"Good morning. Thank you for—"

He cut me off before I could finish. "We need to leave in an hour for your physical therapy appointment. I made you eggs and toast. You have to eat it all before we can go."

Maybe he was trying to save me from having to thank him for placing me in his bed. Or saving us both from having to acknowledge we were still broken in unique ways, to the point we needed the reassurance of the other's presence to sleep soundly through the night.

"So bossy this morning," I grumbled. "Fine, but can you fix me a cup of coffee to go with my required nourishment?"

I could have sworn there was a hint of his amused smile on his lips when he placed the plate, heaped with food, on the granite island countertop in front of me. But sadness still lingered in his eyes, and I hated myself for it. My words yesterday at brunch still caused that unhappiness to linger.

"Listen, Weston." I sighed. He set a steaming cup of coffee on the counter, then leaned against it, looking to me expectantly. "I'm sorry you had to hear all that yesterday. I really am, but you're the one who wouldn't let me have one damn second of privacy."

"Kate, it's…. You do what you need to do, okay? Don't worry about me. Your safety is more important than having to hear you lie to your friend about me."

"Is it going to bother you?"

The glare he shot me said he understood exactly what I was referring to.

"When I go to these events or out with other people, I can get someone else to shadow me if it… you know, makes you uncomfortable."

"Will me being around, knowing our history, bother you while you flirt and flaunt yourself?" he snapped, sending my temper flaring.

"No, why would it? I'll be fine. I'm the one moving on."

He stood staring, burning a hole through me.

"I'm not going to leave you. You focus on you. Don't worry about me."

"Focus on you."

"Don't worry about me."

Each word was a sharp knife slicing through my heart.

Maybe *I* wouldn't be fine.

6

The short black lace cocktail dress I ordered for the charity event was gorgeous online but even more stunning on. The delicate fabric clung to my fuller-than-normal breasts and hips, showing off the new curves I'd gained these past few weeks, which I surprisingly didn't mind; they made me feel feminine. Sexy. The dipping V of the neckline made the dress racy while the fabric around the shoulders—the main reason for buying the dress since it covered the bright pink scar—made it less suggestive, classier.

How I was going to work the zipper in the back without assistance was something I didn't think through when purchasing the beautiful dress.

My shoulder wasn't healed enough to maneuver around to raise it on my own. Hell, it took fifteen minutes just to get my bra on. In an effort to maintain the independence of dressing on my own, I stood with my back to the dresser, attempting to get the zipper to somehow hook on the edge and zip up as I squatted. Weston was the only other person in the house, and he was *exactly* who I didn't want help from. The mere thought of his fingers being close, potentially brushing against my bare skin, made my stomach tighten and the hair on my arms rise in sensual anticipation.

After ten unsuccessful and frustrating tries at the do-it-myself zipper plan, I succumbed to defeat.

With an exasperated sigh, I yelled down the stairs for help and waited on the landing right outside my door. His footsteps were slow coming up the stairs, showing his own reluctance. When his frame came into view, I cursed the damn zipper.

Damn.

He looked amazing with his hair styled, which highlighted his strong jaw and soulful brown eyes. And the suit he wore, with the light blue dress shirt slightly unbuttoned, highlighted the parts of him I admired most. Where *and when* had he bought a suit that fit him so perfectly? Everything combined, he looked… irresistible.

Why am I mad at him again?

"Kate," he said, pulling me from my lusty daze, pointing to my hands clutched against my chest, holding the dress up. "Why are you holding your dress like that?"

"I need your help." I turned so he could witness my zipper dilemma. "Can you zip me, please?"

The silence was heavy as I waited with my back to him, wondering if he would help or turn and leave. A shudder ran down my spine at the brush of his fingertips against the bare skin of my lower back, making his touch retract.

"Please, Weston. I can't do it on my own," I begged.

He sighed through clenched teeth.

The catch of the zipper sliding up was the only sound between us outside our mirrored frequent breaths. Once the zipper was secured, the floor creaked beneath his shifting weight.

"Done."

"Thank you." I turned my upper body to find him halfway down the stairs in what seemed to be a hasty retreat. "I like the suit, by the way."

Understatement of the century.

He paused and turned back to me. Running an assessing eye up and down my frame, his eyes narrowed at my bare feet. "What shoes are you going to wear?"

"A pair of snakeskin pumps. Why?"

Sighing, he looked up to the ceiling like he was praying for strength to endure this conversation. "Nothing too high. When you pass out from overdoing it, because going out has to be the worst idea you've ever had, I don't want you to be farther from the ground than necessary."

"Stop worrying. I'll take it easy. No dancing, just... mingling," I said, fluttering my hands in the air. "Besides, I have to wear heels for people to see me. It's hard being this short."

This time the raking gaze was slow and devouring. Somehow, the heat of his look was like his calloused hands were brushing against the skin beneath my dress even from several feet away. When his eyes found mine again they were slightly hooded and glazed. "Believe me, *you* could *never* go unnoticed, heels or no heels."

———

THE OLD RED Courthouse was beautifully decorated for the evening's festivities. Each floor had a different color and flower theme but somehow flowed together seamlessly. It was a popular event; limos and town cars were backed up for blocks as drivers tried their best to get the passengers to the party.

The event supported the large children's hospital located down-town. It helped raise money and awareness for children who needed treatment but whose families couldn't afford it; donations from the event would help bridge the monetary gap for many deserving families. It was a great cause and one I gladly supported with the entrance ticket purchase and various raffle prizes. Big donors had delivered on the auction items up for grabs: several weekend stays in private lake houses, long weekends at the Four Seasons with all-inclusive spa packages, and—the biggest one I found—twenty-five rounds at the Dallas Country Club. The live-auction packages were even more ostentatious with private plane experiences, European trips, and more.

As I surveyed the items listed, I began to think maybe I'd been a fool to refuse all those other event invitations the past few years. But as I started mingling about, keeping Weston in my periphery, I was reminded why I avoided them at all costs. The bullshit small talk, gossip, and fake friends—this wasn't me or anyone I ever wanted to become. If it weren't for Project SAND, which brought me here in the first place, I would grab Weston and run home to the sweats I desperately wanted to put back on.

But I couldn't, not yet. Not until I had a chance to see Chase and find a moment to interact with him.

After a few more minutes of mingling, Courtney and I snagged an empty high-top to perch ourselves against. Weston tucked into a corner with the best vantage point, staying far enough away to allow us some privacy but still close enough to get to me quickly if all hell broke loose. I greatly appreciated the small allowance of freedom, but the way he glared at all the men who passed by with that twinkle in their eyes, it was obvious this was difficult for him.

"You look gorgeous, Kate," Courtney mused as she took in the dress and paused on my pumps. "And those shoes are to die for. Where did you get them so I can go home and order them tonight?"

They were pretty great. I angled my head down with a smile and rotated a foot, admiring them myself again. "Neiman Marcus. I love your dress though. That color looks amazing on you."

Her eyes shifted to Weston. "Okay, I need to know something. What is going on with you and that guy from brunch? Why is he here with you, standing in a corner—which is so weird—and can't keep his eyes off you?"

Okay, so small talk is over. Noted.

I really didn't want to lie to her again.

"I lied," I admitted with a cringe. "He's not a friend from college. I met him last year." *Damn, I need a drink to explain this.* I tapped the shoulder of a passing waiter, requesting two glasses of champagne before turning back to an expectant Courtney. "Long story short, a case my dad was assigned last year was bad news. The people who were involved pulled me in too. So now I need private security to keep me safe at all times." I waved a hand in Weston's direction. "He's my one-man brute squad."

She glanced to Weston, who looked like he fit in with this beautiful crowd—yet didn't, as he glowered at every person who walked by—then back to me, her expression contemplative, like she was piecing it all together.

"He's the guy you're trying to get over?"

Damn, was it that obvious?

"Yes, we became... close before the shooting—"

"Shooting?" A fair hand clasped over her gaping mouth.

"Oh yeah, that. I was shot last month on my way to the gym." I gave a very unladylike shrug. It was old news at this point. I was getting over it, my body healing. Well, at least the latter was true.

She didn't move. All that had changed since the word "shooting" were her eyes, which had grown to near saucer size in disbelief.

"How... what... why didn't—"

"My dad kept it out of the news since it's tied to an active trial. Anything reported retracted my name for security reasons."

The hand at her mouth dropped to the table between us. "Wow, and I thought I had it bad."

My abdomen was throbbing from the walking and standing, and the heels didn't help. I tried to relieve some of the pressure by leaning against the table so I could focus on what Courtney was saying. "What do you mean? What's going on with you?"

Now it was her turn to look anxious. She nibbled on her lower lip while her eyes darted around the room, avoiding my questioning gaze. "Things have been better, I guess. I recently broke up with this guy, and, well, he hasn't made it very easy to get over him."

The waiter appeared and deposited two flutes of champagne on our table.

"He was great at first. We dated for almost a year. I fell in love and thought he loved me too, so I looked past some initial red flags."

The scowl Weston shot across the sea of people when I grabbed the full flute from the table had me raising the glass in his direction, toasting him and his annoyance. The glorious bubbles slid down my throat easily, filling my stomach with the instant happiness only champagne can deliver.

"What do you mean?" I asked and took another long sip.

Courtney shifted on her feet, and it had nothing to do with the four-inch heels she was wearing. Whatever made her leave her ex still haunted her.

"At first, I thought he was playing when he 'joke' criticized me. That was the first red flag. The second was his temper. He kept it reined in the first six months, but once he saw I was falling in love with him, he let it slip more and more each day. He never laid a hand on me, but I could see the writing on the wall." She paused to take a quick sip of her champagne. "The manipulation games, how everything always seemed to be my fault, were enough to push me away. The final straw was one night he wrapped my brand-new car around a tree, which he walked away from with hardly a scratch, and blamed me for the accident, claiming he was out getting inebriated because of me and my actions.

"When I broke it off, he wasn't happy about it. I think he was more upset at losing future access to my trust fund. Since then, he shows up unannounced, texts me at all hours of the night, anything to keep me from moving on."

"What a fucking tool. I'm glad you broke up with him. He better hope I never meet him."

"Me too. I wouldn't want *him* to be the person who finally pushes you over the edge to homicide."

I laughed, draining the last of my champagne. It tasted great and made me feel lighter than I had in weeks, so I flagged down the waiter again to order another round even though Courtney had barely touched hers.

Courtney shook her head, smiling down. "You know, the fierceness you have... I remember it from high school. We all knew you were one comment or look away from kicking all of our asses, no matter how tiny you were."

Daring a look, I found Weston scanning the crowd for any threats. He loved my feisty side. It might have been the champagne, or the dizziness from standing too long, but deep down I longed to put the past couple months behind us. Move on. If he would only apologize, or at least explain why he left and then felt compelled to come back.

He could be waiting for me to be ready, waiting for any indication I was ready to hear him out.

Maybe now I am.

"Well." I heaved out a deep, clearing sigh to bring my thoughts back to the conversation and grabbed the new glass of champagne. "Cheers to you leaving his sorry ass and having the strength to do it."

We smiled as our glasses clinked. As I took a long sip, the reason for this outing came through the door, shaking hands while he made his way to the middle of the room, a gaggle of women trailing behind hoping for any type of attention.

"Who's that?" I asked, angling the champagne flute in the direction of my target.

Leaning forward to get a better view, Courtney peered through the crowd and let out a low whistle when she saw who I was asking about. "You know how to pick them. That's Chase Smitson, the most eligible bachelor in Dallas right now. Not my type, but you seem to like them tall, dark, and handsome with a side of danger."

I snorted. She did have a point. He was tall, dark, and handsome with an edge. One you couldn't put your finger on, but whatever it was made him dangerously more attractive.

Unfortunately for him, I already knew what that edge consisted of. He dabbled in the business of exchanging women for money. There was a lot of dark I could handle, and potentially like, but that fatal flaw of his made me want to rip off his balls with my bare hands.

"Do you want me to introduce you?" she asked, catching my lingering stare at Chase as he made his way to the bar.

"No," I said too quickly and immediately cursed myself. "Maybe another time."

Three of Courtney's charity-circuit friends approached, cutting off our conversation, thankfully. We talked, but I made sure to keep an eye on Chase, monitoring what and how much he was drinking. A couple times our eyes connected across the room, and each time I held his gaze for two seconds before glancing away, dismissing his attention.

I had forgotten how much fun this was.

AN HOUR LATER, I made my move; his highball glass of whiskey was nearly empty, meaning he would start to the open bar soon enough. Each step I took, weaving through the crowd, made me see stars. Standing the entire time, in heels, was not ideal for my still-healing wound, but I wasn't about to ask Courtney and her friends to sit down for my sake. The champagne had dissipated some of the near-constant tension in my gut, allowing me to move through the crowd without overwhelming fear for my safety. It also helped that Weston was at my back, dutifully keeping three steps behind.

I paused at an empty high-top to wait for Chase to start for the bar, which was now a few feet from where I stood.

Weston's arm wrapped around my waist, sending warmth to pool low in my abdomen. I desperately wanted to lean into him, nuzzle his chest, and breathe in his musky, male scent.

"You're swaying. You shouldn't have had the third glass. Hell, you shouldn't have had the first two. Switch to water."

Ass. The moment of wanting him was over.

I shoved his hand from my waist, taking a step to put the table between us.

"I'm fine. One more drink and we can go."

"What are you doing here, Kate? These people, they aren't.... You're not these people."

My nostrils flared in annoyance at his judging tone. Pulling my gaze from monitoring Chase, I glared at him. "You don't get to stand here and judge me or them. You don't know who I am."

"Like hell I—"

From my periphery, Chase started toward the bar. "I'm going to get a drink," I said over my shoulder, then walked to the same bar for our predestined meet-cute.

I couldn't have timed it better. I shimmied up to the bar right before he did, putting us shoulder to shoulder, leaning against the bar.

Time to set the plan in action.

"Tequila on the rocks, please."

Chase's eyes darted my direction.

"You like tequila?" he asked, half turning, resting his arm along the top of the bar.

"I do." I kept my eyes on the bartender fixing my drink, ignoring him.

He leaned closer, offering a strong waft of his designer cologne that must have made most women weak in the knees. "You should try Bebida Del Diablo. It's good."

"I've had it. Not as good as some of the others. Terribly overpriced too."

"Ah, well, most women I've met wouldn't know what good tequila tastes like anyway."

Finally I turned my attention to him with my best unimpressed look as I said, "Well, the tequila you're talking about tastes like spring break in South Padre. Best used for body shots and miserable hangovers." I had to suppress a giggle as I turned back to the bartender, tipping him with one hand, grabbing my drink with the other.

"Wow, brutal honesty," he said, making me pause.

"Why do you care?"

Oh, I knew why he cared. If he knew how much time it took me to plan this conversation, it would boost his ego way too high.

"Because it's my line. My company distills it."

"I'm sorry." I began to walk away.

He followed.

"It's okay. You didn't know who you were talking to."

The snort I gave was a real one; he really was arrogant. Turning to face him, I was very thankful for the heels; my head was right at his shoulders which meant I only had to look up slightly to meet his amused gaze. "I wasn't apologizing for what I said. I was saying I'm sorry you have to admit to people you make that shit."

When I turned away from him, faking to get away, he wrapped his hand around my wrist. I looked down at his hand and back up, quirking a brow.

"You're very opinionated."

"Yes, yes I am."

"I haven't seen you around before. Are you new to Dallas?"

"No, I'm not new to Dallas. And if you don't let go of my wrist right now, the night will end terribly for you." I angled my head in Weston's direction, who was elbowing his way through the crowd trying to get to me.

Chase dropped my wrist, looking from me to Weston and back again. "I don't think I've ever met someone so unimpressed by me."

I shrugged and gave him a wicked smirk. "If you're looking for someone to fawn over you, then I suggest the long-legged blonde in the corner." I pointed my near-empty glass toward the opposite side of the room, drawing his attention to the woman I was referencing. "She's been eye-fucking you since we started talking."

He smiled down at me, the first one I'd seen him give all night. "Tempting but no. You're far more intriguing. Is he your boyfriend?" he asked, giving a pointed look in Weston's direction, who had backed off—slightly.

"My brother. My very overprotective brother," I lied. Like with Courtney, I didn't want my crazy life to scare him away. No, I had too much information to gain from him before that could happen.

"Let me get you another drink."

Shit. My glass was empty. When had that happened?

"I'm fine, thank you."

"One more drink. Please. I meant what I said. You're far more captivating than anyone else here. What's your name, by the way?"

I smirked, making him think he won. "A glass of red wine, please. Anything but merlot."

A look of male triumph filled his face. He took my hand, kissing the back tenderly before returning to the bar to fetch our drinks. As soon as he turned, I moved quickly through the crowd to the exit; leaving him wanting, wondering, was part of the game plan.

Before I fully slipped through the exit door, I glanced back to where he'd left me waiting. He stood right where I'd been, a drink in each hand, and when he found me through the crowd, he shook his head with a cocky smirk on his lips.

I smiled back as the door closed, cutting me off from his view.

7

———

The glass of tequila on top of the three quick glasses of champagne hit on our way home. The blurring streetlights outside the window made my alcohol-fuzzy brain spin as we sped through the downtown streets. Needing a stationary object to focus on, I smiled down at the hands in my lap and reveled in how well my devious plan was falling into place. Thinking about the entire night's events, my mind wandered to Courtney's admission about her ex-boyfriend. If we were going to be friends, maybe Weston should be prepared in case he showed up unannounced, ready to make trouble for Courtney or me.

I turned in my seat to face Weston and cleared my throat to gain his attention. Reluctantly he pulled his protective gaze from the window to see what I needed.

"Um, would you look into Courtney's ex-boyfriend for me? Not a full dossier or anything like that, but she mentioned something tonight that made me think knowing what this guy looks like might be a good idea. You know, just in case."

"Just in case of... what did she say? Did she mention he might come after you?"

"No, nothing like that. It was just... it sounds like he has a worse temper than me—don't say a word, Weston—plus a tendency for aggressive mind games."

His smirk faded into something more serious. "I'll look into him. What's his name?"

"Not sure."

"So all you're giving me to go off is he used to date your friend Courtney."

"They recently dated, so that's something. But yeah, that's all I have for you. Happy hunting."

The world dipped and tilted as I stepped out of the SUV onto the sidewalk in front of the townhome. But I caught myself on the door before falling on my ass; the last thing I needed was for Weston to notice my stumbling.

With a curt nod, Joe was out the door, and the now-familiar beeping sound of the alarm being activated echoed through the townhouse. A loud grumble erupted from my stomach, reminding me I hadn't eaten anything since lunch, another reason those drinks went straight to my head.

Weston slammed the control panel door shut and strode to the kitchen. He looked pissed.

"I'll make you something to eat," he grumbled.

Not sure why he was frustrated; he knew beforehand what would happen tonight. I followed him into the kitchen, pressing against the wall for stability, and stopped beside him. "I can do it on my own. I'm not helpless, you know."

He whipped around, sending me staggering backward, my back arched over the edge of the countertop, fighting for more distance from his fuming face only a few inches from mine. His cheeks were flushed, nostrils flaring with each deep breath he took.

"For fuck's sake, Kate, I know. I know you can do it on your own. Can't it be enough that I want to do it, that I want to do what I can while you heal from... from something that wouldn't have happened if I would have been there with you?"

Between the alcohol and his agony-laced words, all I could do was blink.

"Now, please go sit down before you topple over. Actually, let's fix this right now." He slipped his hands under my arms, carefully lifting me, and sat me on the cool granite countertop. His rough hands skimmed down my arms, my waist, my thighs, making my heartbeat pound in my ears, pushing aside all other sounds and making the throbbing between my legs almost unbearable.

"I've been wanting to take these off all night," Weston murmured. He skimmed his hands down my calf and roughly grasped my ankle only to pull off one gorgeous pump, repeating with the other, letting both clatter to the tile.

A deep groan escaped as he wrapped both hands around my right foot, then left, gently massaging the arch with the soft, demanding touch that made me remember how he had once done the same between my legs.

Every muscle in his arms and chest was strung tight as he dropped my foot and braced his hands on either side of me, grasping the edge of the counter with a white-knuckled grip. My head was just fuzzy enough that if he made a move, I wouldn't stop him—how it would affect Project SAND was the last thing on my mind. The thought of his soft, full lips pressed to mine had me licking my own in anticipation. His eyes followed the movement, shifting his frustrated demeanor to a more predatory focus. On me.

His eyes were still locked on my lips when he asked, "Did you have fun tonight?"

While he was busy memorizing my lips, my gaze was fixed on the bit of ink-covered chest peeking through his slightly unbuttoned shirt. Every part of me, certain parts more so, wanted to reach out and undo the remaining buttons, then push his jacket and shirt off his shoulders to the floor to give me a full view of the strong chest and arms I knew were hiding under all those clothes.

Wait, did he ask a question?

"Yes, I did. Did you?"

Reluctantly his skeptical gaze pulled away from my lips.

"No, Kate, I didn't enjoy having a front-row seat to every guy there watching you, wanting you. And knowing they all wanted to be the one to take that dress off you tonight."

With the alcohol as my reassurance, I slide my bare toes up and down the inseam of his suit slacks, inching a little farther north with each pass. "What about you, Casey? Were you wanting the same thing?"

He hung his head between his tense shoulders to study each inch I touched.

"Kate, you're drunk," he said, his voice guttural. "And I... we...." He trailed off, clearly not knowing how to finish the sentence.

Neither did I.

The deep throbbing between my legs tried to persuade me to beg him to touch me—anywhere—but deep down I knew it would be a bad idea for several reasons. For one, there was the charade with Chase I needed to keep up. I needed to make Weston believe I was into Chase, that I wanted to pursue other men while I sorted out my feelings for him. Second, I still hadn't fully moved on from his abrupt departure on Christmas Day, and I couldn't move on until he explained.

When he left that day, without the decency of a goodbye, it dented my heart in a way I wasn't sure would ever be repaired, especially by him. I still wanted him, that was clear, and maybe I even loved him, but could I trust him with my heart? If I did put my whole self in his hands and he left again, it might ruin me forever.

Just thinking about it made me frustrated at our screwed-up situation.

"Yeah I know. You're right, I'm drunk. It doesn't mean anything."

He winced at my words like I'd slapped him. Sliding off the counter, I started toward the fridge, but he stepped in front, blocking my path.

"Do you really mean that? You *clearly* want me right now. Does it not mean anything? And while we're at it, did you really mean what you said to Eric and to Courtney? Are you moving on?"

No.

Hell no.

He didn't get to ask that question. He was the one who left.

Words that had been bubbling near the surface since I saw him in that damn hospital room erupted.

"Screw you, Weston." I pushed a long finger into his chest again and again. "You don't get to ask me that. You're the one who fucking left, okay?" I gripped the side of the counter as the room swayed.

"What we had... what we had even before Vail meant something to me. Us together meant everything. Did you not see that? Nothing will ever compare to how you make me feel, how you *made* me feel about myself. Then, one day, you took it all away. You just left when I begged you not to, pleaded with you to let us figure it out together. I don't know if I will ever get over that, Casey. You broke something in me I wasn't even aware could be broken. You did that. Not me. So you don't get to stand here and ask me if I'm moving on when, if I had it my way...." I shook my head, not knowing how to finish as utter exhaustion slammed through me. I turned to head upstairs, hunger now the last thing on my mind, too tired to continue with this conversation.

A gentle hand wrapped around my wrist, urging me to wait.

"If you had your way, what?"

I stared at the floor, hiding my reddening cheeks as I rattled off the foolish hopes I'd been clinging to.

"If I had it my way, we wouldn't have those weeks we were apart. If it were up to me, we wouldn't be sneaking into each other's room at night because we would already be there, wrapped around each other, chasing away each other's fears. But it's not up to me. Not anymore."

His arms enveloped me, crushing me to his hard chest, before my final word. And before I understood what was happening, my arms wrapped around his back, squeezing, holding me tighter against him.

This was not in my plan, but standing here stealing the warmth from his body, I couldn't pull away. Maybe somewhere deep down I knew I would give him another chance if he dared to take it. He would have to be the one to take the risk, to take us back into a relationship, because now he knew what was on the table—what I was risking if he walked away again.

My fragile heart.

A warm breath brushed against my neck as he buried his face in my hair, breathing in every ounce of my scent.

"I didn't know how to handle what happened that night. One minute you were the best thing that ever happened to me, then... then the next... that bastard... he could have easily taken you away from all of us. I already knew I didn't deserve you, but that night made me realize not only did I not deserve you, but I was poison for your life. I let you down. I couldn't even fucking face myself, much less you. I didn't want to be around when you realized it was all my fault too."

"Men are such illogical idiots." I sniffled, nuzzling my face against his hard stomach. "What made you come back?"

"It took me a while, but I sorted everything out, realized what I had done, what I had walked away from. I was on my way back to Dallas, ready to tell you everything, to apologize and beg you to hear me out, when I got the call that some woman wearing dog tags with my information on them was en route to the hospital. I wanted to apologize, to say I was sorry—for everything."

"You saying you're sorry isn't going to make up for the way you walked out or give back the weeks I could barely function from missing you. I deserve more than a simple apology."

Cool air brushed against my chest as he pulled back. His brown eyes pleaded with my hazel ones, begged me to tell him what needed to be done to prove this was still a possibility, that we could come back from his stupidity.

His mouth opened, but then his head snapped to the front door and a strong arm instinctively tucked me behind him before he could say another word.

8

I held a breath, straining my ears to be as keen as his.

Nothing. I heard nothing except the quiet hum of the refrigerator.

I strained again, listening, waiting, but the townhouse remained quiet.

Something had put Weston on high alert, but I had no clue as to what.

"What is it?" I whispered from behind his back. The idea of being tucked behind someone who thought I was too weak to protect myself would have sent me over the edge pre-shooting. But now I *was* the weak person I never wanted to be. Plus, I did recently lose an organ, so I would stay safely tucked behind him without a single complaint.

"I don't know. Something feels *off*."

Just as he said it, a pounding knock from the front door echoed through the house.

I watched with aroused fascination as he pulled a gun from the shoulder holster hidden beneath his suit jacket.

Yep, definitely a little drunk when all I could focus on was how sexy he was holding the gun instead of focusing on *why* he now had a gun in his hand.

In a daze brought on by tequila, champagne, and the visual display of masculinity, I barely registered enough to move my feet when Weston pulled me toward his room.

"Kate, snap out of it."

Another pounding, demanding knock boomed through the house.

After he pushed me into his room, Weston pulled a second gun from his holster, cocked it, and placed it in my waiting palm.

"Lock the door behind me. Do not come out until I tell you it's safe. Do you understand?" He started toward the front door, paused, then turned and tossed his phone onto the bed. "Just in case. Now close the door behind me, Kate."

Right.

It had been a long time since he'd used that commanding tone toward me.

I closed the door most of the way, keeping it open a sliver. Sweat beaded on my forehead and upper lip as I peered through the crack, waiting. Who would show up at this hour? Would someone who came here to kill me really knock on the door? But then who—

The corner of the hallway blocked my line of sight, but I could make out mumbled words being exchanged through the front door.

After a minute, a beep signaling the alarm had been disabled chirped in my ears. Whoever it was must not have been a threat.

Okay, now I really wanted to know.

Since the person didn't pose a risk, Weston wouldn't mind if I ventured out of the room for a quick peek down the hall to see who was at my door. Right? Right.

Gun in hand, I padded to the opposite wall and peered around the corner but still couldn't get a clear view of the door. I needed a better vantage point.

This location, however, was great for eavesdropping.

"What are you doing here?" Weston demanded.

"I need to talk to you," said the stranger, his voice full of arrogance and hostility.

"I didn't know you were in town. I can't believe you would show up here unannounced. I'm fucking working."

"You made her sound cool. I'm sure she won't mind."

Weston's open palm smacking against the doorframe sent my head snapping back around the corner to safety. Whoever this person was could get under his skin—fast.

Weston's deep, annoyed sigh poured down the hall. Even without a visual I knew he was running his hands through his hair in visible frustration.

"Are you in trouble again?"

"No. I'm not always in trouble, Casey, even though you seem to think I'm some kind of fuckup who can't do anything right."

"I don't.... Listen, you need to go. I'll call you tomorrow."

"Typical Casey, putting his work and duty before family."

Family?

I forgot myself, and Weston's very clear instructions, and started for the front door. Weston hadn't noticed my approach behind him, too focused on the male in front of him, but the mystery man did.

He smiled, which I noted looked vaguely familiar, when our eyes locked under the arm Weston had raised to hold the door ajar, preventing the man from entering the townhouse.

"Hi, Kate," he said, pulling a hand from the front pocket of his worn jeans to offer a tentative wave. "Sexy dress."

I had to hand it to Weston, he'd learned to expect me to defy his demands. His entire back tensed, but he didn't turn to reprimand me. My eyes widened, mouth gaping as his strong arm dropped from the edge of the door and motioned for the man to come inside.

Now the earlier conversation would go unresolved. Currently all I wanted to discuss was who in the hell this person was.

The silence grew as we walked deeper into the house, pausing in the kitchen. The stranger turned, his grin widening as he ran an appreciative eye up and down my body. Weston gave a low growl and stepped closer to my side.

"I'm Ryan, by the way. Casey's brother," he said, still staring.

"Kate Wheeler." I stepped around Weston and handed him his gun before shaking Ryan's hand. "Nice to meet you."

"What are you doing here?" Weston asked, rubbing the bridge of his nose with his thumb and forefinger.

"I need a place to stay, only for a few days, and was hoping I could crash at your place."

Weston's eyes danced between me and his brother, who was now getting comfortable on one of the kitchen stools.

"I.... My lease was up last fall."

"So you're homeless," Ryan deadpanned.

Weston rolled his eyes. "I'm not homeless. I've been staying here since and haven't needed to find a new place."

I asked the next question. "Then where is all your stuff?"

He ran both hands through the long section of his hair, disturbing the gel that held it in place. It seemed my questioning exasperated him as much as his brother's did.

"I have a garage where I store my truck during long assignments, so I moved it all there."

No idea why not knowing all this hurt, why I found out simply because his brother decided to show up unannounced, but it did.

"When did you move it?" I asked, shifting closer to Ryan, conveying which side of the current argument I was on.

"Last fall when I went to sort out his"—he waved a hand in Ryan's direction—"arrest with the DEA—"

Ryan interrupted, holding both hands up, palms out. "Misunderstanding with the DEA. Charges were never filed."

I pursed my lips to hide my smile at Weston's return growl. "*That* only took a few days. When I got back to Dallas, I wasn't in a rush, so I took a few days off and moved it all myself."

Huh, why wouldn't he have...? Oh... because he was pissed at me for leaving Joe behind that one day when I snuck out for the gym.

Dick.

Fucking prick.

Wait a second. If he didn't have a place to live, where was he staying those weeks we were apart before the shooting?

"Weston, if you're homeless—"

"Damnit, you two, I'm not homeless."

"Fine," I continued. "If you're between living arrangements, then where were you staying those weeks between Christmas and the shooting?"

He stared as awkward silence filled the room. Even Ryan knew now wasn't the time to make a snide comment. Did he not want to tell me in front of his brother, or did he not want me to know at all?

I hissed as Ryan interrupted the silent standoff; now I would have to wait to find out.

"As much fun as this is"—Ryan waved a hand between Weston and me—"that leaves me without a place to crash while I'm in Dallas." His attention shifted from his brother back to me. Sliding off the stool, he stood in front of me, so close I took a cautious step back. "Would you mind if I stayed for a few days? I promise I won't be too much trouble—"

Weston's loud, sarcastic laugh from behind made me jump. "I've never known you to *not* be trouble for one thing, and two, you're not staying here. I'm working. This isn't going to be some—"

"It's fine, he can stay here for a few days," I said, cutting Weston off. Yes, it would be an inconvenience, but maybe Ryan could distract Weston while I retrieved what I needed from Chase. "Under one condition." I took a step toward Ryan, forcing me to angle my head up to meet his twinkling gaze. "Don't be a pain in my ass."

His eyebrows shot up. Glancing at Weston, he said, "She's a feisty little thing, isn't she?"

"You have no idea," Weston grumbled, drawing my attention back to him. He looked exhausted as he rubbed his eyes with the heels of his palms. "Kate, why don't you go upstairs and change? I need to talk to my brother alone for a minute."

"Fine, but—" *I need help getting out of this dress, remember? You helped me get in it, now help me get out of it.* "—I need your help."

Ryan's hand wrapped around mine in an attempt to pull me

toward him. "I would be more than happy to help you out of that dress, Kate. You know, from the moment I saw it, I thought it would look much better on the floor."

Before I could retort with a smart-ass remark, Weston had me scooped up in his arms and was striding toward the stairs.

"Shut the fuck up, Ryan. I'll be down in a second to deal with you."

I smiled back at Ryan, happy that Weston's annoyance was directed at someone else for the moment. With an exaggerated eye roll, Ryan walked to the fridge, and before he was out of my line of sight, I watched him pull out a beer and twist the top off.

"Maybe I should have said no," I mused once we were in my room and my feet met soft carpet.

"You've been on a long streak of making piss-poor decisions, why stop now?" he grumbled as he gripped my shoulders to turn my back to him. There was nothing intimate in the way he hastily unzipped my dress, his mind on the issue downstairs instead of the fact that he was undressing me, which didn't sit well.

He was almost to the door when I called out, "It took me fifteen minutes to get this bra on, and it'll take me another fifteen to get it off. Can you do it for me?" I dared a glance over my shoulder. He stood unmoving from his spot in front of the door, a hand still perched on the knob. "Please? My shoulder really hurts."

Yep, still tipsy.

He still didn't move.

Maybe he didn't hear me.

"Weston?"

"Kate."

"Please."

His shoulders slumped like he'd just lost some internal battle with himself. The floor creaked under his weight as he approached, his focus solely on my back as if he told himself he would do this one task, then leave and not look back.

The tips of his fingers skimmed down my spine, sending a shudder through my entire body, stopping at my bra clasp. With a flick, the strap released, but his fingers remained, softly brushing along my bare skin. Almost as if he were unable to pull them away on his own.

"Thanks," I whispered and turned to face him, clutching my dress and bra tightly against my chest so neither would fall to the floor.

His face was drawn, eyes looking... conflicted. But conflicted about what, I didn't know.

"I need to go deal with my brother," he murmured. "Change and come back down. I'll make you something to eat."

"I can make it myself."

"For fuck's sake, Kate, are we really going to do this again?" he growled, taking a step away, then another.

"Fine. I'll be down in a few minutes."

A faint smirk pulled at the corners of his lips—he had to be the only man I knew who loved my sass, enjoyed the challenge even— before he turned and headed back downstairs, shutting the door behind him.

I stared at the closed door, holding my breath, wishing he would come back.

TWENTY MINUTES LATER, their heated conversation died as I slowly descended the stairs.

"Don't stop on my account," I said, making my way to the fridge.

Water. I really needed water. And maybe some Excedrin for preventative maintenance. All the meds were stored in the cabinet above the stove, well out of my normal reach.

"Need some help?" Ryan asked as he pulled another beer from the fridge.

I hitched my chin up to the cabinet. "Excedrin, up there."

He reached up and began rummaging through it. "Why do you have a full bottle of hydrocodone up here?" He handed me the bottle of Excedrin with one hand and inspected the hydrocodone with the other.

"Because she was shot," Weston answered from behind me, standing so close I could feel annoyance radiating off him. "Put it back, Ryan."

With a nonchalant shrug, Ryan tucked the medicine back into the cabinet and closed the door like it was nothing. But the shine in his eyes when he saw how full the bottle was told me something different. I'd seen enough addicts and dealers roll through the emergency room to know that look and identify it quickly.

"What do you want to eat?" Weston broke in as he heaped spoonfuls of coffee grounds into the paper filter.

Him knowing I would want coffee right now, not caring that it was past midnight, made me want to hug him for the thoughtfulness. The only thing that stopped me was his brother studying every interaction between us from his perch on the stool.

Something warm sounded good, to shake the chill that hadn't left since the car ride home.

With the sappiest smile I could muster, I said, "Eggs, toast, and bacon. Oh, and waffles."

"Protector and shorthand cook. Ah how the mighty Casey has fallen," Ryan mused into the beer bottle at his lips.

My blood simmered in my veins, which felt... distantly familiar.

"Still a better man than you," I snipped while staring him down, challenging his aggravated gaze.

The bottle in Ryan's hand thudded against the counter. "Based on your vast knowledge of me?"

"Based off the fact that in less than an hour with you, not only would I not trust you with that cabinet full of narcotics, but I would also need a full can of mace and a loaded gun before being left alone with you."

A serpentine smile grew on his face, stretching his attractive features. He glanced to Weston, then back to me. "Oh, we are going to have fun these next few days."

"Ryan, stop instigating," Weston commanded. "And, Kate, he's trying to get under your skin—it's his only skill. Don't let him." When he turned to face me, his cheeks were flushed red. Ryan's comment must have hit home. "I'm not making you a full damn breakfast. What else do you want?"

"Fine." I sighed, feigning annoyance. "A grilled cheese will work."

"Done. Now please go sit on the couch. You've been standing too much tonight, and you need to rest. I'll bring a cup of coffee when it's done."

Faking an obedient bow, I swiped my phone off the counter and plopped down on the couch. As much as I hated admitting it, he was right; my side was killing me, and my feet were throbbing from being shoved into those tiny torture chambers.

It was past midnight. No idea if Eric was even awake, but I had to update him on the night. He was going to freak out.

***

Me: Hey, you up?

Me: Wake up. Weston's brother showed up tonight.

Me: He's an ass. Attractive but not as hot as W.

Eric: Tell me everything.

Me: Hi

Eric: Spill it, lady.

Me: So tonight, after the charity thing, W and I were home fighting, and there was a knock at the door and it was Ryan, his brother.

Eric: What were you and Weston fighting about?

Me: That's what you're taking away from all this?

Me: I was kind of drunk and opened up about us. Then he did too but we were cut off by his brother. Who is standing in my kitchen right now because he needs a place to stay, and Weston is between living arrangements, so that leaves him staying here for a few days.

Eric: Weston is homeless?

Me: Odd, right?

Eric: This could get awkward quick. You said attractive, describe.

Me: Tall, as tall as W. Short dark hair, light brown eyes. Not as bulky as W, leaner, sporty-like. But there is something that makes him look, I don't know, restless, angry even. Can't put my finger on it. But he knows how to push W's buttons.

Eric: Again, this could get awkward. Siblings are hard to understand when you're an only child. Don't get in the middle of their fights. Do not insult his brother, even if Weston just said the exact same thing. And more than anything… do not trust him.

Me: WHAT.

Eric: Trust me.

Me: Okay.

Eric: You were drunk?

Me: Slightly overly buzzed.

Eric: Sounds an awful lot like drunk.

Me: I'm fine.

Eric: You shouldn't be drinking, and if I know you, you were drunk wearing five-inch heels. I'll come check on you tomorrow.

Me: I'm fine.

Eric: Be excited to see me.

Me: Yay.

Eric: See you tomorrow.

Me: I love you.

Eric: I know.

9

I *don't want to die.*
Not like this.
Not here.

I bolted awake once again from the same damn nightmare. Soaked in cold sweat, my body trembling, I took a quiet minute to wrap my irrational thoughts around what was reality and what wasn't.

Deep breath in. I'm safe.
Deep breath out. I survived.
My bed. My home. I'm safe.

Even with the reassuring chant, my heart raced on, and I knew I wouldn't settle down until I saw him, because if he was near, then I was safe. The sheets clung to my damp skin as I scooted across them to climb down. I changed into fresh dry clothes and snuck down the stairs.

Ryan was asleep on the makeshift bed Weston created on the living room couch, making me tiptoe the last few steps to his door. Like the other nights I had snuck into his room—unfortunately, this had become a bad habit—the bedroom door opened silently as I slipped through and shuffled to the love seat, where I would fall asleep but not wake up. Each time I'd snuck into his room for comfort, I fell asleep on the love seat but woke up in his bed, having been carried there at some point in the night to sleep more comfortably.

"Get in the damn bed," Weston said groggily, his deep voice shattering the silence, sending my shin slamming into the side of the love seat as I jumped three feet.

Thankfully he couldn't see my tentative smile. Me in bed with him, knowing I was in bed with him, was a bad idea, but technically I only needed to keep him at arm's length, I reminded myself, as I slipped into the cool sheets on the opposite side of the bed. Far away from him and his strong arms that I desperately wanted wrapped around my waist, holding me against him.

I lay awake staring at the ceiling for several minutes, no longer tired. There was an invisible tug between us, urging me to scoot closer and closer until we were in each other's arms.

"I gave your father my word," he said into the darkness, startling me, "that nothing would happen between us." The bed shifted under his weight as he rolled over in the dark. "I promised I wouldn't be distracted by you again, and I know you did too. But know this, Kate: I'm not going to sit back and let you move on without a fight. When the trial is over, I want you. I'm not going to lose you again."

Holy shit.

Arm's length.

He wants to fight for me.

Arm's length.

I want to let him.

What the hell am I doing?

This could get ugly quick.

This will *get ugly quick.*

FUCK, everything burned and ached.

My feet were still tender from standing all night in those gorgeous shoes, and my abdomen, hell, I could barely get any air into my lungs through the pain. With a muffled whimper, I rolled onto my back and splayed my arms across the empty bed, my fingers dancing along the space where he should have been. I had hoped he would wake up beside me since he invited me into his bed last night, but he wasn't there. The space in the queen bed where he'd been was cold to my touch. Maybe he didn't end up sleeping beside me after all.

Fine, that was good. I had enough shit to deal with.

I sucked in a breath to clamp down a moan from the aching in my abdomen as I leaned against the stiff headboard. Two minutes. I would give myself two minutes to gather up the courage to crawl out of bed, up the stairs, shower—ugh it even *sounded* exhausting. To top it off, my phone was upstairs, so no way to text Weston to ask for help, if he would even give it. Fighting to win me back or not, he wouldn't miss the opportunity to gloat, saying he told me so.

The only option for making it out of this room was on my own.

At first, I believed pulling my legs out of the covers and planting them on the floor would be the worst of it, but each step I took toward the door was like walking on a bed of nails. Before opening the bedroom door, I did a quick once-over to make sure my pajamas covered enough to be presentable; Ryan was out there, after all.

I cringed. Of course the door would squeak *now*.

Ryan was staring as I stepped out, wearing a knowing smirk while he drank his coffee. "Good morning, Kate. Isn't your room upstairs?"

In the kitchen, Weston had his back to me. His bare back. That strong, tattooed back.

He never walks around the house without a shirt. What's going...
Oh! He plays dirty.

Flipping Ryan the bird, I wobbled toward the stairs.

Halfway there, a hand grabbed my wrist, pulling my arm around a lean waist, and a small arm hooked under my shoulder. Blush seeped into my cheeks when I looked up and saw Ryan smiling. We were halfway up the stairs before he said anything.

"I'd do anything to not prove him right too." He winked and continued to haul me up step by step. Once we hit the landing, he unhooked my arm and trotted back down the stairs without a look back.

He was a jerk, yes, but maybe having Ryan around would prove to be entertaining, helpful even.

The shower's near-scalding water helped ease some soreness from my abdomen and greatly aided my feeble mental state from *all* the previous night's activities. Standing, mingling, pretending to care about vapid stories, avoiding Weston's gaze, making sure Chase and I met... plus Weston's declaration to fight for me. I was beyond exhausted.

The only thing on the agenda today was lying on the couch and watching trashy TV.

Even though the majority of the pain had subsided, my abdomen still ached enough that I needed a short break on the last stair before venturing into the living room was physically feasible.

"You okay?" Weston asked, glancing up from his laptop, not reading for once. Ryan was nowhere to be seen.

"I'm fine, just need a minute," I said, leaning back on the stairs. If I could stay here all day with no movement, no conversations, only peace and quiet, I would be perfectly happy.

I leapt from the stair, gasping and grabbing at my splitting side, at a loud knock on the door. Weston's hand was gentle on my shoulder, urging me back down. I hadn't heard him approach because of his stealth skills or from the sheer exhaustion.

"I'm sure it's nothing," he whispered, stroking my hair.

I immediately missed his comforting touch when he started toward the door, gun in hand.

The familiar voice of my favorite deliveryman floated down the hall. Okay, it was nothing. No need to flip out.

Wanting to see what he was delivering, I pushed off the step and started toward the front door, but halfway I was stopped by Weston already walking back, carrying a large gift basket. The cellophane wrapping crunched with each step he took.

"What in the hell is that?" I asked, rising to my tippy toes to steal a glimpse of what was in the basket as he walked by.

He set the basket on the island and peered in with both brows raised. "I have no idea. Looks like tequila."

Interesting.

Cellophane crinkled as I untied the black ribbon around the top. My smile grew as the packaging unfolded. I shouldn't have been excited, but I really wasn't excited about the gift; I *was* thrilled my plan had worked. And fast. The detailed effort he'd put into finding my name and address meant everything had gone right the night before.

Weston flicked a curious gaze between me and the now-unwrapped gift. It wasn't a simple gift. No, it was a full selection of adult debauchery. Three bottles of Bebida Del Diablo lay in the fake straw surrounded by limes, multiple cans of colored salts, and, of course, two shot glasses.

My smile grew wider, making my eyes crinkle at the edges.

A light knock rapped at the door as I reached for a card tucked behind a bottle of tequila.

Weston started toward the door, mumbling something I didn't understand, clearly frustrated by another visitor. Eric's voice echoed down the hall. I turned from the gift, forgetting the note, to greet him.

"Wow, what is that, and who sent it?" Eric asked, eyeing the package in front of me.

I reached out, beckoning him for a hug before I would answer. Snuggled in his arms, I mumbled a good morning and nuzzled his soft chest. Even though he was in street clothes, he still smelled like the hospital, making my gut tremble at the recent helpless, pain-riddled memories it conjured.

With a tight squeeze, he released me, turning his attention to the coffeemaker, which had a full fresh pot courtesy of Weston. "So, who's the ridiculous gift from?"

"I was about to open the note when you came in. Make me a cup too, please." I hitched my chin toward the coffeemaker. Coffee made everything better; maybe it would clear the lingering fog that clouded my thoughts, help make the events from last night a bit sharper.

Pulling the card from the gift once again, I examined the expensive, thick card stock and embossed monogram before sliding open the seal. My cheeks reddened at the inscription.

Here's the tequila. Now about those body shots.... We can get creative on where the salt goes. I have some suggestions on where I'd love to lick.

Oh, he was clever. Not even a signature at the bottom, simply his address, as if he expected me to show up wearing nothing, carrying the bottles of tequila in each hand. The cocky bastard knew I would know who the gift was from, and if I didn't know about his other life, this type of cat and mouse game would pull me deeper into his façade.

Eric set a mug of coffee on the counter and ripped the card from my grappling fingers. "What are you smirking about?"

His mouth gaped at the inscription, and a hint of blush dusted his cheeks too. "WTF, Kate! Who sent this? And why in the hell is he talking about body shots?"

"I... uh...."

Weston reached over the island and grabbed the card from Eric's hand.

Shit.

Weston's lips pursed together until they lacked any trace of color as he read the card.

"A guy I met last night. This is his tequila. I... we... exchanged words about it over a drink," I said with a shrug.

Frustration, annoyance, disappointment, agony all swirled behind Weston's pointed look.

Eric's stare was more dumbfounded. "That doesn't make sense. Some guy you exchanged words with at a charity function doesn't just send you a note like this."

I took a step back from the two scowling men, prepared to run once I told them this tidbit. "What's crazier is I didn't give him my name, much less my address."

The two looked at each other, then back to me, both men looking like they could take on a bear and win based off the anger and agitation rolling off them.

It was Weston who spoke next.

"I don't like it, Kate. This guy doesn't seem.... Eric, help me out here."

"Yeah, Kate, it all seems a little creepy. Getting your information in less than twelve hours is a little... much." He took a step toward me, making me retreat a step.

Holding up my hands, I said, "Listen, I get it. You two are way overprotective and see this as some kind of threat, but he's fine. Arrogant as hell and playing some fun games, but that's it. Nothing harmful." Lie. "He is harmless." Lie. "He really seemed like a nice guy." Bullshit.

The tense silence was broken by yet another knock at the front door.

Damn, I'm popular today.

Weston motioned for Eric and me to stay in the kitchen as he made his way to the front door. I loved his commanding, domineering side. It was very attractive—when it wasn't directed at me. And thank goodness he'd pulled on a shirt before Eric arrived, or else keeping him at arm's length and from Eric mauling him would be near unattainable.

Dad's deep voice poured in as he greeted Weston at the door. I expected him to walk straight in, searching for me, but instead he and Weston paused in the entryway. A minute later they were still talking.

Hmm... what are they discussing?

"Hi, Dad," I called out with an eye roll, making Eric chuckle into his mug.

"Hey, sweetheart," he responded, coming around the corner, both of their faces grim.

This couldn't be good. What if it was about the people who shot me or something worse? My stomach twisted in the same cadence as the hands in my lap. "What's wrong?"

Dad's arms wrapped around my shoulders, carefully pulling me close to him. "It's nothing. I simply wanted to stop by and see you. To see how you were doing," he said, his attention focused on the basket on the counter. "Who is that from?"

Ugh, not another domineering male opinion.

"Um, just some guy I met at a charity function last night. You might have heard of him. Chase Smitson."

The three gaped, Eric going as far as mouthing, "OMG."

Dad finally found his words. "Chase Smitson. Isn't he—"

"Dallas's most eligible bachelor, yeah. Apparently, he and I hit it off last night when I mocked him about his nasty tequila."

It wasn't a good idea, but I dared a glance at Weston and immediately wished I hadn't. The earlier flush of anger was gone; now his brows were furrowed, lips in a thin line as he stared down the basket. I didn't want to know what was running through his head in that moment. Even my curiosity knew not to inquire, knowing it would likely break my resolve to pursue Chase. If I knew his internal negative thoughts, I would most likely wrap my arms around him, like I'd wanted to since seeing him shirtless this morning. But if I did, then he would know my pursuit of Chase wasn't real, that none of it was real.

Nothing *had* felt real since the day he left.

The smile and gaze my father held was one I hadn't seen since the day I made it through residency and was offered a position at Baylor. "Well, that's great. I'm glad you're finally interested in someone who deserves you."

He was proud I'd snagged Chase, which didn't sit well.

Eric and Weston exchanged a brief tension-filled glance capable of cutting through a soul. *My* soul, to be exact.

"We'll see how it goes," I grumbled. "Why did you stop by again?" The look on Weston's face had turned to sheer devastation. I needed to draw the conversation from Chase.

"Ah, well, I stopped by to give Weston an update on the trial. Seems we might be done with all this sooner than later."

"Oh," I said, surprised and a little disappointed. Unfortunately, everyone heard both in my voice and gave me a questioning look. "Thanks for stopping by, Dad."

Needing to lie down, I headed for the couch with the note from Chase and iPhone in hand. I needed advice on how to navigate all this, and who better to help than the biggest flirt I'd ever known —Meagan.

Me: Hey.

Meagan: Hey, you!

Meagan: I've missed you. How are you feeling?

Meagan: Is it bad to say Austin is still hot even though he's a complete jackass?

Me: He is still hot. Despicable but hot.

Meagan: Doesn't that make him hotter?

Me: Not in my book. Listen, I have a question.

Meagan: Shoot.

Me: I met a guy last night.

Meagan: Yay, you! Shot and still working it.

Me: Anyway... he sent me something this morning in the mail.

Meagan: Intriguing, go on.

Me: Do I respond back or wait until I see him again or ignore it?

Meagan: Don't ignore it, that's boring. Respond back. Did he send you something clever?

Me: Yes.

Meagan: Then send him something clever back. Make him see you can play games as well as he can. Don't give him too much though, like don't send him lingerie with a blinking sign that says "do me."

Me: Yeah, that wasn't on the list of possibilities, but thanks for the heads-up.

Meagan: I'm just saying teasing can happen over text, gifts, Amazon, whatever. Have fun with it.

Me: I'll try to channel my inner Meagan and have fun with it.

Meagan: Can I see you soon?

Me: Depends, are you still sick?

Meagan: It was only the flu. You and Eric make it sound like I had Ebola.

Me: For someone who just lost an organ that helped produce white blood cells, yeah, the flu is kind of like Ebola.

Meagan: Going all doctor on me. Fine, I'll wait a few more days.

A steaming cup of coffee was shoved between my face and phone. Eric slouched on the couch beside me, took a few sips of his coffee, and propped his feet on the coffee table.

"You have a lot to explain, little lady."

I tucked my cold feet under my thighs and rested my head against the back of the couch.

"It was nothing really. I mocked his tequila. He didn't like it, so I mocked him again, just to put him in his place, and I don't know...."

"It appears he liked it. Who is this guy anyway, Kate? What are you doing?"

I rolled my head along the back of the couch toward the kitchen.

Weston was making his own coffee, staring at the open gift on the counter. This sucked, hurting him, but one day he would understand, forgive me even. Maybe that would be the deal for us to move on from all this—together. I would forgive him for leaving if he forgave me for this teeny tiny little thing of risking my life for a group of people I didn't know. And not looping him in.

"I'm having fun, Eric. It's nothing. Just fun. Don't I deserve it right now? Haven't I been through enough the past few months that I get some time where I don't have to think or have a plan?"

His warm hand wrapped around my thigh, giving it a gentle squeeze. "I get it, Kate. You've been through a lot, but just remember while you're having fun... moving on... whatever you're calling it, some things might not be fixable if you want to go back to the way things were."

I turned to face him to whisper, "Last night he said he wants to fight for me."

Eric dropped his head and shook it back and forth in visible disappointment. First Weston and now Eric—I wasn't sure how long I could lie to both of them.

My dad's hands rested on my shoulders, and his lips connected with the crown of my head as he murmured a goodbye, briefly pausing our hushed conversation. When he was headed toward the door, Weston close behind, Eric started with his probing.

"Do you want him to?"

"No."

"No?"

"Maybe."

"Maybe? Wait, is that why you're doing this, to make him jealous? That's shitty—"

"No, I'm not doing this to hurt him, make him jealous, or anything like that. You're right, it would be shitty of me, but that's not what's happening here. I just need time."

"Fine, do whatever. But you need to be smarter than you were last night and not drink so much. Weston told me you were swaying by the end of the night."

My eyes darted to Weston, who'd joined us in the living room, sitting on the couch and working on his laptop. "Tattletale," I hissed and stuck out my tongue.

Without glancing up from the computer screen, even though I could tell he wasn't doing anything, he shrugged. "You won't listen to me. Maybe if it comes from a doctor you will."

"I'm a doctor too, remember?"

The glare he shot me dripped with jealousy, but his words, spoken out of hurt or disappointment, pissed me off just the same. "Then act like one and know your own damn limits. Stop making me remind you to slow down or take it easy or even fucking eat. I'm not a babysitter."

Eric sank back into the couch beside me.

"Then stop caring so damn much."

I held Weston's glare and he held mine, neither of us blinking. This was a battle of who could rein in their temper enough to be the one to back down. His frustrated growl reverberated in my chest, and I knew he was holding back a slew of words that would hurt me, hurt our future. Words he didn't mean but wanted to shout in the heated moment.

And because I wasn't the one trying to win the other back, I tossed gasoline on Weston's fiery temper.

"I can take care of myself. I've never needed your help."

Before he could retort with words he would eventually regret, and make me regret pushing him that far, someone banged on the front door again and again; their impatience pounded through the town-house with each beat of their fist. The laptop in Weston's lap slammed shut, making me and Eric jump at the sound and force.

Eric groaned as he leaned forward and set his mug on the coffee table. "Kate, stop being a dumbass." He pushed off the couch and moved for the half-bath in the hall.

Grabbing the iPad from the other end of the couch, I settled back. If these men were only going to piss me off all morning, I would simply ignore them. I had better things to do than bicker with them, like figure out what to send in response to Chase's gift and write a clever message. Even though I already had an idea, as soon as Meagan suggested I send something back, I knew what it would be, and Amazon's two-hour shipping could get it to him before the end of the day.

Ryan's harsh laugh filled the house, making me thankful he was back from wherever he'd been all morning to provide some relief from the swarming tension. He was pestering Weston as they emerged from the hall, but it was clear from Weston's stiff walk and the hardness in his face that he was not in the mood.

"What crawled up your ass, Casey? I was gone for a few hours. Not a big deal. It's not like I'm the one with a price on their head."

The living room walls shook with the force of Ryan's back being slammed against it. I cringed, watching the normal restraint Weston had on his anger snapping as he held Ryan against the wall with one hand firmly pressed on his chest, keeping him in place. As quickly as it happened, it ended. Weston dropped his hand but kept an arm extended toward Ryan, letting him know now was not the time to retaliate.

Eric ran in from the hall, skidding to a stop at the scene.

"What the fuck, Casey? What has gotten into you?" Ryan's eyes flicked to mine, scanning for any sort of insight as to why his brother was practically foaming at the mouth with rage. Maybe it was the lingering anger in my own eyes or the dismissive half shrug I gave in return, but realization flooded his face. "What's going on between you two?"

Weston sat on the couch and rested his forearms against his thick thighs while running both hands through his hair. "Drop it, Ryan," he seethed.

Wisely, Ryan obeyed. So did Eric.

The weight of the three men's accusing stares bored through the crown of my head as I played on the iPad, ignoring them. Nothing good would come from engaging with them right now, and quite frankly, I was pissed they'd ruined my planned calm, relaxing day.

With a final tap on the screen, Chase's two-hour delivery gift of Pedialyte and Excedrin Migraine was on its way with a note that read:

You'll need this after our body shot fun. Doctor's orders.

I GRINNED at the order confirmation screen. Everything was going as planned, even better really. I had expected it to take several of those charity events for Chase to notice me; maybe my short stature didn't make me as unnoticeable as I thought.

The next event was in a week, and it was formal attire, which I hated, but it did give me a good excuse to buy new shoes and a fabulous dress. I would need to find one soon, since everything I ordered needed to be tailored to fit. Plus, I needed to think about what Weston would wear. Unless he was the gorgeous male version of Mary Poppins, there was no way a tux had been packed in that duffel bag of his.

"I'm going," Eric called from the kitchen, startling me so much that hot coffee spilled down the front of my University of Texas T-shirt. "I'll call you later."

"Wait. There's another event next Friday night. I know Courtney could use a plus-one," I said, wiping at the spilled coffee. "That way you can see for yourself that I'm the picture of responsibility instead of having to hear about my so-called antics from an unreliable third party."

A low growl resounded from Weston's direction.

No way Eric could refuse; he loved a good party and would swoon at the idea of getting dressed up. He looked to Weston, who was too focused on the show Ryan had flipped on to notice, then back to me, seeming hesitant.

"It's formal," I mused.

"I'm in. Send me the details. Bye, Weston," Eric yelled over his shoulder as he walked out the door.

Weston was on his heels to lock the door after him and secure the townhouse once more.

When Weston reappeared, he avoided my tracking stare, ignoring me completely. Unfortunately, Ryan noticed Weston's obvious silent treatment and pounced on the opportunity to annoy his brother once again.

"I'll be your plus-one, Kate. I look damn good in a tux, if I do say so myself." Ryan grinned, showing off his straight white-toothed smile. There was no doubt he would look good in a tux, just not as good as his brother. "Unless you have someone else in mind."

My thoughts turned to the package still sitting on the kitchen island. "I'll be fine going alone, I think. I plan on meeting someone there."

When I looked to Weston, his deep brown eyes were narrowed, glaring.

"What?" I crossed my arms and sat farther into the couch. I was too exhausted and really didn't want to fight again.

"I'm not wearing a tux."

With a deep sigh, I shut my eyes and leaned my head back against the couch. This man either brought so much color to my life I didn't know how to handle it or was killing me slowly with his stubbornness.

Hell if I knew which.

10

Lying in bed, I stared at the ceiling unable to fall asleep. It'd been several weeks since the shooting, but being alone, going to sleep alone, continued to be a struggle. Weston had noticed the subtle changes in my behavior—he noticed everything—but nothing had been said, letting me deal with the rolling emotions on my own. The need for a constant visual on him to feel safe had eased slightly, day by day, but this moment, staring into the darkness, all my hidden fears—ones I could normally push away in the light—moved to the forefront of my mind.

My breathing turned heavy, every sound causing me to hold a shallow breath with tense anticipation. The buzz of my phone on my nightstand pulled me out of the downward spiral my mind was taking me into.

Weston: You up?

Me: Yes... Everything okay?

Weston: Yeah, just wanted to say good night.

Weston: And see you later.

Me: Ah, maybe tonight is the night I don't need to sneak downstairs. Ever think of that?

Weston: Doesn't mean I won't.

Me: I've never asked, you've never asked, but what do you dream about that pulls you upstairs with me?

Me: Hello?

Me: Come on, you started this whole thing.

Me: You suck at life, you know that?

Me: Now I can't sleep. Tell me. Is it that bad? Or is it of me, your memories from Vail of the bed, floor, wall…

Weston: Stop it. Now.

Me: Hi.

Weston: They are of you, but nothing good. That would be a dream, not a nightmare.

Me: Aw, I'm a dream!

Weston: Sometimes it's that night in Vail ending differently. Other times it's you standing over me telling me all the ways I failed you. The ways I wasn't there to protect you.

Me: Well, this just got serious.

Weston: You ASKED.

Me: I take it back.

Weston: You're insufferable.

Me: Good thing I'm pretty.

Weston: That's one word I would use.

Me: Gorgeous, witty, smart, beautiful,
charming... Do I need to go on?

Weston: Humble.

Me: You don't get to add words.

Weston: Good night, Kate.

Me: Good night, Weston.

Me: Wait.

Weston: What?

Me: Your room or mine?

Weston: Damnit, I wish that meant something
different.

Weston: Mine.

THIS HAD to be the stupidest show I'd ever seen. Of course, Ryan and
Weston were all into it. It had guns and heavy machinery.

My iPad vibrated on the couch beside me.

Weston: What are you doing?

Me: Watching this stupid Alaskan hermit-
people show just like you.

Weston: It's pretty awful, but look at Ryan.
He's enjoying it. I think he's enjoying their
misery while he sits on his fat ass.

Me: Oh, his ass is anything but fat.

Weston: Watch it.

Me: What? I mean... those jeans.

Weston: Stop it.

Me: His ass is pretty perfect, but…I think you're giving him a complex walking around shirtless all the time. You need to stop.

Weston: It's happened only a few times. It's hot in here. Are you complaining?

Weston: Have I just stunned the smart mouth of Kate Wheeler into silence?

Weston: I'm taking a screenshot. This shit needs to be documented.

Me: Not complaining. Maybe I should start doing the same thing? If it's that hot in here, maybe I shouldn't bother with a bra. Those things are suffocating. Oh, so are colored shirts, so no bra and a white tank top.

Weston: Stop.

Me: Maybe to cool me down, I can pour some ice-cold water down my top too. I'm sure Ryan wouldn't mind the entertainment. You know, lock the visual away for… a later date.

Weston: Please stop.

Me: It would feel so good, that cold water running down my chest, making my shirt completely see through. Mmmmm… brings back memories, right?

Me: Wait!

Me: Where are you going?

Me: Why are you walking funny?

Me: Did you stuff your gun in your pocket?

Weston: I hate you.

Weston: Give me a minute.

Me: I assume it's been since Christmas, so I guess a minute is about right.

Weston: Careful, Kate, or you'll push me to show you just how wrong you are.

Me: Sorry I can't help it. You said it yourself to my father—a promise is a promise.

Me: Weston?

Me: It has been since Christmas, right?

Me: Weston...

Me: Okay bye.

I RUSHED to brush my teeth after getting dressed for physical therapy, knowing Weston didn't like to be late. Another package had arrived earlier from Chase, which meant I had to respond, causing the delay in getting ready and putting Weston in a shitty mood.

As I brushed, my phone vibrated on the countertop by the sink.

Weston: Are you serious about that guy? The stuff he's sending you is borderline stalker.

Me: Jealous?

Weston: YES.

Me: Oh, well, that didn't work out like I planned.

Me: If you fighting for me is you doing THAT all day and night, I'm never going to forgive you.

Weston: It was pretty amazing.

Me: I think I purred.

Weston: You did. I'm surprised you didn't feel the effects with your head.

Me: I was wondering...

Me: Who knew, you reading to me and playing with my hair could be so... calming.

Weston: After the trial we can do it every day if you want.

Me: Weston...

Weston: I know, you haven't said if you're going to even take me back. But a man can hope, can't he?

Me: Just let me figure some things out.

Weston: Figure things out with Chase.

Me: He's just a distraction from all this mess, can't you see that? Can't you let me have a distraction and let me enjoy it?

Weston: No, I can't. Not with him. Not with anyone other than me. You thought today was great. Why can't that be distraction enough?

Me: Because.

Weston: Because why, Kate? Tell me what I need to do. I'll do anything you want, within the boundaries of keeping you safe and keeping my promise to your father.

Me: That's just it, Weston—too many obstacles right now with us. Just give me some time, okay?

Weston: Are you trying to punish me? I
understand if you are.

Me: No, damnit. This isn't about you. Stop
being so self-absorbed.

Weston: Yes, Your Majesty.

Weston: Good night, Kate.

Me: Good night, Weston.

Me: See you shortly.

Me: Your room.

ANOTHER DAY of lying around with the two boys.

It was nice having them both around. Even if Ryan wasn't as big as Weston, he looked scrappy enough to hold a bad guy at bay while I retrieved one of the multiple loaded guns in the house. The only negative was he always demanded to have control over the remote, which meant we were watching yet another *Undeniable* with Joe Buck.

Boring.

Thankfully, my ass vibrated, and I knew exactly who the incoming text would be from. I could see him on the other couch, watching his phone, waiting for a response.

Weston: Don't forget about your appointment
tomorrow with Austin.

Me: Ah, good old Austin.

Weston: I cannot believe you ever fell for his
shit.

Me: Man bun. I don't need to say anything
else. Half of the women in America would
have swooned just the same as me at that
hair.

Weston: And the other half?

Me: Swoon at mine.

Weston: You are a cocky little thing, aren't you.

Me: Having men as good-looking as you and Austin after me, I think I can be.

Weston: So you're saying…

Me: Meh, average.

Weston: You're killing me.

Weston: HA! Ryan just texted me asking what we're laughing about. He knows we're texting each other.

Me: Send me his number or add us in a group chat.

Weston: Hell.

Weston: No.

Me: Killjoy.

Weston: I've sworn to keep you safe from all dangers. Including my brother.

Me: He wouldn't hurt me.

Weston: No, but the way he keeps eyeing your legs in those short shorts of yours is about to make me beat his ass.

Weston: Speaking of which, hasn't anyone taught you how to sit like a lady?

Weston: That's NOT what I'm talking about.

Weston: I swear if you do that again… Close your fucking legs.

Me: Where are you going?

Me: I just had an itch on my inner thigh.

Me: Damn, Weston, you need to get laid.

Weston: Are you offering?

Me: Are you willing?

Weston: Good night, Kate.

Me: It's three in the afternoon!

Weston: I'm taking a nap. You kept me up all night snoring.

Me: I do not snore.

Weston: No, you don't. You look pretty damn cute while you sleep.

Me: You watch me sleep? And you called Chase the stalker.

Weston: Do not mention his name. That gift… and I can't do anything about it. You're not mine.

Weston: Yet.

11

───────

I wasn't sure which was worse, knowing Weston was fighting for me or witnessing him fight for me. It was brutal. On top of the fun texting the past several days, he'd done everything he could to turn my eye, even installing a pull-up bar in his doorway and using it —without a shirt, of course—anytime I was around. He cooked for me, let me sleep in his bed after my nightly nightmare, and best of all, we were finally back into the comfortable routine pre-Vail. When Ryan wasn't around, we talked, really really talked, and it was perfect. The project with Chase was ongoing, but it was nice having my friend back.

Especially on a brutal day like today.

It started out with a follow-up appointment with Austin. My stomach lurched the moment we stepped into the hospital. The smells brought up too many fresh memories—ones I really didn't want to relive. Austin prodding around my incisions hurt like hell, making me stifle a whimper. Weston held back his reaction, but from the stillness that leaked from him, he was a second away from losing his shit if Austin didn't hurry. But we all made it through, and I was rewarded with Austin's approval to increase activity. Nothing too strenuous like abs or weights yet, but slight jogging was fine and at this point might even help speed up the recovery process.

Two additional weeks off work before he would grant me partial work release, meaning half shifts for a few weeks to get my body back in shape.

Good. Two more weeks of being home should be plenty of time to wrap up the Chase project.

Hopefully.

But it also meant two more weeks of lying to Weston and Eric.

Right now the lies were painful, heartbreaking at times, but it was all necessary. For now. Someday Weston and I would be past all this and be what we were meant to be.

Together.

"I HATE YOU, YOU HATEFUL BASTARD," I yelled as my physical therapist stretched out my shoulder an inch past my breaking point. Tears lined my eyes as I screamed more profanities at him. Since he knew me personally, Tom was used to this, unfortunately, and started booking our therapy sessions when everyone else was out to lunch.

Weston was a different story; he wasn't used to my screaming and begging for someone to end my life—to put me out of my misery. Every session, he furiously paced the length of the gym, only pausing when my yelling became borderline abusive.

"If I didn't know you, Kate, I might be offended by all this talk of wanting to kill me. You're fine. I promise, I know how far to push you. I did go to school for this, not you, so shut your damn mouth."

I sobbed on the padded table as he pulled my arm back a second time. Weston paused his pacing, turning his full intense, intimidating focus on Tom. The ferocity in his eyes made me think he was half a second away from tackling the man inflicting my pain.

At the end of the session, I was left lying on the table, having been given a few minutes by myself to recover. I couldn't move my arm; sharp pains radiated through my shoulder to fingertips if I even thought about trying. My wet cheek pulled against the vinyl covering as I rotated my head in search of Weston.

I didn't know whose eyes reflected more pain, his or mine. His face was ashen and tense as he stared, unmoving, giving me space or simply being standoffish, which I wouldn't blame him if he were. The back-and-forth gifts between Chase and me were wearing on him. The worst was the black lingerie Chase sent yesterday with a note that said:

For the after-party.

"You okay?" Weston called from across the room, crossing his arms and leaning against the wall. That spot along the wall, between the only two ways in and out of the therapy room, was where he perched each session—when he wasn't pacing, that was.

"That one hurt, not going to lie."

"You took it over the line when you said you hope he dies at the stake."

"Well, he shouldn't have pushed me past my breaking point. I can't be held accountable for what I say when I'm in pain."

"You shouldn't have yelled at his aide either."

"She was an accomplice," I mused as I sat up on the table.

"It's her job. You made her cry, for fuck's sake. And I bet she's changing her address as we speak, afraid you'll follow up on your threat of killing her. Slowly."

"Okay, maybe you're right about that one. She doesn't know me like Tom does. I should send her a cookie bouquet or something to apologize."

He smirked, shaking his head in amused disbelief. "I have some pain meds in the car if you need them. Today did sound... worse."

Wincing, I swung my legs off the table, allowing them to dangle over the side. "Thanks, but I'm okay. It hurts worse in the moment than it does after. Are you ready?"

He gave a curt nod but held my gaze, allowing me insight into the array of emotions rolling through him.

Sliding off the table, I tried to focus on anything other than the throbbing in my shoulder. "Are you okay with everything tomorrow night?"

"You'll be safe," he said, gently gripping the elbow of my good arm to offer support.

I paused and turned. Toe to toe, I had to tip my head back to gauge his reaction. "That's not what I'm asking and you know it."

"It's fine, Kate. I've told you keeping you safe is most important. I'm not going to stop you. I'll be fine."

"Okay, if you need someone else to—"

"I'm going and that's final. End of discussion."

My anxious stomach eased at his statement. Okay, so maybe I *did* still need him to be close to feel at ease, to feel safe.

So, that settled it. Weston was going to have a front-row seat to me trying to woo Chase.

Lovely.

I REALLY WISHED I'd learned to whistle as a kid; it would have come in handy right about now. If I could, I would have at my reflection in the bedroom full-length mirror. The red one-shoulder dress, tied in a large bow on the right shoulder, conveniently covered the entrance and exit wound, which was my main concern while searching for evening gowns the past few days. The slit up the side stopped short of my hipbone, making the strappy, jeweled Christian Louboutins stand out with each step I took.

The soft perfect wave of my hair took over an hour to tame and style, and Courtney spent no less than thirty minutes doing my eye makeup, giving me the perfect smoky-eye effect to enhance my almond-shaped hazel eyes. I stood in front of the mirror, not recognizing myself, while she did the finishing touches on her own makeup.

I looked beautiful. But even with makeup, the dark circles under my eyes, the worry lines that seemed permanent on my brow, and my now-dull eyes were all visible in the woman staring back.

The past few months hadn't been good to me.

Looking past all that, I stared into my reflection, at the dress, the shoes, hearing—but not listening to—Courtney give tidbits on the different people who would be attending the formal benefit this evening. I could have easily been this person. Hollow, beautifully hollow, floating from one event to the other thinking that was all I had to offer in life.

Money, especially inherited money, swayed your grasp on reality, making you think this type of thing was the norm, and the more you surrounded yourself with people of the same money and mindset, the deeper you dove into the lie. This was the life I was destined for but fought against with every step, every breath. Me and my mother. We both knew there was more that could be done than spending a thousand dollars a plate at a fancy charity party.

So instead of falling into this life of parties and low expectations, I did something with purpose and quantitative positive results on the lives of others. Until recently, that was. Now even work seemed... not enough. I longed to get back to volunteering, but not until I was healed. That kind of emotional and physical drain would set my recovery back tenfold.

"Not sure how Weston plans on holding himself back when he sees you looking like that."

Shifting my eyes, I watched Courtney move around the room as she packed her small clutch with the lipstick she recently applied.

She knew everything about me and Weston now, and it was nice having an outside opinion on the whole messed-up situation. Obviously, I told her me wanting to date Chase was because I was scared of trusting Weston again. The truth about my intentions would stay with me. And *only* me.

My gaze shifted back to my reflection, self-doubt slowly creeping in. "Let's hope Chase feels the same way."

The three men stood around the kitchen island, chatting among themselves as they waited for us to be ready. The banter about who the Cowboys should choose as a backup quarterback slowed and died completely when we came into view.

Not wanting to witness Weston's reaction—either way it would slay me—I found Eric and kept my eyes on him. He looked adorable in a classic black tux and bow tie, his blond hair styled to fit the classic look, forgoing the disheveled style he normally donned.

With a deep breath, holding it in for courage, I risked a glance at Weston. My held breath whooshed free. Undeniable longing lurked behind his hooded dark eyes, the want and desperation radiating off him and through his heated gaze.

He looked damn good too.

He'd given in to my relentless pestering and agreed to wear a tux to the event, even though he was "working." Somehow the cut of the fabric made his shoulders look broader, and with the way the pants hung, no one could miss the strong, muscular thighs they concealed. And damn, that haircut. He had it fixed again, showing off his strong jaw and handsome face.

The others quieted around us.

Seconds, maybe even minutes passed with the two of us simply staring. No words were spoken, but none needed to be. We both knew exactly what the other was thinking. He wouldn't break the promise to my father or put me in danger, and I, well, I had a job to do. One mission. And it was to get Chase to invite me over, gain access to his home. To find... oh hell, I didn't even know what I could find. But I had to try.

Eric cleared his throat, forcing my attention to shift to him. "Courtney, you look stunning. Weston, doesn't Kate look beautiful?"

Courtney cut in before Weston could respond. "Kate, aren't you excited about seeing Chase tonight?"

Okay, so Eric was clearly Team Weston and Courtney was Team Kate. And Ryan... well, Ryan was probably Team Ryan, but he would play instigator in our little game as long as we would let him.

The beer bottle in Ryan's hand paused midair, halfway to his thin lips, as he surveyed the four of us and smirked. "Sounds like you kids are going to have an interesting night. Wish I could be there."

I shot a glance at him, conveying that I was nothing short of annoyed, on the verge of being pissed off. "Please don't destroy my house while we're gone."

"Don't destroy my brother while you're out parading around looking like that, trying to make him jealous."

Wow, maybe Ryan was Team Weston after all.

Sighing loud enough to break Ryan's and my icy stare, Weston headed to the door shaking his head.

With one last warning look at Ryan, I followed Weston out with Eric and Courtney, ready to get the night started.

———

THE MOMENT we were loaded in the Mercedes, my clutch vibrated.

Weston: You do look stunning. That dress... I don't think stunning even covers it.

Me: Thank you. So do you.

Weston: Nothing I could ever wear could put me in the same category as you.

Me: You're right. You look much better without anything at all.

Weston: Please don't drink too much tonight. It's hard monitoring what you're consuming and the people around you.

Me: Eric will make sure I'm on my best behavior too. I wouldn't want to stress you out any more than you already are on a constant basis.

Weston: And don't talk to any other men. That would stress me out too.

Me: Nice try.

> Weston: If Chase grabs your wrist again, I will take him out. If he touches you, I can't be responsible for my actions.

> Weston: I can't see that. Him touching you in any way.

> Weston: Touching what should be mine.

> Weston: If I wasn't such a dumbass and fucked it up the first time around.

> Me: I'm not doing this to hurt you, Weston. Your brother was wrong, I'm not trying to make you jealous.

> Weston: It doesn't make this less frustrating.

PRE-DINNER COCKTAILS and mingling were first on the agenda. The ballroom was full, but Eric scoped out an empty high-top close to a wall for Weston to perch himself against, then headed off to get the first round of drinks.

"You good?" Courtney asked, leaning against the table with a pointed look, brows raised toward Weston.

I sighed through my nose, keeping my gaze in the opposite direction of her stare. "Yeah."

"So you don't care that in less than three minutes five women have approached him?"

It was an instinctive response, the immediate swivel of my head in his direction. Three women were standing close to him, peeking over their shoulders to see if he was watching, then turning back to their friends, giggling.

Women in their late thirties, early forties, giggling.

At my Weston. Looking. At *my* Weston.

It took every last ounce of inner strength not to snarl at the flirting.

None of it sat well. He wouldn't take anyone home, or sneak away for a coat-closet quickie. No, he wouldn't leave me... but did he want to? Even with everything he'd said, it had been a while for him—I hoped—and he was a guy. And guys had certain needs. Did he remember enough of what we had together those few days in December to prevent him from wanting to move on physically?

Just the image of those calloused hands, soft lips, and talented tongue on someone else had my heart pounding as I tried to swallow against a dry throat.

He gave every woman who approached a polite smile but turned his attention elsewhere. Our eyes met across the room. Every worry and traitorous thought dissipated. His look—damn, that look; how could I have ever doubted—conveyed everything I needed to know. And his blazing I-would-fuck-you-right-now-if-I-could stare was only for me.

"So," Eric said, setting our drinks on our table, breaking the heat-filled gaze, "what is tonight—" He was cut off by a stranger who'd approached the table, attention solely on Courtney.

He was a stranger to me, but given the way Courtney's arms folded across her chest and her shoulders curved in, there was no mistaking who he was to her. Giving him a once-over, I didn't understand what she ever saw in him. The ex and I were eye level, thanks to my four-inch heels, and he looked like he lived at the gym. His shirt and jacket were way too tight; he obviously wanted everyone to notice his bulging arms. The sneer on his face didn't help his look either, but honestly, even a smile wouldn't have made him attractive.

"Courtney, good to see you're out and about again," the man said, his voice low and soft, trying to convey concern, but the smirk on his lips said something different.

Shoulders that were normally high and back, showing confidence, were rounded and slacked beside me. Courtney's gaze was anywhere other than the man in front of us. "Hi, Alex," she mumbled.

"Looks like you've been eating your feelings again. It must be hard attending these events alone. If you would have listened to me, we could still be together—happy. But no, you had to make another one of your stupid decisions and leave me. I'm more than happy to reconsider, but it will take enormous amounts of begging."

What. The. Fuck.

Eric was too busy gaping from the man's comment to say anything back, and I knew better than to make a scene with what I wanted to say—something along the lines of "Fuck off, you cuntcake." It would only embarrass her further.

The condescending look on Alex's face faltered at movement behind me before Weston appeared, draping an arm over Courtney's slack shoulders, pulling her close to press his lips into her dark hair.

"Hey, sweetie," he murmured, pulling back to gaze lovingly into her eyes.

Tears welled in the corners of my eyes for many, many reasons.

Turning his eyes from Courtney to Alex, Weston said, "She's with me. Back the fuck off now before I make you." The agitation and anger pouring through the glare he had locked on Alex let everyone know he would follow through with the threat if needed.

I smirked, mirroring Eric's, as the asshole took a step back, mumbling discontent at the way things had turned out before shrinking away from Weston's glare. He was across the room when we turned to face Weston and Courtney.

"Thank you. You didn't...." Her eyes were lined with unshed tears as she looked away, flush spread across her cheeks.

In slow motion, Weston gently gripped her chin to bring her gaze back to his own. The world stilled, the chatter around me going silent. Courtney was my friend, and he didn't have intimate feelings toward her, but touching her instead of me.... My hands fisted at my side.

"You deserve better than him," Weston whispered as he held her chin firm. "No one should talk to you that way. No one. You are beautiful inside and out. Never forget it. If he comes back when I'm not around, kick him in the balls and tell him to go back to the kids' table where he belongs."

A single tear rolled down her cheek, pulling a line of dark eye makeup with it.

"I know. Damnit, I know." Was she trying to convince Weston or herself? "Thank you for stepping in." She wiped at her cheek, frowning when she saw the dark smudge on the back of her hand. "I need to freshen up. Kate, come with me?"

Perfect, I needed a breather myself after *that* scene.

As we weaved in and around the crowded ballroom, a hand gripped my waist halfway to the bathroom, pulling me to a stop in the middle of the crowd.

My breathing stopped.

Either Chase or Weston.

I couldn't look behind me. What if they were back, back to finish what they promised months ago?

No. I shouldn't be afraid.

Chase or Weston. Chase or Weston.

Fight it. Fight it, Kate.

"I was hoping you would be here tonight," Chase whispered into my ear.

I sucked in a deep breath, finally able to get air in my lungs. He pulled me close, pressing my back flush against his chest, to let a waiter carrying various drinks and appetizers pass through.

Turning slightly, I smiled. "How could I not? It's such a good cause."

"Ah, there you go hurting my ego again. Insinuating I'm not the reason you're here tonight. Do you enjoy breaking men, Dr. Wheeler?"

To the right, the crowd briefly parted, drawing my attention. Weston stood a few feet from us, staring—glaring. Out of my periphery, I saw Chase follow my lingering gaze and scowl when he found Weston as well.

His grip tightened around my waist. "About that," he said, inclining his head toward Weston. "I've read multiple articles on you, on your family, and it all indicates you're an only child. So tell me, Kate"—*this can't be good*—"why did you tell me the night we met he was your brother? What kind of games are you playing?"

I started to answer, but with the loud chatter and laughing around us, it was too loud and there were too many nosy-ass people to tell him everything here.

Gripping the hand at my waist, I tugged him to the banquet room where the dinner portion of the night would happen. The privacy it offered was perfect. Only a few servers milled about, putting the finishing touches on tables and the room before the cocktail hour ended and people began filing in.

"He's my individual safety controller," I breathed, leaning my back against the cool wall for support.

Chase stood, arms crossed over his lean chest, in front of me but a foot away—keeping his distance. "He's your bodyguard?"

"Of sorts, yes."

"Why didn't you say that before?" His arms fell and he tucked his hands into the pockets of his tuxedo pants. The tux looked very, very expensive—one of many in his collection, I was sure.

I pulled at my lip. "Because of the reason *why* I need him. A case my father is working got out of hand, so this guy's been with me the past several months."

"And you thought... it would scare me off," he said, taking a step closer. Both hands wrapped around my waist and began drawing tiny circles along my abdomen with his thumbs. He skimmed the scar along my abdomen, sending an unnatural tingling sensation crawling under the skin. I tried stepping to the side, to shrug out of his grasp, but his hands held firm.

Movement at the door snagged my attention.

Weston.

He caught my wide-eyed look, smirked, and casually leaned against the wall, clearly prepared to stay there for the remainder of my private conversation with Chase.

Bastard.

When I shifted my eyes back to Chase, his face had lost all kindness as he waited, impatiently, for me to continue with my story. "Sorry. Earlier this year, I was attacked on my way to the gym." Carefully I pulled the shoulder fabric down for him to see the entry wound, his eyes widening at the pink scar. "And here." I grasped his hand and traced the scar on my abdomen with the tips of his fingers.

His face was unreadable as he processed everything I was telling him. It was a lot to take in, but I needed him to. I couldn't let my recent life events push him away before I got what I needed from him.

"So," I said softly, peering up through my long dark lashes, "you'll have to be gentle." Taking a step closer, I held his wrists in my hands, pulling his arms around me. "Doctor's orders."

His hands pressed on my lower back, joining the lower half of our bodies, holding us flush against the other. His breath hitched at the contact. "I can do that," he said as he lowered his lips to mine. "But not here. Have dinner with me."

Men are too easy.

"It's hard going out right now. He"—I nodded in Weston's direction—"would have to come with us and stay very, very close," I breathed against his lips as I worked to keep my stomach contents in place.

"Fine." He pulled away, clearly frustrated at the roadblock. "We can do it at my house. I have guards on the property and the best security system available. Saturday, seven o'clock. You already know my address."

My back was still pressed against the wall when he started to walk away. He turned before heading back into the crowded room where the cocktail hour was still going strong. "Don't be late. I hate that. And stop doing that." He flipped a hand to my face, where my fingers were playing with my lip. "It's very unattractive."

He passed through the doors, disappearing into the crowd.

The wall at my back vibrated; even with my eyes closed, I knew it was Weston. That musky scent of his along with the boiling low in my gut at his closeness were the first giveaways. Neither of us spoke. But by the way he was fidgeting, fingers rapping along the wall, he was holding something back.

Maneuvering my head to face him, I opened one eye. "What, Weston?"

He didn't respond, which was fine. I was done with all this shit tonight anyway, even if it did take longer to get ready than I was actually going to stay at the event. The purpose of the evening had already been accomplished, and now all I wanted was to go home, take a long bath, and sleep.

"I think I've had enough tonight." I sighed. "Let's go home."

Those fingers stopped their drumming to slide against the wall and encase my own. Skin to skin, even if it was only our hands, was intense. The warmth of his hand, the way it trembled slightly at our touch, was too much. But that didn't mean I was going to let go.

It appeared we both enjoyed torturing ourselves.

"You okay?"

"Yeah, I'm fine, just really tired. Let's go tell Eric and Courtney so they don't worry about where we've disappeared to. Oh, and one more thing...." I peeked up at him with my best mischievous smile.

"Why am I nervous?" That sly smile flashed, making the warmth in my core start to throb with the beat of my pulse.

"I'm starving. Let's stop by McDonald's or something on our way home."

My knees buckled at his rumbling laugh. It killed me. I wanted to hold him against me so I could feel it vibrate from his chest to mine. I missed that laugh, missed being the one who made him laugh.

One day. One day it would be all mine again. I only had to do one more thing.

For those women out there who didn't have anyone else fighting for them, I would fight. I would risk everything I had, everything I was, for them.

12

"You two are home early," Ryan called out from the couch, eyes glued to the TV in front of him. He really was making himself at home. A collection of empty beer bottles—my beer—sat on the coffee table. The asshole didn't even bother to use a coaster.

Plopping on the stool, I reached into the McDonald's bag and pulled out three fries, shoving them into my mouth. Eric and Courtney had stayed behind for the event's festivities, but here in my kitchen, eating fries with Weston, was where I wanted to be.

Weston reached across the island, grabbed the food bag from my hands, and dug around in search of his *two* quarter pounders.

As I munched on my delicious fries and burger, my thoughts drifted to Chase and the first date we had scheduled—not planned. What would his expectations be, and what would I be *willing* to give of myself to keep up the charade of wanting him?

"Kate?"

A quick glance up found Weston's brows furrowed and his lips dipped in a slight frown as he stared over.

"What are you thinking about?" he asked.

"Chase asked me out tonight," I said, shying away from his stare.

"Saturday night. He knows everything about the case now, so he invited me over to his place instead of going out."

"Who's Chase?"

I jumped off the stool at Ryan talking from directly behind me. I hadn't heard him approach.

Weston leaned against the counter and nodded for me to fill Ryan in.

"This guy, Chase Smitson. I met him at a party and—"

Ryan retreated one step, then another, the color draining from his face at the mention of Chase's name. "Wait a second. You're going out. On a date. With Chase Smitson. Do you know what that guy does, who he is—"

Shit, time to think fast. Apparently Ryan knew everyone in the underworld.

"Yes, Ryan," I said, cutting him off. Weston's narrowed eyes stayed locked on his brother, waiting for him to finish. "He's a self-made millionaire."

For being half brothers, they had the exact same accusatory stare. And both sets of eyes were directed at me.

Ryan's questioning gaze scanned my face like he was looking for answers. I widened my eyes slightly, hoping he would get the hint to keep his mouth shut about Chase. The slight twitch of his lips was the only indication he picked up on what I silently asked.

"What were you going to say, Ryan?" Weston asked, his eyes darting between me and his brother.

A sinister smile grew on Ryan's lips. Great, his silence was going to cost me.

Ryan shrugged and walked to the fridge, reaching for another beer. "Just what Kate said. I guess I was surprised she would go for someone like him." He stopped beside me on his way back to the couch. "You're almost out of beer. Can you get some more tomorrow?" he asked, smirking.

Damnit. What had I done making a deal with one devil so I could date another?

THE USUAL NIGHTMARE came back in full force, but tonight's was slightly different. I was racing toward the gym and glanced back only to find Chase casually walking but catching up quickly despite his pace. When I turned back around to run faster, I slammed into someone, knocking me to the ground. The man's face was fuzzy, but when he bent to pin my shoulders to the concrete, Ryan's sinister smile became clear. I screamed for help, but not even a squeak would escape. Chase stopped, stood over me, and pointed a gun at my head. Before he pulled the trigger, he laughed with a mumbled "Nice try."

The bang of the gun jolted me awake. I pulled my sleep shirt off my clammy chest and back. How much longer could I survive like this? I looked to the wingback chair, hoping to find Weston watching over me.

I shot up, back slamming against the headboard.

It wasn't Weston.

"I didn't mean to scare you." Ryan's voice trailed through the darkness. He leaned forward in the chair, allowing the pale light coming from the windows to highlight his face. "I need to understand what you're doing, Kate. What are you doing with Chase? You stopped me tonight from telling Weston who he really is. Why?"

My breathing was still erratic from the nightmare and finding him in my room. It was just a dream. Ryan would never hurt me, would he?

"I don't know what you're talking about," I said evenly, trying to sound calm even though I was anything but.

"Fine." He slapped his hands against his thighs as he pushed out of the chair. "Then it's okay for me to tell Weston that Chase has been known in other, less socially acceptable circles... tied to human and drug trafficking."

My mind spun, lingering fear and grogginess making it near impossible to think straight.

He strolled to the closed bedroom door, giving me time to make my choice. There wasn't a good one in this situation; I would have to go with the lesser of the two evils.

"Why does it matter to you what I'm doing and why?" I whispered as loudly as I dared. Even though Weston was downstairs, those supersonic, army-trained ears could hear a mouse peeing.

"No, I don't care about you. You do whatever you want with your life. But Casey...." He sat on the edge of the bed, closer than I felt comfortable with, but I held my ground. "Casey is the only family I have. and if something were to happen to you, it would break him. For good this time."

This time?

"Did you know he came back for me?"

Eyes wide, I shook my head.

"He aged out of the system a few years ahead of me, and with as much trouble as I got in, I figured he would just leave and not look back. But he didn't. He could have gone to college, you know, he made good grades in school without even having to study, but instead he got some low-paying construction job the day he graduated and started fighting to get custody of me. I never understood why. I still don't know why."

My eyes swam with unshed tears at the love and reverence in his voice for his brother.

"He's different with you, Kate," Ryan said, clearing his throat. "I can see it, your friends can see it, and I know you can see how much he cares for you. I can also tell some shit went down with you two earlier this year, but don't do something stupid like go after Chase just so my brother has to rescue you. I'm not going to lose him. He's survived enough, don't you think?"

That was what he thought of me. Someone who wanted to be a damn damsel in distress, risking his brother's life. With that eye-opening prejudice, any lingering anxiety from the nightmare and unease from being alone with Ryan were chased away by rising bitterness.

"You're an asshole, you know that, Ryan?" I said, no longer caring if I was keeping my voice down. "I would never do that to your brother, and the fact that you think so little of me...." I sighed into the hands now covering my face. "I have other reasons for pursuing Chase, okay? And it has nothing to do with your brother. I can promise you that. In fact, I'm doing everything I can to keep him *out* of this situation I've gotten myself into."

A few seconds of silence ticked away. When he still didn't respond to my vague explanation, I pulled my hands away. He was staring, smirking.

Damn that smirk. I hated it. Nothing good could come when that smirk was on his face. I was at his mercy and he knew it.

"What's my silence worth, Kate? How much are you willing to give to make sure this little nugget of information stays with me and doesn't find its way to Casey?"

I pushed away too fast, the scar across my abdomen burned as the healing skin pulled. "Ryan, I'm not going to... I don't know what you're asking for—"

It took him a few seconds to catch on. When he did, he shot from the bed and was across the room in half a second. "What? No, I'm not asking you to— Damn, Casey would murder me and enjoy it if he found out I coerced you into screwing me."

I blew out the breath I'd been holding in one long stream. "Then what do you want?"

"You know what I want."

My meds.

The bedroom door flew open, banging against the wall behind it. Weston stalked over the threshold and paused in the middle of the room, anger, hurt, and confusion radiating off him. He wouldn't hurt me, but I tugged the comforter closer to my chest, protecting myself from his agitation.

"What the *hell* are you doing in here, Ryan?"

Thankfully, Ryan was wise enough to keep his smart mouth in check. "I heard something and came up to check on her. She was awake when I came in."

"It was one of my nightmares." Half-truth. "We've been talking to distract me." Another half-truth.

His shoulders and back remained tense. I couldn't tell if he was believing our lie or sensing our deception.

Weston glanced between us, assessing. "Ryan, get your ass back downstairs. Now," he growled. He watched Ryan back out of the room and followed him to the door, watching his brother's back like he had a target on it until he disappeared downstairs.

Once Ryan was out of the room, Weston's anger and frustration dropped a level, but he couldn't settle down beside me or in the chair. Was he pissed because he knew we were lying to him? Or maybe, for a brief second, he thought Ryan and I were *together* behind his back?

"Are you okay?" he asked, running both hands through his bedhead hair and finally settling on the opposite end of the bed.

"I'm fine. It really was a nightmare." I pulled at my lower lip. Now that the conversation with Ryan wasn't providing a distraction, various pieces of my nightmare started replaying. "They... the dreams aren't going away. Shouldn't it be getting better by now?"

Angling his body so he could face me, he stared at me—through me—before responding. "You need to talk to someone, Kate, or at least.... I had this guy tell me once it helped to get it out in any way possible. Putting it all out there helps release it, and since he knew I couldn't see him often, he suggested I write it all down."

"Did it help?" I whispered. A small part of the lingering anxiety was wondering if this was now my life, stuck in constant dread, nervousness—feeling vulnerable.

Weston stood from the bed and paced around the room, but this time not from anger, more to aid him in gathering his thoughts. "At first I thought it was making me worse, having to think about each of those memories in detail, but... what I struggle with is the guilt. That's what I can't let go of. Of what I had to do in the army, the deci- sions I made that affected other men's lives and families back home, of how I'm home—alive—and so many weren't as lucky." He took a deep breath in and held it. I waited in the silence of the night, giving him as much time as he needed to rid himself of whatever was now running through his mind.

With a shake of his head, Weston continued. "Writing out each scenario helped walk me through it, helped me understand that in most situations, I didn't have a good choice. I was making the least bad choice for the unit. I still struggle a lot, more than I want to admit, but it started to help, and one day I realized I'd gone a few hours without smothering guilt. And as I continued, it only got better."

I tucked my legs against my chest. "You think it will help me?"

He sat on the bed, pressing his back against my legs. The bed dipped under his weight, causing me to lean against him. "I think it's worth a try."

"I'll try. I'll really try. I don't want this. I think it's breaking me. I can't sleep, I'm constantly on edge, I can't get my emotions under control." I didn't know when I started crying, but warm tears rolled down my cheeks and neck. "Make it stop, Casey," I begged. "Please. *Please.* Make it stop. I can't live like this. I don't want to live like this anymore."

His rough hands wrapped around my petite face, thumbs brushing away my streaming tears.

"You're stronger than this. I don't think anything could actually break you, Kate. You're.... It's going to stop, but you have to talk to me. Let it out. Tell me what's going on. It's the only way I can help, and I want to help. You have no idea how much I want to fucking help. Talk to me."

My shoulders shook with a rattling sob. "I couldn't breathe when you were gone," I confessed. Maybe if I freed this bit of truth, it would help one broken piece of my heart heal. "I missed you so much it physically hurt. How could you leave me when you knew, you *knew* I was falling for you?"

He pulled me to his chest, holding me tight in his arms, stroking his fingers through the hair that hung down my back.

"I know, baby, I know. I promise, when I can, I'll make it up to you. And if you let me, I'll never stop trying to make it up to you. Every day we're together, I'll fight for you. And fight with you. Together we can get through anything."

He pulled me off his lap and laid me down against the cool

sheets. A warm, hard body pressed against my back as he tucked me tightly against him. "Go to sleep, baby. You're safe. I'm here."

For the moment, I could forget the charade with Chase, Ryan's demands for secrecy, shootings, and even the ever-dwindling anger toward Weston and allow myself to relax against him. With a long, deep breath, I closed my eyes and drifted off to sleep.

Smiling.

13

Eric: Are you nervous?

Me: Nah, it's just a date.

Me: Wait, should I be?

> Eric: I'd be more nervous Chase might make a wrong move and Weston will take his head off with a random lamp.
>
> Eric: Then carry you out, over his shoulder, home.
>
> Eric: Smacking you on the ass the whole way.

Me: Um… your fantasy is strange since it's about me and Weston.

Me: Nothing to do with you.

Eric: I just want to see you happy.

Me: And Weston smacking me on the ass, then getting charged with manslaughter would do it.

Eric: I didn't think that through.

Me: Clearly.

Eric: Have fun tonight. Don't do anything I wouldn't do.

Me: Which is…

Eric: I don't kiss and tell.

Weston: Ready?

Me: Soon.

Weston: Didn't he want you there at 7? It's 7 now.

Me: Yep.

Weston: Good to know you're exhausting with everyone, not just me.

Me: I'll be down in a few minutes.

Me: I don't know how to handle all this with Weston.

Me: He said he would make it up when he could.

Me: What does that even mean?

Eric: He knows what he did wasn't the right move, and when all this shit is behind you, he's going to screw your brains out every second of every day to make it up to you.

Me: Another one of your fantasies?

Eric: Nope, direct quote from him. Minus profanities.

Me: Seriously?

Me: Eric. Answer me.

Eric: Okay, not a direct quote. I read between the lines.

Eric: You're not wearing a dress, right?

Me: I'm not a freaking amateur.

Eric: What are you wearing?

Me: Leggings, boots, sweater.

Eric: Good, the boots will deter him.

Me: Huh?

Eric: It looks like a lot of work to get it all off.

Me: Interesting. I liked the outfit, good to know I won't tempt him to take me to bed on the first date.

Eric: Be safe.

Me: Always.

Me: Love you. I'll text you when I get home.

Eric: Love you too.

Me: I think you should wait in the car tonight.

Weston: Hell no.

Me: He has a security system, guards on the property. You can stay outside and keep watch.

Weston: I'm not going to leave your side.

Me: I'm asking you, please. Stay outside so it's not awkward.

Weston: No, now come downstairs, we need to go.

Me: Fine, but what you see tonight you cannot hold against me. And if I ask for it, give me some privacy.

Weston: I'll be fine.

A deep breath in and I started for the stairs. I'd lied to Eric, and I was nervous as hell. Now that my plan was this far in, I had no clue what to do next. How in the hell was I going to find the evidence needed to indict Chase? And what if he *did* try something? Was I willing to take all this *that* far? Was I willing to give up an intimate piece of me to get this information?

Somewhere deep inside, an inner voice was screaming, too distant and distorted to understand. But another voice was ringing loud and clear, convincing me if something did happen, I'd been through worse and made it through, so anything Chase could do would be easy.

Right?

THERE WAS a slight tremble in my hands as we stepped out of the car. I flexed them a few times to stay my nerves; it helped slightly until I caught Weston's hawk eyes fixed on my hands. His gaze floated up to meet mine, and he arched a brow. Of course he didn't understand why I was nervous; he had no idea what tonight was really about. This was my chance to get inside Chase's house and find evidence that would incriminate him or point me in the direction of his partners in crime.

An armed guard was at the gate when we pulled up, another at the door with some kind of assault rifle strapped to his chest. The massive Spanish-inspired stucco home would best be described as a compound plopped down in the middle of Dallas. Chase seemed to be a little zealous with his security. What monsters chased him to need all this to feel safe?

As I raised my hand to knock, the door swung open, revealing Chase standing in the doorway. He really was handsome in a serious-type way. At least tonight he'd ditched his typical expensive suit and donned a pair of navy slacks with a light blue dress shirt—no tie—with the sleeves rolled up to his elbows.

"Glad you could finally make it," he said, flashing a smirk behind the steepled fingers against his lips.

It was seven thirty, after all, a whole thirty minutes after he *told*—not asked—me to arrive.

With my own cocky smirk, I replied, "I'm worth the wait, don't you think?"

With a nod in agreement, he gripped my hand and guided us through the open dark wood double doors into his home. The Spanish theme continued throughout with a large open floor plan. Terra-cotta tile covered the floor and some of the walls, and the distant trickle of water indicated an indoor fountain close by. It was tastefully decorated too, keeping to the theme of the home with large leather chairs and solid wood tables in the various rooms I saw.

I etched a mental map with each room we passed, and right before we entered an expansive living room that opened into a busy kitchen, we went by his office. Doing a quick double take, I noted the large desk, floor-to-ceiling bookshelves, and leather chairs positioned throughout. If any damning evidence was in this house, that was where it would be.

Done with the brief tour, Chase led us to a tan leather couch in the large living room. When we sat, he pulled me in close, the length of our thighs pressed tight side by side. An older white man in a tailored suit appeared, carrying a tray lined with six wineglasses, three filled with white and three with red.

"None are merlot." Chase beamed. He was very proud of himself for remembering that small detail from the night we met. "But I wasn't sure what you *did* like, so here's an assortment."

The man holding the tray pointed and named the various wines in his hand. Selecting a cabernet of some sort, I took a tasting sip and nodded my approval. Another man approached, but only one drink sat on his tray—a highball glass filled with square ice cubes and some kind of caramel-tinted liquid.

"Bourbon," Chase said, inclining his head toward the glass now in his hand. A curt nod and both men were dismissed, leaving us alone —well, alone plus Weston. A fire roared in the corner, warming the room and cutting the cold that seeped up from the stone floor. "So, Kate, tell me something about yourself that I haven't uncovered through my extensive research."

Reaching across him, I set my wineglass down on the end table to his left. His breathing hitched and a smile pulled at his lips when I paused, our faces inches from each other. Without breaking eye contact, I accepted the highball glass he offered and took a long sip before returning it to his awaiting hand. "I like bourbon too." His eyes followed the movement of my tongue as I slid it along my lower lip.

"You're full of surprises, aren't you? I don't know if I've ever met anyone like you, which is probably why I was smitten from our first meeting." Without looking away, he called for one of the men, telling him to bring another highball glass. "I think you're the first woman I've met at one of those awful charity functions who didn't fall at my feet."

"If you're looking for someone to fawn over you, you're right, I'm not your girl."

Weston shifted in my periphery, walking the room like he was assessing the surroundings, and stopped behind Chase—in my direct line of sight. My gaze briefly flicked up. He had a cocky-as-hell smirk on his handsome face. Bastard knew exactly what he was doing.

Chase draped an arm over the back of the dark leather couch, his fingers grazing my shoulder. "I'm liking the challenge so far, and I'm pretty good at reading people, so I can tell you are too."

"It's been very diverting, yes. Which is good since my life seems to be a mess right now. Thankfully, I go back to work in a little over a week, so some things will get back to normal."

Chase's gaze zeroed in on Weston, who was now walking about

the room like he owned it, distracting us both. "When will you be done with the bodyguard?"

I sighed, keeping my attention on Chase, avoiding Weston. "Whenever this trial is over and they have some decent leads on who shot me. I'm not quite sure when that's going to be. It's not that big of a deterrent, is it?"

"For me, no, but my security team isn't happy about it. They know he's armed and looks to pose a risk even if he wasn't." His attention shifted back to me to gauge my reaction.

Hell yeah he can. He's a fucking badass, so you better get your damn fingers off me was what I wanted to say. But feisty Kate wasn't the role I was playing tonight, who I needed to be for the next few hours. I shrugged to feign indifference and took a sip of bourbon; it burned going down. Damn, I hated bourbon.

"He's fine as long as I am. I talked to him before we got here. He knows what to expect from tonight, and if we need... privacy, he'll respect that."

The arm slung over the back of the couch wrapped around my shoulders, pulling me in close. The strength of his designer cologne clogged my nose, making it a struggle to breathe. His lips brushed against mine. "And why might we need privacy?"

The few sips of bourbon made me brave, or stupid. Leaning in close, my lips grazed the rim of his ear. "In case the body shots get out of hand." He chuckled, then jumped when I bit his earlobe hard enough to hurt. I pulled back to gauge his reaction; his eyes were dark and hooded, a look that told me if we were alone right now, I would be on my back in half a second. But with an audience, he was restraining himself.

His mouth opened, but the ringing cell phone in his pocket stopped him short. Sighing, he leaned against the couch to fish it out of his slacks, his eyes narrowing at the number on the screen.

"I have to get this. Excuse me," he mumbled, still staring at the phone.

"Okay," I said and sat forward to retrieve my purse from the coffee table, knowing I should record his conversation in case it proved useful. Sliding my phone from my purse, I moved my thumbs as if I were texting but instead pressed the voice recording app and angled the speaker toward an unaware Chase.

Damn. The conversation had flipped to Spanish. I would have to translate it later.

With a searching glance to where I sat, he mumbled an apology and walked from the room to gain privacy.

Damnit.

"Are you enjoying yourself?" Weston asked from his spot in a corner of the room.

"Yes. Are you?"

Weston's growl was still echoing when Chase returned. He glanced between us and plopped down on the couch beside me.

"Everything okay?" I asked with soft eyes, faking concern.

"Yeah, having some issues at the border with a few of my shipments. It'll be fine. I'm flying down to San Diego in a couple days to sort it all out." He sighed, rolling the highball glass against his forehead. "Sorry for the interruption, but most of my products are perishable and can't sit in Mexico for weeks while they figure out the paperwork."

"It's okay. What's for dinner, anyway?"

The break in our earlier conversation was a relief. Teasing him to the breaking point wasn't the best plan, but what else was I to do? We had nothing in common to talk about.

My question pulled him from his introspective mood. With a real smile, one I was positive few people witnessed, he explained the authentic Mexican food we would be served.

***

THE FOOD WAS delicious and the wine even better. Several courses were served in the large formal dining room, and now that we were done, we sat sipping our wines, waiting on dessert to be served. The conversation through dinner had flowed easily since I kept turning every question he asked back around for him to answer. Like I expected, he enjoyed talking about himself.

Between bites, he spoke about growing up in San Diego; his parents moved there from Northern California for the weather. When I asked where he learned to speak Spanish so fluently, he said it was something he picked up here and there in school but really began learning when he started his own business. Importing and exporting authentic Mexican goods was a lucrative business he noticed growing up, so when he was old enough, he started his own.

Unfortunately, not one mention of human or drug trafficking, but maybe it wasn't a polite first-date topic.

His phone buzzed against the wood table, distracting him. Now would be the best time for snooping if I was going to do it. Excusing myself for the powder room, I left Chase, still focused on his phone, in the dining room.

I discreetly dashed to the living room for my purse and started toward his office but stopped short. Weston was behind me, following from room to room.

"I'm going to the bathroom. You can stay in here. Give me two minutes alone, please."

He narrowed his eyes, assessing, but nodded in approval and resumed his spot in the corner of the room—which I was sure gave him the best vantage point for the entire first floor.

With only a few minutes before both men would start to wonder where I'd disappeared to, I had to act fast. I said a silent prayer of thanks that there was a powder room directly across the hall from the office. This way, if I did get caught, I could say I got turned around. It would be a piss-poor lie, but maybe it would work if things went sideways.

My hands and heart shook as I closed the glass-paned wood doors to the office behind me. The large leather chair rolled noiselessly across the soft rug when I pulled it out from under his desk. Reaching for the side drawers, I pulled once, twice.

Locked.

They were all locked.

Mentally groaning with frustration, I started rummaging through the various files on his tidy desk, but nothing looked suspect. Maybe this wasn't the smartest plan. What would I actually find in here?

I was about to call the whole night a loss and head back to Chase so he wouldn't suspect anything when my eyes landed on a corner of paper sticking out from under his appointment book. Sucking in a tentative breath, I slid the paper out, glancing up every half second to make sure no one was about to burst in and catch me snooping.

Through the minimal light, the paper looked like a purchase order of some kind with a company logo, a small security camera, in the top right-hand corner. Even though I couldn't read what it said, my gut said it could be the type of information I needed.

The phone wobbled in my shaky hand as I angled it over the paper. I didn't dare use the flash as I snapped the pictures, even with the chance the paper wouldn't be legible with so little light.

Hurried, stomping footsteps against the Spanish tile echoed down the hall.

Shit. I'd been gone too long. It was either Chase or Weston coming to check on me—I prayed for Weston. The footsteps paused. I tucked the paper back where I found it and sat in the deep leather chair, leaning back with my feet propped up on the desk just as the door opened.

"What are you doing in here?" Anger and annoyance in his tone boomed across the room.

Hidden behind the desk, I wiped my clammy palms against my leather leggings. I didn't dare move more than that; if I did, it might seem suspicious. Lowering my voice to a beckoning whisper, I said, "Waiting for you."

"Oh?" Chase's tense walk relaxed with each step farther into the office, closer to me.

I crooked a finger with a mischievous smile, urging him closer.

Sweat again beaded on my palms. This was an idiotic move. I'd now put myself alone with Chase, egging him on at that, with no escape plan.

He gripped the heels of my boots, lifting my legs, and dropped them to the floor. "Now that you have me in here, Kate, what's next?"

Surprisingly, my wobbling legs held strong as I pushed out of the chair and wrapped my arms around his waist, pulling him against me.

"I like desks," I whispered, struggling to look as aroused as he did. *Damnit, what am I doing?*

One minute I was standing, and the next my ass was on the desk, legs spread wide, allowing him to stand between them. His fingers ran roughly through my hair. I groaned to cover the painful whimper that almost escaped instead. His lips pushed against mine, his tongue parting them instantly, invading my mouth.

The way he held my head, keeping my lips firmly sealed against his... bile rose in my throat.

Tears threatened, but I held it together, pushing my rising panic down where it would stay hidden from Chase. His hands brushed down my sides, the slope of my breasts, and clenched around my waist. With a strong tug, I was on the edge of the desk, flush against him—the growing hardness in his slacks pressed against my abdomen.

Light, wet kisses trailed across my jaw and down my neck. I brushed away the single tear that escaped, rolling down my cheek, with the back of my hand before he could notice. Not that he would have. His focus was not on me, only on where he wanted this to end.

Pulling his face up to meet mine, I said, "Chase, we need to stop. I'm not cleared from the shooting until next week. I can't... we can't...." It wasn't true, but maybe my injury would make him stop.

He groaned. "Then what are you going to do about this?" He reached for my right hand and wrapped it around himself through his slacks, thrusting into my hand.

What am I going to do?

"You're a grown man. I'm sure you've come up with some ways to take care of it yourself. I hear most involve lotion and a tube sock," I said teasingly. Maybe he would get the hint this wasn't going to happen.

He didn't.

A dark, low laugh rumbled through his chest. "I bring you into my home, have a wonderful dinner and delightful conversation, if I do say so myself, and this is the thanks I get? When *you're* the one who lured *me* into my office for privacy."

Where the hell is Weston? If he popped his head in, the moment would break and all this would stop.

But I *had* asked him to give us privacy. *Of course, the one time he listens.*

Damnit.

I clenched my eyes shut and swallowed down the bile rising in my throat at the sound of a zipper being pulled down.

Again he gripped my hand and brought it against him, this time skin to skin. "Don't make me ask you again. What are you going to do about this, Kate?"

A battle raged. Should I tell him to fuck off or give in? If I balked now, he would either suspect my true intentions or get pissed and never see me again. Neither would help me get what I needed.

So there I was, on his desk, legs spread and hand on his cock. Maybe it wouldn't be that bad. It wasn't like I hadn't done this kind of thing with other guys before. Images of all the abused, broken women who'd come through Second Chances flashed in my mind. For them I would do anything. If doing this helped me see him again, gave me another shot to dig up information, then it was worth it.

Losing some of my own self-respect for the chance to save them was worth it.

14

I *have to get out of here.*

I was going to vomit all over the entryway and all over *him* as he hugged me saying what a wonderful time he had.

Fucking bastard. Of course he was saying that.

Thirty more seconds. I could hold on for thirty more seconds.

Chase kissed my cheek one last time with a murmured "Good night."

My stomach lurched, but I swallowed it down.

The asshole wouldn't even kiss me after all that. I'd *never* been so used, debased in my life. I wanted to hit him, then smack myself for allowing it.

Shit, I'm going to puke right now. I need to get out the door. Now.

The flat boots made my hasty escape easier as I hauled ass to the waiting Mercedes, Weston close behind. Chase called out from the front door before I could climb into the SUV, making me swallow my stomach contents once again. I wasn't going to let him see me lose it; then he would know, and I hadn't just done *that* to show my cards now.

"Hey," he said, jogging to catch up to us. "I was thinking, why don't you come to San Diego with me next week? You mentioned you're going back to work soon, so this could be a fun trip away before. Plus, you'll be cleared by then."

I so wanted to puke on his thousand-dollar shoes.

"I'll think about it. Thank you again for tonight, Chase. It was fun," I said, turning toward the car.

"Here's my number." He tucked a card into my hand. "Text me soon and let me know. We can take the company jet."

A nod was all I could muster before jumping into the SUV. Weston was barely in, the door not even closed behind him. I smacked the driver on the shoulder, yelling at him to go. Thankfully he did. With a quick glance behind me, I saw Chase walk back into the house, showing no concern that I couldn't get out of there fast enough. After all, *he* had gotten what he wanted.

Two blocks.

I made it all of two blocks.

Once again, I smacked the driver, but this time for him to pull over. But I couldn't talk; if I did, there would be no more holding back. His questioning eyes flicked up to the rearview mirror, but not understanding my silent demand, he didn't pull over.

Shit. This is happening.

I grappled for the door handle and shoved, but it wouldn't open. Again I shoved the door with my entire body weight. It finally swung open, and with my hand still gripping the handle, I went with it.

An arm wrapped around my waist, saving me from falling out of the moving car.

"What the hell—"

I vomited onto the moving pavement below.

Again and again.

Weston's hands still gripped my hips, keeping me in the car even after we'd pulled over onto the shoulder.

The shaking started in my arms and spread.

"Kate?" he whispered, fear and concern wrapping my name.

I shook my head, still out the door, not able to handle the trembling in that normally strong voice.

"It must have been the food. I'm fine." Pushing off the door, I sat back in the seat, closing my eyes. Every vent in the SUV was pointed my direction with the AC blowing full blast, even though it was forty degrees outside. That little act of kindness, his attention and concern…. He was the one I wanted, but once he found out about Chase and what I'd done, what would he do?

I gagged and leaned out the door again.

He wrapped his hands around my hair, gently holding it back. "We need to get you to the hospital."

"No," I insisted and sat back in the chair, closing my eyes once again. "No, I'm fine. I can make it home. Just take me home. Please."

His scent enveloped me when he reached across to close my door. Like I was fragile glass, he carefully buckled me in, adjusting the seat belt before commanding the driver to get us back. Now.

The entire drive, he held my hand, his thumb caressing along my knuckles, and I could feel his eyes on me.

Seconds.

I was seconds away from throwing up again as visuals of the night involuntarily replayed over and over again behind my eyes. As soon as the SUV pulled to a stop in front of the townhouse, I pushed the door open and tried to climb out, but the seat belt held me in. Pressing the release button while still leaning out of the car had me falling to the pavement, landing on my hands and knees.

Distantly, Weston yelled, "Fuck, Kate, let me—"

No, he couldn't help me. Not now. Not anymore.

Pushing to my feet, I stumbled to the front door only to find it locked. Angry hot tears trickled down my cheeks as I pounded on the door, silently begging Ryan or Joe to open it.

The lock clicked. I pushed the door open, shoving a shocked Ryan aside, and ran to the half-bath down the hall. Locking the door behind me left me little time to make it to the toilet. My knees hit the tile and I hugged the toilet, throwing up the remainder of my dinner.

All concept of time was lost. How long had I been lying on the cool tile floor? By the loud banging against the door, someone—or two someones—thought it'd been long enough. Weston would demand an explanation. He knew I wasn't sick; he saw my face as we left tonight. He would piece everything together sooner or later.

Drawing my knees to my chest, my wet cheek pressed against them, I stared at the wall.

I'm in over my head. Why in the hell did I think I could do this alone?

Chase hadn't really forced me to do anything; he thought I was enjoying it as much as he was. Maybe my minimizing it before was wrong. Or not. Damnit, I couldn't tell. Everything was so messed up in my scrambled mind. Where was the truth?

Anger, deep and white-hot, began to simmer and boil in my veins with no way to let it out. The pounding and shouting at the door, the two men fighting, plus the insistent disgusting thought of myself was my breaking point. Reaching on top of the vanity, I searched around the rim and grabbed the first thing my hand could wrap around. And I threw it. Threw it as hard as I could against the door. I screamed from the forceful movement of my still-healing shoulder.

Glass shattered against the door, then silence.

Deafening silence.

Then it wasn't.

A thud—the door shuddered.

Another. The cracking of wood, the lock splitting, and the door flew open.

Weston and Ryan stood in the doorway staring at me on the floor, keeping their distance, not daring to cross the threshold of the bathroom.

"What the fuck is going on, Kate? I know it wasn't the food." Weston's hands gripped above the doorframe, torso angled into the small space, like he was restraining himself from coming to me.

"I'm fine," I said, meeting his gaze but quickly turning, burying my head against my knees.

"Like hell you're fine," he yelled. My head jerked up at his menacing tone. "What did that bastard do to you? If you don't tell me *right now,* I'm going back and will make *him* tell me. I swear, Kate. Damn this shi—"

"Stay out of it, Weston!" I screamed. "This has nothing to do with you."

His boots crunched against the broken glass on the floor as he dared one step, then another into the bathroom. Even from where I sat, the anger in his eyes flared. "If that piece of shit hurt you, if he laid a fucking finger on you, it has everything to do with me. I'll kill him, Kate. I'll fucking kill him."

"No."

Turning, he shoved the destroyed door, making me jump and Ryan swear, as he started toward the direction of the front door.

"Shit, Kate, tell him. If you don't, I will," Ryan shouted.

"You bastard! You said you wouldn't say anything."

He blanched at the pure fury in my quiet tone.

Weston stepped back into view, his face nearly purple, eyes only on Ryan. "What the hell are you two talking about?" he said in a dead-calm voice.

At that point I did kind of fear for Ryan's well-being, even if I was pissed at him. Weston looked like he might kill him before thinking of the consequences.

"Ryan, get out. You need to leave now. Let me talk to him. I'll explain everything, but you need to go. Now."

I tried to push off the floor, needing to stand for this conversation with Weston, but I was so tired. So damn tired. Of everything. Mostly of my head being so jumbled I couldn't trust what it was telling me. Staring at the floor, at the mess I would now have to clean up, my attention landed on a large shard of glass.

It would be so easy, if I really did want all this to end now, to silence my overactive brain. Maybe that was the only way for me to get back to normal.

My chin jerked upward, taking my focus from the glass to Weston's alarmed face. The fear behind his searching eyes, it was like he knew every single thought I just had.

"Stop it, Kate. Whatever it is, we can fix it. We can get through anything together, remember?"

I nodded in confirmation. He was right. I still had him.

For now.

He lifted me from the floor, carried me over the broken glass, and lowered me onto a stool in the kitchen.

Needing to brush my teeth and change, I told Weston as much and headed up the stairs, trying not to let his concern shred what was left of my heart.

Three minutes later, I found him on the couch, his forearms braced against his bouncing thighs. My heart ached seeing him so worried when everything that happened I did to myself.

All of it. That night in Vail, the shooting, tonight with Chase—all of it was somehow my fault, a result of my actions.

I chose a seat, the farthest from him, and settled in, tucking my cold feet under me on the couch. This was going to be bad. I should have made coffee first.

"I'll start from the beginning," I said. He nodded his agreement and leaned back against the couch, his clenched fists resting on his thighs. "Okay, wow. This is.... In the hospital—"

Weston shot from the couch and began pacing furiously around the room. "Fuck, Kate," he groaned. "This... whatever this is, you've been keeping it from me since then?"

"Just sit down and listen, you big brute, before you make permanent tracks on my floor. I'm trying to tell you. Sit down." He glared, not loving me ordering him around, as he settled back on the couch. "As I was saying, in the hospital, Shelly came to see me. You remember her stopping by, right?" His head bobbed with the same rhythm of his knee. "She mentioned one of the girls we helped last year came back saying she recognized one of her captors who brought her here to the US against her will. Shelly told me this thinking I would give the name to my dad, but instead... I knew the legal system couldn't or wouldn't do anything without evidence, and since this guy was here in Dallas...."

His face paled. His knees stopped bobbing. Hell, was he even breathing?

"So I learned everything I could about him, going as far as getting an old high school friend to get me into the various events he would also be attending."

He broke in, partly talking to me, partly to himself. "That night, at the fundraiser. You knew he was going to be there. You didn't randomly bump into him. And somehow you knew being an ass would attract him to you."

"Yes."

"What the fucking hell, Kate?" he yelled and turned, placing his back to me. In an eerily quiet tone, he questioned, "You 'learned everything you could,' and then what? You chose to get close to him, to put yourself in danger with someone who, what, dabbles in human trafficking so you could trick him into giving you evidence? Do you have any idea how asinine that sounds? You know who I work for. That I have resources. Why the hell didn't you come to me for help? Hell, for intel, at least."

"I knew you wouldn't—"

"For fuck's sake, Kate!" he roared.

He stalked toward me but paused a few feet away. A mix of fury and hurt strained his features. If there were even a glimmer of a thought he would do anything to hurt me, he would be intimidating like this. But I wasn't afraid of him or what his actions might be. Never of him.

"Of course I wouldn't want you to get close to him. We'd have found another way. But at what point are you going to realize I don't *let* you do anything? I am well aware that when you put your mind to something, you're doing it, regardless of the consequences. I couldn't stop you if I wanted to, so at least let me in. Let me at least protect you when you throw yourself into danger! You can't leave me in the dark."

"I didn't—"

"Nope, still my turn. I don't know what all happened tonight, but from now on, you let me in, damnit. I would do anything for you, Kate, and I thought... fuck, I thought...."

I dared a step closer. "You thought what, Weston?"

"I thought you knew that. I thought you *trusted* me. I thought I was more to you than just your damn bodyguard. That we were more than that to you."

"Casey... I... I do think of you as more than someone here just keeping me safe, but you have to understand when all this happened, I didn't trust you. You had just walked back into my life after four damn weeks of being gone. Not a single word. Not a single text with where you were or if you were even thinking about me. So you don't get to sit here and yell at me about how I don't trust you when you're fucking right, I didn't. I had to shove you back into that bodyguard category just to survive without you."

He took a step back. Then another. My return anger and confession seemed to surprise him. All his fury had dissolved; now only sadness clouded his features.

He ran both hands through his hair, his head drooped. "Do you know what kind of people this guy surrounds himself with if what that girl said was true? If they find out you were trying to expose—"

"That's what your brother was trying to warn me against. The night you found him in my room, I was kind of buying his silence." I shrugged; hopefully he wouldn't kill Ryan for helping me.

Those brown eyes widened, realization flaring, as he stared through me. "Wait, does this mean... all that talk about you needing to move on, needing to get over me, was shit? It was all a lie? You don't want to be with him?" He started toward me, but I held my palms out, stopping him.

"Let me finish. Tonight... I thought tonight would be a perfect night to search for the information I needed. I... after dinner...." I stood from the couch and paced the length of the room. "After dinner, I excused myself, and instead of going to the bathroom, I snuck into his office." I paused to gauge his reaction. I'd just admitted that I'd lied to his face to get that moment of freedom. But he was looking past me, burning a hole into the wall. "I found something, but I took too long, and he caught me. I played it off, making him think I lured him in there for a few minutes alone."

My stomach was rolling again at the memory of what I did to maintain the charade—of what I would now have to admit to Weston I had done. Rushing to his bathroom, I barely made it to the toilet in time. Half a second later, his fingers brushed against the back of my neck as he held my long dark hair away from my face.

"What did he do?" That deadly, intense voice he used with Ryan, that he used to use with me, was back—directed at me.

"He didn't know. I had to make him think—" My head whipped back to the toilet as I gagged.

"I'm going to enjoy killing him."

And I knew he would. If I even gave the slightest indication I approved, he would be out the door, across town, and snapping Chase's neck before the next hour chimed.

As much as I hated bringing him into this mess and telling him about tonight, confessing it all was like lifting the weight that had been sitting on my chest slowly suffocating me. No more lies. And now that I had support, I wasn't going to do this alone.

"I'm shocked. I figured once I told you, your anger would be directed at me rather than him. He's an arrogant bastard, but I'm the one playing him. Or trying to, that is."

Flushing the toilet, I stood at the sink splashing cold water on my face and rinsing out my mouth.

"Oh I'm... I'm beyond mad. But for some reason not as pissed at you as you might think. I'm a little impressed, in a way, that you could do all this under my nose and I had no idea. Maybe my ability to read through bullshit is getting rusty," he grumbled.

Good. Not angry with me.

Maybe we could make it through this after all.

With a relieved sigh, I turned to face him, pressing my backside against the vanity. "Want to look at the stuff I found tonight?"

"Are you okay? Thirty minutes ago you were throwing up everything from the past forty-eight hours on Northwest Highway. I can't believe you're ready to move on from that."

Not wanting him to see exactly how *not* okay I was with all this, I turned, putting my back to him. If I were being honest with myself, I was ashamed of how I assumed he would react. It seemed I misjudged this overprotective, aggressive teddy bear. Not the first time or the last.

"No, I'm not okay. I'm in way over my head, and I don't know what to do next. I've gotten this far and just did... well, whatever, and now I don't know where to go from here. I didn't do all this to stop now. Yes, I feel disgusting. Yes, I want to maul his eyes out of their sockets for what he did. Yes, I want to curl up in a ball with a bottle of wine and forget about tonight. But that's not going to happen. Like you said with the nightmares, I'm not going to let this break me. It won't break my resolve to get justice for all those women and stop it from happening to more. Their lives and the lives of future women are more important than giving in to a meltdown."

Our eyes connected in the mirror. His head was shaking back and forth, but he also wore a lopsided smile, one I'd never seen before, conveying amazement. Like he couldn't believe everything that had transpired in the past hour. From realizing I wasn't moving on to learning how I was putting my life in danger and why I still had to push forward with my stupid plan. That look, his astonishment, sparked tears in the corners of my eyes. Never had anyone made me feel so loved and understood with a single look.

"Kate Wheeler, you... you are relentless, arrogant, stubborn, and have zero self-preservation skills, but all of that is what makes you so incredible. I thank God every day that I've had the chance to meet you. That I've gotten to know you, who you really are, and see that... that there is someone out there worth fighting for, because of how hard you fight for others who can't. You amaze me. Every damn day you amaze me. And what you're doing is courageous. Risky, but courageous."

What did someone say to that? A simple "thanks" didn't really seem to cut it.

"But you need to know your own damn limits. I cannot believe you left me out of this. If you *ever* do anything like this again on your own, I can't be held responsible for my actions."

A smirk pulled the corners of my lips upward, remembering

exactly what those actions would be. He demonstrated them that first night in Vail. Who knew spanking would be so... fun.

"I seem to remember you showing me a side of those actions already, and I also seem to recall saying I would find something naughtier to warrant more. Maybe I've missed that palm of yours and this was my plan all along."

In one fluid motion, he pushed from the wall, his eyes never leaving mine. With a large step, his solid chest pressed against my back, forcing my hips to dig against the granite vanity top. His chest rose and fell with ragged breaths, mirroring my own. Eyes still glued to mine in the mirror, he bent down and brushed his lips against the shell of my ear. His warm breath sent my stomach fluttering, tensing and releasing in a rapid pace.

The whole world stopped around us. The distractions of Chase. Second Chances. The trial. All gone, absorbed in the body heat pouring from him into me. He was doing this on purpose, knowing I needed a distraction. Something to trigger me to move forward, move past tonight's events.

"And I told you, baby, it would be worse the next time. If I were you, I would be nervous the next time that bare perky ass of yours is within reach."

"Looking forward to it." My words were barely a breath, barely even audible over the thudding of my heart, but by the arch in his brow in response, he heard loud and clear.

Yes, this is what I need.

Distract me.

This, he, can heal this festering wound in my mind that won't let me go.

We stared at each other, both wanting more from this moment, but we couldn't. If we started there would be no stopping. We knew how good it could be again, how incredible we were together. There wasn't a day that went by that I didn't think about those two nights in Vail, and from his lust-filled, hooded eyes, he hadn't forgotten either.

Two rough hands drifted up my waist, palms skimming under my sweater against bare skin. The tips of his fingers swept across each rib as his hands continued their ascent. My eyes closed, head thudding back against his chest, as each hand reached my breasts and dipped long fingers into each bra cup, massaging skin to skin as his thumbs circled my peaked nipples.

His wet lips pressed against my throat. There was no holding back my jumbled curses, making his lips curve against my skin, as I lost myself in his touch. He was enjoying this. And so was I. But I needed more than this.

His teeth clamped around a tender area along my neck at the same time he pinched each nipple. I sucked in a startled breath as my eyes flew open, only to find him staring down with a devious smile.

"And that's for those relentless, teasing texts."

Both hands slid from my chest to grip my hips and turn me, setting me on the countertop. Even like this we weren't eye to eye. I tipped my head back, waiting for his next move.

"If you don't want Chase, if you aren't ready to move on, what does that mean for us, baby?"

Okay, didn't expect that. Talking was the last thing I wanted to do. And by the bulge in his pants pressing against my thigh, he felt the same.

But if he wanted to talk, might as well get everything out on the table tonight.

"Weston, I'm not sure. You still haven't told me the whole truth about why you left. You haven't really explained why I shouldn't be terrified to trust you with my heart again."

The breath from his deep sigh brushed over me. "Protecting you stopped being a job a long time ago, Kate. It moved to being a necessity. And something in me snapped when I had to watch that bastard hit you over and over again, unable to stop him from beating the shit out of the girl I.... I don't deserve someone like you, and I didn't want to be around when you figured that out too. When you realized it was my fault. The only thing I could do was cut you out altogether. There was no way I could protect you like you needed, not when every time I looked at you.... You deserved better. You needed better—"

"So you gave up. Turned and left without a single look back."

"No, not at all. Damnit, Kate, how do you not know...? I know you can't forgive me for walking out. I don't expect you to, but at least know a part of me died when I walked out that door knowing I was leaving the woman I...."

The smooth skin of his forehead pressed against mine, his hands gripping the countertop on either side of my thighs, boxing me in. When his eyes opened, reconnecting with my own, the shame that swirled had me gripping his face between my hands and holding it close.

The truth. And just like that, another weight lifted as I let go of the remaining pain I'd clung to in order to keep my healing heart arm's distance away.

"I'm ready to forgive you, Casey, I really am. I've been holding on to this resentment because I didn't understand. I thought if it was easy for you to walk away the first time, what would keep you from doing it again? Each morning I woke up alone in your bed or in my own, my heart ached for you. Maybe once the trial is over, we can move past all this and start fresh. You know, maybe have a normal relationship with dating, taking it one day at a time. That's what I want with you. And I'm willing to risk my heart again for a shot at a future with you."

His soft lips molded against mine, holding all the promises of our future. In that single kiss, we dropped our anger and regret, clearing space for all the new feelings and thoughts of what was to come. Now we only had to wait until the trial was over.

Easier said than done.

Ryan and Joe eyed us as we emerged from Weston's room. The three men exchanged several glances before Joe got the hint and showed himself out.

"Damn, what did I miss?" Ryan asked, leaning against the countertop acting casual, but the nervous glances he kept shooting Weston's way told me he was anything but. "Did you two work everything out, or should I be prepared to fight for my life?"

Weston grumbled something noncommittal back as he began making a pot of coffee. The aroma of fresh grounds filled the kitchen, shifting my mind from Weston's teasing to the future glorious cup of scrumptiousness.

"I told him everything," I said to Ryan when he came to sit beside me on the stool. A sidelong warning glance from Weston said I was sitting a little too close to his brother from his perspective. "We're good, but I can't promise you he won't kill you in your sleep at a later date for taking my bribe."

"Let me worry about Casey."

My deep sigh made my shoulders slump as I picked the label off Ryan's beer bottle. "Where do I go from here though? What else can I do?"

"You need to stop, that's what you need to do," Ryan reprimanded. "Nothing good will come from you seeing Chase again. I don't know what you're doing with him and what you're trying to accomplish, but someone will find out, then report back to Chase, and you'll end up dead. Take it from me, these guys... they're the worst out there, and I would know. Even I don't associate with them, and that's saying something."

An abrasive, chopped laugh erupted from Weston, which forced a pained smile to appear on Ryan's face. He knew his lifestyle wasn't up to par for Weston, but it didn't seem Ryan was planning on making changes anytime soon.

Exhausted, I folded my arms along the island and laid my head against them. I prayed everything I'd done during the past month hadn't been for nothing. Even though the project had gone exactly as I'd planned, I still didn't have anything plausible from my efforts.

My warm breath pushed against the granite back into my face as I spoke. "I get it, he's bad." Heat from a ceramic mug being pressed against the back of my hand had me opening my eyes and raising up, propping my head in my hands. "But now I know he's mixed up in all this, I can't drop it."

"You mentioned earlier you found something. What was it?" Weston asked, blowing across the top of his own steaming cup of coffee.

Mug in hand, I walked to the entryway where my purse was lying on the floor from my hasty entrance. It took a minute to locate my phone in the large handbag, but once I found it, I went back to the kitchen where they were waiting for a response.

"First there's this." I pressed Play on the recording of his phone conversation. From the looks on their faces, neither spoke Spanish.

Now Ryan was the one anxiously stripping what was left of the beer label. If he was nervous, maybe I should be more terrified than I was. But I wasn't. "I caught a few things, but I did hear somethin' about San Diego."

My eyes flew to Weston. San Diego was where Chase wanted to take me. Maybe....

Like he had many times before, Weston read my mind. "I'll get it to one of my friends. He can translate it for us and keep it confidential."

"Are you sure you trust this guy? If we're going to have any hope of breaking up this ring... grouping... gang... whatever you call it, having the surprise factor is the only way it could happen."

The smirk on his face told me enough, but still he nodded. "He's one of my army buddies. I would trust him with my life, have on multiple occasions actually."

"Great, I'll text it to you. Then there was this." I pulled up the multiple dark pictures from Chase's office. Bits were legible, but the majority of the paper was too dark to read, making my optimism slip a rung.

A calloused hand gripped and squeezed my slumped shoulder. It really was amazing how well he could read my body language. "I know someone who can help with that too. Send both to me, and I'll call my buddies now." With that, he walked to the hallway, set the alarm, and went to his room for privacy while he made the necessary calls.

Ryan and I sat in silence for a few minutes before he spoke up.

"Is this real, Kate? Or is what you're doing some fling because of convenience? Because if it is, he's.... I've never seen him like this with anyone else. Not even with Anne."

My head whipped to Ryan, eyes wide, not knowing what to say regarding the reference to another woman who was in Weston's life at one point. And not only in his life; the way he made it sound, this *Anne* had been important to him.

The quick reaction and surprise written on my face gave me away, making Ryan stand from the stool and head to the living room.

"Not so fast, Ryan. Who is Anne?"

"No one, nothing. He hasn't told you about her?"

"Obviously with me asking the question 'Who is Anne?' no, you dumbass."

He smirked.

I loved the playful smirk he and Weston shared. It made my heart happy knowing something about me could bring humor to both men's lives.

"Well, then forget I mentioned it. He'll tell you when he's ready."

"Why don't you tell me now, save him the trouble?"

"Nice try, tiny one." He smacked his palm against the top of my head as he patted me like a child. "What I was getting at was he's different with you, and I can tell he really likes you. It might even be past that for him. But with Casey, just give him time, okay? He's not an open person, so be patient, let him come to you with stuff. Like with the Anne story. It's his to tell, not mine. Give him time and space. He'll tell you."

A strong breath pushed against the back of my teeth in a hiss and I pulled away from him, now more curious than ever. Okay, it did make sense, but who was this Anne person, and what if, in some way, he was comparing me to her? Or maybe she hurt him and she was the reason he was closed off.

Not able to handle the thought of Weston being with another woman, I focused on Ryan's original question.

"I do like him, Ryan," I said into my empty coffee mug. "A lot actually, and now that this stuff with Chase is out in the open, I'm so glad I can stop fighting it. Stop trying to avoid him and my feelings for him. I'm not sure where we'll go from here, because ultimately he'll leave, and my home is here. My life is here."

"Your life. Tell me about your life, Kate," he said with his head in the fridge. There was an edge to his voice I couldn't quite place. It almost sounded like he was mocking me.

"Well, I have my job, my friends, my dad, volunteering," I said defensively. "With my job, I don't have a lot of time for anything else."

After pulling another beer from the fridge, he sauntered over and draped a lean arm around my shoulder, pulling me close to his side. "What would you give up to be with him?" he whispered down to me.

One breath in and one breath out as I thought about my response. But I already knew what it would be. "Everything," I breathed, looking up at him and meaning it with every bit of my soul.

Very ready for sleep, I groaned into my pillow and slid down into the cool, soft sheets, but the bedroom door swung open, pushing bright light from the hallway into my room, illuminating Weston's large frame in the doorway.

"You asleep?" he whispered, waiting before venturing in.

"No." I fluffed my pillow, trying to get it the way I wanted it. "Did you hear back from either of your friends?"

"Yeah, both, but the one who's looking into the pictures needs a little more time. The one who could translate the call, I just got off the phone with him."

"And?" I asked, sitting up and pressing my back against the headboard.

He crossed the room and fell into the large wingback chair he'd slept in so many nights.

"And... I don't want to tell you."

"Why?"

"Because I know you. And I know what you'll want to do with the information."

"And...?"

"And I'm tired of you being in danger. You already have people after you because of the trial. Why do you want to add more?"

"That's not your call, Weston. Didn't we just get done discussing how you won't stop me from doing what I need to do?" I asked, crossing my arms over my chest, frustrated at this whole conversation. "Tell me or you know I'll translate it on my own tomorrow."

He groaned and leaned back into the chair, covering his face with his hands. I heard his deep sigh when he finally made his decision.

"When he goes to San Diego, that trip he invited you on, he's going to meet with someone to discuss new trade routes. My buddy said it sounded like the guy Chase was talking to was his partner and they were going to hash out some details at this in-person meeting."

I started to say something, but he raised a hand, stopping me.

"I know what you're going to suggest, but I have a plan. One that will give us both what we want."

"And what is that, Weston?"

"You want to get enough information to put this bastard in prison, which I agree with, but I need to know you're safe."

"Okay, are you going to tell me your master plan, or will I have to figure it out along the way?" I asked sarcastically. His evasiveness was starting to grate on my nerves.

"Tomorrow. Tomorrow I'll tell you everything, and we'll start to set the different parts in motion. But tonight, get some sleep." He settled back against the chair once again and reached for the blanket slung over the back.

"What are you doing?"

"I'm going to stay up here until you fall asleep." I could hear the confusion in his voice.

"Get in the damn bed with me. Don't sleep in the chair."

"Kate, now that I know... what we did earlier... I don't think it's smart for me—"

"Keep your clothes on if that makes you feel better." I sighed as I rolled over, placing my back to him, letting him hear every ounce of annoyance I felt. "Just get in the bed."

I waited. There was no way he could resist, right?

The bed dipped against his weight and a strong arm wrapped around my waist, pulling me against his chest.

"Did you really keep your clothes on?"

"I'm not taking any chances."

"Didn't know I was that irresistible," I crooned into my pillow.

"Well, you are, and being this close to you, I'm having one hell of an internal battle to keep my hands off you."

I rolled over to face him. His eyes were open, staring back, and I could have sworn I saw that battle raging through his gaze.

"So, just wondering. What are you against? Touching me? Sex? Kissing?"

His growl made me smile in response. Teasing him had to be my new favorite thing. "All of it, anything that would pull my focus from potential risks. It happened once. I'm not going to let it happen again."

"I get that, but what if you kept one ear open? You know, not letting yourself become completely immersed in the moment."

"I don't think that's possible with you."

"Want to try?"

"Go. To. Bed," he hissed and rolled me over, tucking my back against his chest once again.

"Fine," I huffed. "You're a party pooper."

The breath of his genuine laugh brushed against the back of my neck, sending chills down to my toes and back up again, warmth settling in my core. Damn, I wanted him. Bad.

"Soon, baby. I promise."

16

Even coffee sounded awful, which was how I knew my nerves were at an all-time high. That and the skin on my fingers was nearly raw from wringing them over and over in my lap. My packed bag sat on the floor beside me.

All I could do was wait.

Wait and worry. So much could go wrong. I needed to play everything right the moment Chase walked through that door or everything Weston and I had been plotting the past couple days would fall apart.

My co-conspirator was leaning against the wall in the living room, staring at me, worry lines etched into his forehead, looking like he wanted to call it all off. But he knew better. He knew my resolve on this, and nothing was going to stop me.

At least with his plan, I wouldn't be alone in San Diego. The day after we translated the voice memo, we started the ball rolling. The first piece we put into action had been letting Chase know I *would love* to attend the San Diego trip with him. The excitement in his voice when I told him I was coming would have made me feel bad for lying if he'd been anyone else.

Two nights in San Diego with him. Most of the daytime, he would be dealing with work obligations, which I told him was fine.

Now here I was waiting for Chase to pick me up, waiting for the right moment after he arrived, before we left, to let him know Weston would be tagging along with us as my personal protection. Since the trial was still ongoing, we had a valid excuse for Weston to accompany me, and if he didn't concede to it, then I wouldn't go. But I knew the hopes of sex would make him give in to the demand.

That part I was still a little unsure on. How in the hell I was going to avoid sleeping with Chase for the two nights we would be gone was still beyond me. It was beyond Weston too—that was the part he was most concerned about—but I assured him we would figure something out. Having a headache two nights in a row wouldn't be hard to fake.

At least Weston would get what he wanted out of the plan—me being protected the entire time I was around Chase. And I got an extra set of eyes and ears to notice anything out of the ordinary. With the business meetings during the day, I figured Weston or I would follow Chase hoping to get a picture of his partner. Weston didn't know that part of the plan, but maybe he wouldn't mind my slight adjustment.

A loud knock at the front door had me jumping a foot off the stool and stumbling back, where two strong hands were at my shoulders to steady me.

"Are you sure you want to go through with this? You're pale and sweating. I've never seen you this wound up before." His assessing eyes ran up and down my face, the corners of his lips dipping with each pass.

"I'll be fine. We'll be fine, I'm only anxious to get this first part over with."

The gentle skimming of his knuckles down my cheek helped me breathe easier, but all the anxiety came back in full force as he stepped away to answer the door.

"Good morning, beautiful. You look.... Are you okay?" Chase

asked as he rounded the corner into the kitchen, his smile taking a downturn when he took in my appearance.

"I'm fine. I just hate flying." My smile must have looked as fake as it felt; from the corner of my eye, Weston grimaced.

He reached for my bag with one hand and clasped my wrist with the other. "Great, let's go. I can't be late for my first appointment."

Weston cleared his throat loud enough to make Chase pause his tugging on my wrist. "Mr. Smitson, I—"

I held up a hand to stop him; it needed to be me who broached the subject of him coming to San Diego with us. "Chase, Weston needs to come too. The trial is ongoing, and I need additional protection outside of your security detail. They're focused on you, and I need someone focused on me."

The look Chase shot Weston was nothing short of icy. He was not happy with this new development. Not that it mattered.

"My security team will be fine. You'll be perfectly safe. If it'll make you feel better, I'll hire more men while we're down there to watch only you. But this guy, I don't know him."

"I know him," I said, taking a step back, away from him. "He's been my security detail since the trial started, and I really don't want some new guy hanging around who doesn't know my routine. Weston gives me privacy because I've earned it. He knows I won't run away from him."

Weston covered his audacious laugh with a fake coughing fit.

"Really? If he's that good and knows you so well, how did you manage to get shot? He must not be so great at his job if he allowed that to happen." The question was directed to me even as Chase was staring down Weston in some kind of battle for control.

Weston's eerie calm radiated aggression at Chase's stare and his words. This needed to be broken up now before it turned into a full-on brawl and Chase ended up in the hospital, or worse—the morgue.

"Weston was gone during that time. It was another person in his place. Stop being an ass, Chase, and say yes to him coming along and let's go."

That icy glare shifted from Weston to me, making me shiver at the sheer dominance in it. "What if I say no?"

My shoulders rose and fell in a half shrug. "Then I say no."

He looked back and forth between Weston and me. Coming up short with whatever he was looking for, he inclined his head toward the front door and mumbled, "Fine, let's go."

Halfway down the hall, we all paused at the knock at the door. Chase looked to me. I looked to Weston, who pushed forward for the door, breaking Chase's and my locked hands apart. Gun out and resting on his hip, he peered through the peephole.

"Interesting," he mumbled as he holstered his gun and opened the door, revealing my father standing on the welcome mat.

"Weston." Dad barely acknowledged him before pushing past, then stopped in his tracks when he found Chase standing beside me in the entryway. "Sorry to interrupt, but I wanted to catch you before you left, Kate."

He moved around us and headed to the kitchen. The three of us exchanged glances before trailing behind.

"What is this about?" Chase whispered as we followed.

One positive to this intrusion: my overactive nerves were now calmed by the overwhelming sense of curiosity. "No idea. Wasn't expecting this," I mused.

Why is my father here unannounced?

Once we were all in the kitchen—Chase with his arm around me, Weston on the opposite side staying close, my father on the other side of the island—and our attention was solely on him, my father clapped his hands together and smiled.

"It's over," he cheered, his eyes only on me.

"Uh, what's over?" I didn't understand what he was referencing. But with a quick glance beside me, Weston's pale, horrified face indicated he knew. And it wasn't good.

"The trial. The trial is over. The accused woke up from his coma a few days ago and has decided to change his plea to guilty. I can't go over all the details now, but it's over, and everyone seems to think the people who were after you and me will be more focused on keeping his mouth shut than coming after us."

"It's over," I whispered as my smile grew.

It's over. Now things will go back to normal. Maybe....

Wait. If the trial is over—

"Great," Chase exclaimed, the excitement from earlier back in his voice. "Now Weston doesn't need to tag along on our trip."

"But...."

Think, Kate. Think.

I stared wide-eyed at Weston. He stared back, no emotion in his pale face. There was nothing we could do. Everything we had planned was just wiped away by the announcement.

Dad crossed his arms over his chest and beamed. "Which is why I wanted to catch you before you left. Have a great time, pumpkin, and we can talk about the rest when you get back."

Neither Weston nor I could have expected this, and now our argument for why he needed to come with us was a moot point. Now I would be going to San Diego alone. Which was terrifying and fine at the same time.

"We need to get going, Kate," Chase said, grabbing my hand and pulling me toward the front door. My feet blindly followed; everything was numb from my brain to my toes. With one final glance back, I saw Weston and my father talking, but Weston's eyes weren't on him. No, they were on me. He held my gaze until we rounded the corner and were out of sight.

A new level of fear—from the unknown—made my stomach dip.

I was back to being alone in this, except unlike before, there was no mistaking I was in way over my head. And the only thing left to do was go along with the plan, minus one.

***

THE PRIVATE PLANE was amazing with its light leather seats, small galley, and bathroom. It was significantly larger than the one we'd chartered to Vail last year. Even with the large cabin and multiple seats, the plane was packed with us plus the security team and staff.

To my surprise, Chase let me have the window of our row of seats. Once we were situated, he clasped my hand, summoned the stewardess over, and ordered two bourbons on the rocks. While we waited for our drinks, Chase took the free moment to chat with the man sitting across the aisle from him, and I stared out the window, watching the activity on the tarmac. The crew below was busy getting us ready to take off; mindlessly watching them took my mind off everything, allowing a short reprieve from my endless stream of thoughts.

"Here." Chase wrapped my hand around the highball glass and lifted it to my lips, forcing me to take a drink. "This will take the edge off."

The bourbon burned as it flowed along my tongue and down my throat. I gagged but kept the drink down; I did need it to take the edge off before Chase noticed my despondency. I stared at the tarmac once again, thoughts drifting. What was Weston doing? What was he thinking? What had he done the moment Chase and I left? He seemed calm, but there was no way he actually was.

Mindlessly, I took another sip. The trial was over. But instead of celebrating with Weston by not leaving the bed for days, I was stuck playing girlfriend with Chase.

Maybe Weston had reached out. I glanced at Chase, who was deep in conversation, and dug my phone out of my purse. With a nonchalant shift in my seat, I angled my body so he couldn't read my screen if he happened to glance over.

> Me: Tell me everything will be okay.

The pilot came on, informing us we would take off shortly.

> Me: I need to know that you're okay with this, that you'll be there when I get back no matter what.

Me: Casey?

Me: Casey, where are you?

"Put your phone away, Kate. You're here with me, and I don't like being ignored for a screen." He adjusted in his seat to fasten the seat belt and get comfortable for the flight. "Who were you texting anyway?"

Seriously?

"My best friend Eric. I wanted to let him know we were headed out and I would send him pics from San Diego."

"Your best friend is a guy?"

"Yep, since med school." I watched his lips dip in a displeased frown. "Does that bother you?"

Chase didn't respond, choosing to ignore my question.

"I asked you a question," I bit out. The sharpness in my tone, the anger that rose from somewhere deep in me, was a pleasant surprise. I hadn't felt like feisty Kate in a long while.

His honey-brown eyes flicked open, his amused gaze settling on my tightly pressed lips. A devious smile played on his. "Ah, there's that smart mouth." He gripped my chin and leaned over to press his lips hard against mine—more possessive than passionate. "I like it," he whispered against my lips before dropping his hand and settling back in his chair once again.

I tipped my glass back, allowing the bourbon to burn away the taste of him. The engines roared, and I was pressed into my chair from the force of the plane taking off.

Once we were in the air and Dallas was a speck below, I leaned my own chair back and shut my eyes, but not to sleep. No, I needed to make good use of this time and form my own plan. One that didn't involve Weston's help—and it would be good. Maybe even better than the one he came up with. Okay, probably not, but still, a plan was the best way to keep me safe, and that was exactly what I was going to devise.

17

———————

After we landed and had begun the deplaning process, I checked my phone to see if Weston had responded. He had. Several times, in fact, making my racing heart slow and everything around me dissolve into the background as I read his messages.

Weston: Sorry, your dad stuck around to talk about the case and going forward. I couldn't respond with him here.

Weston: Of course you'll be fine. You'll do great. I was always an extra in the plan anyway. I know you. You're strong. Smart. Resilient. It'll be fine. Text me with updates.

Weston: I mean updates on you. I want check-in texts every hour to make sure you're okay. As soon as you land, let me know.

Weston: I'm going out of my mind knowing you're alone with him. If he touches you, I'll likely go to jail for murdering him.

Weston: Please text me back and let me know you're safe.

> Weston: Does that douchebag not have Wi-Fi on his dumbass plane?

> Weston: Kate.

> Weston: Please. Anything. Let me know.

My heart swelled. I hated and loved a worried Weston. Somehow his worry made me feel... cherished. The rest of the group was still deplaning; I took the unnoticed moment to check the group texts from Eric and Meagan.

> Eric: Hey, how's the trip so far? Did y'all do it on the plane?

> Meagan: Oh, I've always wanted to join the mile-high club.

> Eric: You haven't already?

> Meagan: I know right!

> Eric: Truly shocking.

> Eric: So, Kate, are you a part of the MHC now?

> Meagan: Maybe she's busy earning that badge now.

> Eric: Ewww.

> Meagan: Wait, does this mean Captain Sexy As Hell is back at her place? Alone?

> Eric: Don't get any ideas, Meagan. Kate will kick your ass when she gets back if you do.

> Meagan: Yeah, but Weston would be worth it. I mean, have you seen his tattoos? Yum. And those soulful chocolate eyes. Edible. I can only imagine what else he has that's begging to be nibbled on.

> Meagan: Thinking about it... maybe I should pop by and say hi. You know, be neighborly.

Eric: You're not neighbors.

Meagan: Details.

Meagan: I mean, how pissed could she be?
She's on a private plane, doing it with some
other guy. Who is hot and rich as hell, I
might add.

Eric: I thought you were all into some mystery
man? Go hound him.

Meagan: I'm not dead yet, and McHottie is
alone. I'll take my chances.

What the hell? I stared at the phone, not knowing who to respond to first. Weston was worried, but Meagan was about to head his way and throw herself at him.

Before I could write either back, I was being tugged to the front of the plane by an impatient Chase.

The majority of the security team went to the hotel to check us in, drop off the bags, and secure the rooms, leaving Chase and me mostly alone for lunch. The light breeze and warm sun on the patio of the sushi restaurant we chose was perfection. I had forgotten how much I loved Southern California and its year-round amazing weather. The faint smell of the ocean and the warm sun on my cheeks was soothing, and for a brief moment, my agenda was forgotten.

The people-watching was fantastic from our table, the sidewalks busy with runners, bikers, and businessmen and women sharing the space. We sat silently watching them pass by, going on with their lives, as we ate delicious sushi.

Halfway through the meal and my second glass of wine, Chase spoke up.

"I really am glad you came, Kate. I enjoy my time with you. Which came as a surprise. I don't date much, more one-night type things. This talking, getting to know one another, isn't something I'm used to." He sat back in his chair, after a final bite of salmon tempura, with a highball glass in his hand, swirling the dark liquor it held.

"I've noticed," I teased. "I'm glad I came too. It's nice to get away from the chaos back home and have some time to myself before I go back to work."

He leaned forward, bracing his forearms on the metal table separating us. "Do you think you're ready? To go back to work, that is."

I pulled at my lip as I thought about his question, without noticing until Chase gave a pointed look at my hand. I dropped my hand to my now-empty wineglass and sighed. "I'm not sure. I think physically yes, but mentally.... The other day when I was there for a follow-up visit, the sounds and smells reminded me of the shooting. The place now reminds me of those days lying in bed, the pain and being helpless, instead of a place where I used to feel safe and in control."

He smirked behind his glass. "I'm sure you gave everyone on that floor hell those days you were in the hospital. Even shot I can't imagine that smart mouth being tamed."

"I'm glad you like my... confidence."

"Is that what we're calling it?"

"Fine, my smart mouth, like you labeled it. Why is that, when you could have any woman in Dallas who would comply to your every word?"

"I don't know, I guess it's nice to have something different. I like the challenge you've presented." He drained the last of his drink, the glass landing hard against the metal table. When his eyes met mine, they danced with wicked amusement. "I'm also hoping that that resistance, that fight of yours, doesn't stop when the lights go off."

I stopped breathing. Was he saying...? No, there was no way he was that kind of guy, right? But thinking back, he was the one forcing me that night in his office. I complied, yes, but he'd seemed more turned on when I'd pushed back.

"What are you saying, Chase, that you like a little challenge in the bedroom?" I quirked a brow, feigning confidence while my stomach twisted in knots.

"I'm saying I like it when a girl says no but I know she means yes."

Fuck.

His phone rattled on the table, saving me from having to come up with a response. After a quick glance at the screen, he shoved his chair back and excused himself to take the call far enough away for privacy—for both of us.

I slid my phone out of my purse and tucked it under the table to not draw Chase's attention. There hadn't been a moment since we landed to text everyone back, and it was literally making my hands shake, itching to respond. Texting Weston was top priority; Eric and Meagan would have to wait.

Me: Landed and out to lunch. I'm safe
for now.

Me: Flight was good. He left me alone, but
we just had an interesting conversation.

Weston: Good. Going forward I need you to
text me every hour to let me know you're
safe.

Weston: What conversation?

Me: Well…

Weston: Kate. Tell me. Now. I'm going out of
my mind not being there with you.

Me: Okay, but don't go all alpha crazy
protector guy on me.

Weston: Interesting description, but I can't
make any promises. You're in another state
with a guy known for having zero value for
others' lives. I'm already in your so-called
'alpha crazy protector' mode.

Me: He said he likes it when a woman says
no but she really means yes.

Me: Weston?

Me: Crazy alpha guy?

Me: Told you.

Weston: Get out now. Just walk away. Head to the airport and get on the next flight to anywhere.

Me: You know I'm not going to do that. I don't quit.

Weston: Do you know what kind of guy says that?

Me: The kind of guy who's okay with human trafficking?

Weston: This isn't a fucking joke. It won't matter what you say, do you understand that? He's not me. He's not like any other guy you've dated. He wants you to say no. He wants you to put up a fight. He likes the thought of taking advantage of you.

Me: I know.

Weston: Baby, please walk away. This is so much more than we thought. Even if I were there, I would be telling you the same thing.

Me: No.

Weston: Stop being so damn stubborn, damnit. Missions are aborted all the time because of changes with their target. It says nothing about you. Get out now. That's an order.

Me: That's cute. You think you can order me around.

Me: I'll be fine. Trust me.

Me: Don't be mad at me.

The sound of Chase's voice growing louder had me tucking the phone into my purse and leaning back against my chair, staring out into the crowd of people. My phone vibrated again and again with what I assumed was Weston's response.

"Everything okay?" I smiled up at Chase, squinting in the bright noon sun.

He stayed standing, thumbing through his wallet. "Yeah, my meeting got moved up. I'm meeting him in half an hour. Are you okay with getting back to the hotel on your own?"

"Yes, I know how to get there. It's only a few blocks, right?"

"Correct, I'll be meeting my... my meeting might run late. I'll try to meet up with you before the vendor dinner I have tonight, but I can't guarantee anything." Without even a goodbye, he turned and headed down the street.

I smiled as I watched him walk away.

And waited.

When he was almost out of sight, I stood, grabbed my purse, and followed him. I tossed the very identifiable scarf I wore on the plane, leaving me in dark-wash jeans, gold flats, and a black sweater. But something else was needed to help disguise me in case Chase turned around. I purchased an "I love San Diego" ball cap from a street vendor and pulled it low on my forehead.

It wasn't hard to keep up with him. He strolled down the streets like he had all the time in the world and not a single worry. Not once did he turn around; he had faith in the two security guys who stuck close to his side. Even if they were to turn around, there was no way they would recognize me among the swell of people on the sidewalk enjoying the beautiful California day.

When he crossed the street, I ducked behind a brick wall and watched. It was my lucky day; he sat at a table on the patio of a sports bar, and from where I stood, I could see him but I was hidden from his view. Chase pulled out his phone while he waited, so I did the same.

Weston: I'm not mad baby. I'm terrified you'll
need me and I won't be there.

Weston: I don't know if I've ever felt this helpless.

Me: I'm safe, followed him to his meeting. I'm pretty stealthy, if I do say so myself. Forget being a doctor, I'm going to be a spy when I grow up.

Weston: You're kidding me.

Me: The following part or the spy part?

Weston: Kate.

Me: He's waiting on a patio across the street. Don't worry I'm hidden, and I bought a hat. You know, a disguise.

Weston: You think this is a game?

Me: No, but it's fun, right? Me chasing the bad guy. It'll be fine. It's not that big of a deal.

Weston: So it'll be fun when he catches you and makes sure you disappear for good?

Me: Dramatic much?

Weston: This isn't funny, Kate.

Me: I know, but you're kind of being an ass right now.

Weston: I'm fucking pissed. What do you want from me?

Weston: The way I see it, there isn't a way this is going to end well. Either he finds you spying on him and he kills you, or tonight he'll force himself on you, then I'll kill him.

Me: Give me a little credit. I could kill him too.

Weston: I'll pay you back for the holes in your wall.

Me: Seriously? Stop being a brute and act like you're housetrained. Wish Ryan was still around to calm you down. Can't believe he just up and left with no warning.

Weston: I'm done talking to you. And I'm not surprised. That's Ryan. Don't worry, he'll show up the next time he needs something.

Weston: Text me with updates. I need to know you're okay.

I rolled my eyes at the phone and tucked it into my back pocket. Yes, this was a shitty situation, and there were a lot of ways this could turn out badly, but I was here and I needed to see it through. But even as I thought it, something seemed off. Was Weston being dramatic, or was I making too light of the situation?

Those thoughts faded to the background as a man approached Chase's table.

The man had fair skin, dirty-blond hair, and was average build; nothing unique about him to help identify him later on. Thankfully, my new phone came with a camera feature with advanced zoom. I angled it at the two men and clicked. The zoom was amazing; it was like I was right there with them. The pictures were a little grainy, but they would have to do; there was no way I would risk getting any closer for more clarity.

One picture the man was talking to Chase, the next he was facing my direction. Squinting. At me. Whoops. With my cover blown, I should have run, but with his full face in view, I couldn't miss that kind of opportunity. Snapping one last picture, I turned and ran. Fast. In the final picture, the man was yelling at his security team and pointing across the street in my direction, so someone—probably many someones—were about to be after me.

As I ran, weaving in and out of the meandering people, I tugged off the hat and tossed it in a nearby trash can. I didn't dare look behind me; they were chasing me, and nothing good would come from seeing how close they actually were or giving them a clear view of my face. I had to keep moving, put more distance between them and me. Or... I skidded to a halt, almost tripping over my own feet, and dashed into the clothing store I'd almost run right past.

Panting, sweat dripping down my temples, I started grabbing shirts and pants off racks and beelined to the dressing rooms. The pounding of loud, running footsteps grew louder outside, pushing me faster to the back of the store.

"Can I help—"

"I need to try these on. Now." I shoved the clothes into the shop worker's hands and kept walking. With the tall woman at my back, following me to the dressing rooms, there was no way the men outside could see me. She was my tall savior by blocking their view, but I still held my breath until I was safe in my own little curtained-off alcove.

I stared at the phone in my hand for a full minute, wondering if I should tell Weston what almost happened, knowing that would only make him worry more. But he did want me to check in....

> Me: Safe and sound, trying on clothes at a local store. Super cute clothes.

> Weston: What happened to your stakeout?

> Me: Got boring.

> Weston: I don't believe you.

> Weston: You're hiding something from me.

> Me: Stop driving yourself crazy. I'm fine.

> Me: I'll text you later.

Between the running, warm temperatures, and my sweater, I was slowly being suffocated. I yanked the oppressive sweater off and was rewarded with my first deep breath since we landed. There was no way I could put it back on though.

Good thing I was in a store full of clothes.

18

Me: Meagan, don't you dare go over there. Keep your hands to yourself. For once.

Eric: Damn, woman, I was beginning to think we needed to send out a search party.

Meagan: Well... you texted too late. I kind of already stopped by. You know, to make sure he was okay with you being in another state. With a hot man. That you have the hots for.

Me: You didn't. I really don't want to kill you, Meagan.

Meagan: No prison time for you, friend. He didn't answer.

Me: Really? That's strange. I was just texting with him and he made it sound like he was home.

Meagan: Should I go back and make sure he's okay?

Me: NO!

Eric: For goodness' sake, woman, take a flippin' hint. She still loves him.

Meagan: Really? Huh. Interesting. Why?

Meagan: He broke your heart, Kate. He left you.

Me: Thanks for the reminder.

Eric: Meagan, please stop talking.

Me: I don't know. I couldn't stop thinking about him. Even when I hated him, I wanted him there with me. Even now.

Meagan: Do I need to be the one to point out the obvious?

Eric: What?

Meagan: She is in ANOTHER STATE with ANOTHER GUY. I'm all up for games, Kate, but this is taking it to the extreme if you're trying to torture Sir Hunks-a-Lot.

Eric: Yeah, Kate. If you know you still love him, why are you there with Chase?

Damn these two and their perceptiveness. Good thing I had the perfect distraction.

Me: My father stopped by this morning before we left. The trial is over. And everyone thinks I'm out of danger.

Eric: That's awesome news!

Meagan: Does that mean our eye candy is leaving?

Eric: Oh, yeah. What are we going to do about that?

Eric: We could tie him down.

Meagan: Yes, keep going.

Eric: Use the most delicate handcuffs.

Meagan: I have a pair of leopard fur ones.

Eric: And we each get a turn.

Me: So hold him hostage and turn him into
our own personal sex slave.

Meagan: I'm giggling.

Me: I don't know what he'll do. I don't know
what I'll do.

"What are you doing down here drinking alone?"

The phone flew from my hands and thudded down on the wooden bar in front of me. Chase reached over my shoulder to grab it and placed it back in my hands before sitting on the stool beside me.

"It's happy hour." I shrugged and downed the last of my beer.

"I thought I would stop by and hang out for a bit before I have to meet up with those vendors for dinner. I'm sorry I can't take you out tonight, but tomorrow night is our night, and all day tomorrow is yours. I pushed everything to today so we could enjoy San Diego together."

How I managed a smile back at him was beyond all reason. All day tomorrow... maybe I should reconsider Weston's suggestion on aborting this mission.

"Do you want something to drink?" I asked, waving a hand for the bartender to grab me one more beer.

We sat at the bar for an hour talking about the hospital, Eric, Meagan, and his life growing up here. And after a while, him being the bad guy in all this slipped my mind. He was calmer than that night at his house, and after his third glass of bourbon, he was kind of funny. Or maybe the sixth beer I was on helped him seem that way.

By the time he left for his dinner, the kiss he planted on my cheek wasn't repulsive. But when he whispered, "I'm looking forward to tonight. Don't drink too much. I want feisty, remember, not compliant," it sobered me. It was an abrupt reminder that I was not safe with him. Anywhere near him.

Only when the glass door of the hotel was closed behind him and he was climbing into a black SUV did I dare flip my phone over and begin scrolling through all the missed texts. There were several from Eric and Meagan but nothing from Weston. Strange. It had been a while since I last checked in, and I couldn't believe there weren't multiple anxious texts.

Me: Wrapped up happy hour with Chase. He left for dinner with vendors. Not sure what else I can get from tonight. Already searched his bags when the security team wasn't watching. Nothing useful there.

Me: I'm going across the street to grab dinner, then turn in early. Hopefully if I'm asleep, he won't expect anything.

Weston: Okay, be safe.

Me: That's it?

Weston: I hope the food is good?

Me: Okay, what's up with you? Earlier you were punching walls and now you're all nonchalant. What gives?

Weston: Nothing. Be safe.

Me: Fine. You're being weird and not telling me something.

Weston: Sucks, doesn't it?

Me: Do you really want to know what happened earlier? I think it's best if you don't know, but if you're going to punish me... I'll tell you.

Weston: It's always best to know.

Me: The guy caught me. I had to run a few blocks to get away, but I did. I ducked into a store, bought new clothes, and walked out safe.

Me: Told you. Now you're pissed.

Weston: Go eat. And grab a jacket.

My stomach growled loud enough for the person sitting two stools down to hear. After paying the tab for mine and Chase's drinks, I jogged across the street to a packed sports bar. It was perfect. Since I'd left Weston standing in the kitchen this morning, I had felt alone; maybe being around all these people would change that.

After pushing through the crowd, I snagged an open seat at the bar and ordered a beer. It was a madhouse. Some big basketball game was going on, and the noise level when either team scored was deafening. The man and woman to my left seemed to be a new couple, firing off questions to each other about little things they would know if they'd been together a while.

With as little as I knew about Weston, besides his childhood, it was like we were a new couple. But we'd been living together for so long, knew each other's routines, knew pieces of the other that made us not so new. I wasn't sure what we were, really. I knew what he looked like when he was anxious, that he loved watching commercials, how kind and caring he was under that hard armor the world had made him construct, and how his sly smile was only for me being me. But I didn't know his favorite color. Or favorite foods. Or his friends.

He sure as hell knew a lot more about me. It seemed he could get me to open up about anything with his patient silence. Weston knew more about me than anyone ever had, deeper than I'd ever allowed myself to share. Until recently, that was. I didn't want him to know how messed up I was inside after the shooting. He already felt bad enough for it happening; I didn't want to add to it by him knowing the repercussions still lingered. Though he probably already knew since he could read me like an open book. And just like Weston, he was letting me work through it all at my own pace, letting me come to him when I was ready.

That was the thing about Weston that I appreciated the most. I was crazy, hotheaded, fun, flirty, unpredictable, and so much more, and yet, even with his obsessive need to control everything and everyone around him, he always let me be me. Maybe that was why I fell for him in the first place and why I never stopped loving him even when he broke my heart. Shattered it, really. Deep down, my heart told me we would find our way back to each other somehow.

The crowd roared at the game, making me jump, the beer bottle between my hands teetering on the bar.

"You're a jumpy little thing, aren't you?" a man said as he sat on the wooden stool to my right. He pointed a long thin finger at the remnants of the beer label I'd almost completely peeled off and torn to pieces. "And anxious too."

I nodded in acknowledgment to be polite and motioned for a bartender to place my food order. The man continued to talk, to me or himself, after I placed my order, but my gaze stayed on the basketball game, hoping he would take the hint I wasn't in the mood for idle chitchat. The pine scent of his aftershave stuck in my nose when he leaned toward me in an attempt to get his stool closer to mine.

The chuckle he gave to the "back off" glare I shot him made my cheeks flush hot. "Settle down, tiny. I'm just trying to give the big guy here on my right more room. I'm not hitting on you." Even with my eyes on the TV, I could tell he was still staring, smiling. "Why are you here alone, anyway? A pretty girl like you—"

I kept my now-narrowed glare on the TV as I spoke. "Listen, I appreciate you trying to chat. But I can guarantee you I'm not lonely, I am not bored, and I will not sleep with you tonight or any night. So please, stop with the small talk. I really want to eat in silence."

"You don't have to be a bitch about it. Fine, have it your way. Eat in peace." He pressed his hand against my lower back to steady himself as he stood from the stool and sulked off into the crowd.

The food I'd ordered arrived, but I only stared at it. My previous hunger was gone. Damnit to hell all these new emotions that swirled and fought inside me. Tears I was attempting to hold back burned behind my eyes and down my throat. I was lonely. I wanted Weston. And I had no idea how to escape the inevitable tonight.

I continued to stare at my food while I tried to figure out what was going on with me when another man, much larger than the previous one, sat in his vacated seat.

Maybe if I only let it happen once tonight, or if I didn't fight back, it wouldn't be that bad. I'd already debased myself in one way with Chase and survived. Would sex be any different?

"You need to eat."

I knew that voice.

My head whipped to the man sitting beside me. There was no holding back the tears that rolled down my cheeks. "How… what… when?" I couldn't put a thought together as I stared at Weston sitting beside me.

His dark eyes on me, he responded, "Do you want the details now?"

"No," I whispered.

He stood and tossed several bills on the bar top. "Then get your food to go and meet me outside."

Wide-eyed, I watched him move through the crowd, still trying to process the fact that he was here.

Here for me.

19

———

To-go sack in hand, I found Weston outside the restaurant leaning against a street sign. His back was to me, giving a full view of his amazing backside. He really was perfect. Even with his jeans and jacket, anyone could tell there was something amazing underneath. And I was the lucky one who would one day get to feel that body pressed against my own again.

Not even a flinch from him when I appeared beside him. When he shifted his eyes down to mine, I couldn't read his expression. It almost looked pained, but there was also relief mixed in.

Last year he mentioned something about needing a physical connection with me after long spells apart to chase away those dark fears of losing me. The plastic bag rustled as I switched it from one hand to the other. His shoulders slackened and the worry lines along his forehead eased when I interlaced my fingers with his. A simple touch, that was all he needed to know I was still here with him.

My smile dipped, not understanding, when he dropped my hand after giving it a gentle squeeze. The questioning look I gave him said as much.

"Not here. Chase is at a steakhouse a few blocks over, but I don't want to risk anyone seeing us and reporting back to him."

"Okay, then what are we doing out here?" I asked as I rubbed my hands up and down my arms to keep the chilly night air from seeping through my sweater. Seconds later, his black North Face jacket was slung over my shoulders. It swallowed me whole; my short arms didn't even make it to the end of the sleeves.

"Head up the street, take a right at the light. There will be a hotel entrance on your right. Walk in, go straight to the elevators, and press the 8th floor. I'll be right behind you."

My curiosity went into overdrive. How did he get here? What did he have planned? And a hotel....

What the hell?

"Are you going to tell me what's going on once we get there?" I asked as we walked down the sidewalk. I turned my head enough for him to know the question wasn't rhetorical.

He didn't answer.

"How did you get here, anyway? You made great time."

Still no answer, even though I knew he heard me.

"Answer me, damnit." I stopped on the steps of the hotel and turned to face him. But he continued inside, gripping my upper arm as he walked through the lobby straight to the elevator. Which dinged immediately after he slammed his fist against the button.

The grip on my arm didn't loosen until the elevator doors were closed. But before I could get another question out to him, my back was pressed against the elevator wall and Weston's lips were covering mine. It was desperate, like he needed me to breathe—maybe even live. The bag in my hand thudded to the floor, and I wrapped my arms around his neck. Not wasting any time, he cupped my ass, lifting me so I could wrap my legs around his waist. I started to sweat from the heat pouring off him coupled with his heavy jacket. There wasn't a single area of him I didn't want to touch. My hands greedily roamed everywhere from his face, gripping his shoulders, down his solid biceps—feeling the power he had, yet his grip on me was utterly gentle.

When the elevator doors opened on his floor, I tried to pull back, but Weston held me firm. He pulled away from the wall, one arm wrapped around my back and holding me against him, keeping his lips on mine, and walked down the hall, pausing only to fumble in his back pocket for what I assumed was his room key.

The door slammed shut behind us, but Weston being Weston, he took the time to lock and secure the door. It was quite impressive that he could do all that with me biting at his neck and lips, my hands desperately fumbling with his belt buckle.

Only when I was safely on the bed did he pull back, leaving me panting, as I stared up at him. The tug on the hem of my sweater was welcomed, and I didn't resist when he gripped the edge to pull it over my head. His fingers brushed up and down my chest and belly, sparks of fire flaring in their wake. With a flick of his fingers, my bra clasp released, and with a fascinated smile, he looped the straps around his fingers to pull them from my shoulders and down my arms.

For a moment, he simply looked me over, half naked, flushed, and desperate for him. His eyes stopped their scrolling at my breasts, which were already begging for his mouth. But not yet. I wanted to see more of him too. It'd been too long since I'd gotten to touch his bare chest, been close enough to be able to.

I pushed off the bed to grab the bottom of his dark T-shirt. Without breaking eye contact, I pulled it over his head and tossed it to the floor.

Damn. I wanted to lick and nibble every inch of his chest and perfect abs. His body trembled with the light brush of my fingers as I traced the dark lines of his tattoos. I followed each curve of the ink, scraping my nails along his chest in certain areas, making him purr, until... the texture of the ink changed; this spot looked to be lettering hidden among the other designs.

My hand had paused right over his heart, its pounding beat fast beneath my fingertips. I rose to my knees to get a better look at what was now written across his chest.

My name.

In bold typed script were the four letters in my name. Right over his heart.

I couldn't pull my eyes away. There was something amazing—and terrifying—in the fact that he'd permanently marked his body with my name.

I traced the letters over and over while I processed it. He didn't speak, but I could feel his anxious stare on the crown of my head.

"When?"

He didn't answer. When I looked up, the expression on his face was either one of embarrassment or relief. Was he glad I saw it or not?

"The day after I left."

This. This was how he expressed himself. He wasn't verbose or open with how he felt, but this was his way of telling me I'd always been with him. Even when we were apart, I was with him. Forever I was with him. Close to his heart.

I pulled my hand from his chest and wrapped both around his face to pull it down to meet my own. This kiss, my kiss to him, I wanted to convey every emotion that had welled up inside at the sight of my name on his skin. And it seemed he wanted the same. His arms wrapped around my shoulders and back, pressing our naked halves together.

Gently he laid me back against the bed, his lips never leaving mine as he pulled at the button on my jeans. His fingers brushed against my lace panties, and I couldn't stop the desperate groan that passed from my lips to his.

That tiny sound was his undoing—gone was patient, take-it-slow Weston.

He ripped my jeans off my hips and pulled them down my legs, my panties immediately meeting the same fate. Not so silently panting from the bed, I watched his every move as he pulled down his jeans, then his boxers. He was exactly as I remembered—every masculine inch. The need for him on top of me sooner than later almost had me pulling him to the bed before he could finish rolling on a condom. I knew what we were like together, what glorious things he could do to my body. And I wanted all of it, now.

The bed dipped with his body weight, and with one swift movement of his hips, he was deep inside me. We both stilled, savoring the moment we'd long waited for.

He moaned against my neck as he pulled out and slowly eased back in. "Fuck. This is even better than I remembered."

In this moment, nothing else mattered. It was us enjoying each other.

His lips pulled away from my neck for him to lock eyes with my own, and I couldn't pull my eyes away. With each swivel of his hips and deep thrust, we kept our gaze locked. This was more than sex. It was more than anything I'd experienced before; this was even beyond our time in Vail. He was making love to me, pouring every ounce of the words he couldn't find or say into this connection.

"Casey," I whispered when I began to quiver beneath him. "Casey, this is more for me. More than anything. Ever."

The wide smile my words put on his face was beautiful. It was a smile that was only for me, one of true undiluted joy.

"I love you too, baby," he whispered back. His lips crashed into mine, and his hips began rocking faster against me.

Those five words, combined with his expert movement, had me crying against his lips as I shattered beneath him, clenching tight to prolong every magnificent sensation. The feel and sound of me urged Weston deeper and faster until he found his own release, pressing his sweat-slick chest against mine.

Slow, delicate kisses filled the next several minutes with him still on top and inside me. Neither of us wanted to break the moment. Once we did, the reality of where we were and what was to come would swoop in.

The groan that escaped when he pushed off the bed told me he hated pulling away as much as I did. While he cleaned up in the bathroom, I tucked myself under the covers and snuggled in, hoping to ward off the conversation we both knew would happen next. Only after I was tucked in beside him, his arm wrapped around me and my head resting on his chest, did I dare break the spell.

"How did you get here?" I murmured against his chest.

He began trailing his fingers through my hair. "Your dad isn't the only one who can charter a jet."

I pushed off his chest with one hand and propped myself up on the bed with the other. "That must have cost a fortune."

"It was worth it. You're worth it. You're worth it all, baby—everything I have. Nothing could have kept me from being here."

Aww, how sweet was that?

With a kick of my leg, I tossed the covers back and rolled on top of him. I traced the outline of my name with the tip of my index finger. "What are you doing here? Did you think I couldn't do this on my own?"

His arched brow and wide eyes told me he either had no clue what I was asking or I was an idiot for not knowing the answer to my question.

"I came here for you. I came here to take you home."

I pushed both hands against his chest to put distance between us. "What? What do you mean, you came to take me home?"

"I mean I came to bring you home so you don't have to stay the night with that fucker. You know and I know what he's going to do. I can't stand back and let someone hurt you like that."

I swung my leg off him and lay back on the bed to stare at the ceiling. *This is a joke, right?* "Weston, this isn't your call. You don't get to swoop in and rescue me. I don't need to be rescued. I've got this. I know what's going to happen, and—"

"Do you, Kate?" He raised up on his elbow and looked down with a mix of frustration and terror coating his features. "Do you really understand what'll happen tonight and how it'll fuck with your mind for months, even years after this?"

My attempt to roll over was stopped by his hand on my shoulder.

"It'll be fine. Do you know what those women who are trafficked go through on a daily basis? They're ripped away from their families, from their lives, to be sold into slave labor, or worse, sold to be raped repeatedly, given drugs they don't want on a daily basis, then tossed aside when they're too sick or used up to be profitable anymore. What Chase would do—what he *will* do—will pale in comparison to that. And it's not like I'm going to walk in there and spread my damn legs for him. I'll do everything I can to avoid it, but I can't not go back. Don't you see that? I have this one opportunity to save them. Even if it's only a handful. I can get more infor—"

"What other information can you get from him? Do you think he'll walk you to the fucking warehouse where they're keeping the girls? Maybe give you a blueprint of his whole operation? This is so insane. Do you hear yourself? He's not going to give you anything, and you'll be left feeling used."

I yanked my shoulder from his grasp to sit up and threw my legs over the side of the bed. A sliver of me, which I didn't want to listen to, knew he was right.

"I'm worried about you," he said and pressed featherlight kisses along my shoulders and neck. The soft touch, his warm breath, was almost my undoing. With the drop of my head, my hair fell forward like a curtain, keeping the outside world at bay a little longer.

"I think…," he started but stopped mid-thought.

I turned to ask, "Go on. You think what, Weston?"

"I think you're showing signs of PTSD and have been since the shooting. The nightmares, the inability to concentrate, high anxiety, being on edge and now… now *making* rash decisions, in a way minimizing the impact of those decisions and their long-term effects. You need—"

"Seriously, you think I have PTSD? What makes *you* such an expert, *Doc*?"

He retreated to the other side of the bed with hurt and anger behind his eyes, making me cringe at my insensitive accusation.

"You were fucking gunned down in the street. Do you think that wouldn't affect *even you*? I know the symptoms, and, well, Eric brought it up to me a couple weeks ago too. And now tonight, what you're thinking about walking into and thinking it won't affect you long term, that's not the rational Kate I know."

"I make irrational decisions *all the time*, even before the shooting," I said, not sure if it was a good point to make or not.

Weston sighed like he agreed, which pissed me off even more, and began massaging his eyes with the heels of his hands. "True, but this…. You normally think things through. About what will happen next. But you aren't in this case. You believe you'll walk in there tonight, let him fucking *rape* you, and then you'll go back to your normal life after. It won't happen that way, and I think you know it too. You need to look past tonight."

I pushed off the bed and started yanking on my clothes from the floor. I needed out of this tiny hotel room, away from him and all his male logic. Something inside me knew he was right, that my plan was outrageous, but not until he shoved my flawed plan in my face did I realize it.

Too fucking late. I'd gone this far. There was no way to turn back now.

"Listen, I know you want to protect me, but I'm not asking your permission, Weston. You don't have a say in this. You can either support my decision to continue on or leave." The words clogged in my throat; the idea of him not being with me at the end of this mess made me nauseous. My hand paused on the door handle as I waited for his answer.

"I can't walk you over there, to *deliver* you when I know what's going to happen. I also know if I tie you up and force you home, you'll never forgive me. What do you want from me, Kate? Either I lose or you do. But if you're asking me to choose—"

"I'm not asking you to choose, Weston. I'm *telling you* I'm going. You have to let me go."

The hands that covered his face swept back into his hair and interlocked his fingers behind his head. "I'll be here if you need… *when* you need me. I'm not leaving this town until you do."

So this was it. I was really going to walk out on the man who was desperately trying to save me from myself.

"Thank you for coming. Tonight was…. I love you, Casey."

WITHOUT HIS OVERSIZED jacket for protection, the cool ocean breeze bored through my lightweight sweater and chilled my cheeks. Even though he said he wouldn't, I knew he was only a few steps behind me. There was no way he would let me walk back alone at this hour—standing his ground on not delivering me to Chase only went so far before the overprotective gene kicked in.

I was now lost and empty, the complete opposite of how sated I'd been only twenty minutes earlier in his arms. When we were together, nothing else mattered, and it was exactly where I wanted to be right now. But his reason for coming to San Diego, thinking he could scoop me up and carry me home, was absurd.

Or was it?

All he wanted was for me to be safe, and he knew I wasn't when Chase was around.

Weston loved me. I couldn't fault him for being so protective.

I bit back my growing smile. He loved me.

Damn, he loved me.

Loved me enough to let me walk out of that room, to make my own dumb decision, even if every instinct he had was roaring at him to stop me.

And I told him I loved him too. Then walked out. Fuck, I was a mess when it came to relationships. Pretty sure telling him and then leaving wasn't the best scenario to drop that little nugget of emotion on him.

"Hey, Casey, I love you too. Now I'm going to go sleep with someone else. Byeee!"

At a crosswalk, pausing to let the traffic clear, I tipped my head to stare into the dark night sky. What the hell was wrong with me? Weston was right, and I knew he was right, but why couldn't I shake this need to continue? Would I really let Chase take advantage of me tonight over and over for the chance of getting additional information? And still have to relive the same nightmare tomorrow night?

"Damnit," I murmured to myself. He was right. Since the shooting—maybe even since being woken up in my bed in Vail with a gun to my head—I had been slightly unhinged. Like I was running from my own fate or believing my actions weren't as drastic as they actually were.

But I was here. I needed to see this through.

No. That was the lie my mind was trying to force on me. There was another option. And he was lurking somewhere in the shadows, protecting me from afar. I could get out of this now. Unharmed. No additional emotional scars.

So, I had my decision. As I went through the revolving glass doors into my hotel, I started to text him.

Me: You're right. About everything. I don't want to do this. I'm not going to do this. But not for you, for me. For us. Because I know if I were to let everything unfold tonight like it will, I would risk never forgiving myself.

Me: I'm going to grab my stuff and will be back down in a few. Wait for me.

Me: I love you. Thank you for stopping this. Thank you for loving me enough to save me from myself.

Weston: Do you want me to come up with you?

Weston: I know I can be overbearing, but if anything were to happen to you… I wouldn't be able to live with that, baby. You're all I need in this world, and I'm going to do everything I can to make sure no one ever hurts you again.

Me: No, Chase won't be back for a while. I'll be fine. See you in 10.

Weston: I love you too. If you're not down in 10, I'm coming up. What's your room number just in case?

I smiled at the phone and nodded to the security guard at the door to our room as he opened it for me. Write a quick note, grab my still-packed bags, and in ten minutes I would be with Weston. Maybe we could even stay the night here in San Diego, go back to the hotel room, where we could take our time exploring each other, familiarizing ourselves with each other once again. Earlier had been great, but rushed by our need for that physical connection after too many months apart.

Phone in hand to text Weston our room number, just in case, I pushed open the door to the bedroom and stumbled to a stop. The phone trembled in my tight grip at the sight of Chase at the end of the bed, highball glass in hand.

His angry gaze only on me.

20

———————

My feet were like lead weights keeping me from running out the door. I couldn't move. Hell, even blinking was a challenge as I stared back at Chase on the bed. His tie was slightly undone, hanging loosely from his neck, the sleeves of his blue dress shirt rolled to mid-forearm. He must have been waiting a while to be that comfortable, and there was only a sip or two left of the drink in his hand.

Fuck.

Think, Kate. You can get out of this. Think and play his game.

"You're back early," I teased. The phone slipped in my damp hand, but I held it firm to press the Video Record button before laying it facedown on the desk beside me. I leaned against the doorframe for support, my legs and knees shaking so hard they could give out at any moment.

Chase downed the last of his drink, his questioning eyes scanning my face. "Where the hell have you been?"

"I ran across the street to grab something to eat. I guess the time got away from me. Plus, you said you wouldn't be back until later, so don't go acting like you're pissed."

A corner of his mouth twitched up in faint amusement.

"Listen, Chase, while I was at dinner, I started thinking and—"

The thought left as he stood and stalked closer, my mind and body shifting into survival mode. The problem was he needed to know I wanted out now, but I had to be careful how I worded it; if he knew I'd been playing him this whole time and why, I wouldn't survive to tomorrow.

He stopped, putting us toe to toe, gripped a fistful of hair, and yanked it down to make my eyes meet his. I sucked in a breath from my hair pulling at the root, my scalp screaming. Not too long ago, I'd suffered through this same situation in my room in Vail, which was where the memory of the pain started to transport me back to. The corners of my eyes darkened, but passing out was not an option. I couldn't fight if I were unconscious. Instead of getting lost in the burning sensation in my scalp, I focused all my attention on his wolfish grin.

"Don't think about this, Kate. We both know this is only something fun for right now. Don't fight it."

With my hair in his grasp, I couldn't shift away as he kissed down my neck and back up again, nipping at my earlobe. I pressed against his chest, but the harder I pushed, the harder his lips smashed mine. Resisting him was turning him on, but was I willing to give in in the hope it would make him stop?

"Chase, stop. We need to talk." My voice was too high-pitched.

I pushed against him again, but he only stepped closer.

"No talking, Kate, not now. Now I just want you, I've wanted you since you pissed me off at the charity event. And now that I have you here, alone, I'm not going to let you go until I get what I want." His free hand grazed down my waist only to trail back up, this time under my lightweight sweater. The boldness in his touch sparked an ember of anger within me.

"Enough," I shouted and pushed harder than before against his chest.

This time Chase wasn't prepared for my strength, fueled by my growing contempt for him. He stumbled back, the grip on my hair breaking free. He stared, brows and eyes narrowed, but shifted back to a devious smile that had me inching for the door, toward freedom.

I needed to get out. I lunged toward the living room, but he lunged too and gripped my wrist to fling me backward, deeper into the bedroom. Stumbling a few steps, I turned in time to see him shut the bedroom door and heard the lock click into place.

"I love that you're playing along, Kate, I really do. But don't push me off again. I was just getting started."

Each step he drew closer, I retreated two. My panic rose when my back met the wall. Nowhere to go. This time when he reached out, I shifted right, avoiding his grasp.

"Nowhere to run, Kate. Give in now. You know it'll be fun." He chuckled to himself.

My only escape was through the door Chase now blocked. I needed a plan, needed a way to get through him. Beating the shit out of him seemed like a solid plan but one that might end up with me being charged with aggravated assault. Plus, I was still too weak; there was no way I could fight him off long enough to get away. Five months ago, yes, he would already be on his ass, but not now. Not this wimpy version of myself.

"Chase, I'm not playing your games right now. I'm being serious. I want to leave. I'm not ready for this—for you and me tonight. I'm not there, okay? The past few months have been long, and I'm tired. Damnit, I'm tired. Now I want to go home and sleep for the next few days. Please understand this has nothing to do with you. It has everything to do with me and my fucked-up life."

He shook his head back and forth as he reached out toward me. "You're a very good actress. Now stop putting up so much of a fight. It's not fun if I don't get to touch you."

"I'm not kidding, Chase."

"Neither am I."

"I want to go home."

"Too late now, baby."

Weston's term of endearment coming from his lips made a hidden part of me crack open. The fire that had been smothered for too long blazed inside, burning through the layers and layers of numbness I'd held onto all these months. And, unfortunately for Chase, it was directed toward him. For the first time in a long time, the old me was simmering at the surface. The Kate before having her face beaten to shit. Before having a broken heart. Before being shot in the street. And it felt fucking fantastic.

"If you touch me again, I will take you down, Chase. I've given you fair warning. Do not take another step toward me or you will regret it. I'm going to grab my things and leave now."

In a standoff of wills, we stared each other down. Gone was the playful Chase; now angry, frustrated, and confused Chase was in his place.

"No, Kate. I'm not sure if you know how all this works, but you came here with me, and you're not leaving until we leave together. We're going to enjoy our weekend, or at least I will, we'll go back to Dallas, and we can go our separate ways then. But now, tonight, you belong to me."

"Fuck you. I am not yours. I don't belong to anyone. Now get out of my way."

Done talking and staring at his smug, pompous face, I pushed around him toward the only exit in the room. Two feet past him, a scorching hand wrapped around my wrist, yanking me to a stop. I tugged forward, but his vise grip only tightened. In one forceful pull, my back was against his chest, my arm screaming in pain from the jolt to my still-healing shoulder.

An involuntary whimper escaped when he reached around to my chest and forcefully palmed my breast through my sweater. Bile rose in my throat at his touch even over the clothes.

"I can't wait to get you undressed," Chase hissed into my ear. His breathing was erratic, and I could feel him hard against my back; the fight was a major turn-on for him. What in the hell had the women before me put up with? What had he done to them if he believed he could get away with this?

"Get your hands off me," I pleaded. My shaky voice matched the rest of my body. If I didn't calm down, I would pass out from the adrenaline. I needed to get out of there. Now.

His hand began descending over my stomach and stopped at the waistband of my jeans, where he stroked lackadaisical lines back and forth before stopping to pop the top button. There were ways to defend myself, and I had learned them all. And if it took every last ounce of energy to get out of this unharmed, I would do it. There was no way I would let him force himself on me. Before, it was going to be me giving in, but now that the threat was real… game on.

With every ounce of weight in my tiny body, I pushed my hips back against him and leaned forward to force him backward. He stumbled, which gave me enough space to turn and draw my arms up in the defensive move I'd used many times at the gym. This time when he lunged for me, I was ready. One smooth move to the left, but when I turned to punch him, he was already upright, coming at me again. He slammed his chest into mine, gripped my arms behind my back, and pressed me against the wall. I was trapped. There was no way to get free from his death grip.

Hair stuck to the back of my slick neck and forehead as I struggled against him, using my hips and shoulders, anything to get out of his grasp, but it only drained what little energy I had left and made his hold tighten.

"I knew you were feisty, Kate, but this is a whole other level. I like it." He kept his face pulled away to gauge my reaction, or maybe to keep me from biting off his nose. "I can feel how angry you are. The heat is radiating off you. Can you feel me?" He ground himself against me. Tears burned, blurring my sight as I begged him to stop. "Oh no, why stop now? It's just getting fun. But if you could keep up with the pleading and drop the pushing, we can get this over with sooner than later. Stop delaying the inevitable."

Tears rolled down my cheeks as he continued to rub himself up and down my inner thigh. What would Weston think of all this? What would he tell me to do?

Somehow in my panic-laced thoughts, a moment of clarity surfaced.

Wait. It's not what Weston would do but what he trained me *to do all those months ago.*

The next moves were second nature thanks to his relentless coaching.

Raise foot up and slam on top of attacker's foot. Check. Chase grunted in pain, but his hold tightened, nearly suffocating me.

Slam forehead forward into attacker's face. Check. His grip released as he staggered back, holding his nose. Blood already ran over and between his fingers.

Raise foot backward and swing forward, nailing assailant in the groin. Check. The sound of his pain and knees hitting the floor were glorious. But unfortunately, this last burst of defense had taken nearly everything out of me. My breaths were short and fast, and my head spun. I needed to get out now; if he came after me again, there wouldn't be anything left to fight him off a second time.

I rushed past him as he lay on the floor, toward the door that led to the living room and freedom. There was no time to grab my suitcase, only my purse and phone. I had already been up here long enough. Who knew what Weston thought at this point or what he was doing in an attempt to find me.

The security team at the door shot me a questioning look when I burst through and bolted down the hall. Too much adrenaline to wait for the elevator, so I took the stairs—two by two—down toward the lobby.

I swung the door to the lobby open, grateful for the coolness it swept over my now-damp sweater and skin, but stopped short. There was shouting to the right. A male voice.

Shit, did Chase beat me down here?

Tentatively I peeked around the corner and let go of the breath I was holding in anticipation.

Weston was at the front desk yelling at a cowering employee. From the pulse in my ears, only every other word was understandable.

"Room... danger... tell me... kill... now...."

The flashing of red and blue lights snagged my attention from

Weston to the glass doors. Multiple police cars were pulling through the circular drive. And stopping.

"Oh hell," I murmured.

With the police climbing out of their cars, there was only a half second to make my decision. I bolted toward the front desk, grabbed Weston's hand, and started toward the bar area.

"Follow me, you impatient brute," I shouted over my shoulder.

At happy hour earlier, I noticed the door to the kitchen, which the staff came in and out of frequently, and the kitchen would have a way out through the back. At least they always did in movies.

Multiple rushed feet filed into the lobby behind us. I pushed harder with each step to put more distance between us and them. Weston caught on quickly to where I was taking us and pulled ahead, hand still gripped around mine. We pushed through the staff-only door into the kitchen, shocking about a dozen or so employees. They all stepped back as we made our way down the line, our eyes only on the back door we could now see.

The door behind us slammed open, and multiple voices rang out, instructing us to stop.

But we didn't.

Evading the police, if we got caught... oh, Dad would be so pissed. Nothing like the DA having a daughter with a felony on her record.

Weston shoved the door open with his shoulder and pulled me into the alley behind him before he took off again toward the busy street. The door to the kitchen banged open as we rounded the corner out of sight. Still in danger of being caught, we kept with the fast pace, attempting to put more and more distance between us and the police officers who continued to pursue. It seemed we were going in circles, but I trusted Weston.

The cool air burned down my throat and felt like glass in my lungs with each heaving breath as we ran. At least the inability to breathe was a decent distraction from the throbbing in my shoulder from being yanked around by Chase and now pulled down the sidewalk by Weston.

But eventually I slowed, my breaths now heaving. Weston shifted his focus from the street ahead to me and frowned.

"Damnit, I'm sorry. In all this, I forgot you can't.... One more block, okay? Can you make it one more block? I promise you can rest once we get to the car."

"Yes," I wheezed, hoping it was the truth. The last thing I wanted was to get caught because I passed out on the sidewalk.

True to his word, one block later, he helped me into a dark SUV in a pay-by-the-day parking lot. He started the engine before he was fully in the seat and began to back out. With our hasty escape, I expected him to peel out of the dark parking lot and speed out of town. But instead, he pulled out into the light traffic like a normal driver would and began driving below the speed limit.

My eyes drooped and closed completely as the car warmed and he drove us onto a highway.

THE SUV PULLED TO A STOP. Teetering between awake and asleep, my eyes remained closed. The driver door opened, then closed. Seconds later, a cool breeze brushed through my hair when the passenger door was opened.

"You're safe, baby, I promise. We're safe," he murmured into my ear as he lifted me from the seat and pulled me out into the cool night air.

Safe. Always safe with him.

Involuntarily, my arms wrapped around his neck as he started walking, and the steady beat of his heart in my ear quickly lulled me back to sleep.

"BABY, WE'RE HERE," he whispered as he nuzzled his nose into my hair with a deep inhale.

Exhaustion still wrapped around me like a thick quilt. Everything was blurry when I opened my eyes. Blinking a few times still didn't help. "Where is here?" I asked groggily.

He brushed a few strands of hair away from my face. "Dallas."

"How did we get here?"

"A plane. It's time to get off. I'll help you to the front."

When I was back in his arms, he carried me down the short aisle of the plane and set me on my feet. Both hands rested around my waist, giving me a minute to gain my balance.

My legs were like rubber and my shoulder throbbed as I descended the short flight of stairs into a dim hangar. "What time is it?"

"Early morning. A little longer, baby, and you can sleep as long as you want."

Once our feet were safely on the ground, I was in his arms again, being carried toward a fenced-off parking lot where only a few cars were parked. From behind us, someone yelled a quick goodbye and thank-you that Weston chose not to acknowledge.

Through the gate, he paused beside an old SUV and dug around in his pockets. The passenger door creaked, and he lowered me onto the seat. After buckling me in—and checking the lap belt was tight enough, twice—Weston leaned the chair as far back as it could go, which allowed me the angle and room to curl up on my side, and draped a cold blanket over me that he'd pulled from somewhere in the back seat.

I fell back asleep before he'd even closed the door.

21

———————

Dust and trash whipped and swirled outside my window. There was nothing out here except us, a Whataburger, and miles and miles—and miles—of flat dry land. Hell, I hadn't seen another car since we turned off I-20 about twenty miles back. The same scenery played over and over again through the passenger window as the last twenty-four hours replayed in my mind.

What Weston said about my PTSD symptoms was a hard one to process. When he initially said it, I brushed it off as him overreacting or saying whatever to keep me from sleeping with Chase. But now, after last night, now I *feel* a part of me that had been missing all these months. Maybe he was right. Not once on the plane or in the car did I have a nightmare. Maybe it was because Weston was close, or maybe I'd stopped running from the monsters in my mind and was now ready to face them head-on. With him.

It wasn't over—nothing was ever that easy—but the dread and unease seemed settled somehow. And what pissed me off was I had Chase to thank for it. Smug, sadist Chase.

I screeched and stretched against the cloth seat beneath me. Weston's amused chuckle drew my attention from the window to him in the driver seat. We hadn't spoken since I'd woken up an hour or so ago and found us somewhere between Dallas and Abilene.

"I smell," I said out of nowhere. Okay, I didn't smell, but if I didn't get a shower soon, I knew I would. "Wherever we're going, I hope it has a shower and a Target."

He smirked and continued to stare silently out the windshield.

I turned in the seat and curled on my side, laying my head on my arm to stare at him. The sun had risen behind us, the morning light pouring into the SUV highlighting his tan skin. There was something beautiful in his masculine profile—I could stare at it all day.

A smile crept up my cheeks. The trial was over. There was no more pretending, no more holding back. If I wanted to stare at him all day, every day, I could.

And I will.

His dark brown eyes cut over to me. "What are you staring at?" The strain in his voice made him sound exhausted. He had to be.

"You," I said softly and continued to stare.

That sly smile I loved pulled at his lips. "Well, stop. You're creeping me out."

"Really? You're the one who kidnapped me and won't tell me where we're going. I woke up in this old car and have no idea what's going on."

"Classic," he mumbled under his breath.

"What?"

His sigh was deep, like the conversation was pointless. "My truck. It's a classic Ford Bronco. If you're going to make fun of it, might as well get it right."

"Was I making fun of it? I just said.... Never mind. You're very grumpy when you don't get sleep."

He frowned out the window. "I'm not grumpy."

"Whatever. So this is your classic Bronco?"

"It is. I've restored it myself over the past several years. I started with the parts that mattered, like the engine and the body. I'm still working on the inside. Sorry about no radio."

Wow. Now *that* was hot.

The visual of him with no shirt, sweaty and covered in grease was enough to beg him to pull over now for a quickie. "Your hands are very... *talented*, aren't they?" I couldn't hold back my smirk as I watched for his reaction.

The cocky smile he shot my way had me pressing my thighs together. "Glad you think so, baby. And I didn't kidnap you."

"Where are we going, then?"

That smile fell as he sighed. "You need some time away to process everything, and I want to be with you while you do it. No expectations, just letting you have some time away from it all. To put you first for once."

I waited for him to continue. When he didn't, I sat up and said, "That still doesn't tell me where we're going."

"A friend of mine is getting married this weekend—tomorrow night, actually. I was invited but said no because I didn't want to leave you in Dallas. But now that everything is over, I thought it would be fun and give you a few days to relax."

"A wedding."

"Yes."

"Tomorrow night."

"Yes." He shot me a questioning look. "And meeting a few of my friends. If you want to, that is. They're all getting together at my buddy's house tonight, just sitting around a campfire drinking beer and hanging out." He shrugged to indicate it didn't matter either way to him, but the anxiety behind his eyes as he stared ahead told me something else.

"I don't have any clothes, or makeup. Hell, I don't even have clean underwear!" I cried. "How am I going to meet your friends and go to a wedding with nothing but what I have on? And I'll remind you, I stink."

"Who knew you were so self-conscious? I promise they'll smell worse than you."

"No, I am not meeting your friends looking and smelling like this." I pulled the visor down and groaned at my reflection in the mirror. My eye makeup was smudged, making me look even more tired than I felt, and my hair... oh hell, my hair was perfect if I was about to model for an '80s rock video. "Casey," I whined into my hands, now covering my disheveled face.

"There's a mall ten minutes from their place in Brownwood for more clothes, and you don't need makeup. You're beautiful without it."

Now my hands hid my flushed cheeks.

When I dropped them from my face, the beginnings of civilization had started to appear through the front windshield. We rode in silence, him focused on where we were going and me staring out the window at all the beautiful old buildings and houses.

I loved West Texas. It had a unique beauty about it. Harsh and unyielding from the heat, dust, and wind, but these buildings and people stood strong in the elements, surviving, and still managed to be friendly while they did.

It was the complete opposite of Dallas. I had to hand it to Weston, he knew what I needed —here, out of the city, in a part of the country where who you were and how you treated others mattered more than the label on your clothes.

We pulled into a busy Walmart parking lot. He parked and turned in his seat to face me, his arm propped up on the steering wheel. "The mall won't open for another few hours, and the hotel won't let us check in until early afternoon. So our options are sleep here in the car for a few hours or go roam around Walmart and buy a bunch of random shit we don't need."

MY CHOICE WAS BUY random shit at Walmart instead of sleeping, even though I felt like I could sleep for weeks and still be exhausted. This was way more fun than sleeping. Casually we trailed up and down every aisle, tossing stuff into the basket that looked cool—like all the as-seen-on-TV crap—but would never buy under normal circumstances. But here in the middle of nowhere, at Walmart, why not? When we stopped in the beauty-product aisles, I wasted over an hour carefully selecting new makeup, face soap, body wash, shampoo, and so on.

While I picked through other aisles, Weston stationed himself at the blood pressure chair outside the pharmacy and proceeded to take his blood pressure no less than ten times. With each try, he attempted to relax himself further to see if he could get the number lower. It was quite hilarious to watch, except his blood pressure reading the first time he sat down had me worried about him stroking out.

Maybe he needed this weekend away as much as I did.

When we made it to the toy section, the real fun started. We chased after each other with Nerf guns, had several hula-hoop contests, and at one point abandoned our cart to test out a couple skateboards that were on display. It was childish, yes, but so much fun. This was us dating, goofing off with each other without a care of who was around. There were many sides to Weston I knew, yet this one surprised me with his kid-like actions. And it made me aware that what I was questioning at the bar last night was a mix of both— we weren't a new couple, but we were still learning new things about each other.

For someone like me, who normally ran or pushed others away to keep them at arm's length in a relationship, the revelation was amazing. From the smile on Weston's face that hadn't fallen since we entered the store, I bet he felt the exact same way. We were both new at this, getting this close to someone, and there would be roadblocks in the future, but not right now.

Waiting in line to pay, I dropped a few magazines into the basket and a variety of snacks from the display. The lady in front of me had just finished paying when Weston jogged up and tossed something into the basket. He took one look at the candy and snacks I had snuck in, grabbed a handful of Slim Jims, and tossed them in as well.

I leaned over to see what he'd added.

A box of condoms.

I took a quick glance behind us to make sure no one could hear our conversation, then leaned my arm against the basket to face him. "You know, unless you aren't telling me something about your health, you don't have to bother with those." I hitched my chin toward the box.

"Really? I've never noticed you take a pill, so I assumed you weren't on birth control."

Damn, he was observant.

"Because I don't take a pill, I have an IUD."

His brows knitted together. "Why did the conversation move to bombs, and how or why do you have one?"

Bombs?

What the hell is he talking...?

When I figured out his mistake, I wanted to double over with laughter, but that would embarrass the hell out of him. He wasn't the type of guy who enjoyed being laughed at, that much I had learned these past several months together.

"An IUD, an intrauterine device. It prevents me from getting preg-nant without all the fake hormones and lasts about five years."

I loaded the last of the items from the cart onto the conveyor belt and held up the box of condoms to Weston with an arched brow. "Your call, but I'm healthy and have the birth control part taken care of. I mean, if you like them and—"

The box was ripped from my hand before I could finish.

"That's what I thought." I smirked and slid my card through the machine to pay. "After all this and not eating last night, I'm starving. Where are you taking me for breakfast?"

"I'm not sure what's out here, but I could always go for a Whataburger breakfast taquito, and they still serve them for the next thirty minutes." With the hopeful, little-kid look he had, how could anyone say no?

After everything was put away in the back, I climbed into the Bronco and turned, angling my body toward Weston, who was holding the door open. He leaned forward, wrapping his hands around the top of my thighs. The warmth of his hands and firm grip made my heart rate pick up and butterflies flutter in my stomach.

"Walmart and Whataburger. You really know how to show a girl a good time on a first date, Casey Weston." I tipped my head back and found him smiling down.

His broad shoulders rose and fell in an exaggerated shrug. "Not sure what you were expecting, but I had fun."

"Me too. You have no idea how much fun I had being with you, and I hope...." I ran the tips of my fingers up and down the inside of his leg. His gaze blazed brighter with each long stroke of my fingers. "I hope this afternoon you'll show me an even better time."

Long fingers wrapped around my chin to hold me in place as he gave me a hard, passionate kiss. My lips immediately parted for him, giving him access to take full possession of my mouth with his lips and tongue. My hands roamed from his legs up to his taut stomach, over his shoulders, and into his hair. I gripped tightly, pressing his lips harder against my own.

His hands wrapped around my hips and pulled, sliding me across the seat to position me flush against him. Instinctively my legs wrapped around his thighs, trying to push our bodies more firmly together. I needed any kind of pressure to relieve the relentless pulsing between my legs. Damn, I wanted him here in the parking lot. If he were to ask, there would be no hesitation—damn the consequences of being caught.

A hand slid from my hip to between my legs and began circling as he pressed firmly with the heel of his hand. My lips stopped moving at the intense feeling of relief, but it only lasted a moment before my body demanded more. I whimpered into his mouth. I was at my breaking point. This wasn't enough. I needed more. Now.

He smiled against my lips, which I reveled in, until he popped the top button of my jeans. My eyes flew open as he began pulling down the zipper, finding his eyes gazing down.

"Don't worry, I won't let anyone catch us." He chuckled and moved his lips down to my neck. "This show is only for me."

He slid his hand beneath my panties and applied the same movements and pressure as before, now much more intense without the barrier of clothes. Our hearts raced and the desperation in the kiss grew as he moved his hand farther down.

A deep growl rattled through his open mouth when his finger easily slid in.

Sweat beaded on my forehead despite the cool breeze that came in from the open truck door. Another finger entered me, joining the first. It was too much but at the same time not enough. I lay back against the center console, giving him a better angle. He answered, pushing deeper and faster. On the edge of somewhere between reality and bliss, I wrapped my hand around his wrist in a silent plea for him to never stop. When he curved his fingers, stroking back and forth, I shuddered with release around him, squeezing his hand tight with my thighs and arching against the seat.

"Holy hell," I panted.

When I opened my eyes, he was staring down, smirking with his lips wrapped around those two fingers. His eyes shuttered closed briefly as he sucked on the essence of me. Everything stilled; all I could do was watch, partly embarrassed, another part wildly turned on.

"Damn, you taste good," he mumbled around his fingers before pulling them from his mouth with an exaggerated popping sound. "I can't wait to have the rest."

My eyes still wide, he pulled me up, kissed me hard and quick, then pulled away to shut the door.

While he rounded the hood toward the driver seat, I fixed my pants and attempted to act normal. But I wasn't. No, even though I should have been sated, I wasn't. I wanted more, so much more of him, the urge almost unbearable. There was no way in hell I would make it through breakfast, shopping, and getting to the hotel he'd arranged. Maybe I could sneak him into one of the dressing rooms at the store for some additional fun this morning.

The driver door slammed, bringing me out of my daydream. He glanced over, pursed his lips, and turned back to stare out the front windshield. "Fuck. Don't look at me like that, baby. I'm barely hanging on as it is."

I batted my lashes, feigning innocence. "What?"

The answering snarl as he slammed the truck into Reverse had me turning to the window to conceal my stupid happy grin.

22

———————

The only decent store at the "mall" on the outskirts of town was a JCPenney. It wasn't what I would normally turn to in Dallas, but thankfully it had everything I needed from clean underwear to a dress for the wedding. The dress wasn't anything fancy, but I loved its simplicity. Jeans, shirts, socks, and shoes for any occasion were also bought and lugged around by a patient Weston. Anyone could see shopping wasn't his thing, but he never complained, and he commented on clothing options when asked.

After the successful shopping spree, my self-conscious mood about the impromptu trip and meeting his friends was lifted. However, the mood shifted back to gloom when we pulled up to the only hotel Weston could find with availability.

It wasn't a hotel at all. Calling it a motel would have been kind.

Under most circumstances, I wouldn't consider myself a snob, but in the sleeping category I was. I needed a soft bed, good sheets, and a great shower—so sue me. This motel would, without a doubt, fail to provide even one of those luxuries.

Saying something about the accommodations he arranged might hurt Weston's feelings, but I didn't care. I was not sleeping in a place where tiny rodent eyes might stare at me all night.

"Weston... I...."

He glanced over and grimaced. "Fuck, I know. Give me a minute." He pulled out his phone and stepped out of the Bronco.

While he paced back and forth beside the truck, I watched the motel and its occupants. The doors faced the outside, so I had a great view of all the activity.

One guy moseyed out of his room in only his tighty-whities with an ice bucket in hand, smoking a cigarette with the other. He caught my stare, tipped his ball cap, and kept walking.

My curt laugh came out as a snort.

I scanned the other rooms, now very entertained with my people-watching. Another couple hung out on the second level walkway smoking and talking. They weren't doing anything interesting, so I moved on. Movement at the end of the row of rooms on the first level caught my eye. A woman was storming down the walkway, purse clutched against her chest. Oh, she was pissed. A man, just as mad, followed closely while yelling, but with the window rolled up, I couldn't make out what he was saying.

The man rushed to catch up with the woman, gripped her upper arm, and jerked her back against his chest. The way her eyes darted around, looking for help, those desperate moves to break out of his hold.... Sweat trickled down my temple. Too recently I also had to fight, until I barely had an ounce of breath left to get free.

I was out of the Bronco and stumbling across the parking lot, unable to turn away, angry tears streaming down my face.

The woman found her footing and pushed off the man only to have him grasp her shoulder and shove her against a metal door. The echoing rattle and the smack of her slim back slamming against it sounded through my head. My feet felt like lead, same as last night when I first saw Chase, preventing me from rushing to help.

However, the woman gave little time for me to jump into action. Seconds later, she was in his arms, legs wrapped snug around his waist, having given in to his pleading for forgiveness. With her in his arms, he strode down the walkway to their room.

I jumped and swore at the blaring of a car horn, but I was frozen.

The replay of last night was all I could see, hear, smell—sending my stomach rolling. If things had turned out differently, if I hadn't fought and won, I would still be in San Diego, trapped, instead of here experiencing the best morning of my life with Weston.

The angry driver swerved his car to avoid hitting me, flipping me the bird out the window, but still I didn't move.

A warm, calloused hand interlaced with mine and began urging me out of the parking lot toward the Bronco. Even as I crawled into the seat, I couldn't take my eyes off the door the couple had disappeared through.

Weston slid into his seat, the door slamming shut behind him, but he didn't move toward the keys dangling from the ignition.

Minutes of tense silence passed.

"What happened, Kate? Last night with Chase, I promised myself I wouldn't ask, that I would let you tell me when you were ready, but...." He ran his hands through his disheveled dark hair as he turned to face me. "What happened? Tell me."

"You don't want to know." My exhausted eyes stared unseeing out the windshield. "I made it out okay. I made it out to you, and that's all that matters."

My voice, completely void of any emotion, was one I hadn't heard before.

His hand moved across the console, the warmth a striking contrast to the icy clamminess of my own.

"*Obviously*, you're not okay. I saw what made you bolt out of the truck." His voice trembled. "You froze in the middle of the parking lot, staring. Just... just tell me. It'll help, I promise."

"It won't help you though."

His tone flattened. "I'm not fucking worried about me."

"Well, *I* am, and I'm not going to do that to you." Anger seeped in, filling that emotionless pit I'd started to slip back into. "Or us. I don't want you looking at me, only seeing what might have happened. It's bad enough in my own mind. I don't need you reliving it too."

"Kate—"

"No!" I screamed, slamming my fisted hands against my thighs.

"Stop asking. Now, where are we staying tonight? *Obviously* we aren't staying here."

I squinted against the sun pouring in from the windshield, but still I stared ahead, not wanting to meet his glare.

"We're going to stay at my buddy's house. He lives a little way out of town." He turned the ignition and started to back out, pausing when he again faced me.

"Gotta be better than staying here," I grumbled and turned to the passenger window.

THIRTY MINUTES LATER, we pulled off the highway onto a long gravel driveway in what seemed to be the middle of nowhere. Outside the window, mesquite trees and open fields passed, but I didn't really see anything, my vision too blurred as I stared. The fact that we hadn't spoken since my outburst at the hotel was all I could focus on.

The entire property seemed to be around fifty acres, based off our drive, with a small ranch-style home perched in the middle. The house had a wraparound porch with about five dogs lazily lying along it in the sun.

A man appeared out of the front door, rousing the sleepy dogs, and started toward us. He was about Weston's size but had a roughness Weston didn't have, like the wind and dust of West Texas had stripped away any soft edges he might have had. His hair was buzzed short, military style—*okay, so there's a clue on how Weston knows him*—and from the looks of his arms and waist, he stayed in decent shape.

The man stopped in front of the Bronco and arched a brow at Weston, who killed the engine as if on cue.

"Ready?" Weston asked, reaching across the center console to grip my hand, brushing his thumb across my knuckles soothingly, as if he sensed my growing panic. He turned back to his friend, and a genuine, wide smile spread across his face. To put that kind of ease and happiness in him, he must have been a good friend, which made my unease worse—I was about to meet someone very important to Weston.

I stank.

And had greasy hair.

No makeup.

I'm going to kill Weston. I'd *never* been this self-conscious—which was saying something since middle school was a shitshow.

"Ready," I replied. "But one thing. I get a shower, and soon."

He nodded, shoving the door open, and slid out of the truck to greet his friend.

But I stayed in my seat as Weston rounded the hood of the truck, observing the two men before climbing out.

The clap of their hands smacking together was loud, even from where I sat. After a minute of talking and laughing, his friend's eyes moved from Weston, locked on mine, then slid back to Weston's with raised brows, inclining his head to the truck.

That's my cue.

I shouldn't have stayed in the truck; he probably thought I was some kind of loon or a bitch or worse. Damn, my palms were sweaty; hopefully he didn't want to shake hands. The moment he touched their clamminess... shit.

"Hi," I said meekly with a half-smile and a small wave before tucking my hands into the back pockets of my jeans.

My shoulders relaxed when the friend kept his hands in his pockets.

"Aiden. Nice to meet you, Doc. He tells me you need a shower."

I nodded wearily with a side glance to Weston.

"Guest bath is down the hall on your right. Help yourself." His West Texas drawl was mesmerizing; each word sounded like it had an extra vowel added.

At that, I turned my attention to Weston, finding him already smiling, watching me chat with his friend. "I'll bring the stuff in. Go ahead."

It was a little odd walking past Aiden and into his house, and normally I wouldn't dare be this rude, but I needed to get clean. A hot shower would help wash away the traces of Chase's touch that still lingered along my arms and neck.

THE NEAR-SCALDING water of the shower revived me. It helped shift my focus from what could have happened last night to the fun weekend ahead with Weston. The men's voices carried down the hall seconds after I stepped out of the shower.

"Why the hell did she go and buy all new clothes?" Aiden asked.

Weston's voice lacked the amusement Aiden's had. "It's a long story. I'll tell you later."

"Why didn't she just bring stuff from Dallas?"

"She was asleep when I stopped by the house on the way out of town, okay? I didn't want to leave her alone in the car long enough for me to pack her stuff."

"Damn, you're whipped."

The bathroom's wood door was cool against my warm ear as I strained to hear Weston's response.

"Yep. And you're one to talk. You're the one getting married tomorrow."

Aiden's response was muffled as they moved toward the front of the house and out of my hearing range.

With the tiny blue towel clutched against my chest, I carefully opened the bathroom door, looked up and down the hall, and tiptoed until I found a room with Weston's duffel bag on the end of the bed and all the plastic bags stuffed with the shit we'd purchased.

With the closed door against my back, I sighed at the sight of the bed; it looked so comfortable, almost like it was begging me to lie down for a few minutes.

So, I did.

Too soon, exhaustion swept in and my lids grew too heavy to keep open.

"Baby."

Weston's deep voice reverberating against my dry lips pulled me awake. His soft lips grazed along mine before brushing down my neck and collarbone, while his fingertips dragged up and down my bare inner thigh, sending a jolt of pleasure down to my core.

"How long have I been asleep?" I asked with a yawn, stretching my arms above my head, my back arching off the bed in an attempt to shake the grogginess.

Silence.

My eyes opened and found him unabashedly staring at my naked breasts. With all that stretching, the knot I'd secured must have loosened. The blue towel now lay on the bed beneath me, leaving me fully exposed to his intense perusal. But with the way he was visually devouring and appreciating every inch of my naked body, who would mind? Especially since it was me—*only me*—who had him adjusting himself over his jeans to accommodate his growing erection.

"Damn, you're gorgeous. The things I want to do to you...," he murmured as he lay beside me. One hand propped his head up and the other caressed the curves of my breast, down to my waist and hips, and up again. The touch was gentle and slow like he wanted to cherish each part of me, memorizing me. "I've no idea how I got to be the fucking luckiest man alive who gets to be with you, but I thank God every day I am."

He kissed along my jaw, down my neck, sucking and nibbling on his way to my chest.

"Where's your friend—" I gasped as his lips wrapped around one peaked nipple while he teased and pulled the other. "Never mind, I don't give a shit." With a deep, pleasure-filled groan, I threaded my hands through his hair, holding his mouth tight against me.

The loss of his warm mouth and flicking tongue had me whimpering. "He just left for the rehearsal dinner." Tightening my grip, I attempted to pull him back, arching my back to close the space between us. "It's just you and me, baby. You can be as loud as you want. I know I will." His tongue lazily circled my nipple before he lightly clamped down with his teeth; the mixture of pleasure and pain had me squeezing my thighs tightly together, trying for some kind of relief.

He chuckled, moving to the other breast and continuing with the arousing torture.

"Fuck, I love kissing your body. Every time I see you, I want my lips on your skin. I love everything about you." He trailed his hand down my abdomen, over my hip, and down my leg. In one quick move, my leg was hooked over his shoulder and his palm smacked my raised backside, leaving a stinging handprint. "Even when you drive me nuts with your antics."

Lowering my leg, he kissed and sucked down to my navel, Brushing light kisses from hipbone to hipbone before dipping lower. He lay between my legs and gazed up with a mischievous grin. I swallowed against my dry throat, panting on the bed, staring down at him. His eyes shifted from mine to the apex of my thighs. A deep, throaty moan rumbled as he pressed his nose against me and inhaled deeply; once again he met my heated stare and blew a warm stream of air up and down, teasing me.

The comforter crumpled in my fisted hands. "Casey, please," I whimpered, begged, pleaded with what little breath was left in my lungs.

"No need to beg, baby. It's going to happen. This is more for me than you. You have no idea how I've had to hold myself back every damn day from putting my head between your legs. I want to take my time. I've craved tasting you again for months."

Blood thundered in my ears as he shifted his intense focus between my thighs. My blood boiled in my veins when he flicked his tongue against my small bundle of nerves before wrapping his lips around it to suck me between his lips. His moan was pure euphoria. He idly licked and sucked, taking me to the edge of pleasure before slowing to torment me again and again.

He slid lower, eyes never leaving his meal, bending my legs and pushing them farther apart to accommodate his broad shoulders. Now that he had room, his control slipped; it seemed the idea of savoring was gone.

His tongue plunged inside, sending my hips reflexively arching up, demanding more. A hand wrapped around my hipbone, holding me firm against the bed. Sweat glistened on my forehead and neck, my skin flushed. Two fingers glided in where his tongue had been, sending sounds I didn't know I could make or would ever make pouring from my lips. His tongue and fingers quickened their pace, pushing me over the edge. The world faded to the distant background as I shattered, screaming, around him. The convulsions that racked through me were gloriously painful, but Weston held me tight, keeping his mouth on me, prolonging my pleasure.

My heavy panting breaths slowed, and after a quiet minute, floating back to reality, I opened my eyes to find him smirking. *Damn that cocky-ass smirk.*

Eyes still on me, he gave one last long lick before I jolted up, gripped his face in my hands, and pulled his lips to meet mine.

I loved the way he kissed, like I was something he needed in order to breathe, and tasting myself mingled with his unique flavor was enough to make the throbbing between my thighs return. Fumbling at his belt, I whimpered against his lips; the buckle wouldn't budge. Lips locked with mine, he scooted us to the edge of the bed to have room to remove his pants and shirt.

Our lips separated as he pulled the black T-shirt over his head. I placed my hands over his, pausing them at the metal of his buckle.

"Stop." My voice was shaky, still not fully recovered from the soul-shattering orgasm he'd just given me. "I want to do it."

Naked, I kneeled on the bed before him and traced the black lines of the tattoos along his chest and shoulders. When I first met him, I'd thought the tattoos were simple swirls, no particular design, but now, with the intimate views I'd had, I knew they were several pictures and symbols molding into one another. I traced my fingernail along the detailed wings of an eagle, wings spread, and beside it the "Come and Take It" flag rippling, like it was caught on a strong breeze.

"I love these," I whispered against his sweat-slick skin as I kissed the four letters of my name inked over his heart. "You have no idea how much I love these. So damn sexy." My hands traveled across his washboard abs, down to the waistband of his jeans. Making quick work of his belt, I yanked it through the loops, tossing it to the other side of the room. The jeans popped open with single pull against the button. His erratic breathing, the heaving of his chest tried to distract me, but my eyes never left his as I slowly lowered his zipper.

The guttural groan was my aphrodisiac, knowing *I* could do this to him.

"Baby, I don't know how much longer I can wait." He moaned, eyes shuttering closed.

Smirking, I threw his words back at him.

"Casey, no need to beg. You know this is going to happen. It's more for me than you, believe me. Let me enjoy licking you."

I gripped his backside, kneading handfuls of his perfect ass. Having my fill, I slid my hands toward the floor, pulling his jeans and boxers down. I wrapped my fingers around the base of his thickness as I circled my lips around the tip. I stared up through my lashes, wanting to watch his reaction. It had been months since I'd been able to savor him like this, to send him over the edge with my mouth, and now I understood why Weston wanted to take his time earlier.

This, pleasing him, was... amazing.

I tortured him exactly like he did to me, teasing, licking, swirling my tongue before taking all of him in my mouth. He lost all restraint, weaving his hands into my hair to hold me while he slowly thrust in and out.

"Fuck," he hissed through clenched teeth. "I... I need you to stop, baby. I don't—" I sucked hard, catching him off guard. "Shit!" he yelled and stepped out of reach. "Not like this, I want to be buried inside you. I want to feel you. It's all I've been able to think about since you tossed the fucking box of condoms out of the cart."

"Yes." It wasn't the most eloquent reply, but he didn't seem to care. Crawling backward on the bed, making room for his massive frame, I paused. He didn't follow, instead just stood taking deep breaths in and out.

I waited, but he still didn't move.

"Casey?"

With my plea, he knelt and crept across the bed, placing his full weight over me. His nose nuzzled into my hair and his lips began kissing down my neck.

"Patience, baby. If you want this to last longer than thirty seconds, you need to have patience."

His soft lips skirted over mine before connecting, tasting like salt from my sweat-covered skin. Our kiss was demanding, like he was attempting to pour every ounce of love he felt into it. I dragged my nails down and up his muscular back, enjoying the feel of it flexing and moving.

But he still wasn't inside me. My hips reflexively arched, trying to find him.

Pulling his face from my neck, he wrapped both hands around my cheeks, slowly brushing them with the soft pads of his thumbs. My breath hitched, and I was unable to look away. Only love—pure, genuine, terrifying love—lay behind his eyes.

"I love you, Kate. I love you more than I could ever explain. More than I've ever thought was possible." Those hooded deep brown eyes locked with mine as he shifted his hips forward, pushing deep inside me.

I couldn't breathe.

Neither could he.

The air pulsed between us.

My eyes shuttered closed, unable to stay open a moment longer at the intense sensation of the skin-to-skin contact. The fullness of him, stretching me, was exquisite, and based on the slew of whispered curses from Weston, he felt the same way.

Achingly slow, he withdrew to the tip and eased back in, repeating the motion over and over.

My arms stretched above my head, sending my back arching off the bed.

"Casey, you have to go faster. Please," I whimpered.

Damn, it felt good, but every time he pushed, I needed more.

The begging worked.

One hand gripped both my wrists, restraining them above my head; the other supported his weight as he thrust deeper and faster.

And that was when he started talking. Telling me everything he'd been thinking the past few months. What he'd been planning for me. How beautiful I was. How good I felt clenching around him. I couldn't help but blush at some of the darker things he murmured.

I bit his lower lip when he leaned down for a kiss, trying to hold back a scream that would have been loud enough for the next town to hear.

He growled against my teeth and slammed in hard, pushing me over the edge once again. I quivered and tightened around him, aiding him to gain his release with a barked curse.

We lay together, catching our breath for several minutes before he looked down with a satisfied smile.

"Damn. That was... feeling you squeeze me.... *Thank you* for being on birth control. It's always been great with you, but that was...."

"Mind-blowing. Fantastic. Perfect because it was with me."

"Exactly."

"Agreed." I hooked a leg over his thigh to flip him to his back and straddled his hips. "So... question. It'll be a while before Aiden gets back, right?" The tips of my fingers traced the outline of his red, swollen lips. He really was amazing in so many ways; I loved all these unguarded moments with him.

As I gazed down at him, I was thankful there weren't any additional hurdles keeping us from each other. We could now love each other openly, without the risk of someone taking advantage of Weston's new weakness—me.

"Probably another hour or so, why?" By the arch of his eyebrow and that damn cocky smirk, he knew why I was asking.

"I want to do that again."

His grin grew as his hands skimmed their way up to my breasts, cupping both in his palms and teasing each nipple between his fingertips. "Do you now? I think we can make that happen, baby."

My eyes fluttered closed to focus on each inch his hands roamed along my body, discovering and worshipping all of me.

Even our time in Vail couldn't compare to this moment. In Vail, there were still doubts in the back of my mind on where we would go from there, almost preparing myself for him to leave. But now, now I knew he didn't want to go anywhere, that I was a part of his life. And he was a part of mine. Wherever we went from here, we knew we would have each other.

23

───────

There weren't many choices on what to wear since I'd only purchased a few outfits, plus the dress for the wedding. The plastic bags rustled as I dug around until I found a pair of jeans, underwear, a white V-neck T-shirt, and white Converses which were a last-minute purchase. The tags were still on everything. I glanced around but didn't see anything to use to cut them. With a shrug, I raised the thin plastic to my teeth, but thankfully Weston walked into the room carrying a pair of scissors before any dental damage could be done.

Damnit, he was good. He seemed to know everything I needed and when.

About ten minutes ago, the laughing and talking of people pouring into the house had woken us from a short nap. From the multiple pairs of boot heels walking across the floor, it sounded like more than a few of his buddies were here.

Weston pulled his dark-wash jeans, the ones that hugged every edible inch of his perfect ass, over his hips and tossed on a short-sleeved plain white T-shirt. The white shirt highlighted his tan skin and brought out his dark hair and eyes.

And those tattoos. Damn, I loved the tattoos that peeked from under his sleeves and continued down to his elbows. So damn sexy and masculine.

Swiping the new jeans off the bed, I pulled them on before I could tackle him for another erotic round. Not that he would mind, but he did want to see his friends.

"Listen, I thought tonight was going to be low-key, but Aiden texted and said more people are coming over than he expected."

"Like who?" I asked as I secured the top button of the new jeans. Damn, they were snug. I lunged around the room to stretch them out a little while Weston stared, completely confused as to what was going on.

He shook his head, trying to remember my question.

"The whole wedding party, for one, plus some of his friends from high school. He grew up here. Both he and Tracy did, so there might be a lot of people looking for an excuse to hang out and drink free beer."

I started to respond that it was fine, but a man bellowing through the house cut me off.

"Where is he?" the man shouted in an excited boyish tone.

Rushed footsteps pounded down the hall before the door to our room flew open and a man not much taller than me marched in.

Startled, I grappled for my T-shirt lying on the bed to cover myself from the man now smiling wildly at Weston.

"There you are, you fucking prick," he said, taking a few steps toward Weston before realizing I was also in the room. He gave me a lazy once-over, not caring to stop at Weston's warning snarl, and turned to face me, completely forgetting about the person he'd come in to see.

"Hi." He extended a hand, his honey-brown eyes twinkling with amusement. "I'm—"

Weston shoved him against the wall, the hanging pictures and the dresser rattling from the force. Even with Weston's large hand wrapped around his thin throat, the man smiled, eyes only for me.

With an annoyed grunt, Weston released him only to grab the back of his collar and pull him from the room, slamming the door shut behind them. The breath I had no idea I was holding released with a whoosh. But the awkward incident made me smile; maybe, hopefully, all his friends were that rough and easygoing. Maybe then I would learn a little more about Weston and what all he'd been through with this group of guys he called brothers.

My stomach grumbled loudly, reminding me I hadn't eaten anything since Whataburger, and with all the *exercise* this afternoon, I was famished. Thankfully Weston had brought in the bag with all the random snacks we'd piled into the basket at Walmart. Opening a few of the Slim Jims and potato chip bags, I sat on the bed and tucked my legs under me to text Eric while I snacked. He was probably wondering what the hell happened to me.

> Me: Hey, so random turn of events. I'm no longer in San Diego but now in West Texas with W about to meet his friends.
>
> Me: I'll tell you all about what happened another time.

With an ungraceful flop backward, I stared at the ceiling, waiting for him to respond. I bit off a piece of Slim Jim, my mind wandering. Maybe Weston was right and I needed to talk to someone about last night and everything else that had happened since Christmas. Eric and Meagan would listen, but they wouldn't know what to say, and Weston, well, he was out of the question. If he knew what happened in that hotel room, nothing would stop him from killing Chase. And that wasn't what I wanted; my goal was never to make Weston jealous or have to defend me.

What I did need was an unbiased opinion to listen. Once I got back to Dallas, I could find a shrink to spill everything to. From Vail, to the shooting, Chase... okay, so the past eight months really. I had a lot to get off my chest.

The phone vibrated beside me.

> Eric: What the hell. I need to know everything. Spill it, Wheeler.

I couldn't help but smile, though the tears on the verge of spilling over made the screen go blurry. Damn, I loved my best friend. Meagan was... Meagan. I loved her, but Eric was my best friend and one who knew everything about me. Except the past few months with Chase. I wished Meagan and I could be as close, but it never seemed to happen, and I didn't force it. She had her life and I had mine; it seemed we were more each other's backup friend than anything.

Me: So... things with Chase didn't work out. Weston flew to SD to bring me home. Then he decided to bring me to his friend's wedding. Now we're here.

Eric: A wedding?

Me: I know, it's all spur of the moment. He was invited a while back but said no because of the case and me. But he said I needed to get away, so he brought me here.

Eric: I love him.

Me: Me too.

Me: He did mention you two had a nice little chat about my mental health. Thanks for the heads-up.

Eric: I wasn't sure, love, and I'm not an expert in that field, but I have noticed you acting different. Not the Kate I know and love. Sorry if I you think I went behind your back. I wasn't trying to. Just want you to get better.

Eric: I mentioned it to W one day, and he said he was thinking the same thing. IDK. Are you mad?

Me: How can I be mad that you were concerned about me?

Eric: Are you going to talk to someone? You know, about the shooting.

Oh, so much more than that, Eric.

> Me: I guess when I get back to Dallas, I will.
> Speaking of which, when am I back on the
> schedule?

> > Eric: Sunday night. Looks like they have you
> > on a 5-hour shift. Better than nothing right?
> > You're still excited about coming back?

No.

> Me: Yes, I've missed you.

> > Eric: We've missed you, that's for sure.
> > Nothing has changed though. People are still
> > getting sick, pissed at us for not being fast
> > enough, and saying we charge too much. You
> > know. The usual.

> Me: Oh no, sounds like someone is having a
> tough shift.

> > Eric: I miss my best friend.

> Me: Soon, love. Okay, I need to go out and
> meet these friends of his.

> > Eric: If they're hot, take pictures or video so I
> > don't have to use my imagination later.

> Me: Love you.

I stood from the bed and groaned at my reflection. I was a hot mess, to say the least. Rummaging through Weston's duffel bag, I found an old Texas Rangers baseball cap—just what I needed to cover my unruly hair. Next, a quick few layers of mascara and nude lip gloss. Not bad, not great, but I had an inkling none of his friends would care. Which made me like them already.

At least I smelled better than before. Not being the stinky new girlfriend had been priority one on my list.

Silence in the house as I crept down the hall told me I was alone, but a sudden noise from the kitchen said otherwise. A tall, slender woman had her head buried in the fridge, rummaging around for something; she jumped when she turned and found me standing behind her.

"You must be Kate," she said, her free hand on her heart, the other holding a bottle of water. My mouth watered at the sight. After three Slim Jims, chips, and a bag of trail mix, I desperately needed something to drink.

"Hi, yes." I stuck my hand out, which she gripped for a firm handshake. "Do you mind if I grab one of those?" I pointed to the bottle she held.

"Of course. Help yourself. I'm Tracy, Aiden's fiancée. It's nice to meet you finally. I've heard a lot about you."

A little dribble of water escaped down my chin from the bottle, but I didn't wipe it away, too focused on what Tracy had said. How in the hell had she heard about me? When did Weston...? Damn, there was still so much I didn't know about him, that he wouldn't open up about.

"Hopefully all good things."

She smiled, not answering my obvious question. "We all wondered if he was going to bring another girl around one day."

Um, say what? Another girl? Is she talking about that Anne chick Ryan mentioned a while back? The tips of my ears and cheeks burned.

"How long have you known Weston?" Maybe she could fill me in on these other women if she'd known him for a while.

"Oh geez, let me think. Aiden and Weston went through basic together, which was 2001, I think. Then Special Ops together, so Weston has been a part of our little family for a long time."

"Family?"

"Aiden and I have a daughter. She's six now. Staying with her grandparents tonight since we knew it would be a late one with all the boys in town. And I figured I wouldn't stick around to watch them drink themselves into oblivion, so I'm heading out to stay with one of my girlfriends."

The guys must get together often if she knew what was going to happen by night's end.

I tilted my head toward the back door. "Are they all outside?"

"Yep, Aiden insisted on having a keg and Cuervo for shots, so be ready for a long night. I'm going to pack and get everything ready for tomorrow."

I nodded in response and started to turn, but her calming voice stopped me.

"He really is a great guy, Kate. Don't hurt him. What he's done for Aiden, and in turn for me and our family has been...." She sighed and looked up at the ceiling, obviously searching for the right words. "He's family, and it's going to be hard. What the boys went through, what they sometimes remember or flash back to... just be patient with him, okay? He'll open up eventually."

"I love him." No idea why I said it, but it seemed she knew Weston well, and I wanted her to know. She needed to know this was real for me too. "And I've never said that about anyone and meant it as deeply as I do when saying it about him. I'm pretty difficult myself, and he's put up with me, pushed through every damn wall I put up. I'm thankful he's been patient with me."

She moved, and out of habit, I widened my stance, preparing for a fight. But instead she wrapped her arms around my neck, pulling me against her. When she didn't let go, I relaxed and wrapped my arms around her waist, loving the feel of instant friendship. It was strange to not put up a fight or wonder when she would stab me in the back. My gut told me she was genuine with her happiness and concern for Weston.

"Have fun tonight," she murmured as she pulled away to arm's length and held my shoulders. "I'll see you tomorrow at the wedding. I'm so glad you two could make it." A quick squeeze of my shoulder and she was gone, heading down the hall to their room.

"Huh." *Interesting.* Swiping the half-full bottle of water off the counter, I turned and headed out the back door.

The patio was packed with people, and as soon as I walked off the step, I was lost. I couldn't see anything from being too damn short, and the stupid hat restricted my line of sight. Matchbox Twenty's *Push* album played from a nearby stereo as I pushed through the crowd, making me already like Aiden more for his choice in music.

I found an empty spot, and if I stood on my tiptoes and angled my head up, I could somewhat see among the crowd. There was a large group of men and women, all about my age, to the right where I assumed the keg was by the red Solo cups in their hands. To the left were a few picnic tables, also surrounded by people, but as the people shifted, plates with wings, chips, and other food appeared laid out on the red-and-white checkered tablecloths.

A drink. Yes, a drink was the first order of business, then find Weston. Or eat wings. Beer. Wings. Weston. Yep, in that order. A drink would help shake the uneasy feeling rising in my gut about meeting his friends. His *good* friends.

A man I didn't know slowly sauntered up, smiling a smile every woman knew all too well.

Great.

His hands were tucked into the front pockets of his jeans, and the bill of his hat was pulled so low I could barely make out his face.

"You look lost, sweetheart. Are you looking for something? Please don't tell me you're looking for someone."

"Um, yeah, I'm looking for my boyfriend."

"Well, he's not that great of one if he's not with you now. How about you come over and let me pour you a drink?" He extended a hand to me with a beckoning gesture.

"I don't think that's a good—"

A heavy arm draped around my shoulders and pulled me close, signaling the person I was searching for had just found me.

"Hey, you." I took a step back to look up at him. Damn this hat. I was going to have a crick in my neck tomorrow from having to look up at everyone to fucking see them. "I was looking for you but got distracted by booze."

Under Weston's intense back-the-fuck-away glare, the man retreated two steps and bolted to where his friends were watching by the keg.

"There are some people I want to introduce you to. Then I'll get you a beer." His grip was strong as he guided us toward a large firepit several yards away. "Nice hat, by the way. Looks better on you than me. How in the hell does it even fit?" I assumed he was smirking when he said it since I couldn't see anything; my eyes were glued to the ground, watching where I was stepping.

"The hair. I have a ton of it."

We stopped a few feet from a firepit, where some guys were sitting in lawn chairs, watching us. Waiting for us, I realized. Weston's long fingers pulled on the hand at my lip and tilted my head up so our eyes could meet.

The way his eyes searched mine, the bob of his throat... as if he were nervous.

Shit. What in the hell am I about to walk into?

He opened his mouth to speak, but a voice from the firepit called out, "Come on, Romeo, we don't bite. Unless, of course, she wants me to."

A chuckle erupted around the fire.

"Fuck off, Mouse," he growled, which made the men laugh harder as he tugged us toward his friends.

Three men sat around the fire, all staring at me. And my impression of their stares was more assessing and sizing me up, maybe even trying to gauge my feelings for their friend, than ogling.

"The loud-mouth fucker over there"—Weston pointed to the man who'd barged into our room earlier; he was lying out on a long lawn chair, that same mischievous smile on his lips—"is Tyler."

Tyler—or Mouse—stood to grab my hand. He was only a little taller than me, lean build, and had unruly light brown hair. His carefree smile had me staring, his white teeth perfectly straight; the way the corners of his lips turned up beckoned me to laugh with him. With that smile, I knew he was the rogue of the group, the one no one could tame. His light-wash jeans hung low on his narrow hips with a black button-down, the long sleeves rolled up to his elbow.

"Sorry about earlier. If I would have known you were changing"

—he glanced at Weston with a wicked smile—"I would have come in sooner."

With a cackle, he dodged Weston's swing toward his gut.

Weston's grip on me tightened, and with the other hand, he pointed to the average-looking redheaded man now standing in front of Tyler, protecting him. "That's Kyle."

Kyle stepped forward and shook my free hand but held on when I tried to pull away. His light green eyes bored into mine, and for some reason, it felt like he knew everything about me from that one look. Hell, maybe he did.

Kyle was tall like Aiden and Weston but built lean like Tyler. They all had a presence about them, like they were on edge, ready to jump into action if needed. But Kyle... he seemed more calculating, analyzing the entire situation. He had to be the planner of the group.

"And you already met Aiden." Weston gestured toward Aiden sitting to our left. "Now, I'm going to grab her a beer. No one says anything until I get back. Understood?" he barked. Turning toward the patio, he stalked toward the crowd.

I strummed my fingers along my thigh, mind racing, trying to think of anything to talk about. Weston had said to wait in silence, which it seemed the men were more than happy to do, but who was I kidding? I was never good at following his orders.

"What's up with him?" I nodded toward the patio where Weston had disappeared to.

The three looked between each other, their lips clamped tightly into thin lines. Kyle went so far as shaking his head at Tyler, like he might be the one to break Weston's command.

"You have to be kidding me. Don't tell me you're going to listen to him and not say anything until he gets back. That's ridiculous. I'll start. I'm Kate Wheeler. Well, Dr. Kate Wheeler, if you want to get technical about it—"

Aiden broke my rambling.

"So we finally meet. I've heard a lot about you, Doc." He leaned over the armrest of his chair, holding a bottle of Cuervo and two shot glasses in his hand when he righted himself.

I walked to his chair, Kyle and Tyler glancing nervously back and forth, and grabbed a shot glass. "Then it seems I'm at a slight disadvantage. Weston isn't very... open, if you haven't noticed."

Aiden filled my glass to the brim before tending to his.

We clinked our glasses in cheers. "Here's to you, Doc. I sure as hell hope you know what you're doing."

I tipped the full shot back at the same time he did, neither of us dropping the other's gaze. I shoved my empty glass toward him once again with a nod to the bottle in a silent request. He smirked but didn't say a word as he again filled mine, then his.

This time the toast was mine.

"Me too," I whispered and tossed the shot back. The slow burn down my throat warmed my body, chilled from the cool night air.

"What the hell are you doing, Tex?" Weston growled from behind me. He didn't sound too happy to find me leaning over his friend's chair taking shots. "Have you forgotten how to *obey* a direct order?"

Aiden smirked, pointing his empty glass at me. "She started it."

"Yeah, but I expect that kind of thing from her. She hasn't obeyed a single fucking thing since we met."

With a wink to Aiden, I turned to Weston.

He placed the two Solo cups he was holding on the ground before slouching into a lawn chair and beckoning me to sit in his lap. Silence once again wrapped the group. Aiden was the only one who would look my direction for longer than a few seconds. They all seemed to understand how deep Weston's protective nature went.

Maybe even deeper than I understood if his friends were this nervous to open up.

Someone needed to lighten the mood, and since the two shots of Cuervo were already doing wonders, that person should be me.

"If I'd known the army looked like this"—I gestured to the men around me—"I sure as hell would have enlisted."

Their relaxed laughter released the tension from the air.

"Baby, don't make them any more conceited than they already are," Weston said behind me. He had his arm wrapped around my waist, holding me close to him. With each breath, his stomach and chest rose and fell against my back.

This could be fun.

Wiggling a bit along his lap, like I was trying to get comfortable, had the hand surrounding my waist tightening a fraction.

Finally, Kyle relaxed enough to sit in his chair opposite me and Weston.

"Us, conceited? You're Romeo, remember? The one who could walk into any bar and be found by the flock of women around him."

I turned with an amused look; Weston simply shrugged his broad shoulders and took a long sip of his beer. A cocky smile played at his lips; it seemed he loved that Kyle made that little revelation while I was here. *Cocky bastard.*

"You always managed to take them home, so I'm not sure why you sound put out by it, Miss Ginger," Tyler said from his lawn chair. He was completely relaxed, laid out staring at the stars, beer in one hand and a cigarette in the other.

What the hell is up with all these names?

"Okay, what's up with the nicknames? Mouse? Miss Ginger? What the hell?"

They looked to each other and busted out laughing, Aiden was clutching his stomach, Tyler was practically crying, and even Kyle was smiling. Apparently, the memories behind the nicknames were hilarious.

"Each has a long story attached to it. One day we'll tell you. Promise." Weston chuckled beneath me, sending a nice vibration from his chest heating my core. Automatically, my legs squeezed together and my hand skimmed up and down his thick thigh. His eyes met mine, and I knew we were both wishing the same thing—that we were alone and clothing was nonexistent.

Tyler cut in, breaking our lusty moment. "Let's go back to this whole 'you not obeying Romeo's orders,' Doc. How in the hell are you still alive? Pretty sure if anyone in our group did it, they would find themselves dead or wishing they were."

I smiled, the flickering flames of the fire holding me in a peaceful trance. It was funny hearing him talk about Weston like that. He was a hardass, yes, but it was such a contrast to who he was with me. Even when I defied his orders.

"I think he likes the challenge." I tipped the red Solo cup back, draining the last of my beer, and stood to grab more. Not surprising, Weston stood as well, took the cup from my hand, and walked in the direction of the keg with Aiden at his side.

Kyle and Tyler started talking about some guy Axe and how he was doing, not engaging me, so I took the opportunity to relax. Sitting in the chair Weston vacated, I leaned back and closed my eyes, focusing on the crackling of the firewood.

Nowhere to go, nothing to do but hang out with friends around a fire. It was comfortable. This wasn't something I normally enjoyed but maybe should consider.

Perhaps a few hundred acres somewhere outside Dallas was in my near future. It wasn't like I had other things to spend all the money I'd made over the years on, plus the multimillion-dollar trust fund which had sat untouched, gaining year after year.

The crackling of the fire faded and my eyes grew heavy as the two men talked.

A hand gripped my shoulder.

My eyes flew open. I stumbled out of the chair, sending it flying only for me to trip over it, my ass hitting the stone pavers hard. I panted, scooting away from the threat I still couldn't see.

"Doc? It's just me. It's okay. You're safe," Tyler said, concern lacing his words.

Both Tyler and Kyle stood by the upside-down chair, staring apprehensively. Tyler spoke up again. "Sorry to scare you. We aren't going to hurt you."

My cheeks flushed as my hands trembled beneath me. *Damn this... this fear that still controlled me.*

I stood on shaky legs to brush the dirt off my jeans. There wasn't any on me, but it was a good excuse to not meet their questioning eyes as I said, "Yeah, I'm fine. Sorry, must have dozed off."

I peered at them from under the hat. The two exchanged a glance, then looked behind me in the direction Weston had gone. When they looked back, the sympathy in their eyes....

"Is that your professional opinion?" Kyle asked, keeping his gaze locked with mine.

Seemed fucking chatty Weston thought it was fine to tell everyone about the state of my mental health. He was going to get an earful for this one.

"Not sure what Weston has told you, but I'm fine. Really." I righted the chair and sat back down, my heart still thrumming in my chest. "It's not as bad as he thinks it is. He's just being his usual over-protective self. It's becoming smothering, actually." I grumbled the last part to myself and closed my eyes.

The lawn chair squeaked beside me as Tyler sat back down. "That reaction you just had isn't normal and you know it. He's just trying to prevent it from getting worse. We've all seen what can happen if you don't deal with it. You have to face it head-on. Trust him. He's spent so long looking out for us, for others, he knows what to spot."

Their eyes shot behind me, indicating Weston was on his way back with my beer. And that was when it was clear. The way they looked at him, such respect and almost adoration in their eyes, for the infuriating man I loved. It was like a little boy would idolize their big brother, but there was no way the two men were much younger than him. My bone-dry throat made it hard to swallow. What had they been through together for them to see Weston that way? A large part of me never wanted to know.

"What were y'all talking about?" Weston asked, handing me my beer. He lifted me out of the chair, sat down, and pulled me back into his lap.

No way I wanted him to know about the scene I'd made; it would only prove his point more. "You, and how adorable you are," I said quickly, making sure Tyler and Kyle couldn't tell him the truth.

"Fuck, baby," Weston groaned from behind me, "are you trying to emasculate me?"

I turned to gauge if he was joking or not, but his eyes were closed, head resting against the back of the chair.

"Would you rather I tell them how much I love your dick and talented hands?" I grinned, waiting for a reaction.

The other boys spewed out their beer, Aiden cackling so hard his chair tipped back, making him flail his arms to keep upright.

"Yes!" Weston exclaimed and pulled me in for a chaste kiss. "And how things go very wrong when you don't listen to me."

"Like when?" I pouted.

"Let's see here. There was that time you stabbed yourself, in your kitchen, with your own knife."

The boys started howling again.

Eyes wide, I turned to Kyle, Aiden, and Tyler, pointing behind me accusingly. "He took my gun! What else was I supposed to do? He ran off with my gun, leaving me alone in the house with not one but two armed men. I had to defend myself, and my spare gun was five drawers away. I thought it was quick thinking to use a knife. Very MacGyver of me, if I do say so myself."

"MacGyver would have fashioned a knife out of a splinter from the cabinet in less than a second. Grabbing a knife was just quick thinking," Kyle chimed in.

Thanks, jackass.

Aiden leaned forward, bracing his forearms on his thighs. "How many guns do you own, Doc?"

"Three." I winced; Weston didn't know about the third tucked away in my bathroom vanity drawer. You know, just in case.

"Tell us how you ended up knifing yourself," Tyler asked, blowing out a long breath of smoke.

"After your boy here shot a guy, he was down but not out. He reached for me, grabbed my ankle, and pulled me off my feet. I accidentally cut myself in the thigh on the way down."

"Too bad. Hopefully it didn't scar that pretty little thigh of yours," Tyler said, smiling, that damn amused twinkle back. "That would be a shame." He glanced to Weston, waiting for a response. But I spoke up first.

"It did. Would you like to see? I can give you a private viewing."

"I—"

"Knock it off, you two," Weston said, caution lacing his words. His fingers began playing with my hair, slowly pulling through the dark strands which lay down my back. I purred, my eyes shuttering closed.

Kyle pulled my attention from Weston's touch. "Who's going to tell me about the cryptic pictures you sent a few days back?"

I sat up in Weston's lap, gripping his knees.

"Did anything come from them?" I asked, my words dripping with hope.

The shake of Kyle's head had me sinking against Weston's chest.

"But," he said, perking me back up, "I'm trying one last thing before giving up. I was about to do it, then had to hop on a plane and head out to middle-of-nowhere Texas."

"Hey," Aiden said, "this is home. Watch it, Miss Ginger." His eyes shifted to mine, narrowing. "I guess that voice recording sent for me to translate also came from you via Romeo."

"Yep, and thanks for doing it. It was helpful. Hey, Kyle, do you think you could look at a few more pictures? They're kind of blurry, so they'll need to be cleaned up before I try to find someone who can identify this guy." I clasped my hands in front of me in a silent prayer.

"I could probably make that happen. Do you have the picture on you?"

Weston grunted in discomfort as I shoved out of his lap and stumbled to Kyle while pulling out my phone. Bending over Kyle's chair, I flipped through the various photos I had taken of Chase's mystery partner.

Kyle grabbed the phone from my hands to swipe through on his own. "These are pretty far away. How'd you get these, anyway?"

Yeah, that. Not daring a look to Weston, I kept my focus on Kyle. "I... um... it's not important. I just need to know who this guy is."

Kyle paused on the final picture, pulling his fingers across the screen to enlarge it. "Okay, send them all to me. I might have some friends who can run it through facial recognition when I'm done."

"Some friends. Do you know a lot of people with that kind of software access?" I snorted but leaned in, hoping he would tell me.

"Yes" was his only reply.

"He won't tell you," Aiden said from beside me, drawing my attention away from my phone still in Kyle's hands. "He won't tell you who he works for, so don't even try. If Romeo can't get it out of him, no one can."

"Kate." Kyle startled me; they'd only called me Doc since I arrived. "What the hell is this?" My phone was against his ear like he was listening to something.

Shit, the recording from the hotel room.

My stomach dropped, the beer and tequila on the verge of making a reappearance.

24

F *uck.*
   Fuck.
Fuck.

Think, Kate.

"It's nothing, Kyle," I said, stretching for my phone, but he held it out of my limited reach. "Damnit, give it back."

While struggling for the phone, I glanced to Weston, who was watching us with an amused smile, his head cocked to the side, not understanding what we were fighting over.

"That was your voice, but it wasn't Romeo's," Kyle said loud enough for the group to hear. I dared another glance at Weston; his amused smile was gone and replaced by a tight-lipped glare. "Who were you begging to—"

"Please." I pulled on his sleeve, frantically trying to get my cell before Weston did. "Don't do this to him."

That did it.

Kyle glanced at Weston, who was now standing. Slowly, not looking away from Weston, Kyle placed the phone in my palm.

One step to my left, two back, I stood behind Aiden's chair, using him as a human shield.

Weston took a calculating step. "You recorded the whole thing."

A log from the fire shifted, causing the entire thing to fall around itself. Kyle jumped from his seat, eyes assessing.

"Yes, just in case," I said loudly in an attempt to sound braver than I was.

"Will someone please explain what the hell is going on?" Tyler shouted from where he sat perched on the edge of his lawn chair, ready to pop into action if needed. "Because if I didn't know any better, I'd think Romeo was about to murder the pretty doc any second now."

"I second that," said an unknown female voice. "Is this a bad time?"

A tall, full-figured woman stood behind Weston, smirking. She was striking, radiating from the glow of the fire, with her long pitch-black hair and her stunning blue eyes.

I hated her instantly, not for her natural beauty but for the way she was looking at Weston as if she were about to pounce on him and wrap her legs around his waist.

"No," Weston barked without a glance behind him; he didn't seem surprised by the woman's intrusion. "You talk some sense into her. Apparently she doesn't think I have enough control over my reactions to know the whole damn story. Fuck, she won't even let me listen to it."

Hesitantly, Kyle spoke up. "I agree with the doc's assessment, Romeo. You're about to lose it, and you didn't hear her scared voi—"

The look I shot him, which promised death if he continued, had him stopping midsentence.

"I'm kind of enjoying the show. I haven't seen you this riled up since... well, maybe now's not a good time to talk about it," the mystery woman mused, smiling up at the star-filled sky.

"Who the fuck are you?" I demanded.

Weston flinched.

This couldn't be good.

None of the men would meet my gaze.

Shit.

Aiden stood, angling himself between Weston and me.

"Anne, meet Kate—or Doc, if you will. Doc, meet Anne."

The distant sound of people laughing from the patio, the crackling of the fire, the world faded at that name. *What the hell is going on? Why doesn't Weston seem surprised to see her here? Why didn't he warn me she might be here tonight or even at all this weekend?* Hell, if it weren't for Ryan's slip a few days ago, I wouldn't even know the name Anne and know she was affiliated with Weston. It seemed there was a lot that Weston still held back.

All eyes were on me. Well, except Anne's, who stared at Weston.

My Weston.

Seeing my confusion and slight rage, Weston ran a hand through his dark hair. "I called her."

"You called her." My tone was void of all emotion. It sounded eerie even to my ears.

"Yes. You need someone to talk to, and I figured you would want to talk to someone who's been through something similar. She... Anne can relate to everything you need to talk about."

"You called her. For me to talk to."

"Yes, we've already established that." He took a step closer, but Aiden held out a hand, stopping his advancement.

"You called your ex-girlfriend to come here, not even fucking warning me, for me to talk to. Are you that ignorant?"

"Fiancée," Anne piped up, her voice cheery knowing I was dumb to their relationship.

"What?" I growled.

Tyler bounced from his chair to stand beside Anne.

"I was his fiancée, not just his girlfriend. And yes, he's that ignorant. I tried to tell him this was a bad idea, but you know men. They see a problem, find a solution, and move on without thinking about anything else."

My mouth gaped open. *A fucking fiancée. This is too much.* And *he wants me to talk to her? Open up about my nightmares, the fears that eat away at me every waking hour? Oh. Hell. No.*

"Seriously, Casey? Does that sound anything like me? Spilling my guts to some woman I don't know, much less one you've fucked?" Okay, that was a little harsh, but I was pissed. Hopefully he would let it slide.

Weston's head shook in disbelief, his brows knitted together. "I don't understand. You need someone to talk to about what happened last night and the shooting—"

"Shooting!" Tyler and Kyle exclaimed in unison.

I sighed. This was getting confusing.

Weston glared, signaling them to shut the hell up, which they did instantly. "Anne was coming tomorrow anyway, so I asked her to come up a day early. You'll feel better after talking to her, so—"

"Hell. No," I said, taking a step toward him only to have Aiden's other arm shoot out and press against my chest, keeping me from inching closer to Weston. Aiden understood the anger and disbelief in my voice; nothing good could come next. "I'll feel better after I punch you in the fucking throat."

"Why are you mad?" Weston sighed and rubbed at his eyes. His head shot up, those brown eyes bright like a brilliant thought struck him. "Wait, what's the date? Are you about to...?"

Anne's unamused huff made me like her a bit more, but the boys, it took them a little longer to catch on. When they did, all three chuckled quietly.

But me? I was beyond pissed.

He was dead.

Even if I died trying, I was going to do everything I could to kill him.

That was a fact.

"You're a fucking prick, Weston." I turned and strode away from the group, away from the party, into the dark where I could privately sort out what had transpired in the past ten minutes.

Weston's voice bellowed through the night, and the sounds of a scuffle filled the air at my back. "Kate, come back here." But I didn't turn. "You're going to get lost or hurt. Come back here. Now."

My feet stopped at the pure command in his tone.

Five seconds. I'd give myself five seconds to rein in my lethal level of anger. The cool breeze floated over my sticky neck and palms, calming me enough to turn and walk back.

Weston was restrained by Kyle and Aiden; each had an arm, holding him back from coming after me. Tyler stood vigil by Anne, whose smirking face I wanted to punch after I was done with Weston.

Kyle and Aiden continued to hold Weston as I stalked back to the group and stopped in front of him.

I tipped my head back so he could see, feel the fury rolling inside me.

"I don't need you to watch out for me. I don't need your protection. The trial is over. I'm no longer your client, I'm your damn girlfriend. Start acting like it. This whole trying to corral my life, the commanding, the thinking you know what's best for me, is fucking smothering. I did pretty well for myself before you came along, so stop treating me like I don't know how to get through life without you barking orders or trying to fix me."

I turned to walk away but paused, turned, drew back my arm, fisted my hand, and punched him hard against the cheek, only wanting to inflict pain, not break anything like I had with Austin.

Tyler moved from Anne, gripping my arms behind my back.

"That's for the damn PMS comment, you moron," I seethed.

Tyler's lips graced the shell of my ear. "Damn, you're feisty, Doc. It's... I love it."

Shaking out of his grasp, I directed a final death glare at Weston and started back toward the dark end of the property.

Raised voices, shouting, then Aiden appeared at my side.

"Leave me alone, Aiden," I snarled.

"Um, I just thought you should know—" He gripped my upper arm, but I wrangled out of his grasp to keep storming into the dark.

"I should know what? That your friend is an oblivious male or that he's infuriating or has major control issues which he should focus on instead of focusing on what others need help with?"

"There's that, and I thought you should know you're about to walk into a tank."

"A what?" A few feet ahead, the reflection of the moon shined and shifted along the top of still water. "Oh, thanks." Dropping down, my ass plopped against dry grass and I leaned back on my elbows to lose myself in the expansive night sky.

Aiden grunted as he sat down, wrapping his arms around the shins of his bent legs.

Neither of us said anything, letting the peaceful night clear my clouded mind.

"Want some?" he asked minutes later, holding out the half-empty bottle of Cuervo.

Exactly what I needed.

I wrapped a hand around the neck, pressed the opening to my lips, and tipped it back.

"How long?" I rasped, the burn from the tequila stealing my voice. With the back of my hand, I wiped away a dribble of tequila from my chin.

Thank goodness Aiden didn't need additional explanation. "The engagement or the dating?"

"Both."

From the corner of my eye, I saw him take a long pull from the bottle before settling back on his elbows to stare up at the inky sky. "He met... well, we met her during basic. There was something between them instantly. But nothing happened until they were in separate units. Even then they couldn't be together much, only when their leaves aligned, or the rare occasion neither was out on deployment. It went on like that for years, both of them thinking it was the real thing."

"But you didn't?" I sputtered.

With a slow shake of his head, he pulled his gaze from the stars to me. "No, I never did, but I wasn't going to tell him that. I had the real thing back here, so I knew what it looked like, what it felt like. What those two had, even until they broke up, was more of a wanting to have someone. Anne didn't have family, and Weston only had Ryan, so having each other gave them a sense of belonging. Like all they really wanted was to know someone was missing them, cared if they came home or not. And the engagement was a bunch of shit. There wasn't even a ring.... It happened after a particularly hard deployment. And I don't know, something flipped in Romeo, I guess. He asked her to marry him the day we got back."

I snagged the tequila bottle from the ground.

"So you don't think he loved her."

"I didn't say that. I think he loved her but not really. I think he was more in love with the idea of her, the idea of coming home to someone, of having someone to think about when we were up for days and not knowing if we were going to make it out alive. And even if I saw it then, would you've wanted me to shake some sense into him? Or let him keep on believing in it because it helped him survive."

Survive.

He survived.

That word, sometimes I forgot.... With a deep sigh, I lay back against the grass. "I'm thankful for anything that helped him make it through it all. Anything that made him the man he is today with me. But damnit, he can be a fucking jackass."

Anger and hurt laced my words. We hadn't fought like this in a long time; the guilt was eating at me for storming off like I did.

Aiden chuckled. "He's a guy so... it kind of comes with the territory."

"If you and Tracy knew each other in high school and have a daughter together, why are you just now getting married?"

Crickets chirped in the dark. I gave him the time he gave me earlier to gather his thoughts.

"I wanted to wait until I was the man she deserved, that they *both* deserve. I wasn't that man for a long time, Doc, and Romeo was the one who pulled me out of it. I owe him my life in so many ways." He paused to gnaw at his lip. "He came here, after that shit in Colorado, did you know that?"

Eyes wide, I barely shook my head.

"He came here completely lost, and I welcomed him into our home. No questions asked from me or Tracy. And we gave him the time to process everything, but we both knew."

So here, with his best friend and his family, was where he'd been those few weeks between Christmas and the shooting. He was here sorting himself out, though trying to decide what, I didn't know.

"You both knew what?"

"That whoever this Kate girl was who he left behind, he was in love with her. And the real love that makes you so fucking crazy when you're with them and even crazier when you're not. Every night he would sit out on the porch drinking, attempting to push away the memories of you two, of that night. And each morning he'd wake up, help us around the house, work on his truck, until our daughter went down, and he was right back on that porch drinking. It was Tracy who got him to open up about you. One night he let it all spill out about the assignment, those nights your life was on the line and what it did to him.

"Doc, he and I have been through a lot of shit together. That night on the porch with Tracy when he finally talked about you, damnit, I hated you. Hated you for making him feel that way. For making one of the toughest men I know cry like a fucking baby, wrapped in my woman's arms, asking for help on what to do."

And that was all I needed.

What I had needed for *months*.

Pushing off the ground, I turned toward the fire, toward the man who drove me fucking crazy, but the kind of crazy when the love was real, it seemed. Aiden called from behind me, but I didn't turn back. Rocks and roots caught my feet as I sprinted to the fire.

Weston pacing between Kyle and Tyler, who also still seemed on edge, came into view, making my breaths come a little easier, a little deeper. He was still there; he hadn't left. The three of them froze, eyes wide, when they caught me sprinting toward them. In a protective move, one I was sure he'd done multiple times in the past, Kyle jumped in front of Weston, becoming a human shield. Having none of that, Weston shoved Kyle aside just as I leapt into his open arms, wrapping my legs around his waist and my arms around his neck.

Weston's lips pressed hard against mine before I could find his, like he was trying to express an entire apology with this one desperate kiss.

"I'm sorry, baby, I wasn't thinking. I didn't—" he murmured against my lips.

Pulling back to see him, I cupped my hands around his strong jaw. "*I'm* sorry. I'm sorry I hit you. You were just trying to help—"

Soft, wet lips again pressed against mine, cutting me short. A hand held the back of my head, the other wrapped under my ass as the sounds of the party grew soft in the background. I had no idea where he was taking us, but it didn't matter. The way his body felt against mine, the way his fingers dug into my ass as he carried me, was all I wanted to focus on.

We paused and my back pressed against something hard and cold, sending a shiver racing through me from the contact with my overheated skin.

He loved me. Really loved me.

We didn't know a lot about the other's past, or even what the future might hold for us, but it didn't matter now; he loved all the crazy, explosive, mind-numbing pieces of me.

Our desperate kisses slowed, and his mouth moved to kiss and nuzzle my neck. "I love you, and I'm so sorry, baby. I really am. I didn't think it through, I just thought.... Please don't leave me." Those last words were barely a whisper against the shell of my ear.

With a deep sigh, I relaxed my tense shoulders and neck, my head thudding against the metal behind me. "I'm not going anywhere, Casey. I'm just as bad at all this as you are. This is a first for me. What I feel and how I process it, it's all new. You'll have to be as patient with me as I am with you, but you have to give me something to work with. Tell me enough about yourself so I'm not blindsided by your past like I just was. Hell, if Ryan hadn't mentioned Anne a few days ago—"

"Fucking Ryan. Can't keep his damn mouth shut."

My eyes rolled at the loving irritation Weston had for his brother.

"If it hadn't been for Ryan, I wouldn't have known there was an Anne, and he didn't tell me much, obviously, since I had no idea y'all had been engaged. I need more, Casey. I want more with you. To understand you and know why you're so driven to protect me like some damn helicopter parent."

"I'll do whatever I have to do to deserve you. I have no idea why you chose me, how I'm the lucky one standing here right now—"

"Casey, stop it with this bullshit that you don't deserve me. I won't let you keep thinking so shitty about yourself, thinking I'm somehow better than you. *You are amazing.* You're kind, thoughtful, an amazing listener, strong, you love to read. Stop putting yourself down. It's annoying the shit out of me."

Silence hung in the air.

Did I upset him by being so direct? But he really needed to understand how amazing he was and that any woman was lucky to be loved by him.

With his bottom teeth tugging on his lower lip, he whispered, "You don't know what all I've done, and not just in the army. I'm not sure I'm the good guy you think I am."

My heart fell into my stomach for this beautiful, broken man pressing against me.

"I don't need to know it all. Some but not all if you're not ready, but if you ever want to tell me, I'm here. No judgments. Whatever happened in your past is in the past, and if what you went through made you the man you are today, the one who would give his life to save mine, who thinks of others before himself, then I'm thankful for that terrifying past of yours, Casey."

His warm lips brushing against the shell of my ear sent my heart fluttering with hope.

"Okay, I'll try. I'll try to give you what you need. Just don't go. Don't leave without giving me a chance to fight for this, fight for us."

The tip of his tongue slid along my lower lip, begging me to open for him, which I did willingly. With a tilt of his hips, I groaned. It felt amazing and I wanted him, but too much had just happened for me to move on to sex that easily. A hand skimmed along the waistband of my jeans and popped the top button.

I gripped the hand that was now starting on my zipper. "Um, no. I'm not 'I want to kill you in your sleep' mad anymore, but you don't get to invite your ex-fiancée here, expect me to spill my whole life story to her, say I'm PMSing, and then fuck me against your truck. It doesn't work that way, Weston. You should be glad I'm thinking of allowing you to sleep in the same bed with me tonight. Earlier I was going to banish you to the floor."

His brows pulled together—was he annoyed or concerned? "But I thought we were good. You just said—"

I pressed two fingers against his lips to cut him off. "You're being a total guy right now, and before our amazing moment is ruined by your guyness, I'm going inside and going to bed."

"I'll come with you," he said, looking chastised.

I shook my head. "No, you go hang out with your friends. They want to see you. I'm not going to be selfish and take you away from them. Just promise me one thing."

"Anything," he murmured against my lips.

"That I'll wake up with you beside me. These past few months… it's been killing me waking up without you."

His demeanor shifted to something playful, his brown eyes dancing with mischief as his sly smile pulled at his lips. "How about on top of you?"

I rolled my eyes and shook my head.

Slowly he lowered me from around his waist. He was disappointed, that was clear by his puppy-dog eyes, but I really was tired. Even with the two naps, exhaustion kept a hold on me.

As we walked toward the house, I wrapped my arm around his waist and leaned against his chest, savoring the strength and rhythm of his heart.

He's mine. Somehow through all this, he's mine. And I'm his.

He paused at the front porch steps.

"I really did…. I thought it would help, you talking to Anne, even with our past. She's been through more hell than you could imagine and could understand what you're going through. This afternoon, after seeing you at the hotel… she lives in Austin, and…. When we were together, there was a time when I couldn't reach her. Something had happened and she wouldn't open up even to me. Anne mentioned then that all she wanted was someone who would understand, tell her she wasn't crazy for how she felt. The shrinks on base weren't what she needed at the time. I get it—well, now I do—that I should have warned you, but—"

I shook my head and started up the wood stairs. "Yes, you should have told me—about her, calling her, why you called her—but I get it, Weston. You're trying to protect me from myself, and I need it. I'll find someone when we get back to Dallas. I'll get help."

He planted a gentle kiss below my ear, conveying gratefulness and relief.

"I love you, baby."

I GASPED AWAKE.

But my heart wasn't racing from fear. It was different than the other nights I'd woken due to a nightmare. It was a rapid beat from excitement, like I would have on the mat at the gym. And there was no cold sweat along my skin.

I lay back down, trying to remember the details of the dream. My eyes moved back and forth behind my lids, searching for answers. It started the same, I remembered that much—me walking down the street at night with a knowing sense something was off. I had tried to run, but like before, my feet wouldn't move, stuck waiting as the person in the dark approached.

But this time it was... damnit, who was it?

After a few seconds of replaying the images over and over, I sat up again with a jolt.

My heart beat frantically.

I remembered.

The man, from that night in Vail, had been walking toward me with a gun like the others had in previous nightmares. He said nothing when he stopped in front of me, holding the gun against my chest.

Tears slid down my cheeks. Waking up with a racing heart now made sense.

Because this time...

For the first time in *months,* night after night of this same nightmare...

I fought back.

And won.

"BABY, YOU 'WAKE?"

Damn, he smelled awful. A mix of campfire smoke, cigarettes, cigars, and tequila.

"What time is it?" I groaned and reached for my phone on the bedside table. Cracking an eye, I checked the time. "Five in the damn morning. Have you been out there this whole time?"

He ran his nose along my cheekbone before nuzzling in my hair and taking a deep breath in. "Are you still mad, or can we have fun?" he asked, giggling and then hiccuping in my ear.

"How drunk are you?" I asked, pushing him off with a single shove.

He rolled on his back, arms splayed across the bed.

"Drunk. I love Cuervo. Cuervo loves me. But I give you full permissions to take 'vantage of me."

Oh hell, he's hammered. And adorable.

Maybe now was a good time to get some of the answers I'd been wanting.

"Good to know. So, Casey...." I sat on top of him, straddling his hips. He gripped my hips, fingers digging into the bare flesh he found beneath his T-shirt I'd thrown on before climbing into bed. "I have a few questions for you."

His eyes were closed, but he was smiling. "Mmkay."

"A month or so ago, my father asked you if you knew who beat the shit out of that guy who attacked me at the hospital. You said you didn't know. But you do, don't you?"

His hold on me tightened, almost painfully. "Yes, he was very bad. I stopped, knew... wouldn't want to make Kate mad... stopped for Kate. Wanted to kill him. He hurt my Kate."

Okay, so that was a nice little revelation. What else could I ask while he was being... open?

"Aiden's getting 'arried," he slurred, then hiccuped, the force almost knocking me off him.

"Yes, I know."

"I'm gonna marry 'one too."

He couldn't see my questioning gaze with his eyes closed. "Oh really, Weston? Who are you going to marry?"

"Can't tell. It's a surprise."

"Surprise for you or her?"

"Hungry. I need pizza. Do you have pizza?"

"Um, no, not on me. Now, who are you going to marry, Weston?"

"I know, she doesn't. Yet. I love Kate. She...." He sighed, his smile growing. My heart was on the verge of breaking apart right here for him. "Perfect... great ass... fucking brilliant... tiniest feet. How does she walk on those tiny feet?"

Random.

His eyes flickered open and focused on mine, and somehow that happy smile grew, making the edge of his eyes crinkle.

Holy hell. This was him with all his guards down, nothing standing in his way of the happiness he deserved.

"Hi, baby. When did you get here?" he asked while his unfocused gaze raked over my face and down to my hips.

I yelped in surprise when he flipped us, pushing my back against the bed as he trailed kisses down my T-shirt-covered chest. Not so gently, my underwear was yanked down my legs and tossed to the floor, his predatory gaze now locked on the apex of my thighs. I couldn't suppress the shudder when he wet his lips, like he was about to devour the best meal he'd ever had.

Roughly, he pushed my legs apart to accommodate his broad shoulders. At the first flick of his tongue, my eyes closed with a deep moan.

Mental note: stock up on Cuervo.

25

———————

The next morning was as brutal for Weston and the others as I expected. Which meant I was the only one around to take care of the four very hungover men and one puking female. The three who weren't originally staying at Aiden's were too drunk to drive home and ended up crashing in the living room. Anne had passed out on the couch, trash can close to her head. Kyle slept on the floor, and Tyler had somehow curled up and slept on an ottoman—still wasn't sure how he fit on there.

After a run to the convenience store for Pedialyte, Sprite, and Excedrin Migraine, I settled on the couch, content on reading and watching them suffer until the wedding. But just as I pulled up the Kindle app, Aiden tossed his phone in my lap, mumbling for me to read it. I flipped the phone over on the couch. A text to me, from Tracy, via Aiden.

> Tracy: Give your damn phone to Kate.
>
> Tracy: Kate—told you they would drink too much. Come brunch with us.

As I read the text, Weston and the boys whined again, asking for more toast and water. Without a second thought, I texted *hell yes* back and waited for the address to meet her.

———

THE RESTAURANT WAS a hole-in-the-wall located in old downtown Brownwood. The brick on the outside was crumbling in places, and the tile along the floor had to be decades old. It was beautiful in its old-school charm. The food was amazing and the company better. Tracy's friends were just as nice as she was and did their best to make me feel included. Afterward they all insisted I come with them to get my nails and hair done at the salon across the street. In no hurry to get back to my self-inflicted ill boyfriend, I went willingly.

Now here I stood in front of Aiden's guest bathroom mirror, putting the finishing touches on my makeup with the small amount I'd bought. The dress was simple, navy with a high neck to cover the still-visible entry wound scar near my shoulder. The top section fit snug but flowed out at the waist, giving it a casual look. At the salon with the girls, I had my hair blown out; it now hung over my shoulders in beautiful dark waves.

The dark circles under my eyes were still visible, but less apparent, and some of the light had come back into my hazel eyes, chasing away the dullness.

Ready to go except for shoes, I headed back to our room only to find Weston fully dressed in his dark suit, eyes closed, lying on the bed. The door clicked closed as I lay my back against it, staring at him. Even hungover he was handsome. Maybe a little paler than normal but still my soft-hearted, chatty, drunk badass.

He cracked open an eye at the noise of plastic bags rustling beneath my fingers as I searched for the shoes I'd bought to go with the dress. "Never let me drink that much again," he groaned, whined, begged... kind of a mixture of the three.

I tossed the navy wedges aside to crawl on the bed beside him, my head propped up by one hand while the fingers of the other traced the outline of his jaw. "Do you still feel that bad?"

He gave a pained nod. Of course he did. They all still felt that bad. Why in the hell they thought they could drink like they were in their twenties when they were in their thirties was beyond me.

"Baby, can you get me something to eat, maybe more toast? Oh, and more water, and maybe another jug of that baby shit you bought?" He moaned like the effort to talk was too much, or maybe the sound of his voice was too loud for his still-pounding head.

I stared down at the pitiful man before me. Every man—big or small—was completely helpless when they didn't feel well. In the emergency room, this was very apparent, some of us female doctors going as far as drawing straws to decide who would be assigned to the male patients. The men always yelled the loudest and complained about the intolerable pain even if it was something as simple as a bee sting. The bigger they were, the worse it was. The female patients, however, were tough as shit. I'd seen a woman hobble in on a shattered ankle without a single word about her pain level and asked if we could wrap it really quick because she had errands to run.

Pushing off the bed, I left to fetch him everything he requested, hoping it would help him feel better. And soon. If not, the wedding— and our fun night—was really going to suck.

A West Texas sunset was hard to beat under any circumstances, but when it was also the backdrop to Tracy and Aiden's ceremony, it was breathtaking. It was a small ceremony, only about one hundred people sitting in a semicircle of white folding chairs watching them exchange their vows. Tracy was gorgeous in a simple white lace dress that hugged her thin frame. The bridesmaids all wore dark purple, which made their flowers of varying greens and whites stand out against the pinks and purples of the beautiful sunset.

I couldn't help but replay what Weston had said in his drunken ramblings about wanting to get married one day. He was talking about me based on the rest of the conversation, but that left me...

confused. Marriage had never been on my radar. Maybe it went back to the fact that I'd never let anyone in—until Weston, that was.

Out of the corner of my eye, I watched him smiling broadly up at his friend.

Maybe with Weston, marriage could be a possibility. I certainly loved him, and he loved me, but was that enough? Was our kind of love enough to help us get past our drastic differences? More time was needed to decide that for sure, not that a decision was needed today—he mentioned it in a drunken state, after all, not a proper marriage proposal. I had time; we had time. And hopefully we could both open up enough to make the idea of marriage one day a real one.

The reception was a ways down a dirt path that led to an opening in the mesquite trees scattered with large white tents for the occasion. After numerous long toasts, we grabbed food from the buffet and sat at a table near the bride and groom. The rest of the squad followed, leaving only a couple empty chairs at our table. They had all recovered enough to not be puking in the bushes, even Anne, but no one at the table was drinking except me.

"So, Aiden is your best friend, right?" I asked, taking a sip of red wine.

The forkful of food paused in front of Weston's mouth. "Yes, why do you ask?" he answered and continued eating. Even nauseous the man could put away food.

I brushed the rim of the wineglass back and forth against my lip as I thought about my next words. "If you're his best friend, then why aren't you his best man?"

"I was."

"You were?"

"I was."

"What happened?"

"You."

Wine caught in my throat, sending me into a coughing fit trying to dislodge it. Behind my napkin, I asked, "What do you mean, me?"

Weston set down his fork and turned in his seat, gripping my thigh between his hands. "I told you before that I wasn't planning on coming because of the trial. There was no way I was going to leave you to come here, and I didn't want to bring any trouble to their wedding by bringing you with me, so I told him I couldn't come."

"You could have come down here for one night. I would've been fine with Joe."

"Oh really?" He arched a brow and gave me a smirk. "Tell me how that previously worked out for you."

"I... the first time—"

"Listen, I don't want to fight about it. I made the decision then, and I'd make the same decision now if needed. We're here now, and I'm very glad to be here seeing my best friend marry his. But more than anything, I'm very happy to be here with you. Now eat." He gave a pointed glance at the plate of food in front me, which I'd barely touched, before turning back to his own.

My heart sank to my gut. What had I put this man through with my indifference to my own safety? Tears welled in the corners of my eyes.

"I'm so sorry, Casey. It's all my fault. Vail, the shooting, Chase—"

"Stop," he growled. The anger in his voice stopped my tears immediately and drew my gaze up to meet his. "Those sick bastards are the ones to blame for what happened in Vail. They're the ones who sent that fucking piece of shit, not you. They're the ones who fired that gun, not you. And Chase...." He smiled around the spoonful of mashed potatoes in his mouth. "Okay, that was you."

I sniffed and wiped my eyes with the white napkin. "But if I hadn't done all that, you would have felt free to be here, to leave me."

"Don't feel bad." Without looking up from his plate, he reached across and pulled my fingers from my lip. "Aiden understood and so did Tracy. They both just want me to be happy, and you—safe—make me happy, so there you have it. Now eat."

A little while later, our plates were cleared and the bride and groom moved to the dance floor for their first dance as a married couple. "At Last" by Etta James poured through the speakers as we all watched. I couldn't stop staring at their stupid happy smiles. It was beautiful. When the song ended, Tracy asked Weston to dance with her, and Aiden did the same with me.

Elvis singing "Can't Help Falling in Love" played in the background as he moved me easily across the dance floor.

"If anyone can do it, it's you, Doc," Aiden said with his thick Texas drawl, smiling down at me in his arms.

"Do what, Tex?"

He laughed at my use of his nickname. "If anyone can get to him, make him see there's so much more out there to be excited about, to look forward to, it's you. You will be that person, but don't break him in the process, okay?"

"I think it's breaking me more than him," I whispered and rested my head on his strong chest.

"Then you're not seeing what I am." He pulled me close as we danced and listened to the music. When he spoke again, it was more of a laugh. "I can't believe you hit him."

I pulled back to look up at him and shrugged. "It wasn't the first time, and I'm pretty sure it won't be the last."

The song trailed off, morphing into another, and a strong arm wrapped around my middle, hauling me away from Aiden.

"Get your hands off my girl, Tex. Your *wife* is waiting for you."

"My wife," Aiden breathed with a smile of pure bliss.

Weston released his grip around me to shake Aiden's hand, which ended with a tight hug as he mumbled something I couldn't hear in his friend's ear. When they were done, Weston pulled me against his chest. "Dance with me," he whispered, his words a mix between a command and a plea.

We skirted along the dance floor, talking and laughing, both enjoying the feeling of being free and safe. As we danced, what Aiden said nagged at me. The idea of me helping Weston see life in a new way, a brighter outlook, was a lot to ask—to accomplish. Was I up for that kind of... responsibility? Was I even the right person for the task?

Aiden seemed to think so.

Deep down, Weston seemed to think so too, based off his talk of marriage last night. But what about me? My own outlook on the world, my multiple failed relationships, my uncertainty about the future, it was all as much of a cluster as anyone's. Most times it seemed he was guiding me through life, helping me find my way, rather than the other way around. When he was around, things were clearer, more focused. Or maybe it was that nothing else mattered. I didn't need a plan when I was in his arms; I just needed to exist and take it all in. When he was around, he was my world.

Whatever it was we had was fierce, that was for sure. I went from having no emotional attachments to being so wrapped up in him I couldn't think about a future without him. And it seemed he felt the same way. He was happy. I was happy. For now that was enough. We could figure out the rest along the way. Together.

THE COLD WATER running over my hot, swollen hands was amazing. With all our dancing, sweat dripped down my back and temples despite the cool Texas night temperatures.

The bathroom door creaked open.

Anne.

Our eyes met in the mirror.

"Hey," she said, not looking surprised to be meeting me in the bathroom.

I chose not to respond. What was there to say?

"He really did mean well. Last night. And if you do need—"

"Thanks, I'm fine."

"Sure you are. I was sure I was too at one point. But I wasn't. There are some things that never leave you no matter what you do. When you realize I'm someone you can talk to, who will listen and under-stand… give me a call. I'll do that for him." She leaned against the cinder block wall. "He fought for me one time, did you know that? I'm not sure I'd be here today if he hadn't."

Her blue eyes swirled with regret, sadness even, as she stared past me—staring into nothing.

"You still love him." A statement, not a question.

Anne shook her head, breaking out of the trance she was just in, and turned to the door. "You know him, Kate. I'd be a fool not to."

The metal door closed behind her.

She was right. About everything.

THE KEYS DANGLED from the dash after Weston cut the ignition to the Bronco in front of Aiden and Tracy's home. All the lights were off inside, and only a single light on the front porch shone through the dark. No one was home. We'd said our goodbyes at the reception since they were driving to Dallas tonight to make their early morning flight to Cabo tomorrow.

"That was fun," Weston said, resting his head against the headrest and closing his eyes. "I'm happy for them."

"Me too," I whispered, staring at him in the driver seat. In his suit, hair fixed, his handsome profile lit from the porch light's soft glow, how could I not stare?

He opened his eyes and rolled his head to me. His deep brown eyes conveyed contentment and happiness, which made my heart happy—full. Hopefully he was finally realizing he deserved to be happy, no matter his past.

We stayed like this, staring in comfortable silence, for a few moments before I couldn't take it anymore. I kicked out of my shoes and unbuckled the seat belt restricting me from crawling over the center console to him. Straddling his hips, I wrapped my hands around his shocked face, brushing my thumbs over the soft skin of his cheekbones.

This entire night made me want to show him how much I loved him. How I cherished him and what his love did to me.

He shivered at the first caress of my lips against his. I moved down the length of his jaw to his ear before stopping on the sensitive skin of his neck. He groaned as my lips, teeth, and tongue teased him. His hands gripped my bare thighs and started sliding up, pulling me harder against his growing erection. But this was my moment; I was in control of what happened and when. Reaching down, I gripped his hands and pulled them behind his head, making him grasp the headrest.

"Don't let go," I whispered against his neck.

"Are you trying to torture me? I want to touch you, baby. Fuck, I want to touch every inch of you, inside and out."

I shook my head, smiling.

My eyes locked with his, I kneeled on the seat and began brushing the tips of my fingers up and down my inner thigh, each stroke upward inching my skirt higher and higher. I hooked my thumbs around my lace underwear and slowly pulled them down my thighs. His brown eyes were nearly black with lust as he watched each move of my hands. When I couldn't go any lower, I shimmied out of the lace thong and tossed it to the passenger seat.

In a flash, he released the headrest and was desperately pulling at my waist, hauling me against the strain in his pants.

"Nope," I tsked and positioned his hands back on the headrest.

"You're killing me," he groaned.

Aware of every move, I deftly untied his tie and began unbuttoning his dress shirt, making sure my fingertips grazed against his sculpted chest and abdomen between each button. I couldn't help my sinister smirk at the groan I was rewarded with as I gave a forceful tug to pull the tails of his shirt free of his pants. Each kiss I planted on his chest made him wiggle beneath me, arching his hips, trying to tease me while I teased him. I kissed and nibbled each inch of inked flesh, more for me than him. His tattoos were something I longed to touch with the tip of my tongue every day.

As I kissed along his collarbone, I unfastened his belt and worked on getting his pants undone. Weston's breaths were long and labored by the time I wrapped my hand around him. So were mine. This was torturing both of us, and I'd had enough of it. My eyes shuttered closed as I lowered myself on top of him; I couldn't stop the gasp as I shifted in the seat, allowing him to sink deeper.

I couldn't breathe or think. I could only sit there, giving my body time to adjust. But Weston had enough and knew too well how to spur me into action. With a buck of his hips, driving himself deeper, I fell forward, running my hands through his hair, cursing in his ear.

Enough of being in control.

"Casey," I whispered. "Take me, Casey."

"With pleasure. Hope you're not fond of this dress, baby," he growled into my ear before gripping the neckline and pulling. The snapping of threads and ripping of material sounded through the truck. Roughly he pulled the dress over my head and tossed the shredded material to the side. My bra quickly followed.

His hands started at my spread knees and glided up my thighs, feeling every dip and curve of my body. His worshipping touch made me believe I was beautiful and precious. Both hands cupped my breasts, teasing and pulling my hard nipples. I yelled his name, eyes slamming shut as he flexed his hips, catching me off guard, hitting a sensitive spot.

"Open your eyes. Watch me," he demanded.

I obeyed, prying my eyes open to meet his. My hands wandered over his chest and shoulders, my nails digging into his slick skin with each thrust of his hips. His breathing grew fast as I responded, pushing down to meet each thrust.

A faint smirk appeared on his lips in response to my whimper at the loss of his hands on my breasts. One wrapped around my waist, holding me tight against him as he moved faster; the other weaved into my thick hair, pulling my lips to his. I shifted and adjusted, trying to gain pressure right above where our bodies connected.

What I was trying to accomplish didn't go unnoticed. Nothing ever did with him. The hand in my hair brushed down my neck, tugging a nipple as it continued to descend past my waist. His thumb softly pressed on my tiny bundle of nerves, making me pull from his lips with a gasp and reach up to grip the same headrest I'd banished his hands to just so I wouldn't fall against him.

His sensual, cocky laugh only made it worse.

"Like that, baby?" he crooned, running his nose up the shell of my ear. "What about this?" He applied more pressure while lazily circling his thumb. I had zero control left. There was no stopping my hips from the movements of his thumbs, shifting and swaying with him inside. Weston cursed, his breathing shifting from deep and controlled to quick pants.

His thumb moved faster, as did my hips, until we were both moaning and pleading for more. With one deep thrust, I fell over the edge, moaning various versions of his name and calling out to nonexistent gods. I lay limp against his sweat-slicked chest as he gripped my hips holding me firm, driving deep several times before finding his own release with adulation.

When I could finally open my eyes, every window was fogged around us. His were still closed, allowing me a brief unguarded moment to take him in. It really was amazing that we'd found our way to each other. From our rocky introduction to the assault over Christmas in Vail, the odds were stacked against us. But we overcame those odds and now were lying skin to skin, thoroughly wrecked and wrapped up in each other.

Is this normal though? Is this how everyone feels when they're in love or when they decide to give their full trust to someone else? Maybe what Weston and I have isn't that special. Maybe it's just another run-of-the-mill puppy love that will fade as time goes by.

It didn't feel that way.

His hand began skimming up and down my bare back. When his eyes finally opened, he smiled his sly smile at finding me staring.

"Tell me this is different," I whispered. "That what we have is beyond what anyone else could ever hope for."

Those thick brown brows furrowed at my question. "People pray for this kind of thing, baby, and most never get it. What we have is... it's unexplainable. Are you doubting it?"

I sighed and turned my eyes from his, nuzzling my nose against his neck. "You know me. I've told you about my... issues. You know this is the first time I've ever gone this far emotionally with someone. I don't know if this is typical. It doesn't feel typical. It feels...." I paused and took a deep breath of his unique musky scent. "It feels like I can't breathe when I think about how much you mean to me. And just the thought of us not being together is terrifying."

As if my words were like a warm blanket to his soul, he gave a deep relieved sigh and closed his eyes. "I've dated a lot. I've thought I was in love before too, maybe even more than once. But you and me, what we have together is like... the difference between a revolver and an assault rifle." *Strange analogy, but I'll allow it.* "When you're not with me, I can't stop thinking about you. When you're with me, I can't stop thinking about you. You make me happy, baby, plain and simple. And I can't say that about anyone else, ever. You take away the baggage I've carried for so long just with one of your challenging looks. I don't know how you do it, but please don't stop."

His eyes flicked open, his hands wrapping around my face, making me look at him. "I don't want to go back to being the me before you."

Warm tears rolled down my cheeks. Those words. I had said those exact same words to him in Vail before he left. Weston knew what kind of power they would hold, how they would help explain and describe how his life was better with me in it.

"I love you, Dr. Kate Anne Wheeler, and I'll do whatever it takes for however long to deserve you." The anguish in his voice.... My tears streamed faster. I started to dispute his words but instead was pulled forward for a soft kiss. "I'm done talking. Get your tiny ass up and let's go inside and do that all over again, except this time I'm in charge."

He set me in the passenger seat and shook off his dress shirt, letting it fall behind him in the seat. After situating himself back in his dark boxer briefs, he zipped up his pants, grabbed his shirt, and strolled over to open my door. The dress shirt was draped over my shoulders, providing some protection from the chilled night air. The shirt swallowed me, my arms only going down half the length of the sleeves. And damn did he look like a romance novel model with only his suit pants on, showing off his perfect abs and inked pecs.

"How do you stay in such good shape? Don't most men need to go to the gym for hours a day to look like this?" I waved my arm, which ended up being a floppy cuff of the shirtsleeve, up and down his bare chest.

"Sit-ups, push-ups. You look sexy as hell in my shirt. If we don't go now, I'll have to fuck you against the truck."

Well, when you put it that way....

He pulled me from the seat, tossed me over his shoulder, and strode toward the house.

26

———

The townhouse felt weird. Like I was an intruder instead of having the sense of being home. Weston unloaded the truck while I meandered around downstairs trying to figure out what was off besides the three massive fist-sized holes in the living room wall. Damn brute.

But maybe it wasn't the townhouse itself that was off. It could have been me or Weston. About halfway between Brownwood and Dallas, our phones lit up with old voice mails—the service at Aiden's apparently wasn't that great. He'd checked his while I checked mine. Mine were from Eric, Dad demanding an explanation on where I was —not sure how he knew I wasn't with Chase—and one from Chase himself. The one from Chase simply asked me to call him so he could apologize, and when I told Weston, his face went hard and his grip on the steering wheel tightened; the metal looked close to bending under the force. Even though he was clearly pissed about Chase reaching out, he said to delete the message and we would figure it out later.

With a few hours to burn until my first shift back at the hospital, doing absolutely nothing sounded perfect. I grabbed the iPad and curled up on the couch, ready to do just that.

The garage door slammed shut and the beeping of the alarm being activated sounded.

"Weston?" I called from the couch. *What the hell is going on?*

He stopped pacing, the obvious frustration on his face shifting to concern at the look of uncertainty on mine.

"I'm sorry, it's just hard not thinking you're in danger. I'm back in full-time protection mode being here." He plopped on the couch and tucked me under his strong arm. "It'll take some time for me to adjust, baby. Be patient with me."

He was lying to me, that was certain. It could be a partial truth, but it wasn't all of it. Something else was bothering him, but he was holding back. He could just need space and time like everyone had been saying.

He'll tell me, eventually. I think. Hopefully.

THE MOMENT I walked through the hospital doors, the scent of antiseptic filled my nose, stopping me in the middle of the doorway. The nagging feeling from earlier had been pushed aside and was overtaken by a sudden panic attack. My clammy hands trembled, not enough air could fill my lungs from my labored breaths, and my stomach rolled, bile rising up my throat. People pushed past, making their way down the halls to see loved ones or find medical help, but I couldn't move. My eyes were open, but all I could see was the hospital room where I lay for days, connected to machines keeping me alive—confining me. And the pain, ugh, I had just started to forget the constant level ten pain—part of that my own fault for discontinuing the pain meds too early. Lesson learned.

The edges of my vision started to darken; passing out was near.

Nope. No way could I allow that at work. I had a badass, woman-of-steel reputation to uphold.

Shuttering my eyes, I focused on anything other than my body turning against me. The image of a brown-eyed man with dark wavy hair popped into mind, taking enough of the edge off my panic for my breaths to deepen. The sly smile he only showed me made my hands stop shaking and helped steady my legs. And then, much to my surprise, remembering him saying he intended to marry me made all the fear fall away.

My vision had cleared when I opened my eyes again, the patients and visitors still scurrying about, but I was different. There was a confidence within saying I wouldn't be back in that bed, wouldn't be in pain like that again, and I had Weston to thank for it. It seemed even when he wasn't around, he was protecting me. The memory of him stating he wanted to marry me was what pushed everything aside. It was surprising as hell, but maybe it meant this was more than I even knew.

"There she is," Eric called from across the room. He darted forward with his arms out, almost knocking a little old lady over in the process. After a tight hug, he pushed me out to arm's length, his smile turning downward and his brows furrowing with concern. "Hey, what's wrong? Aren't you excited to be back with me?"

"I am. Just hard, you know. It's been a while, but I am excited to see you. You have no idea how excited I am to see you."

He gave me an uncertain once-over, like he knew I was holding something back but wasn't going to push it. "Well, good thing you have an easy shift. It's going to be hard getting back into work shape. And later, if we aren't too busy, I want to hear all about this weekend with W and his friends."

"Deal." Eric kept an arm wrapped around my waist as we headed to the computers to clock me in. "I will say they were nice. Really nice. Maybe more than nice? I don't know how to explain it. It's like now I'm their little sister or something. Now that I'm associated with Weston, they would lay down their life for me just as they would him."

"Cowboys?"

"Um, not really. More just military."

"Hmm, did they wear camo?"

"No... where are you going with this?"

"Just a question. Are you their type or maybe someone with

different"—he waved a hand toward my chest and between my thighs —"equipment."

I hung my shaking head, my hair forming a dark curtain hiding my smirk. "I see them liking more of my equipment, but it's not like we talked about our sexual orientation by the campfire."

He gave a frustrated sigh, which only made my smile grow.

After I clocked in and reacquainted myself with where everything was, I headed to the charge nurse. This particular charge nurse, who before the shooting would have wished me to die a slow death, now gave me a warm hug in front of the entire staff. The emergency room had never been so quiet.

As I started my rounds, the sense that something was off wouldn't kick, just like earlier in the townhouse. From patient to patient, my curious, anxious thoughts wandered. Weston had tried to act normal on our walk to work, but he wasn't, and I didn't push it.

As the hours rolled on and there was only an hour left of my short shift, my unease turned to full-blown worry. It didn't help that the Advil I'd taken thirty minutes prior wasn't doing shit for the pain radiating in my side and shoulder.

Five hours on my feet, taking care of patients and filling out charts, was much harder than I'd expected. Perhaps the time in residency was about physical as well as mental training to get us ready for the real world of being a doctor.

"You good?" Eric asked, his lips against my ear, hands massaging the knots in my shoulders.

I didn't want to tell him it felt like my appendages were about to fall off at their joints; he'd already worried about me enough these past few months.

"You were right though about me being out of work shape. There is no way I could do another five hours of this. Right now, the only thing I think I can accomplish is making it home and hopping into a hot bath."

"I don't think you're back on the schedule until Tuesday night, so at least you get a couple of days to recover. I'll remind them to keep up with the easy schedule until you're up for full time again." His hands dropped from my shoulders and grabbed the stack of charts I was holding. "Now, go home and kiss that hunky boyfriend of yours before I do."

With a quick peck on the cheek, he turned me in the direction of the locker room and gave a gentle shove. Smiling, I weaved in and out of people on the ER floor. I bumped into someone accidentally and looked up to apologize only to find aqua blue eyes staring down. One of his hands rested on my shoulder, tightening slightly.

"Good to see you're back. How's your abdomen? Any pains after working a shift?" Gone was the cocky Austin. He was shifting uncomfortably on his feet, which was very unlike him.

My head cocked to the side, and I narrowed my eyes up at him. "What's with you?" Never was good at beating around the bush.

"Nothing." But his quick glance away, avoiding my questioning stare, said otherwise.

"Fine, I'm too tired to try and get it out of you. Bye, Austin. See you next time." I turned, but what he said next stopped me from continuing to the locker room. Stopped everything, really.

"I slept with Meagan," he blurted quietly enough so only I would hear.

When I turned back to him, to respond to his statement, he took three very large steps backward. I couldn't help my smile. He was scared. But surprisingly, I wasn't mad. The anger that burned in me last Christmas, which made me break his nose, wasn't even an ember inside. I couldn't care less what Austin did. And Meagan, well... Meagan was Meagan. I was disappointed that she had such low standards that she would sleep with Austin after everything, but I wasn't mad. Weston took away the anger when he came back for me. What we had together took away giving a shit about Austin and his promiscuity.

"Okay, and you're telling me this because...."

"I thought you would want to know." He shrugged, keeping his eyes on the old linoleum at our feet.

I sighed, rubbing the bridge of my nose with my thumb and forefinger. "Austin, listen. What was between us was nothing. We both knew that. What you did with me, pursuing me while you were engaged, was a shitty move, but I think we dealt with that on Christmas Day, don't you?" His hand flew up to his nose at the mention of that day. "You two have fun, I have no emotional involvement in whatever y'all choose to do."

Austin stared with an amused look for a second before responding. "You love him—Weston. You love him, don't you?"

"I think what we have goes beyond love," I said, tucking a loose strand of dark hair behind my ear.

"Well, good luck, I guess. See ya around, Kate. And don't tell Meagan I told you. She was nervous about how you would react."

"Okay. Bye, Austin."

As I walked back to the locker room to change, I couldn't help my smile. Even with the pain in my legs and the draining conversation with Austin, I was about to go home to Weston, and that made any day better.

Maybe I should take a shower here so I could jump on him the moment I see him outside. Or I'll shower at home so I can see him quicker. Decisions, decisions.

Deciding on a quick shower here, I changed into street clothes, grabbed my backpack, and headed to where he instructed he would be waiting to walk me home. But I didn't find him in the waiting room. I headed out the emergency room doors; the weather was nice, so he could be out there instead. But he wasn't.

My insides twisted and tensed, and the unease I'd carried all day came back with a vengeance.

Where was he?

I dug through my backpack for my phone. He might have changed plans last minute or was too tired to come walk me home. Neither excuse sounded like him, but I needed them to keep me from freaking out at work.

When I swiped my screen, several missed texts from him popped up.

Weston: Something came up that I need to take care of tonight. Not sure how long it'll last. I won't be able to walk you home like we planned. I'll be back soon.

Weston: I know you want more. I'm not good at opening up to you—or anyone—but I need you to know how I feel. What I've been through, what I've felt, the past several years is yours. I want to share it with you. You won't like everything you see, I know I don't, but it's me. All of me and what has gotten me to this point. I left something on the kitchen counter. It'll give you access to everything you want to know.

Weston: Everything will be fine. Promise. But if something were to happen… I want you to know when it all started for me. What you are to me.

Weston: My buddy James is going to stop by while I'm gone. Be nice to him while he waits for me to get back.

Weston: I love you.

My stomach churned; something was off. He wouldn't have been all concerned about my safety this afternoon and then be okay with me walking home alone at night. Plus, a friend stopping by without him there. It was odd. Right?

I glanced around as the lights beaming from the hospital shone through the darkness; it was one in the morning after all. Walking home at this time of night wasn't the most responsible idea.

See, Weston, I do have some shred of self-preservation in me.

With a click, an Uber was on its way to deliver me the few blocks home. I waited. Anxiously. Terrified of what was going to happen in the next few hours. If my body was correct, whatever it was… it wasn't going to be good.

27

It was a short ride home, but even in that little amount of time, I had somehow peeled enough of my lower lip that when I pulled my hand away, traces of blood dotted my fingertips. I tucked my lip in and winced at the stinging sensation just as the townhouse came into view. The car slowed its approach, and every internal warning alarm started sounding, yelling that something wasn't right, making me ultra-vigilant as I stared out the window.

"Wait," I said to the driver. "There's an alley in the back where I go in through the garage. Drop me off there. Please." My whole body trembled. The driver gave me a confused look through the rearview mirror but honored my request and drove around to the alley. I directed him five or six houses down in case my instincts were correct. After thanking him for the ride, I quietly shut the door and ducked into the shadows.

No lights were on in the house I stood outside of, which was good since Texans were more of a "shoot and ask questions later" type when suspicious people were lurking around their property. I leaned against the cool brick, only my labored breathing sounding in the dark. I needed to focus, to get my shit together. Deep breaths in and out, easy, rhythmic cadence. Thinking of puppies, kittens, the snow falling on the deck in Vail, wine... nothing helped. In fact, the longer I stayed stationary, the worse my unraveling thoughts became. A full-fledged panic attack was knocking at the corners of my mind. That same feeling of unease which followed me on the street that cold January day wrapped itself around my lungs, suffocating me.

Tears filled the corners of my eyes. I cursed at myself. Being scared and weak was infuriating because I couldn't do anything about it. Every little thing sent my pulse racing or made me overthink every scenario. Like this one. I needed to get a fucking grip and move on. All this unease was probably in my head anyway, my PTSD-scattered brain making me see danger or worry when everything was fine at home. Maybe Weston and his friend were there waiting, ready to joke about me blowing it all out of proportion.

It's nothing

Weston is fine.

I'm fine.

There is nothing going on at home.

Pull yourself together, Wheeler.

Right or wrong, now I needed to know if I was crazy or if there truly was danger waiting at home. At least now the rising curiosity smothered the panic. That was one thing I had going for me.

It was difficult keeping to the shadows with the bright streetlights and motion-sensor floodlights on almost every house. After what seemed like miles, I paused and listened at my neighbor's fence.

Nothing.

One Mississippi, two Mississippi, three Mississippi, four... fifty-nine and sixty.

Sixty miserable seconds of waiting and listening, but still nothing. Craning my neck around the fence that separated my driveway from the neighbor's patio, I looked up my driveway.

It's nothing.

I'm overreacting.

I'm just paranoid.

Everything is fine.

With a forced sigh, I turned to head up the driveway, but before the streetlight fully exposed me, I was yanked by my backpack. A large, rough hand clasped across my mouth, silencing my scream.

I kicked and bucked against the person at my back. In pure desperation, I sank my teeth down into the soft flesh of the hand covering my mouth. The person holding me hissed and pulled me tighter against their chest.

"Be quiet. Romeo sent me. We need to get out of here. Now," the unknown man whispered harshly into my ear as he walked us backward. I could sense his head swiveling from one side to the other watching for danger. But what danger, I still had no clue.

The guy used Weston's nickname, so he must have been telling the truth; plus, he was pulling me *away* from the danger my subconscious had been trying to tell me was waiting at the townhouse the whole time. *Note to self: always side with gut feelings.*

He dropped his hand from my mouth to grip my upper arm and pull me alongside him down the alley. We reached the end, both of us panting. He motioned to the passenger door of a small black truck. I pulled on the handle and slid inside just as he did on the driver side.

Okay, so this was James. But why would he be pulling me away from the house when Weston said he would be coming to hang out? With a side glance, I noted the man's shoulders were still tense, almost at his ears, and he kept glancing in the rearview mirror every half second, so maybe now wasn't the best time to ask questions. Many more miles were needed between us and the threat before either of us could relax, so we rode in silence for several blocks.

A few minutes later, he visibly relaxed, unleashing my questioning.

"Who are you? What was going on back there? Where is Weston?" I demanded.

"Damn, woman, how about you ask one question at a time? Then I'll decide if I'm going to answer."

I glared at him through the dark cab. We pulled up to a stop light, which illuminated the truck enough that some of his features were visible. His jaw and chin were covered in a short, dark, scruffy beard that looked like he hadn't shaved in days rather than it being kept long to be trendy. His ball cap was pulled down low on his brow, shadowing his eyes, and he looked thin, unhealthily thin for a male. The way his fingers anxiously tapped the steering wheel and his left foot bounced insistently hinted there was something unstable about him. If he was Weston's friend, he was the complete opposite of the others I'd met. This guy seemed dark, even a little disturbed, one to be wary of.

"Fine, let's start with what the hell was going on back there?"

He gripped the brim of his hat and shifted it back and forth before resting his hand back on the wheel. "Romeo asked me to stop by tonight and keep you company until he got done with whatever he's doing. I don't know what's going on, all I know is I showed up waiting for you and found multiple guys lingering around. Not sure why or what the hell Romeo and Mouse have gotten themselves into, but me against all them weren't good odds, so instead of waiting at the house, we're going to them."

What was Weston up to if he felt he needed to send this guy to check in on me? And how did Tyler get caught up in all this?

"Where are they? Where is Weston? Is he safe?" Fear made my voice barely a whisper. He had to be safe. Of course he was safe. He was Weston. Nothing could hurt him.

The man laughed uncomfortably. "Ask me another question, hon. I can't answer that one just yet."

Seriously? Hon? What the fuck? "You will tell me what I need to know or—"

"My hand fucking hurts," he mused, looking down at his palm before flicking the right turn signal and turning into an outdoor self-storage facility. He rolled down the window, punched in a code, and waited while the gate slowly opened. "I know you want answers, but I can't give them to you, not that I would if I did know. All I know is Romeo called in a favor, so I came. Things didn't go as planned, so I texted Mouse and we changed the plan. Which is how we find ourselves here."

He had talked to Weston recently—that was a good sign—but

then Tyler changed the plans? Why didn't Weston? This guy was holding something back.

"Tell me something you do know, like who the fuck are you?" I asked, facing the window, watching the storage units pass. The truck came to an abrupt halt, making the seat belt catch to keep me from flying forward, in front of a large storage shed, one that looked large enough to fit... a Bronco.

Ah. So this was where all of Weston's things were. Maybe we had a few minutes before the other two boys showed up and I could snoop around a bit. You know, look for high school yearbooks or embarrassing pictures.

"James Steel." He sighed and leaned his head against the headrest like this conversation was draining what little patience he had.

"And...."

His eyes rolled behind his lids.

"Do you always have to talk?"

"Do you always have to act like an asshole?" I spat back.

"Damn, woman, hasn't anyone ever told you to bite your tongue to hold back that mouth of yours?"

I grinned. Annoying him was a new fun distraction. "I tried once, but I had to bite too hard to stop mouthing off, and I don't particularly like the taste of blood. Never tried again."

"Maybe you should reconsider."

"Maybe you should tell me what the fuck is really going on, and don't say you don't know. You do. You're just being a twatwaffle and not telling me."

His head rotated to me, but with that damn hat on, his facial expression was hidden. A death glare was probably being shot my way, but no way to be sure.

"Twatwaffle, that's a new one. I've been called a lot of things—"

"Most derogatory or unflattering, I'm sure."

James pulled his hat off, tossed it with force on the dash, and ruffled his military-cut dark hair. "But that is a new one. I think I like you, Doc." His grin was not happy. In fact, it made the earlier assessment of him being unstable flash to the front of my mind. "I met Romeo in the army. We've... we're friends. When he can hang out, that is. Lately he's been so pussy-whipped by some client that he only calls when he needs something, like babysitting said kitty cat from what I bet is some pissed-off ex-boyfriend or play at making him worry about you."

Ass. Why Weston would even keep in touch with this jackass was beyond me. "What is your fucking problem? Have I done something to offend you? If this is about me biting your hand, get the fuck over it. Do not talk to me that way or you'll regret it."

"Weston wouldn't hurt me."

"I'm not talking about Weston, you fuckstick."

He shot me a dismissive look and climbed out of the truck.

Deep breaths in and out. Calm down. Don't go after him. This guy was one to stay away from; I wasn't positive he had an off switch if we were to take it to the physical fighting level.

The clock on the dash said two in the morning. Exhaustion from the shift, panic, and running made my eyelids heavy. The window was cool on my forehead when I rested my head against it, just for a minute. Hopefully when I opened my eyes, this nightmare would be over.

BRIGHT LIGHT FILLED the cab from an approaching car, pulling me awake. A quick glance down at the dash told me it was fifteen after two. The truck stopped twenty feet in front of ours. James sat unmoving from his perch against the front hood.

That could only mean one thing.

Weston.

Relief made a slightly hysterical laugh bubble up. With a shove against the door, it flung open, and I stumbled out, rushing to where James stood leaning against the hood. His face, now highlighted by the light, was hard, unfriendly, like a real smile hadn't passed his lips in years. There was something sorrowful about him now that I had a good look, like a sad movie was constantly playing in the back of his mind, never allowing him to forget the pain he'd been through.

"Well, I can't say it's been fun, Doc. But thankfully before we kill each other, your ride's here."

The driver door swung open and Tyler came into view. Both James and my eyes shot to the passenger side, expecting it to swing open as well, but it didn't.

"What the fuck, Mouse? Where is he?" James growled.

And just like that, the brief moment of relief was overtaken by fear, suck-the-breath-from-your-lungs fear.

Tyler stayed silent as he approached, stopping a foot from us, hands tucked into his camo pants. Mud was smeared across his thighs and black T-shirt like he'd been lying or crawling on his stomach.

He shifted on his feet and kept his gaze on James, making the anticipation ten times worse. Gone was the carefree instigator I had met just over forty-eight hours ago. Now a deep crease marred between his furrowed brows, and his lips pressed in a thin line, almost white from the pressure.

"Something went wrong, very wrong, and..." He dared a glance to me and blanched at my wide-eyed stare. "We need more help. We need to get him out tonight."

What the hell have these boys gotten themselves mixed up in?

"What happened?" James spoke up before I had the capability, still too stunned to speak. His intensity had shifted from menacing to focused, intent on finding a solution that would bring his friend home.

I leaned against the truck for stability as Tyler recounted the night's events. Guilt settled high in my stomach, making me want to vomit to ease the pressure.

Chase had called Weston after he couldn't get ahold of me. He wanted answers, and Weston, being the jackass hero, went to settle the score while I was at work. All for me. He'd walked into a trap at some abandoned building for me, foregoing his own safety. All to get Chase away from me and get the information that only a few days ago

I was willing to sacrifice myself to get. My throat burned with unshed tears of frustration.

"...then whatever Chase said set Romeo off. There was nothing I could do, man. I didn't have a clean shot, and I knew if I started picking off the guards, there were too many of them. They would shoot him dead. Romeo took out two guards before going after the fucker again, and that's when...." Tyler looked over, sympathy in his eyes. "Doc, I'm not sure you want to hear all this."

"Tell me now," I demanded with what little breath wasn't being squeezed from my lungs.

James snorted. "Why don't you go play Candy Crush or whatever you women do and let us figure out a way—"

"Fuck you, James." I shoved a finger against his chest before turning to face Tyler, widening my stance just in case. "Tyler, tell me now. You know I'm not going anywhere until I know the truth."

"Fine." He held up his hands in a motion of surrender. "But don't take my head off when the truth isn't what you want to hear."

I nodded and crossed my arms over my chest, bracing for the worst.

"One of the guards shot him. I couldn't tell where, but it was enough to make Romeo stumble. They took that opportunity to pistol-whip him—he was out when they dragged him to the waiting SUVs."

Aching silence filled my ears, but the two men's lips were still moving like they were talking.

Shot, and not only shot but taken somewhere. *Is he alive now? What if they've already killed him? What if we're already too late?*

"We have to go get him," I breathed.

"It's not that easy, princess. Shot, seriously? Who are we dealing with? What the hell did Romeo get himself mixed up with?"

Tyler stepped closer to us, angling his body slightly between me and James. James didn't know all this was my fault, and based off Tyler's protective move, he would most likely lash out once he learned the truth.

"It doesn't matter, Axe," Tyler snapped. "What matters is I tailed them as far as I could. But they went through a maze of warehouses off 635, and I couldn't follow without being compromised."

"We have to go get him," I said louder, with more conviction this time around, but neither heard me.

James stared at the pavement, focused like he was trying to piece together a plan in his mind. "How many warehouses are in the general area?"

"Hundreds. It would take us hours to search, and I don't know how long he has with the gunshot—"

"We have to get him out!" I screamed and shoved Tyler hard on the chest, sending him stumbling backward. "Stop standing here and let's go get him. Now."

"Don't you think I know that?" Tyler yelled back, his face inches from mine. "We've been in this type of situation before, not you, Doc, so let us handle this. We will get him out, but let us figure it out." He took a step back, then another, putting space between us like he knew the leash on his anger was dangerously close to snapping.

I stared at the bright headlights, my gaze unfocused, as the two men started discussing different rescue scenarios. What if...?

So, the danger back at the townhouse had to be Chase's guys. They wanted me too. Why though? Did he find out what I was looking for? But it didn't make sense why he would take Weston. Unless Weston told him it was all his idea, which wouldn't surprise me. He went in my place, so maybe they were still hoping to get me, but why? What could I offer that Weston couldn't?

Tears welled.

Leverage. I was leverage.

"Use me," I said, staring at the asphalt as the various details of my idiotic plan pieced together. Risky, but it might work.

The two men stopped talking. James sneered, not understanding why I would be of use, but Tyler knew what was going on. And based off him stuffing his hands in his pockets and taking a step back, he knew what I was going to offer up.

"Use me," I said again. "I'll go back to the townhouse, where they'll be waiting for me. One of you will follow from there, and one of you will already be stationed around the warehouse area where Tyler lost them. They'll take me to him. They want to use me as leverage against him."

Neither spoke, which was good; it meant they were considering it. Probably because they couldn't come up with a better solution that would get us to Weston quickly.

"I can handle myself in there." I took a step toward Tyler. "You two can handle everything from the escape angle. Once we're safe, I can treat Weston on the spot so we don't waste any time."

"Doc, Romeo went to a lot of trouble to keep you out—"

"Tyler, I got him in this mess. I'm going to get him out of it with or without you. But I'll fail on my own, so I need your help. Help me save him."

Tyler looked to James, who was glaring at me with the threat of violence behind his eyes. The muscles in his jaw twitched; he now knew his friend was shot and held hostage because of me.

"If we're going to do this...," Tyler started but trailed off like he couldn't believe what he was saying.

James finished the thought for him. "We need to act now. I sure as hell hope you know what you're doing, Doc. But know this. If it comes down to saving you or Romeo, my brother comes first."

Tyler flinched at the clear hatred that laced James's words.

"Fine. He's priority, I get it. I'll go call an Uber to take me back. We can't have one of you just dropping me off, now can we?" I turned and started toward the gate we'd driven through just forty minutes prior. In those minutes, my whole world had turned upside down. My phone shook so badly I couldn't type in the password.

The sound of jogging footsteps approached.

"We will get him out," Tyler said through deep breaths. "But promise me one thing." *What in the hell could this be about?* "Once you're both out and safe, do not let Romeo murder me for allowing this. He gave me strict orders on what to do if he didn't get out, and I'm breaking every one of those right now."

"Promise." I attempted to smile, but a grimace surfaced instead. "Now let's go bring him home."

He jogged back to James, who was in the process of opening up the storage unit, which, I assumed, was to raid Weston's belongings looking for more firepower. I was betting my life and Weston's that these two would be able to get us out alive. Maybe they would call others to come help, but who would walk into a gun battle with someone like Chase? All to save their friend.

Most of his friends, probably.

But he wasn't just a friend to me.

He was more than a lover, really.

He was my lifeline.

My hold on the good the world had to offer.

The reality that seemed like a dream.

The next few hours would be terrifying, but a calm washed over me. This time when I pulled out the phone, my hands weren't shaking. They were steady as I entered my password and called for a stranger to drive me, willingly, into jeopardy.

Now was the time to prove to myself what I could do, who I was. That this person I had become these past few months was not me, that the effects of the shooting would not be my identity. No. Now was the time to prove to myself and everyone else what I was made of.

I would get him back.

Tonight.

This time when the Uber driver approached the townhouse, I wasn't afraid. Even when I stepped out onto the sidewalk and headed for the door, my legs were stable, my hands hanging relaxed by my side. My ass vibrated with the notification of an incoming call, but I ignored it and continued to the front door. *Will they grab me on the street or be waiting inside?*

My back pocket started vibrating again. Someone was really trying to get ahold of me, but when I pulled it out and checked the screen, it was an unknown Fort Worth number. When the phone stopped vibrating, it said I had ten missed calls from that same number. And one text.

Unknown: Do not go in that house. We found another way to find him. We're on our way to get you.

"Shit, shit, shit, shit," I whispered, whipping my head back and forth. I backed down the few stairs of my front stoop. The screech of tires startled me, throwing me off balance. My hip hit the pavement hard, and the palms I threw out to soften my fall burned from scraping against the rough sidewalk.

I stood and swayed, desperately trying to regain my equilibrium. Three men stepped out of a black Suburban—no plates—and started in my direction. They were on me before I could even think about running; two gripped my upper arms in their massive hands and a hand clapped over my mouth tightly to muffle my yells for help. They hauled me toward the car. I dragged my feet in an attempt to slow them down. The other guy reached for my feet to help his buddies.

His mistake.

Using the leverage of the men holding my arms, I swung both feet up directly at the man's face. Behind the sweaty palm, I smiled at the stream of profanities that came when my foot connected with the side of his face. When he glanced up, gripping his jaw, it looked like he was going to lunge for me, but he didn't, just simply grunted, scooped both my legs into his hands, and helped haul me into the awaiting SUV.

Hands and feet bound, my head bounced off the floorboard as I was tossed in the back. I strained to hear anything that might help me later. Three car doors opened and closed, the engine started, and the SUV slowly pulled out onto the street going north... wait, maybe south... nope, for sure east. Who the hell knew. It was dark, and the dickheads were talking about the damn Rangers like they didn't have a woman bound in the back. All I could do now was wait.

Too soon the Suburban stopped and the engine died. When I got my hands on the damn driver.... With every bump and quick turn of the SUV, I'd been flung around the back area. Bruises from head to toe were a sure thing tomorrow.

If I made it to tomorrow.

No overhead light clicked on when the trunk opened and I was scooped out. The larger of the three tossed me over his shoulder, which meant I couldn't see where we were headed, only what was behind us. Through the dark, I searched, mentally pleaded for a trace of light or movement from James and Tyler, something that would let me know they were there, that I wouldn't be doing this alone. But I saw nothing.

The man pushed through a door and stopped, the door slamming shut with such force it would have broken my face if he'd stopped half an inch closer. The building was metal of some kind, looked like a warehouse, which made sense based off Tyler's story from earlier about where he'd lost the tail of Weston and Chase.

The sound of clapping echoed through the small space. "There she is. And look, we get to see her best side first." Chase's voice carried through the room, but I still couldn't see him—only the guy's fat ass and the door we'd just come through. But that view stopped when I was dropped into a plastic chair.

The guard shifted. Weston was in my direct line of sight. Before I could visually assess his injuries, Chase stepped in, blocking my view. He stood too close. I angled my head up to meet his eyes, which were slightly purple and his nose swollen from... well, me. I stifled the proud smile that was trying everything to pull at my lips. No need to taunt him... yet.

The swollen nose and eyes were different, but there was something off in his demeanor as well. He seemed more... hateful, evil almost. Like he'd lifted the damper of his façade and now this was the real Chase.

"Hello, beautiful." He wrapped a hand in my long hair and pulled it back, bending my neck from the forceful pull. "I'm sorry you had to be brought here like this. I promise we won't harm you if you tell us the truth. If everything checks out, then you can go home and go about your life like nothing ever happened."

"What is he doing here?" I attempted a nod in Weston's direction, my scalp screaming at the movement. That tug, the pain of my hair being pulled from the root against my will, flashed me back to my room in Colorado. Everything faded to the background, and for a moment I was back in that room, giving myself up so Weston wouldn't be harmed. The blood drained from my face, and my stomach rolled, wanting to throw up the seven cups of coffee I had earlier at the hospital. The room started to spin; I was seconds from passing out.

"I needed some answers from him," Chase responded to the question I'd forgotten I asked. I was too busy trying to hold myself together, keep myself in this nightmare instead of slipping into a past one. "Are you okay, Kate? You don't look well." His hand dropped from my hair as he took a step back, still staying between Weston and me. The moment my hair was released and I gained the freedom to move my head, the pain in my scalp fading, reality pieced back together, reminding me of why I was here. "Now let's get this started, shall we? I would really hate for him to bleed out before I get to have some fun—"

"Let her go, you motherfucker." Weston's deep voice, still his own but weaker, ignited my will to fight.

"What do you want to know, Chase?" I asked, trying to peer around him to see Weston, but it was a lost cause. He stepped close once again and ran his fingers down my cheeks until he was gripping my chin with unnecessary roughness.

"First, I want to know who told you to start looking into my business, investigating me."

Well, shit. Didn't see that one coming.

Think fast. No way I can tell him the truth.

"A case that came across my father's desk mentioned something about suspicions of you being tied to human and drug trafficking. I told him I would look into it." It was a weak lie, but hopefully he would buy it.

Chase turned, strode to Weston, and punched him so hard blood sprayed across the cement floor. Again. And again.

"Stop it!" I screamed.

He was still blocking my line of sight to Weston; all I could see were his legs, the small pool of blood under his chair, and Chase's back. "You want me to stop, do you? Then tell me the truth."

"I am. I swear, Chase."

"See, I know you're lying. If your daddy had any inclination I was into this kind of business, he wouldn't have freely given Casey's information earlier tonight. Since you weren't picking up, I still needed answers. I hate to tell you this, Kate, but I don't think he approves of you and Weston. He seemed all too willing to give me his information to get him the hell away from you when I used the excuse of wanting him on my security team."

Chase motioned for one of the guards, took his side arm, and pointed the barrel of the gun at Weston's heart. He shifted, giving me full view of Weston, but my eyes were locked on the gun in Chase's hand. One flick of his finger and the future I had recently started hoping for would be gone.

"You have three seconds to tell me the truth."

"I...."

"Don't do it, baby," Weston rasped.

"One."

"Chase, I don't know what to tell you—"

"Two."

"What do you want from me?"

"The truth, Kate. All I want is the truth."

"I found out, okay? It doesn't matter anymore. All you need to know is that I know everything and have what I need to get you indicted." Slight lie.

My shoulders shook with a relieved sob as Chase dropped the gun he held at Weston and handed it back to the guard.

"Oh really, Kate? Tell me what you have that would suffice as proof?"

My narrowed, furious eyes shifted up to meet his. "I followed you, in San Diego. I have pictures. Not to mention what I gained from your office that night."

He stepped to the side and angled his body to face Weston, finally allowing another view of him. This time I took the opportunity to look him over. I kept my expression calm for Weston's sake. His face was a bloody mess, and a small pool of blood had collected under his chair, but nothing that would signal he was on the verge of bleeding out now unless he lost substantially more earlier. I could sense his stare burning into me, begging me to look at him, but I didn't dare let my eyes meet his as I took in the paleness of his skin and lips.

Not in great condition, but we had time. Tyler and James would come through. Weston had time.

"Casey," Chase said, smiling, "do you know there are still some nights I lie awake thinking about her lips on my—"

"It's Weston, you dipshit," I growled, saying anything to stop him from tormenting Weston with the details.

Weston tugged and lurched against his restraints. "It was me, Chase. She doesn't know what the fuck she's talking about. It's me you want. I have all the information."

Chase crossed his arms over his chest as he looked back and forth between us. From the look on his face, he was trying to decipher who was telling the truth. After a minute, he threw his hands up and sighed.

"Fine, you both know everything, which means you both will have to pay the consequences. I can't risk any of this information getting out. I've worked too hard and evaded the authorities too many times to be taken down by some washed-up army fucker and a dumb cunt."

Weston shouted, begging for Chase to listen to him. But Chase's predatory gaze was on me. Only me. And mine was only on him. This was a standoff. The past few months boiled down to this, and I was going to use the opportunity to get what I'd been striving for the entire time.

"Why, Chase? How did you get mixed up in all this?"

"You want to know my story, Kate?" he mused as he walked behind me, rested his hands on my shoulders, and began massaging them with an intimate touch. "Everything I told you about me was true in the way I started my business, but with a slight side path. During the recession, my business began to fail. I was on the verge of filing bankruptcy, and I was willing to do anything to keep that from happening. My now business partner approached me with a side business plan that would make enough to keep my business afloat, plus some. All I had to do was allow my trade lines to be used for... things other than consumer goods. It was an offer I couldn't refuse. Plus, I reasoned I would be providing these women and children with safe passage. They wouldn't have to worry about starving to death or dying from dehydration on their voyage here. I provide them with safe passage—"

"To their own fucking slavery, you fucking ignorant piece of shit,"

I shouted, jerking my shoulders forward to get his hands off, but his grip only tightened. "You were delivering them to a lifetime of forced labor or being raped and used every day. Women, children. The kids —how can you live with yourself when you're delivering children to...?" I couldn't finish the sentence, the horrors too much to even voice.

"That's the way you see it, but I see it as a way for me to keep my still-underperforming company in business. Besides, it does have its perks. You see, Kate, I can't always find someone who is as... open-minded to the way I approach sex. With this little arrangement, I have access to as many unwilling partners as I want."

My chest and shoulders shook from an uncontrollable sob.

"Shhh, it's okay, Kate. You won't know anything. The drugs help us with that and keeping you... amiable. We wouldn't want that fight of yours to come out on a client, now would we?"

I startled as he ran his nose along the rim of my ear, inhaling deeply against my hair.

"No," Weston choked. "You wouldn't do that to her. She's the daughter of the DA. You're a fucking lunatic for bringing her tonight, much less—"

Chase's warm breath brushed along my neck as he chuckled at Weston. "Don't you think I've already thought of that? There was no way I was going to let either of you leave here tonight knowing as much as you do. Isn't it going to be so unfortunate for Daddy to learn the group from the trial didn't give up when it was over? Too bad for him, he'll never know what really happened."

He stepped around the chair and scooped me into his arms. I bucked as forcefully as I could, but his hold on me only tightened. "Oh, and, Casey... I know before the pretty little doc got here I promised if you told me everything I needed to know, I wouldn't make you watch, but... well... I lied."

No. My thrashing stopped as I stared wide-eyed up at him. *He can't be serious. There's no way he's going to—*

In the distance, Weston begged for Chase to let me go, and my heart cracked in two at the desperation and panic in his voice. My bound arms and legs bounced as he strode across the warehouse. If he wanted a fight to turn him on and to torture Weston, then that was exactly what I wouldn't give.

Even though my mind was screaming to tense up, to fight, I worked against it, focusing on relaxing my body, starting at my legs and working up.

My feet hit the concrete floor first; then my chest and face were pushed into the warm metal wall of the warehouse. But still I didn't fight, stayed relaxed. His hands wrapped around my bound ankles and released the zip tie, letting blood flow back into my nearly numb feet. With a chuckle, he picked up one foot and then the other, spreading my legs. My eyes slammed shut as his hands traveled up my calves, caressing my thighs and ass before settling on my waist.

He pushed flush against me, his hard-on pressing against my back, but still I didn't fight. No way in hell I would give him what he wanted.

Both of his hands slid under my T-shirt and inched their way up to my breasts, but still I didn't react. "Come on, Kate, what are you waiting for? Try to get free. Fight me." He breathed against my neck, forcing an involuntary shudder to run down my spine.

I said nothing, my focus on the men guarding the back door, who were talking among themselves like it was every day they witnessed a woman being assaulted.

The room spun when he flipped me around to face him, sending my back slamming against the metal building. I dared a glance at Weston, against my better judgment, and immediately regretted it.

He was still yelling at Chase, but now it was more of a rasp, and tears were streaming down his cheeks.

Weston was crying.

Crying for me.

I sagged against the wall. Forcing Weston to watch was breaking him, and there was *nothing* I could do to stop it. Only wait for the two slow-ass jackasses to get their shit together and make it all stop. Until then, I would not fight back. I repeated it over and over in my mind as Chase's hands continued to roam.

"Maybe this will change your mind," he growled just before the back of his hand collided with my cheek, sending my head whipping back so hard the sound of it banging against the metal wall echoed throughout. "I've been wanting to do that since you fucking head-butted me."

I cleared my vision, blinking once, twice, and turned to meet Chase's frustrated gaze, but I didn't react, only stared back emotionless.

"Come on now, Kate. Show me a little of the alley cat who was in our hotel room that night. The way you fought so hard, damn." As he talked, he gripped my thigh and hooked it around his hips, then began pushing himself on me. Behind Chase, Weston started going ballistic, shouting all the ways he was going to torture Chase. "Let's see if you're worth all this trouble you've caused me." His hand slithered between us and dropped to the waistband of my jeans.

This was really happening.

Chase licked his lips as he stared between us.

No. There was no way I could sit back and let this happen, right? At what point would I fight back, even with my arms bound? It would be suicide, but that was better than being assaulted while the man I loved was forced to watch.

The first button of my jeans popped open under Chase's fingers.

And the entire room exploded.

***

FLASHES OF LIGHT flickered from every direction as smoke filled the air, making me cough and try to drop to my knees, but Chase still had me pinned against the wall. The room looked like someone had turned on twenty disco balls and turned them on high speed. Men bellowed through the smoke as gunfire popped all around.

Chase shoved me against the wall and hissed into my ear. "You'll pay for this, you fucking bitch." Then he ducked and ran into the smoke.

I tried to track where he went through the chaos, even took a step in the direction he fled, but a bullet ricocheted off the wall an inch or two from my head. *Shit.* My ass slammed against the concrete as I dropped to the floor, tucking my head to my thighs.

Someone will come for me.

The pops and shouting became less frequent as I stayed wrapped in my little cocoon of false safety.

Two strong arms engulfed me.

"Baby, it's me. You're safe," Weston whispered against the back of my head. But was I? Several rounds of an automatic weapon fired outside the warehouse. "Look at me, Kate." No. I couldn't. How could I? What he just witnessed, having to watch Chase... my stomach lurched. "Kate, look at me. Now." His tone shifted from worry to pure command.

That did it.

Slowly I raised my head, blinking back tears to clear my vision. He wrapped his sticky hands around my cheeks, tucking his thumbs under my chin, urging me to look up at him.

"What happened?" I asked, staring over his shoulder.

"I don't—"

James and Tyler emerged through the smoke, dangling assault rifles from their sides and wearing black bulletproof vests.

"What the hell are you two wearing?" I asked.

Tyler smiled as he crouched behind me with a small knife in hand. My fingers tingled as blood flowed freely with the zip ties now gone from my wrists.

"Let's just say we phoned a friend, or a friend phoned us, really. We told you we had another way," Tyler said, standing and resuming his position beside James.

"How... who... what?" I pushed out of Weston's grasp and stood to look around the chaos. Twenty or so men in black wind jackets, slacks, and ties were walking around assessing the carnage.

Tyler started to reply, but Weston's groan as he pushed from the floor to stand cut him short.

Girlfriend and doctor of the year right here.

"Sit back down, Weston, and lay your leg out straight. I need to look at your GSW," I commanded, pointing to the ground. Thankfully he didn't put up a fight, not that he could have if he tried based off his clammy skin and pale face.

First I needed to get to the wound, but his jeans were caked with dried blood, preventing any visibility. "James, toss me your knife," I said, extending my hand without looking.

I was expecting something small like a Swiss Army knife, but instead a miniature machete was placed into my outstretched palm. I stared at it for a long moment. Could I maneuver this thing without cutting Weston's leg off?

Tyler chuckled from where he was crouched down beside me. "What, Doc, never had something so big and hard in your hand?"

"Fuck off, Mouse," Weston and I said in unison, which made both Tyler and James laugh.

Carefully I sliced through his jeans. Every few inches, I prodded around with my fingers until they sank into open flesh. Weston hissed through his teeth as I applied pressure to certain areas, searching for the exit wound. A hysterical laugh bubbled up from my chest, making the three men stare back confused.

James kicked my thigh with his boot. "What's so funny, Doc?"

"The wound is on the outer thigh, a through and through. It doesn't look like any major ligaments or tendons were ruptured, and the femoral artery runs along the inside of the leg, so that's safe."

Still, I couldn't look at Weston. Touching him was hard enough. The second my eyes met his, all this became real, and I would have to deal with what almost happened in front of him. No, we would work through all this later, but right now wasn't that time. "He's lost a lot of blood, but if we get this wrapped and pressure applied, he should be fine until we get him to a hospital."

Weston tried to pull his leg from my grasp. "I'm not going to the damn hospital. Just bandage it up. I'll be fine."

I glared at James since I couldn't glare at the idiot with the gunshot wound. "You're going to the hospital. You need antibiotics, stitches, and for someone to look at the head wound Tyler said they gave you. You're going." I pushed off the floor to face James and Tyler.

They each looked to me, Weston, then back to me, not knowing who to listen to.

"You can't make me—" he started but was cut off by a loud commotion coming from the other end of the warehouse, snagging everyone's attention. A younger-looking agent jogged up and glanced between the four of us. James stepped forward and asked what he needed.

"There are women here, in the back. Has to be a dozen or so," he said, his voice harsh, void of any empathy.

My brows shot up with realization at what he was saying. All of this was worth it. We saved them. Everything I had done to get here had been worth it. The feeling was... rewarding, something I hadn't genuinely felt in a long time.

"We don't know what to do with them, so I guess we'll take them downtown to the police—"

"Hell no," I said forcefully as I took a step toward him. "You're not going to take them downtown and treat them like they're the criminals in all this. Tell your guys to take them to Second Chances." I took a deep breath in and rattled off the address before continuing with my orders. "Tyler, go out and get a field medical kit from one of the SUVs. Wrap Weston's leg tightly so he doesn't lose any more blood before we take him to the hospital." Weston started to voice his disagreement, but I moved on, ignoring him. "James, find us a car. You'll drop me off at my place before taking Weston to the hospital. I'll call Eric to let him know you're coming."

The four men stared. James had a look of amusement or disgust on his face, I couldn't tell which. Tyler grinned ear to ear, seeming to love my bossy ass.

"How about you calm down, Tinker Bell, and stop barking orders. You could ask nicely, you know."

Tyler tried to cover his laugh with a fake cough. "Tiny, bossy, feisty as hell. Yep, Tink it is."

Fine. As long as they listened, more for their sake, they could call me whatever they wanted.

29

———————

By the time we hauled Weston into the SUV James had commandeered and started toward home, it was close to 5:00 a.m. Tyler drove, James sat in the passenger seat, and Weston and I were in the back. We were all cranky and tired, plus a layer of animosity hung in the air.

Halfway back, Weston broke the tense silence by stating he would not go to the hospital, that I needed protection at Second Chances, and he would go with me to ensure my safety. He. Wouldn't. Let. Up.

"Weston," I said, trying to keep the annoyance out of my voice. After all, he was beat to shit and had a bullet wound. "There is no need for security. They caught Chase, and after the gunshot wound he got while trying to escape, plus the beating you handed him, he won't be moving without assistance for a long time."

A grumbled approval for his actions came from the two men up front. It was... generous of the agents to look the other way while Weston had a few minutes alone with Chase before hauling him away for treatment and questioning. Chase was lucky; if Weston had been at full strength during those five gifted minutes, he would probably be eating through a tube the rest of his existence. Which I hoped wasn't long. It was bad for me to say that as a doctor, but what he was capable of, what he almost did to me... overlooking some basic morals for him was okay in my book.

"We're going with you and that's final, Kate. Now go get your bag and come right back. If you try to leave without us, we'll just follow you." Restrained anger, not toward me but at the whole morning, made his tone harsh and unyielding.

Turning from the window, addressing him to assure him he didn't need to worry about me or my safety, would be best to calm him down, but that was something I still hadn't done and wasn't planning until we were alone.

Tyler pulled up to the townhouse, leaving the SUV idling, and glanced back through the rearview mirror, a worried expression pulling his brows together.

With a louder-than-needed grunt to let everyone in the car know how annoyed I was, I opened the door and headed inside to grab the stocked medical bag I always brought to Second Chances. After securing the house once again, I kept my gait even, breathing steady, trying to seem normal so the very observant Weston wouldn't catch on to my scheme.

Tyler shifted the SUV into Drive, but he paused from pulling away from the curb when I asked him to wait so I could administer Weston's needed antibiotics. I pulled out a vial of clear liquid, a new syringe, and began filling the syringe to the amount someone of Weston's size—minus several pints of blood—would need. Weston's focus on what I was doing never wavered, nor did the other two men's up front.

Blindly reaching across the seat, I grabbed his arm, held it flat, and searched for a good vein in the semi dark. He didn't hesitate as I slid the needle into his arm, which was good; I had played my innocent act well enough to fool him. After placing a folded square gauze over the small puncture wound, I glanced up at Tyler, my lips pursed together. How would those two react to me drugging their friend?

In less than a minute, the effects of the sedative began to kick in.

"I'm sorry, Casey. I really am, but you gave me no choice. You have to go to the hospital, and I'm wasting time sitting here fighting with you about it," I whispered to the floorboard.

He didn't respond, his body and mind now too relaxed to understand what I was saying. When he slipped into sleep, his body slumped and his head softly hit the window. I opened the door and stepped back onto the sidewalk.

James jumped out and gripped my upper arm so hard it hurt.

"What did you do to him?" he yelled into my face.

I gave a forceful shake to loosen his grip. "I sedated him. You and Tyler take him to the emergency room at Baylor. I'll have Eric waiting for you." Turning on my heels, I started toward the front door.

"He won't forgive you for that, you know."

Maybe, maybe not, but I would rather him be pissed and alive than dead. Or having his leg amputated because of infection that could have been prevented. But instead of acknowledging James with my reasoning, I continued up the same steps that only a few hours ago I had fallen down before being taken into this nightmare.

I pulled out my phone once I was safely inside. The kitchen was eerily quiet, making me miss Ryan's and Weston's gruff voices.

> Me: Hey, Weston is on his way to the ER.
> James and Tyler are bringing him in.
>
> Me: Gunshot wound to the right outside
> thigh. Through and through. Maybe some
> facial fractures. And possible concussion.
>
> Me: Oh, and he is sedated, so might want to
> get a wheelchair to lug that massive frame in.

I swayed on my feet, the adrenaline effects wearing off quickly. Maybe a quick shower would help revive me enough to go help out at Second Chances. A few more hours; then I could sleep and process everything. And apologize to Weston. Damn, he was going to be so mad when he woke up—which made a smile pull at my lips.

Something on the counter, where I had tossed my phone, caught my eye. It looked to be a sliver of paper with Weston's handwriting on it. *What in the world?* Reaching over, I dragged it close and held it up to see what was written. It didn't make sense, only an email address and what looked to be a password underneath it.

My phone rattled on the counter, stealing my attention.

> Eric: What. The. Fuck.
>
> Eric: Who is James! Who is Tyler!
>
> Eric: You have a lot of explaining to do.
>
> Eric: I'll take care of him.

Great, now Eric was pissed too.

Elbows on the counter, I rested my face in my hands and sighed. The past twelve hours were brutal. Weston was hurt because of me. Eric was pissed. James wanted to murder me for multiple reasons. And me... well, I was barely hanging on by a thread after everything at the warehouse. Thankfully my mind was too tired to keep replaying the events over and over.

A shower. Everything would be better after a shower.

Grabbing the shred of paper and my phone from the counter, I trudged up the stairs.

WITH THE HELP of another doctor, who Shelly had called in, it only took us a couple hours to examine all the women and get them to a secure location. A translator was brought in from the agency—I still had no idea which division of the government they actually worked for—and started gathering information on where they'd come from and how they could contact family members.

The midmorning sun warmed my face on the ride home; it wasn't smart to be driving the bike this exhausted—past exhausted, really—but it was relaxing. I was free on my bike, like nothing could catch me, especially the memories from the past twelve hours.

I didn't know what to expect when I opened the garage door of the townhouse, but I really hoped Weston wasn't waiting to hash everything out now. Thankfully it was quiet as I walked through the house.

Just as the feeling of relief washed over me, my stomach dropped again. What if he wasn't here at all? He could have been so pissed he stayed somewhere else. A new panic knotted my gut.

His room. I needed to check his room.

The door pushed open without a sound. For the second time in thirty seconds, deep relief calmed my racing heart. He was sprawled out on the bed completely naked, a white sheet draped across his backside. Either James or Tyler didn't want to lug him up the stairs or he was sleeping down here to put space between us. But it didn't matter if it was the latter; after everything, curled up beside him was the only place I wanted to be.

After a quick shower in his bathroom, I slipped on a T-shirt of his and slid into his crisp, cool sheets beside him. I sighed and shut my eyes, so ready to get some sleep.

The bed shifted beside me, and I stilled.

"You fucking drugged me." His voice was hoarse with sleep.

I didn't turn to face him. "Sedated."

The bed shifted again under his weight, like he'd rolled over to face me.

"Look at me, Kate."

I shook my head and curled my body into a tight ball to enforce my answer. His rough hand gripped my shoulder and tugged, trying to roll me over, but I pulled against him, not allowing it. His answering growl was loud in my ear.

"Enough of this shit, damnit. Look at me. I need to know what you're thinking. We need to talk about it."

"Let's just go to sleep, Weston. We can talk about it later, okay? I'm exhausted."

"No." This time when he gripped my shoulder, he tugged on my hip as well, flipping me to my back. Before I could roll back over, he flung his leg over my hips and pulled himself up so he was straddling me. "Look at me." He gripped my jaw with one hand, angling my face toward his, but I stared at the ceiling instead of him. "Baby, please, please look at me. Just look at me."

Warm tears crested and spilled from the corners of my eyes. I clenched them shut and shook my head side to side, internally fighting against what he was begging me to do.

Gentle fingers wiped away each tear in silence, allowing time for me to figure out what to say. He was forcing me to face this head-on, and it seemed he wouldn't let up until I did.

"I'm afraid of what I'll see," I whispered, my voice cracking.

"It's just me, baby. What are you afraid of?"

It took a minute to figure it out, how to put it into words that would make sense. Even to me it was confusing, but I would try for him.

"I'm afraid you're going to see me differently and I'll know it. That you'll see me as a victim in all this, that what you saw at the ware-house... what almost happened... changed the way you see me. We saved eighteen women tonight and countless more by stopping this one ring. It was worth it to me. Everything that's happened and I've been through has been worth it. But if I open my eyes and find I've lost you in the process...."

I trailed off, not knowing how to finish the thought. "And when I look at you, you see me. All of me. And I know what you'll find when you do. Maybe I don't want you to see me this scared and vulnerable. Because that's what I am right now. I'm so fucking terrified of what's going to happen when I stop and have to think about it all. I'd just started to get through the shooting and now this. What if I can't handle it? What if I can't handle any of this?"

My body shook from the sob that finally broke free. I gasped for air from the tears that couldn't fall fast enough, getting caught in my throat and slowly suffocating me.

With each tear, the shreds of who I was started piecing back together, cleansing each wounded memory. When the tears slowed and my mind cleared, I opened my eyes to find him staring down. The look in his eyes made all the sad tears stop. There was no pity, no disgust or shame, only awe and understanding.

"There you are," he croaked. It sounded like he was holding back tears of his own. "You amaze me every day with how strong you are. The way you juggle everything and put others before yourself, it's incredible. There isn't a doubt in my mind you can handle this. It'll take a while to sort it out, yes, and you'll need to talk to someone. Not Anne, obviously."

My huffed laugh made the worry lines on his forehead and around his eyes loosen.

"But you're stronger than some of the men I've known, and it's okay to be scared and vulnerable. You have to let me see it, baby. I love you more than I ever thought was humanly possible, and I'm not going to let this take you from me. I will fight for you. That's what I'm doing right here, right now, is fighting for you. For you and me. There is no me without you. That person who was shut off and didn't deserve a future is gone. And I'm scared too. I sure as hell am vulnerable when it comes to you. Don't let them win. Talk to me. Keep talking to me. Please don't shut me out."

His warm forehead pressed against mine, and for a minute we lay just like that, taking in each other's confession and giving the moment the silence it deserved. When he climbed off me, I missed him, but the view of him walking to the dresser naked was a nice consolation. When he came back to the bed, he had a box of tissues in one hand, which I immediately grabbed to wipe my hot mess of a face, and two white pills.

I downed the two pills with a glass of water from the bedside table without a second thought. The smirk on his face, giving away his evil plot, told me I should have thought it through.

"What were those?" I asked suspiciously.

"Your sleeping pills."

"You drugged me?"

"Sedated."

"Asshole. I'm tired. I don't need help going to sleep."

"Ah, but you're exhausted, and you'll need help staying asleep so you can get the rest your body needs." He crawled over the bed, settled under the covers, and pulled me tight against his chest.

"Don't worry about anything, baby, just sleep. I'm right here. I'll always be here."

LOUD VOICES from the other room pulled me out of a deep, restful sleep. Those pills were amazing; I felt rested physically and mentally. Maybe I was wrong not taking them after the hospital. With a glance at the clock, I saw it was three in the afternoon. Good, I didn't want to sleep the entire day away, even though it felt like I'd been asleep for way longer than a few hours.

After a long stretch, I tossed my legs over the side of the bed and stared at myself in the mirror over the dresser. There was no sugarcoating it, I looked like hell. My hair was just waiting for a rat family to take residence, my eyes were bloodshot like I'd pulled an all-nighter, and my cheek was red and swollen from Chase's backhand at the warehouse.

"Dick," I mumbled and stood to check out who was in the living room making so much racket. It sounded like multiple people shouting, but not in anger, more like an excited discussion.

I tossed on a pair of Weston's boxers, tight-rolling them eight times just to get them to stay on my hips, since it sounded like we had company. Resting my hand on the doorknob, I paused to listen before venturing out.

"...I know, I'm just glad I got to Mouse in time. Sorry it was too late to keep Doc out of this."

"She would have jumped in somehow either way. Not your fault, Miss Ginger. It's good what she gave you helped after all."

"Back to what you were saying, Miss Ginger, what about us helping you?"

"Damn, Mouse, give him a fucking second to breathe. He just walked in the door."

"It's fine. What you guys did last night didn't go unnoticed—in a good way. They want to contract you out to help with other situations like this. Where we don't have any evidence, just... suspicions."

"Would we get paid?"

"Yes, we could set you up with a business and pay you a consulting fee. Plus expenses."

"Y'all have to admit it would be fun working together again."

Interesting. Kyle was here—not sure why—plus Tyler, James, and, of course, Weston. What Kyle was suggesting sounded amazing. But one small catch: what they did last night, how they found out about Chase, was because of me. No way in hell I would let them do any of this without me.

Maybe this was my chance to do more and be more, what my mom always knew I was destined for. My medical background could come in handy too.

"How long do we have to decide?" the voices continued outside the door.

"Whenever, but I can tell you we need the help now. One of the guys who survived last night has already started to talk. He was new to the group, just moved here from Hawaii. Said some stuff has gone down there recently, leadership change, and he had to get out. We've heard the same thing. It seems one of the groups out there has decided human trafficking is more profitable than the drug trade. We've had an alarming amount of chatter from there. But we don't know who, where, or how they're doing it. We need help."

I'd heard enough.

Every eye turned to me as I meandered into the room, the smell of coffee drawing me to the kitchen before everything else. Weston appeared at my side as I poured a large cup of steaming beauty. I took a deep whiff to wake my brain cells before looking up at him.

"You heard all that, didn't you?" he said, smirking.

Of course he'd heard me moving the moment I stepped out of bed.

"Yep, and I have some thoughts on the matter."

He gestured for me to lead the way and sat beside me on the couch, an arm draped over my shoulders.

No one spoke, only watched, as I took a scalding sip of coffee. "So, you were saying we would gather information and hand it off to the authorities or you, Kyle, right?"

"Um, yeah... but not sure this involves you, Doc."

Tyler cut in, "It's Tink now."

Kyle gave me a quick once-over and smirked. "That fits better."

"Right?"

"Seriously, you two, back to the point. Yes, it does involve me. I got us to this point with Chase, and I can help do it again. Not involving me isn't an option."

James was leaning against the wall glaring. "Yeah, way to go, getting us to the point of a gun battle."

"So I hit a snag," I said with a shrug.

"Romeo was shot and kidnapped. They threatened to sell you into a prostitution ring," James snapped.

"Okay, a big snag." I turned to Kyle, who was watching me warily. "I never said I was perfect. This was my first go at it, okay? Give me some wiggle room to make errors."

"Big fucking error," James grumbled.

"Knock it off, Axe. She did get us here, and if you want my help in all this, then she's a part of it too."

I looked up at Weston and smiled. Why did I initially think he would try to hold me back in all this? Putting me in harm's way wasn't something he would want to do, but he knew it was what I wanted. Maybe he even remembered our conversation from months ago out on the deck in Vail about wanting to find my purpose, something more than what I am now.

"Now that that's cleared up, when are we going to start?" Tyler was lying on the floor with a pillow from the couch tucked under his head, staring. Something he always did when we were together. It didn't bother me, but I definitely noticed. "I'm game anytime."

Weston's voice carried through his chest, rumbling against my cheek that was pressed against his side. "Let's talk about it tonight. A lot needs to be figured out before we say yes."

"I'll go get changed and we can talk over dinner," I said, scooting off the couch.

"Um, you have to work tonight, baby."

I turned with a confused expression. "I don't work until tomorrow night, Tuesday."

"It is Tuesday."

"What the fuck, Weston? You let me sleep for over twenty-four hours!" I smacked him on the shoulder, hurting my hand more than him. "Fine, you guys talk it over, but include me in the plans."

"And if we don't?"

Fucking James.

"Well, Hawaii is beautiful this time of year, and I'm told I need some time away to decompress. So Weston and I are going to Hawaii. It's your call if you want to come help or not."

MORE THAN A HOPE

MORE THAN A THREAT BOOK 3

1

This was a joke. A waste of time.

I mean, clearly I had issues, sure. Too many to list, really. The most prominent concern in the current moment was the immediate violent deliberations toward the person annoying me. *That* was a problem, because the person I wanted to throat-punch was the therapist who my father and I selected to help me work through said violent tendencies.

Well, help me moderate my anger issues and the collection of other mental instabilities which I'd gained from the shit show with Chase and being gunned down in the street.

See? Issues galore. My middle name should have been Issues, first name Serious.

What I put myself through to uncover evidence of Chase's involvement with human trafficking had infected every thought since that terrible night. The fear and paranoia which were now my constant companions even slithered into my dreams, shifting them to nightmares filled with the possibilities of what could've happened if Chase had gotten his way. An authentic threat of being sold into a human trafficking ring would do that to anyone, I'd like to think. It wasn't just me being weak.

Not that the old-ass clown sitting patiently across from me knew about my mission to uncover Chase's side business or what happened that night in the warehouse. Neither he nor my father knew how close I came to never being seen again. Both assumed my inability to morph into the pre-Chase Kate was because of the shooting earlier this year when I was gunned down in the streets because of a case my father was working against a notoriously violent cartel. Little did they know that was just the tip of the iceberg. I wasn't about to tell them the real reason I was now so royally fucked in the head.

I tightened my fingers into fists at my side as I glared at the ceiling, silently counting down the seconds until the session was over. Every visit was the same: he'd ask questions, I would evade, maybe even sometimes respond with a hostile or bitchy answer. But I made a promise to Weston to see someone once we got back to Dallas, so here I was.

Not that I had more pressing things on my daily schedule. I just couldn't deal with this guy's fake concern and patience. If I was honest with myself, I couldn't stand to be around anyone for long periods of time anymore except Weston.

The corners of my lips tilted up at the thought of him. Even hundreds of miles away, he could still somehow make me smile.

"What are you thinking about?" the therapist asked, leaning forward in his large wingback leather chair. My chart dangled from his hands—my very thin chart. Did I mention I wasn't very forthcoming with processing my feelings?

"Oh, you know, same old, same old. Thinking about the coffee I'll buy seven minutes from now when I get to leave."

Long, dark silky strands slid along the red velvet chaise lounge as I shifted to see the frown on his finely wrinkled face from that response.

He released an exasperated sigh. Trying his patience had become a new fun game. At least I was getting something out of the near thousand-dollar session, even if it was enjoyment at his expense.

"Kate." Using two fingers, he rubbed at his temples like he was trying to keep a headache at bay. "You're not getting any better by avoiding my questions."

"I'm not getting any worse," I countered with a fake smile.

"That's your opinion," he said. "I see things differently."

Joints popped as he stood, sad eyes locked on where I lay several feet away. Tentatively, he stepped across the small office, closing the distance between us. I watched, eyes widening as he drew closer. Fear surged, jolting my pulse into overdrive, blood pounding through my veins, building heat beneath my now clammy skin. Hands on the plush cushions, I shoved myself back, scrambling out of the chaise to recover the acceptable distance between me and the man encroaching on my personal space. Pain radiated up my tailbone as my ass slammed to the floor in my hasty retreat. I scurried to get both feet under me and leapt to stand, shifting backward until my back hit the wall of windows.

His weary gaze tracked my every move, not missing a single moment of my near panic attack. "See? Kate, this is no way to live. Living in fear, with your emotions strapped down tight, will ruin any amount of joy you have in life. Talk to me, open up about what's going on inside that mind of yours. It will help." After a long pause, with no snarky comment from me, he continued. "Let's talk about the nightmares."

I tensed. "What about them?"

"Are you still having the nightmares?"

"Yes," I said through clenched teeth. "Any time I can actually fall asleep."

"Want to talk about the details? Opening up about the details, letting that fear out—"

"No." Which was my standard response every Tuesday for the past month when he asked me to relive those nightly horrors. "I don't want to talk about those."

With a disappointed shake of his head, he turned and stomped back to his chair. The slip in his emotions, displaying his obvious annoyance with me, felt like a breakthrough from my side of things. At least now I knew he *had* emotions.

"Then why are you here, Kate? Why come see me every week, pay my fees, if you refuse to talk to me during our sessions?"

Twisting around to look out the window, I studied the high-rise condo building next door, like some creepy stalker searching for activity on the hundreds of balconies. Pulling at my lip, I debated how to answer him. In the end, fessing up to the truth seemed better than another evasive, slightly hostile response.

"Because I made a promise to talk to someone about my... issues." A promise I made to Weston not that long ago and regretted every Tuesday. "I know I'm not fine. I might never be who I was before everything. Plus, just because I'm not talking to you doesn't mean I'm not talking about it with someone."

"And by someone, you mean him." I shot him a side-eyed glare at the frustration in his tone. "Based on your reaction moments ago, clearly he's not helping." Yep, I was totally going to throat-punch him. "Your father and I—"

A scoff vibrated up my throat as I rolled my eyes. "My father—" Emotions clogged my throat at the title. "—is not a part of this conversation, nor should he be involved in my treatment or notified of our sessions' outcomes. Patient confidentiality and all."

I swallowed hard at the pressure from a knot forming in my chest. The absence of my normally ever-present father this last month left a crack in my heart that oozed sorrow and grief any time I mentioned him. What made it worse was he didn't know why I continued to avoid his calls and push him away. He attempted to reach out daily, either by stopping by the townhouse or calling throughout the day, but I wasn't ready. Not when I felt betrayed by him and his insistent belief that he knew what was best for me. Dad gave Chase, Weston's contact information—which was the catalyst to Weston almost dying to protect me—in hopes Weston would leave me to join Chase's security team.

I couldn't forgive Dad for that betrayal, for going behind my back, because he assumed he knew what was best. Not yet.

Plus, when we spoke, for those few seconds he would question what happened between Chase and me for it to end overnight. Somehow Kyle had kept the media away from reporting that a well-known businessman seemed to up and disappear, his business frozen. Kyle—aka Miss Ginger, if you were one of the boys—told us they took Chase to a secure black site for questioning and to never discuss what happened that night in the warehouse with anyone other than those who were there. Fully understanding the implications if I let the truth slip, I followed the direct order, which made Kyle happy and shocked the hell out of Weston.

"I know what my father believes," I continued as I watched a woman water the various potted plants along her balcony railing. "The man he thinks is the reason why I can't move on is the only person I trust with the truth, with the details of my nightmares and memories. Casey Weston has, many times, kept me from falling apart and has continued to keep me safe. Only Weston can help me through this. Not my father, and certainly not you. And he saves me every fucking day by understanding what I've gone through."

My chest rose and fell in quick succession as each labored breath came in harsh pants with the heavy truth in my words. Weston did —*does*—save me. When he's home, he listens and wraps those strong protective arms around me, holding me tight while I cry, and when he isn't close, the long-distance texts and phone conversations keep me from... from shattering.

"That's just it, Kate. Can't you see it's not helping? In fact, it's making things worse. You're exploiting your old bodyguard as a crutch, holding on to him because he was your hero, the stable ground you needed during the situation with the gang threat. But you don't have to be worried anymore. Your father assures me the case is over and you're safe now. You don't need him anymore to feel safe. Your life before the case, before the shooting, your friends and work are the solid ground you need, or this free-falling feeling, of not having control, will continue. You're clinging to the man who's keeping you anchored in the storm that's slowly killing you. Get out, Dr. Wheeler, while you still can."

I glanced at the clock and watched the second hand tick around and around while remaining silent. There was nothing to say. Yes, the case was over, but not the memories or the feelings of guilt and shame. The heaviness of what I did with Chase sat on my chest like a damn ten-ton elephant.

This idiot sitting across the ornately decorated office from me in his fancy-schmancy cashmere sweater with that dopey soft look on his face would never understand what roared inside me. Neither would my father or my best friends. This anger and resentment were a twisted form of survivor's guilt.

But *they* did.

Kyle, Weston, Tyler, and even the jackass James. When I was around them, I didn't feel as broken. Maybe because they were a bit broken in areas too, and being surrounded by others who understood the pain from witnessing the worst humanity offered and surviving was the only form of therapy that could actually repair me.

I might never be the same Dr. Kate Wheeler I was over a year ago, and maybe that was okay.

The minute hand ticked to the hour mark, signaling this oh-so-helpful session was finally over. Without a word, I picked up my cross-body purse from the desk by the door and strode from the room, not losing one additional second of my life to that waste of time.

The moment I stepped through the revolving doors, I inhaled in a lungful of fresh hot summer air and tipped my face up to the expansive cloudless Texas sky. As I moved from where I currently blocked the door to the business building, a vibration tickled against my hip, signaling an incoming call or text. Forgoing my armored G-wagon parallel-parked three spots down from the Turtle Creek Business Park, I headed in the opposite direction, knowing deep in my soul that only a venti coffee from Starbucks would shift my current foul mood from unbearable to barely pleasant.

While digging for the vibrating phone as I started the two-block trek, my fingers brushed against the cool metal of my concealed .22, sending a wave of ease over my tense muscles. The weapon offered the only sense of safety while Weston was gone. I didn't leave home without it these days.

Lifting the phone, I squinted at the screen to see past the glare from the blazing noon sun.

Casey: Only two more days of this bullshit training, then I'll be home.

Casey: Miss Ginger has something for us. We're all meeting at your place after we're done here to discuss what he's learned and where we go from there.

Casey: How did the shrink visit go?

Casey: Did you actually talk to him, or did you ignore him while daydreaming about me and coffee?

I snorted and shook my head. He knew me too well.

Before I replied, I checked the other missed messages.

Dad: How did your visit go with Dr. Bart?

Dad: I really wish you'd talk to me.

Dad: Dinner tonight like old times?

Dad: Pumpkin, I don't know what I did, but tell me so I can make it right.

Tears welled in my lower lids, causing the screen to blur. I clicked out of the thread and went to the most recent group text conversation with Meagan and Eric, hoping for a new message I missed despite my borderline obsessive checking.

Nothing.

I swallowed back the tears I refused to let fall. *Damn these stupid emotions.*

These days, Meagan was too busy with Austin to text like we used to, and Eric... well, Eric was still pissed. After that night, when I texted him about Weston headed to the ER where we worked with a gunshot wound, things hadn't been the same between us. He wanted the full story of what happened that night and with Chase. Even if I could tell him what went down those few months, I wasn't sure I wanted to admit to what I'd done. My best friend would see me, see it all if I opened up, and I didn't want him to know what raged inside me these days.

Even Weston didn't know how much shame and guilt I harbored because of my selfish actions. He was shot, beaten to a pulp because of me. And forced to watch—

I shook my head to dislodge that line of thinking. I couldn't let myself go there, not on the busy uptown sidewalk where everyone could witness my panic. It would have to wait till later, in the dark, when I was alone and no one could see my tears or hear my sobs.

Me: Just wrapped up. Another riveting visit.

Me: I mean, I said words... so yes, I talked to him?

Casey: Are you asking me or telling me?

Me: Asking?

Casey: You're impossible.

Me: Agreed.

Me: Can't wait to see you.

Me: What does Kyle have for us? We going to Hawaii soon? I need a beach in my future, stat.

Me: Get it? Stat. A little doctor humor for you this afternoon.

Casey: Funny.

Casey: He gave no other details other than needing to meet up and that he had something for us.

Casey: You sleeping okay with me gone?

Me: Yes?

Casey: You're killing me, Smalls.

Me: Sorry?

Casey: I'm done with this conversation until you can give me a straight answer.

Me: Okay?

I cringed as I reread his sleep question. Weston knew how tough it was without him close. When I slept tucked in his arm, I slept peacefully. When he wasn't home, the nightmares woke me up in a pool of sweat. Once or twice, I'd actually fallen asleep in the corner of my bedroom with a gun squeezed between my hands. Part of the fear speared from past events, the other from the real danger I was still in. Kyle said Chase was somewhere secure and couldn't reach out to his contacts to seek revenge against me, but that did nothing to quell the constant fear that felt like a heavy blanket slowly suffocating me.

Even now as I stepped into Starbucks, the calming scent of fresh ground and brewed coffee swirling around me, I sensed them—eyes watching, waiting.

A figment of my imagination or not, it felt real as the hair stood along the back of my neck and a chill sent goose bumps along my arms.

Very real.

WITH A SHARP TURN, I whipped the SUV into the two-car garage and slammed the gearshift into Park but left the glorious AC running for a few more seconds. Sweat still clung to every inch of my skin, my thighs and the exposed areas of my upper back and shoulders sticking to the smooth expensive black leather from my only beneficial therapy: kickboxing. Every time I left the gym, some of the heaviness lifted from my chest and left my steps a little lighter. That was one thing that hadn't changed about me—punching the shit out of a dummy or sparring partner could still lighten a cranky mood.

Maybe I should be in a true anger management program instead of traditional therapy.

I shrugged off the thought, cut the growling engine, and leapt from the high seat. The moment I stepped over the threshold from the garage into the townhome, I paused. The sense of something being off inside perked my overactive paranoia. Without making a sound, I lowered the gym bag to the floor and pulled my trusty SIG SAUER from the purse still slung over my shoulder.

Heart thundering inside my chest, I stalked with silent steps down the short hall, gun gripped between both hands, the barrel aimed to the floor. At the corner of the hall leading into the open kitchen and living room area, I sealed my back to the wall to peek around.

Lungs burning from a held breath I refused to let loose, the blood thrumming in my ears dulling all sounds, I scanned the area.

Kitchen, empty.

Living room, empty.

On the balls of both feet, I moved silently through the kitchen, sliding a butcher knife free from the wooden block as I rounded the island, just in case double weapons were needed, and moved toward the guest bedroom. Palms clammy, I tightened my hold on the gun's rough grip in one hand and the smooth wooden handle of the massive knife in the other.

Overkill? Maybe. But who knew what lurked in my house, waiting for the moment I let my guard down? The reality of Chase somehow making good on his promise from that night in the warehouse, to sentence me to a life of captivity and horrors, lingered like a dark omen penetrating every thought.

"Kate?"

A petrified scream scratched up my throat, piercing my ears as I whirled around to face the confused male voice, gun and knife raised. A finger twitched over the trigger as I frantically searched the living room I swore was empty half a second ago.

A familiar head of floppy blond hair popped over the side of the couch, eyes wide with alarm as he flicked his focus from the gun pointed at his head to the knife raised high above mine.

"Holy fuck," he wheezed.

"Holy fuck," I yelled, my trembling voice giving away my fear. "What the hell are you doing here, Eric?" The gun trembled in my still outstretched hand. I couldn't bring myself to lower it just yet, the panic coursing through my veins still too strong for me to drop my guard.

"Kate," he said in a calm voice. "It's me." Both hands rose over the back of the couch, palms out—trembling. "You can put the gun down now. I'm friend, not foe, remember?" His gaze slid to the knife, his brows furrowing. "Seriously, a knife? I thought you learned your stabby lesson last year. You only hurt yourself, not the intended victim."

In a rush, the adrenaline whooshed out of me, leaving my legs weak with fatigue. I lowered both weapons, careful to not stab myself in the thigh—again—and fell back against the wall. The picture frame beside my head rattled with the impact.

For what felt like hours, we stared at each other disbelievingly as a heavy silence stretched between us.

There were no words, no comebacks or funny remarks like I used to have for my best friend, which made me sad. I was never at a loss for words with Eric, yet here I stood without a clue how to bridge the wide canyon that formed in our friendship these past few months.

"How'd you get in?" I asked, the only thing I could think of to say. The answer hit me before he could respond, as I moved to rest the gun and knife down on the coffee table. My nerves were still a little twitchy; best not to have a gun or a pointy object in each hand. "Let me guess: Weston." Eric nodded, blue eyes wary—guarded, even.

Jealousy flared, knowing those two had spoken recently. "How long have you two—" I circled a hand in the air as I searched for the right words that would portray the betrayal I felt at them talking behind my back. "—been conspiring against me."

Eric sighed, dropping his hands to the leather couch with a smack. "I'm not conspiring against you, Kate, and neither is he." I gingerly sat on the couch beside him and leaned forward to rest my elbows on each thigh, keeping a good foot between us. "I think you're handling that on your own."

"What's that supposed to mean?" I flexed my hands, working out the stiffness in my joints from the earlier sparring session and holding the handles of both weapons in a death grip.

"It means...." He blew out a breath and mirrored me. "I'm not ready to forgive you for leaving me in the dark. I know there's a lot that happened those few months with that hottie Chase and the bad-boy bodyguard Weston that you're not telling me, and I resent you for that. I resent the fact that I'm not the person you trust enough with the truth."

I released a long breath through pursed lips. "I do trust you," I admitted truthfully. "You're still my best friend, Eric. Even if things have been awkward lately."

"Don't get your granny panties in a twist," he huffed with a small smile. "He called me today. It's the first time we've talked." I twisted to rest a bent knee on the couch and hugged a throw pillow to my chest. "He's worried about you. Hell, I am too. You're not the same fierce tiny storm you were before, and I have no fucking clue why. Even though I'm mad, I can still be worried about my friend Kate."

I sank my teeth into my lower lip to hide the quivering. "I've made a mess of things," I admitted in a hushed voice. "A selfish decision put his life and others in danger. It worked out, but that confidence and fierceness you called it, I lost... that part of me is still vacant. And the guilt of what I did is suffocating me slowly day by day." I held his concerned stare. "Chase wasn't a good person, despicable actually, and I knew that when I pursued him at that charity function. I wanted to help others so much that I didn't think about myself or the others who loved me, others who could get hurt because of my rash decision."

"Kate." Eric sighed and reached over, wrapping my hand in his. "That's you. Rash Decision-making is your middle name." I huffed a laugh and dipped my chin in agreement. "That's what makes you this amazing spunk of a tiny person who I gladly call my best friend." His lips twitched in a smile. "Answer me this. Did you end up helping those people you risked your life and others for?" I nodded. "Then focus on that. I've never known you to second-guess yourself. Even in med school, when you made a mistake, you considered it a learning moment and moved on. One truth about you, you never make the same mistake twice."

I sat up straighter as his confidence-boosting words sank in deep, reminding me of who I was at the core. Something I'd desperately needed the last month. A reminder of *who* I was.

"Listen, bestie. I'm fine with pushing the 'What the hell happened, Kate?' discussion off," he said with a pointed glare. "For now. As long as you do two things for me."

I flopped back against the couch and closed my eyes with a fake annoyed groan. "What?"

"First, tell me where you're hiding the beer."

My lips quirked. "I'm not hiding it. I drank it all and haven't been back to the store." At his exasperated sigh, I peeked one eye open and found him fiddling with his phone. "What are you doing?"

"Ordering some beer. And chips. Oh, and dip, yes." He tipped his face to the ceiling like he was deep in thought. "Plus wine, ice cream, popcorn, and porn."

I barked a genuine laugh and kicked a heel against his thigh.

"Okay, the last one was a joke. Unless...."

"Why all the snack food and booze?"

He shot me an incredulous look. "Because we haven't talked more than a few sentences to each other in weeks, mostly about patients, and I need a good catchup session. And if I get you drunk, maybe you'll finally give me the juicy details about you and that hottie with a naughty body."

He smiled widely while prodding at my hip.

Just like that, the easy conversation and joking came back, and the thick wall of tension that had separated us crumbled. Launching forward from where I lay, I tackled him and wrapped both arms around his neck. His back smacked the couch under our combined weight.

"I missed you," I said, squeezing him tighter. "I'm sorry I lied to you. I'm sorry I didn't tell you. I'm just so fucking sorry for everything."

"Can't. Breathe."

Hand to the leather cushion, I pushed up and grinned down at my friend. My best friend. My best friend who was here, ready to fight for me. And maybe with him and Weston by my side, I would have enough strength to fight for myself, for confident Kate. Badass Kate, who ensnared a human trafficker and gained enough evidence to put him behind bars.

"I said two things," Eric said beneath me. Snaking his arm around my own, he pinched his nose. "You reek worse than the gerbil I pulled out of a patient's ass this morning."

My cheeks burned with the broadest smile I'd worn in what felt like months.

"Shower, got it. You order the food, and I'll wash this stink off. No one wants to hang around someone who smells like gerbil dingleberry."

Eric's features softened.

"There's my bestie. Welcome back, Kate. I missed you." I jerked and yelped in surprise when his palm slapped against my ass. "Now go shower before I vomit."

Halfway up the stairs, I paused and turned. Eric's full focus was on his phone, no doubt putting half of Eatzi's into the delivery cart.

"Hey, Eric?" He peered up through his blond lashes and raised both brows in question. "Thank you. And I'll tell you—everything. I think... I think I'm ready."

Without waiting for a response, I jogged the rest of the way up the stairs, hope building in my heart.

Maybe this was the starting point to shifting course, turning my life back around. I had two choices: either stay sad and scared, or suck it up, actually talk to my bestie and others about what happened, how it consumed me, and move on.

Moving on.

That sounded fucking fantastic to me.

2

____

What a fucking day.

Each fatigued step shot a jolt of pain up my tender shins. Last night's shift seemed longer than normal from the sheer number of patients plus the anticipation of what the day would bring. The guys' training ended yesterday, which meant Weston could arrive at the townhouse at any moment, along with the others. After two weeks of training at some black site in DC, whomever had to approve them as a consulting group for the upcoming trial assignment did so, finally.

Weston hadn't gone into detail during our infrequent calls or constant texts about what the training entailed, just that its intent was to prepare them for anything they might encounter on the types of missions the government would send them on. Such as their potential assignment in Hawaii.

Per Kyle, these groups were the vilest of all smugglers, and agents needed to be prepared for anything. Anyone and everyone was in their pockets, meaning once you landed, the only people you could trust were the ones who came with you—maybe not even the ones who sent you.

Not a comforting thought.

But I trusted Kyle wouldn't send his friends, or me, without knowing every single detail of the mission, and he'd do everything in his power to ensure we came home safely. That was the only reason I wasn't completely freaking out about tagging along on the mission. Sure, I'd demanded I go on the mission with them, to be part of the team, but after the initial shock wore off and reality set in, I worried I was getting myself in over my head once again.

Too late to back out now, though. Not that I wanted to, not really. But the anticipation built with each day and morphed into uncertainty.

The keys jingled together as I reached for the deadbolt, hovering just outside the lock as something caught my eye. Swiveling on the balls of my sore feet, I eyed the two black SUVs parallel-parked down the street with scrutiny. Their matching dark tint and government-issued license plates drove my heart into overdrive.

Shoving the thin metal into the lock, I twisted and pushed the door open in one move. The front door swung open, banging against the wall. Depositing my bags at the threshold, I raced down the short hall toward the ruckus of arguing male voices.

Their argument stopped the moment I barreled around the corner. My stomach flipped at the sight of the men crowding around my living room. I scanned the room, searching for the one my heart was desperate to see.

Kyle's intense gaze locked with mine from where he stood in front of the TV, lording over the others. He offered an acknowledging nod. Tyler smiled from his spot leaning against the wall, that damn mischievous smile parting his lips. James, as always, looked pissed as hell—at me or the world, fuck if I knew.

My breath hitched at the tense features of the man who paused his obvious frantic pacing along the far wall.

Weston.

My Casey.

A soft, pitiful, desperate whimper crawled up my throat when our eyes met. We moved at the same time toward the other with the same sense of urgency. Thick powerful arms encircled my shoulders, hauling me against a solid chest with a desperation I felt deep in my soul. I wrapped my arms around him, hands fisting his snug T-shirt as I inhaled his unique masculine scent.

Utter exhaustion consumed me from the inside out at the sense of ultimate security in his presence. The little strength I had left vanished, turning my leg muscles to useless noodles. Only his firm hold kept me from sliding to the floor in a happy, content Kate puddle.

Weston shifted his hold, lifting me higher until only my toes brushed the floor. Eyes closed, face buried in the tight muscle of his shoulder, I didn't see the room spin as he turned.

Then we were moving.

"Go somewhere else for a while," Weston said over his other shoulder as he climbed the stairs.

"Can I stay and listen?"

My lips brushed the soft black cotton as a smile grew at Tyler's inappropriate comment.

Weston's movement paused, and he half turned. The look he shot Tyler and the others must have conveyed annoyance and the promise of death, because it sent the boys into action. The sound of grumbling and moving feet reached my ears as we hit the landing at the top of the stairs.

"Pussy whipped."

I peered over Weston's shoulder and flipped James the bird. I returned his scowl until we rounded the corner of the master bedroom.

The door slammed shut behind us. With the tension thrumming through Weston's strained muscles, I expected to be tossed on the bed and ravaged. Maybe hoped more than expected. But he didn't do either. Not loosening his hold, he toed off his boots and kneeled on the comforter.

A pillow molded around my head as he laid us along the top of the unmade bed.

"Casey," I whispered against his skin, exhaustion clear in my weak voice. Yet I wanted him. Craved that connection that only came when we were skin to skin. Now if I could muster up enough energy to take off my scrubs and his clothes, that was debatable.

"Shh, baby. Sleep. Then we... talk." I felt his smile along the crown of my head. "You're safe with me. I'll chase the nightmares away."

A soft sigh escaped my parted lips at the thought of sleep—good, deep sleep in his protective hold. Snuggling closer, finding just the right spot curled against him with his chest as a pillow, I allowed my heavy lids to flutter shut.

This.

Us.

I would never get enough.

I AWOKE WITH A START, ripped out of a vivid dream of unwanted hands caressing my trembling body and restraints preventing me from breaking free. Breaths coming in quick pants, I squirmed against the heavy presence keeping me pinned in place. Panic raced through my veins, turning my movements frantic as I tried to break free.

"Baby, it's me. It's Casey. You're safe." I stilled my desperate attempts at freedom. Blinking away the haze, I searched the face hovering an inch above my own. Weston's features were tight with worry. His dark brown eyes narrowed as he searched my face. "You're safe."

I nodded my understanding, unable to speak from my bone-dry throat. Weston stayed hovering, his nose brushing my own until I relaxed against the mattress and each breath came easier than the last. Only then did his own tension fade.

"I'm okay," I breathed. Reaching up, cupping his scruff-covered cheek, I rubbed a thumb along his cheekbone. "Just a bad dream."

"They're not getting better." A statement, not a question. "Kate," he chastised like I was in trouble.

"Don't start." I slipped two fingers over his parted lips before he could suggest, again, that I abort the crazy idea of accompanying them on the Hawaii mission. "Just kiss me."

His features softened before a heated gleam lit behind his knowing eyes. "You giving the orders now, tiny one?"

I smirked and nodded. "What happened to 'Your Majesty'?"

His soft chuckle vibrated along my ribs, where his chest pressed against my own. "Yes, Your Majesty." I exhaled at the first brush of his lips, which morphed into a moan as a bite of pain burst from a quick nip to my lower lip. "But as much as I want this to go further, the boys are back and waiting."

An annoyed whimper slipped out. "It's been weeks Casey." Eyes wide and pleading, lip stuck out in a full-on pout, I batted my dark lashes. "I need you, now."

So much truth filled those words.

"As if I could say no to you," he murmured as he planted soft kisses along the column of my neck.

Well, that was easy.

I smiled up at the ceiling as warm fingers dipped beneath my top. Hot calloused skin skimmed higher and higher along my stomach. A needy groan vibrated in my throat when he palmed my breast, squeezing almost to the point of pain.

Wiggling along the bed, I urged him to continue his exploration. Abandoning my neck, Weston pressed his lips to mine in a possessive, hard kiss, parting my lips with his tongue, demanding entry. I melted into the bed, savoring the sheer domination of his lips and hands, giving him full control. Dipping beneath my tight sports bra, he brushed a short nail over my pebbled nipple before pinching it between two fingers.

Air caressed my ribs and back as I arched off the bed.

More.

More.

More.

I needed so much more to feel that connection with him, for his presence to chase away the remaining panic from the horrible dream.

"Casey," I pleaded. "I need you, us. No more playing around."

Without leaving my lips, he yanked the elastic bands of my scrub bottoms and underwear down to my knees. My lips parted on a gasp when he plunged three fingers deep inside me without warning.

"Fuck, baby." Leaving a trail of my wetness along the inside of my thigh, he ripped the scrubs off and tossed them to the floor. Twisting, he turned us, hooking one of my legs over his thigh as he lay back on the bed. I ground my damp center against his erection, still confined behind his dark jeans. Weston hissed through clenched teeth. "Lift up, baby."

The bed molded around my knees. Immediately two fingers sank into my wet center, his thumb circling my swollen nub. I ground against his hand, loving the heat and passion flaring in his dark eyes as he flicked the button of his jeans and hastily ripped the zipper down.

I waited impatiently for him to slam into me the moment his hard cock sprang free. Instead, he palmed himself as he watched his fingers slip in and out between my thighs.

Praise and filthy promises whispered past his lips as he tugged on himself and teased me with curling fingers, hitting a certain spot that made my legs weak.

Enough of him teasing me. He shouldn't be the only one having a bit of fun.

Pitching forward, I shoved my bare ass high in the air and lowered my face to his rippled stomach, kissing each flexing muscle as I moved farther down. Hazel eyes locked with his, I flicked the tip of my tongue along the slick head of his cock before wrapping my lips around it to lap at the drop of precum along the slit.

With a barked curse, he gripped beneath my shoulders and jerked me higher, positioning my entrance just above his head, wet with my saliva. He thrust upward while hauling me down with a firm grip on both hips.

Our combined groans mingled in the warm bedroom. Needing movement, I pressed both palms to his chest and tried to rise up, but his tight grip on my hips kept me sealed to him.

"I love you so damn much, Kate." With those words, he lifted me until only the tip of his cock stayed snug inside and then jerked me down, impaling me in the best way possible. Over and over, he lifted my slight weight, controlling our cadence.

Warmth bloomed in my lower belly, twisting and tingling as he filled me over and over. Chasing that feeling, I pressed against his chest, picking up the pace, chasing the orgasm I'd craved since the day he left for training. Sweat slicked along my forehead and the back of my neck as I worked myself up and down his hard length.

Releasing one hip, he cupped my jaw, his gaze locked on his thumb as he shoved it between my parted lips. I sealed them around him, sucking and flicking the tip of my tongue against the soft pad. Darkness clouded his already hooded gaze as I rode him, his attention darting from my mouth to where our lower halves joined.

Popping his thumb free, he pressed the slick digit against my swollen bundle of nerves and flicked.

The coiled pleasure burst within me, my stomach hollowing out as I squeezed around him. A soft cry crept up my throat as I tipped my head back, savoring every glorious sensation. A hissed curse met my ears as his hard thrusts slowed.

A sweaty palm cupped the back of my neck, tugging me forward until our foreheads sealed together.

I smiled.

He smiled.

And in that moment, I knew even with my fucked-up-ness, everything would be okay, because we finally had each other.

After a shower—then another to clean up from the sweaty quickie against the tile wall—I pulled on a pair of lounge pants and an oversized sweatshirt before whipping my long dark hair into a messy knot on top of my head. Ready to see the others and hear what Kyle offered, we descended the stairs, the yummy aroma of pizza and garlic bread greeting us halfway down.

My stomach growled as I eyed the display along the bar. With a squeeze to my hand, Weston urged me toward the food to rummage through the four open pizza boxes. Choosing to ignore the sudden silence that blanketed the room the moment we emerged and now the sense of eyes on me, I bypassed the food for the coffee maker.

"About time."

I clenched my teeth in annoyance at the sound of James's grating-ass voice. And that tone. He was damn lucky I just got off twice, or I'd use the spare gun one drawer over and cap his ass.

"Good to know the time apart didn't do shit for your jackass personality," I cooed over my shoulder. After filling the filter with fresh grounds, I tapped the Start button, then turned and leaned against the counter with a single raised brow in James's direction.

He sneered and lifted a water bottle to his lips.

I narrowed my eyes, scanning his features to figure out what was different about him. The asshole appeared to be the same jackass, yet... not. There was a healthy glow to his previously sickly complexion, his eyes less dark and tormented. If I wasn't mistaken, he'd also gained weight, which was needed. Even his hair looked healthier.

I shot a questioning side-eye look to Weston as he handed me a plate topped with two slices of cheese pizza. He simply nodded, acknowledging my observation, and shoved a whole slice of supreme pizza into his mouth.

Men.

"Are you two ready, or do I need to distract the kids a little longer?" Kyle's heavy tone drew my attention back to the reason they were all sitting in my living room.

"If I'm disruptive, will Tink be the one to punish—"

"Shut the fuck up, Mouse," James and Weston barked in unison.

"Party poopers." Tyler's eyes danced with humor as he rolled a brown glass bottle between his palms, its peeled label littering the coffee table.

Tendrils of steam rose from the white ceramic mug as streams of dark liquid splashed inside. Despite the scalding temperature, I lifted the mug to my lips and took a tentative sip, savoring the bold flavors that wafted up my nose and slid across my tongue.

With a hand pressed against my lower spine, Weston guided me toward the group waiting impatiently in the living room. His thick jean-clad thigh brushed against my own as we settled next to each other on the leather couch. Fully aware of the growing tension in the room, I wiggled until I was snug against Weston's side before gesturing to Kyle.

"You may proceed." His red brows rose along his forehead, forming three thin lines along his fair, freckled skin. "What?"

Thin lips pressed into a tight line as he shook his head. "I'm not sure you're taking this seriously, Kate. What I'm about to ask the guys—"

"And me."

Kyle's face pinched with a grimace. "That's still to be determined—"

"Like hell it is," I snarled through gritted teeth. "I either go with you guys and am a part of this mission, or I go on my own. I thought we covered this already?"

Kyle reached up to massage the back of his neck. "We did, but now that you've had time to think about it, we'd hoped you would've thought this through and changed your mind." His green eyes bored into me. "The shock has worn off now, Kate. Are you sure you're ready to put yourself back into the line of fire knowing what happened in that warehouse—"

I startled at Weston's snapped command for Kyle to shut the hell up. Reaching over, I laid a hand over his thigh and gave it a gentle, comforting squeeze. Sometimes I forgot that what happened that night didn't just change me. Sure, I lived with the memory of Chase's roaming unwanted hands, but Weston, a born protector, was forced to watch while restrained across the room, unable to make the horrors stop.

What nightmares haunted him at night?

"You're a smart woman, Kate. Are you ready to potentially give your life or more pieces of yourself to help a bunch of women you don't know?"

I stared at him, never dropping his hard stare as I thought over his words. It wouldn't be easy or without more bumps and bruises— mentally and physically. What Kyle and the others didn't know about me was I'd wanted something more for my life for a while now. Wanted more than the hospital, more than Dallas, more than being an oil heiress.

A growing part of me needed to be more than those labels and titles.

Shifting my gaze to Tyler, I searched his face, which held a hint of worry beneath the cocky exterior. Sliding to James, who still sat pressed against the wall with his knees bent and forearms resting on top, I only found contempt and anger, yet maybe a flicker of hope.

"What do you think?" I asked.

A cruel smirk danced along James's full lips. Instantly I regretted asking him that question, but I knew he'd shoot me straight.

"I think you're a fool believing you'd walk out of this unscathed. No sane person would willingly sign up for this. Not with what we'll witness."

"You willingly signed up. What does that say about you?"

"Honey, I've already seen and experienced the worst we humans can do to each other. Those images are already branded into my brain." He thumped the heel of his palm against his temple. "And I'd do fucking anything to unsee it all."

I smirked behind my coffee mug. "So you're trying to protect me?" That cruel smile fell to a frown. "It's okay. I know you're still the same miserable prick." Dismissing him completely before he could respond, I twisted on the couch to face Weston. "And you?"

He released a resigned sigh and set his empty plate on the coffee table. "I want you safe. That you already know." I opened my mouth, but he pressed three fingers against my lips, stopping me. "But I also know when you set your mind to something, there's nothing stopping you. I'd rather you be with us where I can keep you safe by my side than coming up with your own plan and ending up somewhere I can't save you."

A swirl of emotions squeezed my chest, shortening my tight breaths.

"Well—" I cleared my throat. "—there you go." Turning back to Kyle, I dipped my chin in confirmation. "I know it won't be easy, and I understand the risks. This is what I want, to help those who can't help themselves. To free those who are out there right now, this very second, praying for someone to save them from the world someone trapped them inside. The reward, what we'll accomplish—together— far outweighs the risks."

"You're not trained," James grumbled. "You'll be a liability. Putting us at risk. You okay with that, Doc?"

"Sure, I don't have y'all's training, but I'm not completely ignorant. Look what I did with Chase." I grimaced just saying his name. "I'm resourceful and can handle my own. I know I won't be as involved as you guys, but I will not be left behind either."

"Enough, Axe," Weston growled. "She's coming with us. Accept it and move on."

I smiled fiendishly at the win, rewarding me with a middle finger from the grumpy man. Snickering to myself, I looked to our redheaded leader.

"Now that that's taken care of, what do you know, Kyle?"

My courage and happiness fell at the grief that flashed across Kyle's fair face before his typical emotionless mask fitted back into place.

Fuck. That can't be good.

3

———

I swallowed down a gulp of coffee and leaned forward, everyone's attention on Kyle as he paced in a brief clip.

"We have little on the traffickers we believe are operating out of Hawaii. What we've been able to gather is that seven months ago, this group moved their operations from the Philippines to this new location. Apparently taking tourists and locals around the various islands is easier than transporting women from abroad to the States." With that tidbit, he stormed to the kitchen, returning moments later with a steaming cup of coffee in one hand. "We don't know how they're targeting the local victims or how they're moving those and others off the island. Smitson's involvement was only a fraction of the transportation plan."

"Are they getting them to the mainland and selling them here?" Tyler questioned, his normally mischievous attitude now grave with the heavy topic.

"Yes and no." A soft hum of approval sounded through the room as Kyle took a long sip from the full mug. "This is damn good. Better than the shit I have to drink at the office." I nodded, accepting his compliment, desperately wanting to ask him more about this office he never told us about. "Half of the victims are shipped, which is where that fucker Smitson came into play. He was their transporter, taking the girls from Hawaii to all along the West Coast. We assume they have another lined up for the East Coast. After questioning Smitson, we discovered he first started working with a cartel moving drugs, but a better deal came across the table with the human traffickers."

"Are you saying the cartel allowed some unknown to come in and use their smuggling channel without a fight?" Weston mused beside me.

Kyle shook his head. "They made a bargain."

"What in the hell could a new trafficker offer a cartel?" James asked. "That makes little sense."

"A piece of the profits," I whispered, knowing exactly why this would happen. "The cartels are getting smarter. They can sell a brick of coke once or a woman multiple times a night for years. There's greater profit in the exploitation of women than drugs."

"Exactly right, Kate. As sick as it sounds to us, all these bastards see are dollar signs." A sadness enveloped him like a gray cloud as he stared at the wall. "We've worked to shut down as many of these human trafficking rings as possible, but new ones keep popping up ever damn day."

"Who's this 'we'?" I asked. Maybe he'd finally open up and tell us exactly which agency he worked for. Even the guys were clueless, which eased the sting of not knowing.

That sadness evaporated with a sly smile. "Nice try, Doc."

"And the other half?" Weston asked. "You said half are shipped to the mainland. What about the other half?"

"They're sold in Hawaii."

"That should make them easy to find. I've never been to Hawaii, but I'm pretty sure the island can't be too big." Tyler's features shifted from a hopeful smile to a disappointed frown at the shake of Kyle's head.

"They're sold in auction-type settings to the highest bidder, never to be seen again." The room went quiet. "Only international businessmen, and some women, are invited to attend these auctions.

They're virtually impossible to find since they change locations and dates with each event. We don't know when they'll happen until it's too late and the girls are sold, then vanish with their buyers. At that point it's the buyer's responsibility to smuggle them out, but considering these fuckers are known in the underworld, they slip out easily with their new purchases."

"Fuck," James huffed. "How is this happening on American soil?"

My muscles tensed at the anger trembling in his voice.

"Because there are always people willing to buy."

The depressing silence that filled the room made the ball of dread rolling in my stomach grow larger.

"Where does that leave us?" Weston stood and began pacing along the back of the couch. I didn't fail to notice that he stayed within arm's reach of where I sat. "Sounds like you know the basics, which won't help shit. We don't have a clue how to infiltrate this group."

Infiltrate.

That word stuck with me as I processed everything Kyle revealed.

"Have you tried to get anyone on the list to the auctions?" I asked, my stare locked on the now empty coffee mug cupped between my hands.

"Yes, but nothing has worked. We lost the last agents who went in undercover. We found their bodies—"

James's, Tyler's, and Weston's objections to the unknowns and hazards of this mission drowned out whatever Kyle said next.

Agent.

Another word that stuck in my head.

"What if it wasn't an agent at all though?" I mused loud enough to be heard over the three fighting male voices. Their arguing stopped as they all turned their attention to me. "Isn't that why you brought this group into the picture?"

Kyle tipped the white mug back, downing what was left inside before nodding. "But we still don't know how to access the auction or how to get one of the guy's names on the list. We don't have a contact who would vouch for whoever we sent in. These bastards are ruthless, and if they discover the person who vouched for a fed, he and his family would be tortured and scattered around the globe as a warning to future rats."

I grimaced and nestled farther into the couch.

"What about Smitson?" James asked. "You still have him at that black site, right?"

"We do, but I can't risk any of his contacts knowing we're investigating this operation. You'd be captured the moment you stepped off the plane. Everyone knows everyone in the smuggling world."

I nodded. Even Ryan knew—

My cup clattered to the rug as I jolted up and turned to face Weston. The sound of several guns being cocked filled my ears. Slowly, hands up in surrender, I turned and took in the three men at my back. All had their guns raised, each barrel aimed at a different point of entry.

"Jittery much?" I breathed with a forced chuckle. "I just had a thought. No imminent danger, guys." One by one, they each holstered their guns. "I have an idea, but you might not like it."

"You're not putting yourself in danger over there. I will not allow you to be caught—"

"What?" I scoffed.

"What?" Weston glared down at me and stepped closer until we were toe to toe. "I figured you were about to suggest using yourself as bait."

I tilted my head one way, then the other, weighing his assumption. "Who, me? That's absurd."

"It's not like you haven't done it before, Tink. As in recently."

Behind my back, I raised a middle finger at Tyler. His rumbling laugh made a smile tug at the corners of my lips, despite the heavy topic.

The tension on Weston's handsome face slipped. "Okay, then. Prove me wrong. What's this idea of yours?"

"Hear me out before you say no." That tension returned in a flash to his pinched features as he crossed his arms over his chest. My traitorous eyes studied the movement of his flexing tatted muscles to the armband of his T-shirt stretched to the max.

"I'm listening."

I wrangled my hormones back under control, dragging my gaze upward. A spark of heat flashed in his brown eyes. Oh yeah, he knew exactly where my mind had drifted.

Oops.

But we'd been apart for so long. I hated the time we wasted—no, *I* wasted away from him while I devised and executed my takedown of the fucker who was shipping women.

"Your brother."

That heat in his gaze vanished.

"What about my brother?"

"Remember how before you knew about my ultimate, amazing, slightly flawed plan to take down Chase, Ryan did?" His lips pursed. I'd take that as a yes. "Well, one night, he told me to stay away from him. That he knew the people he dealt with, and they weren't the best of people."

"So?"

I pulled my brows together and narrowed my eyes. "So that means we have someone to vouch for us. We can send in—"

"No." Without another word, he turned and stomped to the kitchen. Glass bottles clinked against one another when he jerked the fridge door open. "We are not pulling my brother into this."

"Shouldn't that be his decision?" I pressed.

"I said no, Kate, and that's final."

I swear you could've heard a mouse fart, the room went so quiet and still. I wasn't even sure the other guys were breathing. Like they knew Weston had just lit a fuse tied to an unpredictable, extremely destructive bomb.

"What did you just say to me?" My voice was steady with an edge of crazy to it.

He didn't turn, just slammed the fridge closed and twisted a cap off a beer bottle.

"You heard what Miss Ginger said about what happens to those who open the door for the feds. They die, as does everyone they've ever known. You're asking me to put my baby brother's life on the line, and I said no. End of discussion."

"Wow," I mouthed, unable to get the actual word out. Closing my eyes, I took several deep inhales and slow exhales to calm the many slightly overreactive responses running through my head.

"Casey, I get it's your brother, but is it not worth the risk? This could be the one shot we have to get behind enemy lines, so to speak. If anything goes wrong or they leak his name as the source to get us into the auction, Kyle's employer can protect him." I looked to my right, brows raised in question. "Right?"

"Yes and no. He'd have to leave that life behind after all this was said and done. There would be no going back. Which, from what I know about Ryan from Romeo here, wouldn't be a bad thing."

I turned back to Weston with hope written across my face. "See, it could be a win-win. Ryan is a good guy who's just made a lot of bad choices in his life. Maybe this could be his chance to free himself, to start over. At least be open to the idea of giving *him* the option to say yes or no. You know he won't turn on you if he decides this isn't the right path for him. He wouldn't leak our plan. There's nothing to lose."

"There is if he says yes," Weston said into the bottle pressed to his lower lip.

"We're giving him the option, and that's final." I dared him with my hard stare to say something back.

His shoulders slumped, and he scrubbed a hand over his face.

"Knew that comment would come back to bite me in the ass." He huffed, almost in defeat. "Just thought the consequence would be me not making it to tomorrow."

I smiled and turned to Kyle. "Okay, that's taken care of. What next?"

The blood seeped from his lips as he pressed them together, suppressing a smile. "Now we wait. Again." I deflated a little at the idea. "But while we do, we can make a few preparations."

"Such as?" Tyler asked.

"Such as if we can score an invitation to one of these auctions, we need to create an infallible background for the person going. My tech guys can take care of the online search history, but we need to determine who from this group will be the potential buyer."

I glanced between James, Tyler, and Weston, who'd joined us once again in the living room. "Any volunteers?" I asked, hope lifting my voice.

"I'll do it," James grunted.

"You would play the part of arrogant asshole well." My smile widened at his answering curse. "Joking aside, you fit the idea of a dark, demented businessman better than these two."

"Thanks?" Tyler laughed from his spot on the floor. He fluffed the throw pillow behind his head and closed his eyes. "What about me and Romeo?"

"And me," I added. "Security." Three sets of eyes focused on me. "You two as his personal security, and I can play—" I thought for a second. "—his personal doctor. You use me to take care of your purchased girls back home." I shivered at the thought of what all that would entail. I'd seen enough from Second Chances to know a full-time doctor would be needed for a larger operation.

Kyle rubbed at his chin, seemingly deep in thought. "Possibly. Right now we'll focus on Axe as the buyer and start his background and these two as his personal security. Until we hear from Romeo's brother, that's about all we can do."

I cocked my head to the side. "What about you in all this? Will you be with us on the mission if it all works out?"

Kyle shook his head. "No. I'm best utilized to run point from here."

Well, at least we had something.

Hopefully Ryan would respond sooner than later.

And be open to risking his life to help us.

We'd know soon enough.

"I NEED A COFFEE IV DRIP," I grumbled to Eric, who blocked my way to the computer. "Is it just me, or are our shifts getting harder and longer?"

"We're just getting older and slower," he said, sounding just as tired as I did. "Medical school was a long time ago, friend."

Seeing as many patients as we did this shift would do that to you. There had to be a full moon, because the strangest cases came out of the woodwork tonight. At least I hadn't run into Austin, which was the only positive I could say about the shift.

Eric and I talked—more like mumbled—while we finished up the charts and entered everything into the system. The moment we both wrapped up, we hurried out the door with a quick hug and air kiss before parting ways.

I pulled at my lower lip. An unknown worry had my stomach in knots as I walked the short distance home. Something besides the strange and long shift had me worked up, but I couldn't put my finger on it. Maybe it was the waiting and unknowns regarding the mission that tried my patience daily. It had been over a week since Weston reluctantly reached out to his brother, asking him if he'd help us out, even with the potential consequences. Ryan said yes, eager for the chance to start over. Apparently he'd grown tired of drug running, cartel wooing, and crime evading but didn't know how to get out. Then out of the blue we offered him the opportunity of a lifetime.

Go me.

Well, go us. Kyle and his merry band of friends with whichever agency he worked for would do the hard work of relocating and erasing Ryan Weston from existence. I was just the cute, brilliant, stunning, courageous woman who thought of the idea.

So yeah, go me.

Even if Weston was still slightly irritated about the whole thing, I counted it as a win.

Since Ryan accepted his part of the mission and began asking around the crime underworld about human auctions in Hawaii, the guys had been bored. To say it was getting cramped and annoying in my townhome was an understatement.

Hopefully we'd find out some information soon to give the guys something to do besides lie around watching survival shows all day.

At the front door, loud voices vibrated through, signaling the guys were waiting inside, again. Not ready to be around them just yet, I spun on the balls of my feet and plopped down on the top step. My bags dropped to the sidewalk with a loud *thunk*. Elbows on my knees, I rested my face in both open hands. Out here, it was quiet, no stinky men filling my space and making sounds that belonged in a damn zoo and not my townhome.

Out here, even with the sounds of a bustling city, it was peaceful.

The door behind me clicked, and a gust of cooled air brushed along the back of my neck.

Well, it *was* peaceful.

"What are you doing out here?"

Dropping one hand, I patted the small square space of cement beside me, beckoning Weston to join me. The door clicked shut a second before a pair of black boots stopped next to me. "Not the same as Aiden's place, but peaceful in its own way, I guess."

The bright morning sun warmed my face as I tipped it up to Weston and smiled. With a few groans and pops, he settled down beside me, tossing an arm over my shoulders to pull me against his side.

"Bad day?" he asked after a few minutes of silence.

"Yes, but no. Just exhausting. I don't know how much longer I can take waiting to hear from Kyle. I'm in this constant state of limbo, and I hate it. I need a plan. I've always had a plan and been in control." I pushed away at his scoff. "What? I have."

"Baby, none of us has control over life. We can plan, but shit happens."

"Like a death note from a notoriously vicious cartel that leads a sexy bodyguard into your life?"

His eyes narrowed at the question. "Yes," he ground out. "Exactly like that."

"But this limbo is killing me slowly. I'm tired."

"You're sleeping better at night, right?"

I smiled at the worry in his tone. "Yes, now that you're here."

"Well, I hate to tell you this, because it's not good news," he said with a resigned sigh. Reaching over, he stroked a finger down the side of my face. "No more waiting. Ryan got back to me. We have a lead."

His hand dropped to his thigh when I leapt up. My toe caught the edge of the stair in my hasty retreat, tipping me forward. I slammed my palm on the front door, catching myself before I could face-plant to the faded brown welcome mat. Ignoring Weston's chuckle at my expense, I hurried inside, leaving the door wide open behind me.

My sneakers skidded along the tile as I pulled to an abrupt stop at the full attention of the three men. Kyle appeared pensive, Tyler worried, and James... well, James looked fucking smug.

Oh, I hate him so much.

"What?" I asked. "Wait." I held up a finger and stepped to the coffee pot, only to find it already freshly brewed. Twisting at the waist, I shot Weston an appreciative grin as he came into the kitchen, dropping the bags I'd forgotten on top of the island.

"Figured you'd want some."

Yep, he's totally getting laid tonight.

"What's this not good news?" I asked, busying myself with retrieving a mug and keeping one ear open to hear a response. But one didn't come. The empty mug dangled from my fingers as I leaned against the counter. "What is it?"

The other three ignored my question and avoided my pointed look.

"Come on, guys, just tell—"

"The plan won't work." I whipped my head in Kyle's direction. "The auction we have a lead on is... different from the others. Fuck, we didn't know anything like this even existed." Kyle ran thin fingers through his red hair, making it frizz with the movement. "It's a dead end."

"No." I refused to accept the fact that we'd waited, that they'd trained—hell, that everything we'd put into this was for nothing. "Explain. Why is it different?"

Again the room went silent.

"It's for couples and their current pets." I narrowed my eyes at James. "The next auction is for couples who are looking to upgrade or add to their collection."

I cringed at the word "pet," even though it was 100 percent accurate.

"This... this is what Ryan brought to the table?" I questioned, my voice weak.

"It's the only one he could get a lead on," Weston said as he sat on a stool and pressed both elbows to the granite countertop.

"And we're sure it's the same group you've heard about, been trying to track down?" I asked Kyle while thinking through the different options they might have overlooked. I thought outside the box, unlike my military-trained friends in the room.

"Yes. This auction, though slightly different, should be operated by the same traffickers. They've taken over the trade there in Hawaii, so I can't imagine they'd allow competition to host an auction on their soil without backlash."

Nodding, I turned back to the coffee maker and stared at the black, scrumptious liquid inside the glass carafe, hoping it held the answers we needed.

"So your concern is that we only have James's profile created and not a couple's?" I questioned.

"Among other things." I glanced over my shoulder to Weston. Tension radiated off him as he gripped the edge of the island.

"We could do it."

"Kate."

I bristled at Weston's chastising tone.

Turning back to face the group, I leaned against the rounded corner of the counter. "Hear me out. Could you alter James's new profile by adding a low-profile wife?" I asked Kyle.

"Well, yeah, but we don't have anyone."

"Don't you dare suggest yourself, Kate."

Ignoring Weston's order, I stared Kyle down as another name popped in my head. "Of course not me. Like someone of my caliber would be married to that jackass." I hooked a thumb in the scowling man's direction for emphasis. "What about Anne?"

Kyle's eyes bounced from me to Weston and back. "We could ask, but I think she's working in Austin already." He massaged his chin, thinking through my suggestion as he slowly nodded. "But that could work."

"You're fucking kidding me. You're actually considering this?"

I held up a hand to shut Weston up. A bolt of jealousy weaseled its way inside my head, wondering if he didn't want Anne on the assignment because he didn't want her hurt, still protective of her like he was with me. I didn't want my grumpy, overprotective, sexy body-guard worrying about any woman but me.

I shook my head to dislodge the thought.

"But that still leaves us without someone to take as their current... acquisition."

I nodded, thinking that tiny problem over in my head.

Then it hit me.

"What about me?"

4

A mix of curses, a loud scoff, and a very inappropriate slow clap filled the kitchen. I laughed at Tyler, the slow clapper, and rolled my eyes.

"What's the applause for?" I questioned wearily while pouring myself a cup of coffee.

"You never cease to surprise me, so I just thought that shocking offer deserved an applause," Tyler said, smirking like always.

What in the hell did he find so funny all the time? It was almost like seeing the best in any situation. The joy in the world was a part of him, in his soul.

That 100 percent was not a quality I held.

"You're too old, princess." James scoffed with a humorless huff. "No one in their right mind would buy a woman in their forties."

Coffee sloshed over my hand, burning the skin, when I slammed the mug to the counter. My thigh muscles bunched as I bolted around the island to punch the smirking fucker in the balls. An arm hooked around my waist, stopping my attack.

"I'm not forty, you asshole," I hissed, fighting to get out of Weston's hold. "And I don't look old."

James tilted his head as if considering my statement. "Yeah, maybe with some Botox—"

"You're dead," I yelled. Abandoning any sense of decorum, I upped my efforts to dislodge Weston's arm. Instead, Weston stood and hauled me off my feet, my legs kicking through the empty air. "Let go of me, you damn brute. Let me kill him."

Weston's chest vibrated against my back. I twisted in his hold to scowl at my soon-to-be ex-boyfriend if he didn't quit laughing.

"No death and dismemberment today, baby." He pressed a kiss to my forehead. "He's just being the prick he always is. He's not worth the jail time."

"I don't look old," I grumbled.

"No you don't." Weston's lips tugged into an almost smile that had the fight draining from me.

"Romeo's just saying that because you're fucking him."

"Shut the hell up, Axe," Weston snapped at his friend. "I'm trying to save your damn life here."

James's scoff filled the room. "She could try."

Closing both eyes, I took several deep, calming breaths to ease the blood thundering in my ears from the anger spike.

"I'm petite," I said as calmly as I could. "Change up my clothing, hairstyle, and without makeup, yes, I could pass for someone much younger than me." Probably. But I couldn't let them see a hint of doubt. I had to sell this. "That could be the reason for our fake couple to be at the auction, to upgrade to a younger girl." My stomach soured at the words, knowing that actually happened daily around the world. "Before you shoot me down, at least give me a chance to dress the part."

"Baby, you're not putting yourself in that kind of situation again. I don't want—" Weston shook his head and blew out a heavy breath. "I can't watch that again, can't sit back with you in a direct line of danger."

"But would I be?" Having collected myself—somewhat—I wiggled out of Weston's hold and turned in his arms to face Kyle. He was the mastermind; if I could convince him, then maybe we had a shot at seeing this through. "Hear me out. You said it was couples who were looking to upgrade their current captives. Right?" Kyle nodded, checking with Weston to verify. "So how would I ever be in danger? The couples wouldn't allow their current captives out of their sight until they had a replacement. The risk of being without would be too high for these assholes. So that means I would truly just be playing the part, under all of your watchful eyes. Hell, you could even put Weston as my personal guard, telling them I was a flight risk, tried to run before. So how would I be in danger?"

The four men exchanged wary glances.

Kyle was the first one to speak up, as expected. "What about at the auction? What if they're looking for the buyers to offer their current captives as trade-ins? What then?"

I picked at my lower lip, eyes focused on the floor.

Think, Kate.

Think.

"If that happens, well, it could benefit us."

"How?" Weston shoved both hands into the front pockets of his jeans and leaned a hip against the granite counter. "How could you being out of our sight with human traffickers who have no fucking morals work in our favor?"

I reached out and gripped his forearm, sliding my hand down until he held my hand.

"Because then I'd be taken back to their holding location, or better yet their training or preparation site."

"What's that?" Tyler asked, his nose scrunched in confusion.

Disgust sealed my throat, making my next words raspy. "Where they break the girls. Beat them into submission and there's nothing left of the women they used to be. All traffickers have some kind of housing site like that. It has to be remote or at least in an area where the neighbors won't call the cops."

"She's right." Pride flared in my chest at Kyle's words. "It would get us deeper into the inner workings of this group, making it easier to infiltrate." Weston's fingers squeezed around my shoulder. "But if—and that's a big fucking *if*, Kate—this gets approved and Romeo here doesn't kill me for agreeing with your crazy idea, you being alone with any of those fuckers won't be a part of the plan. It's too dangerous to consider unless it's absolutely necessary."

He blew out a heavy breath and tipped his head back, eyes closed.

"It's unorthodox, but that could be the reason it works. I'll call Hawk—"

"Hawk?" I asked.

"Anne."

"Okay... why Hawk?"

"Because she has eyes like a damn bird. She's one of the best snipers I've ever met." I raised a brow at James, surprised by not only his praise for the woman but also the pride that leaked through his steady, gruff tone. "Which is why I suggest we find someone else to play my partner. We need her outside watching our backs."

"Wow. That's...."

"Intimidating? Scared, Doc?"

"Hot." Weston tensed behind me. "Don't get any ideas," I grumbled and playfully elbowed him in the gut.

"I'll see if we can come up with an agent willing to play your counterpart, Axe. Good idea about Hawk. She'd be nice to have ensuring shit didn't go sideways while you're there." Kyle dug into the front pocket of his gray slacks and slipped his phone free. "I need to make a few hundred calls. We probably won't know anything until tomorrow."

At that, he wandered into the guest bedroom and quietly shut the door behind him.

The exhaustion from the earlier shift and the heaviness of the conversation hit me full force. I melted against Weston, allowing my lids to flutter closed as his naturally scorching body heat seeped through my shirt, relaxing my tight muscles.

"Come on." The words brushed across my ear, fanning along my cheek.

Without protest, I followed his slow steps as he guided me up the stairs and into the bedroom. Helping me sit on the bed, he crouched in front of me and worked off one tennis shoe, then the other, chucking them into their usual home in the corner of my room. "Shower or no shower?"

I let out a pitiful whimper. Even though I'd showered and changed into clean clothes at the hospital, I still felt dirty. "Shower."

A startled gasp pushed out of my lungs when he yanked me upright. "Then get to it."

At the bathroom door, I turned. The thought of inviting him to join me flickered, but I was too tired to be any fun. "Will you be out here when I'm done?"

A smile tugged at the corners of his lips. "Sure, baby. I'll wait."

His frustrated tone had me leaning against the doorframe instead of heading to the shower. "What are you thinking?"

His wide shoulders rose and fell in a slow shrug. "I'm not sure." He shook his head as if his feelings were waging war in his head. "Loving you comes with... challenges." At that, his smile widened. "I want to tell you no, to forget the conversation downstairs—hell, forget the last several months—but that's not you, and I fell in love with you. All of you. And this, you risking your life for others, wanting to be a part of this mission is the real you. How can I be mad or upset at this selfless act because of your lack of self-preservation?"

"Casey." No other words followed. What was there to say to that? Like always, he was spot-on. What I suggested, what I would do, was crazy, yet I knew I had to do it.

"I won't stop you, but that doesn't mean I like it. Or that I won't be glued to your side with my finger on the trigger, ready to take out anyone who I deem is a threat. You're just now recovering from... *him*." He growled the word and clenched both hands into tight fists. "Promise me that if it becomes too much, that if this affects your mental health, you'll step away."

The wooden edge dug into my shoulder when I pushed off the doorframe and covered the short distance between us. Using my knee, I spread his legs wide enough for me to step between. I slid both hands over his shoulders, barely covering the wide area.

"I know it's crazy, and who knows, it might not even work out, but I promise if it becomes too dangerous or I slip into my nightmares, I'll walk away. We can figure out a way for me to 'die' or something if we're in the middle of the mission." The skin of his forehead slipped beneath my brushed kiss. "And thank you."

Tipping his face up, he stole a kiss before pressing our foreheads together. "For what?"

"For loving me for me. Knowing I'm difficult and being okay with that and loving me anyway."

"Baby, you have it wrong." Our noses brushed as he stared into my eyes. "All that spunk and crazy is *why* I love you, not in spite of it."

"I love you too, Casey. So much it scares me sometimes."

For several seconds, I allowed the silence our conversation deserved to fill the room before standing tall and making my way back to the bathroom for a quick shower.

Damp hair cascading down my naked back and a towel tied around my chest, I emerged from the bathroom several minutes later, a billow of steam following me out. Weston still sat on the edge of the bed, hands clasped between his legs as he stared at the floor, looking deep in thought.

The soft rug fibers pressed between my still damp toes as I tiptoed over and sat beside him on the bed.

"You look deep in thought," I said, nudging his shoulder with my own.

Without responding, he reached for the phone lying on top of the duvet and held it out to me. Frowning at the ominous feel in his actions, I input his passcode—my birthday, which was super cute and easy to remember.

"What am I looking for?" I asked as I flipped through the pages of apps.

"The text your father just sent me."

Dread coiled in my gut, making me somewhat nauseous. "Oh?" I swallowed hard and pressed the messaging app.

> Client—Wheeler: With the case closed, I expect you to do the right thing and step away from my daughter's life. Her therapist and I believe your presence keeps her trapped in the fear she felt during the case and being gunned down in the street. She deserves better than what you offer. Please vacate her home so she can heal.

Sorrow and anger battled for the winning emotion as I read the text again. His words about Weston not being good enough made me wince, knowing that exact concern was what my man battled daily. The audacity of my father's words, that he thought it was okay to infiltrate my love life, step over the boundaries I set in place, sparked my growing frustration.

"What a know-it-all asshole," I muttered. Picking at my lip, I tossed the phone aside but refused to look at Weston. If I found hurt on his face from my father's words, there would be no stopping me from going over to Dad's house and cutting all ties.

"Yeah."

My heart clenched at the pain that one word held. How Weston could believe my father, or anyone who said he wasn't good enough. They didn't see the man I saw. The protective, courageous warrior who loved fiercely and would move mountains for his friends and family. That was what mattered to me and what should matter to my father. Not because I loved Weston, but because I would always be loved, truly loved, like he and my mother had.

Didn't he see that my entire life I'd longed to find what they had together? And with Weston, I had it.

True, messy, never-failing love.

I wasn't delusional—well, in this area—to think it would be easy. Nothing worthwhile ever was.

The edge of the towel dug into the tops of both thighs as I slung one leg over Weston's lap to straddle him. Palms pressed against his cheeks, I forced his dark eyes to meet my own.

"You know what's worse than his lies?"

"What?"

"Believing them. Casey, I know your value. Who gives a fuck if that asshole doesn't? His opinion doesn't matter. It's you, it's me, it's us, and *that's* all that matters."

"It used to matter to you, though. I'm driving this spike between you and your father, and I fucking hate it, Kate. I hate that I'm the reason—"

Slipping both hands forward, I pressed the pad of each thumb to his lips. "It's me driving that wedge, not you. It's me who won't tell him what happened with Chase, what I did. He wants to keep me in this little gilded cage, sitting pretty and being the daughter he can tell others about without cringing. My entire life, he's wanted me to be softer, be more ladylike. But that's not me. You're not trying to change me, Casey, he is."

His soft sigh whispered past my fingers. Leaning forward, I pressed a kiss to his lips, intending it to be short, but a hand glided up my spine and dove into my hair, pressing me closer.

"What happens when you realize it's true?" he asked, peppering my lips with soft kisses. "That you could do better than someone like me. Or you get distracted by a tool with a man bun... again."

I laughed, my smile growing. "I have a thing for man buns." I yelped when his teeth latched on to my lower lip and tugged. "Kidding."

"No you're not." That hand fisted into my hair, arching my face to the ceiling. "Maybe I'll just have to grow mine out. Even though it's frizzy as fuck."

Weston with a man bun? Hell yes, but I couldn't think about that while he nibbled up my neck and kissed behind my ear. The soft cotton slipped beneath my bare knees as I widened my stance and settled lower. We both groaned as I shifted back and forth, rubbing my bare, damp center along the hardness still restricted inside his jeans.

"This needs to go," Weston murmured against my shoulder. The towel tightened painfully around my chest before slipping away. Pulling back, he slowly took in my naked body, from my tight nipples to my already slick center. "Fuck, you're perfect."

"For you," I whispered like a prayer. "And not old."

"Not old. Perfect."

Calloused palms caressed down my sides and gripped my waist. In a fluid motion, Weston stood, ensuring I was steady on my own feet before releasing me. Teeth digging into my lower lip, I watched with rapt fascination as he worked the top button and tugged at the zipper, absorbed in the show like it was his first time undressing in front of me.

His hard cock sprang free the moment his zipper slid down. Immediately I reached out and wrapped both hands around the base and squeezed, knowing he liked it tight, almost to the point of pain. The desperate need to chase away those lingering self-loathing thoughts dropped me to my knees in front of him.

Before he could protest, I sealed my lips around the thick head and sucked, hollowing out my cheeks as I took him deeper until he nudged the back of my throat. Weston's pleasure-filled hiss sent goose bumps along my damp skin. His coarse leg hair scraped beneath my palms as I skimmed both hands along the backs of his thighs before taking handfuls of his firm, bare ass. Up and down, I sucked and licked at his thick cock, savoring his unique flavor and the flex of his hips as he pushed himself deeper down my throat.

Daring a look up, I found his dark eyes locked on me, teeth sunken into his lower lip, looking sexy as fuck from my position on the floor.

"Enough," he ground out. Two hands tucked beneath my armpits and hauled me upright. With a couple of kicks, he flung his jeans across the room, where they smacked against the wall.

I expected him to turn and toss me to the bed, but instead he backed me across the room until the door rattled against my spine. His hands engulfed both ass cheeks, lifting me until I could wrap my legs around his waist. Gripping both wrists in one tight hold, he pressed them high above my head. Keeping me sealed to the wall, he shifted to line up with my entrance and then slammed into me in one hard thrust.

My head thumped against the door at the glorious sudden fullness. The warm, damp skin of his forehead pressed against mine as he thrust in and out, pulling out to the tip before pushing back inside.

"You're coming to Hawaii," he said, words strained. "No matter what. I couldn't live without this for long."

"Yes," I whimpered. His flexing ass shifted and moved beneath my heels as I urged him harder and deeper. "I'm close."

"I know."

A soft whimper escaped at his cocky tone. Fuck, I loved him and how only Casey Weston could dominate me with ease.

Pushing deep, he swiveled his hips, rubbing against my clit. Cool air slipped along my sweat-slick spine as I arched away from the door. Taking the opportunity, Weston dipped forward and nipped at one nipple, then the other, sending delicious ripples of pleasure-filled pain straight to my already quivering center.

Slamming my eyes shut, I cried out as the world around me faded away with the flood of ecstasy. Tight muscles went limp in Weston's arms as his thrusts turned quick and forceful, making the door rattle on its hinges. With a hissed curse, he slammed deep one last time, sealing our sweaty bodies tightly together.

For several seconds, our harsh breaths mingled as we slowly came down from the post-orgasm high. Locks of damp hair slipped through my fingers as I raked them through the longer portion of his dark hair.

"I need another shower." I chuckled, not caring one bit. "And then we're leaving."

That got his attention. He pulled back, his brows furrowed, a deep line forming between them. "Where are we going?"

"My father's." Trepidation flashed across his features. "We're setting his pompous ass straight on how important you are in my life and how he needs to stop thinking he knows best."

His lips pursed into a tight line before he said on a sigh, "Well, this should be fun."

My thoughts exactly.

5
___

The constant hum of the private jet's engines gently vibrated through the cabin. Under normal circumstances, the soothing sound and gentle vibration would lull me to sleep within minutes after takeoff. But that was not the case for this trip. I would categorize nothing about this flight in the 'normal circumstances' box. Never had I flown to Hawaii with enough guns, ammo, and other gear to take over a small country. Nor had I ever ridden with highly trained —and currently insanely tense—ex-military men and one woman. In this luxurious cabin, I was the only one who didn't know how to kill someone with their pinky finger.

Intimidated, sure.

Intrigued, fuck yes.

Outside the small oval window, fluffy white clouds in the shapes of large cotton balls blanketed the air below us, just as they had for the past five hours now. The vibrating tension from the other four in the cabin grew stronger the closer we came to the island, where our performance and the mission would begin the moment our wheels hit the runway.

The rounded edge of the crystal glass pressed against my lower lip before I tipped it back, draining the last few drops of high-end bourbon, needing it to calm my overactive mind. A calloused hand slipped up from where it was resting on my knee and tightened around my thigh in a comforting gesture. Stealing a side-eye glance at Weston, I found him leaned back in his chair, eyes closed, looking to be asleep, but the foot bouncing along the floor making his knee bob up and down told me he was not only awake but on edge too.

Turning to look back out the window at the baby blue sky, I thought back to the past few days and how we all ended up here on this plane, headed to Hawaii on a mission to save lives.

It was ten days ago that I straightened things out with my father over dinner. The healing relationship was still rocky, but the lines of communication were back open, which was good for both of us.

Nine days ago, our ragamuffin crew and suggested plan of attack against the human trafficking group in Hawaii was approved by whatever agency funded this unorthodox mission.

Eight days ago, I snuck out of the house for the dermatologist to inject several units of Botox along my forehead and eye wrinkles to help look the part of the younger girl I would have to portray.

Seven days ago, Anne arrived, full of sass and, to my surprise, laughter. Somehow, in only a matter of a few days, Weston's ex grew on me.

Four days ago, we hashed out the details and solidified the plan.

Three days ago, I put in a long-term leave of absence at the hospital and said goodbye to my best friend.

Two days ago, I packed a few bags and said goodbye to my father.

Yesterday, I puked all day from nerves and self-doubt.

This morning, I sucked it up, put a game face on, and boarded a plane that could be taking me to certain death.

A stinging pain and taste of copper paused my plucking fingers along my lower lip. Yanking my nervous fingers from my mouth, I tucked both hands beneath my thighs, sucking on my lower lip to dull the sting.

"Having second thoughts, Tink?"

Cutting my eyes across the aisle, I shook my head at the relaxed Tyler. Legs manspread wide, taking up most of his area, and hands cupped behind his head. It looked like he didn't have a care in the world, but I knew better. There was a sharp edge to his smile, a dimness in those bright eyes. Even the happy-go-lucky one of the group was tense, knowing full well the danger we were about to walk into.

We planned everything around Ryan's intel and the connection he set up to meet us in Hawaii. There were no certainties of what might happen the moment we landed. If someone found out we were going in undercover, they could shoot us on sight, or if Ryan double-crossed us... No, that wouldn't happen. Ryan wouldn't do that to me or his brother. This would work out.

A cackle of laughter drew my attention away from the staring Tyler. Soft leather groaned under my ass as I twisted around, searching for Anne.

Along the couch in the back they sat side by side, Anne talking and laughing at whatever story she was reminiscing about. It appeared he wasn't paying attention to the chatty female, but a small smirk tugged at his lips, showing he enjoyed whatever story Anne told. When she caught me staring, she sent back a grim smile, offering me a brief insight into her own concerns about the mission.

Even she was nervous, it seemed.

Anne boarded the jet in a pair of ripped jeans and a black tank top that made her look as badass as she was in real life, but she'd changed moments ago, transforming into her role as James's wife. Decked out in the latest designer fashion, she wore a flattering cream Chanel pantsuit with a low-cut black silk top and red-soled black heels. She looked filthy rich. James had also transformed into someone I almost didn't recognize. For the first time since I'd known him, he looked decent. Okay, fine, he looked good. In a sharp black Armani suit and black dress shirt plus the new haircut, trendy scruff, and annoyed scowl—which was currently directed at me—he looked the part too.

Tyler and Weston boarded the plane in what they currently wore. Both wore nice but much cheaper suits than James, thin black ties, and crisp white dress shirts plus visible shoulder holsters and hidden knife sheaths strapped to both calves. They perfectly portrayed the rich asshole personal security team with an air of confidence and haughtiness about them.

Then there was me.

I looked like their kid sister playing dress-up. When going over the details of the plan and the importance of that initial meeting in the hangar, Kyle stated I needed to be seen deboarding the plane and appear unassuming. Apparently the rich deviants who purchased girls for their personal playthings didn't enjoy showing them off to those they didn't know or trust. Their pets only appeared for private parties or personal use. So the dress I changed into about an hour into the flight was sweet, innocent-looking almost. One size too big, with the cap sleeves and the hem hitting just below my knees, it gave my petite frame a frail appearance. Navy not black, with flat brown sandals on my feet, along with thin gold cuffs secured around each ankle and wrist.

Turning back in my seat, I held the gold bangles up to the window, allowing the sunlight to highlight the flawless metal. It would be a beautiful piece of jewelry if it weren't for what it represented—captivity.

A soft crackle sounded from the speakers before the captain announced that our arrival at the private airstrip would be in less than an hour.

Puffing out a heavy breath, I relaxed my arm, allowing the bracelet and hand to drop onto my lap. Too soon my focus would be trained to the floor at all times. I'd be forced to follow James's lead and somehow confine my confident attitude enough to appear broken and demure.

"Ready?" Weston pitched his tone low to not draw the attention of the rest of the group.

"Yes?"

The seat vibrated with his soft chuckle. "It's not too late, you know. To back out."

"Yes it is," I whispered. "Not that I want to. It's just... I used to feel the same way before starting a shift. It's not really trepidation, more eager to jump into the action. I'm just ready to get it all started so we can know how it plays out." I inclined my head toward the back of the plane where James and Anne sat. "James is right about all the unknowns in this plan, which I hate. I want to know what to expect. That's what I'm nervous about, not so much the danger part." Looking Weston in the eye, I offered a smile to put him at ease. "My middle name is Danger."

Leaning over the armrest, he pressed a chaste kiss to my lips. "Now *that* I believe. The past year was interesting...."

"The best of your life."

"That too." His cheeks bunched, making small smile lines burst from the corners of his dark eyes. "But also interesting." I shoved his shoulder, not even moving him an inch. Those eyes shifted to where I touched him. "Remember, you can't do that once we land."

"Touch you?"

"Show any emotion, any reaction. Even if Axe screams in your face, you cannot react."

"You think he'll have to?" Just the thought made me itch to grab something sharp.

Weston's wide shoulders rose and fell in an exaggerated shrug. "Maybe, but don't worry. If he does, I'll beat his ass later for it."

"My hero." I batted my eyes for emphasis.

The long layers of his hair shifted along his forehead as he shook his head. "If I've learned anything from my time with you, it's that Dr. Kate Wheeler doesn't need a hero. You need a partner." He waggled his brows in an attempt to ease the weight of our conversation, but the tightness in the move, the tension that crept into his dark eyes, told me the truth of how he felt.

"Hey." I snagged his hand off his thigh and interlaced our fingers. "It will be fine. We'll figure it out day by day."

"It might not be fine, Kate, and that's what concerns me. In missions like this, nothing is guaranteed. I've seen enough well-planned missions go to shit and my friends get hurt." Dread rolled in my stomach, making my breath catch. "But if I demanded you stay behind, you'd hate me forever and then come anyway just like you said you would." Tightening the hold on my hand, he brought my palm to his lips and gave it a quick kiss. "Just promise me one thing."

"That makes me nervous," I said with a forced laugh.

"Do nothing that purposefully puts you in danger. I'll kill anyone who hurts you, Kate, without regrets." *That should not be hot. That should not be hot.* "Even if it messes with the mission. So when you want to act without talking to us first, think about all the women we're trying to save. If we blow our cover because I go apeshit, then those women's chance at freedom is ripped away."

I swallowed hard and nodded. "I promise. I'll be the dutiful trafficked girl when out in public. But in the house...." House was an understatement. To keep with the 'multimillionaire pushing toward billionaire' façade, we leased an estate along the beach for two months, unsure how long the mission would last. "I'm free to be me, right?"

"Once we check the house for bugs and cameras, yes, but only when shutters are closed. And no going out on your own. That would be a major red flag."

Good thing this wasn't my first time on the island, or I'd be pissed I was in paradise but stuck inside hiding from traffickers we were trying to fool.

Fuck, just thinking it made the entire plan and mission seem crazy as shit.

A small smile tugged at the corner of my lips. Good thing I thrived on crazy. You couldn't be a successful ER doctor without needing the pressure and unexpected cases to keep you interested.

Hopefully this would be just like the ER on a Saturday night with a full moon.

Insane, exhausting, hilarious, and overwhelmingly rewarding.

Rewarding. That was what I had to focus on while keeping my cool in this submissive, weak role.

Less than forty minutes later, the cabin jostled as the wheels slammed against the runway, spurring everyone into action. Without a single word, the click of four sets of seat belts disengaging and falling to the side sounded over the roaring engine as the plane slowed. Each dug into their own carry-on, strapping various weapons along their bodies, including Anne, though all of hers were well concealed.

She caught me enviously watching as she secured a knife to her calf.

"Don't worry, we can get you one." She winked and went back to strapping a different blade to her other calf. "But not today. You ready for this, Doc?"

"It's Tink, remember?" Tyler said absentmindedly as he inspected the clip of the nine-millimeter in his hand.

"And I've told you I'm not calling another woman Tink. She worked for that damn doctor title, and I intend to use it." She paused. "Except when she's meant to be our purchased party favor." A look of disgust washed over her pretty features. "I really hope I get to kill some of these bastards."

"I like you," I said with a nod. "We should hang out."

A half smile and a nod were her only response. Sure, we started out a little rocky that night at Aiden's, but that was then. Now that I knew she enjoyed pushing the boys' buttons, which was what she did that night at Aiden's, I found her humor funny. Likeable even. Well, as likable as your boyfriend's ex-fiancée could be.

The smooth metal latch of the seat belt slipped several times before my shaking fingers could unlatch the contraption. Fuck, I was nervous. Closing my eyes, I inhaled deep through my nose and held the lungful while vigorously shaking out my hands to chase away my growing nerves.

At the third breath, a looming presence had me peeking one lid open to see who was standing over me.

James stared down from where he stood in the aisle with an unreadable look.

"What?" I asked, annoyed that he'd interrupted my Zen moment.

"Don't make me hurt you."

What the hell?

"What?" My annoyance morphed into a rush of anger. Heat flared beneath my skin as I gripped the armrests to keep me from launching from the seat to strangle his arrogant ass.

"Don't break character. If you do, I'll be forced to punish you for those who are watching. The promoter's assistant is waiting for us in the hangar to vet us out. Don't speak, don't look up—"

I held up a hand, cutting him off. "We've been over this a hundred times, James. I get it. Don't worry. I'll be the perfect submissive, brainwashed doll."

"Good." The plane shifted as it turned into the massive hangar. With his free hand, James pressed four fingers to the low ceiling to stay upright. Bending closer, he reached out and gripped my entire face in one large hand just as the sunlight winked from the windows from the shadows of the private hangar. "Because the show starts now."

My eyes widened as my heart raced with a fresh surge of nerves. Cutting my gaze, I tried to see out the oval window to get a glimpse of how many people waited in the shadows. Before I could see anything of importance, James stretched across me and slammed the shade closed.

"You're not allowed to look at anything other than the ground. Do nothing unless I directly tell you to. Don't even follow me unless I've given a direct order to you or the guys. I'll give you direction while we're in this as much as possible. Just listen for my cues and we'll be good."

I nodded as much as I could in his hold without jerking my face from his light grip, even though that was exactly what I wanted to do.

His gaze slid to look at something over my head. He nodded and stepped away, straightening the cuffs of both his sleeves as he did.

"Don't give me that fucking look, Romeo," James said under his breath. "She wanted in, so she's in. Deal with it." He cut a death look to the seething Weston, who had paused his gun inspection to carefully monitor our interaction. "I'm keeping her alive."

Without a word, Weston gave a stiff nod and looked at me with raised brows.

"I'm good. I get it. The show started the minute we landed." My return smile was forced. "I'm good."

"Say it again, Tink, and I might believe you." Tyler stepped around Weston and squatted, putting us eye to eye. "You've got this, little badass. Don't let the overly protective ass and the... well, just plain ass make you doubt yourself. None of us would've allowed you on this mission if we didn't believe you could do it."

"Even him?" Keeping my hand pressed to my thigh, I hooked a thumb in James's direction.

"Even him." He cast a worried glance James's way. "Don't let him fool you. He's a good guy, he just doesn't want anyone to know it. He's been through—"

"Shut the fuck up, Mouse."

Tyler's head snapped forward, almost hitting the seat when James's hand collided with the back of it. The promise of death shone in Tyler's eyes when he turned to James and stood.

"Stop it, you two," Weston snapped and stepped between his friends. "Mouse, I'll go out first to secure the hangar and vet the waiting assholes. I counted eight, but there could be more in their SUVs. Seven are openly carrying. The other, who I'm assuming is the one we're meeting, is probably armed too, just concealed."

He took a step, hand raised to cup my face, but paused and clenched his fist. "Fuck, I can't... Baby, listen to Mouse and Axe. They know what you mean to me and understand that if something happens to you, they die." A sinister grin spread across his face as he looked the other two males in the eyes. "See you soon, fuckers."

Dark eyes locked on mine, his features softened. "I love you."

The low hum of the automatic stairway almost smothered those whispered words as they peeled away from the side of the plane. Instantly, warm, humid air swept through the cool cabin, bringing with it the scent of jet fuel, burnt rubber, and a hint of the ocean.

Weston stepped into the opening, hand casually by his side as if this were a normal day in the life of a high-profile guard. After a beat, he nodded to James and started down the stairs. His heavy footfalls thundered in my ears with each stair, not knowing exactly what he was walking into. None of us did, but Weston being the first to step into the unknown danger had tears of worry burning in my eyes. I stared at my hands, tightly clasped in my lap, and blinked back the unshed tears to hide any trace of emotion. The earlier light snack rose up my throat, but I swallowed hard to keep it down.

"You're in excellent hands." Anne's voice came from somewhere behind me. "We've been in worse situations. This shit is easy street."

She was right. They were pros at this danger thing, unlike the wannabe heroine I'd played my entire life. These four were the real deal, and this, this crazy plan, was nothing.

"Now, we've never pretended to be rich fuckers who enjoy buying girls, but it can't be that hard to infiltrate a trafficking ring, right?" A pulse of worry clouded her last word.

Oh fuck.

"No more talking," James growled from where he stood like a statue beside my seat. "Who knows what they can hear."

"Come on, dear," Anne said loudly with a high pitch that was nothing like her normal low tone. "Let's get this party started. I need a fucking drink if I'm going to deal with your grumpy ass." Her soft suit brushed against my arm as she squeezed between James and me, making her way toward the front of the plane. At the doorway, she turned and flicked her wrist toward me. "Have her hurry the fuck up. I'm over her lazy ass."

Slipping large Chanel sunglasses over her eyes, she gave me a dismissive scoff and started down the stairs. Unlike Weston, I could barely hear the click of her heels hitting the stairs, almost like she was taking care to make as little noise as possible.

A large hand engulfed my bicep and yanked me to a standing position. Forgetting myself, I tipped my face up to Tyler, who now wore a cruel, emotionless mask. He didn't look down as he hauled me toward the front of the plane and jerked me to a stop in front of the stairs.

Tyler turned to where James still stood in the middle of the aisle. "We're good to go, sir."

Even with my face tilted toward the floor, out of the corner of my eye, I watched James tug on each cuff before slipping both hands casually into the side pockets of his slacks as he meandered down the aisle toward us.

I shrank away when he reached for me, but two fingers snatched my chin, tipping my face upward. Instead of meeting James's gaze, I kept my eyes downcast, focusing on what bit of floor I could still see.

"Don't cause any problems and maybe we'll reward you." My head snapped to the side when he released me with a dismissive push. "Make sure she stays quiet."

Beside me, Tyler gave a single nod, acknowledging his boss's request.

Only when James was all the way down the stairs and the introductions had started between Mr. and Mrs. Bartwright, aka James and Anne, and the assistant did Tyler urge me toward the first step.

I did not have to force the shake in my legs and tremble of my lips, the full weight of it all engulfing me as I carefully descended the stairs. Fear locked away all rational thought, and all I could think about was how this could go bad fast. I missed the last step, too lost in my own spiraling thoughts, causing me to stumble. My ankle rolled, pitching me forward, but Tyler's tight hold on my arm kept me upright.

"Stay on your damn feet," he growled while practically dragging me toward a black Suburban.

My stick-straight shoulder-length hair swayed forward, offering a curtain of privacy as we hurried across the hangar. The passenger door almost flung off its hinges from how hard Tyler yanked it open before shoving me inside. Ready to be away from prying eyes, I hurried in, not needing much prodding.

"Wait here, and don't make a sound." The entire SUV bobbed with the hard slam of the door.

I watched Tyler's back through the dark tinted window as he stormed back across the stained concrete floor, retrieving the bags the crew had already begun unloading from the plane's underbelly. Two duffels in each hand, he marched back to the SUV and tossed them all into the back of the Suburban. I didn't dare turn to watch as he loaded bag after bag.

Only when the last bag was tossed inside, the trunk closed, and Tyler behind the wheel did I relax back against the seat. Grumbling under his breath about swamp ass, he turned the SUV on and cranked the AC to the max. Within seconds, the chilled air blasted through the vehicle, cooling the sweat already building along my upper lip I was too nervous to wipe away.

That relief quickly morphed back into fear when James turned our way and pointed.

I swallowed hard as the unknown man nodded and started our way with James and Weston hot on his heels.

Fuck, what is happening?

6

F ull-body tremors racked through me, shaking me in the seat as their slow, confident steps grew closer. The unknown man's unimpressed gaze seemed to slice through the impenetrable tint to stare directly at me. Unease washed over me on the off chance he could see me watching his approach, and I quickly averted my eyes to the floorboard. All color seeped from my interwoven fingers, leaving them ghostly white from their death grip, but still I held on for dear life to keep me from doing something stupid like running.

The door opened without a sound, allowing a gust of sticky air to sweep inside the SUV, taking away the cool crispness I'd barely gotten to enjoy.

"This is her." I swallowed at James's words and dismissive tone. Why would they care about me? I was only here as a prop to prove their nastiness and previous buying habits. "She's outgrown my tastes."

"And the lady of the house?" I'd yet to see this guy up close, but he sounded ugly and weak with that slightly high-pitched voice and presumptuous tone.

"What about me?"

Fuck, I liked Anne. That impassive bitchiness toward the vile man made me want to hug her.

"What did she do for you?" he asked, leaning deeper into the SUV.

The overpowering aftershave he must have bathed in before meeting us caught in my throat, making a cough tingle in the back. I squeezed my fingers tighter to keep from leaning away from him.

Anne's laugh was cruel, even in a pretentious way. "Kept him from touching me."

An unfamiliar soft laugh filled the cab. "I understand."

Would I get in trouble if I stabbed him? Just once, nowhere important like the heart or neck, maybe just his crotch area. Inflict pain but not mortally wound him. That seemed like a great diversion to our plan to me, but I promised Weston I wouldn't deviate from the mission. So no penis stabbing for me.

For now.

"I do like to watch," she mused, almost as an afterthought. "The first few times when they're more—" Anne paused as if she were searching for the word. "—willful against his particular needs."

"I see," the man said, now only a few inches separating us. Too close, way too close. "Are you wanting to trade her in for a new purchase or purchase outright at the auction? We can accommodate either need."

"Purchase," James replied. "If I get bored with the new one, I can still fuck this one. I enjoy having the option of which pussy or mouth to rip apart."

Another dark chuckle rumbled through the inside of the SUV.

Forget not mortally wounding him. I'm going straight for the jugular.

"Are you sure? We have many buyers who are open to second-hand merchandise. Some see it as the less willful they are, the better."

A pause.

A motherfucking pause, like James was actually considering the option. I so wanted to shoot a scathing look in James's direction and scream at the top of my lungs, but I didn't do either. Instead I stayed completely still, eyes downcast and head down, mentally plotting the many, many ways I'd make him pay for that damn pause.

"Maybe," he mused, yet somehow sounded bored with the entire conversation. "I'm not attached to her, but it's not like I need the money."

"Where did you purchase her?"

"Canada."

"Does she speak English?"

"Yes. She was an American college student visiting the Falls when they procured her for me. I was specific about my particular needs."

The man hummed as if he found that suspicious. "Why not return to them for a new girl?"

"Fucking feds. I had another one lined up, but they lost her in transport in a Texas raid." His voice rumbled with annoyance. "After that, I found somewhere I can buy and walk away with the product that night. No more waiting. I'm fucking ready for fresh blood to shed."

"Understood. Do you mind?"

Does he mind what? My heart raced at the feel of clammy skin caressing along my cheek before tucking the curtain of dark hair behind my ear. Internally I screamed at the unwanted touch, but outwardly I stayed calm, keeping that placid mask in place. Thin, bony fingers pressed beneath my chin, tipping my face upward.

I was right. Ugly-ass vile man.

I didn't meet his searching gaze as he scanned my face. I only glimpsed greasy, slicked-back fair hair, pockmarked skin, and a crooked nose. Needing a place to keep my gaze trained, I focused on the driver's headrest. Those uncaring fingers prodded around my face, slipping between my lips, checking my teeth like I was a damn prize mare. A shiver I couldn't hold back tracked down my spine as his hands slipped lower and settled on my shoulders.

"You took care of her," he mused as he continued to inspect every inch of my face. Taking a lock of hair, he rubbed it between two fingers. "If you change your mind, we could make you an offer. She'd do well in our group. Clients love the little ones."

"Boss." Weston's clipped voice rang through the hangar.

"Right," James answered. "We done here? I have other business on the island to take care of."

"And I need a damn drink," Anne added.

"And my wife"—that word was more of a hiss—"needs a pill and a bottle of whiskey. When will I get the details?"

"Soon," the man replied. "Until then, our guards will accompany you to your residence out of utmost precaution."

"Until when?" James snapped. "I have enough security to protect me and my property."

His glassy, mud-brown eyes bored into me. "Until we can trust you. Our men will stay with you until we see fit. For our protection, you see. We don't allow just anyone to attend an event. Only those thoroughly vetted make the cut."

"They're not staying anywhere near my wife," James hissed and yanked the disgusting man out of the SUV with a hand gripped around the back of his neck. "They can monitor us from the outside, but none are allowed inside. My house, my rules. I don't give a fuck who you think you are. I'll find someone else to buy from."

"Understood." Out of the corner of my eye, I caught the man stepping away from James and dusting off his ugly-ass Hawaiian shirt. "I'll be in touch with those dates and details once you've cleared our security measures. Until then—"

The door slammed shut, jolting me an inch above the seat and cutting off the man's next words.

"Easy," Tyler whispered so low I almost didn't hear it over the blasting air and the blood pounding in my ears. "We've got you."

Inhaling in and out, I focused on controlling each breath to calm my erratic pulse and help fight back the nausea. My fingers twitched in my lap, desperate to scratch away the filthy film that bastard left along my skin. I counted the seconds as we waited.

"We're good to go," Tyler said. The SUV slowly eased forward before accelerating fast, throwing me back against the seat as we raced out of the hangar.

Daring a look over my shoulder, I searched out the back window for the other three. A murdered out Range Rover with full blackout windows followed us, plus two other black SUVs following them.

Deep longing squeezed my heart from the need to feel Weston's arms wrapped around me, to hear his voice and syphon his unending strength from his body into my own. Wrapping both arms around my chest, I leaned back against the seat and closed my eyes.

Based on what the guys went over on the plane, it was a thirty-minute drive, maybe more with traffic, to the estate. Which meant thirty more minutes until I could shower and shed these clothes—hell, I might even burn them on the beach tonight.

A sharp ringing filled the enclosed area, snapping me on high alert once again.

Fuck, my nerves were shot. I needed a cup of coffee and an orgasm or two, stat.

Coffee first, for sure.

"We'll need to plan around our new company." Weston's voice filled the air, making my stomach flip. "Once we get there, I'll secure the house before you bring the girl and the boss inside." My brows rose at his words. Surely he didn't think they bugged the SUVs... right? "After, we'll both walk the perimeter, set up each guard where we need them, and vet them out. This isn't just a one-way fucking street."

"Agreed." Even with his dark sunglasses on, I could feel Tyler's gaze flicking between the road and me. "You sweep first."

"Agreed. Then you do a second pass to ensure I didn't miss anything." My fingers twitched to reach up and tug at my lower lip. "The girl okay?"

"Fine. Think the boss will trade this one in? I liked how broken in she is. Less of a damn headache."

"Not sure. Depends on what's offered, I guess." Weston's words were clipped, giving away to the anger coursing through his body. "See you soon."

The line died, bringing a heavy silence to fall over us.

"Maybe if you act like a good girl, he won't sell you to the highest bidder." Tyler's grimacing face flashed in the rearview mirror. "You understand all this? What's going on?"

Ah, that was what he was doing. Trying to communicate without blowing our cover in case those creeps *had* bugged the SUVs before we arrived.

"Yes," I whispered, just loud enough for him to hear.

Tyler's shoulders visibly relaxed from around his ears. "Good. Be there in twenty. Boss might want some time when we get there. Take a nap. You look like shit."

Truth or lie?

Hmm, it really could go either way. No doubt all the stress was showing on my face, and the damn humidity did nothing for my hair. It had grown an inch outward since the plane landed. Maybe while I was here, I'd pull a Monica and get braids.

Taking Tyler's advice, I laid the seat back and curled into a small ball. Little by little, the tension drained away, leaving utter exhaustion in its wake.

Just before the whirling of the tires soothed me to sleep, a question circled through my mind, refusing to leave.

If they demanded the trade, would it save others' lives?

Maybe it was being shot, or what happened with Chase, or hell, maybe the fact that I was deeply in love with a man I wanted to spend the rest of my life with. Whatever it was, for the first time in my life, I wasn't sure I'd be willing to take that step.

But in the end, the choice might not be mine to make.

The sound of a car door slamming snapped me awake, groggy as hell and utterly confused.

"We're here."

I buried my face in the seat to hide my cringe at Tyler's impersonal voice.

Right. Time to play my part in this mission once again.

Leather slipped beneath sweaty palms as I pushed against the seat to sit upright. My tongue stuck to the roof of my dry mouth as I scanned the estate grounds. Ten-foot concrete walls surrounded the small green area where a fountain with water flowing from fat concrete fish sat in the middle. The house itself was what I expected based on the pictures I'd seen before we left. Large and beautiful, with well-kept grounds and plenty of colorful flowers, yet it somehow radiated cold. There was no personality in the block, modern-style building, or maybe it was because the house itself would be my temporary cage during our stay.

"Wait here."

I drew my attention from the window to Tyler as he climbed out of the SUV, grumbling about the heat. The door slammed shut, enclosing me alone inside. Without turning to stare obviously at Tyler, I followed his movements out of the corner of my eye as he marched for the Range Rover that parked in front of us on the round white concrete drive.

I watched Anne and James climb out of the door Tyler opened for them, but no Weston. His words from before I fell asleep reminded me he was probably already inside, securing the house and doing the first bug scan.

Tyler leaned against the SUV, watching the surrounding area, acting casual but clearly on full alert as he stared down the drive in a direction I couldn't see unless I twisted around.

After several minutes of waiting in the warming SUV, I saw Weston emerge through the double dark wood front doors and offer a clipped nod to Tyler, who started toward the house behind James and Anne.

"Go get the girl," James said over his shoulder, loud enough for me to understand every word. "Secure her in a room and get her some damn food. I forgot to have her fed on the plane."

"Yes, sir," Tyler clipped as he changed direction.

Fisting both hands, I rotated them into the seat cushions until a slight burn erupted along my knuckles. That sting somehow centered me, calming the overactive nerves pulsing through my veins, threatening to force me into a catatonic state.

A burst of saltwater-scented air brushed along my cheeks when the side door swung open. Taking that as my cue, I immediately accepted his extended hand and stepped out into the blinding sunlight.

The moment my feet hit the driveway, my legs buckled from falling asleep on the ride over, sending me tumbling into Tyler. He grunted when my shoulder slammed into his stomach but recovered quickly and shoved me off him. Well, to anyone else looking, it was a shove, but really he eased me against the side of the SUV to help steady me until the tingling down my legs subsided.

"Let's go," he ordered and gripped my bicep. The hold was tight but not painful, but I still winced, acting as though I was in pain or hating the harsh touch. I should get an award for the level of acting I was putting into this mission, or at least a Starbucks gift card for my efforts. I took in all I could around me while watching my feet shift along the pristine concrete as we moved toward the open doors. A cool ocean-fresh breeze brushed across my sticky face, catching a few strands of hair. The sound of crashing waves in the distance signaled the beach was just on the other side of the property.

Up three stairs, past a set of polished black shoes, and over the threshold, I dutifully followed Tyler inside the house. Two steps into the marble-floored entry, I heard the heavy doors behind me whoosh closed, and the sound of a lock clicking into place echoed through the quiet.

"All clear, Romeo?" Tyler asked, loosening his hold on my arm but not letting me go completely. "You okay?"

"Yeah." The single word rasped from my parched throat.

"Clean from my initial sweep. You go on and start your own to make sure I didn't miss anything. Kate?"

At my name, I finally raised my face from the floor, blinking as I searched for Weston. Raising those dark glasses, he scanned me from head to toe, visibly relaxing when he found me unharmed. "You okay?"

I nodded and shrugged at the same time. I wasn't really okay, but I wasn't not okay. I was tired and sick of shoving myself away to play this part in the mission. I just had to wait for Tyler to do the second search until this act could fall away and the real Kate could emerge once again. Real, fantastic, badass Kate. Because she was in here, fighting to get out and disgusted that we were one, put in the back seat—*nobody puts Baby in a corner*—and two, couldn't speak our mind.

Shit. Cracking under the pressure, splitting into two personalities could be a legit concern.

I stifled a laugh at the possibility. Soon I'd be able to be myself again, even for just a little while behind closed doors.

But first, coffee.

My little coffee-loving heart pitter-pattered with joy the moment we landed knowing the delicious coffee this island was known for was within reach.

Someone needed to get me a big-ass cup of Kona.

Stat.

THE ROOM ASSIGNED AS MY 'SECURED' room was smaller than mine at home but had a private bathroom with a large walk-in shower, which I used the moment they brought my luggage up to wash the nasty-ass man's grime off my skin. The private bath was my one requirement when the room assignments were planned so I wouldn't have to share a bathroom with the guys. After the few weeks they stayed at the townhome, I quickly realized living with a bunch of guys was not for me. I was a doctor, yet some of the smells and sounds they emitted turned me green.

Clean and alone, I fell against the bed, the soft light pink comforter molding around my back and shoulders as I watched the ceiling fan go round and round. After being deposited inside the room, they instructed me to stay put until told otherwise. Which was fine by me. I could use the alone time, especially since Tyler snuck a steaming cup of coffee up the stairs when he brought up my bags.

It was delicious, but now I was jittery, antsy, and locked in a damn gilded cage in the shape of a beautifully decorated room. I lost track of how long I lay alone, wondering when someone would come get me, when quiet footsteps sounded down the hall, the distant squeak of rubber against hardwood dragging my gaze from the rotating fan.

A shadow appeared in the gap between the door and the floor. The brass knob turned slowly, almost as if someone was checking to see if it was locked. Pressing up to my elbows, I watched with fascination as Weston's dark head of hair popped through the small gap when he peeked inside, dark eyes searching.

The moment he saw me on the bed, he maneuvered the rest of his massive body through the gap, quietly closing the door behind him. Keeping some distance between us, he leaned a shoulder against the far wall and crossed both arms over his massive chest.

"What?" I asked, my voice rough from lack of use. I cleared my throat and lifted my chin. "You look"—I waved a hand in his direction—"upset. What got your panties in a twist? I was the perfect little captive today, wasn't I?"

His thinly pressed lips curved down into a deep frown. "Yes, you did your part perfectly." Reaching up, he scrubbed a hand over his face and groaned. "I'm not pissed, Kate. I'm... affected."

The cotton comforter bounced under my palm as I patted it for him to come join me on the bed. "What do you mean, affected?"

With a shove, he popped off the wall and sat on the edge of the bed, still a respectful distance away from where I lay. I frowned at the space between us.

"I had to sit there and listen to that fucker talk about you, talk about the other women like they were nothing more than property. Trash, really. I bet the disgusting asshole treats his cars with more respect than he treats the girls he's taken or bought." Rolling over to my stomach, I propped my head up, propping my chin on the heels of both open hands. "Then seeing him touch you." He let loose a deep sigh. "I'm not sure I can do this."

The smooth material of the suit pants slid beneath my fingers when I tried for a comforting squeeze. "My job is over now. We're good. All they needed to see was that James had done this before and was a legit buyer. Don't worry about me. You know when it comes down to it, I can handle myself."

"That's the thing, Kate. I don't want you to have to handle yourself. I want to destroy any threat against you. I want to protect you."

Pushing up, I sat with my legs folded and rested my chin on his shoulder. "I know what being alone is like, Casey, and since you stormed into my life, I haven't been. It has nothing to do with your physical presence, it's about knowing you're always there looking out for me, loving me, thinking about me."

"Especially in the shower," he quipped. Finally that frown was gone, replaced with an almost smile. "Come on." He stood from the bed and held out a hand. "There's food downstairs. You haven't eaten anything but coffee in hours."

I narrowed my eyes. "See, you're a rule breaker too." Referring to the one rule I made up when he first arrived.

That barely there smile grew to a crooked grin. "Only with you, baby. You'll never stop being my exception."

"Are you sure it's safe for me to go down there? What if those guards see me?"

After sliding my hand into his, he pulled me off the bed and wrapped an arm around my waist.

"We closed the shutters and curtains so they can't see inside. Mouse and I cleaned the house of any bugs and cameras and will do a new sweep every morning and evening. We're good to act normal in the house as long as it's just us five."

I breathed a sigh of relief. "Great."

Muffled voices and male laughter greeted us as we descended the stairs. A sense of family wrapped around my heart and squeezed when we rounded the corner. Anne sat on the counter, a wide smile on her face while Tyler talked animatedly in the center of the kitchen. James had his head tossed back, laughing.

I tugged Weston to a stop. He looked down, brows raised in question.

"I get it now."

"Get what?"

"Remember when we first met, and you said the military gave you a family? I get that now. I see it and I feel it."

His fingers tightened around mine. "You're one of us now, Kate."

Suddenly the heavy feel of eyes on me had me turning back to the others. Tyler and Anne wore smiles on their faces, and James... well, it was more of a grimace than a smile, but I'd take what I could get.

This was different from what I had with Dad or Eric and Meagan. This was deeper somehow, forged by the danger and trusting the others to keep me safe—alive.

As I followed Weston into the kitchen, I couldn't help but grin.

Whatever this feeling was with the ragamuffin team, I never wanted it to stop.

7

A worn narrow path indented along the white rug covering the living room floor.

Okay, maybe not a literal path, but it sure as hell felt like there should have been one. For the past two days, we'd done nothing but eat, drink, sleep, and repeat, never leaving the confines of the secured house. Tyler and Weston were the only two lucky ones allowed to venture outside these prison-like walls to monitor the guards and make sure they were an appropriate distance away from the main house.

There was nothing to do while we waited, hence the path I'd worn along the rug. Even now we were all bored out of our damn minds, needing something—anything—to do.

From where he lounged along the couch, legs hanging over the armrest, Tyler tracked me back and forth while munching on an apple. Across from him, Anne sat quietly on the loveseat with an array of weapons laid out on the coffee table in front of her while cleaning the one in her hand with reverent care. The other two sat at the twelve-seat dining room table playing a game of cards, their conversation hushed.

They appeared relaxed, but tensions were high for everyone.

Waiting to hear from the promoter's assistant on the next set of hoops to jump through to gain an invitation to the auction was draining.

Until then, all we could do was wait—again.

"Let's go do something," I suggested, flopping onto the couch beside Tyler.

Instead of glaring at me for disrupting his peaceful snack, he smiled and offered me a bite.

"No," the other three said in unison, irritation in their tones.

"I'm game," Tyler said with a grin. "What do you have in mind?"

I shrugged and pushed the apple back toward him, declining his offer. "I don't know, just something before I lose my damn mind."

"We could always go monitor that warehouse Miss Ginger mentioned as—"

"Shut the hell up, Mouse," Weston snapped, standing so fast the chair nearly toppled backward. "We agreed to stay inside for everyone's safety."

And by 'everyone,' I had a sneaking suspicion he meant me.

Arm slung over the back of the couch, I turned to glare at my boyfriend. "I didn't agree with that plan."

His shrug was stiff. "Majority wins."

"I change my vote," Tyler said as he stood and stretched his arms overhead. "I'm bored."

"You can't just change—"

"Me too." We all turned our attention to Anne. Without looking up from the rifle, she flicked two fingers toward Tyler. "For once, I agree with him. I'm bored."

"We're not going—"

"Me three." My jaw dropped as I turned my stunned stare on James. "You can't keep us from doing our job because you're worried about her. If she dies, she dies."

"Thanks?" I tilted my head, confused whether I should thank him or punch him. With a head shake to center my thoughts, I turned my focus to Weston. "Well, there you go. Majority wins."

His lips pursed into a thin line as he stared me down. "And how do you propose we get everyone out of here with the guards outside?"

"There's a weakness along the northwest fence. Too much property to cover and too few of their dumbass guards."

I nodded as Tyler spoke. "See?" I said to Weston while pointing at his friend. "Piece of cake."

"Until they shoot you," Weston growled. "We're not leaving. It's not safe for anyone."

"You and I could take the Range like I'm going to a business dinner. Make a show of it so they see it's just us two in suits. They wouldn't consider that out of the ordinary for someone like me," James mused as he leaned back against the wooden chair, balancing it on the two rear legs. "Those three could meet us down the road once we're out of sight with the gear and made sure no one is tailing us."

"Just one warehouse?" I asked, since I wasn't privy to that information from Kyle.

"He gave us a list of ten," Anne said, finally looking up from her meticulous cleaning. "We could take care of three tonight, then the others in a few days. You know, spread out the fun."

"Fun?" Weston snapped.

"You used to be fun," Tyler said with a sigh. "Stop worrying so much. We'll be fine. I'll keep my hands on Tink at all times."

"You mean eyes," I corrected.

"Sure," Tyler said. He whooped with delight as he dashed around the gun-covered coffee table to avoid Weston lunging with both hands out, ready to strangle him. "Listen, it's not dangerous, you know that. It's not like we can leave her here with those assholes outside. We have a job to do, Romeo. It's why we're here."

"And getting paid," James huffed.

I raised my hand. "Um, we're getting paid?"

"Not you."

I frowned at James. "Why not me too?"

"Because you're not an official part of the group. The government is paying the temporary company we set up, and we're dividing the amount evenly between the four of us."

It's not like I needed the money, but it still kind of stung that I wasn't really part of the group. I opened my mouth to tell him how unfair all this shit was when Weston spoke up.

"Fine. Mouse and Hawk, go with Kate through the fence and wait for Axe and me in the Range. If we're going to do this, let's do it. Leave several lights on so the assholes outside think the rest of the group is still inside."

While they converged to hash out the finer details of this impromptu plan, I snuck upstairs to change out of my lounge wear and into something a little more 'badass spy.'

Hopefully tonight would go off without a hitch, proving Weston wrong.

Hopefully.

A LITTLE MORE THAN an hour later, we slipped out a side window into the late evening darkness. Anne and Tyler dressed in badass tactical gear, each carrying a duffel with weapons, and I was in black leggings and a long-sleeve black shirt. I didn't look as official as them, but at that moment, I didn't care. Grinning from ear to ear, heart racing with excitement, I followed Tyler as we hugged the edge of the house, keeping to the darkest shadows.

Was I a little intimidated and scared, sure, but this was also the most excitement I'd had in days, which trumped everything else.

Behind the tall plants, the constant breeze whipping off the ocean was nonexistent, making the temperature and humidity nearly suffocating. Sweat slicked along my spine, making the long sleeves cling to my damp skin.

Suddenly Tyler stopped. My face slammed into his back, eliciting a low grunt from me at the impact. With a glance over his shoulder, he shot me an amused look before turning and backing up to monitor through a gap in the bushes. Without realizing it, I fisted the back of his shirt as we waited. Waited for what, I had no clue. After a minute, his taut back muscles relaxed beneath my tight fists, and we were on the move again.

With Tyler in the lead and Anne watching our backs, we dashed across the yard, only slowing once we found cover in the thick hedges. Unlike the greenery around the house that were shorter, softer, these bushes were planted as another line of defense for the estate. The little bushy bastard snagged at my shirt and pulled at my long ponytail, but thankfully Tyler, being in the lead, took the brunt of the bush's anger.

Panting from the excitement and heat, I focused on putting one foot in front of the other as I cowered behind Tyler. Cooler air whipped along my sweaty face when we emerged, stumbling from the tall hedges' grasp, only to come face-to-face with a solid stone wall. Without a word, I tapped Tyler's shoulder to find out how in the hell we were supposed to get over the monstrosity, but he was already scaling the thick blocks jutting out from the smooth wall where two larger sections met.

Jaw slack from my astonishment, I followed his moving form as he vertically crawled up little by little. At the top, he slung a leg over to straddle the wall before tossing the other over, dangling the front half of his body my way with a hand extended down toward me.

With a quick flick of his fingers, he beckoned me up.

I shook my head, gaping, knowing there was no way in hell—

A muffled, surprised screech hummed in my chest when a set of hands wrapped around my shoulders and turned me away from the wall. With a smirk, Anne pointed up to Tyler, then cupped her hands.

Oh. Right. Teamwork.

Maybe they were right in not including me in the team pay. Clearly I was a terrible team player and the weak link. Not that this was a new revelation.

The moment my black tennis shoe landed in Anne's interlaced fingers, she counted softly under her breath and lifted. Using the wall as balance, I basically scratched my way up the side, base leg trembling, until a solid hand wrapped around my forearm and hauled me up the last few feet.

I winced when the edge of the wall pressed into my tender belly.

Flipping my legs over the wall, I held on to the edge, dangling myself as low as I could manage before releasing my hold.

The free fall only lasted half a second. My feet slammed into the earth, jolting me so hard I stumbled back, landing on my ass with a grunt. A soft, amused chuckle sounded above my head. I flipped my middle finger up in the air in response, quietly cursing as I stood and dusted off my ass and legs.

"Heads up" was whispered before a duffel bag dropped several feet away, followed by another.

A feminine grunt and furious whispers filled the quiet night moments before the other two landed on this side of the wall. I sneered in disgust with myself when both stuck the landing.

Inclining his head to the right, Tyler gripped the two canvas handles of the duffel bags and jogged toward another row of hedges that lined a portion of this side of the wall. The space between the wall and branches was narrow, and I hugged the stone as much as I could, but with the fast pace Tyler set, a few branches smacked me in the face and neck, leaving stinging scratches in their wake.

The bright flash of oncoming headlights had us all skidding to a halt. In a stealthy move, Tyler and Anne stepped in front of me, pushing me until my back smashed against the stone wall. The blinding light seemed to beam straight into us, giving away our location. I held my breath and said a quick prayer that whoever was driving didn't notice three shady people in all black hiding in the bushes. The last thing we needed was the cops called on us, revealing our attempted escape to the world.

Soon an engine-revving roar filled the night air, growing distant as the headlights also faded.

I slowly released a lungful of air in relief.

After a few more feet, we freed ourselves on the other edge of a thick line of shrubs and dashed across the road, weaving behind tree trunks to maintain some cover. When we rounded a neighboring security wall, my stomach dropped at the shape of a SUV idling along the side of the road in the shadows of the trees with its lights off.

The door swung open, and a familiar frame stepped out of the driver side.

"Thank fuck," Anne muttered behind me. "I need some AC before I sweat completely through these pants."

"Swamp ass?" Tyler tossed over his shoulder.

"Don't you?"

"Of course, but there's a lady present. I don't use that kind of language."

Anne and I both snorted, knowing that was the furthest from the truth as we hurried the short distance toward the Range Rover.

Changed out of his suit, Weston wore familiar black tactical pants and a tight black short-sleeve shirt. A shoulder harness secured two handguns to his sides, with another strapped around his thigh.

"Took you long enough," he grumbled to Tyler as we all piled into the SUV.

"Hawk fell when I tried to pull her up," Tyler said nonchalantly.

"I didn't fucking fall. You dropped me, you weak—"

"Can we just go?" I said, not enjoying being squished between the two while they argued. "And turn on the AC."

The leather beneath Weston groaned as he turned and reached out, cupping my face. "What happened here?" He swiped his thumb along my cheek and pulled it forward so I could see the streak of red.

"An assassin in the disguise of shrubbery," I deadpanned.

To all our shock, a bark of laughter rattled from the passenger seat. Every eye turned to James.

"What? It was funny," he said, still chuckling. "Shrubbery assassins. And here I thought I'd heard of everything."

The corners of Weston's lips twitched, but he steeled his features. "We good?"

"Good," the other three said in unison, like they'd done this a thousand times before. Hell, maybe they had.

"Golden," I added to not feel left out. "Let's go spy on some bad guys. Maybe take a few out. Pew, pew, pew."

"What the fuck was that, Tink?" Tyler laughed, his body shaking against mine in the tight space.

"A gun. Duh."

Weston groaned and flipped back around, gripping the steering wheel with more force than necessary. "This was a terrible idea."

"Of course it was." Tyler laughed, elbowing me. "But that's how all our best stories have started. Tink, did I tell you about this one time in..."

While Tyler started into a mission story I absolutely had not heard before, Weston pulled away from the curb and flipped on the headlights. Adjusting the vents, I directed the gusting cold air toward myself and Anne while Tyler was distracted with his story. Whether or not he noticed I hoarded the AC, he didn't let on, never missing a beat.

In the front seat, James stared at his phone and murmured directions to Weston as he drove through the darkened streets. We passed estate after estate as we maneuvered out of the neighborhood. Soon the larger homes faded into cuter smaller cottages with small yards filled with toys and playscape equipment. Fifteen more minutes and the family neighborhoods changed to worn, dilapidated shacks stacked on top of one another.

"What does Kyle assume happens in these warehouses?" I whispered. Not sure why, but it just felt right in the current situation, even though Tyler was talking loudly, more to himself at this point.

"Remember how he said a group merged with local dealers?" I nodded when Weston's eyes met mine in the rearview. "Well, these warehouses were on a list of suspected storage or dealing locations of those dealers. It's a long shot to find the girls or the trafficking operation, but we were asked to monitor the locations while we're here in case of recent activity. Drug or human trafficking related."

"Okay," I whispered. "So we're just going to watch for a while and then move on to the next one?"

"Yep. If there's any activity, we'll take what photos we can, then send them off to Miss Ginger," James said, sounding annoyed by the lack of excitement in this stakeout mission.

But me? I was beyond excited just to get out of the house. Add in a legit stakeout of an assumed drug dealer's lair? Hell fucking yeah.

Eagerly, I rubbed my palms together with a wicked grin. "This is going to be epic, I just know it."

THE SUN'S warm rays sprouted along the horizon, dusting the dawn in pinks and oranges just as Tyler helped me through the window of the house. My mud-covered tennis shoes slipped on the clean hardwoods as I shuffled toward my room. What I assumed would be an epic night of hunting bad guys and kicking ass turned out to be more boring than sitting around the house watching Anne clean her guns. The most thrilling part of the night was getting out and back into the house undetected.

All three of the warehouses were dead. Zilch activity minus a few stray dogs sniffing about.

Disappointment, exhaustion, and hunger weighed on me, making each step sluggish as I ascended the stairs. Clutching the banister, I forced myself up to my room and slammed the door shut behind me.

"What a damn waste," I muttered to myself. "Was just one guy doing something nefarious too much to ask?" I toed off one shoe and then the other, leaving them in the middle of the room as I trudged toward the en suite bathroom for a much-needed shower. Not only did I reek, but my muscles could use the pounding of steady scalding water to ease the tension.

The sound of the other door slamming echoed in the bathroom, signaling the rest of the team felt as frustrated and disappointed as me. Desperate to rid myself of the sweat and dirt-covered clothes, I ripped the T-shirt over my head, the healed bullet wound in my shoulder stretching with a pinch of pain. My pants took more finagling, considering they were nearly suctioned to my skin. With more anger than warranted toward the stubborn leggings, I kicked them violently off a foot until they flew across the bathroom and smacked against the wall.

I huffed in victory, knowing the damn clingy leggings just learned their lesson.

Inside the glass shower, I twisted the chrome handle all the way to the right, needing the hot water to rinse away the layers of grime. A blasted stream of cold water jolted my lagging mind wide awake before quickly transitioning to scalding my skin. Face under the spray, I shut both lids and held a shallow breath, allowing the steady flow to beat across my scratched cheeks and sweat-soaked hairline.

The bathroom door opened, bringing with it a waft of cool air, but I didn't turn, knowing full well who would enter this bathroom unannounced. The sound of shoes clattering to the floor echoed over the water rushing past my ears. Less than a minute later, the glass door whooshed open and a hot, hard body slid against mine.

We didn't exchange a single word as we washed away the evidence of the unsuccessful venture off the estate grounds. This shower had nothing to do with intimacy, only getting clean enough to fall into bed and not feel disgusting.

Both done with the speedy shower, I shut off the water and turned to wrap both arms around his waist.

"Tonight was not what I expected," I muttered against his skin.

"I know, but we won't see action every time we're out. I'm thankful as hell that we didn't. Getting into a firefight with a bunch of gang-bangers with you in the mix is not something I ever want to do."

I nodded in agreement. "I just feel so useless. I hate this feeling when I'm used to being active either working at Second Chances or at the hospital."

"Want me to stab Axe or Mouse so you can have something to do?"

I chuckled against his chest, skimming my lips over a small dusting of chest hair. Pulling back, I stared at my name tattooed just over his heart and placed a soft kiss along the ink. "If anyone gets to stab James, it's me."

His responding chuckle tickled where my bare skin met his.

Exiting the shower, I wrapped a fluffy towel around my chest and snagged another to begin the tedious process of towel-drying my thick hair. Watching Weston in the mirror, I squished the long dark strands between the cotton fibers, transfixed by how ruggedly gorgeous he was.

With a low-slung towel secured around his hips, dark tattoos decorating his chest and arms, and tousled wet hair, he looked like every woman's wet dream. Well, if we had wet dreams. Which we could, I guess, but I never experienced one.

My reflection tilted her head as I thought it over.

"Do you think women can have wet dreams?"

Ever so slowly, those dark eyes met mine in the mirror. I raised both brows, showing it wasn't a rhetorical question.

"Pretty sure you're the one who took all the anatomy classes and are also a woman."

I shrugged and went back to drying my hair. "Good point."

"I don't even want to know what made that question pop up in that head of yours."

"You." I hitched my chin toward his reflection. "You're all bad-boy model hot in your towel right now."

A soft grin spread up his cheeks, making my heart flutter. Damn, I loved his smile.

"I'm your reality, baby. No need to dream about me." He yawned, covering his open mouth with a fist while stretching the other high above his head. His towel dipped even lower, dragging my focus to his almost exposed crotch. "Fuck, I'm tired."

I nodded and yawned too. "You sleeping with me?" After all we'd been through together, I didn't even try to mask the hope in my voice. I needed him with me to keep the monsters away while I slept. Somehow, even the men who haunted my dreams were too scared to appear when Weston was beside me.

"Of course. Nowhere else I'd rather be." With that, he tugged off the towel, dropped it to the floor, and marched out.

I watched, gaze trained on his muscular bare ass, until he slipped through the door and into the bedroom.

With that view, I suddenly wasn't tired anymore.

Hopefully, with a little encouragement, Weston wouldn't be either.

8

G rogginess weighed my thoughts, making the hushed male voices a struggle to comprehend. Slowly I blinked, forcing my lids to stay open to see who in the hell was waking me up so damn early.

Ugh, when was the last time I was this tired?

Vision glossy, I searched the room from where I lay, warm skin pressing against my curved spine. Rotating along the sheets, I rolled to the other side and draped an arm across Weston's chest. A blurred figure moved along the wall, attracting my attention.

James fucking Steele.

An annoyed-looking James with his frown and furrowed brows.

"Why are you in my room?" I muttered and swiped at the corners of my lips to ensure they were drool free. "What time is it?"

"Ten."

I grumbled and rolled back over, putting my back to him. "Go away, James."

"Told you she's not a morning person." A heavy arm draped over my side and tucked me tighter to a radiating warmth. Soft lips pressed to my temple. "Good morning, baby." A hand slipped beneath the covers, fingertips dancing just below my belly button.

Heat flared, twisting my stomach.

"I don't give a fuck if she's a morning person or not," James snapped. "We need a game plan. I'm not winging this shit because she needs her damn beauty sleep."

"Watch it, Axe," Weston rumbled with warning in his tone. "What exactly did he say?"

Those naughty fingers walked lower. I sucked in a breath, not daring to move.

"The assistant called. His boss wants to meet at one of his clubs later. I guess this is another one of their damn vetting sessions to make sure I'm legit before giving me the details of the auction. These guys might be depraved, but they sure as hell aren't dumb."

"Agreed." A single finger dipped into the wetness already gathering between my thighs. I stifled the urge to wiggle against the hard length pressing against my ass. "Miss Ginger mentioned there have been several hits to the fake profiles they set up. Deep ones too. They're doing everything they can to prove we're not who we say we are."

How he could tease me and keep his tone even while he discussed the mission details was beyond me.

"Oh, and in case you're wondering why I'm in here, he wants me to bring her too."

Those teasing fingers stilled and disappeared completely. The bed jolted when he sat up. Glancing over my shoulder, I watched him tediously secure the blanket to my neck, keeping me covered.

"Fucking hell, Axe," Weston snapped. "I knew you shouldn't have said you'd be open to trading up for the next girl."

Beneath the covers, I placed a hand on Weston's bare thigh, trying to keep him from leaping from the bed and strangling his friend. His body trembled with restraint beneath my hand.

"I didn't have a damn choice," James yelled, throwing his hands in the air. "What sadistic asshole would be too emotionally attached to the girl they're currently looking to replace to not be open to trading with her? Huh? They had eight of their fuckers surrounding us with automatic rifles. I had to say something that day in the hangar. Your life and the others' were in my hands."

Weston relaxed beneath my touch. Whatever James said struck a chord with him, but I wasn't sure which part.

"Fine, you're right. You did what you had to do, but now so am I. She's not going." I dug my nails into his skin and turned to glare at his profile. Weston hissed, shifting out of my reach, and turned his scowling face down to me. "What if they want to sample you, huh?" A fiery rage roared behind his dark eyes. "What if they want to test the product?"

"I...." *Fuck, what do I say to that?*

"We can manage that if it comes up." I blinked up at James, surprised at his words. With the way he didn't want me on the mission at all, I expected him to be on board with the 'Kate not attending this important meeting' command Weston threw down without my say-so. "I won't let them touch her or any of you. She needs to go, play the part she signed up for, and then we leave with the information we came for. We have to do it to get an invitation to the auction, Romeo. There's no other way."

"What kind of club?" Based on past research and documentaries, I had a sick feeling I already knew the answer.

"Strip club." James finally looked at me and raised a brow. "Full nude. That bother you, princess?"

Making sure not to slip a nip, I crossed both arms over my chest and rolled my eyes. "I'm a damn doctor, James. I've seen more naked ladies than you ever will. Second—" I smiled, knowing this next one would throw them both for a loop. "—I've been to one before. They're fun." Slight lie. I've never been to a full-nude strip club, but the other, sure. How different could it be?

Both men blinked slowly. Weston opened his mouth like he had something to say before shutting it again.

"That's surprising considering your stance on all this."

I scoffed at James's ignorant comment. "Yes, some women in the seedier places are there against their will. Those clubs, I'm against. But women trying to make a living the only way they can without turning to selling their vaginas to anyone willing to pay, I'm good with it if they are."

James pressed his lips into a thin line.

Weston scrubbed a hand over his face. "Hawk coming too?"

"No, which means it would just be me, Mouse, and your girl here. You're not coming either." He held up a scarred hand when Weston sat up, ready to protest. "You're too emotional with her around. I don't trust you not to kill any fucker who even looks at her wrong."

Picking at the edge of my lower lip, I nodded. "He's right." Weston's head snapped in my direction. "You know he is. You're great at schooling your features, but this, this is a different level. You've trusted these men with your life before, right?" He gave a single confirming nod. "Then trust them with mine. It's not ideal, but it is what it is at this point."

"Either we all go, or no one goes and we fuck this mission." That steel look in his dark eyes that drilled into my damn soul told me he wouldn't bend on this. "They wanted couples for this auction, so everything you do needs to be as a couple. Who knows, maybe asking you to come alone was a test to see if your wife is as committed to the purchase as you are."

James grimaced. "I hadn't thought of that."

As the two dove right into planning the details, I nestled back down into the bed, hoping for a few more hours of sleep only for the insistent pressure in my bladder keeping me from getting comfortable no matter how many times I twisted and turned. With an annoyed huff, I smacked the comforter, drawing their attention.

"Get out. I need to pee." James blinked and tilted his head in confusion. "I'm naked under here," I said, waving to the sheet and blanket. "So unless you want a little peep show—"

Faster than I'd ever seen a man react to the mention of a naked woman, he spun on his heels and strode out of the bedroom, slamming the door closed behind him.

The moment the door shut, I leapt from the mattress and hurried to the bathroom. When I returned, way more comfortable but very much awake, I found Weston sitting up in bed, eyes trained on his phone.

"If that's your other girlfriend, just know I'll cut her, bury the body, then come back for you."

Without moving, Weston lifted his gaze to me, peering up through his long dark lashes.

"Baby, you're all I need and want. I can barely handle you most of the time. Why would I—"

Before he could finish, I raced the remaining few steps and pounced on the bed, straddling him in a single leap. A grunt rushed past my ear as I leaned in close and nuzzled his neck. Toeing at the sheet, I dragged it down until we were skin to skin.

"Good morning, baby." He chuckled as I pressed soft kisses along his neck. His abs flexed as I trailed a hand between my raised thighs, sweeping my fingers along the rippled muscles. "Fuck," he groaned, shifting along the bed when I wrapped my fingers around him, squeezing tight. Up and down, I pumped my hand along his cock while staring deep into his hooded brown eyes. Positioning his thick head just outside my slick entrance, I slowly lowered until our hips connected.

Our combined groans filled the room as I adjusted, moving my knees wider to take him an inch deeper.

Palms to his tattoo-covered pecs, I smiled down at him, loving the way my hair seemed to protect us from the outside world. In here, it was just us. No traffickers, no team, no terrifying memories.

"It is a very good morning. Now, Casey, finish what you started earlier with your friend in the room." A wicked gleam and smirk told me he enjoyed teasing me, knowing I couldn't do a thing about it. "Show me how much you want me."

Gripping my hips, he raised me up, lifting my slight weight, and then brought me back down hard, slamming into me with a flex of his hips.

Oh fuck.

A very good morning indeed.

THE CARESSING SILK of the one-size-too-large dress floated in the early evening breeze, flicking against my shins as we walked into the club. My stick-straight hair—which took me over an hour to achieve, since humidity was still being a bitch—swept across my face, sticking to the light shimmering gloss coating my lips.

Beside me, James strode a single step ahead, a firm grip around my bicep like he was dragging my reluctant ass to the meeting. Anne looked gorgeous as always, having dropped the badass combat outfit and donning a black Prada pantsuit and low-cut black silk tank beneath.

Our two guards, Weston and Tyler, stayed close behind. Before we left the house, I watched each strap on at least four different guns plus a knife along each calf, then stuff switchblades in their slacks' side pockets.

We were prepared for anything.

We hoped.

Everyone looked ready for this shady business meeting, whereas I looked like I was playing dress-up in Anne's clothes. But that was what we were going for. The smaller I appeared, the more they'd believe I was mid-twenties instead of my true mid-thirties. The Botox injections along my forehead and around my eyes helped the younger appearance. Not that I'd admit that to James. Turned out that shit was legit, and I liked it enough to add the quarterly sessions to my beauty routine when we got back home.

James tugged me to a stop in front of the dual twelve-foot-tall glass doors, the tint so dark it hid any hint of movement on the other side. I startled when the door swung open, allowing cherry-scented air to escape the large club.

From the outside, the building looked like something you'd find in New Orleans, the old architecture more Creole style than tropical with its arches, white trim, and dark green façade. At first I thought we'd arrived at the wrong place since there was no blinking sign with a kicking female leg or bright neon letters advertising nude girls.

But apparently this was a classy, fully nude strip club. If that was a thing.

Beside me, James nodded to a suit-clad man who opened the door for us and shoved me inside first. The toe of my ballet flat caught the edge of the red carpet, making me stumble forward. I fought the urge to turn and glare at James, knowing full well that would give us away.

The man who opened the door told us to follow him and started down a long, dark hallway. Soft light barely lit the floor from the wall sconces placed every few feet. At the end of the hall, the man swung open another door, this one groaning under the heavy weight.

The stench of sex, sweat, and vanilla clogged in my throat, making me choke. Stifling the urge to cough, I tipped my face to the floor and forced a hard swallow. The strip clubs I'd been to in the past all had this same smell, but those few times I went during college with friends, I was wasted. I wasn't this go-round, which was a mistake. Maybe a strong drink before leaving the house would've helped my heart not burst from my chest.

Shit, what if I was having a heart attack? I had been pretty stressed out lately.

Okay, maybe my whole life.

I gave myself a quick check, making sure no other heart attack symptoms were present as we descended a short set of stairs. To my left and right, movement along the stages and flashes of colored light caught my eye, but I refused to look up from the floor. All around me, dance music thumped, seeming to vibrate along my spine all the way to my toes.

Dutifully following James, I slid onto the black leather couch beside him, careful to leave at least a two-inch gap between us, and placed my folded hands onto my lap. The cushion popped on my other side when Anne eased onto the couch beside me, never glancing up from the game she played on her phone. Even though her eyes never strayed from the device, I knew she was aware of every person in the room.

Warmth ignited at my back, indicating either Weston or Tyler's hovering presence.

"He'll be with you soon," our guide said. "Enjoy the entertainment while you wait. Drinks are on the house."

I followed his black shoes until I couldn't see them anymore without lifting my head.

James adjusted along the couch, manspreading and tossing an arm over the back like he owned the damn place. This was his role though, acting like a douchenozzle who'd be completely relaxed waiting to meet someone who auctioned women for a living.

A server came by, her five-inch red heels my sole focus as she asked James if he'd like a drink. Anne spoke up before he could and ordered a triple vodka on the rocks. James ordered a Blanton's on a cube. As if I or the two men behind us didn't exist, she left with only the two drink orders, not caring if we were thirsty or not.

I ground my teeth in annoyance. I was fucking thirsty. Maybe I could sneak a sip of Anne's at some point. Throat suddenly dry, I swallowed hard and adjusted along the couch.

One song after another blared through the overhead sound system, and still the promoter didn't come.

What felt like hours later, James stood from the couch and hauled me up with him. After adjusting his pants, which I assumed was to make others think he was hiding an erection that he clearly wasn't, he stormed across the room, dragging me behind him.

"Stay with her," James commanded over his shoulder.

Oh, Weston would not be happy about that.

At a closed door, a man stepped in front, blocking our entrance.

"I need a room." I trembled at James's words, the low gruff tone of his voice almost husky. "Now."

There must have been something on James's face or in his tone, as the guard immediately opened the door and held it so we could maneuver through.

"All are open," he muttered at my back. I could feel his leering gaze as James dragged me past one curtained-off room after another.

James stopped suddenly and ripped back the curtain, the thick velvet soundless as it slid along the high metal bar. With a hard shove to my back, I stumbled inside the small room, James hot on my heels.

Half a second was all I gave myself to acclimate to the new surroundings as best I could with my mind playing catch-up to what the actual fuck was going on.

What the hell was James thinking bringing me back here? I knew deep in my gut he wouldn't harm me in the way every other man in the building and the guards assumed.

But again, why with the whole charade?

As smart as I was, I couldn't come up with an answer.

Turning in a quick circle, I found a single deep leather chair in the corner, a pole with a small stage in the middle. Beside the chair stood a side table with neatly folded white hand towels, a sweating pitcher of ice water, and a single glass. I shifted to face James, finding him watching me while he tossed back the remaining dark liquid from the highball glass between his fingers.

That dark, calculating gaze flicked upward, almost scanning for something. He continued tipping the glass back, even though nothing remained as he searched the ceiling and corners.

Cameras.

James's random behavior with the empty glass was a cover as he searched for cameras.

When he slipped the glass from his lips to dangle it by his side, a sliver of tension around his eyes lessened. Without a word, he nodded and shifted to lean back against the wall. With a crook of his finger, he beckoned me closer and closer until we were toe to toe. This close, I could almost feel the animosity and resentment pulsing off him as I searched his face, hoping to find answers.

I jumped when the crystal glass slipped from his fingertips and tumbled to the floor, the soft carpet cushioning its fall. In a smooth motion, one calloused hand wrapped around my waist and hauled me against him while the other slipped beneath my hair and grasped my neck.

Fear soared through my veins, my instinct to fight out of his hold kicking in. With everything I had, I pushed and shoved against him but got nowhere under his tight hold.

"Stop," he hissed, bending close to put his lips close to my ear. "I don't like this any more than you do, princess."

"Why?" I asked, my frantic breaths bouncing off his suit coat, fanning back against my face. A thin streak of gloss glimmered in the pulsing light along the lapel of his jacket from where my coated lips brushed against him in the scuffle.

"Well, we obviously wouldn't get a tour of the place, and I wanted to see what these bastards were hiding behind door number two."

The way his breath brushed across my ear made my muscles twitch, ready to break free of his hold. Only the reminder that this was for the mission, not him, kept me frozen in his arms.

"Was that a joke?"

"Maybe. I noticed two girls, wobbly on their feet, led back here while we were waiting out there. Neither ever came back out, which I found odd considering we've been here for over two hours." *Two hours? Ugh, feels like ten.* "Since you were being the perfect little submissive and kept your gaze down, you didn't notice the door next door. But I sure as fuck did. It's why I put us in this room specifically."

"Is it different?" I whispered.

"Very different. It's a solid door, not a curtain like the others. There are two more too."

I frowned, thinking over his words. "Odd."

"I watched a few of the girls out there—"

"Ew, do not need to hear—"

"It's called research, princess."

"Still TMI, asshole."

"Just fucking listen for once. The dancers on the various stages, the girl behind the bar, and those waiting on us all seemed into their jobs. Not one hesitation. Made me wonder if there are women against their will here on site, considering why we're using this place for a meeting to discuss auctioning stolen women. Where would they be hiding them?"

"The back rooms." James nodded. "One more question. Why in the hell are you touching me?"

His chest ballooned, and an almost laugh brushed through my

hair. "Because if anyone looks in here or I missed a camera...." He trailed off, letting me fill in the blanks.

"Smart."

"You sound surprised."

"Well...."

"You and that mouth of yours," he huffed. "How Romeo puts up with it, I'll never—" He cut himself off and straightened against the wall. "Fuck, someone's coming."

Just like that, his tension and tone snapped me into hyper-drive. I strained to hear what he heard, but came up with nothing.

"I'm sorry about this."

Before I could question what he meant, I was tossed across the small room to the opposite wall, my chest colliding with a thud and palms smacking to the smooth surface before my face could connect. Just like that, memories soared to the forefront of my mind, terrible memories of Chase and the warehouse and almost being....

I sucked down gulps of air in desperate attempts to keep from passing out. Sweat collected, dripping down my forehead and between my breasts. A pitiful, terrified whimper croaked up my throat when his heavyweight pressed against my back, pushing me harder into the wall.

"I won't hurt you," he said softly into my hair. "I'd never hurt a woman, but especially not my best friend's girl."

I knew that. I fucking knew with every ounce of my being that James would rather die than hurt me. He was a conceited, arrogant asshole, sure, but not deviant like the bastard he portrayed for this mission. Even knowing all that, I couldn't stop the spiraling panic attack as it squeezed in my chest and threatened to swallow me whole.

The clink of a belt being undone tipped me over into unending, peaceful darkness. Everything went numb. I slumped against the wall as all my fight and emotion fled.

Through the roaring in my ears, a grumbled curse sounded close yet far away.

Slowly, I began sliding down the wall, my legs no longer holding my body weight.

James snaked an arm around my waist, holding me steady, and rested his chin on my shoulder.

"You're okay, Doc. It's just me, the sexy asshole. Say something so I know you're still with me."

Words wouldn't form in my mind, not even a sassy comeback to his 'sexy asshole' comment.

"Weston saved me." Just his name cleared a bit of the all-encompassing darkness. "Many times, in fact. Most recently by putting me on this team. I owe Romeo my life."

"Mr. Bartwright." James lifted his chin to, I assumed, look over his shoulder where the voice came from. "We're ready for you two."

"Fuck off," he snapped, as any guy might do if he was interrupted. "I'll be done when I'm fucking done."

The pressure on my back returned, and a hot breath fanned through my hair.

"Almost done, Doc," he said, almost too low for me to hear. "When I step back, I want you to shrink into the corner, try to look disheveled." *Try? Is he serious?* Pretty sure I looked disheveled already with a sweaty face, hair growing by the second, and silk dress clinging to my sticky skin. "I'll send Romeo back to take care of you. You two look around while I entertain the fuckers."

All I could manage was a single nod, but it was enough confirmation for him to release me with a barked curse.

"Fuck," he grunted and shoved away from the wall. With a not-so-hard push, he urged me toward the corner between the wall and the leather chair. I cringed as I curled along the carpet, feeling how stiff it was from... Ew. Not going there.

Cowering in the shadows, I heard rather than saw James storm off. "Get my damn guard to get her. Fucking pathetic."

And then I was alone.

I wasn't sure which was better.

Alone in a club where human traffickers worked and did business, or with James acting like he was having sex with me all for show.

Unfortunately, I didn't have time to debate the lesser of the two evils before someone yanked the curtain back and an unfamiliar man stepped into the small room.

Well, fuck.

9

The unfamiliar black eyes glared from where he stood holding the curtain open, a look of disgust on his thin face. The overwhelming urge to jump from the floor and into a fighting stance warred through me, every muscle twitching from the fight with myself to stay cowering in the corner.

He took a single step deeper into the room, a small evil smile now contorting his face, allowing his depraved thoughts to shine through. Bile rose up my throat as the fear of what was to come rolled in my stomach.

"Now that he's done—"

"What the fuck do you think you're doing?" The building fight and freezing terror drained from my veins at the sound of Weston's booming, pissed voice blaring down the hall. "Get the hell out of here. I'll deal with her."

Through the strands of hair curtaining my face, I watched as Weston shoved him out with a hand gripped around his throat. With one last snarl at the man as he tossed him out, Weston ripped the curtain closed. In two quick steps, he crouched in front of me, concern bleeding through his searching gaze as he scanned my face.

"Cameras?" The single word was more of a breath, so quiet I almost missed it.

I shook my head.

"You okay?" The low, menacing vibration in his voice paused my erratic heartbeat. Tilting my chin, I stared into his dark chocolate brown eyes, looking for the cause of his anger. "Are. You. Okay?" Each word hissed through his tightly clenched jaw.

"Yes," I whispered back. He visibly shuddered, as if my response sent a tidal wave of relief washing over him. "We need to get back there. James said—" A menacing look flooded Weston's face at the mention of his friend. I swallowed hard and inclined my head toward the few rooms James mentioned were strange. "The rooms that way are different. We need to check them out." Neither of us moved. "Weston?"

"Give me a second, Kate," he grunted, closing his eyes. "Did he touch you?"

"Not the time," I snapped. "Say you're trying to find a bathroom for me to clean up."

A perfect excuse for wandering around, if you asked me.

Gentle fingers wrapped around both shoulders, lifting me off the ground as he stood, releasing me when I was steady on my own two feet. With a grimace, he slipped a hand through my hair and gripped the back of my neck in a proprietary way. We both knew the type of show that was needed once we left the little room. With a single nod, he turned, urging me through the part in the curtain and back into the narrow hall.

Learning more about the rooms was a priority. To ensure Weston understood which direction we needed to investigate, I shifted my slight weight to the right, silently urging him the way we needed to snoop. Without a hint of hesitation, he turned to the right and pushed me forward. Each step was slow, like Weston gave me time to keep my footing along the unfamiliar hall, but in reality we moved hesitantly to center our focus on the four rooms with solid doors instead of curtains.

And locks.

A deadbolt on each door that locked from the outside, plus another with a key inserted inside.

What the hell kind of horrors happened behind those doors for two locks? I chanced a worried look at Weston. Face grim, he dipped his chin and reached out to try one of the door handles.

Unlocked, the door swung open without a sound.

The hand on my neck tightened as Weston poked his head inside, keeping me from seeing through the gap into the room. Not that I wanted to see inside. Based on the foul smells of body odor, body fluids, and the unmistakable scent of blood, I had a suspicion what happened behind these menacing doors. The others with curtains were for lap dances and private shows. These four secure rooms were for those clients who wanted more from the girls—willing or not.

A shiver of disgust rushed down my spine.

How could we do this to each other? How could evil be so ingrained in someone that they would allow this to happen to another human being?

With a quiet snicker, the door clicked shut. Not saying a word, we moved to the next door. That one was also unlocked and empty. But at the next one, the door didn't open with a flick of the handle. Locked.

Releasing his hold on me, Weston kept one hand near his concealed sidearm and flicked the deadbolt. I held a shallow breath, watching with nervous anticipation as he eased the door open.

"What the hell do you think you're doing?"

Shocked at being caught red-handed, I whirled around toward the angry voice. My wide eyes met the man's suspicious gaze before I remembered my role and dipped my face to the floor.

"Finding a bathroom to clean her up," Weston said nonchalantly. "Where the fuck is it?"

I could feel the man's heavy stare as silence filled the hall.

Shit.

Shit.

Shit.

"This way." Weston's hot palm slipped behind my neck once

again, the grip soft and comforting as he led me in the direction the club's security guard pointed us. "This area is for approved clients only."

"I'm certain my boss is on the fucking approved list."

"We'll see about that soon enough."

I swallowed hard at his ominous tone.

Inside the single powder room, I stumbled toward the sink and gripped the black porcelain like my life depended on it. My hands shook as I twisted the cold water tap. Glancing up in the mirror, I eyed Weston in the reflection. Stance stiff, arms crossed, brows furrowed—oh, he was pissed.

"I'm fine," I whispered. Who knew if they had listening devices in here, so I couldn't say much, but I needed to ease the pain and worry in his dark eyes. Leaning forward, I splashed the cold water on my cheeks to calm my frayed nerves and wipe away the salty remains of dried tears.

His return nod was stiff, almost like he didn't fully believe me. Flipping around, I pressed my back against the edge of the sink and cocked a brow. With another stiff nod, he yanked the door open and stormed out. With an eye roll, I trailed him to where he waited just outside the door.

The blare of bass and techno music assaulted my ears the moment we stepped back into the premier room. The hand around the back of my neck pulled me to a stop. Brows furrowed, I chanced a glance, only to find the room empty—our group was gone.

Shit. Where are they? Straining my eyes, I looked as far in my periphery as possible, searching for the team.

"This way."

I jumped at the closeness of a male voice—too close. I didn't dare look up when he wrapped a meaty hand around my bicep, squeezing to the point of pain. I winced, my shoulder lifting as I fought the urge to rip my arm away.

"Hands off what's ours if you value your life." Another strong, much gentler grip encircled my other arm.

Unable to stop myself, I watched nervously as they faced off with me between them.

With a humorless huff, the man shoved me into Weston's side and held up both hands in surrender.

"Fine, keep your toys to yourself. Follow me." Turning on his heels, he strode in the opposite direction of the door James took me through earlier. "Hurry the fuck up. He doesn't like to wait."

A thumb brushed along my shoulder in a comforting sweep as we hurried to follow. I turned my gaze up to Weston, who shot me a guilty grimace. Of course he thought that guy's hand on me was his fault somehow.

Down a maze of short hallways lined with similar doors, it felt like they led us in circles until familiar voices sounded, signaling we were close. The door to the room where the team waited was open, offering a glimpse of the situation before we crossed the threshold.

I swallowed the gasp that wanted to erupt at the sight of Tyler draped between two men, face swollen and blood dripping from several shallow cuts. The grip around my bicep tightened before Weston tugged me safely behind him. Just before the scene before me disappeared, I caught Tyler's pointed look at Weston and slight shake of his head.

Peeking around Weston's side, I surveyed the room, trying to understand what the hell was going on. Neither Anne nor James said a word as a third guy punched Tyler in the gut. He wheezed, slumping forward when his knees gave out.

"That's enough," James said in a bored tone. "He knows his place now. As does yours."

A pain-laced moan from the floor drew my attention to what I hadn't noticed before. My eyes widened to the size of saucers. One of the other guards lay flat on the floor, barely twitching like he was just coming to.

What the hell?

"Bring her here," James snapped, his voice a direct command. "Let's get this shit done."

Reluctantly, Weston moved me back around to his side, helped me step over the still moaning man, and pointed to the seat beside James—the farthest from the man sitting on the opposite leather couch.

With the slick material of my dress, only the puff of the cushion molding beneath my backside sounded as I eased onto the couch. Based on the vibrating tension and testosterone in the room, I knew better than to draw more attention to myself than there already was.

"Look at me, pet." Everything in me roared with disgust and annoyance at the haughty command, but I fought through my natural urges and slowly lifted my face. Blank mask firmly in place, I hid my disgust as the man inspected every inch of exposed skin, his gaze lingering a little too long on my throat for my liking. He licked his thin lips as he nodded. "Very nice. Older than our normal product though, which is a concern for resale."

"She's been with me a while. Boring as fuck now." A heavy hand landed on my shoulder, and I flinched away. "No fight left in her."

"Hmm," the man mused as he leaned back into the couch, fingers tapping along the armrest. "That's a plus for some of my clients. Too lazy to work for it, if you will." A knowing, sinister grin spread across his face.

I choked back the disgust threatening to erupt from my throat. Everything about this man was sleazy. With slicked-back black hair, beady eyes, and a beak-like nose, he looked like the perfect villain—which he was to the many women he sold to deviant buyers.

"Mind if I sample the product before I offer a trade-in value for your next purchase?"

"Yes," James said with a laugh. "I don't know where you've been, and I go in bare. No sampling—any part of her."

The man cocked his head as he studied James with an unnatural stillness about him. A rush of fear raced through my veins, my breath catching. Was this when we were discovered? These could be our final few seconds of living. I held a shallow breath at the thought, holding it until the man's snakelike grin slipped across his face.

"Smart man. Possessive too."

A glass with a few ice cubes thumped on top of the side table next to his arm, drawing my focus to the completely nude woman who delivered it. The glass decanter clutched in her hands trembled as she poured his drink, a few drops sloshing over the side from her tremors.

The man sneered in clear disgust at the mess and flicked a dismissive hand toward something behind me. "You two go." Only then did he shift his penetrating gaze from me to James. "Our pets shouldn't be present for this next part of our discussion."

Then why the hell did you make me come today? I wanted to shout in his face while punching him in the balls. The need to inflict harm on the disgusting man roared inside me. Only the few useable pointers from that therapist helped calm my need for blood.

One of the other men who'd dropped Tyler at his feet grabbed the now-cowering naked woman by the upper arm. A shriek of pain or fear bounced off the walls when he hauled her across the room, disappearing behind me. Another guard started toward me only to stop dead in his tracks, eyes going wide when a distinctive click of a gun engaging reached my ears.

I froze when, in the next breath, the others pulled their guns free and trained them on us. The uncontrollable shake started in my toes, moving up my ankles, to my knees and thighs. Soon my entire body visibly shook with terror.

Anne let out an amused laugh as she took in the room, shaking her head, then turning her bored face back to the phone in her hand. Tyler, who lay on the floor barely able to see out of one eye, had his own gun raised.

I watched in astonishment as James ignored the scene unfolding before us to brush off some lint from his slacks. The icy glare he sent the now serious man sitting across from us chilled me to the bone. "Are you trying to steal her from me?"

The man steepled two fingers beneath his chin and glanced around the room. "What kind of business partner do you think I am?" He had the audacity to sound affronted by James's accusation. "I wouldn't think of it. Now kindly have your men lower their weapons."

"Not until yours do," James countered, leaning back and resting both arms along the back of the couch like he owned the place.

He gave a single nod to one of his guards, and the other men slowly lowered their guns. Weston and Tyler followed suit but didn't holster their weapons.

"Now kindly tell your pet to go with mine while we discuss the finer details of this business meeting. There is still much to discuss."

Oh hell. I had zero desire to go anywhere alone, but if this fucker wouldn't talk about the auction details with me in the room, how could I refuse? I turned to James for direction on what to do. He waved a hand, motioning for me to stand.

"Go. But he'll go with you." He inclined his head to Weston and turned his attention back across the room. "I don't trust you or your men to handle her with care while she's away from me. I might be ready to purchase an upgrade, but until I have a replacement pussy ready to rip apart, I need her whole."

Lovely. What lovely fucking words.

But he'd finagled Weston in the room with me, so I couldn't be too pissed.

Weston shifted to stand in front of me, not giving the other man a chance to deny James's request, and helped me stand. Instead of tugging me along, he pointed to the door the other woman walked through.

Only pressing the tips of my toes to the rug, I moved quickly while dodging the splatters of blood.

A tsk sounded at my back, making my hackles rise. "You're leaving you and your wife defenseless," the promoter said in a chiding tone.

"You're a fool if you think they're the dangerous ones in the room."

Oh snap. I sent James a mental high five as I stepped into the adjoining room. With the light much lower than the office, I forced several hard blinks to help my vision adjust. With a hand pressed between my shoulder blades, Weston guided me deeper into the room as my vision cleared. In front of me, the other woman sat on the edge of a black leather couch, her head bowed and arms tightly wrapped around her stomach.

The door clicked closed behind us, cutting off the voices from the other room. For the first time since we walked into the club, silence engulfed us. Not a single beat or vibration from the club's sound system reached inside. I shifted on my feet, unsure what to do, where to go, or if talking was even allowed. Half turning, I looked at Weston with my brows raised, hoping he'd offer some insight.

"Sit down," he said, pointing to the chair opposite the clearly distraught woman who now rocked back and forth, mumbling quiet words to herself. "It might be a while."

I grimaced at the stickiness coating the expensive leather as I eased onto the cushions and leaned back. Keeping both hands clasped, I studied the woman directly across from me, only a coffee table separating us.

As if she could feel my scrutiny, her bloodshot baby blue eyes shot up and locked on me. Her breathing grew more rapid, her naked chest rising and falling faster and faster.

Purple and black bruises littered her neck and arms, and if I wasn't mistaken, a heavy layer of makeup concealed a healing yellow bruise along the right side of her jaw.

The more I studied her, the angrier I became. Not just at the visible abuse her thin body had taken but at the fact that all I could do was sit and stare. I couldn't inspect her injuries, couldn't prod around to find out why she was holding her stomach in a death grip. Couldn't do one fucking thing my brain and body demanded I do to help the woman who obviously needed a doctor.

Her lower lip trembled before she tucked it between her teeth.

"Help me," she whispered before sucking in a breath and groaning, curving over until her forehead smacked her knees. "Help me, help me, help me," she repeated over and over.

Slowly, I turned my head to where Weston leaned against the far wall, my eyes pleading with him to allow me to do something—anything. He pursed his lips, clearly feeling as helpless as I did and hating it.

"How?" I questioned the woman, not waiting for Weston to respond to my unspoken question. He visibly tensed and took a step closer to the couch. "How can I help you?"

That wasn't terrible. Didn't give anything away. It's not like I said, 'Hey, guess what? You're in luck, because we're actually here to save you from this shithole. Not today but soon.' That would've been bad. But I held my tongue—James would be shocked—and asked a blanket question.

I'm totally killing it at this undercover stuff.

Next stop CIA, where I'll become the female version of Jason Bourne.

But the woman didn't respond with words; instead she groaned in pain, rocking again along the edge of the couch.

That was it. I couldn't take it any longer. My medical training rushed to the surface. Pushing off the chair, I maneuvered around the coffee table and sat beside her. She jumped, her face twisting in pain with the movement.

"I just want to help," I said with both palms up in a placating stance. Her wild eyes moved to Weston as I tracked her line of sight and grimaced. He did not look happy. "Don't worry about him. He won't tell because I'm not doing anything to hurt myself or escape." That sounded like a legit excuse, right? "Come here, let me help you."

Instead of moving closer, she narrowed her eyes in clear disbelief.

I sighed, knowing they had abused her too long for her to trust me in the first few minutes of us meeting considering the circumstances.

"What hurts?" I asked, watching her arm constrict around her middle. "Your stomach?"

She gave a reluctant nod, thin blonde hair slipping over her rounded shoulders.

Fuck. That could be one of a dozen things, and that was just what I could come up with off the top of my head. Maybe she was hungry or about to start or....

"Are you pregnant?"

Horror blanketed her features, face going deathly pale.

"No, no, no, no," she said over and over like she was trying to convince herself. "Get me out of here," she begged. "Take me with you."

I sucked in a breath and bit my lip so hard a sharp sting told me I'd bit through the flesh.

"I can't, but you need a doctor," I said through clenched teeth. "Will he get you medical help? Mine does when I'm sick."

Lunging forward, she grabbed onto both my shoulders with unexpected strength. Her nails snagged at the dress and dug into my skin.

"Take me with you. Get me out of here. Please."

Guilt wrapped around my heart and twisted, sending barbs of pain through my chest and up my throat.

One second she was pleading for us to save her, the next those fear-filled eyes rolled into the back of her head and she fell limp onto the couch before sliding to the floor in a heap of tangled limbs.

"Shit," I snapped and dropped to my knees beside her. Hand pressed to her shoulder, I rolled her over with ease and pressed two fingers to her neck, desperate to find a pulse. "She isn't dead, so that's a good thing." Next I prodded at her stomach, trying to find what was causing her pain. It could be anything from a failed miscarriage to a bowel obstruction, and I couldn't fucking tell what was wrong with just my damn hands. "She needs a doctor. Make them get her to a doctor."

A loud pounding vibrated around the room.

"Get off the floor," Weston commanded. Reluctantly I pulled myself away from the convulsing girl and leveraged myself back up onto the couch half a second before the door swung open. "Your girl is down. Said something about her stomach."

With little urgency, a suited guard moved past the one holding open the door and scooped up the woman with an arm beneath her neck and one under her bent knees. Within a minute of her collapsing in front of me, she was gone.

Tears lining my lower lids, I followed their retreating backs until the door slammed shut, sealing Weston and me inside.

"Don't look like that," Weston said under his breath from where he stood guard along the wall. "You couldn't have done anything."

He was right, but it still didn't make the feeling of failure any less heavy in my heart.

For the first time since we started this mission, I wondered if everything we were doing was actually worth it. If I couldn't help one woman who was dying in front of me, how in the hell was I supposed to save others?

10

―――――

"I said I'm fine, Tink," Tyler grumbled beneath my prodding fingers for the thousandth time as I inspected the swollen facial tissue, checking for any breaks that might need resetting or worse, a hospital visit. "I've had worse, believe me."

"Don't tell me that," I chastised. "I'm a doctor first, and hearing about anyone hurt—well, anyone I like—makes me hurt too. Instead of complaining about the free health screening I'm providing, how about you tell me what happened in the damn office before Weston and I arrived? One guy knocked out cold and you beat to shit—"

"I'm not beat to shit," Tyler grumbled before hissing when I pressed on a tender area along his nose. "Will I still be pretty?" Those innocent eyes blinked up at me, full of light and humor.

"As pretty as you ever were," I said, finishing my inspection of his face before trailing my hands lower. "Now this might hurt," I warned with a grimace of my own.

It would hurt. There was no might about it. I'd had bruises along my ribs like his, and anyone even breathing on the area hurt, so my poking to check for rib fractures would most definitely be painful.

"One of those asshole guards grabbed Hawk," James said. Pausing my fingers, I peeked up through my lashes. His features hard, anger rolled off him in waves. He'd barely spoken since we left that awful club over an hour ago. "She mouthed off about something, he grabbed her arm, and Mouse here knocked him out cold." A smile pulled at his thin lips. "Nice work, by the way."

The cut along Tyler's lower lip split deeper at his widening smile. "Thanks."

"That's when we came in?" I asked as I moved my fingertips along each of Tyler's ribs.

"They wanted a punch for a punch," Tyler grumbled. "Good thing none of them knew how to land a single—" He hissed, cutting himself off.

"You were saying?" I raised both brows and shot him an incredulous look before turning my focus back to his ribs. "Was it at least worth it?"

"What?"

"Any of it," I clarified.

"He was about to give me the information on the auction when his girl OD'd," James said.

My hands trembled with restrained anger. "She didn't OD. I know those signs. It was something...." I shook my head. The signs were strange, off almost. Who knew what she was on and what was going on in that weak body of hers. "It was something else. And I couldn't help her."

"You did what you could," Weston said from where he sat, barely perched on the back of the couch. I didn't dare to look over at him. I hadn't been able to meet his gaze since we left the club. I didn't want to answer the questions he was no doubt dying to ask.

No, I didn't know James's plans to pull me in that back room.

Yes, I freaked out when he pretended to pin me.

No, he didn't touch me in that way.

No, I wasn't mad at him.

No, his body wouldn't show up floating in the ocean tomorrow.

Well, maybe. Still debating that last one; we had a few more hours in the night to get through.

Satisfied nothing was broken on Tyler's beaten body, I sat back on my heels and peeked up at Weston. His dark eyes were on James, and if looks could kill....

"Hey," I said, snapping my fingers to gain his attention. "We're all good." I waved a hand, gesturing to our merry little band of killers. "No one died. We got some basic information out of our little outing and met some terrible people. I wouldn't call that a win, but it sure as hell wasn't a damn loss."

"What happened back in that room?" Weston asked, sliding his glare back to James, who straightened at Weston's icy tone.

"Nothing, Romeo." If I wasn't mistaken, there was a hint of remorse in James's tone. "We needed a reason to see down that hall. What did you find after I left?"

The muscle along Weston's jaw twitched. For several seconds, he remained silent, staring James down like he was moments from launching across the room and taking him out.

"Nothing definite. The rooms with the doors had locks on the outside and inside. The smell—" He cut himself off and shifted his gaze to a dark corner of the room. "There's no doubt in my mind what goes on in those few rooms. The last one was locked from the outside, but one of those fuckers stopped me before I could get a good look to see if anyone was inside."

"Do we think that's where they hold the auctions?" I asked absentmindedly as I stood to make my way to the kitchen to wash Tyler's dried blood off my hands. I shivered as the cold water splashed over my fingers, turning pink. The need to bathe my entire body in sanitizer after leaving that place was strong. "That would make our mission easier, wouldn't it?"

"I don't think the club is where they hold them or have the auctions." Weston pushed off the wall and took a step toward James, who retreated. "But I think that's where they bring a few women for clients who want more than a damn lap dance. My guess is they bring one or two there for the night, then take them back where they're holding them when they close." Reaching out, he pointed at James. "You, outside. Now."

Without waiting for an answer, Weston turned and stalked

outside, throwing the door wide open before disappearing on the dark back patio.

"Oh, someone's in trouble for playing with Romeo's girlfriend."

I cut Tyler a 'shut the hell up' look.

"I wasn't fucking playing with her," James grumbled and strode toward the back door, shoulders rounded.

"Wait," I said, stopping James in his tracks. "What about the guards? Won't they hear you?"

He cast a wary look outside before turning back to me. "They were called off. Apparently whatever they needed to see from me, from us, was met today."

That seemed strange. Unease tightened in my stomach. I wanted to push him on it, ask more about why they would suddenly call off the guards, but James stepped through the door and closed it behind him.

A painful groan chased away the oddness of the guard's removal. Hawk helped Tyler off the floor, hands hovering until he stopped swaying and stood steady.

"I'm going to take a shower," he muttered and staggered down the hall to his room.

I watched him to make sure he made it there okay. It would really suck if he didn't break anything earlier but to run into a wall now, shattering his nose.

"Hey." I jumped at the sound of the close voice. "Sorry, we're all a little jumpy after today." I turned to Anne, the rag I was using to dry my hands now pulled tight between my clenched fists. "You did good today."

"Thanks." I sighed and leaned forward, pressing both hips to the counter. "I freaked out back there. With James." Chewing on the corner of my lip, I held back what was desperate to spew out of my mouth.

"Want to talk about it?" I stayed silent while studying the marble counter. "I know I've offered this before, but I really am here if you want to talk. Unlike everyone else, I know what it's like."

I scoffed and shook my head. "You know what it's like to be almost

—" The word closed up my throat. "—in front of your boyfriend? To have almost gotten him killed because of something you did?"

Her weary sigh pulled my attention to her. Eyes unfocused, she stared at the wall. "Well, yeah. Not exactly the same situation, but similar. I know what it takes from you, how vulnerable you feel after being in a situation like that. And how fucking shitty that feels because there's nothing you can do about it. I know what it feels like to be made to do shit you had to but didn't want to. I'm a woman in a man's world, Kate. Don't for one second think I've never been manipulated, taken advantage of, or forced to...."

Wetness slicked her lower lids.

I swallowed hard, chasing down the guilt riding up my throat.

I should've known someone like her would understand.

"I need a damn drink," she muttered and closed her eyes, tilting her face to the ceiling. When she reopened them, she cut her gaze over and smiled. "Wanna get out of here?"

"Girls' night?" I said, a tilt to my voice showing my excitement about the idea. Leaning to the right, I peered around her shoulders. "Think they'll let us go?"

She scoffed. "Who says we have to let them know? Go change. We'll sneak out in twenty minutes."

"Sneak out?" I said behind her as we ascended the stairs, me one step behind her.

At the top, she shot me a wicked smile. "Well, yeah. Where's the fun in going out the front door?"

For the first time all day, my lips parted with a wide smile. "Make it thirty. I need a shower."

"There's a dive bar I saw within walking distance from here, so wear something comfortable."

At my door, hand on the knob, I turned. "Please tell me there's karaoke."

The sadness and frustration from earlier had vanished from Anne's beautiful face, her smile mirroring my own. "I think I like you, Kate Wheeler."

"Same," I said back. "See you in thirty."

I COULDN'T BREATHE. Holding my stomach, I sucked down deep gulps of air between silent shoulder-shaking laughs. Anne shoved my shoulder and grumbled something about not laughing at her as she dusted off her dark jeans.

"I did not fall."

"Yes," I wheezed. "Yes, you did."

Groaning, she ran her fingers through her nearly black hair. "Fine, but don't tell Mouse. He already thinks I'm clumsy. Don't need to go verifying his assumptions."

"How in the hell did you make it through basic training?"

"With lots of bumps, bruises, and nearly shattered kneecaps. Now hurry. I need that drink more than ever."

"Will I have to carry you home? If you can't walk sober—"

Anne shoved my shoulder playfully.

My backside vibrated with an incoming text as I shuffled to the side to not fall like she did. "Oh no," I groaned.

Immediately, Anne's shoulders tensed. Head on a swivel, she scanned the darkness.

"What?"

Reaching back, I snagged my phone and pressed the Home button.

Casey: Where the fuck are you?

"Ugh, Dad texted me. He knows we're gone."

Anne snickered. "He always was the overprotective type." Jealousy grew, hampering my good mood and fondness for my partner in crime. "Tell him you're with me and he'll be fine."

The echoes of loud bass and shouts drifted down the street, drawing my attention from the phone in my hands like a siren's call. Anne and I sped up, hurrying toward the blinking neon sign in the distance.

At the front door, Anne beat me to it and held it closed, turning to face me. Both brows rose along my forehead in silent question.

"I know he loves you, and I know you love him," she said. "I won't get between you two, but know when I mention something about our past, it's exactly that—the past."

I dipped my chin. "Thanks."

"Now that that awkwardness is out of the way"—in a flourished move, she swung the door open and gestured for me to enter before her—"let's have some fucking fun."

The stench of stale smoke, sweat, leather, and beer wafted up my nose, but instead of recoiling, I inhaled deep, savoring each smell. The patrons didn't pay us any attention as we weaved through the crowd toward the bar in the middle.

Two male bartenders worked the three-sided bar, slinging drinks and pouring drafts as fast as possible.

"What day is it?" I asked as I slid onto a barstool, Anne taking the empty one beside me.

"Saturday. I think."

We both laughed at the ridiculousness of my question and her response.

A bartender made his way to us, adding a bit of saunter to his walk when he saw Anne. Mid-length dirty-blond hair, light eyes, and a deep tan that said he preferred being outdoors, the man was attractive and knew it. A slight smirk pulled at his pink lips when he leaned against the bar, closing the distance between him and Anne.

"What are we having tonight, ladies?"

"Shots," I said before Anne could get anything out.

"I like your style," he said and stood straight, waving to the array of bottles behind him. "What will it be, sugar?"

Sugar. Really? Fucker.

"Goldschläger. Four, and two IPAs."

He blinked. Anne cackled.

"I think I might love you, Doc." I shifted in my seat to turn toward Anne. She tossed an arm around my shoulders and pulled me in tight. "If you get me hammered, I'm 100 percent okay with you taking advantage of me later."

Out of the corner of my eye, I saw the bartender stand straighter, as if he heard Anne's comment, his shoulders dropping a bit in defeat.

"I'll get your drinks," he grumbled as he walked away.

Once he turned, Anne dropped her arm and twisted to face the bar.

"Want to tell me what that was about? Pretty sure you don't swing my way."

She shrugged. "I have a boyfriend." Her face pinched in a grimace. "Well, not a boyfriend, but someone I'm seeing, I guess."

"Oh yeah?"

"It's new." She shut me up with a look out of the corner of her eye. "Don't ask questions. I won't answer. I'm not someone to girl talk with, Kate. Drink, have fun, maybe start a fight or two, I'm your girl. But girl talk?" She scrunched her nose. "No, thanks."

Four shots clinked to the bar, followed by our two beers.

Raising one shot, I turned to her. "To no girl talk," I said and tapped my glass to hers.

Anne smiled and tipped hers back at the same time I did.

A sharp hiss escaped from her clenched teeth. "Oh, that's good stuff."

"Right?" I exclaimed. Taking the second one, I tapped the bottom to the bar before shooting it back. "So damn good."

The vibrating phone I'd laid on the bar drew my attention to the bright screen.

Casey: Where. The. Fuck. Are. You?

I sighed and picked up the small device.

Me: Out.

Casey: Get home.

Me: Didn't know I was grounded, Dad.

Me: I'm with Anne. We're good, just needed a drink.

Me: A break. Today was tough for all of us.

Me: Give me tonight to forget about it all. You know I'm safe with her.

Casey: Are you close?

Casey: Having her there doesn't make me feel any better. She gets herself into as much trouble as you.

Me: Not anymore. She has a boyfriend.

That little thought bubble popped up, then disappeared. Twice. Eyes on the screen, I chugged half the beer, waiting for his response on that little nugget of information.

Casey: Interesting.

Casey: What are you wearing?

Biting my lip, I smiled at the phone and typed out my reply.

Me: Just those cutoff shorts and a tank top.

Casey: My favorite cutoff shorts I told you never to wear out of the house again because they show half your ass when you bend over?

Me: Oops.

Casey: I'm tracking your phone.

Me: I'm kidding. Jeans and a tank, and a hat to be inconspicuous.

Casey: I don't think you could ever be inconspicuous.

Me: I'm a great spy.

Casey: Sure, baby. Fine. Just text me every so often so I know you're okay.

Casey: And keep an eye out for anyone you might recognize. Just because they released their guards doesn't mean we're still not being followed.

Me: Hence the sneaking out and disguise.

Casey: Disguise?

Me: The hat.

Casey: You really went all out.

Me: It's all I had!

Casey: Even more reason to not go out. We had beer here.

Me: Are you pouting?

Casey: No?

Me: Well played, sir. Well played.

Casey: Keep calling me Dad and sir and I'll show you how well I can play, baby.

I gaped at my phone. Sure, we'd had some super awesome sex—the best, really. Even broke a door once. Oh, and that dent in the wall. But never had we played like that.

Is that considered role-playing?

"What's considered role-playing?" I asked out loud.

"I don't even want to know where that question just came from," Anne grumbled beside me, making me laugh. She finished her beer, smiling around the bottle pressed against her lips.

"Anything that plays into a fantasy, not reality." I startled at the masculine voice near me. Swiveling to glance over my shoulder, I stared at the man about my age, rough around the edges like he could've been attractive but lived a too hard life. His hand brushed against my shoulder as he reached for the beer bottle the bartender slid toward him. "What's your fantasy, little thing? I can make all your dreams come true."

My skin heated with the flash of annoyance that flooded my veins.

"Not interested, twatwaffle," I snapped and turned back to my phone, but my attention stayed on the man, who hadn't moved.

"I wouldn't talk to me that way."

"Kindly fuck off," I said over my shoulder.

"You'll pay for that smartass mouth, bitch," he grumbled low. "No one talks to me that way." The rounded edge of his bottle clipped my shoulder as he turned.

"Dick," I said, loud enough for him to hear over the music.

"You make friends fast, I see." There was a tightness to Anne's voice, making me turn to face her straight on. I expected her to be smiling, but her face was dead serious as she stared over my shoulder.

I turned and followed her line of sight. The dick had sat down at a table with two other guys, all three dressed in leather vests with some kind of emblem stitched on the front.

"I'm not scared of those *Sons of Anarchy* wannabes." I grinned and gave a little middle finger wave to the dick, who was scowling our way. His face flushed red.

"Oh hell." Anne cackled. "You're going to get us in trouble." I jolted forward when she slapped between my shoulder blades. "I like it. More shots before we start a bar brawl?"

Forgetting about the three annoyed men and the grumpy guy back at the house, I grinned and flagged down the bartender. We came out tonight to forget all the shit around us, and that was exactly what I planned to do.

11

"Anyone understand this... situation?"

Pain radiated in my skull like a high school marching band from the shouting voice hammering through my ears. Everything hurt. My head, my stomach, my skin.

How in the hell does my skin hurt, and what is with the yelling?

"All I know is it's fucking hot."

Squeezing my eyes shut even tighter, I curled the comforter up and over my head.

"She's alive. What about the other one?"

The other one? Peeking one eye open, I immediately closed it again, shutting out the light that was too bright even through the comforter.

"I might be dead," I said into the bed, my voice raspy like I'd yelled all night. My tongue stuck to the roof of my mouth, feeling as dry as the desert.

"You might be later once Romeo is done with you two."

You two?

Slowly I pulled the blanket back down, blinking past the squiggles blurring my vision.

"What are you talking about?" I said, squinting so tightly I couldn't make out a single thing.

"You. Your bedmate. The blood."

That perked me up. Fear adding to the rolling in my stomach, I twisted to see who this bedmate was. A relieved sigh brushed over my dry, cracked lips.

Anne.

"What the hell happened last night, Tink?" I shot Tyler the bird, or where I thought Tyler was, at the laughter in his voice. "Even hungover you're still feisty."

"Back off, Mouse."

Blinking, I shifted toward Weston's voice. Leaning against the far wall, a smirk pulled at his lips. "Care to share what you two got into last night?"

"I, um...." A loud groan stopped me from repeating the story I really couldn't remember. The mattress shifted as Anne leapt off the bed and raced to the connected bathroom. The sound of her vomiting made my stomach turn. "We went out drinking."

"Yes, and then?"

"Um, we drank a lot. I remember that part."

"Don't forget about dancing on the bar," Anne yelled from the bathroom before puking again. "I think there was a hula hoop involved somehow."

I snorted and whimpered. My knotted hair tugged against my fingers as I tried to run a hand through it.

"I look like a mess, don't I?" Weston's smile only grew. I scowled his way. "Okay, the drinks, dancing, and then, um...." *Shit, what happened next?*

"You texting me about wanting to role-play."

"Oh damn." I groaned and fell back onto the bed, covering my face with both hands. "Someone kill me now."

"Can't do that, Tink. For starters, I need you alive to tell me all about this role-playing idea you texted Romeo here, and the second reason you can't die is we have an auction to attend in a couple days, and your attendance is required."

I sat up so fast my head spun. Slapping a hand over my mouth to keep the lingering alcohol in my gut down, I breathed in through my nose.

"What?" I said around my hand, my breath so putrid I gagged. "Water. I need some water."

Something hit the bed beside me. I felt through the folds of the comforter, sighing in relief when my fingers grazed a cool plastic bottle. The cap cracked as I hurried to get it open and downed half the contents.

"Let me remind you boys," I said, wiping the few escaped drops of water from my lips with the back of my hand, "I took care of your sorry asses when you were hungover at Aiden's. So no making fun of me."

"Give us a minute," Weston commanded and pushed off the wall. "You too, Hawk."

"Can't," she groaned from the bathroom. "I'm dead."

Tyler's face dropped, losing the earlier humor. Before any of us could say another word, he strode into the bathroom, closing the door shut behind him.

"Interesting," Weston said, looking across the room to James, who hadn't said a word yet. "That leaves you. Out."

But he didn't. Turning on the bed, I blinked lazily up at the man staring at me with... was that concern?

"You look like shit."

"I feel like shit."

"Whose ass did you kick?"

When I tried to raise my brows in question to his question, pain pinched.

"Ouch." Reaching up, I brushed careful fingers over my face. "Is my cheek swollen?"

"And you have a cut above your eye." Weston sat on the bed beside me. "Last night, when y'all stumbled home, you were both bleeding, laughing, and could barely walk. We were halfway down the driveway, ready to come find you both. After we made sure you were okay, we got you both to bed—"

"Oh hell," I whimpered, flexing my hands in front of my face. The slices along my knuckles cracked open, weeping fresh blood. "What happened?"

"I think I stabbed one." I slowly turned to Anne's voice. Using Tyler as a crutch, she looked terrible. A dried cut darkened the middle of her bottom lip, a bruise already developing along her temple.

"Nice," Tyler said beside her with a smile. "I'm sure they deserved it."

"Was it that biker gang?" I asked, still drawing a blank.

"Biker gang?" James and Weston said in unison, both sounding super pissed.

I waved off their anger and concern.

"We survived, obviously."

"Maybe?" Anne said on a groan. "I'm going back to sleep. Someone get some of that baby juice Kate gave us last time. And crackers."

"And Excedrin Migraine," I added.

"Already ordered and—" Weston glanced at his phone, "—will be here within the hour."

"Glad you didn't die, princess," James grumbled. His own wince when he started toward the door drew my notice.

"What's wrong with you? Did you get in a knife fight with a biker gang too?"

He waved me off and kept going toward the door. "Romeo handed me my ass for yesterday. But knowing we're on a mission and I couldn't just show up with a bloody face, he kept it all lower. Fucker." He grumbled that last part when he was halfway down the hall.

Weston grinned at the floor. Someone seemed pleased with himself.

Anne and Tyler followed James out and closed the door behind them.

"Casey, I'm not up for this talk," I groaned. "You were right. I was wrong. I shouldn't have snuck off. I won't do it again. Are we good?"

"Not even close." Turning on the bed, he rested one knee on the mattress and placed a hand just above each shoulder, hovering over me. "You're smarter than this."

"I'm really not. I mean, look at my track record." I forced a smile. "I just needed to get away."

His brows pinched together. "From me?"

I shook my head, sliding it along the pillow. "No, not from you. From this. The mission, why we're on a mission in the first place, from my memories." A gentle hand wrapped around my wrist and pulled my fingers from my lip. "You were right. She understands, just like she understood last night that we just needed a few hours. Not to forget, but to just...." I searched for the right words. "To not be the women who have it all together. To be stupid, and careless, and free for just a little while. Always being on guard, watching and preparing? It's exhausting, and we just needed a break."

That line between his brows deepened. "I could've gone with you."

My hand trembled from exhaustion when I reached up to cup his face. "I know, but thank you for not. If I truly felt in danger, I would've reached out. Thank you for trusting me enough to stay home."

His nod was clipped, but some of the worry eased from his features. "How drunk were you when you texted me about role-playing?"

"So drunk I don't remember texting you about role-playing?" Squeezing my eyes shut, I tried my hardest to remember. "Please don't tell me I said anything dumb."

The bed jolted as he shoved off the mattress and stood. Grabbing my phone from the nightstand, he tossed it to the comforter beside me.

"I didn't think it was dumb. I was, however, ready to play out some of your suggestions, but someone had about four shots too many and somehow got into a fistfight on the way home from the bar." His words were chastising, but the almost smile on his lips eased the sting. "We'll talk more about that part later, when you don't feel like death warmed over."

"Pretty accurate description."

"Been there before. I know how it feels. I'll bring you up something to eat."

I scrambled for my phone before he was even halfway to the door. Rolling on my stomach, I pushed up onto my elbows and clicked the phone on.

Several missed texts told me Weston wasn't the only one I drunk texted last night.

> Eric: What the hell did I miss while on shift? Okay, I'll answer allll your strange, kind-of-creepy texts. And side note, we will discuss all this in person the next time I see you. Which will be when again? I miss you. Okay, here we go.

> Eric: As much as I'd love to give you pointers on that, I think that's kind of awkward.

> Eric: Nope, never done that before. How drunk are you? You sound more like Meagan than Kate.

> Eric: Now that's just gross.

> Eric: What about a hula hoop?

> Eric: I'm booking a flight to Hawaii. I think some alien has taken over your tiny heinie.

> Eric: Actually, I might like the alien better. Think you two can share that body?

> Eric: Um, no, I don't think you should render aid to someone you just stabbed.

I groaned and gently smacked my forehead into my pillow. Whimpering pitifully at my own antics, I flipped over to the text string with Weston. And scrolled up, and up, and up, and up some more until I found the last message I remembered sending him while at the bar.

> Me: I mean, role-playing could be fun.

Me: Daddy Casey?

Me. Yes, sir.

Me: Hula hoops are so fun. I need one at
home.

Me: Just ordered two hundred hula hoops.

Me: You get a hula hoop. You get a hula
hoop. Everyone gets a hula hoop.

> Casey: Oh fuck, you're drunk.

Me: Is that a no on daddy play?

> Casey: That's a 'let's talk about that when
> you're not hammered.'

> Casey: Please tell me Anne isn't drunk too.

> Casey: KATE! Tell me there is at least one
> responsible party there.

Me: Already getting into your daddy role,
I see.

Me: Will I be punished when I get home?

> Casey: Fuck. I'm coming to get you.

Me: No, we're about to leave.

Me: We're good. Anne has a knife.

Me: She's kind of hot. Like scary hot. She
might kill you, she might not.

> Casey: Sounds like you're talking about
> yourself.

Me: Yeah, but she's the real deal. I bet she
has a certificate of badassery.

> Casey: I don't think that's a thing.

> Casey: So back to this punishment idea.

Me: Spankings?

Casey: You're killing me.

Me: You could ground me to my knees. That could be fun.

Casey: I just spit out my beer.

Me: Oh snap.

Casey: What?

Me: Nothing.

Casey: Kate.

Me: Urm, gotta run. Literally. Be home in a bit, Daddy!

Casey: If you're not home in 10 min, I'm coming to find you.

"What the ever-loving fuck?" I grumbled into the pillow with a hoarse, frustrated scream. Flopping to my back, I squeezed both eyes shut with a loud groan at my dumbass actions. "Kate. You're a damn adult. Get your shit together. You're a doctor, for fuck's sake."

My stomach lurched with the movement, ready to empty itself of the liquor that remained sloshing inside. The sheets wrestled with me, fighting to keep me in bed. After several attempts, I freed myself of the sheet restraints and fell to the floor, almost bear crawling as fast as possible to the bathroom just in time to vomit into one of the dual sinks. Daring a peek at the mirror, I cursed and averted my eyes from the scary monster staring back at me from where my reflection should've been.

Slipping to the floor into a Kate puddle, I pressed a cheek to the cold stone tile, savoring the way it calmed the rolling in my stomach.

Sleep.

Yes, more sleep, and then maybe when I wake up, all this will have been a bad dream.

Well, a fun bad dream. Because even though I couldn't remember the exact details of the night before, I knew we had fun.

I just hated paying the consequences for those few hours of crazy, no-responsibilities fun.

Dozing in and out of sleep, popping up once to vomit again, I wasn't sure how long I lay on the cool floor wishing for death or someone who knew how to pump stomachs to burst through the door when a set of arms scooped me into the air. The feeling of floating almost had my stomach revolting again, but I held down my nausea with several hard swallows.

Crisp cool sheets greeted my sensitive skin as my body molded into a plush mattress. Daring a one-eye peep, I found a concerned Weston staring at me with a glass of pinkish liquid in hand.

"Baby," he rasped, like my pain was his. "I need you to sit up to take a few sips. Do you need help?"

I slowly shook my head and pushed up on a shaky elbow, each muscle protesting at the exertion. Removing the two white pills from his outstretched palm, I popped both onto my tongue and downed several large swallows of the electrolyte-infused drink.

"Thank you," I rasped and fell back to the pillow. "Remind me to never drink again." His deep chuckle raised my hackles, not liking that he was laughing at me. Doing the only thing I could while at the brink of death, I stuck out my tongue in response. "Don't be a dick. I'm dying a slow, cruel death here. Feel sorry for me."

"I seem to remember you saying men were the babies. You're not acting any better than we did that morning at Aiden's."

"Whatever." Not the best comeback, but my brain was mush. Every thought hurt. It would be in everyone's best interest to not get injured over the course of the next few hours; there was no way my slow-ass mind could conjure up any medical knowledge if they did. "I really am sorry. For everything last night."

The bed dipped, rolling my limp body toward where Weston sat, perched on the edge of the bed beside my shoulder.

"It was difficult not coming for you," he admitted. "But I didn't because I assumed you or Anne would be responsible enough to keep a head on your shoulders and not get that hammered without someone looking out for you." I could almost feel his chastising glare. I burrowed deeper into the covers like a coward. "Don't expect it to happen again."

Fuck, he was pissed.

"Okay," I whispered when I finally found my voice.

And why was his response to my actions hot instead of demeaning? He just said I wasn't responsible enough to go out on my own, like a little kid. Yet heat replaced the nausea in my lower belly instead of annoyance.

"Are you alive enough to discuss the texts or fight?"

"I'm not sure which I'd rather avoid more," I admitted with a cringe. "Can we just pretend nothing happened and move on? Tyler mentioned the auction. When is it?" My lids popped open as the realization of what we did last night smacked me in the chest like a hard punch. "Oh fuck, my face. Anne's face. How will we explain that?"

Weston shook his head, the longer portion of his hair slipping across his forehead. A knowing grin pulled at his lips.

"We're talking about the texts and fight at some point. There's no glossing over that, so don't get your hopes up. Maybe when your memories come back."

"Oh, I really hope I keep this amnesia. I really don't want to remember making an ass out of myself."

"Maybe it'll help remind you to never do it again. Well, that and your punishment will drive that idea home."

Somehow, even feeling like death, my heart raced at his words as a tingle zinged along my skin.

"Punishment?"

"If you don't realize I'm going to wear your ass out for putting yourself in that kind of danger, then you're not as smart as all those degrees say you are." I narrowed my eyes, faking annoyance that I didn't feel. "And don't give me that look. You know I'm right. You could've been hurt, taken, or worse. You knew better than to let both of you get that drunk, and then the fight." He inhaled deep like he was trying to control his anger. "I'm going make sure you understand my expectations going forward. You want freedom, girls' nights, going out with friends, great. I'm not a possessive ass. But I am a protective asshole, and if you ever put yourself in that kind of danger again, we're done."

I sucked in a breath. Dark eyes pinned me to the bed, and I knew without a doubt he was serious.

"Okay, okay, I get it. No more danger for Kate. I won't do that to myself again."

"It's not just about you anymore, Kate. We have this conversation more than we don't. You're not alone. It's not just you that your actions and subsequent consequences only affect anymore. If you were hurt or worse, I'd blame myself. I'd be lost without your damn mouth telling me off daily. There wouldn't be anything left in this world that would be worth protecting if you were gone. We're tied together. Our lives are connected. Stop being so selfish in thinking your irresponsible actions will only reap consequences for you."

My lip trembled, and tears built along my lower lid.

Fuck, he was right. But I didn't intend to get that crazy last night. It just happened.

"I'm sorry, Casey," I whispered, emotions making the words soft. "I really am, and I promise to try to stop my... jackassery?"

He scoffed and rolled his eyes. "Jackassery or Kate-assery."

I huffed and stuck my lower lip out in a dramatic pout. "I deserved that one."

Reaching over, he swiped the pad of his thumb along my lip. "Get some more sleep. We have two days to figure out the details for the auction. Axe and I have a basic plan in the works. And yes, the bruises on Hawk's face aren't ideal, but I think I have a workaround for that problem."

"Tell me more," I prompted and snuggled deeper into the bed.

Gripping the edge of the comforter, I adjusted it around me until I was situated comfortably. "It'll be like a creepy bedtime story."

That earned me a bark of a laugh, making me smile. Some of the tension around his tight eyes relaxed as he stared down at me. I fluttered my lashes, playing up the innocent card.

"Fine. You always get your way with me, don't you?" I shot him a sassy smile and nodded. But it immediately faded, and a breath caught in my throat at the flash of unending love behind his soft gaze. "Always, baby. I'll be wrapped around that little finger of yours until I'm just a memory."

"Casey." Nothing else would come out. Unshed tears clogged my throat, blocking my voice.

"What would you say if I asked you to make this official?"

I felt my eyes go as wide as dinner plates. "Like *official* official?"

He nodded, never taking his eyes off me, gauging my reaction.

"You're asking me this while I'm hungover and look like absolute shit?"

He shrugged. A shy grin tugged at his lips, making his face look innocent. "I haven't asked you anything, just more of a preliminary line of questioning."

"You sound like a lawyer."

"I sound like a guy who's scared shitless that the tiny little thing that has stolen his heart and soul might say no if he ever gained the courage to ask her to spend the rest of his life with him."

"Yes," I blurted. "I'd say yes. No hesitations. I'd say hell fucking yes, Casey."

That grin widened to a wide, radiant smile. I couldn't help but smile back, even as happy tears leaked from the corners of both eyes and slipped into my hairline.

"Good to know." After a brush of his lips along my forehead, he settled into the bed beside me, tugging me to his chest with an arm around my shoulder. "So, you want a creepy bedtime story, huh? Well, here's the preliminary plan..."

12

——————

The smooth material of the black mask moved as I shifted in the seat, brushing against my cheeks, catching on the healing cut along my brow. Reaching up, I adjusted the black lace covering half my face, ensuring it still covered the remaining reminders of our wild and crazy night. In the rearview of the Escalade—the Range too small to hold us all comfortably for a billionaire like James—I met Weston's dark sunglasses' reflection and offered a shaky smile, knowing his gaze behind those lenses was flicking between me and the road.

"Ten minutes until arrival at the site," James announced to us in the SUV and those listening in through the earpiece hidden inside his left ear. "Were you able to get everyone into position at the location?" He nodded at whatever response he received, obviously what he wanted to hear.

I sighed, pressing my forehead to the tinted window, and watched passing cars.

It was only an hour ago that we waited in the living room, all staring at the phone, willing it to chime with the incoming message with the location of tonight's auction. We were told to be dressed and ready at a certain time, and then a location would be sent just before the event. Dressed in designer labels, all black suits and dresses matched with the masks, we looked ready for a fancy masquerade party instead of a human auction.

A shiver of revulsion mixed with nervousness sent goose bumps flaring down my arms. I fisted both hands and ground them into the leather seat. Tonight was the night. Everything we'd worked toward, all the planning and energy and waiting, it all boiled down to tonight's outcome. We had to get it right. Which was why no one would make a move blowing our cover until we verified the girls were on-site and other buyers were present. At that point, James would give the signal, giving the green light to the local cavalry to swarm the premises.

The local agents supporting this mission were obtained with a single text from Kyle to a sister agency. Whatever that meant. Either way, we were relieved for the reinforcements and firepower waiting along the perimeter, hidden from sight until we needed them.

My role was to play the perfect pet at James's side until they gave the signal and all hell broke loose. Once the other agents swarmed the location, I was to ensure the girls knew we were the good guys and to help lead them away from the firefight to safety. Anne would cover my back, making sure I didn't get shot while my focus was on the trafficked women.

Pulling my gaze from the passing building and cars, I turned to Anne where she sat in one of the two captain's chairs. Back stiff, she studied the headrest in front of her, completely still except for the rise and fall of her slow, even breaths. Gone was the still slightly hungover friend, the woman who danced on the bar and stabbed someone to help us escape the brawl we started. A badass, focused, and determined warrior sat in the chair, mentally prepared to do whatever it took to complete the mission.

They were all focused, menacing, even in their stillness.

Taut silence filled the inside of the SUV, pulsing waves of energy and nerves into us all. Not even Tyler joked like usual, which said a lot about the dangers waiting for us.

I swallowed hard as the minutes ticked down, drawing us closer to the auction. Flipping my right palm up, I angled the skin along my wrist into the light offered by the full moon and passing streetlamps. A slight shimmer caught my eye with each fracture of light that hit a certain spot, revealing the almost-invisible-to-the-naked-eye tracker adhered to my skin. We all had one on various parts of our body, just in case the worst happened. A nagging thought told me they wore theirs to make me feel less like the weak link—the one who might get taken if shit went down a different way than we expected.

Plus a few voiced their concerns about me being a flight risk. Which, I mean, I understood their worry. I tended to run into danger without thinking about the consequences. But with my four team-mates and the location soon to be surrounded on all sides, what trouble could I get myself into?

As I would soon find out... a lot. I could get myself into a hell of a lot of trouble.

Tyler's lips pressed into a thin line as we parked the Escalade under a dilapidated, rusted metal-covered area in the pothole-infested parking lot beside a warehouse that looked on the verge of collapsing in the next powerful storm. More panes of glass were missing or broken with jagged edges than whole. The graffiti deco-rating the sides of the cement block structure added to the desolate, abandoned appearance. This was exactly the type of place I expected to hold a human auction—void of any life or warmth.

"They went all out on the location," James grumbled. After a beat of silence, he blew out a hard breath and gripped the door handle. "Let's do this. Everyone comes home. No stupid shit. I'm talking to you, Mouse and Princess. Follow my lead and we'll all be headed home in the morning knowing we completed the mission and saved some fucking lives."

With that pep talk, I leaned forward, hand extended for us all to stack and shout "Go team."

That did not happen. Instead, James shot me a disapproving glance and shook his head with what looked to be pure exhaustion at my innocent gesture.

Weston opened James's door at the same moment Tyler tugged

Anne's open. Using Weston's offered hand, I ducked to maneuver around the SUV and step out into the crisp night air.

Above us, the bright full moon highlighted the surrounding foliage that grew more dense in the distance. Several other black SUVs and a few sports cars dotted the covered section of the parking lot.

Shards of glass and loose gravel crunched under my towering heels as I followed James, the tight grip on my bare bicep a visible display of his ownership over me. Eyes tracking the broken asphalt, I maneuvered around the deep holes and larger debris to avoid falling face-first. Tyler shot ahead, marching forward like he owned the place, while Weston hovered behind.

A few times I wobbled in the heels when they caught on a deep crack or stumbled on a large piece of broken asphalt, but James's hold kept me upright. His fingers dug into my bicep, pulling me to a stop just as a set of matte black shoes appeared in my line of sight.

"Name and password."

I almost snorted at the ridiculousness of it all, but somehow I held it back. We'd gotten this far; I couldn't blow our cover now by snickering at their childlike rules. Not when in a few brief hours the mission would be completed successfully. Kyle mentioned on one of our several calls that he wanted one apprehended alive to learn the location of the prepping house, with some strategic convincing. I knew he meant torture but said 'convincing' for my benefit.

I preferred the former and told him so, several times, considering what these bastards did for a living.

What did it say about me that I hoped these deviant bastards would meet a painful end? They were bad people, so didn't that mean they deserved to be put through the same type of pain and agony they inflicted on others?

The moment the door clicked and whooshed open, all thoughts vanished.

We were in.

The low murmuring of others gathered within greeted us as we stepped inside the warehouse. Daring a peek through my cascading hair, fury ignited in my chest at the various groups similar to ours scattered around the warehouse floor. Too many groups. Too many people who were here to buy a person for their own pleasure.

My entire body trembled with the need to scream, to throat and dick-punch every one of these fuckers standing around waiting for the auction to start. The clamp around my bicep squeezed, showing James somehow sensed my rising temper and need for vengeance. Forcing my gaze back to the dust-covered floor, I followed one step behind him and Anne like a good little pet.

This mission, this role, couldn't end soon enough. I was ready to be vocal, smart, independent Kate again with no recourse.

"Take her," James grunted and callously handed me off to Weston. "You, get me a tablet to look over the evening's selections."

I bit back a smile, keeping my face blank at Tyler's barely audible disgruntled grumble before he stalked off.

"Where are the drinks?" Anne asked casually, but there was a dip of annoyance in her voice. "And why the fuck am I suddenly not getting a signal?"

"Precautions." I tensed at the somewhat familiar, seedy voice. The three of them shifted to face a new direction. "We have a blocker in place to ensure all information stays here for the evening."

"This is a hellhole," James commented, sounding bored. "When does this start? I want to get out of here as soon as I fucking can."

"Soon. I see you brought your current pet again. She does look lovely all dressed up in that fantastic dress, almost edible." *If I kick hard enough, could my stiletto puncture his black heart?* "However, I would bet she's more beautiful with nothing on at all and covered in black and blue." The hand at my bicep tightened almost to the point of pain before it relaxed, like Weston remembered who he was holding. "Have you reconsidered trading her for an amount toward your new purchase? I have an interested buyer."

"I told you—"

"Since she's used but beautiful for someone older, we're willing to offer half a million."

First, what the fuck? Half a million? Not sure whether to be disgusted or preen.

Second, 'we?'

I just assumed he was the one in charge of it all—the head honcho.

Guess not.

The long pause before James's response had me gritting my teeth. *That motherfucker better not trade me in like a damn used car.*

"Depending on what I find here tonight, maybe. I'm still not sold that I'll find a new purchase to my liking."

"We brought extras ensuring everyone leaves with a purchase of their liking. Two were newly gained and not quite broken yet. That might intrigue someone like yourself."

"It does. Ah, took you fucking long enough," James snapped over the approaching footsteps.

"Sorry, boss," Tyler said, not sounding sorry at all. "Long line."

"Are we able to see them first, in person, before the bidding? I don't trust you haven't made some of these out to look better in the pictures provided than they do in person."

I felt the man bristle beside me. "Of course, sir, but we wouldn't do that. Once you've been chosen as the winning bidder, you head for that door in the back right corner. There you can pick up your purchase and make payment. Tonight you will leave with the product and new identification and papers of health."

Like a damn show animal. I gritted my teeth so hard to keep from screaming at the man, the muscle along my jaw trembled.

"Now if you'll excuse me, we'll start as soon as all the guests arrive, which will be around midnight. We staggered your arrival to avoid suspicion."

The clip of his dress shoes on the dust-covered cement floor faded as he walked away.

"Fuck," James grumbled. "They're blocking the radio signal too. I hate these overly prepared fuckers."

Glancing up through my long lashes and over the rim of the

mask, I watched James swipe his finger along the screen of an iPad of sorts, a deep scowl lining his face.

"Was it fine outside?" Weston's voice grumbled as he stepped closer to my side. James nodded in response. He was the only one with the earpiece to communicate with the other agents since we didn't want the added risk of all of us having one—more chances to be caught. "Then we need to get outside to let the other team know what's going on. They'll just have to time it correctly and come in blind."

"How?" was James's only response, tilting the screen toward Anne. She frowned at what she saw and shook her head before going back to looking bored as fuck.

"Not sure yet without it looking suspicious." A wave of unease made my stomach drop. We had a plan, and now it was all fucked up. "First, we need an eye on the girls."

James nodded, continuing to swipe a single finger along the screen.

Awesome. More waiting.

I fucking hated waiting.

The minutes ticked on and on as we waited for the rest of the buyers to arrive, the noise in the warehouse growing louder with the building anticipation. I wiggled my toes to keep the blood flowing. The ache in the balls of my feet worsened with each passing second. With the mask covering my face and my hair curtained around me, I carefully watched those nearby. A few of the couples looked like James and Anne, the others seedier somehow. Not that they were dressed bad or dirty. It was the air around them that sent a shiver of unease down my spine any time I skimmed my gaze their way.

"Fucking finally." My hope perked up at James's words. "Let's get this shit done and get out of this hellhole."

I smothered my agreeing smile.

"Ladies and gentlemen, the auction will begin shortly. Please ensure your information is logged into the bidding system on the device each of you received. This auction is silent, and only bids sent through the system will be counted. When you've won your desired purchase, please step through the door here to collect your merchandise and complete the money transfer. As always, we only ensure the health and physical well-being of the product while they remain in our care. Once they walk out the door, they are yours, no returns. If you break them, that is on you." I gritted my teeth at the chorus of soft male chuckles that hummed through the warehouse. "All paperwork is credible and will provide easy entry anywhere around the globe. If you have a certain name you'd like to give your purchase, that will need to be done on your own terms. All identification provided here is final. Regarding the money transfer, all money is due up front, as I've discussed with each of you individually. The product will not leave this warehouse until all funds are transferred into our accounts. If you have questions, there is a Google Docs form link on the device. Please ask it there. Thank you."

"Of course they have a Google form," I hissed.

A hand clasped around the back of my neck and squeezed.

"Quiet, pet," Weston whispered into my hair. "You've gone this long without running that sassy mouth of yours. Try to hold it a little longer."

Tipping my face to the floor, I shielded myself from the crowd. I was officially over this. All of it. Sure, it was fun at first, the anticipation and excitement, but now it was just gross. I wanted to go home, to be normal Kate and... be with him. Maybe we could find a mix of me being a part of the mission but not in the middle of it next time. As long as I could help and be with Weston, that would fulfill the urge for more in my life, wouldn't it?

A hush fell over the room, calming my circling thoughts on what might be next for us. Vibrating energy rippled along my skin with the cresting anticipation pulsing through the warehouse. Assuming all eyes would be on the stage, I dared a peek to see what held everyone's rapt attention.

I really shouldn't have.

I might have been a doctor, but sometimes I was dumber than a sack of rocks.

My knees wobbled as I watched the woman—no, girl—teeter in

the middle of the makeshift wooden stage dressed in a sheer black long dress, completely see-through with nothing worn beneath, and sky-high midnight heels. Waves of long blonde hair swayed with the constant movement of her thin frame.

Drugged.

Her glassy eyes flicked from one corner to the other, face slack as if her mind couldn't keep up with what she was seeing.

I thought I could do it. Thought I'd be strong and that my normal temper would give me some kind of backbone. But it didn't. Turned out I wasn't strong at all.

Pitching forward, I gagged, stomach heaving up what little I'd eaten earlier.

Whispered shouts sounded over the rush of blood pounding in my ears, something about someone staying with her. With help, I moved through the crowd, a large body parting the other buyers with ease. Snaking my arm around my middle, I squeezed, urging my body to stop, but another wave of nausea had bile rising up my throat instead.

We paused for half a second at the door we'd entered through earlier in the evening. Low words were spoken, a commanding snap, and the door snickered open. My skin pebbled with the contrast from the warm warehouse to the cooler night air as it swept across my skin the moment I stumbled outside. Without the two firm grasps on either bicep, I'd be eating asphalt.

"You're okay, baby." A thick arm wrapped around my shoulders and a hand fisted my hair, keeping it away from my face as I dry heaved. "Breathe through your nose."

The steady crunch of footsteps grinding into the dilapidated parking lot had me shifting, preparing for the worst. Two feet away, James paced, a look of fury on his face, yet... I squinted, barely able to make out the movement of his lips.

Well, there you go. I gave us a way out without even meaning to. High five to me.

"Do I get a bonus?" I whispered. "For being the distraction?"

Weston's hard body pressed to my back, offering more comfort.

Without realizing it, I leaned back into him, soaking up his unending strength.

"The fuck are you doing?" James's voice rattled through the night. He stomped over and gripped my face in one large hand. I glared up at him, making his lips twitch in the corners as he fought a smile. Leaning in close, he let that smile loose. But there was an evil edge to it that his words didn't convey. "Nicely done, princess. But next time try not to puke on my shoes." He frowned, looking at the splattered leather. "They're Ferragamo."

I snorted and flinched away when his hand raised like he was about to backhand me. He let it fall, his fingertips barely whispering over my skin. Knowing we were putting on a show for the guards at the door who reluctantly let us outside, I fell to the side, only staying upright because of Weston's hold.

"Get your shit together or I will trade you in." With that lovely parting line, James turned on his heel and brushed past me. "Get her inside. I don't want to miss the one I want."

But Weston didn't move, tightening his hold instead.

"You okay?" I nodded. "If you need out, we're out. Take it if you need it. I can toss you in the Escalade and—"

"No," I rasped. "I'm fine. It's almost over. I can do this."

"I know you can," he said, his lips moving against the top of my head. "I just wanted to make sure you realized that too."

Fuck, this man and his belief in me. Even when I was limp in his arms and smelling like vomit, he believed in me. How did I get so lucky?

"When are you going to ask the real question?" Where the hell did that come from? This was not the time or place for this conversation, yet I needed to know right this second.

His chest vibrated against my back as he held me closer, helping me stand upright.

"Soon, baby. Now come on. Let's finish what we started."

13

The caress of expensive suits and soft exposed skin pressed around me, like walls slowly closing in as we weaved through the crowd back toward Anne and Tyler. The unnerving sense of eyes on me had the hairs rising along the back of my neck and alarms blaring in my head. One man snapped a hand out, reaching for my ass, only to curse, snatching his hand back to his side after being knocked away.

"Not yours," Weston growled and stepped even closer, acting as a volatile protective shield. Even when we were surrounded by our friends, he kept me close to his side. "We fucking done yet? I'm over this shit."

"Wish I knew." Anne sighed and went back to studying the ends of her hair. "I'm bored. Let's just buy one and get out of here."

"Soon. The one I'm good with is next," James said, sounding just as bored. "If we get her, then we can discuss exchanging her." I caught his nod in my direction. "Fucking weak."

I knew he didn't mean it, but still his words, combined with the uncertainty I already felt, made me flinch. His dark brows furrowed as he studied me. Did he care that I took a sliver of his words to heart, or was he more worried about what Weston would do to him for hurting my feelings?

"Now," said a loud voice that boomed through the warehouse. "Number nine is coming up on the stage—"

The floor vibrated beneath my heels half a second before every window shattered, shards of glass raining down through the air. Women screamed, men shouted commands, and it seemed every person in the room drew a gun.

Oh fuck.

In the next shaky breath, several smoking cans flew through the window frames. The metal cans rained down over us, filling the entire area with smoke. It burned my eyes, making tears leak down my cheeks in an attempt for some kind of relief.

A hard shove between my shoulder blades urged me down to the ground. Shards of glass sliced into my palms and knees when I collided with the concrete. But the chaos surrounding me kept the pain from registering. All around us, feet slammed against the ground in a desperate attempt to escape, but the standing wall of bodies kept others from trampling me to death. Another boom shook the building, shaking my bones and rattling my teeth with the force. I covered my ears a moment too late; the noise pierced my eardrums.

Everything fell quiet, muffled, as if the chaos around me lowered several decibels. Blinking through the tears, I tipped my face to stare through a set of legs, disoriented without my hearing. Beneath my knees, the floor vibrated as if a herd of elephants raced toward us. Within seconds after my hearing faded, a sharp ringing filled the silence.

Still attempting to find my bearings, I pushed to stand, my legs shaking, wobbling in the high heels. Something tickled along my neck. Cautious fingers swiped at the annoyance. The silky ribbon that once held my delicate mask across my battered face now hung limply beneath my chin. Pinching the end, I ripped it off completely, feeling a rush of relief as it fluttered to the floor.

Anne turned, searching over her shoulder until she found me. Bright red lips moved, but with the ringing in my ears, I shook my head, not understanding what she said. Her perfect brows dipped. Skimming her eyes over my shoulder, she moved her lips once again, talking to someone behind me. Looking past her, I watched in shock as agents dressed in full tactical assault gear raced from one area of the warehouse to another, guns at the ready.

Along the side wall, several earlier patrons, all dressed in suits and dresses unlike the agents, were shoved against the wall. Multiple bodies lay still on the floor, puddles of dark liquid pooling beneath them.

Normally the sight of blood rushed the need to help to the forefront of my mind, taking over every other thought. But not this blood. At the sight of the crimson puddle, victory and joy swelled in my chest. Smiling, I turned, looking at other parts of the warehouse, my gaze landing on the side door where buyers were to pick up their purchases.

The girls.

"Where are the girls?" I shouted, my voice barely audible to my own ears. A hand twirled me around and slammed something into my blood-speckled palm. The weight and feel were familiar, and I knew what I would see before I set eyes on the nine-millimeter Glock. Brows raised, I glanced to James, who still had a steadying hand on my shoulder.

His answering grin was maniacal. Shifting, he turned to Anne, who grinned back like a crazy fool and turned to Tyler, who was already jittery with excitement. As one, we four turned to Weston, who wore a calculated smile. His lips moved as he said... well, I wasn't sure what he said since hearing was still a slight issue, but I assumed it was something like 'Let's go,' because the four moved at once.

As a herd, we raced toward the side door I'd spotted moments ago. With a stiff arm pressed to my collarbone, Tyler urged me back, sealing me against the wall while Weston kicked the door open—there was something wrong with me that, despite our surroundings and danger, I grew wet at the sight. James rushed through first, arms straight, gun raised to put a bullet between the brows of anyone who stood in his way.

At the go tap to my right shoulder, I lifted the borrowed gun, finger hovering over the trigger, and trailed behind Anne with Tyler to cover my back. The lights flickered along the ceiling, barely lighting our path down the wide hall.

Anne checked over her shoulder and pointed down. Following the direction, I nodded and carefully stepped over the prone body she'd pointed out. Up ahead, the quick movements of James and Weston as they cleared one room after another were fluid, as if they'd done this before a thousand times. Which they probably had during their several deployments together as Rangers. This action and danger were second nature to them, to all of them—except me.

At the end, the two men turned, scowls wrinkling their dirty faces. I gave myself a second to appreciate the way the disheveled suit and gun in Weston's tight grip made him somehow sexier than ever before.

Not now, Kate.

"Where are they?" The words scratched up my throat with the force to get them out, this time more of the sound bleeding through past the insistent ring.

"The warehouse has several sections where they could hold them. Many more places to clear, princess. Don't worry, we'll find them. Let's go."

James hurried past, but Weston paused, using a knuckle under my chin to tilt my face up to his. Those dark eyes searched every inch of my face.

"You good?"

"Good," I apparently shouted based on his wince. "Good," I said again, much softer. "Let's go find them."

A warm confidence-inspiring kiss sealed to my slick forehead and quickly disappeared along with the man. Taking a moment, I inhaled a deep breath to center myself. I followed the backs of Weston, Anne, and Tyler as they raced back the way we came, no doubt expecting me to be hot on their heels, ready for action like normal. But not yet. I needed a quick reset and to do a quick assessment of my own physical well-being.

Rotating my wrists, I inspected the slices covering my palms. A few shards of glass embedded in the delicate flesh shone in the light, but nothing that needed immediate medical attention. Both ears still rang, but it's high pitch was more of a background noise, allowing some of the other sounds to filter through. Great, as that meant no permanent damage. Again, not urgent.

My knees were scraped, but not too deep.

I winced as I wiggled my tender toes. Blisters rubbed along the top of my toes where the thin strap worked hard to keep the stiletto secured to my foot, along with the strap around my ankle. Another nonemergency injury, but it hurt like hell.

So, I was good. Time to get my head in the game and get this mission over with. Once all this was behind us, hopefully Weston would ask the question we were both clearly ready for. If he didn't, well, maybe I'd just have to ask him.

That would go over well....

I snorted and rolled my head, stretching the tight tendons, searching down the dim hall. The others were long gone by now, but the sounds of the ensuing battle still vibrated along the walls and floor from the main warehouse area.

Unease crept up my spine as I searched the empty office to my right. Yeah, time to go and not be alone in a creepy abandoned warehouse. Standing straight, I squared my shoulders and hurried as fast as I could with the damn heels in the direction the guys and Anne disappeared.

Movement out of the corner of my eye had me pulling up short outside another unassuming, empty office. I took a single step closer, squinting to see through the filth-covered glass pane for whatever caught my eye. Careful to keep the click of my heels quiet, I maneuvered around the trash littering the floor toward the window to get a better look outside.

As I peered through a gap in the glass, a gasp caught in my throat at the sight of two people bent low, as if they didn't want to be seen, hurrying away from the madness inside the warehouse. Even with the darkness and distance, I immediately recognized both.

The sleazy promoter from the club and the woman who'd collapsed in my arms just days ago.

Even from where I stood, several yards away, his hand tightly gripping her arm was clear as he hurried her along the perimeter of the property toward the dense pocket of trees and underbrush I noticed when we first arrived.

My heart stopped. He was taking her.

My breaths turned frantic as I scanned the area outside, hoping to spot an agent or one of my teammates, but came up empty. No one was around to help her as she and the bastard disappeared into the lush foliage.

No one but me.

"Fuck." Using the butt of the gun, I shattered a few remaining pieces of window, glass shards raining over my feet and onto the floor. The embedded glass in both palms dug deeper, a hiss of pain pushing past my clenched teeth as I hauled myself onto the windowsill and swung both legs over. The rip of the expensive fabric sounded just before the slice of pain registered along the back of my thighs as I leapt from the window to the soggy ground.

My ankles rolled as my feet hit the soft dirt, the spiked heels sinking deep into the ground. Damn shoes. Pretty but not at all functional in this setting. My fingers shook with the rush of adrenaline as I worked the small buckle of the straps securing the shoes to my ankles loose. Both free from their tiny restraints, I hurried on bare feet in the direction I last saw the pair before they disappeared. Two sets of deep footprints marked the mud, one large leading, another small following close. Without a second thought, I slipped through the greenery, following the tracks they didn't seem to care they were leaving behind.

Hushed voices up ahead had me pushing harder, shoving through the face-slapping limbs and leaves. Mud oozed between my toes with each step while sticks and roots cut the soft skin of both soles. Maybe losing the shoes was a terrible decision after all. Not that I could've run in those things, but at least they would have provided some protection.

As quickly as the overgrowth of trees and plants started, it ended, giving way to a clear, open dirt road. I skidded to a halt as I tried to reorient myself with my surroundings while searching for the two I was chasing.

A sound had me whirling around, gun raised out of instinct toward the looming danger.

Bingo.

Chest heaving from the exertion, I brushed the hair stuck across my forehead and dangling in my eyes away with my forearm before alerting them to my presence.

"Let her go," I called out. Pride burned in my heart at the steady sound of my voice.

They froze their scurry to get inside the older model Jeep Wrangler parked alongside the road about fifty yards from where I stood. Despite the pain, I dug my feet into the soft dirt, planting my stance in case I needed to fire. The man stole a long look at the woman. I tilted my head, confused about what in the hell was going on.

Her head dipped in submission, face focused on the ground. Turning from her, he leveled those evil beady eyes my way, nose scrunched as he studied me. I knew the moment he recognized me, a sour look crossing his pinched features.

"You," he said, venom coating the single word. "I knew there was something off about your group."

"Oh?" I questioned.

"FBI?"

A single-shoulder shrug was the only answer I offered him.

"Doesn't matter. We never lose. Not tonight, not ever."

There's that 'we' again.

Whirling around, he drew a large handgun from the small of his back and pointed the barrel in my direction.

In a single heartbeat, two shots reverberated through the night. A thin tendril of smoke highlighted by the golden moonlight rose from the barrel as I continued to stare down the length of my gun at the now prone body beside the Jeep. Each breath was a struggle. Full-body tremors had my knees knocking together.

Shit, I almost died. If he would've been a better shot....

I swallowed to suppress the fear, desperate to shut down my body. Only when the cowering woman turned wide eyes my way did I lower my gun. I could almost see the wheels working before she scrambled to the ground, grappling for the dead man's gun.

"Hey," I said, voice weak. The dirt road squished between my toes with each step I took closer to the clearly terrified woman. "It's okay. We're here to help you. You're free now. See?" I prompted as I lowered my weapon in hopes she'd do the same.

The metal of her gun caught the beams of moonlight as it wavered between her clasped hands. Eyes glued to that finger that hovered just over the trigger, I cautiously crept closer.

"Stop," she shouted. My muscles tensed at the sudden halt of movement. "Don't come any closer."

I nodded, holding my hands up in surrender. With only the faint light, I scanned her for any injuries or signs of drugs. Eyes bright, cheeks flushed—even in distress, she looked healthier than the other day in the club. Which was... odd. I thought she'd died, and now here she was with a healthy appearance. Hell, even her hair was shiny.

I angled my head in an attempt to pinpoint what was off.

"You're safe now," I drawled. "The others are at the warehouse, liberating the rest of the women. You're free."

"You're alone?" Her gaze shifted to over my shoulder, searching the overgrowth.

My heart dropped in my chest and my lungs froze as a menacing grin spread along her perfectly painted deep red lips.

Her next move happened too fast for me to react, my brain locked on trying to process the sudden turn of events. "Good girl. I love the dumb ones who run off on their own."

A cry crawled its way up my throat, barely piercing the heavy night air before her steady hands slammed the butt of the gun against the back of my skull, making everything fade to black.

A STEADY BEAT hammered against my skull.

Oh hell, I really need to stop drinking Goldschläger. Shots are for college kids. This old liver can't handle that direct poison anymore.

My tongue, fat and dry, stuck to the roof of my mouth, my burning throat demanding I find water. Every muscle and joint ached as I rolled over in bed in search of the nightstand, intensifying the beating drum in my skull.

"Fuck," I rasped.

What the hell did I do last night to feel this poorly? It wasn't until I breathed deep to calm my rolling stomach that it registered that something was off. Mildew and the unmistakable stench of body fluid now coated my lungs.

What the... Why does my room smell like an abandoned meth house?

Agony shot through my skull as I peeked one eye open to search my room, validating what I already suspected.

This wasn't my room.

Gasping down tiny breaths, I willed my pounding heart and rising pulse to settle enough for me to think clearly. Panic crept in, making my thoughts race with one terrible scenario after another. Unable to move, I frantically scanned the area again for anything that looked familiar. Darkness blanketed the room except for a few slivers of the full moonlight cutting through boards nailed over the only window.

Designs and block letters decorated the peeling cinder block wall in various shapes and colors. Slick, glinting slime collected in the far corner and climbed the wall. Or maybe it was vines. Crawling over there to find out was not on the priority list.

If crawling was even an option, since I'd need both hands free for that. Trepidation washed away with the wave of relief when nothing restricted the movement to shift both hands and feet.

Not restrained—good.

Captive—not great.

Clearly whoever took me didn't know that while I might be small, I packed one hell of a punch if they got close enough.

Tentative fingers danced along the back of my neck, slipping beneath the hairline where the steady throb stemmed from. My prodding fingers immediately shied from the enormous knot at the base of my skull.

"Bitch," I hissed as the memories of the manipulative woman's gun rising in the air and her victorious smile filtered through.

But that made little sense. She was a captive, a trafficked victim... right? Or was she in on it all from the start, only acting like a victim to gain our sympathy?

That didn't make sense, though. How could a woman be a part of a business that sold other women to a life of horrors? Maybe that was a sexist comment, but it never crossed my mind that a female would actively sell other women to the seediest of ick on our planet.

Gingerly sitting up, I scooted along the ground until my spine hit the wall across from the only door. Flicking my attention between the door and the boarded-up window, I contemplated the best way to escape. The window seemed like the best option, in case they guarded the door on the other side. If I could get a board free, I could wiggle through the gap, but what if there was a drop? I had no way to determine if I was on a main level or stories high.

Squinting, I studied the gaps in the slats, doing my best to gauge the position of the moon for a way to tell the time. Too bad I was a doctor and not a damn astronomer.

"Idiot." Gently, I rested my head against the wall and cast my eyes to the ceiling to keep the fear-fueled tears from falling.

Panic threatened to lock me down, freeze every thought, which, in this scenario, was deadly. I needed to be ready, not scared and cowering. There was still hope.

Swiping a thrum along the inside of my wrist, I used the reassurance of the tracker and the others knowing my location as a grounding comfort that all hope wasn't lost. They would find me.

Escape was out of the question, then. Too much of a gamble of dying before they could gather the forces and liberate me from this hellhole. Plus, who knew *where* I was. If it was still night, I had to be on the island; not enough time to move me anywhere else. Unless I was out for days. Just the thought caused a lump of tears to lodge in my throat.

Either way, I just had to wait, bide my time until Weston and the others swooped in to save the day. Which they would. That I knew.

Yay, more waiting. It was like the universe was determined to teach me patience.

Based on the rolling nausea and location of the head injury, a concussion was likely, which meant I needed to stay awake. Which was the opposite of what I wanted, my body feeling as heavy as my lagging thoughts. Using my elbows instead of my injured palms, I crawled up the wall. The room swayed. Or maybe that was my body. I fell backward, slamming my upper back against the wall to keep from crumpling back to the floor.

It took a full minute to feel steady enough to attempt moving without support. Each step toward the window thrust bits of debris deeper into my feet. Tears from the sharp stabs wet my vision, making the moonbeams waver. Careful to keep one eye on the door, I pressed a cheek to the rough, damp wood and peeked out through the slats.

Trees, trees, and more trees.

Nothing remotely remarkable about the surroundings except that I was deep in the jungle somewhere. Wait, was it a jungle or a forest? I'd have to ask Alexa when I got home. Either way, we were hidden, far from anyone who would render aid if I screamed.

Awesome.

At least now I was certain escaping was out of the question. Between the looming darkness in the trees and the significant drop from the room, it was too much of a risk. If the drop didn't break a bone, who knew what animals lurked along the perimeter ready to give chase the moment I ran from my captors. Hard pass for this girl. Which was saying a lot because, I mean, look at my track record.

I huffed and leaned against a waterlogged board as I continued to stare out into the night.

At least this time it wasn't my fault. Well, not really. I didn't mean to get taken or run out there alone; it just kind of happened. Hopefully, Weston wouldn't be too pissed when he saved me.

I physically cringed knowing the excuse was just that, an excuse for my actions.

A lot of apologizing was in my future, no doubt. Maybe some of those role-playing hints would come to fruition. That kind of punishment and begging I'd be totally down for.

The approaching click of heels and stomp of heavier footsteps snapped my attention toward the door. Anticipation mixed with dread weighed heavily on my chest, making each breath difficult. I licked my lips and stood straight, ignoring the way my head swam with even that small movement.

I had to be strong.

No matter what happened next, I needed to stay alive, giving Weston and the others time to get me the fuck out of here. But as the door swung open and a familiar female face smiled into the desolate room, I worried it was already too late.

My return smile was a little ferocious and wild, showing all my teeth.

"Good to see I didn't kill you," she cooed. "I worried I hit you a little too hard."

"Nope, still alive with one hell of headache thanks to you."

Two massive men followed her inside the room, standing on either side of her shoulders. Her nose crinkled as she inspected the small space.

"I always forget how nasty it is here." She raised a single slim shoulder. "But they usually are. Can't have luxury out here, nor is it needed."

"And where is here?" I asked, thankful my voice was steady despite the nerves vibrating down my entire body. I fisted both hands and tucked them beneath my armpits.

"Far away from where we were," she remarked, lips ticked up in a knowing smirk. "Come." She gestured with a three-finger wave as she turned. "We need to talk, you and I." At the doorway, she cast a narrow-eyed glance over her bare shoulder. "No federal agent has made it past my tests. You've intrigued me. That is the only reason you're still alive. That and"—her narrowed eyes bored into mine—"you might prove useful. Now come, don't make me ask again. I'm not opposed to stepping back into a training role if needed to make you fall in line."

Useful?

Training role?

What the actual fuck?

Nothing made sense, and I wasn't sure if that was because of her evasiveness or my foggy brain.

With no other options, I followed her out of the room toward a well-lit area. With each step, I offered a pleading prayer to any deity who would listen.

Hurry, Casey.

Find me before it's too late.

14

Gray cement blocks crowded the room, trickling random rivets of water from various holes. They'd scattered several shadeless floor lamps around the room, offering bright light, highlighting areas of deep red along the chipped cement floor. Thin, well-worn mattresses lined the wall to my right.

A full-body shiver racked my shoulders at the fear and pain that seemed to pulse in this room left over by the many victims it'd held.

The scrape of something heavy being dragged brought my gaze from the mattresses to where the woman pulled two rickety chairs to the middle of the room. I retreated a step on instinct but slammed into the chest of a meathead's chest, halting my escape. He clamped a hand around my shoulder, engulfing the entire thing, and squeezed in warning.

That smirk only grew on the woman's face, like she was savoring my fear and pain.

"What are you?" I asked before thinking better.

"An entrepreneur of sorts," she said, positioning the two chairs to face the other. She motioned between them with a pointed glance. "Sit. I have questions for you to answer."

"Joy," I muttered under my breath. Not wanting to be dragged, I yanked my arm out of the man's grip and gingerly stepped toward the chair. A creak and groan sounded as I sat and leaned back. Picking up one foot, I rested the ankle on my thigh and squinted to inspect the damage. "You wouldn't have any tweezers in this place, would you?"

"Your feet are the least of your concern." I peered up as she sat across from me and dusted off the once pristine dress that was now streaked with mud and torn in several places. "Simple questions first. Who are you?"

"First," I said, turning my attention back to my foot, "what did you mean by test? Were you referring to that act you put on pretending to be his pet and being sick?"

Those red lips pursed, clearly unhappy I didn't answer the direct question immediately. Well, tough shit. She was the one who kidnapped me. I wasn't the one forcing her to hang out with me.

Her head tilted to the side, the long blonde ponytail draping over her a shoulder.

"Yes. I learned early on that behind closed doors, agents blow their cover when they think someone is hurt or dying." Her face contorted into a sneer. "Except you. Which brings me back—"

"So this is your operation, then?" Giving up on removing the bits of sticks out of my foot with just my ragged nails, I sat up taller and pretended to take in the entire room. "Seems nice. Except for the whole selling people part. How'd you get into this sort of work? Career day at school?"

Despite the quaking in my chest and fear pulsing through my veins, I offered her a smile.

"Answer my question," she hissed. Her agitation showed as she shifted in her seat, clearly not loving the idea that I wasn't intimidated by her. Which I was, but I knew something she didn't, which helped bolster my lagging courage.

My Weston would come for me.

"Sorry, what was the original question?" I pointed toward my head and rolled my eyes. "Concussion is messing with my memory. Speaking of which." Twisting the finger to hover in a 'just a second' gesture, I tilted from the waist and vomited. Ab muscles trembling, throat burning, I heaved up stomach acid until nothing remained.

Between the dry heaves, I heard the chair clatter to the floor.

"Weak," she snapped, now standing several feet away. Probably to avoid any vomit splatter if she was smart. "You want to know how I built this business, a woman? Because I'm stronger than you, stronger than all the ones who came before me. I was forced into this life with nothing, sold countless times until I stopped feeling sorry for myself and gripped the reins of my life. I outsmarted those fools, found their weakness, and fought my way to the top. I've been through hell, and I came out on the other side on top. That's how I do this, because I'd rather be the one making the money than the one fucked day in and day out."

A streak of saliva glazed across the back of my hand as I wiped at my lips. When I sat back and turned my attention to her, a new rush of fear bubbled to the surface. The familiar click of a slide being engaged ricocheted through the empty room.

I swallowed hard.

"Now," she said, back to the calm, collected sex trafficker witch. "I won't ask again. Who are you?" Flicking her hard glare over my shoulder, she hitched her chin. "Go get the girls. We need to move as soon as I'm done here."

That didn't sound promising for my life expectancy.

I watched their retreating backs as they hustled across the room and vanished through an open doorway. The sounds of them yelling and faint whimpers echoed reached the room.

My heart raced. The women, all those victims, were here. More were here to save if I could stall the crazy lady long enough for Weston and the others to rescue them, and me. How, though, I wasn't sure. My quick mouth surely wasn't the answer in this type of scenario.

"I'm no one. Just the prop to help them get inside," I stammered, hoping it wasn't the wrong approach. I needed to stall but also not get shot.

"How did they even know about the auction?" She took a step

closer, keeping the barrel of the nine-millimeter pointed at my chest. "We go by referral only and vet each applicant."

No way would I throw Ryan under this lunacy bus. But I knew one other person familiar with this dark side of humanity. A certain someone I didn't mind mentioning, even if it shortened his days on Earth.

"Some guy they paid off, Chaz... Champ...." I lowered my gaze, searching the floor like it held all the answers to offer the impression that I couldn't remember his name.

"Chase?" she said with a disbelieving laugh. "Of course that fucker did. Always looking out for himself. I heard what happened in Dallas with a particular shipment, but I thought he'd be smart enough to not cut a deal." Her unwavering stare drilled into me. "Rumor has it, some guy-and-girl team took him down. Do you know anything about that?"

I shook my head and grimaced from the way the movement made my brain roll around in my skull. "Just that he gave the name. Why?" I dared, hoping to pull her off track of the Chase incident. Pretty sure she wouldn't think twice about putting a bullet in my brain if she knew I was the one who messed up her shipment. *Sorry, not sorry.* "Why do this if you know what those women go through? Why subject them to that horrible existence?"

Her answering snort sounded too innocent, too young for the situation. "Money," she said, but there was hesitation there too. Like she was holding back from saying more.

"And a way out for you?" I prompted. "For you to be the one inflicting the pain and harm instead of it being done to you. You're in charge now, not at someone else's mercy."

A flash of surprise flicked across her pretty yet haggard face before it vanished, and a stony mask fell into place.

"What agency are they with?" she demanded, taking a step closer. Only three feet separated me and the outstretched gun.

"I don't know," I whimpered. "I don't know, just that they wanted to find the promoter who put on the auctions."

Her brows inched higher on her forehead. "Tom. All they wanted was an ID on Tom?"

He didn't look like a Tom, but sure.

I nodded, licking my lips nervously. "Yes. I bet they assume he was head of the organization. We didn't know about you."

As she thought it over, a frown dipped the corners of her lips. "But now you're gone, and they'll know there's someone else."

"What about the first guy?" I blurted. "The one who met us at the airport. I could blame it on him."

"That's cute that you think you'll live through this to tell them anything." An uncontrollable squeak inched out of my throat. "But you have a point." Keeping one hand wrapped around the grip of the gun, she pulled a cell phone from a small slit in the seam of the dress.

"Hidden pocket," I said, not even thinking. She nodded, not looking away from the phone. "Cool."

"Thanks. In this line of business, I need all the pockets."

Ew. No longer cool. There were probably sedatives and other things a human trafficker might need at a moment's notice stashed around her body.

With her attention on the screen, typing out some message, I had an opportunity to lunge forward, to disarm her. But what about the goons down the hall and the other bad guys creeping around with guns who I hadn't seen yet? So instead of taking the opportunity, I just sat staring while counting each passing second.

"Why you?" she asked while slipping the phone back into its hiding place.

Why me? Why me? Um, because I'm a badass who gets in over her head and regrets the decision to run off into the woods at night chasing after who I thought was the bad guy who turned out to be the evil woman. That's why.

"I'm a doctor." *Much better response.* "They thought I could help any of the women or men we found being trafficked."

"A doctor," she mused. The gun lowered a little, almost like that tidbit about myself made her think I was less of a threat than just moments ago. "That makes sense. In that room, you tried to diagnose me instead of promising to get me out of there. That's why you slipped through the cracks."

Despite myself, I sat up straighter in the chair. Damn straight, I fooled the evil incarnate thing standing in front of me. *Good always wins.*

One of her slim shoulders lifted in a dismissing shrug. "Lesson learned. I'll just have to come up with a new vetting process. What a pain."

"Or you could just quit this line of work. Maybe do something that doesn't destroy a person's humanity."

She glanced at the ceiling like she thought over my idea. "Nah. I really like the money." Waving a hand over her face and down her trim build, she smiled. "I like this person I've become."

"Really?"

Those bright red lips pressed into a flat line. "Yes. I'm only using people like I was used. It's only fair."

"Pretty sure there's nothing fair about human trafficking."

"Good thing I don't care what you think. Now, I'd like to say I'm sorry for doing this, but I'm not. You ruined a month's worth of work and stole hundreds of thousands from me tonight. It's only fair that I take something from you."

"You really need to Google the definition of fair," I blurted. "You use it in the wrong context—a lot."

"Shut up," she shouted, then waggled the gun for emphasis.

"Good luck with getting her to do that." A strange swirl of relief and fear stirred in my chest at the familiar deep voice. In my periphery, Weston stepped from the shadows, or maybe another doorway I hadn't noticed. "Drop the gun."

A flash of panic lit in her wide eyes before she pulled a calm, innocent mask back into place. "They made me do it." Slowly, she lowered her gun and gaze in a submissive move. "Help us. Please, help me."

What. The. Actual. Fuck?

"You're batshit crazy," I yelled and leapt from the chair. With one painful step, then another, I backed away. "It's her," I said, partially turning toward Weston, not daring to take my eyes off her. "She's the one we've been—"

A close, breath-stealing blast shook the entire structure. Debris rained down from the ceiling. Both arms shielded my already injured head as I curled into myself to help maintain my balance while the floor continued to shake. The scattered lamps flickered, making the room seem like a dance club with a wicked malfunctioning strobe light.

Eyes squeezed shut and hands over my head, I startled when a warm body pressed to my side. A familiar scent enveloped me, immediately calming my nerves.

"Are you hurt?"

I shook my head and dared a peek to the middle of the room.

Empty.

"Fuck," I called out. "Where did she go?"

"Kate, I need you to use your words. Are you hurt?" Two firm hands latched onto my shoulders and squeezed. "There's dried blood in your hair."

"Concussion from that bitch pistol-whipping me after I killed her damn partner. My feet are torn to shreds, but I don't care, Weston," I shouted. "Where did she go? She can't escape—"

"She won't. We have the place surrounded." Releasing me, he pressed a finger to something in his ear. "The woman from the club, the one Kate tried to save, is our target. She's in the wind. Do not let her leave the premises. She's armed and—"

A scream tore from my raw throat when the cement block near my head burst into a thousand tiny shards. Bits sliced across my cheeks and neck. Knees weak, they wobbled and gave out completely. A shock wave rattled from the impact, making my teeth clack together.

Ears still sensitive from all the evening's events, I cupped both hands against my head, hoping to muffle the boom of several guns being fired at once.

"Come on." Weston's grip was urgent as he hauled me to my feet and pulled me through the room. Gun raised in one hand and the other wrapped around me for stability, we stalked down a dark hall. The sounds of a battle and screams of pain mixed with the thundering of high-powered weapons.

"Just a little farther." The cool night air was a welcomed relief from the stale air inside the.... I turned to look over my shoulder. House? Storage facility? Whatever it was, it couldn't look more unassuming. Dark paint highlighted by the array of spotlights from various cars and trucks peeled in places but mostly aided in the building's concealment in the dense trees.

A hiss pushed past my clenched teeth when a stick tore through a raw spot on the ball of my right foot.

I felt more than saw Weston shoot me a concerned glance. Without asking for permission, he lifted me in one arm, gluing me to his side. The world bobbed and swayed as he sped past empty SUVs. A familiar Range Rover sat hidden in the back, welcoming me home with its glowing interior light.

Setting me on the passenger seat, he hurried around to the trunk only to return seconds later with a large white hard-shell box. "Here." The red cross on the front had me sighing in relief. "Do you need help with your feet?"

Just as he said it, another smaller explosion shook the building we just ran from. A deep line formed between his brows as he stared off toward the ongoing fight.

"Go," I insisted. "Go help them. Find the other girls. I heard some crying earlier. I'll take care of myself so I can be ready to take care of them during transport to the hospital."

His dark eyes glanced from me back to the fight. The war raging in his mind—to protect me or go help his friends and complete the mission—was clear on his pinched face.

"Go," I said, shoving his shoulder, though it didn't move him an inch. Leaning back, I searched the back seat and pointed toward the bottle of water James didn't end up using on the drive to the auction. Damn, that seemed like days ago. "Grab me that bottle of water, will you? I can wash my feet to see the extent of the damage, but I need—" A massive flashlight appeared out of nowhere. "—better light. Thank you, Mr. Boy Scout." He didn't smile. Wrong time for jokes, apparently. "Go, I'm fine. We're surrounded by agents, you're close, and I know who the bad guy—or girl, in this matter—is now. If she comes close, I'll cap her ass."

A corner of his lips twitched upward.

Winning. Just like when we first met, pride filled my chest at that almost smirk.

"Fine, but here," he said as he tossed a radio into the cup holder and withdrew a gun from a thigh holster, placing it gently on the dash. "Call if you see anything suspicious."

"What's the code word?"

"Weston, it's Kate. I see something suspicious," he deadpanned.

"Well, that's not very creative or quick. How about Code Red?"

"Fine, just say something if—"

"Weston. I'm fine. Go help the others. Save those women. Finish what we started."

After retrieving the water bottle, he gripped my chin and tilted my face to his. Before I could tell him to leave, he planted a hard, desperate kiss on my parted lips, leaving me breathless when he pulled away.

"Be safe."

I followed his muscular back and firm ass as he jogged away, appreciating his hard body.

"Damn," I whispered to myself, inhaling deep to get my racing heart and surge of emotions under control. Shifting my focus to the blood seeping from the bottom of both feet, I scrunched my nose.

Fuck, this would hurt.

AFTER TWENTY MINUTES filled with tears and even more blood, I wrapped both feet with layers of gauze, satisfied with what I'd accomplished with plastic tweezers and a flashlight.

Damn, I really was like MacGyver. Surely this was enough to convince even the critical James of my badass status.

I nodded, agreeing with myself, and grimaced. Well, badass with slight head trauma. Damn, I hoped he wouldn't bring up how I once again encountered a big snag in the overall plan. Last time it worked out fine, and it did this time too. That was what mattered.

Gently setting my foot on the floorboard, I chucked the empty plastic water bottle into the back and relaxed against the leather seat.

Brief flashes of light cut through the darkness, and muffled sounds carried on the cool wind from the direction of the fight. A gust whipped along my bare arms, reminding me of the slinky dress I still wore. Stretching the leg closest to the door, I attempted to hook a toe beneath the door handle to tug it closed but failed miserably. With a half groan, half whimper, I leaned forward, fingers stretching for the handle, when a shadow shifted, redirecting my attention.

I paused, hand hovering midair, halfway in the SUV and halfway out. I stole a look at the gun resting on the dash and radio. Both were too far away to grab quickly. Snatching the flashlight off my lap, I clicked it on and swung the bright beam toward the dense trees and foliage. Squinting, I scanned the area for any signs of something or someone lying in wait.

Nothing.

Maybe my overactive imagination conjured up a monster in the dark, considering the eventful night. To be fair, I had every right to be paranoid; it was a shit day. Not my worst, which was saying something about this reckless lifestyle I'd bulldozed my way into, but not great.

I sucked in a breath, holding it at the rustle of leaves and shift of the tall grass.

Now, *that* was not my imagination.

Wouldn't it suck if I survived this but died by a jaguar?

Did Hawaii have jaguars?

I really need to carry an Alexa around with me.

The beam of light bounced in my quivering hand as I swept it along the perimeter of the car. I completely passed Swamp Thing before realizing what I'd seen and moved the light back.

My heart stopped, lodging in my throat, preventing a scream for help to erupt.

Caked mud streaking her pretty face cracked and moved with her growing wide smile.

The slow rise of her clasped hands drew my attention to the gun.

"No," I gasped.

"See you in hell," she cackled with a manic laugh.

Not wanting to bear witness to my murder, I squeezed my eyes shut and crossed both forearms over my face, like that would protect me from a bullet entering my skull. Many thoughts raced through my mind, but regret weighed heaviest. Regret that I'd never get a life with Weston, never get to see my love-filled marriage like my parents had.

Regret and sadness swallowed me whole as I waited for the pain of a bullet ripping through my skin, damaging organs, and killing me slowly. I knew what it would feel like, that piercing pain that sucked your very life away.

A whizzing sound cut through the silence as the bullet sped toward me before warm liquid splattered across my face, a few drops making their way into my gaping mouth. The scream that was caught finally erupted in a high-pitched, ear-piercing cry.

My lungs burned with lack of oxygen from the held breath I refused to release as I waited for the pain and darkness.

Regretful and unprepared for my premature death.

15

____

But nothing happened. No searing pain from the bullet ripping through my skin. No blinding agony as my body leaked massive amounts of blood to the ground, depriving me of the liquid needed for survival.

Cracking one eye open a sliver, I scanned the area where I last saw the vile woman only to come up empty. Confused as to what in the actual hell was going on, I blinked both lids open wide and let out the breath I held as I waited, fully expecting for it to be my last. The smooth, round grip of the flashlight molded into my hand as I lifted it from the ground. The high beam landed on a gory scene just feet from where I still sat frozen in the passenger seat.

"Oh fuck," I squeaked, my hand rising to cover my gaping mouth. A warm, sticky substance slicked my fingers when pressed against my quivering lips. Slowly I wrenched my gaze from the prone body to the three wet fingertips and redirected the light, highlighting the streaks of crimson.

In a haze, I turned back to the unmoving body oozing the same crimson liquid on the ground, seeping between the chunks of gray gravel and dirt. Hand to the metal frame for support, I stood. Resting the flashlight so it flooded the area with light, I grabbed the gun from the dash and eased down the side of the Range Rover in case my quaking knees gave out completely. Wetness collected along my upper arm and soaked into the fine material of the ruined dress.

Turning, I shuddered at the blood and chunks of gore splattered along the shiny black paint. Afraid of what I might see, yet needing to know, I swiveled back, my focus zeroing in on the gaping hole where half of her head should have been. Gone were the long blonde tresses, those evil eyes now lifeless as they gazed into nothing.

"What the—" Nothing made sense, my thoughts lagging, unable to process the sudden turn of events. One second I waited for my impending death, and the next the woman who threatened me was missing half her skull, and the important contents it held inside coated the gruesome scene.

The crunch and rustle of approaching steps snapped my training with Weston into high gear. Whipping around, gun raised, I prepared to defend myself against this new threat.

A slim frame moved closer in the dim light, camouflaged in all black, a huge rifle peeking over their shoulder. I blinked several times to make the approaching face clearer.

"Anne?" Confusion and hope dipped my tone.

"That's me. Do you mind pointing that thing somewhere else, Doc?" She continued forward despite my raised gun, hands up in surrender. Slowly, recognition eased my pounding heart, and I lowered the end of the gun to the road.

"You good?" Anne asked, concern in her steady voice. "I thought I got my shot off before she could, but... are you? Good, that is?"

I nodded, not able to speak just yet.

Trying to piece it all together, I took in the body, then the menacing long barrel poking over her shoulder.

"You shot her," I said.

"Guilty," Anne responded with a forced laugh. "You okay with that?"

"Yes."

"Good." Anne rubbed her hands together and shoved both into

the front pockets of her black tactical pants. "Just making sure we're good even though...." She waved toward the body.

I cocked my head to the side, not understanding.

She groaned and looked to the night sky. "You save people for a living, Kate. You bring people back to life, and I'm very, very good at taking it without them even knowing they're in my crosshairs, their life in my hands."

I shivered. "Anne," I said after swallowing hard. She visibly tensed and shied away. "I might have a deeper crush on you after tonight." Her dark brows rose along her forehead as her shoulders sagged. "Not only do you look like Lara Croft, but you just saved me from being dead. So yeah, we're good. Just don't be concerned that my strange crush has risen from slightly strange to an awkward level."

A slow smile pulled up the corners of her lips, chasing away the earlier tension and worry. "Cool."

"Cool." Falling against the Range Rover, I dropped the gun to my side. Blowing out a heavy breath through pursed lips, I tipped my face to the sky full of stars. "We did it," I said after a minute. "The woman you shot was the brains of the trafficking operation. I know there are more out there, and we'll never keep up with all the groups, but I feel... I feel good. Minus the concussion, of course."

"Of course." I turned from the stars to find Anne. She pressed a finger to her ear and grinned. "Stop yelling through my private channel. She's fine, you overprotective ass." Anne winced as she took in my face, which was no doubt splattered with blood and.... Ew. Not going there. As a doctor, I wasn't queasy by any means, but brain matter sprinkled in your hair, that would gross anyone out, I'd think. "Is the house cleared?"

I watched, waiting for her to relay the information coming from the other end of the radio.

"How many?" Those dark brows furrowed as she listened, staring over my shoulder. "The others?" I stood straighter, dying to know what was being said. The way her features hardened said it wasn't good news. She zeroed her intense focus on me as she said, "I'm bringing her in." A pause as she listened to the response. "I don't give a fuck what you think she can or can't handle right now." A low growl of annoyance vibrated in my throat. *Dammit, Weston.* "This is what she does. An ambulance is too far out and you know it."

While she continued to debate me going back into the fight to help whoever was injured, I hobbled back to the passenger seat and began collecting the loose medical supplies I used and putting them back into the white box. Everything crammed inside, I tucked it under my arm and turned just as Anne stepped close, her face pale and tight.

"Who's hurt?"

"Mouse." Her voice was tight with strain. Her gaze dipped to my gauze-wrapped feet. "Can you run?"

I wanted to say yes—fuck, I hated being the weak link—but with the soles of both feet shredded, there was no way I could.

Her face softened, as if my answer was written across my own before I said a word. After removing the massive gun and leaning it against the SUV, she turned her back to me and squatted. "It's fine. Hop on my back."

It felt stupid, but Tyler needed me. That was what mattered, not my pride. First aid kit tight in my grip, I held on to her shoulder with the other and leapt. The second my legs wrapped around her waist, she wrapped her own beneath my knees, securing me tighter, and took off.

Each thundering step jolted my brain, making it swim within my skull, but I kept silent, not wanting to slow her down. The concussion wouldn't kill me, but Tyler might run out of time depending on his injuries.

As we drew closer to the cement structure, more battle-ready agents dotted the area. Several stared as Anne bobbed and weaved through the small crowd.

"Romeo," Anne called out and paused, her breath barely labored. "Where the fuck—"

"In here."

Spinning on her heels, she tore down a long hall, checking each room before skidding to a stop and backtracking.

Inside, Weston and James knelt, each on one knee at Tyler's head. Tapping Anne's shoulder, I wiggled out of her now slack grip and slid down her back. Forgetting my pain as my feet hit the cement floor, I hurried over to the pale, sweaty man bleeding out on the floor.

"What the hell did you do?" I chastised as I knelt beside Tyler. Blood pooled everywhere. Popping the white lid, I dug through the medical kit, pulling out a pair of scissors to cut away his clothes.

As I snipped through the thin fabric, he rasped, "He was hiding behind the girls. Didn't see him until it was too late."

Well, fuck.

With one last snip, I pulled open his shirt, scowling at the layer of blood.

"I need water," I said over my shoulder to where Anne stared, still as a statue. "Water bottles, now, Hawk."

Turning back to my patient, I doused one hand and then the other with the small bottle of alcohol.

Blood bubbled out of a wide hole near his clavicle. Leaning closer, I prodded around the gunshot wound, checking to see if the bullet was still inside or a through and through. Tyler groaned but didn't move away. Even with my pushing around the wound, the blood seeping out wasn't enough to think this was the major injury causing all the blood along the floor.

Desperate to find the source, I picked up the scissors again to remove his pants. The material cut easily as I snipped down his right leg, then left. Slowly, I peeled back the soaked pants and barked out a laugh at what I found—or didn't find.

"Seriously. You went on a mission without underwear on?" I said with a forced ease as I actively avoided staring at his penis.

But Tyler didn't answer.

"Fuck," I grumbled under my breath and doubled my efforts in finding the other gunshot wound. Fresh blood bubbled out of an entry wound on the leg opposite where I knelt. Hopping over his naked ass, I held a hand out. "Flashlight."

A bright beam had me squinting and turning to the owner. James ignored me, his face pinched with worry.

"I'll hold the light, Doc. You do what you need to do. The ambulance is five minutes out."

"Why weren't they on standby?" I grumbled as I pressed against the wound.

Anne raced into the room, holding five bottles of water in her arms. Hand raised, I motioned for one, which I caught midair.

A large hand reached over my shoulder for the bottle, twisted the cap off, and handed it back. "We didn't want them to know we were coming," Weston said. "We couldn't risk them killing you the moment they sensed us."

"Ambulances are loud," Tyler mumbled incoherently. "Weow, weow, weow."

All eyes turned to him.

"Right," I said slowly and turned back to the wound needing my attention. "Anne, wipe the tweezers with one of the sanitizing wipes and hand them to me. Also, toss a stack of gauze to James for him to apply pressure to the shoulder wound."

The clear water flowed over the wound, clearing the blood for only a moment before more bubbled up, covering the area again.

"Here, Doc."

Without looking, I held out a hand and waited until the plastic tweezers were in my palm before pulling it back to my side.

"I think," I said, my voice shaking. "I think it hit the femoral artery." Dousing more water on the entry wound, I stuck the tweezers into the hole. Tyler screamed in pain and tried to jolt away from me. "Hold him still," I hissed. "I have to get a clamp on this before he loses too much blood."

Weston stepped to the other side of his friend, placing a hand on his shoulder and one on his leg.

"Thank you," I whispered, worry and fear making my throat tight. "Okay, this is going to hurt." I winced and widened the entry wound to get a better look inside. I ignored Tyler's screams until they stopped. "He's fine," I said when the room went silent and tension pulsed. "He passed out from the pain. Anne, are there any pain meds in there? I didn't see any earlier, but I didn't really look."

The sound of the entire kit being dumped on the floor made me smile.

"Check his pulse," I said with a nod toward James. "But keep the light steady."

"It's there but faint."

"Okay. If I can get this clamped, his pressure should stabilize." Gritting my teeth, I dipped my fingers into the thick thigh muscle. "Fuck. Come on, you slippery sucker." Even with me holding the wound open, there wasn't enough room to work. "I can't do it, not in these conditions." Swiveling on the balls of both feet, I quickly scanned the area for something to use as a tourniquet.

"Help him." Anne's voice was soft, the words almost lost.

"Working on it. I need a tourniquet. If I can't clamp the artery itself, I need to stop the blood flow higher up."

"Here." Weston stood, unlatched his belt, and yanked it through the loops. Holding it out to me, his focus never left his friend.

"I'm going to pass out," James murmured.

"Don't you dare, light holder. I'm sure Tyler would be fucking pissed if I accidentally tucked his dick into this tourniquet all because you slacked on your light duties."

"Please don't hurt his penis. It's kind of the best part."

I peeked through my lashes at Anne. "It makes so much sense now."

"Yep," Weston added.

"What did I miss?" James responded. "She's right. Don't tourniquet his dick." I swore I felt the cringe of every man in the world at that statement.

The black leather slid easily along the blood-coated floor as I pushed it beneath the injured leg. Wrapping it around, I slipped it through the buckle and raised the end toward the ceiling until skin and muscles bulged around the edges and the steady flow of blood slowed.

"You're doing great, baby. The medics are here, making their way to us now."

Sweat beaded and slipped down my face as I strained to keep the tension tight enough to stop the blood flow.

Shouts and rushed steps echoed down the hall. Four men and a woman stormed into the room, medical bags in hand, as a familiar gurney rolled inside behind them.

"Gunshot wound to the right shoulder, no exit wound. Another damaged the femoral artery on the left leg. Tourniquet applied to slow the bleeding. No pain medication administered."

As I spoke, one man dropped the bag to the floor and ripped the zipper open. He withdrew a glass vial of clear liquid and sank a clean needle through the rubber top, filling the syringe before injecting it into Tyler's vein.

"It's for the pain and blood pressure. You a doctor?"

I nodded. "I'll hold the tourniquet tight while you load him onto the gurney."

Careful to keep every part of him supported, we loaded Tyler's limp body. I hopped on too, awkwardly straddling his legs.

"I tore my feet to shit, so I can't walk with you. Let's go," I snapped, feeling their unspoken questions.

The wheels squeaked as they wobbled down the hall, jerking left and right when a rock or piece of trash disrupted the smooth floor. One medic situated a blood pressure cuff over his bicep, calling out numbers as I tried to not fall off with every wayward sway. I wondered how this thing would do along the gravel when the room filled with rotating red lights and the back of the ambulance stopped an inch from the exit door's threshold.

"We'll follow." I heard Weston's deep voice over the medics and agents as they loaded the gurney. "She needs to be checked out too. Lacerations on her feet and head trauma at the base of her skull."

I stole a glance out the back just as the doors swung shut, but not before I caught sight of James, Anne, and Weston. They stood side by side, pain and anger clearly written across their dirty faces. Two hard pounds against the back doors and the ambulance lurched forward, making me sway to maintain my balance. The ride out of the trafficking compound was bumpy as hell, and more than once I had to latch on to a medic's shoulder with my free hand.

"Doctor."

The world blurred as I turned to face the medic.

"You're covered in blood—"

"And bits of brain matter," I mumbled, my lips feeling numb. As I stared at her, my blinking slowed, the urgent need for sleep slowly overpowering my insistence to stay awake.

"Not yours, I take it?"

"Not mine."

"Ma'am." Her voice echoed all around me like I was in a hollow barrel.

"Doctor," another man shouted. "I'll keep the tourniquet tight. You're good to let go now."

Yes. That sounded like a fantastic idea, considering I could barely keep my eyes open.

The moment the transfer happened, I slumped to the side, a set of arms saving me from slamming into the racks of supplies.

"Just a brief nap."

16

———

Hushed voices and familiar smells invaded my senses as I roused from a strange, violent, and gory dream. Gaze still hazy with sleep, I blinked several times to see clearly. Antiseptic and hospital-grade disinfectant burned up my nose, offering a strange sense of relief with the immediate familiarity. The basic white square tile ceiling, ugly-as-hell thin floral curtain, and echoes of barked orders and laughter all pointed to one truth.

I was safe and in excellent hands.

But how I got from the ambulance into the hospital was a black hole in my groggy memory.

The narrow IV tubing tugged at the needle inserted along the top of my hand with my hesitant movement. Weak fingers swept up the back of my neck to check if the wound had been treated. My eyes widened as the unmistakable feel of buzzed hair prickled against my fingertips.

"You've got to be kidding me," I grunted in frustration. The newly cut area was about a three-by-three-inch square, and a knot the size of a golf ball sprouted in the middle. Gone was the flaking dried blood and the crusted hair. A thin line with steri-strips cut through the throbbing mass.

A sudden ear-piercing screech of metal hooks grating along the above rod jolted me off the bed, my hand falling to the bedside. Pulse racing, I sank back into the thin pillow, wary of who was paying me a visit.

Covered in dirt, grime, and some of his friend's blood, Weston shoved through the gap in the curtain, his dark eyes finding mine instantly.

"Sir, I told you she's not awake yet," a nurse said, clearly agitated as she followed close on his heels.

Jealousy rushed to the surface. She would've seen I was in fact awake if her horny stare wasn't glued to his ass.

Back off, lady. That's my ass. Get your gropey little eyes off it.

"Yes she is," Weston grunted and pointed to where I sat glaring. I offered her a small wave when she finally noticed me. "Give us a minute."

"The doctor will want—"

"It's fine," I rasped, the words burning along my dry throat. Hand pressed to the pitiful excuse for a mattress, I sat up straighter. The earlier slow throb picked up pace now, thundering against my skull. "I'd like oral pain meds. Non-narcotic, please."

Grumbling under her breath, she gave Weston one more full-body once-over and twisted on her white tennis shoes before disappearing around the curtain.

Once the barrier to the rest of the emergency room floor was closed, Weston turned, his hands flexing and tightening into white-knuckled fists at his sides.

Right. I swallowed what little saliva I could to prepare myself for all the groveling and apologies.

"Weston, I'm sorry—"

The words vanished, sucked right out of my throat when he crossed the room in two large strides and wrapped his arms around my shoulders in a tight hug. His muscles quivered like he restrained himself from tightening the hold. Which was good. I could barely breathe like this.

"Tyler?" I croaked, needing to know the answer but yet not.

Weston's hold only tightened. Almost like he was protecting me from the upcoming answer.

"No," I cried, tears welling and spilling down my cheeks. "Please, no."

"Shh," Weston hushed, releasing me enough to pull back and cup my face between two calloused palms. "He's still in surgery. The doctors haven't told us anything." My lower lip quivered from a restrained sob determined to erupt. "You kept him alive until he got here to the hospital, baby. You did everything you could to save one of my best friend's lives." His own tears leaked from the corners of his eyes. "Thank you," he whispered, voice hoarse and full of emotion. "I don't deserve someone as amazing as you, but every day I thank any god who will listen that you chose me."

"Casey," I sobbed finally, allowing the tears to fall freely. Pitching forward, I sealed our foreheads together, not caring about the dirt and blood still caking his skin and maybe even mine.

"Marry me," he pleaded, eyes closed. "Please marry me, and I'll make sure that every day you'll see how grateful I am that you chose me as your partner in crime. I'll support you even when you take on too much, when you break down, when you need to let go. I'll be there for all the highs and lows. We'll take on this world knowing nothing can stop us if we're together. Please, baby, please marry me."

I placed both hands over his that still cradled my face. New, happy tears cascaded down my bunched cheeks as I gazed at the man I loved with every square inch of my heart, who my soul connected with the moment we met, seeing not just a match but a companion and partner.

"Yes," I whispered around the tears and sniffles. "Yes, I'll marry you because you see me, Casey. You see all of me and still love me, crazy parts and all."

Dry lips brushed against mine in a whisper of a kiss.

The rip of the curtain startled me, but Weston's hold on my cheeks didn't falter, keeping our faces a hairbreadth apart.

"Kate Wheeler?" a male voice questioned.

"Dr. Kate Wheeler," Weston said, releasing me and turning in a flash to the new male in the small area. His muscles flexed in his black T-shirt when he crossed his arms and widened his stance.

I rolled my eyes with a wide smile. "That's me. Don't mind him." I gestured to Weston, who continued to glare at the doctor with menace. "Let me guess. You cleaned and bandaged my feet, cleaned the head injury, and shaved my hair." I narrowed my eyes at that part, letting him know I wasn't happy about it. "And you want to keep me overnight for observation because of the concussion."

The doctor smirked and closed the metal lid on the clipboard in his hands. "Exactly. Emergency room?" I nodded. "Where?"

"Dallas."

"I'm sure that keeps you busy. We're getting your room ready now. Then we'll get you officially admitted." With a wave of the clipboard, he turned.

"How's our friend?" I asked quickly before he could hurry to his next patient. "The one with the two GSWs. I think he's still in surgery."

"You know as well as I do I can't release that kind of—"

"We're not asking for details, just...." I tipped my face up to the ceiling, hoping to keep the hot tears at bay.

"We are his family," Weston cut in. "He doesn't have anyone else."

My heart ached at that piece of information I never knew for the happy, mischievous man I'd allowed to enter my little circle of friends. *Oh, Tyler. Sweet, sweet Tyler.*

"He's still in surgery," the doctor said and pursed his lips before glancing one way, then the other outside the curtain. "I don't know much, but I heard he's still with us. Now, if you'll excuse me."

Thick, calloused fingers interlaced with my own and squeezed.

"He's a fighter. He'll pull through like he has before."

"It's my fault," I croaked. "It's all my fault. If I hadn't—"

An angry Weston bent over to put his face directly in my line of sight that was still glued to the ceiling.

"That's utter bullshit, and you know it, Kate. We knew what we were getting into with this mission. We wanted this. Hell, the guys want to make our team official and sign up for more assignments." He ran a hand down his face. "Do you know how many women were at the location where we found you?"

Relaxing back into the flat pillow, I shook my head. I needed this story, desperately needed to hear that I wasn't a complete fuck up who might have gotten one of his best friends killed. I swallowed hard and averted my eyes.

Not having any of that, Weston pinched my chin between a finger and thumb, turning my face to meet his.

"Eighteen." An uncontrollable, ugly sob of relief shook my shoulders. "Plus the ones we extracted from the auction location puts it at twenty-nine. Twenty-nine women were saved in the last twelve hours, freed from torture and pain because of us. If Mouse—" He cleared his throat. "If Mouse doesn't make it, he will have died knowing he made a difference with his sacrifice. This is what we do, Kate. We trained to walk into dangerous situations that we might not walk out of. We're used to it."

"I'm not," I whispered. Biting my lower lip, I searched his dark brown eyes. "Don't get me wrong, I'm so damn happy that we saved those women. Even if it was just one, I'd be happy. But the danger, being on the front lines of the action, I don't want to do it again," I admitted. "I want to help, but not like this again."

"Thank fuck," he said with relief clear in his heavy breath. "I don't want you on the front lines with us, baby. I died a thousand deaths in the last twelve hours. I'd much rather have you safe in the background, supporting us in other ways."

I nodded in agreement. "So what does this mean?" I asked, excitement building, chasing away the doubt and sorrow. "That you guys want to make the team official and do this, like, as a job?"

"Maybe. There's a lot to work through with Miss Ginger. This might have been a one-and-done type thing." His shoulder raised and lowered in a shrug, drawing my attention lower.

"Have any of y'all showered?" I asked. "Wait, have *I* showered?"

His long, dark hair shifted with the shake of his head. "But don't worry, I told them to upgrade you to a suite for the night and asked an agent to run by the house to grab us all a change of clothes. Once Mouse is out of the woods, we can think about taking care of our own needs."

I nodded. A wave of exhaustion rolled over me, making my lids heavy.

"Sleep, baby," Weston said as he pressed a kiss to my forehead.

"Go wait for Tyler," I said, slowly slipping into the beckoning drowsiness.

"I'm not going anywhere without you. Sleep and know I'll be here the whole time."

With those final words, I let myself drift. No one, not even my nightmares, could hurt me with Weston close. I felt my soul and heart smile as I settled into the peaceful darkness of sleep, the earlier conversation circling through my mind.

I'm getting married.

"HE'S GOING to be pissed when he finds out you doubted him," Anne commented as she towel-dried her hair in the doorway of my en suite bathroom. "He's been shot before."

"Not like this," James grumbled. "But he's good now, right?" He turned worried eyes to where I lay in my hospital bed.

"The doctor said he made it through the surgery and was stable. I was worried about the blood loss and his leg. I hoped they wouldn't have to take it since it went without direct circulation for so long." Three sets of eyes blinked at me. "What?"

"I didn't know that was a concern, princess."

"That's why I kept it to myself, jackass." I sighed and rolled my eyes to the ceiling. Thankfully, the pain and throbbing had decreased with the pain medicine and a nice long nap. "You guys were worried enough. But they said they were able to restore the blood flow, get a few pints in him, and now he's good as new." I shot him two thumbs up, which he returned with a middle finger.

Weston smirked from where he leaned against the wall of windows, watching.

"So," I drew out. "Anne. You and Tyler...." My forehead wrinkled as I raised both brows.

With a groan, she tossed the towel into the bathroom and crossed her arms. "Yeah, like I told you the other night, it's new."

"Why didn't you tell us?" James asked, sounding oddly hurt. "We keep nothing from each other."

"Yeah, well, this is different," she said as she shot a cautious look at Weston.

That was when it all clicked.

"You two were worried about what Weston would think," I said as a statement rather than a question. It was clear on her face that she was concerned about that piece of the equation.

"That and the team. We work well together, and we didn't want our personal lives to interfere with the mission."

"Speaking of personal lives," Weston added, pushing off the window to come sit on the edge of the bed, "I asked Kate to marry me, and she said yes."

Excitement, pride, and a little bit of nervousness lit in his dark gaze as he glanced over his shoulder and smiled.

"What?" James and Anne said in unison.

"And we're getting married here in Hawaii," I added. "Before we go back home."

Weston turned on the bedside to look down at me. "Really?"

I nodded. "If you're okay with that."

Instead of answering, he leaned forward and placed a soft kiss on my lips. "The sooner the better." His lips dipped in a frown. Reaching up, I smoothed the pad of my thumb over the deep line that formed between his brows. "I don't even have a ring."

"Like I give a fuck about that," I whispered, meaning every word. "All I want is to be yours forever."

"How in the hell did I get so lucky?" The awe and love in his soft tone were nearly my undoing.

Rough scruff scraped against my palm as I slid a hand up to cup his jaw.

"You fell in love with the real me, that's how. You know me at my worst, have seen me break down, and stayed. You stayed even when I wasn't perfect. You stayed with me through it all."

An attention-snagging, slightly annoyed throat clearing had Weston stepping away from the bed, but he didn't go far. Instead he placed his hand on top of my head and began softly sweeping his fingers through the still damp strands.

"Not to be rude—" James glared at me when I snorted. "But what in the hell are we supposed to do until then? Who knows how long it will take you to plan that shit—"

"Not shit, and not long," I cut in.

"Plus, you'll want Mouse by your side, and he won't be healed for—"

"I've already thought of that." I interrupted him again, earning me an 'I hate you so much' glare. "Stop looking at me like that, Jamesy. You know you love me."

"What the hell did you call me?" he snapped, but there was no heat to it. In fact, the level of annoyance and anger he normally threw my way had diminished little by little since this mission started, tapering off to acceptance almost.

"If you continue to call me 'princess,' then I need a nickname for you. 'Jackass' was getting boring and really couldn't be used in certain company."

He groaned and rested his head on the back of the couch he was sprawled along. "Fuck me."

"Anyway, as I was saying, I have a plan for what we can do while I handle the wedding arrangements and Tyler heals. I'll need all of y'all's help, though. I've never worked in construction."

I barked out a laugh, groaning at the pain the noise caused, at their combined confused stares. The three shot worried looks at each other. Which was silly. Like I'd ever tossed out a plan that wasn't well thought out.

Well, okay, they had a right to be worried. But this was different.

Way different. No guns needed, just hammers, nails, and a lot of muscle were needed for this plan.

The wedding planning was also where I was clueless.

Good thing I had a perfect friend to help make the wedding plans happen, and four friends who would help me make the other come true.

17

———

The soles of my tennis shoes squeaked along the newly stained concrete floor as I meandered along the living quarters wing. It housed fifteen rooms down this hall and another fifteen down another. Each room came equipped with a queen-size bed, basic desk and chair, a dresser stocked with clothing of various sizes, and a small bathroom attached. Those bathrooms were filled with yummy-smelling soaps, hair products, brushes, a hair dryer—hell, anything Meagan had suggested I should add to make any woman feel at home.

I paused in front of the last bedroom and leaned a shoulder against the doorframe, staring inside. Meagan was a no-brainer on who to consult on the furniture, layout, and design of the private rooms to make them cozy and welcoming. I wasn't the girliest of girls, but she was. Hopefully, because of her insight and ideas, the women who lived in these rooms appreciated the small touches of home we added.

Construction on the location began two weeks after they released me from the hospital, which was just over two months ago. The guys and Anne helped every step of the way, either working alongside the workers or managing the flow of supplies from the shipping yard. Tyler did what he could, mostly offering comic relief when things were stressful or when that huge hurricane threatened to hit the island, destroying all our efforts. With him recovering, he needed to take it easy, which drove him nuts, but he still listened to the doctor's orders despite his annoyance.

"Hey." I turned to look down the hall toward Weston's voice. "I was wondering where you ran off to."

"Didn't run, not anymore," I offered with a grin and turned to stare back into the room. "Do you think it will be enough?" I asked absentmindedly.

"I know it will." The hand that gripped my shoulder turned me to face him straight on. "You've done amazing work here, Kate. They'll feel safe. That's what's most important."

He was right. The tall fence around the twenty-acre property was more for their benefit than to keep others out. That was what the guards were for.

This new location for Second Chances could house thirty women in the main house and ten males in the smaller house. We also hired two full-time counselors, plus a full kitchen and cleaning staff. Anne built a small garden in the back so the place could be self-sufficient with fruits and vegetables. The solar panels in the rear of the property were her idea too.

James handled the security side, making sure the buildings had the latest and greatest alarm systems, installed panic buttons in each room, and hired the guards who were instructed to stay as invisible as possible to not scare the residents.

We were set to open in two weeks. Technically, the inspectors just left and we could open tomorrow, but no. Tomorrow was for me and Weston. And the following two weeks were for us too as we island-hopped for our honeymoon.

Was it selfish? Maybe, but we deserved the downtime away from danger and work, to just be us.

A hand reached up and encircled my wrist, pulling my hand away from my lip.

"What are you worrying about?"

Leaning forward, I pressed my forehead to his hard chest. "Nothing, just thinking about tomorrow."

"Are you rethinking—"

"No," I blurted and leaned back to look him in the eye. "Not that at all. It's just I'm worried Eric's gone a little overboard with the plans."

An almost smile tugged at Weston's lips, erasing the worry etched on his features. "It'll be great. Just wait. He knows you better than most. He knows you want nothing too big or over the top. Trust him."

I huffed and pushed my lower lip out in a full-on pout. The two had conspired against me and decided I didn't need the additional stress of building this facility in record time plus planning a wedding, so Eric had full control, not letting me in on any of the plans. I knew nothing except for my wedding dress, which I picked out, thankfully. Eric thought it was a little plain, but to me it was perfect. I knew Weston would think so too.

"Fine," I grumbled.

"Have you eaten today?" he asked, smoothing his hand down my arm and interlacing our fingers. I winced. "That's what I thought. Come on, baby, I'll feed you. Then we need to go pick up everyone from the airport."

"Oh joy." I sighed, dragging my feet as he pulled me down the long hall. I smiled when a blond mop of hair poked around a corner. "Hey, bestie." I gave Eric a brief wave with my free hand. We'd been joined at the hip since he arrived last week, needing to be on-site to complete certain wedding details. "We're headed to get some food. Want to join?"

"Is the grumpy one coming?" Eric asked. When we passed by, he hooked an arm around my neck and pulled me to his side. "He's hot and all, but damn, that man needs to get laid."

Weston's booming laugh had Eric and me turning. When his laugh dimmed to a low chuckle, he nodded. "He really does. You offering?" He arched a dark brow but kept his gaze straight ahead.

"Um, no, which is saying something. What's the story about him, anyway?" Eric continued as we passed through the living room area. "There's a dark side to that one."

All humor left Weston's face. I squeezed his hand for reassurance.

"He was a POW." Eric skidded to a stop, tugging me backward with his arm still around my shoulders. "He won't talk about it, which is why he had problems adjusting when we came back from our last mission. It's his story to tell, but he fights a battle daily in his mind that I'll never understand even with my own issues caused by those deployments."

"Drugs or alcohol?" I asked, my eyes searching Weston's. "I noticed when I first met him that he was sickly looking. Too thin, too pale."

"Both, but mostly alcohol. It was his way of dealing with the memories. All of us, Aiden included, tried to help him get clean, but it never took until recently." Something like awe and love washed over his face, softening the lines of worry that had formed. "This assignment, it gave him purpose again, and I told him no drinking or drugs or he'd be off the team. He's stuck to it too. The last two months have aided in his recovery somehow." A hard tug sealed me to Weston's chest. "Look at that, baby. You've saved two of my best friends." That smile of his turned wicked. "However will I thank you?"

Heat bloomed between my thighs as my stomach tightened with want. We'd been so busy lately, alone time with him was nonexistent, or when we were, all we wanted to do was sleep. But here, right now with that heat in his eyes, all I wanted was us skin to skin.

"Later, lovebirds. I'm starving, plus we need to pick up Kate's father and your friend Aiden from the airport." Eric started toward the exit door, pulling me along with him. "It was nice of your dad to let him and Meagan fly on the private plane with him."

"He's trying to make up for being such an asshole to my future husband," I grumbled.

Weston gave my hand a comforting squeeze. Dad still wasn't fully on board with the wedding, but he was getting there. We had another fight just the other night when he emailed me a prenup agreement he approved of and needed Weston to sign prior to the ceremony.

Hellll fucking no.

I said as much the moment Dad picked up the phone after I read the ridiculous and slightly offensive email. In true Dad fashion, he doubled down on making it a requirement or he wouldn't show up, which made me double down and say I didn't give a shit if he did or didn't.

That was a lie, but he didn't know that. What girl didn't dream of their father, who they'd idolized and loved—until the last few months, that was—walking her down the aisle. It wasn't until a few days ago that I knew he was actually coming, despite Weston not signing the stupid agreement. Only time would tell if he'd use this face-to-face time as another opportunity to push the reasons for Weston to sign the document.

I could see why he thought that was the wise choice considering our family's wealth, but he didn't know Weston like I did. I knew deep in my soul that Weston wasn't after my trust fund and the millions that came with it; he wanted me and that was it. The fact that my father couldn't see that spoke volumes and had further damaged our once strong relationship. Maybe one day we'd be able to repair it, but not soon. I needed time to heal from his angry words and distrust of my own choices.

Outside, the thick air stuck to every inch of exposed skin, slicking it with sweat.

"How about tacos?" I asked, trying to break the silence that had settled between us three. "There's that taco cart right down the road on the way to the airstrip." I offered this solely for Eric's benefit. His newest food addiction was said taco truck. He'd eaten it every day since he arrived. I wasn't sure how he'd found it, but it was good and had cold beer, which sold me.

"Yes," he said, pumping a fist in the air. "Then after, let's get you pampered."

I groaned and leaned harder into Weston, hoping he'd save me from Eric's ministrations.

"Airport, Dad, and friends, remember? We just talked about this."

"I can handle that," Weston said with a small smirk. *Traitor.* "You go with Eric. You deserve some time for yourself before tomorrow. Because believe me, baby, you won't get a second alone after we say 'I do' through the honeymoon. I plan to be—"

"No details, please," Eric groaned. "Not unless you 're inviting—"

"No," Weston and I said in unison. We smiled at each other as we stopped in front of the SUV.

Reaching up, he cupped my face, swiping his thumbs along my cheekbones.

"I can't wait to make you mine tomorrow."

I gave him a shy smile and pushed up to my tiptoes to kiss the corner of his lips.

"Don't you know, silly boy? I already am."

"I AM NOT HAVING this conversation with you again," I hissed through my clenched teeth before taking a long sip of my red wine. "I'm getting married tomorrow whether or not you approve."

Dad sighed from across the table, his eyes on the cheerful crowd talking and laughing along the beach. I had to hand it to Eric—he could throw one hell of a party. The rehearsal and dinner after weren't stuffy or long, which he knew I'd loathe. Instead, he gave us all a quick rundown of times for tomorrow, directions to the ceremony spot, and then gave free rein to eat, drink, and be merry.

I couldn't be merry, though. Not with the stubborn-ass man beside me.

"I'm just trying to protect you, pumpkin," he said, exasperation in his tired voice. "You've only known him for—"

"It doesn't matter if I met him yesterday. You should trust me and my decisions. I'm a big girl now, Dad. I can decide without your approval." Turning in my seat, I gripped his wrist. "I want you to walk me down the aisle tomorrow, but if you can't get on board with Casey and me not making him sign the prenup, then I think you should leave."

His hazel eyes searched my own, no doubt looking for the bluff. Too bad I wasn't.

"I'll be there," he whispered. Tears filled his lower lids. "I wish your mother could see you now. Standing up to me, not letting me boss you around." A sad smile tugged at his lips. "You're just like her." Now my own eyes grew wet with unshed tears. "Strong, independent, beautiful inside and out. I'm so damn proud of the woman you grew to become, Kate. And I know without a doubt your mother would be as well."

Lurching forward, I wrapped my arms around his neck and held on tight. For several seconds, we stayed in the near-suffocating embrace, letting the fights and arguments over the last few months fall away, leaving only the deep unconditional love we had for each other.

Still holding on to Dad, I searched the beach, finding Weston's eyes on me, smiling that knowing smile of his. He shot me a wink before turning back to the guys, engrossing himself in their conversation once again.

"I'm going to go see my friends for a bit," I whispered against Dad's neck and pulled away.

Cool wind brushed against my arms, sending a chill straight to my bones. Rubbing my hands up and down them, I meandered through the crowd, making my way toward Weston and the boys and Anne. The moment I was within reach, Weston pulled me against his chest, turning me to face the smiling group.

Heat seeped from his chest into my back, and the powerful arms he wrapped around me helped protect my arms from the ocean breeze.

My smile slipped when I saw Tyler standing beside Anne, his arm slung around her shoulders.

"Tink—" he started, catching my scowl.

"Don't 'Tink' me. Where is your cane? You shouldn't put your full weight on your leg this long, especially with tomorrow—"

"Someone get her a drink," James grumbled, then tipped his own beer bottle up toward the sparkling night sky. "Calm her ass down."

"Screw you, James," I said with little heat. This was an ongoing conversation since Tyler started physical therapy. He was healing but still needed to take it easy.

"I have a human crutch tonight, Tink. Don't go getting in a tizzy."

I snorted and snuggled against Weston. The conversation from earlier seemed to have fallen flat the second I arrived. I scanned the group before tipping my head back to see Weston.

"What were y'all talking about before I walked up?" Silence. "Come on, don't do that to me. Keep me in the loop."

Weston's chest ballooned out, pushing me forward several inches. "Just talking what-ifs. Miss Ginger said he'd tell us more when he could, but until then, we're in a holding pattern. No one knows if we'll be needed again or if this was a one-and-done type thing."

"Oh," I muttered. This was a tense topic these days. They all wanted to stay working together, but how if they didn't have an agency backing them? "Well, maybe he'll give us news tomorrow. He'll be here, right?"

"Landing at 0300," James said. "He had a few things he had to wrap up before he could take off. I think he was closing loose ends on that fucker Chase."

"And securing everything for Ryan," Weston added, sadness in his tone. "I hate that he can't be here with us tomorrow, but it's for the best, considering. Miss Ginger has him all set up with a new identity, background, job, everything up in Alaska. Hopefully, he'll stick to the rules and make a clean break with his old life."

"And when has that ever happened?" Anne said with a chuckle.

"Never." Weston sighed. "Hopefully, this time he knows how much work they put into it all to give him a second chance. That asshole better not blow it."

A comfortable silence settled between us until Eric walked up, talking a mile a minute, slightly slurring.

"There you are. I've been looking for you." I held in a groan. Today was fun getting pampered, sure, but I was really ready to be done with needing to be somewhere or having something to do with the wedding stuff. "We need to get you home," he said, reaching for my hand.

I yanked it back.

"It's nine," I complained. "You said the party lasted all night."

"For them, yes, but for you, no. You're the bride and you need your beauty sleep." I opened my mouth to argue, but he pressed a finger to my lips. "I've seen you hungover, little lady, and it's not pretty. And I also know how cranky your ass can be when you haven't had enough sleep, and no one needs to be exposed to that tomorrow. So let's go." He slapped my ass hard, making me yelp from surprise and the sting.

Three sets of shocked, wide eyes whipped to Weston. Who simply smiled and kissed the top of my head.

"Listen to your friend, baby. He's only looking out for our best interest. I've been around tired, grumpy Kate and agree 100 percent that no one needs to be around that."

I punched his arm, hurting myself more than him.

"You're supposed to be on my side," I said, sulking as I dragged my feet in the sand, reluctant to follow as Eric pulled me away.

"Always, baby. Now go. I'll see you tomorrow."

Digging my heels, I stopped and tilted my head in confusion. "Why? What's tomorrow?" I couldn't stop the cheeky grin that spread up my cheeks.

"The best day of my life."

Well, hell.

Shaking my hand loose, I ran the few steps and launched myself into Weston's awaiting arms, wrapping my legs around his waist.

"I love you so damn much," I murmured against his lips. "We should get married."

"How about you meet me tomorrow, say around two o'clock, up on this pretty overlook a few miles from here? Wear something fancy, white maybe."

I tapped my cheek like I debated his offer. "You'll be there?"

"I'll be the one down front waiting to start the rest of my life with you."

"The best part?"
"The happy part."
And just like that, he made me fall in love with him all over again.
Tomorrow couldn't come soon enough.

18

***

Delicate cream lace hugged my shoulders, chest, and hips before loosening, allowing the soft material to float down my legs. Lounging on the small settee in the bridal suite, I studied Eric and Meagan as they fussed over their hair, both talking rapidly. The smooth rim of the champagne flute pressed against my lower lip as I took a deep sip of the crisp bubbly liquid, the corners curved in a smile at my friend's antics.

Eric had outdone himself with all aspects of the wedding. From this private room to the intimate ceremony that would start in a little over an hour to the celebration after. Not only was everything low-key, very me, but he handled the nitty-gritty details through the last couple months and continued to today. All I had to do was show up. He deserved a best friend trophy or something when we got back to Dallas.

Glancing at the full-length mirror, I inspected the reflection I barely recognized. I asked the stylist to go easy on the hair and makeup, preferring a more natural look for the big day. The way they shaped my eyes, the highlighting of my cheekbones, and bright coral-shaded red lips, I went from regular Kate to stunning.

"You're wrinkling your dress," Eric said, drawing my focus back to my two friends. Both had turned from the mirror over the vanity to stare me down. "And smudging your lipstick."

I offered a one-shoulder shrug and winked as I downed the rest of the glass. "There, no more lip smudging. But you're crazy if you think I'm standing until the ceremony. This is the only time the dress will be worn. Let it get wrinkled. Gives it character."

Eric waved me off and turned back to his reflection, fingers teasing the ends of his blond hair to position them just right. Meagan crossed the room and plopped down beside me, clearly having the same thought as me about standing.

"So," she started, dragging out the word. "You ready?"

"Yep." Raising the empty flute high in the air, I gave it a little attention-grabbing waggle. The attendant hurried over to the champagne bucket, picked up the nearly empty bottle, and refilled my glass.

"But it's forever. One dick, forever. Even when he has old saggy balls." The sound of disgust in her voice had me chuckling into the champagne flute as I tipped it back.

"Not sure if you've noticed or not, but we get old and saggy too. It's not just the males." Leaning forward, I set the glass on the side table before turning back to Meagan. Champagne was dangerous, and I needed to slow down. The last thing I wanted was to show up to my wedding tipsy.

"Damn straight," Eric added.

"Speak for yourself." Reaching up, she cupped her full breasts, weighing them in her palms as she glanced between them. "I'm still quite perky and full. Fuller than normal. Maybe that's a perk of getting older too. I think I'm one of those blessed ones who look better with age."

"Because of the push-up bra," Eric sniped with a wink in the mirror to me. "Or...." Turning, he studied the redheaded beauty beside me. A line formed between his brows, head tilting to the side as he looked her over from head to toe. "Meagan."

"Eric," she huffed, annoyed until he didn't respond. "What?"

"Didn't you say you've been feeling nauseous off and on?"

I twisted to face her, waiting for her answer and to figure out what spurred that random question from Eric. Meagan and I had had little time together, so this was my first time to really look at her. Her normally pale skin seemed almost white, her light sprinkling of freckles standing out along her nose and cheeks.

"How long has the nausea been happening?" I asked. Unease grew in my gut, making me regret that last glass of champagne.

Meagan released a nervous laugh, clearly not enjoying being the center of our interrogation. "Like a few weeks, I guess. It's not so bad. Honestly, I think I've grown an allergy to milk. You know how much I love my lattes in the morning."

"So, you're mostly feeling sick in the mornings." I shot a knowing glance at Eric. "Meagan."

"Kate."

"Don't be dense." Eric sighed. Squatting in front of us, he rested a hand on her bare knee. "Are you still sleeping with Austin?"

"Yeah, so?" She shot me a wary glance. "Is that a problem? She's getting married to—"

"Could you be pregnant?" I blurted quickly, covering my mouth, which was smacked away. Eric frowned at the offending fingers that now had a layer of lipstick along the tips.

"No, that's not what's going on." Except the forced laugh and the way her eyes shifted around the room said otherwise. "Oh shit," she gasped. "Am I pregnant?" Those searching eyes turned pleading, bouncing from me to Eric and back again.

"Hey, lady," I called over my shoulder. I should've asked her name earlier, but now all I cared about was getting her to do my bidding. "Run down to the hotel gift shop and buy us a pregnancy test. They have those right?"

"Um, I'm not—"

"One hundred dollars for the test and your time," Eric added, fishing his wallet out of a front pocket. Pulling a crisp bill from the stack, he waved it in the air toward the attendant, tempting her to say yes. "If it's not downstairs in the little shop, tell your boss you're running an errand for the bride. If he has a problem with it, then tell him to come see me. Or her future husband," he added with a knowing grin. "He's a scary motherfucker. Sexy as hell—"

"Watch it," I warned.

"But scary."

I shoved his shoulder, causing him to tip to the side. He caught himself with a palm on the armrest before he face-planted to the floor.

Taking the bill, pinching the money between two thin fingers like it might bite her, she retreated a step away from our little huddle. "Okay, sure. I can do that for you, Ms. Wheeler. I'll... I'll be right back."

"There's another hundred waiting for you if you can do it in less than thirty minutes," I shouted just as she slipped through the door into the hallway. The pounding of her running steps soon faded away.

Turning back to the pale and distressed Meagan, I interlaced our fingers and squeezed.

"Hey, it's okay. We'll know soon. You really had no clue?"

Her red ringlets swished along her bare shoulders as she shook her head. "I've been working a ton since we're down a doctor." She sent a side glare with zero heat in my direction. "And when I'm not at work, I'm with Austin. This can't be happening." Leaning forward, she covered her face with her free hand. "Things are so good between us. A kid? A kid will ruin everything. And you two know me. I'm not meant to be a mother."

Eric and I shared a look. She wasn't wrong about that. We loved Meagan, but she loved to party, fuck, and do it all over again the next night with a different stranger. But things had changed since she and Austin hooked up. Eric had mentioned a few times through texts that Meagan seemed settled, less restless in a way these last few months. So maybe she was growing up and a baby wouldn't be too much of a transition.

"Distract me," Meagan said, pushing off the maroon crushed velvet cushion. Tugging off one high heel and then the other, she began pacing the room, wringing her hands with worry. "Tell me something—"

A tentative knock stopped her in her tracks. We turned toward the door. There was no way the woman was already back.

"Kate?" The tension in my shoulders eased at the sound of Dad's voice. "Are all of you decent?"

Standing, I teetered on my heels, using Eric's shoulder for support as I gained my footing. At the door, I gave myself a quick second to school my features. Dad would notice something was off immediately if there was an ounce of worry or stress on my face. After three deep breaths in and out, I steeled my spine and twisted the knob.

I offered a forced smile through the three-inch crack I left between the door and frame.

"Hey, Dad." The added lightness to my voice sounded off even to me, too high-pitched and happy. "Did you need something?"

"Can I come in?" I glanced over my shoulder to where both my friends were waving their raised arms frantically in a no gesture. "It's important, pumpkin."

I released a resigned sigh as I pulled the door wide and gestured toward the middle of the bridal suite. I mouthed an apology Meagan's way, who turned and busied herself with the Caboodle full of makeup and hair supplies strewn along a vanity.

"Something going on?" Dad asked as he surveyed the room, no doubt feeling the tension between us three.

"Nope," I hurried to say, hoping to distract him. "All good. What's so important, Dad?" My gut twisted with panic. What if he was here to attempt talking me out of the wedding *again*?

Dad shifted on his feet. My focus centered on that uncharacteristic show of uncertainty. With a resigned glance to Eric and Meagan, he stood straight and reached for my left hand. The pad of his thumb brushed over the area still vacant at the base of my ring finger.

The earlier panic morphed into frustration. Dad knew Weston wasn't the reason I didn't have a ring. I was. Even after all the trips to various jewelers over the past two months, I hadn't found a ring that spoke to me. It drove Weston crazy, but I wouldn't settle on a ring just because it was big and shiny. It needed to mean something to us, to me.

Biting my tongue against all the accusing words I wanted to unleash, I tracked Dad's hand as it disappeared inside the hidden pocket of his suit jacket. Disappointment felt heavy in my heart when he held a small, square red velvet box on top of his extended palm.

"Dad." I sighed, tugging my hand out of his. This was the last fight I needed right now. Him buying me a ring because he assumed Weston couldn't afford one was a low blow. Why was he determined to undermine Weston at every turn? "You know Casey can—"

"Just open it, stubborn girl," he rasped.

I finally peeled my irritated gaze away from the box, only to find fresh tears welling along his lower lids, threatening to spill over.

That sight lessened the growing irritation enough to grab the box from his palm and flip the lid.

A choked gasp caught in my throat at what lay inside, resting on the tiny black pillow. Memories surged at the sight of the beautiful two-carat oval-cut diamond glittering back at me.

My mother's ring.

The presence of someone at each shoulder had me raising the box for both to see the beautiful, priceless gift inside.

"That's gorgeous," Eric whispered, resting a comforting hand on my shoulder.

"It was my mother's," I somehow choked out around the burning ball of unshed tears. I blinked to clear my watery vision and smiled up at Dad.

"I spoke with Casey this morning."

My smile grew, bunching my cheeks. That was a big step for Dad to approach Weston on his own, wanting his blessing before giving me the family heirloom. Love swelled in my chest. My grip on the box tightened. It meant Dad's respect for Weston as my future husband was growing.

"Once I showed him your mother's ring, he agreed it was perfect. I have to believe you not finding one was a sign that this was meant for you all along. I was a fool not offering it the moment you called with the news of your engagement. I was a fool about many things. I hope —" His voice cracked. "I hope one day you'll forgive me for not seeing the special relationship you two have and trusting your decision. Your mother would be proud of you, Kate. I know I sure as hell am, and it's an honor for another strong woman in our family to wear this ring."

There was no preventing the warm trickle of tears that slipped down my cheeks. A tissue-blotted one cheek, then the other with Eric's attempt to salvage my eye makeup. I shot him a wet smile, only to find tears of his own in his bright eyes.

Plucking the platinum band off the miniature pillow, I started to slip it on, but a masculine hand covered mine, pausing the movement.

"I think he should do it, don't you?" Dad said, smiling at someone over my shoulder.

I twisted toward the door, only to melt at the sight of one sexy-as-hell Casey Weston. He filled the doorway with his broad shoulders and overall powerful presence. Hands casually tucked in his black suit pants, tie undone and dangling along the sides of the white dress shirt with the top button open gave him a ruggedly sophisticated appearance.

Edible. My future husband was truly edible in everything he wore. Dirt-covered tactical wear or a Hugo Boss suit, he radiated confidence and strength. And for some reason, he loved me. Really loved me, flaws and all.

"Holy fuck," Eric gushed into my ear with something that resembled a pant. "If you don't eat him, I will."

I giggled, shoving him off me, and started toward the door. Weston met me halfway, his dark eyes sweeping me from head to toe.

"You're stunning," he rasped.

"You're edible."

The returning deep chuckle and shy shake of his head did more to my head than the few glasses of champagne.

Reaching out, he removed the dazzling ring from between my

pinched fingers. The world stilled, my heart pounding in my chest and lungs frozen as he lowered, planting one knee on the plush carpet, looking nowhere but at me. Transfixed by the sight, I startled when his large hand engulfed my own.

"I promise to love you forever and a day. To never stifle your fire, to hold you when you cry, and champion your dreams. Kate Wheeler, will you marry me?"

"Oh my." Meagan sighed wistfully.

"Say yes," Eric called out.

Over my shoulder, I smiled at Dad, who offered a single nod of confirmation.

Turning my full focus back to Weston, I bit my trembling lip.

"Yes." The word was barely audible. "Yes. Forever, yes. Only you, Weston. You stole my heart that day in the rain, and I never, ever want it back."

The metal, warm from his fingers, slipped over my knuckle before settling at the base. In a quick motion, Weston stood, wrapped his arms around my middle, and swung me around.

I'd never forget his smile. The joy and love radiating off him were palpable, and I knew without a doubt it would never fade. Sure, we'd fight, but we would always be each other's only exception.

"I have the pregnancy test."

It felt like the air was sucked out of the room as the attendant dashed inside, holding the box high above her head as she leaned forward, hand planted on her knee as she fought to catch her breath.

"Pregnancy test?" Weston asked, confusion in his tone. He eyed me, then the box.

"Not mine," I announced quickly. The tight hold around my waist loosened, allowing me to slip down his chest until my heels hit the floor. "It's not mine, I swear, Casey."

"Then who's—"

"Mine," Eric and Meagan blurted in unison.

I couldn't help it. With the back-and-forth of emotions plus the champagne, I snorted and laughed out loud, unable to stop as the giggles kept coming.

"Pretty sure that's impossible, Eric," I said between cackles. "But way to cover for our friend."

With a resigned sigh, Meagan took the box from the attendant. "Thank you."

"Oh, I owe you a hundred bucks for making it under the thirty-minute mark."

Without me asking, Casey dug in his pocket, pulled out five twenties, and handed them to the attendant.

She took the money, staring wide-eyed at Weston with a bit of fear and awe. Leaning to see around us, she nodded when she located Eric. "You weren't kidding."

That had Eric and me bursting out laughing.

"What?" Weston asked, clearly confused and knowing he was the basis of whatever was so funny.

"Nothing. Eric just described you perfectly to her." Twisting in his arms, I pointed to Meagan, who stood frozen, staring at the box in her hands. "Go take that test."

Her red hair shifted as she shook her head. "Nah. I mean, it's your day and—"

"Go," the four of us said in unison. I smiled at Dad, finding it awkward and hilarious that he was a part of this drama.

"Fine. But what happens if I am?" Meagan's voice cracked, betraying her calm demeanor.

"Then you go from there," I offered. Stepping out of Weston's hold, I crossed the room and wrapped her in a hug. "But you need to know. Based on all those medical school classes, we know this isn't something you can ignore and hope it goes away."

She huffed a laugh and sighed. "You're right. I need to know."

"Then go pee on that stick," Eric cheered.

We both rolled our eyes, but a small smile at our friend's antics crept up our cheeks.

"Do you want help?" I asked.

"No."

"Okay. We'll be out here ready to support you either way."

"Thank you." She slipped from my arms and made her way to the bathroom, avoiding looking at anyone else. The door snickered shut, followed by a distinct click of the lock engaging.

I released a loud breath and looked to Eric, who shrugged.

"Great, more waiting," I grumbled.

At Weston's responding chuckle, I smiled and turned my full focus to the brilliant diamond sparkling on my left hand. I held it toward the window where the early afternoon sun streamed through and rotated it, allowing the sprinkles of rainbow light to dance along the walls.

"I need to go finish getting ready." Weston's minty breath caressed along my neck before he pressed a soft kiss just beneath my ear. "See you soon, baby."

Dad followed Weston, giving me a quick peck on the cheek and saying he'd meet me downstairs to ride together to the ceremony site. Even before the door shut behind the men, Eric was dragging me to the vanity scattered with all the makeup.

"You're a mess." He sighed. "But hell, that was romantic as fuck." The wistfulness in his voice caught me off guard. "You're a lucky woman. I'd give anything to find a guy like that."

I opened my mouth to tell him it would happen one day, but the creak of the bathroom door snapped both our mouths shut. Swiveling on the stool, I looked to Meagan, brows raised, silently waiting. The slump in her shoulders and fresh tears slipping down her cheeks conveyed the results even before she spoke.

"It's positive," she whispered with a loud sniffle. "I'm pregnant."

WARM HEAT FLARED along my aching cheeks from the wide, joyous smile I'd held the past hour. Adjusting my grip on Weston's hand, I hurried after him as he led me toward the small room, the reception location set aside for the bride and groom. My heels clicked along the hardwoods as we raced, both of us ready to seal the marriage vows we'd just recited with our friends and family watching.

"Fucking finally," Weston muttered under his breath as he shoved the tall dark wood door open and strode inside. He whirled me around, forcing me to hurry my pace as I spun into the room, a happy giggle tickling my chest. When the room stopped spinning, I found him leaning against the closed door. Without looking away, he reached down and flicked the lock.

My breasts pushed against the tight confines of the dress with each heaving breath. All laughter stopped as he stalked closer like a predator ready to devour his prey.

Yes, please.

I backed away, retreating for every step he drew closer, until the cool drywall pressed against the bare skin of my shoulders. Weston sealed both palms to the wall beside my head, caging me in with his powerful arms. My lower belly quivered with want as he leaned closer, his lips hovering a hairbreadth from mine.

"Mine," he whispered like a prayer.

"Yours."

"Forever."

I licked my lips, loving the way he pulled back enough to track the movement. "Forever and a day."

All the air sucked out of my lungs when his lips crashed to mine. A hand peeled from the wall to wrap around the back of my neck and squeezed. The hold tightened, positioning me at his mercy as he poured all his love and devotion from his mouth into mine. Moving lower, he kissed and nipped down my neck, sucking at the tender place where it met my shoulder.

I relaxed into his hold, allowing the grip to keep my head stable. Eyes closed, I focused on the sensations from every place he touched, each kiss and nibble to my skin. The blaze rising low in my core flared hotter with the swipe of the tip of his tongue along the exposed swell of one breast, then the other.

The wall dug into the knobs of my spine as he pressed his hips against mine, applying pressure right where my body demanded.

"Casey," I breathed. Not giving my actions a second thought, I shoved my fingers into his styled hair, disrupting the carefully placed strands, and tugged his face up. "I need you *now*."

"Yes, wife."

A thrill shot down my spine at the title.

I expected him to yank me from the wall or even rip the dress off instead of dealing with the hundred delicate buttons. Instead, he dropped to his knees before me with a wicked gleam in his eye and grasped both ankles. Keeping those dark, hooded eyes locked on mine, he trailed both hands up my calves, slipping over my knees before caressing along my inner thighs.

A look of surprise lit his face when he found no boundary between his searching fingers and my wet center. With a nearly painful groan, he stood, bunching the lacy material around my waist. Excitement and need had my fingers fumbling with the clasp of his belt, taking me two tries before I yanked it open. The second I had the fastener free, I slipped a hand beneath the waistband of his slacks.

"Fucking hell," he hissed when I wrapped it around his stiff cock.

With a quick pop and zip, Weston yanked his pants and briefs down his muscular thighs. Up and down I worked my hand, swiping a fingertip across the sensitive head, slicking the side with the beads of precum.

"Up you go," he grunted and lifted me with ease. Immediately I locked my heel-covered feet around his back, sealing our two lower halves together. With a curse, he pounded a fist to the wall, rattling the picture near my head, as I worked my hot, wet center up and down his cock, moaning at the delicious friction and teasing torture.

With a quick tilt of his hips, he lined up with my center and slowly eased inside. Our combined moans of satisfaction and pleasure vibrated around the otherwise quiet room. Gripping both my wrists in one hand, he held them above my head, trapping me fully with his body.

Desire darkened his gaze as he stared down at where we were connected.

"I'm not holding back, baby. Hold on."

Pulling out to the tip, he slammed deep, his hips slapping against mine with enough force to leave a bruise. I hissed a breath through clenched teeth as he pounded me against the wall. Pulses of pleasure burst through every cell, fogging my thoughts.

"You're mine," he rasped, breath ragged. "Forever. This body, your mind, all of you. Mine."

"Fuck yes," I whimpered. "I'm almost there."

At that, he held our bodies close, pressing his pelvic bone to my clit, and circled. A pitiful moan rattled deep in my throat.

"I wanted it to be you," he whispered into my ear. "I wanted the pregnancy test to be yours." The vulnerability in those words ignited a deep, unfamiliar feeling in my chest. "Someday I'd love to put a baby in this belly." Slipping a hand between us, he pressed against my lower abdomen. "When you're ready."

What was there to say to that?

Before I could come up with a response, he moved that hand lower and pinched my clit, sending a shock wave of tingles dancing along my skin and rushing through my veins.

Tighter and tighter, my body wound as he thrust deep while roughly stroking my sensitive nub until every nerve ending burst into flames. A silent cry caught in my throat as I tipped my head back, unfocused gaze upturned to the ceiling. All the tension from the last few months flooded from my muscles, leaving them lax in his tight hold.

With a muffled curse against my shoulder, Weston sank his teeth into my skin as he tipped over the edge too. Panting as we came down from our high, we didn't move, both of us savoring our first moment as husband and wife.

"I love you so damn much, baby." Soft lips pressed to the indented skin where his teeth marked me.

"Can we just stay in here and do that again?"

His chest rumbled against my own with his low chuckle. Pulling back, he brushed a rogue strand of dark hair off my sweaty forehead. "I think that's what the honeymoon is for." Sticking out my lower lip, I gave an exaggerated pout. "Come on. Let's get you cleaned up and go celebrate with our friends."

The moment he slid out of me, I felt hollow, wanting that connection a little longer. But he was right. Others were waiting for us, and it would be rude to have them fly all this way just for us to spend the night screwing in the back room.

At least we had the honeymoon to look forward to tomorrow. Just us for two weeks. Nothing but skin, sun, and sand for days.

What a way to start the next part of our lives.

Together.

Forever.

EPILOGUE

"Oh, hell yes," I muttered. The morning sun's rays heated my bare skin, but it held nothing to the heat radiating from my hot center where Weston's face was currently buried. As he sucked my swollen nub, I shattered, my back arching off the lounge chair.

The sounds of the waves crashing along the beach just a few feet away slowly came into focus as I came back down to Earth. Peering down, Weston smirked, licking his lips before sucking on the three fingers he just had inside me.

"Well, that's a fun way to wake up from a nap." The mesh indented beneath the heels of both palms as I pushed up.

"You looked too delicious lying out here naked to not have a bite."

My teeth sank into my lower lip as I attempted to stifle my smile. Looking down, I pressed a finger to the skin of my bare breast, checking for signs of too much sun. Sunbathing nude was the way to go. I couldn't do this in Dallas—pretty sure that was a misdemeanor, maybe even a felony—but here on our private patch of beach that came with the house we rented for this stretch of the trip? Hell yes.

Not that I cared so much about the tan lines, but it was freeing, sexy to walk around buck-ass naked. It also provided ease of access on both sides.

"Come swim with me." Pushing to stand, he extended a hand.

I gave myself a second to appreciate his nakedness. Every time I saw him, another wave of desire rushed through me, settling low in my belly. But who could blame me? He was deadly beautiful and all mine.

"Pool or ocean today?"

"Pool. It's only been a few days, but I'm already tired of the sand. It irritates my balls like a son of a bitch." Taking his outstretched hand, he helped me up before sweeping me into a bridal-style hold. He shook his head at my exasperated sigh. "The sand is hot."

I shot him an incredulous look but let him carry me up the beach toward the private pool. Since the moment we said 'I do,' he used every opportunity to carry me whenever he could. He said it was because I felt so good in his arms; I assumed it was because he was too damn protective for his own good and was scared something might happen to me before our forever could start.

Sighing, I leaned against his chest and closed my eyes. Let's be honest, it wasn't a hardship by any means to be carried everywhere by your hottie of a husband.

"What will it be like when we get home?" I mused more to myself. "I guess I'll go back to working in the ER and volunteering at Second Chances." My lips dipped in a frown. That didn't hold as much appeal as it used to. "And you'll go back to the security detail gig?"

I squealed, wiggling in his hold, when the cold water slid along my skin as he slowly glided through the pool toward the deep end. The evil bastard held me tighter.

"Don't you fucking dare, Casey West—" The rest was swallowed up by the water rushing over my head as he sank us to the bottom. Bubbles rose from his spread lips as he smiled at me beneath the crystal-clear water.

Slipping from his hold, I shot him my middle finger and shoved off the plaster bottom, rocketing me to the surface.

"You're an ass." I wiped the water from my eyes to glare at the head that bobbed above the surface just seconds after I did.

"Your ass, you mean." Leaning back, he floated on top of the water, his arms slowly circling to keep him afloat. His naturally tan skin was already a dark brown, but somehow his tattoos still stood out, especially the one above his heart. "And I don't know."

"Don't know what?" Dog-paddling to the side, I pressed myself up and plopped my wet ass on the stone decking with a smack.

"What will happen next? I really don't want to go back to the security firm. It's not that I didn't like it, and my boss was great, but it just doesn't fit anymore."

Water gushed to the stone, running in little rivulets toward the cracks as I squeezed the pool water from my thick hair. "Especially the overseas part. I don't think I could go months without seeing you. Scratch that, I know I couldn't."

Only the sound of the pool's whirling pump and jets filled the silence as we both thought over what would happen once we returned to Dallas.

"Do you want to go back to the ER?"

I leaned back, the warmth of the stone seeping into my chilled forearms. Swirling my feet through the water, I thought over the most truthful response.

"Yes and no. I enjoy it, taking care of people and helping others. But the bureaucracy of the hospital and insurance companies and ungrateful patients, not so much. What that leaves me with, I'm not sure. Medicine is my passion."

"And getting into trouble."

Kicking a pointed foot, I showered him with droplets of pool water. "Well, that's a talent really, not a passion."

"Touché." Flipping, he swept his arms up and over in long strokes. Shouldering between my legs, he rested his arms on either side of my hips. "You don't have to work though, you know."

"I know." I smiled. He wanted to take care of me in every way, but that wasn't me, and he knew it. "But I need to work. If I don't stay active, who knows what kind of trouble I could get myself into."

"That's a terrifying thought," he deadpanned.

He flinched back when I flicked the end of his nose. "Have you heard anything from Kyle?"

Kyle didn't have any news to offer regarding future missions for the small group or if what we did months ago was just a onetime deal. After the wedding, James, Tyler, and Anne went back to Texas, but all expressed interest in keeping the team together if possible. But with no leads on missions or local agency support, it wasn't workable.

When talking to Kyle during the reception, I got a feeling that he had a lead on something but didn't want to share it until he had all the information. Maybe that was me just being hopeful. I wanted the team to stick together. Weston loved it, James was healing, and it brought Tyler and Anne together.

The team was meant to be.

"Nothing yet. I'm trying to not get my hopes up. It's a shot in the dark that the government would want us on the payroll long term. There are only so many times we can go in undercover before our pictures and specifics of our group are all over the dark web. Hell, it might be out there now."

"Maybe, but I doubt it. Everyone who saw us are dead." Thankfully that evil woman ordered the promoter's assistant's death while I was sitting there, held captive in that damn building. "There aren't any loose ends."

"This time." Concern marked his features with a deep line between his dark brows.

"How about you and I switch places and I return the favor from earlier?"

And just like that, all the worry and concern vanished. With a gleam in his eyes, he gripped my waist and tossed me into the pool before hoisting himself up to the side. His cock twitched, growing hard as I slowly swam closer. Palms to the inside of his knees, I pressed them wide and settled between his spread legs.

His coarse leg hair snagged between my fingers as I made my way up his thick thighs, savoring the power and strength flexing beneath my hands. Using the edge as leverage, I pitched forward and sealed my lips around the soft head, swirling my tongue along the top, flicking the slit and tasting the first salty drop.

Strands of my hair pulled at my scalp as he sank his fingers into the wet locks to cup the back of my head. The slight pressure urged me closer, slipping him deeper into my mouth until he grazed the back of my throat. Breathing through my nose, I fought off the automatic gag reflex as he lifted for a shallow thrust, slipping farther down my throat.

His fingers tightened, fisting my hair. Using the hold, he lifted me back before pushing me down until the tip of my nose brushed along his flexing stomach. Back and forth he moved me along his cock with grunts and curses about my fantastic mouth. With a groan, his grip tightened, pulling at my scalp as he came.

Slipping into the water with a mischievous smirk, I wiped at the few stray drops and licked the back of my hand.

"Damn, woman." He chuckled. "That was fucking amazing—"

The sharp ring of a cell phone cut through our peace. With an annoyed grunt, he pushed to his feet. Rifling through the tangled towel along a pool chair, he looked at the screen and turned to me, his brows raised.

"Miss Ginger." He held up the phone in a silent question if he should answer it or let it be until we got back.

"Answer it," I said excitedly as I swam toward the shallow end. "Just no FaceTime."

He smiled at that and swiped the screen, pressing it to his ear with a curt greeting.

Keeping my attention on Weston as he talked in a hushed voice with his friend, I paced through the water, sneaking in a little exercise outside of sex on our glorious honeymoon.

Holding up a finger, he turned and disappeared into the house.

With a huff, I sank back into the water and lay out to float on my back. Puffy white clouds in various shapes floated across the powder blue sky, blocking the full intensity of the sun from burning into my eyes and skin. A soul-settling peace poured over me as I floated alone in the pool. So much had happened over the last year to lead up to this. Some good, some bad, some great. And I wouldn't have changed any of it. Not one second to ensure this was the same outcome.

Him and me, together, working side by side day in and day out.

Everyone assumed I had everything in life because of my fortune and career, but none of that mattered until Casey Weston barged into my life, changing its course forever.

A shadow cast over my face, adding another layer of shade from the sun. Flipping over, I stood, water slipping down my sides back into the pool.

Weston stared me down from his high perch, tapping the phone against his palm in a rapid beat. My pulse raced at the anticipation of the good or bad news that was about to be delivered.

"We have a lead."

I squealed and jumped up and down, sending waves sloshing around me. "What does that mean?"

With a flick of his wrist, he tossed the phone back to the pool chair and jumped into the water. I shied away from the spray, shielding my face with a hand to keep from getting it in my eyes.

"It means we might have an option for more consistent work. Not undercover, more rescue and retrieval." I circled a hand, urging him to tell me more. He laughed at my over-the-top enthusiasm. "Americans go missing every day across the globe. Too many for the various agencies to keep up with. They'd back us financially to take on the higher profile cases, go in, find the target, pull them out, and bring them home."

"Wow," I breathed. "That sounds legit, Weston. What do you think?"

A small smile tugged at the corner of his lips. "It sounds perfect." That smile slipped. "But I'm not sure where you'd fit in since we both agreed you wouldn't be on the front line of action again."

I waved him off. "Not sure if you noticed, but my medical knowledge came in handy twice this past mission. I can go with you guys, stay out of the initial takedown, and be ready in case anyone needs medical help. I'm sure the agency would supply me with all the drugs and medicines I'd need."

He tilted his head one way, then the other. "Yeah, that could work."

"Especially if you're going into remote locations. If anything bad happens, I might be the difference between life and death for you, the guys and Anne, or the person you're trying to rescue."

Wrapping me in his arms, he rested his chin on the top of my head. "Okay, okay, baby, you've proven your point. Like I could've gone any length of time without that mouth of yours." He grunted when my fist connected with his kidney. "It was a joke."

"Not laughing."

Pulling back, he dropped the smile that was permanently on his face these days and searched my face.

"We already have the training, so all they need is our new paperwork with our private security business name. The basic one we chose for the last mission won't work with the international specifics we'll need to incorporate."

"Hmm, a name. That's a tough one. I feel like we need a few drinks in us to come up with a good one."

"You sure about this? If you are, I'll call the others and get the ball rolling."

Holding his face between my hands, I pulled him down to my eye level. "We're in this together, right?" He dipped his chin in a brief nod. "Then yes, I'm good. Go call the others, tell them the news. Get it started, and while you do that"—pressing off his chest, I stepped backward toward the stairs—"I'll go pour the shots. We'll figure out a company name before dinner rolls around."

"You're perfection, Kate Weston."

I shook my head and smiled. "Just close enough to perfect for you, Casey Weston."

Turning, I strode out of the pool and wrapped a towel around my chest. Staring out over the ocean, I wondered what this next chapter would bring. As long as Weston was with me, we'd make it through anything.

But as far as the others who I now called friends—Meagan and the baby, Eric and his search for undying love, James with his recovery, Tyler and Anne's new relationship, and of course, the mysterious Kyle—only time would tell what the future held for them.

FOLLOW ME

Want to stay connected? Follow me on any (or all!) of the platforms below:

FB readers group
Facebook Author Page
Instagram
TikTok
Newsletter
Bookbub

ALSO BY KENNEDY L. MITCHELL

In Clear Sight: A Small Town, WITSEC Interconnected Standalone Series

Safe Haven - FREE Prequel

Guarded by the Marshal

Cherished by the Agent

Saved by the Officers

Hidden by the Doctor

Protection Series: A Dark Romantic Thriller Interconnected Standalone Series

Mine to Protect *

Mine to Save *

Mine to Guard *

Mine to Keep *

Mine to Hold *

Mine to Love *

Mine to Share

Mine to Shelter

*Now available in audio!

SEALs and CIA Series: A Navy SEAL Interconnected Standalone Series

Covert Affair

Covert Vengeance

More Than a Threat Series: A Connected Bodyguard Romantic Suspense Series

More Than a Threat

More Than a Risk

More Than a Hope

More Than a Threat Series Boxset: Complete Series

Power Play Series: A Protector Romantic Suspense Connected Series

Power Games

Power Twist

Power Switch

Power Surge

Power Term

Standalones:

Finding Fate - Dark, Captive Romantic Suspense

Memories of Us - Contemporary, Small Town Romance

ABOUT THE AUTHOR

Kennedy L. Mitchell lives outside Dallas with her husband, son and two very large goldendoodles. She began writing in 2016 and has no plans of stopping.

She would love to hear from you via any of the platforms below or her website www.kennedylmitchell.com You can also stay up to date on future releases through her newsletter or by joining her Facebook readers group - Kennedy's Book Boyfriend Support Group.

Thank you for reading.

ACKNOWLEDGMENTS

Thank you so much to everyone who stuck with me, patiently waiting for this book. I'm sorry it took me WAY too long to get this out to you guys. I meant to write it right after More Than a Risk but A Covert Affair popped in my head and wouldn't let me go.

As always I have to first thank my three biggest supporters. Em, Chris and of course my amazing husband. None of this would happen with out those there. It takes a lot of encouragement, plot sessions over bottles wine, and many many texts to get a book written, these three are there for it all.

And of course to my amazing ARC team, bloggers, and dedicated readers - THANK YOU! You guys have put me on the map with all the posts, shares, comments, recommendations and praises. I can't thank you enough for what all you do for me and supporting this wild author journey I'm on.

Again thank you so much for sticking through the slight down time between books. You guys rock. Thank you for reading me!